✝ Captain from Castile

CAPTAIN
FROM
CASTILE

by Samuel Shellabarger

THE SUN DIAL PRESS
Garden City, New York

To my son

JOHN ERIC SHELLABARGER

Part One

I

On the evening of June 28th, 1518, young Pedro de Vargas, aged nineteen, confessed his sins of the month to Father Juan Méndez. He took them more seriously than the priest, who had been hearing confessions for hours, and was ready for supper. Besides, Father Juan knew the young man so well that he could have guessed beforehand what he would tell him.

"I, Pedro, confess to Almighty God, to Blessed Mary . . ."

Though the wall of the confessional separated them, Father Juan had as clear a picture of the penitent as if they had been face to face. In imagination, he could see Pedro's bronze-colored hair, short and curly; the greenish-blue eyes set well apart; a sunburned face and strong mouth; the high cheekbones with hollows under them. Pedro's folded hands, big and brown, though shapely, held a paper with a list of sins in poor handwriting.

"I accuse myself of forgetting my prayers on the night when Campeador came."

"Who is Campeador, son?"

"My new horse, Father, a good horse, sired by —"

"You must not forget the Blessed Virgin because of a horse, my son."

"No, Father."

"What next?"

"I accuse myself of falling asleep during the Bishop's sermon on St. John's Day."

"Hm-m," said the priest, overcoming a smile.

"I have disobeyed my father by frequenting the Rosario tavern in the mountains."

"An evil place. There is none worse in the province of Jaén. The resort of bandits and rascals."

"Yes, I have sinned. Moreover, I kissed a certain girl there—a dancer."

1

"Amorously?"

"Yes," gulped Pedro.

"And afterwards?"

"Nothing, *por Dios!*"

"Do not swear."

"I'm sorry. . . . No, there was nothing, Father."

"Go on."

"I accuse myself of drawing a knife over cards."

"You did not use it?"

"No, Father."

"What next?"

"I made fun of my sister, Mercedes, for reading saints' legends. I told her that they were not the equal of *Amadís de Gaula.*"

The priest muttered: "Woe unto them through whom offenses come! It were better for them if a millstone were tied around their necks."

"Yes, Father. I repent. I have been impertinent to my mother."

"Alas! What next?"

When Pedro had finished, Father Juan, struggling with a yawn, absolved him. His penance consisted in part of reading five saints' legends that evening and of an interdict against *Amadís* for a month.

The next morning, therefore, on June 29th, day sacred to his name saint and patron, Saint Peter, he was clean spiritually as a hound's tooth, and climbed up through the narrow streets of Jaén with his family to take communion in the cathedral church under the castle.

From the side of the nave, Father Juan, who at that mass had no duties at the altar, watched the procession of the de Vargases down the center aisle. First, a page boy carrying prayer cushions; then Don Francisco with Doña María on his arm; then Pedro with his sister Mercedes, a girl of twelve.

As father confessor, the priest knew them all well. An honorable family, a credit to Jaén. His eyes followed them affectionately. Don Francisco, tall, erect, lean as whip leather, with a hawk nose too large for his face, and his lower lip jutting out. Though sixty and retired, he still looked his reputation as one of Spain's foremost cavaliers; a soldier of the Marquis of Cádiz in the Moorish wars; knighted by King Ferdinand at Granada; stirrup comrade of the Great Captain, Gonsalvo de Córdoba, in Italy; survivor of more forays and pitched battles than anyone in the province. He was well known among the soldiery of Europe. Even such a champion as the French knight, Bayard, called him friend. With a head grown partly bald from the rubbing of his

2

helmet, a stiff knee crushed at the battle of Ravenna, almost every one of his features was a trophy of war. Even his wife, Doña María, might be considered a trophy. Florentine by birth and belonging to the great Strozzi family, she had married Don Francisco twenty years before during a lull between campaigns. She had since grown plump, maternal, and forty; but her husband treated her still with scrupulous gallantry. She walked beside him now like a dignified pouter pigeon beside a falcon.

Father Juan shook his head as he glanced at Mercedes de Vargas. Too slender and frail. Her delicate health gave concern to her family. He liked Pedro's manner with her, protective and smiling, as they went down the aisle.

It was Pedro himself, with his reddish hair and scarlet doublet standing out in the dimness of the church, who most fixed the priest's attention. A man of the world before he had taken orders, Juan Méndez could not but admire the erect figure, narrow hips, and broad shoulders. He realized suddenly that here was no longer the boy he had known, but a young man on the threshold of his career as a soldier. Pedro's naïve confessions the evening before contrasted strangely with the impression he now made.

The Processional began; the priest turned to devotion.

Kneeling between his father and mother, young de Vargas did his best to pray. His eyes rested on the huge, black, fearsome crucifix newly brought from Seville. But his thought drifted to the crusades. There were still infidels—in Tangier, in the Indies. Some of his father's friends had sailed with the Admiral, Christopher Columbus . . .

He returned to prayer, but soon found himself gazing up at the votive banners overhanging the nave. He tried to make out the quarterings. There was León, there Mendoza; that was the banner Queen Isabella left when she held her court at Jaén. Becoming too much absorbed, and gaping upwards, he received a poke in the ribs from the gold knob of his father's cane. On Pedro's other side, his mother frowned and shoved a half of her book at him.

The Bishop took his throne, the celebrant bowed to the altar, the servers kneeled, puffs of incense rose from the thurible.

"Kyrie eleison. Kyrie eleison. Kyrie eleison."

From now on, Pedro did his best to keep his mind on the service. On other days some inattention might be allowed; but today he was receiving the sacrament after confession—if unworthily, to his eternal loss; if worthily, to the fortifying of his soul—and he had been wasting precious minutes, which should have been spent in preparation.

3

Earnestly he followed his mother's forefinger across the page of the missal, as it accompanied the priest's singsong.

A subtle anguish began between his shoulder blades. A flea, with the cunning of its race, was attacking him in the most unreachable spot, and he could do nothing. A cavalier did not scratch in public. He could only wriggle his shoulders, which seemed to provoke the enemy. But a sudden thought struck him. Was it an ordinary flea? Was not Beelzebub himself the lord of fleas? Wasn't it probable that the Fiend had sent a familiar to attack the soul of Pedro de Vargas through the flesh? *Vaya*, he defied the demon! As a result, he did not miss a word of the Epistle, and the temptation passed, a fact which showed that he had gauged it correctly.

Some late-comers took their places among the kneeling congregation, but Pedro kept his eyes on the book. If the devil sought to destroy him this morning, he must not be given another loophole. Only at the *munda cor meum, ac labia mea*, Pedro happened to look up.

Por Dios! That girl who had just passed down the side aisle, wasn't she—? He stared intently. Yes, indeed! Satan still prowled. It was Catana Pérez, the dancer at the Rosario. The wildest girl in the mountains! She could dance a *zarabanda* to make blood boil, could throw a knife like a gipsy, could swear like a man. Church was hardly the place where he expected to see her.

He watched the sway of her hips along the aisle, then ducked his head, glancing furtively at his sister, Mercedes, who knelt on the other side of Doña María, to see if she had noticed his lapse. And of course she had.

"Thou art Peter, and upon this rock I will build my church," intoned the priest. Pedro could hardly feel that he had been appropriately named for the stanch apostle.

Then suddenly his eyes, again straying from the page, widened. Until that moment he had not noticed the girl to his left near the side column. From where he knelt, he could see only the pear-shaped pearl dangling under one ear, and the curve of her cheek. Madonna! That Luisa de Carvajal appeared at early mass on his name-day was indeed an event.

A year ago she had returned from her convent in Seville because her father, the Marquis de Carvajal, was lonely and wanted her at home after his wife's death. For some time, Pedro de Vargas had admired her at a distance befitting her rank and unapproachableness. Once he had met her at the Bishop's palace—an affair of ceremony, but they had had a word or two. Another time he had passed her on the church steps, and she had smiled and looked down.

4

But this morning she seemed nearer, less forbidden. Watching her at her prayers, he felt a delicious tenderness steal over him. That she was here on his name-day seemed very significant. He could not take his eyes from her. If he had admired her before, he now realized that he adored her.

And at that point, a miracle happened.

To his glowing imagination, it could not be called anything else. A ray of light, slanting through one of the narrow windows, rested on her face, illumined it, and then, intercepted by a cloud, gradually faded.

He held his breath. It was a manifest revelation that here was his destined lady of ladies, the mistress of his life. She had been revealed to him on his name-day by a special act of heaven.

"*San-ta Ma-ri-a!*" hissed his father. "Will you attend to the service! Do you have to gape at every skirt!"

With a sense of injustice, Pedro returned to the book. He had never felt so religiously uplifted. He thrilled with a new zeal. In the spirit of his hero, Amadís de Gaula, he now prayed:—

"Holy Saint Peter, gracious patron, I thank thee that by thy intercession Doña Luisa de Carvajal has been designated to me as the lady whom I am ever hereafter to serve and honor as a Christian cavalier. May it be to thy glory and the advancement of chivalry! And herewith I vow to perform this day three deeds for her sake, if thou wilt deign to provide me with the occasion for them. And this I swear by the blessed Cross on the altar. Amen."

They were story-book words, but he meant them. "*Sanguis Domini nostri Jesu Christi custodiat animam meam in vitam aeternam.*" When it came time to approach the altar, he trembled with emotion, and returned to his place a new creature. Or so he thought.

"*Dominus vobiscum.*"

"*Et cum spiritu tuo.*"

Like a runner on the mark, Pedro had one foot under him. At *Deo gratias,* to the concern of his family, he leaped up and hurried out, but stood waiting at the holy-water font in the vestibule of the church.

Having followed the side aisle, Luisa de Carvajal, with her duenna, was among the first to come out. Seeing her approach, Pedro stood lost in admiration.

She was not tall, but beautifully proportioned. In every detail, her small person showed finish—in the arrangement of hair and mantilla, in the modishness of her dress. She carried herself exquisitely. The arch of her eyebrows, the bow of her lips, her pearl-white complexion, were perfect. She had been schooled and polished to become the model

5

of correctness which people expected from the daughter of a grandee.

Only her eyes had not yet been fully disciplined. Even in Andalusia it takes longer than seventeen years for that. They were dark and clear, innocent, angelic. They utterly confused Pedro, who kept just enough presence of mind to dip his two fingers in holy water and present them with a bow. His face was beet-red; he felt gawky as a lout; his salutation stuck in his throat.

"Gracias, señor."

She touched his fingers, made the sign of the cross, and once more her eyes devastated him. He was privileged to read in them almost anything he pleased.

Then she passed on, leaving a momentary breath of rose water. Happily dizzy, Pedro stared after her.

"Have you nothing for me?" said a voice at his elbow.

He had forgotten Catana Pérez. She confronted him now, chin up, her eyes challenging. He could have sunk through the pavement—all the more as at that moment his family emerged from the main body of the church.

He hesitated a moment. Should he pretend not to know her? By God, he couldn't do that to a friend like Catana, whatever people thought! It took high courage, though he wouldn't have called it so, to grin back at her under the eyes of his family, return the greeting, and dip his fingers for her in the font; but he did it gallantly.

"As much for you as for anyone, *querida.*"

He was puzzled by the sudden change in her. The devil in her eyes faded; her reckless, swarthy face grew gentle, and her lips tightened. Looking down, she crossed herself quickly. And leaving him nonplused, she hurried out into the glare of the plaza.

"What the deuce!" he thought.

"Who's that trollop?" his mother demanded in a low voice.

"A country girl," he stammered. It wasn't necessary to be too definite.

"I believe you know every wench in the province," Doña María went on indignantly. "No shame at all! No propriety! And after *el Santísimo* too! At least I thought you might be saluting the Lady Luisa; but no, in the face of the town, you have to disgrace your family with a trull!"

"She isn't a trull, *Madrecita.*"

"What else is she?"

With her head in the air, Doña María waddled out, followed by Mercedes.

6

Don Francisco's lip drooped—a bad sign. But on the point of speaking, he checked himself. Be hanged if he would correct his son in the presence of the town gossips! Hadn't he been young himself? *Cómo no!* To Pedro's relief, he drew himself up, pulled in his lip, and smiled.

"Hombre! A lively-looking filly!" He spoke in a voice for anybody to hear. And taking Pedro's arm, "What's her name?"

"Catana Pérez, sir."

"Catana, eh?"

The old cavalier limped stiffly to the door, and adjusted his flat velvet cap with the short plume, reserved for churchgoing.

A wave of affection for his father surged through Pedro. He would have liked to squeeze the sinewy arm that rested on his. *Por Dios,* it was good to be a de Vargas!

II

THOUGH it was still early, the sun already struck hard along the alley-like streets descending from the church. As became their sex, Doña María and Mercedes rode, while Pedro, the page, and a mule boy walked, leading the animals. Don Francisco, also mounted because of his stiff knee, brought up the rear.

The odors of oil, garlic, wine casks, and other ingredients, thickened; breakfast was in the air; shutters opened, and voices clattered between opposite windows. Now and then a cascade of slops from above splashed the cobblestones. "Look out! Look out!" called the mule boy in perpetual warning. Far off—an occasional vista through the chasm of the street—extended the plain below with its groves of olive trees and, beyond that, the dark wall of the Sierra Morena.

Picking his way mechanically through the litter underfoot, Pedro de Vargas walked in a dream. What did the fuss about Catana Pérez matter! He didn't even care to defend himself on that subject. He knew that it would have pleased his mother if he had told her all that had happened at the holy-water font, but the name of Luisa de Carvajal and his new-found love were too sacred to be bawled out in the common street. He relived his experience in the church: the miracle of the ray of light, his exaltation. He ached with an unspeakable longing. Typical of humanity, he walked with his feet among ordures and his head in the clouds.

Downhill the town opened up, leaving more breathing space than in

7

the crowded district around the castle. Small squares, with a tree or so in the center, were lined with the fronts of newer houses. Upon entering one of these open places, within a stone's throw of home, the de Vargases came upon a considerable hubbub.

In front of the house of Diego de Silva, horses were prancing and fretting under their riders, among whom were several of Pedro's friends; hunting dogs, held back by footmen, yelped and strained at the leash; a crowd of idlers stood around. In the center of the throng, de Silva, mounted on a fine sorrel, was just pulling on his riding gloves.

He was a clean-shaven, still youngish man, with large, reckless black eyes, shrewd and insolent. He had closely knit brows, forming an over-hang to the bridge of his nose, with one of them tilting up at an angle, which gave him a sinister, rather sly look. His large ears, pointed chin, and the strips of hair creeping down from his temples reminded Pedro of a bat, though he was otherwise handsome enough. He had soldiered in Italy, had been at court, and was reputed the richest man in Jaén, richer even than the Marquis de Carvajal. Still unmarried, he was a beau with the ladies and the best catch in town. Pedro admired, without liking, him.

At the sight of fine horseflesh, Don Francisco's eyes lighted up, and he forced his mule through the crowd.

"What's this?" he hailed. "It isn't the hunting season, Señor de Silva. What are you out for?"

"The oldest chase in the world," returned the other with a super-ciliousness that galled Pedro.

"And that is?" Like all Andalusians, the elder de Vargas spoke with a lisp, which was more marked in his case because he had lost his front teeth. "It's too early in the morning for riddles."

"No riddle," replied de Silva. "It's a man hunt." Noticing Doña María and Mercedes on the fringe of the throng, he bowed with two fingers on his heart.

"What man?"

"My servant, Coatl. I gave the dog some lashes yesterday for the good of his soul, and he rewards me by running off. *Hombre!* When I get my hands on him, he'll run no more."

Coatl, the Indian, was one of the curiosities of the town, as yet un-used to natives of the Islands, though savages, naked or in their bar-baric panoply, were frequent enough spectacles in the retinues of home-coming discoverers arriving at the main ports. He had been brought over by a Cuban planter, from whom de Silva had acquired him—a well-muscled, stately man of about thirty, and rather light-colored. His

8

ears, nostrils, and upper lip had been pierced for ornaments which he no longer possessed. Though technically a servant, because of the edict against the enslavement of Indians, he had no effective rights and was virtually a slave.

The young bloods of Jaén, with Pedro among them, liked to draw him out. Though silent and brooding as a rule, he grew talkative with drink, and would then relate a hodgepodge of marvels in his broken Spanish. It appeared that he was not originally from Cuba, though he was extremely vague on this point; but as nothing could be vaguer than Cuba itself, the mystery did not trouble his audience. He told a tall story about being cacique, or chief, in some fabulous country of the West, whence he had been kidnaped by Carib Indians and finally storm-tossed to the Cuban coast, a story which was accepted as credulously as the tales of Prester John. He was an expert tracker, and Pedro had borrowed him once for a wolf hunt, on which occasion they had become friends. He regretted now that Coatl had proved himself a rascal by running off.

"Join us," remarked de Silva with a roving glance. He was evidently impatient to start.

Don Francisco shook his head. "Too old for such pleasures on a hot day. By God, I recall a chase we had once near Gaeta after a French cavalier by the name of . . ."

"Excuse me," interrupted de Silva, "but we have to ride. Your son would like it perhaps?"

De Vargas stiffened. "Perhaps, señor. He can decide for himself. As I was saying when you took the liberty of interrupting me, the name of the French cavalier was Lanoy."

His eyelids drooped slightly. De Silva kept a patronizing smile.

"Vaya, sir, this fellow Coatl has a long start on us and will reach Granada if we do not spur. I have no time for anecdotes. . . . Señor Pedro, are you with us?"

Nettled at the slight which had been put on his father and about to decline, Pedro caught himself. He remembered his vow to Saint Peter, who was evidently putting him to the test. There could be no question that it was a good deed to help a man recover his property.

"I'll saddle in ten minutes."

De Silva gathered his bridle reins. "Good! We'll follow the Guardia Valley, and loose the dogs on both sides of the brook. He was seen heading that way. Catch up with us when you can. . . . Sound the horn, there."

A huntsman blew the call; de Silva's horse reared; the dogs went

9

crazy; the onlookers made way, and the cortège headed out of the square. One of Pedro's friends, Hernán Gómez, paused a moment to shout to him: "Don't miss the 'death.' De Silva swears he'll give Coatl two hundred lashes on the spot and cut his leg muscles. Ride hard."

The sound of the horn and clatter of horses drifted back. The little plaza became silent. Turning his mule, Don Francisco rejoined his wife and daughter, who had been looking on from the background.

"Talk of modern manners!" he grunted. "It's a degenerate time. I can't imagine myself at the age of that puppy cutting short an older man of consequence who was addressing me. It would have been unthinkable. And the fellow wishes to buy my vineyard! He can whistle for it!"

Preoccupied as he was, Pedro felt startled. The vineyard and its pavilion were especially dear to his father. Until now a sale had never been mentioned.

"The vineyard, sir?" he repeated.

"Yes, he wants to round out his property. He offers a good price, but I'll see him hanged first."

"You wouldn't sell the vineyard?"

Don Francisco exchanged a glance with his wife, which expressed annoyance at having talked too much.

"Why, perhaps," he evaded, "sometime. But not to him. And by the way, son, I'm surprised that you're riding with him."

"Not *with* him, sir." During the last minute, Pedro had been thinking intently. "They're following the Guardia. I don't believe that Coatl took that way."

"Ha? And why not?"

"I've hunted with him and know his mind. He's sick for the Islands. He will head for the sea—for Cádiz, not Granada."

"Hm-m," nodded the other. And with a touch of pride, "Well reasoned."

"Besides, we hunted in that direction, through the Sierra de Jaén, not toward the Sierra de Lucena. He knows the paths over there. I wager he let himself be seen along the Guardia, and then cut west. He's shrewd as a fox. I'd like the credit of bringing him in alone."

It was the pretext which would most appeal to his father, a scrap of honor in the offing.

Don Francisco approved. "Yes, it would be to your credit. By the Blessed Virgin, I'd go with you except for this knee. Bring the fellow in alone, eh, while de Silva scours the country with his men and dogs! It would be a feather in your cap and a joke on him. I'm sorry for the

Indian, but servants should not run away. Discipline must be kept. You'll be doing a service to all masters, not merely to de Silva. Remember to take stout cords with you."

"It may be dangerous for Pedro," ventured Doña María, "alone with a savage."

The old cavalier gazed proudly at his son's broad shoulders. "Pooh! The boy can take care of himself. He'll never get forward if you coddle him. . . . Hurry ahead, son. Saddle Campeador, and ride with God!"

III

FIFTEEN MINUTES later, Pedro struck fire from the cobblestones under the arches of the Puerta de Barreras, and waved at Ramón, the gateman, as he passed.

"Hey!" shouted the old soldier, cupping his hands. "If you're following the Señor de Silva, you're taking the wrong road . . . I say, you're taking the wrong road."

But as only a column of dust drifted back, and Pedro continued obstinately to the left, Ramón shrugged his shoulders and returned to the coolness under the tower.

Outside, the heat of the day had begun in earnest. Pedro could feel the burn of it on his shoulders through his long riding cloak. To spare Campeador, he pulled in, when the path turned upward, and continued at a moderate pace. Gradually the patchwork of orchards and gardens and the simmer of the plain on his right, the Campiña de Jaén, leading to Córdoba, were cut off by the first low ridges of the sierra. He threaded a grove of cork oaks, dipped into the greenness of a valley, clambered up again, and at last emerged among the naked mountains.

Meanwhile, the problem at hand absorbed him completely. With the instinct of the tracker, he kept putting himself in the place of Coatl. What would the Indian be likely to do under the circumstances? Apparently he had escaped before dawn. If Pedro's theory was correct, and he had cut over into these mountains from the Guardia Valley, he could not as yet have gone very far in the direction of Cádiz. Moreover, it was hardly to be expected that he would travel by day. The heat, the chance of being seen, his uncouth appearance, and the fact that he was probably moneyless, were all against him. Therefore, he would be apt to hide during the day and travel by night, relying on theft to keep alive until reaching the coast. Once in the dives of Sanlúcar, where the scum of the seaports gathered, he might lie hidden, though he had a poor outlook from beginning to end. The immediate question was where to search for him in these hills.

Breathing his horse at an angle of the road, Pedro thought it over. On the face of it, the task seemed hopeless. Every boulder, every crack in the rocks, might serve as a hiding place. He might ride within a yard of the man without seeing him. But a couple of factors helped. In this heat, Coatl must have water, and water was scarce along the uplands. Pedro knew the location of every spring and runnel in the neighborhood. Step by step, he tried to recall the route which he had followed with the Indian during the hunting trip last winter.

Then, beginning with the nearer possibilities, he tried several places without success. The air along the stony stretches had the hot bite of a furnace. Now and then glimpses of the plain far below, with here and there the *campanil* of a church or roofs of a hamlet figuring the green carpet, offered relief; but for the most part it was only rock and glare. Even Campeador, usually high-hearted, grew listless, hung his head, and left the water holes unwillingly. Pedro reflected that he might spend the day in this region to no purpose. On horseback, he could be seen and heard too easily, provided indeed that he had guessed correctly, and that Coatl was still in this section of the mountains.

At last an idea flashed on him. There was one place of all places that made an ideal hideout from the Indian's standpoint. It was a narrow, shallow ravine about a mile off, open at both ends, and with a good spring of water. In one direction it gave a wide view of the country, and was a favorite stop of Pedro's on a day's hunt. He and Coatl had halted there. He remembered the Indian staring off into distance and his homesick talk about his native country.

But to reach this *barranca* to the accompaniment of horse's hoofs over the loose stones without giving an alarm was impossible. Riding at a walk, Pedro brought Campeador to within a quarter of a mile of the place. Then, dismounting, he tethered the horse between two boulders, and took off his cloak. The cords for tying up Coatl were transferred from the saddle pouch to his breeches pockets. He made sure that his dagger hung right and was loose in its sheath. That he might prove unequal to the Indian in a personal encounter did not enter his mind; for, without vanity, he knew his own strength and knew besides that a Castilian cavalier was the superior of any savage. At the same time dutifully he commended himself to the Blessed Virgin with three *Aves*, and prayed to Saint Peter for help to fulfill his vow in honor of Luisa de Carvajal.

There was a low ridge to cross, and a slope to climb before the ravine; but, from the outset, Pedro walked carefully to avoid displacing any of the loose stones. Instead of proceeding in a straight line, he took a roundabout way, moving from boulder to boulder and listening at each pause. He had never stalked a wolf or bear with such intentness. There was not a sound—only the emptiness of the hills, the blue heat of the sky. In spite of the dry air, he ran with sweat.

Rounding the contour of the slope, which led to the ravine, he stopped again, listened, and then, inching his way, he peered around the corner.

The place was empty. He could see the round hollow of the spring and clear along to the opposite opening. All his precautions and maneuvers had been unnecessary.

Disgusted, he now entered the place to take a look from the vantage point at the other end.

And in the same moment two arms of steel closed around him from behind; he was lifted clear off his feet and brought down with a thud, while a heavy body pinned him to the earth. Quick as a cat, he arched himself, but felt the prick of a knife through his doublet.

"Spanish dog!" hissed a guttural voice at his ear. "I kill."

The knife prodded deeper, then withdrew; Pedro could sense that it was poised. Convulsively wrenching his neck around, he saw the granite face of Coatl six inches above, and the white of his bared teeth. He caught his breath against the blow.

But all at once everything seemed to relax. He heard a surprised grunt; the weight on his shoulders lightened.

"*Señor Pedro?*"

Still half-dazed, he was aware that the Indian had got up. Raising himself on his arms, he returned Coatl's stare.

"I not know," muttered the latter. "I think someone different; I jump and not look."

Suddenly a wave of feeling transformed the man. He flung his knife down and lifted both arms. "Coatl kill Señor Pedro, his one friend. Señor come to help. Coatl kill 'im. Señor, forgive!"

Gradually Pedro's brain cleared. It was evident that he owed his life to a misconception. He had been outwitted and downed, and his pride felt the shock more than his body.

Getting up, he brushed himself off, finding it hard meanwhile to face the quandary into which Coatl's forbearance had put him. A mere step, and he could plant his foot on the other's knife, draw his own, and carry out the purpose for which he had come. But he could not take

13

that step. Shame forbade it; though, on the other hand, conscience assailed him for shrinking from his duty as a citizen and Christian. There could be nothing but scorn for such ill-timed scruples in the case of an escaped slave.

He temporized by saying, "Why did you want to kill anybody, Coatl?"

"People follow me," returned the Indian. "I kill. But not Señor Pedro. You-me eat together on hunt. I tell you of my country. Señor pity Coatl." He drew closer; his hands affectionately clasped each of Pedro's arms and lingered a moment. "Friend," he repeated.

Now was the time to take the fellow by surprise. A sudden blow to the jaw and a leap would do the trick; but the word "friend" cast a spell.

"I thought you would be here," Pedro said helplessly. "You came across from the Guardia, didn't you?"

The Indian nodded.

"Why did you run off?"

In answer the man's face became stone again. With a sudden movement, he was out of his ragged shirt and, turning, showed his back. The flesh gaped open in several long ridges with the blood clotted between them.

To Pedro, the sight of a flogged back was familiar enough in view of the public whippings imposed by the Inquisition. He had seen dozens of such backs pass through the streets of Jaén. But he winced a trifle because de Silva had apparently used a mule whip.

"Coatl no slave," said a choked voice. "Coatl cacique, lord, in his own country. People, towns. De Silva a beggar beside him. He beat me; I kill if I could. Run away, yes."

"Do you think you can get back to the Indies?"

"My gods will help."

Pedro's scandalized conscience burned hotter than ever. His gods! The man was not only a fugitive, but a heretic, an *apóstata*. He had been baptized and had lapsed. After de Silva had finished with him, he belonged to the Inquisitor. And here was Pedro de Vargas, a good Catholic, fresh from mass, fresh from making vows to the saints that he would perform deeds in his lady's honor—here he stood, hesitating to seize an infidel and hand him over to punishment! A moral weakling because the dog had spared his life! He felt bewildered, bewitched.

Resuming his shirt and knife, Coatl now walked the short length of the ravine, and stood gazing toward the southwest. Pedro followed him, grudgingly conscious of his statuesque body and stately bearing.

14

"Look, señor." The Indian pointed beyond the mountains. "Over there, Great Water take Coatl home. Where the sun set. Señor Pedro help?"

Standing behind him, Pedro could easily bring the heavy butt of his poniard down on the man's head. A moment later, he would be securely tied. Young de Vargas's hand stole to the hilt of his dagger.

"Help how?"

"Money. I reach Sanlúcar."

"It's a long road to Sanlúcar."

Pedro intended to couple the words with a blow, but his arm failed him. At that moment Satan—because no saint would have intervened for a heretic—distracted him with a mental picture. It was the picture of Coatl captured and strung up in front of de Silva. Two hundred lashes! The flesh in strips, the bones showing. And what was it Hernán Gómez had said? Cut the tendons behind the Indian's knees? After that he would be a cripple; his legs would wither; he would creep in and out of de Silva's door, fair game for the street boys to trip up. It was queer to think how his fine body would look by evening.

Pedro's hand dropped from the dagger hilt. He had lost his chance, for Coatl now turned with a look of entreaty.

"If I have money, I reach Sanlúcar."

Aware of his madness, but unable to resist, Pedro opened the purse at his belt and fingered its contents. He had two gold pesos, which his father had given him for his name-day. It was a dazzling present; he had never had so much money before.

With an aching heart, he drew out one of the precious coins and handed it to the Indian. "Here, Coatl." But his madness was unappeased; he could not rid himself of the picture in his mind or of Gómez's words. His fingers crept back to the purse, lingered wretchedly, then brought out the other peso. It seemed heavier than the first and more freshly minted. As if no longer in control of his muscles, he pressed it into Coatl's palm.

And now, having made the plunge, he went on recklessly: "I wish I had more. You've got to hurry, Coatl. You mustn't wait here. Put country between you and them. They may cut over from the Guardia. Good luck! I hope you get to Sanlúcar."

The Indian stood silent a moment. Then he caught Pedro's hand, looking him straight in the eyes.

"Coatl never forget," he said hoarsely. Struggling to express himself, he added at last one word that had the effect of an accolade. *"Caballero!"* he said.

And as if anything more would have lessened this title of honor, he turned and disappeared through the mouth of the ravine.

IV

THE RAVINE seemed very empty and silent. It was so quiet that Pedro could hear the minute trickle of the spring. Little by little, the realization of what he had done expanded in his mind.

Whether discovered or not, he felt disgraced. He had cheated a gentleman out of his property, and had aided a heretic, whom he ought to have denounced. Still worse, by failing to perform his vow when the chance offered, he had been false to heaven itself. Yet meanwhile in the unacknowledged part of his mind, the murmur persisted that if he had given Coatl up to torture and perhaps to death, the memory of it would have haunted him always. It was his first experience with moral issues too complicated for the familiar rule-of-thumb, and he felt utterly at a loss.

In this unhappy frame of mind, he rambled absently downhill to where Campeador waited. How would he ever be able to confess these sins to Father Juan? How could he ever expiate them? The horse whinnied and rubbed a velvet nose against his shoulder. Here was a friend who would think none the worse of him. With the resiliency of youth, Pedro decided not to think too badly of himself. He might have done wrong, but Father Juan himself admitted that the flesh was weak.

The idea of breakfast suddenly occurred. He had eaten nothing since last night's supper and had taken no provisions for the ride. But it was impossible to return home for a while, because he must give the impression of having searched far and long for the Indian. The nearest place to get a meal was the ill-famed and forbidden Rosario tavern over toward the Guardia Valley. It struck him too, as an excuse, that he might turn up in de Silva's crowd and thus, so to speak, cover his own tracks.

Cheered by thoughts of bread and cheese, he resumed his cloak, untethered Campeador, and set out at as brisk a pace as the heat and the hills permitted. It would be less than an hour's ride to the doors of the *venta*.

The landscape of Jaén is varied by bleak mountains and fertile valleys. The roads ascend toward heaven and plunge down to the lushness

16

of earth. Perhaps on that account its natives are apt to be sometimes among the stars, and at times in the mud, though, to be entirely fair, one doesn't have to be born in Jaén for that. By the time Pedro had crossed the first sierra and reached the trees and thickets of the valley beyond, the moral anxieties of the last hour were beginning to pale. The thought of a cup of wine dispensed by Catana Pérez inspired him to sing, and he started to hum catches of a popular *romance*.

The road spiraled up to the rocks again, then down in loops that permitted glimpses of the next valley, in which the tavern was located. From this point, he heard dogs and horses in the far distance, and gathered that de Silva's party had broken up into groups, following not only the course of the Guardia, but combing the entire neighborhood. The air was so clear that at one point, looking down, he could see a narrow strip of high meadow flanked by thickets not far from the inn. Then a curve of the road gave him a view in the opposite direction. His ballad burst into full voice:—

> *"Río Verde, Río Verde*
> *Tinto vas en sangre viva . . ."*

Campeador pricked up his ears and put action into his trot. They swept down into the tree line again, wound back and forth, crossed a brook, and at last came out upon the strip of meadow at which Pedro had been looking a few minutes earlier. Here Campeador, with his mind on refreshment at the tavern, broke into a gallop, which his rider did nothing to restrain.

> "Río Verde, Río Verde [Pedro sang],
> Dark with crimson blood thou flowest . . ."

But halfway along, the horse, shying to the left, cut the ballad short. "Devil take you!" cursed Pedro, a little off balance. At the same time, glancing back, he drew up with a jerk. Campeador had shied at a peasant girl's black and red dress lying in the deep grass. A couple of yards farther off appeared the body of a dead hunting dog. It had been newly killed by a gaping knife cut across the throat.

"*Cáspita!*" muttered Pedro, staring.

A faint trail of bent grass toward the thicket at one side caught his eye. Then for the first time he heard a confused sound from that direction; and, curious to know what it was, he guided his horse into the underbrush between the pine trees. As he drew closer, the sound became more distinct. All at once, as if it had been pent-up and suddenly released, came a woman's cry, *"Socorro! Qué me matan!"* accompanied by an outburst of oaths.

At this call for help, Pedro gave spur to Campeador and, regardless of whipping branches, plunged through the thicket to a small clearing beyond.

"Socorro!"

A girl, clad in nothing but her shoes, stockings, and shift, stood knife in hand, confronting a couple of burly, hard-looking fellows, who were circling around and trying to close on her. They wore the badge of de Silva's household. One of them, evidently wounded, clutched his shoulder. He was retching out oaths, while the other, grinning but silent, waited for a chance to spring in. The girl's hair was disheveled; even her shift was torn; but she looked intent as a lynx faced by dogs.

Then, as she turned suddenly and drew back, Pedro saw that it was Catana Pérez.

His view of the scene had taken no more than a second. With the fierce pleasure of battle, he charged in. His riding whip opened the face of one of the men. Campeador, trained to fight, reared and struck with his forefeet. The man who had been grinning went down with a shriek, but scrambled up and scuttled off into the bushes. His companion, with Pedro at his heels, raced for the opposite thicket, but did not escape a second dose of riding whip on his head.

Pedro turned back into the clearing just in time to catch sight of the girl hurrying for the covert on her side. A glimpse of disturbing contours, and the pine branches closed behind her.

"Hola, Catana!" he called, riding over. "Are you all right?"

An urgent, suppressed voice came out of the bushes. "Go away, señor! Go away!"

"The devil! I call *that* gratitude!"

"Do you hear? Please go away!"

He backed off. "Don't worry. Stay where you are. I'll get your dress."

Returning to the meadow, he scooped up the garment and rode back.

"Hang it on that branch in front," came the voice. "Then turn around."

Dismounting, he obeyed instructions. There was a quick snatching movement, followed by rustling sounds. A minute later Catana emerged.

She had put up her thick brown hair after a fashion, and was now at least covered; but she held a long rent in her skirt together with one hand, and a patch was getting dark above her cheekbone.

At her best Catana was not beautiful, and she was certainly not beautiful now; but since her attraction at no time depended on good looks, it was not affected by the torn dress and the beginnings of a black eye. Indeed, if anything, these features harmonized with her peculiar personality.

Her angular, tanned face still had the undercolor of embarrassment. "That was a close call, señor. You came in the nick of time."

"Caramba qué suerte, Catana! What on earth happened?"

She explained that on her return from church she had been sent by Sancho López, the innkeeper, to look for a strayed goat. While crossing the upper meadow, the two men had accosted her.

"Do you know them?" he asked.

"God forbid! They're strangers. I could tell that by their talk. They said they belonged to the Señor de Silva, and were after some poor servant. I hope he gets away."

This was balm for Pedro's guilty conscience. He reckoned that the men had probably followed de Silva from Madrid.

"Go on. What happened then?"

"One of them started to get fresh. I slapped the bastard."

The huskiness of her voice sounded hot.

"And then?"

She shook her head. "Believe *me,* there're some very bad *hombres* in this world! These devils set their dogs on me and laughed."

"Diantre!" growled Pedro.

"They didn't laugh long, I can tell you. I lost my dress, but cut the throat of one dog, and sent the other off in a hurry. I think he will howl a long time."

She added that the men, furious about their dogs, sprang on her, wrenched her knife away, gagged her with a scarf, and then hustled her through the thicket. She pretended to faint, but watched for a chance. When it came, she snatched a dagger from the belt of one of the men, stabbed him, and in the confusion got rid of the scarf.

"I was praying harder than ever in church. Then you and Campeador dropped from nowhere. It's a misery to think what they said they would do before killing me."

"God's blood!" de Vargas muttered. "I wish I'd had a sword."

"No, it's better this way. I'll speak to Manuel about them."

Pedro stared. "Who's he?"

"My brother. Don't you remember? He works in the prison. We have friends, gentlemen of the night, who will oblige us."

She did not enlarge on the point. It was beneath Pedro's rank to carry out vengeance against two lackeys. They should be left to cutthroats. But for a moment de Vargas regretted it. It recalled the distance between the girl and himself. He liked Catana. She was just a wench of course—but fascinating. He would have been glad to manage this for her.

Suddenly she raised her hand to her mouth. "Holy saints! What about Señor de Silva!"

"Well, what?"

"He's a rich lord," she said in a hushed voice. "I killed one of his dogs. We wounded his men. Blessed Catherine! What will he do to us!"

She had indeed good reason to fear; but this was more along Pedro's line. "By God," he exclaimed, "there's such a thing as the King's law! You're just as much his subject as Diego de Silva. The men and dogs attacked you. If he says a word, appeal to the Corregidor."

She looked amused. *"Ay María!* What do you think that a girl like me can get out of the law except hard knocks? The law protects people who are born in big beds. Can't you see me accusing Diego de Silva before the Corregidor! Me, Catana, maid of all work at the Rosario! Why, a good hunting dog is worth three of me. I only hope that Sancho López doesn't catch it on my account. He's been good to me—like a father."

On second thought, Pedro had to admit privately that she was right; but he couldn't resist showing off a little.

"Call on *me* then. I'll look out for you. If de Silva wants satisfaction, he can have it."

She smiled at him. "Thanks, *caballero.*"

All at once the girl's lips seemed irresistible, and he drew her close to him.

"No," she said, avoiding his kiss.

"Why not, Catana? You've kissed me before."

"Yes, but not now."

A strange note in her voice set his blood tingling.

"Why not?"

"Figure it out for yourself, sir. If you can guess, I'll give you one if you want it—then."

"Is it because you don't like me?"

"No."

"Because you're betrothed?"

"No."

"Because—" God in heaven! The curve of her lips, the feel of her body against his arm, set him on fire. "Devil take it!" he said. "I can't guess."

He kissed her anyway, full on the mouth. She did not resist, but she did not return it.

"Please," she said at last.

He let her go, wondering at the ways of women. It did not occur to him to wonder at the ways of men.

"I've got to get back," she said, "and tell Sancho López what happened."

"Then we'll ride together on Campeador."

"Do you mean it?"

He couldn't account for the excitement in her voice.

"Of course."

Mounting, he gave her his hand. Light as a cat, with one foot on the toe of his boot, she sprang up behind the saddle and held on with an arm around his waist. Campeador danced to show that riding double meant nothing to him.

"Steady!" commanded Pedro. "Sorry, Catana!"

"I'm all right."

Glancing down as they rode, Pedro warmed to see her hand with a couple of fingers linked in his belt buckle. It was a strong, capable hand, but smooth and well-shaped.

Then suddenly he remembered Luisa de Carvajal. As if from far below, he now looked up toward her, toward the heights of his experience in the church. He saw once more the ray of sunlight on her face. By contrast, what a spectacle this was! Riding double with a mountain hussy in a torn dress, whom he had just been kissing—a half-wild tavern girl, companion of rogues and boors! With her arm around him! And there on her summit stood Luisa, daughter of the Marquis de Carvajal! *Sancta Trinidad!* What a day! First he connives with a runaway heathen; then he gets mixed up with this. Evidently Saint Peter liked practical jokes.

He could not see the tranced, adoring look on Catana's face. It could not possibly occur to him that this was the supreme moment of her life. She wanted to lay her cheek against his shoulders; her arm pressed tenderly around his waist, she sat with her lips half-parted in an impossible dream.

It was a trait of hers to invent future conversations. She knew that years from then she would be telling people how once she had ridden behind Pedro de Vargas on his war horse, Campeador. . . . "You mean the *great* Don Pedro, Catana—*maestro de campo* of the King?" . . . "Surely, who else? I felt like a real lady that day. It was almost," she heard herself saying, "almost as if he were my cavalier."

21

Much too soon for her, the whitewashed walls of the Rosario came in sight. They turned into the smelly courtyard with its assortment of travel-worn mules and donkeys. Pedro reined up.

"*Gracias.*"

Catana slipped back to earth.

V

IT WAS A SLACK hour at the Rosario. The guests of the night before had pushed on, and the guests of that evening had not yet arrived. Several muleteers were drinking at one of the long tables in the cavern-like room, and a gipsy trio—a man and two women—babbled their own language in a corner. The place was dark, smoky, and had a stale stench of cooking. It served as kitchen, dining room, and sleeping quarters combined; for, though a loft upstairs provided pallets, wise travelers, valuing their sleep, preferred to stretch out on the tables. Coming in from the outside glare, it took Pedro a minute or two to distinguish anything, and to adjust his nose and lungs.

"Señor Pedro, at your service!" said a gruff voice from the dark. And to Catana, "It's good time you got back, long-legs. Did you find Bepé?"

Gradually the squat figure of Sancho López, who had been serving the muleteers, became visible.

"What misery!" Catana burst out. She shook her two clenched hands above her head. "*Qué inmundicia!*"

Discovering her torn dress and swollen eye, López stared. "What do you mean?" he demanded.

"Pigs of men who attack girls! Except for Señor Pedro, you would have seen me no more."

Her voice filled the room. She gave an account of the action with spirit and pantomime. Now and then she remembered to clutch the rent in her dress that showed too much thigh.

A growl of indignation greeted the report. Since no one could boast of possessing Catana's favors, she was a potential sweetheart to every-body, and an attack on her became an injury to all. If her two assailants had been there at that moment, their chances would have been poor, for the Rosario had a bad name for bloodletting. And yet at the men-tion of de Silva, silence descended upon the room. He was a rich lord with a big following. Sancho López looked thoughtful.

"Antonio," Catana went on to one of the muleteers, "when you reach Jaén, you will see Manuel and tell him what has happened."

Antonio, a quiet, flint-eyed fellow, looked proud to be appointed. He answered with a swagger, "I will do so, Catana. But if I meet one of those *cabrones* first, it may not be necessary for Manuel to concern himself. . . ."

"Bah!" interrupted Sancho López. "You let well enough alone, my friend. Tell Manuel from me that sparrows don't make war on hawks."

The innkeeper had a close-cropped, bullet head and a dark stubble of beard around his face. He was a man of clipped, but weighty words. Half-leaning against a table with his arms crossed, he dominated the group. After a pause he went on:—

"Forget it! The girl wasn't raped, so what's the fuss? I knew de Silva when he wasn't cock-a-hoop, and he knows *what* I know. He'll leave Catana alone, but you and Manuel leave his men alone, d'you hear? The score's settled."

He unfolded his arms and started to move away, then stopped. "Besides, lightning doesn't strike cabbages. But aren't *you* planning to travel, Señor Pedro?"

"Not on his account."

"Then be careful." López stood fingering his rough chin a moment, as if in two minds about adding something. But he thought better of it, and said to Catana, "You've got a black eye, long-legs."

"Does it look awful?" She appraised the swelling with her forefinger.

"It is a very black eye," said López frankly. "You can't dance for the patrons until it fades. It does not look feminine. We'll get Dolores Quintero."

"No you don't!" flamed Catana, who was proud of her exhibitions in the evening. They were the chief attraction of the tavern and her main source of income.

"By your leave," came a heavy voice out of the dimness in a corner, "there's nothing like raw meat for a black eye. I have often used it. Beef is best, but goat or pig will do. Bind a good hunk over your eye at once, señorita, and by tomorrow, with the help of God and a little flour, you will dance. Only do not delay."

Attention now centered on the speaker, whom Pedro had not yet noticed. The bridge of his nose was extremely wide, though not at all flat. This feature, combined with the truculent squareness of his face, and bold, large eyes, gave him a bull-like cast. He had a thick neck and huge shoulders. He was clean-shaven, and had a big, purposeful mouth. His hair, bulging from under a round cloth cap, sprayed out in a mop. He might be thirty-five; and, though he spoke with the accent of Jaén, Pedro couldn't remember that he had ever seen him.

23

"There is much in what the señor cavalier says," agreed López. "It is a good remedy. Cut a slice from the newly killed goat, Catana, and bind it on with a clout. I'll serve Señor Pedro. What's your pleasure, sir?"

Pedro ordered bread, cheese, and wine, then walked out to see personally to Campeador. When he came back, the big man in the corner greeted him.

"Do me the honor, señor," he boomed. "Join me. Juan García at your service." And after Pedro was seated, "The son of Don Francisco de Vargas?"

"Yes, sir."

"A great cavalier, Don Francisco. I have seen him—I mean, I have heard of him often. As who has not? Your health!"

He raised the cup to his mouth, but Pedro noticed with surprise that he did not drink.

"In the Indies," García went on, "I have known soldiers from the Moorish wars and several from the Italian. They liked to talk about him."

"The Indies?" Pedro's eyes quickened. Except for Coatl, he had never happened to meet anyone from the New World, and Coatl's broken Spanish did not give a clear picture. Jaén was an inland town and off the beaten track, but rumors of the western seas filled the imagination of every boy. "The Indies?" he repeated. "You have been there, sir?"

"Many years—sixteen, to be exact—and landed two weeks ago on St. Anthony's Day." García paused to slice an onion with his case knife, laid the section on a piece of bread, and stuffed it into his mouth. It did not keep him from talking, but the words came out muffled. "I was around your age when I last sailed from Cádiz with Cristóbal Colón."

"The Admiral?"

"Aye," nodded García. "It was his last voyage—and a very unprofitable one. There was promise of gold at Veragua, but the cursed Indians drove us off. Two wasted years. We flopped around, discovering useless land, and got back to the Islands no richer than scarecrows. Thank God, I've done better since."

Pedro leaned forward. "Tell me about him, sir—about the Admiral."

"Don Cristóbal?" With his fingernail, García dislodged a morsel wedged between his teeth. "Well, sir, to be fair, he was an old man, when I knew him, and full of ailments. But from what I've heard, he had his faults at best. No hand with men, d'you see? And he had a fuzz-buzz of a brother, Don Bartolomé, who got under people's skins. You can't expect Castilian cavaliers to take orders from Genoese foreigners.

24

A seaman, yes. None like him. How he could smell his way around the ocean like he did, nobody knows. But when you've said that, you've said about everything."

García rolled a pellet of bread between his fingers.

"To tell you the truth, Don Cristóbal wasn't of my kidney. I mean he was too cursed strange. I've seen him at the rail by the hour, staring at nothing but the skyline. If you spoke to him then, he didn't see you; he had the look of a sleepwalker. Lived in a dream. Give me practical men!"

García broke off, sat ruminating a moment, then shook his head. "Still, you've got to admit what he did. I guess a practical man wouldn't have put out across the ocean. Takes everybody to make a world."

Pedro's mind was on Columbus's dream. García's disparagement did not lessen the tall, bent figure of the old man, gazing out to sea. What was he dreaming of? Glory? Cathay? The Great Khan? That is what Pedro de Vargas would have dreamed. Or was he thinking of his chains and disgrace, the tragedy that had stirred even heartless Spain? Or was it something else beyond everything, his dream—some grand horizon that only he could picture? Pedro thrilled at the thought of him. He did not share García's enthusiasm for practical men. At the same time, García did not make an ordinary impression either.

"Señor," Pedro asked, "do they still expect to find Cathay on the other side of the Islands?"

García smiled. "You're behind the times, sir. Ever heard of Vasco Núñez de Balboa?"

"No, sir."

"I suppose you wouldn't. He was a good friend of mine, a brave gentleman. Too bad he was executed. The old comrades keep dropping off." García sighed thoughtfully. "But that's neither here nor there. Four years ago, being a man of enterprise and in charge of the new settlement of Santa María de la Antigua, he crossed the mountains of Darién and sighted the great South Sea. Until then, people weren't sure, but that proved it. Big new lands—the Great Khan has nothing to do with them. Belong to nobody but His Majesty. How far Cathay and the Spice Islands are across the South Sea, God knows, but it doesn't matter. It's a new world, my son."

Pedro sat looking at García, his imagination leaping like fire in a high wind.

"Listen!" the other rumbled. "I've stood on the water front of the Habana de Cuba and looked north. You could *feel* the great land over there like a cloud, the land Ponce de León found. Endless. Then I've looked west. Land beyond the horizon in that direction. Hernán de Córdoba coasted it last year. Country of towns and gold. Then south there's Honduras, which the Admiral discovered—and south of that God knows what! Balboa heard of a country on the Southern Sea where gold's cheaper than iron, where the Indian dogs live in palaces and eat their victuals off of gold. And all of that is waiting—kingdoms, empires, mountains of gold—to be taken by the first cavalier that has the guts to venture. *Hombre!* The smell of a strange land when you're putting in! But young fellows like you stick around Spain! God, it's a queer world! Slaves, women, pearls, jewels . . ."

"Your bread and cheese, sir," interrupted Sancho López, thumping the plate down, *"a su servicio."*

But for an instant Pedro forgot his appetite.

"Father says that Italy's the true school of honor. He plans to send me over there next year. My mother's Italian. I don't intend to stick in Spain. Father says a man gets more reputation by fighting against the French *hommes d'armes* and Swiss pikemen than any other way."

For a moment García looked puzzled. Then his eyes lit up like a man's who recalls something which he had forgotten.

"Por Dios!" he grinned. "Doesn't that bring back old days! Spain hasn't changed. You see, señor, I'm just a common man, without crest or ancestors. I was born in a garret and have had to hustle. But I remember that that's the way hidalgos should talk." He smiled fondly. "Well, put it on that score. With all respect to Don Francisco, Italy's old-fashioned. You'd get more honor, I should think, converting heathen Indians to the Faith and winning provinces for the King than in scuffling with the French. But I may be wrong."

With the look of having said his say and not wishing to intrude upon another's business, he now finished in several huge bites, and sat eying Pedro, who began making up for lost time opposite him. When their glances met, they both smiled unconsciously like people who understand each other. Gradually their talk became more personal, but at the same time Pedro was struck by a queer reserve in García. His birthplace in Andalusia, why he had returned from the Indies, his plans and business, remained cloudy.

"Ho, señorita!" García called to Catana, who had returned to duty with a bandage over one eye and her dress stitched together. "Another cup of wine for the *caballero,* if he will honor me."

Meanwhile, his own wine remained untouched. To Pedro's amazement, he quenched his thirst from a cannikin of water.

26

"To the New World!" said Pedro, bowing his thanks across the table after the wine had been brought.

"To the New World!" answered García warmly. But again he no more than touched the brim of the cup with his lips.

The boy's curiosity overflowed. "You do not drink, señor?"

"No," answered the other, "I do not drink save like a donkey. It's a heavy cross. Please do not let it disturb you. I buy wine for the good of the house."

"I see," nodded de Vargas—"a penance."

"Something like that."

García fell into black silence, hacking the edge of the table with his knife. Pedro wondered what sin he was expiating. The man's reserve became a wall. Then suddenly he clapped the knife down in front of him.

"By God, I'll tell you how it is. I'm an ordinary man, when sober; I'm mad, when drunk. And a taste of it gets me started, d'you see? When I'm drunk, I want to kill. That's the story."

For an instant, his bluff face turned ugly; a gleam showed in his eyes. Then he relaxed.

"Born that way. Probably I have a devil, though God knows I've done what I could to get rid of it. Spent a pile of money on priests and candles. But it never worked. So I don't drink."

Pedro felt sympathy and showed it. It was hard on a big, companionable man to be cut off from wine, he thought.

Another silence followed, while García seemed to be noting the effect of his confession. He looked as if he were in two minds about something, glancing up and then down.

Finally he said in a low voice: "I think I can trust you. You have a straight look."

Pedro said nothing, but glanced a question.

"I've been told that hidalgos keep their word, though I've known several who didn't. How about you?"

"I do my best."

"Gad, I believe it," said García finally.

He dropped his hand to his belt and shoved the cross hilt of his poniard over the table. "Hold that and swear that you'll keep what I tell you to yourself."

Their eyes met. It was quiet for a moment in the room, so quiet that Pedro could hear the scamper of a rat across the floor.

"I swear."

The noise at the other table burst out again.

27

García cleared his throat. "The fact is, I was born in Jaén. I killed a man there sixteen years ago—killed him, being drunk. Plain murder, not fight. That's the curse of it. My mother's still alive, and I'm back to see her. If I'm taken—" García gave a jerk of the neck, then added, "I may need a friend. Does it happen that you are riding into town?"

"Yes, sir, at once."

"I'll ride with you, by your leave. We can talk better on the road."

It was evidently not García's style to do things quietly. He now roared for the reckoning, paid it with a flourish, and tried to pay Pedro's as well. There was an altercation over this with Sancho López and Catana, who clamored on their side that they did not choose to be dishonored by allowing Pedro de Vargas hereafter to pay for anything at the Rosario. Then, heaving himself up, and with a clumping of his huge riding boots, García betook himself to the door, carrying his saddlebags over one arm. When his mule was brought, he tipped the stableboy with silver, smote Sancho López between the shoulders, wished him good custom, and finally thrust a coin into Catana's hand.

"Buy yourself a new dress, sweetheart," he boomed, "and to hell with Dolores Quintero!"

"But it's *gold!*" she gasped. "It's a gold ducat. I've—I've only seen one before—once, the time Sancho López showed it to me. It'd buy ten dresses."

"Then buy a trousseau. And if you can't find a husband—which isn't likely—call on Juan García. I like your mettle, girl. We need your kind in the Indies."

They left amid benedictions. Pedro wondered whether this free-handed breeziness was peculiar to García, or whether life in the Islands had something to do with it.

But once in the glare of the empty noonday road, García's exuberance dropped off, and he jogged somberly along with his gaze on the distant walls and turrets of Jaén.

"It's the right hour to pass the gates," he observed. "Siesta time. They won't be thinking of the boy that cleared out from there with the help of Saint Christopher sixteen years ago. The town hasn't changed, from the looks of it. But I hope I've changed. Maybe I can get by if I look sharp and lie low. It's a risky business."

Once again that day, Pedro was floundering morally beyond his depths. He remembered his father's injunction against the Rosario, and admitted that if he hadn't turned in there, he would not have become involved in the present quandary. He must keep his word to García of course; but friendship was different. Like Campeador, who snobbishly

28

eyed the mule askance and kept as far away as possible, the young hidalgo had reservations about the man from the Indies. And yet there was something simple and winning and heart-warming about García. Pedro couldn't help feeling drawn to him.

"Do you know Señora Dorotea Romero?" García asked abruptly after a pause.

"You mean the old"—Pedro caught himself and changed "witch" to "midwife"—"who lives on the Calle Santo Tomás near the Castle?"

"The same, I guess, though she used to live on the Calle Rodolfo—there wouldn't be two of the same name and profession. Yes, she must be old, though I can't think of her that way." After another pause, García added with a certain pride, "She's my mother."

"Holy Virgin!" thought Pedro. But after all he didn't know for sure that Mother Dorotea was a witch. There was always talk about ugly old women who practised the trade of midwife.

"Is she still beautiful and stately?" García asked.

"Well—I haven't seen her for some time."

"She was very beautiful. And a good mother to me—the best anyone could have. By God she had a thin life—poor *Madrecita*—and what I did was cruel hard on her. But from now on she'll go in velvet like the best of them. She'll end her days on roses, *Madrecita* will. I'll move her to another town where she can have a house of her own, and a servant and a mule. She'll eat meat every day. Man, I lie awake nights thinking of it. . . . Which reminds me."

García stopped, but then, swallowing his last hesitation, went on. "I haven't done badly in late years. I had a nice little property in Santo Domingo that I sold out for a fair sum—two thousand pesos."

Pedro felt impressed.

"Some of it's here," said García, slapping his saddlebags. "Some of it's in a bill of change on the Medici house in Cádiz—as good as gold. Now, if I'm taken in Jaén before I get *Madrecita* away, the game's up as far as I'm concerned. But she'll get the money, d'you see? Her name's on the bill as well as mine. Will you look out for her? That's what I wanted to ask. She'll be robbed otherwise, being a woman and ignorant. I'll tell her about you."

He read the demur in Pedro's face.

"I've got no friend here. Lord, man, I'm not asking for myself—though, believe me, I've done penance for that madness sixteen years ago. I'm asking for her. If the son of Francisco de Vargas gave his word to help—"

He broke off with a note in his voice which Pedro could not resist.

29

"I'll do what I can."

"Your hand on it."

The two gauntlets met.

"*Compañero!* Comrade!" said García. Evidently he could think of no higher tribute.

Some spark passed between the two men, one of those spiritual currents that are forever contradicting the materialism of life. Pedro felt warmer and stronger for it—strong with the strength of the big, bluff adventurer who had suddenly become his friend.

"I can hang now with an easier mind," García added—"if it comes to hanging. But let me show you something."

Reaching into one flap of the saddlebags, he produced a small cloth package, and opened it on the pommel of the saddle. It contained a false reddish beard, which did not look false, Pedro thought, when attached to the contour of García's broad face. A lump of wax, inserted between gum and upper lip, altered his mouth. A streak of what might well be dust of travel changed the character of his nose. Several touches gave a new look to his eyes. While Pedro gaped, the overseas rover shrank step by step into an elderly merchant with round shoulders.

"*Ay María!*" he exclaimed.

"Neat, isn't it?" mumbled García, as yet unused to the lump of wax. "There's a rascal I know in Sanlúcar who makes a specialty of such tricks. He tips you off what disguise to use and trains you how to put it on. He's been schoolmaster to the ablest rogues in Spain. I paid him a fat price, but anything that saves your neck is worth money."

It seemed to Pedro that García's chances of survival in Jaén were much increased. Even if the constables remembered Juan García after sixteen years, they would hardly identify him in this disguise with the elderly man of affairs, provided that he didn't forget his role.

"Don't worry about that, my son," declared the latter, when Pedro mentioned it. "If your life's at stake, you don't get absent-minded."

The Moorish battlements of Jaén drew closer, sharp and clear-cut, with the slope of the town behind them. At last the two riders reached the gate and passed through without challenge. At the first cross street, they separated.

"Everyone knows the Casa de Vargas, if you want to reach me," Pedro said.

"And you know the Corona Inn," answered García. "It's a new place since my time. I'll put up there. If all goes well, you won't hear from me until I'm out of Jaén. Meanwhile, think about the West, *compañero.* If you decide for a venture overseas, let me know; I can advise you." García hesitated. "I may even go with you. *Adiós!*"

He turned the head of his mule. Pedro raised his hand. *"Adiós! Good luck! Qué vaya bien!"*

"Holy Saint Peter," he smiled to himself on the way home, "there are my three deeds! I've befriended a pagan heretic, saved the virtue of a barmaid, and given comfort to a murderer. If this was thy will, hold me excused, for I am only a fool."

On his heavenly throne, it may be that the impenetrable saint answered with a smile. For at that moment a soberly dressed serving-man, without badge or livery, approached Pedro in the narrow street outside the de Vargas house, and doffed his cap, while the other reined up.

"Señor Pedro de Vargas?" he said. "A message for Your Worship."

It was a small letter with a dainty seal. Pedro stared at it incredulously. The impossible had happened. He knew without opening it that the note was from Luisa de Çarvajal.

VI

DOÑA ANTONIA HERNÁNDEZ, duenna and cousin to Luisa de Carvajal, was considered too young a chaperon by conservative matrons of Jaén. At the age of thirty, a woman has not yet sufficiently forgotten her own youth. There was a certain amount of gossip about her in the miradors of the town, and perhaps with good reason, for she was lively, pleasure-loving, and resourceful. Though now a fortuneless widow, she had had a taste of court life and knew a great deal about the world. A love affair, even at second hand, especially when it concerned her young charge, Luisa, thrilled and stimulated her.

At the holy-water font, Pedro de Vargas, handsome and vigorous, had made a vivid impression on Doña Antonia. When they were back in the airy gallery, or mirador, overlooking the Marquis's Italian garden, she understood perfectly why Luisa stood dreaming, with her eyes on the far distance of the *campiña.* And at last, coming up with a smile, she slipped her arm around the girl's waist.

"I like him too, Cousin."

Luisa blushed, then leaned her head against the duenna's shoulder.

"He's better-looking than Juan Romer, don't you think, Cousin? Did you notice how his eyes light up when he smiles? And I love red hair! They say he's going to Italy. They say he's the best swordsman in Jaén, that his father taught him."

"They, who? You seem to know a great deal about him, *Primacita*. I hope you didn't forget yourself and ask questions."

"Of course not, Cousin. I heard some ladies talking at the Bishop's the first time I met him."

"Did you hear anything more?"

"No."

"Then it's my duty to tell you, little Cousin. He's young and poor. Your father could not possibly consider him. You know how it is. The Marquis plans a suitable match for you."

"I know."

The words and tone of voice expressed Luisa's attitude. She knew, without resenting the fact, that she must be given to some great lord whom her father chose for her. He might possibly be young and attractive, but the chances were against it. He would probably be years older than she, with a stout beard and bad teeth. He would exercise the authority of a father and the rights of a husband; would possess her body at his pleasure and beget children by God's will. She would be respected for her birth and rank, would go in front of most women at court; she might even, if she married a grandee, be called *prima* by the King. That part of it, from Luisa's standpoint, was most desirable. And then perhaps, according to Cousin Antonia, she might fall in love with a young cavalier, who would risk his life to keep trysts with her. It was a great sin, of course, but exciting and romantic, and women were naturally weak, Cousin Antonia said; they couldn't be expected to resist *every* temptation. But romance, if it came at all, came after marriage, not before.

"I know," she repeated.

Pedro de Vargas's eyes hovered in her mind like candle flames on the retina after the candles are blown out. They were more green than blue, and they had a queer fascination. She had felt almost a shock when he raised them to hers. It was still more of a shock when suddenly now she imagined him in the place of Cousin Antonia with his arm around her waist—a wicked thought, especially after mass. It embarrassed her and at the same time made her tingle all over, though her saint-like face revealed nothing.

"Pedro de Vargas means nothing to me of course," she said in her schooled, limpid voice to cover up the burn of her cheeks.

"Nothing?" smiled Antonia. "That's perfect then. A little flirtation

32

would do you no harm, Cousin. It's taking young men seriously that hurts. In marriage, some experience beforehand is a great advantage. You know better how to please your husband—and manage him."

Luisa, more sophisticated than she appeared, asked innocently, "Experience?"

"Yes, chance meetings at church, *unsigned* letters, a word or two through the grille of a gate. No harm at all. He swears eternal troth. He thinks his heart is broken when you marry. You sigh a little. It's the spice of youth."

"It must be fun," Luisa agreed, careful to keep the eagerness out of her voice. And then, betraying herself, "Do you think he likes me?"

Antonia gave her a squeeze. *"Válgame Dios!* He's mad about you! Any dunce can see that. If you lived in an ordinary house, you'd find him posted tonight under your window. But the poor boy can't besiege the Carvajal Palace. You'll have to give him a lead."

"How?"

"We'll think it over."

Antonia's eyes danced. Whatever happened, it was at least a pastime for an empty summer morning, usually so dull and hot behind the curtains of the mirador. As for Luisa, brand-new ideas were popping in her head like roasted chestnuts. She was being actually permitted by her duenna to think about a boy—not an imaginary boy such as she pictured before going to sleep at night, but a real boy with green-blue eyes and curly, bronze-colored hair! She might be allowed even to talk with him. Perhaps he wasn't so poor after all. That was the one fly in the ointment, because instinctively Luisa did not think much of poor people. Still, he was the son of Francisco de Vargas, and that partly made up for it. Luisa's heart raced under the strait jacket of her stays.

"What fun! May I call Sancha to unlace me? It's rather hot."

Antonia consented. "Yes, she can put me at ease too. The Marquis will not visit us this morning. They told me he was joining a man hunt for one of Diego de Silva's servants. *There's* an attractive man—Diego de Silva."

"Father says he has great holdings," commented Luisa absently.

"Rich as Croesus," Antonia nodded, "and of the first fashion. A relative of the Bishop of Burgos."

With scraping of brocade and creaking of laces, the ladies were divested of their church attire and of numerous petticoats. Luisa's trim figure expanded only slightly, but the duenna's a good deal. Exasperated, Señora Hernández cuffed Sancha for pinching her at the unlacing. They then slipped into the long, negligee gowns of the period,

33

and at the same time, without knowing it, slipped forward in costume several hundred years. Sancha, kneeling, pulled the cruel, tight shoes from her mistresses' feet and replaced them with Moorish slippers. Then, at Antonia's direction, she brought a plate of candied fruit, placed it on a tabouret within reach of the couch, and retired.

Antonia, reclining, selected a fig and toyed with it a moment. A faint, flower-laden breeze stirred the window curtains. Luisa, seating herself on a cushion near by, looked up expectantly.

"That's better," Antonia sighed. "What were we talking about? Yes, de Vargas. In stays, one can't even think about love, can one?"

She nibbled the fruit. Her eyes deepened.

"We'll send him a letter, *Primacita*."

"What kind of letter? I could never write one."

"We'll do it together."

"What fun!"

Señora Hernández gazed at the ceiling. Her lips moved. She smiled.

"Let me hear, Cousin," urged Luisa.

"Just a minute. Get the inkhorn and paper. Write down what I say." And when Luisa was ready, Antonia dictated, while the girl, who was not too handy a penman, labored with the tip of her tongue between her lips.

"Señor Cavalier, It is said that the devil dislikes holy water, which proves that Don Cupid is no devil, because he appears to thrive on it. If you would know more of the matter, you might apply at the gate of a certain garden tomorrow evening at nightfall. Which garden? Oh, sir, let Cupid instruct you."

"Why not tonight?" Luisa let slip before she could catch herself.

"For many reasons, my dove," Antonia instructed. "In the first place, you must not let him think that you are in too much of a hurry. In the second place, you must let him languish. In the third place, the Marquis de Carvajal is invited out tomorrow evening, and we shall be undisturbed. Know, my child, that the art of love is extremely subtle."

"You are very clever," Luisa admired. "But how can we send him the letter? Whom can we trust?"

The duenna nodded. "You're learning. Of course the chief point of love is secrecy. Don't worry, though. I'll send my servant, Esteban. He's carried messages to gentlemen—" She coughed. "I mean he knows me and knows what side his bread is buttered on."

"Thanks, darling Cousin!" Forgetting decorum, Luisa threw her arms around the other's neck. "And you'll teach me what I should say tomorrow night?"

34

"Yes." Antonia was enjoying herself.

"No girl but me has such a darling duenna."

"I'm probably very weak, little rose."

She gave Luisa a long kiss.

VII

Peace after toil, port after stormy seas. No words could better describe Francisco de Vargas's retirement from active life. Though at times— especially after a visit or letter from some old comrade—he still discussed the possibility of returning to the service of king and honor in the arena of Italy, and cast yearning eyes on his weapons, he was becoming happily reconciled to the comforts of home and garden.

In this disposition, Doña María warmly encouraged him. She pointed out that since their marriage in Florence twenty years ago, he had spent little more time with her than was enough to beget their children. She doubted, indeed, whether they would have had children at all, except for the fact that she had passed some of those years in her father's house, and had thus been available between campaigns.

"Honor, sir," she declared with Italian good sense, "is all very well until it becomes an excuse for travel and junketing. You have had all you need of it. A man of your years with a bad knee should not be elbowing young fellows and roaring *Santiago* in a charge."

"Do you call sword thrusts and wounds junketing, my love?" he protested, for she had put her finger on the weak point.

"Yes, sir, I do," she answered frankly. "But wounds and sword thrusts aren't the whole matter. In the service, you meet your friends; there's gossip and drinking, dicing and wenching, as you know very well."

"You talk as if I were a young dog like Pedro," returned her husband with a half-smile. "I trust that I have outlived such sins. As to my knee, you must admit that, once on horseback, I can hold my own against most gentlemen with lance, sword, or mace, as I proved last year in the tournament at Córdoba."

"And my heart was in my mouth every second," interjected Doña María.

"Even on foot," continued the other, "I can still match our Pedro, though I grant it costs too much breath and sweat. He's very promising."

35

At that point, Doña María always clinched the argument. "Yes, and what becomes of his promise if you return to the wars? We certainly cannot afford to keep more than one of you in the army. What becomes of honor for him? What becomes of the dowry for our daughter if she is to be married? What becomes of me who love you, *querido mío?*"

But in truth he did not need much urging. It was pleasant to be one of Jaén's most respected citizens, to be called on as judge in matters of sport or punctilio, and to be the idol of his wife and children. He gradually became almost as proud of his vines and orchard on the western slope beyond the city as he had once been of the Great Captain's favor; and a bumper of his golden wine, the envy of the district, or a salver of purple plums from the orchard, was nearly as close to his heart as the earlier drums and trumpets of fame.

He had built an open pavilion on a terrace, overlooking his trees and vines, and spent many spring and summer evenings there. If at times the approaching obligation of fitting Pedro out for the wars in a worthy fashion counseled the sale of the property, he kept putting it off, as a man who clings to a final luxury. That he might have to sell it was plain, for accouterments and traveling expenses came high, and his small revenue could not meet the charge; but he would not sell this year perhaps. He had won much from ransoms and from the intaking of cities during the Italian campaigns; he had also spent much, as befitted his rank, and he had a casual attitude toward money. Perhaps, after all, a loan rather than a sale might tide things over until Pedro could win a ransom or prize for himself.

On the terrace or within the pavilion, he liked to take the air with his family and eat supper from the generous baskets carried by Mouse, the donkey. At times his twelve-year-old daughter, Mercedes, who had a gift with the lute, would sing favorite ballads; Doña María busied herself with needlework; while often the old cavalier would discourse on campaigns and captains, pedigrees and heraldry, fine points of manners and the code of honor, which formed an essential and fascinating part of young Pedro's education.

In front and slightly below them stretched the plain, rich in olive groves; a neighboring brook grew loud toward evening; the crimson sun withdrew beneath the horizon. Often they lingered until the moon came out and the shrilling of the cicadas filled the night. So the afternoon of Don Francisco's life drew to a leisurely and reminiscent close.

It was only fitting that Pedro's name-day should be mildly celebrated at the pavilion. In their next best, if not their very best, clothes, the four members of the de Vargas family sat on three sides of the small table so that everyone could look out over the landscape. Señor de Vargas was fastidious in small matters. He liked good plate on the table and fine linen. There must be a servingman prompt with ewer and napkin for fingers greasy from the handling of meat. Everyone must have his or her appointed silver cup.

"Like good tapestry," he used to observe, "a noble life is the result of small stitches."

This afternoon, he was richly dressed in black velvet, and he wore a heavy gold chain with a medal of Saint Francis about his neck. Because of the heat, he had removed his cap and sat bald-headed, though a fringe of hair still resisted time. Pedro had resumed his scarlet doublet. Doña María, as became her age, wore purple; and Mercedes had put on her saffron gown. The rays of the setting sun added color to the clothes and a gleam to the silver.

When the last bones had been tossed to the dogs, and when wine and fruit were brought, the old gentleman raised his goblet to Pedro.

"Long life, my son, and fame!" After drinking the health, he added: "Do not be depressed about your failure to bring in de Silva's servant. Not every enterprise succeeds. You laid your plans well, but finding a man in the sierras is difficult. As a matter of fact," he went on, "I'm not too sorry, because I have no great fondness for his master."

Pedro flushed. His pensiveness had nothing to do with Coatl, but concerned a letter, the stiff edges of which he could feel at that moment through his shirt. He was thinking how long it seemed until tomorrow night.

"Thank you, sir."

"Probably," the other continued, "we will not be having many more of your name-days together. Next year, if God wills, we shall drink to you abroad and, I hope, in the field. After beating the Swiss at Marignano, it isn't likely that the young French King, Francis, will rest too long on his laurels."

"They say his court at Fontainebleau is the gayest anywhere," Mercedes put in.

Her father nodded. *"Creo que sí.* There are no higher-spirited or better-bred *caballeros* anywhere than the French. And apparently young Don Francis is most accomplished. The more I think of it," he went on hopefully, "the better your prospects look, son Pedro. We have three young and valorous monarchs in Europe today: Henry of England, Francis of France, and our own King, Don Carlos, whom God cherish. Where youth is, sparks will be flying."

Pedro roused himself. The subject was almost as absorbing as Luisa de Carvajal.

"You know, sir, coming back today, I met a man" (it was not expedient to state where) "who has spent many years in the Indies."

"And I have no doubt he's a notable rogue," grunted the older de Vargas.

It was so near a guess that Pedro felt startled.

"Why do you think so, sir?"

"Because it has been that way from the beginning. When the Admiral made his first voyage twenty-four years ago, he took the prison scum of Palos and Cádiz with him. Even my good friend, Alonso de Ojeda, who went along and was a young man of promise, became corrupted in the Indies and behaved, I understand, no better than a pirate. So it has been always. Rascal seamen, deserters, lawbreakers, gold hounds, young cadets on the loose, and rabble. There are a few exceptions, but not many. . . . What about this fellow?"

"He spoke of new lands, empires, gold."

The elder de Vargas stuck his lip out. "That *proves* he was a rogue. They found some islands with a lot of naked savages on them. I'm told they also found leagues of swamp land further west with more savages. What gold and pearls they found haven't paid for the good ships wrecked or the funds wasted, let alone brought in a return. For a while there was grand talk of treasure from this evil country, but it has amounted to nothing. Empires? Pooh! What has Spain ever got out of the New World but the French Sickness, the cursed pox, that the Admiral's ne'er-do-wells brought back with them!"

"And yet, sir," Pedro argued, "the man said that he left Spain poor and has now two thousand pesos."

"Probably a lie. Make it fifty. Those I have met from across seas are always big talkers."

Pedro clung desperately to his new enthusiasm. "It was only, sir, that I thought it might be possible—it might be interesting—"

"Oho!" said his father.

"To look into the matter."

"What matter?"

"As an alternative to Italy, sir. We have peace with France—"

Don Francisco slapped his palm on the table so vigorously that Doña María jumped. "Exactly! I thought that was in the wind. Every boy in the two Castiles is cracked on the subject of picking up gold and Indian slaves for nothing, not to speak of an empire or so. Listen. I

38

had a friend in Estremadura, Martín Cortés de Monroy, as good a captain of foot as any in the army, a poor, but honorable man. He raised his son—I believe the name was Hernán—to be the support of his old age. He headed him for Italy under Don Gonsalvo himself. Well, the boy, who was an idle scapegrace, got moonstruck about the New World. Empires and mountains of gold or what-not. So he took the bit in his teeth and sailed for the Islands. He was just about your age."

Señor de Vargas cooled his ire with a draught of wine.

"You must not excite yourself, my love," soothed Doña María. "You ought not to accuse our son—"

"I am not accusing him; I am instructing him," returned her husband. "That was thirteen or fourteen years ago. What happened? Well, this Hernán Cortés, after being in and out of jail a couple of times, gets mixed up with a trashy girl in one of the Islands, whom he is forced to marry. He runs a farm there, so his father told me, and has worked up to the wonderful position of alcalde in a twopenny village called Santiago. That's what his empire amounted to, and a deuced scurvy one. I could give you a dozen other examples. No," Señor de Vargas concluded, "let this be understood once and for all. You are not going to the Indies. Get that nonsense out of your head this instant. You will follow the regular army career. It means work, but it means solid advancement."

Silence followed this outburst. Doña María half smiled, because she knew that her husband's rough voice covered up a very gentle heart. Mercedes, excited to hear the discussion of such weighty matters, sat with her lips parted. Pedro accepted what he had been anticipating all along. Italy might not be so exciting as the Western World, but it had advantages.

Almost at once Don Francisco's irritation died down. He fingered his gold chain and cleared his throat a couple of times. Then, with the look of a man who has been keeping a pleasant surprise up his sleeve and decides that this is the moment to spring it, he said with attempted casualness:—

"You're right about the present peace with France. I've had a plan for some time which I didn't want to tell you of until it ripened. No use raising false hopes. I had a letter yesterday from the Señor de Bayard in Grenoble."

The stir that greeted this announcement equaled Don Francisco's expectation. María de Vargas lowered her needlework, and her round face became an O of interest. Pedro forgot momentarily about Luisa de Carvajal. Mercedes's dark eyes, already too big for her small face, became still larger.

"Señor de Bayard!" echoed Pedro. "A *letter* from him?"

The name of the French chevalier "without fear and without reproach" was one to conjure with in military circles of that day. It was already legendary, though Bayard himself had not passed the middle forties. From the marches of Flanders to the mountains of Navarre, from the Alps to Naples, there was hardly a battlefield of the last twenty years which had not seen his pennon. He had slain the Spanish knight, Sotomayor, in one of the most famous duels of the age; he had taken a leading part in the day-long, bloody combat at Trani; he was one of the heroes of Fornuovo, Ravenna, Marignano; he had been selected as the only one from whom the young King of France would receive the order of knighthood. If Gonsalvo de Córdoba was the most distinguished general of the period, Bayard was its most illustrious single champion. Around his crest blazed the glory of departing chivalry.

He and Don Francisco had fought each other with mutual admiration for ten years, and his name was a household word in the de Vargas family. It was one of the old cavalier's titles of distinction that he had lost his front teeth from a blow of the good Chevalier's mace at Cerignola, but had given as good as he got by unhorsing the beloved enemy in a later melee. He liked to describe the charge of the French horse at Ravenna.

"There was a forest of pennons. I knew most of them and in front, as always, I could pick out the Señor de Bayard's. It looked like an old friend. I said to Pedro de Paz, 'See there! We'll have hot work.' He laughed and tossed his lance up and caught it, vowing that no day had ever promised better. We faced the Duke of Lorraine's lances, whom the Chevalier commanded. They came on like a wave, six hundred of them, yelling 'France!' and 'Bayard!' We met them with 'Santiago!' Holy Virgin, what a crash! But I kept my seat and headed toward the lion pennon. Everybody wanted the honor of engaging Pierre de Bayard, and he was hard to reach. All at once I saw a great black horse rearing up on me and heard Bayard's war shout. My horse, El Moro, met him with teeth and hoofs. We could get in no more than a couple of blows before we were swept apart. But he recognized me. He raised his sword and called, 'Ha! Monseigneur de Vargas!' I have never seen him since."

That a letter should have arrived from such a personage was more than enough to stir the family of a retired soldier in southern Spain. A letter from the King would hardly have been so exciting.

"Bayard!" exclaimed Doña María. And lapsing into Italian, *"Che cosa!"*

"I wrote him four months ago," said Don Francisco, "and he has given an immediate answer by the hand of his clerk. The good gentleman never learned to write, I believe, though he can sign his name. He is now governor of the French city of Grenoble, a place most convenient to Italy when the next war breaks out. I have given great thought to your education, son Pedro, because a good schooling is worth more than treasure, and I could think of no cavalier under whom you could study the profession of arms with as much profit."

Pedro's eyes were glowing. Mercedes caught her breath.

"I asked him whether he would graciously receive you into his household while peace lasts."

Having worked his audience to a pitch, Señor de Vargas now tantalized it by removing a travel-stained letter from his pocket with great deliberation. A blob of red wax, stamped with a signet, showed on the outside.

"It's in French, of course," said Don Francisco, pleased with his knowledge of that language. *"Au moult preux et moult valoureux—"*

Pedro could no longer contain himself; he leaned across the table. "What does he say, Father? Does he say yes?"

"Steady, son. Everything in its order. The noble gentleman is kind enough to recall with pleasure our meetings on various fields. It is like him to overvalue my merit, but he was always generous. He remarks truly that we are growing old and that we will never see such pleasant days again." Don Francisco's finger crawled down the page. "He regrets the injury to my knee, but hopes (note this, how gallantly put!) that it will not deprive him of the honor of encountering me in the next campaign. He kisses your hands, María." De Vargas paused for effect. "And he will be happy to welcome our son to his company of lances. He will give him every opportunity in his power. . . . Well, Pedro, how's that? Where's the New World now!"

It was nowhere—blotted out by this magnificent prospect. France, the patronage of the Great Cavalier, the prestige of having been trained by Bayard! Pedro sat with his fists clenched and his cheeks red.

"Pedrito, querido mío!" exclaimed Doña María. "How proud I am!"

Mercedes slipped around to her father's side and gazed at the signature on the letter, bold and rough as if it had been cut in wood.

"Look, Pedro," she said, "look!"

At that instant the dogs burst into an explosion of barking and dashed for the path leading up from the road to the pavilion. Señor

41

de Vargas called them back. An unhurried footstep could be heard approaching. Then, around the corner, appeared a tall, handsomely dressed figure.

It was Diego de Silva.

VIII

PEDRO ONCE MORE had the impression of a large black bat transformed into a man, though nothing in de Silva's appearance, except his small chin and big, pointed ears, accounted for it. He was dressed in the latest fashion, with gold points to his doublet, a touch of lace at the throat, elegant riding boots, and a beautifully hilted sword. As he fondled the latter with a long, tapering hand, the last ray of sunset struck fire from a diamond on his forefinger. His scornful, unquiet eyes looked darker and larger than they actually were by contrast with the pallor of his skin. He moved and spoke with the grace of a finished courtier. But in spite of his glitter, something furtive and deformed, something *nocturnal,* clung to him.

Civilities were exchanged. De Silva raised Doña María's hand to his lips—she made him as low a curtsy as her plumpness permitted; he confused little Mercedes with a couple of compliments; greeted Don Francisco with respect and exchanged bows with Pedro. He explained that he had been inspecting his vineyards, which bracketed the de Vargas property, and couldn't resist the temptation of dropping in.

"We are honored, señor," bowed the elder de Vargas, overlooking his irritation of the morning. "If we had been warned of your coming, we would have provided a suitable reception. As it is, we can offer only meager refreshment. Pedro, fill a cup for our guest. The fruit, sir, is not bad, if I may presume so far."

"Your kindness embarrasses me," returned de Silva.

He drank to his hosts, then took the chair which had been placed for him on Doña María's right. He observed that the weather, while excellent for the crops, was much too warm for riding, and that he felt slightly tired from his hunt for the Indian servant.

"You did not get on his traces, then?" said Don Francisco.

De Silva shrugged. "No, but he'll be picked up. A savage from the Indies won't get far in these mountains. I've sent word to Granada and Cádiz." His black glance rested a moment on Pedro. "You didn't join us."

Perspiring under his doublet, Pedro explained his idea of searching in the other direction.

"Ah," said de Silva.

There was a chilly note in his voice. Pedro thought he knew the reason for de Silva's call and braced himself to meet a complaint about the two huntsmen. But surprisingly the subject was dropped.

"Excellent wine!" continued the other, smacking his lips. "Which recalls something very close to my heart, Don Francisco. Have you considered the offer I made you for your vineyard?"

So, that was his object. It annoyed the elder de Vargas that his guest should bring up a business matter in the presence of the family, a topic that ought to be discussed in private.

"Yes, I've considered it."

"You see," de Silva went on, "except for your land, I own this entire slope. I have acquired it piecemeal over several years. It would greatly convenience me if you sold, so that I could round out my property. And the price offered seemed to me fair."

"Entirely."

"Have you reached a conclusion?"

The de Vargas family held its breath.

"I do not wish to sell for the present, sir."

"Oh, come, sir!" de Silva urged. "The price is no great matter. We won't split hairs. I offered you five hundred ducats; suppose we make it seven hundred. It's an absurd figure, but I've set my mind on the thing. You can't say no to seven hundred ducats."

Hot waves began pulsing along the old cavalier's veins. The fellow seemed to think that all he needed was to jingle money—as if a de Vargas were a tradesman. He not only intruded on a family's privacy, but sat there parleying like a Jew. Saucy malapert! thought the old gentleman.

On her side, Doña María gave him a disturbed glance. With Italian realism, she could see what the proposed sum meant. It would entirely cover the rest of Pedro's education and add weight to Mercedes's dot. Then, with the royal pension and the couple of benefices they held, life would be comfortable enough. Even if it meant sacrificing—

"I do not wish to sell for the present, sir."

"Ah," said de Silva. He looked bewildered a moment; then his eyes kindled, and a white band showed across his forehead. "Ah. Well, we'll drop the matter, señor, for this time, though I'll be cursed if I understand."

He was quite honest. He moved in a world where every value has its

43

price in gold. When that yardstick failed, he was bewildered, angry, and scornful.

"Someone told me," he went on, "that you planned to send your son abroad." His voice had a patronizing drawl that stirred the roots of Pedro's hair. "Which is costly, as no one knows better than I. It seemed to me that perhaps a sale would accommodate you."

Don Francisco was doing his best to remain civil, but he felt the surges of wrath gaining on him. He tried to shut his mind to them. Because de Silva had no manners, it did not discharge him from his obligations as a host. He clung to that.

"As it happened, we were discussing the matter when you came, sir," he answered with more of a lisp than usual. "In view of the peace, I plan sending my son to France. The Señor de Bayard has graciously consented to give him a place in his company."

"Ah?" De Silva did not seem impressed.

"It might interest you to see his letter. We were in the course of reading it."

De Vargas proudly handed over the sacred document, but the other gave it no more than a perfunctory glance.

"Hm-m," he said. "Yes, quite so." And having returned it: "Why Bayard? The choice amazes me. With all respect to the Chevalier as a stanch old war dog, isn't he a good deal of a relic? We're living in modern times. Why not send your son to one of the fashionable courts? I should think the household of Monsieur de Bayard would be as out-of-date as my grandmother's coif."

De Vargas's mouth felt fever-dry. With a shaking hand, he raised his cup and emptied it. Pedro's face was rigid. Doña María looked appealingly at her husband.

"Ha!" choked Don Francisco at last, his head swimming. "The Señor de Bayard is my friend."

"No offense, of course," said de Silva airily. "It's no business of mine. I was only surprised. Or if not a court, why not the Indies? A youngster can pick up experience and perhaps money there. As a matter of fact, I intend to make the voyage myself fairly soon."

Pedro exchanged a glance with his mother. The look on his father's face would have made him laugh at any other time. It implied that of all places in the world, the Indies was where Diego de Silva best belonged.

"Naturally I shall not remain there," the latter continued. "My friend, Diego Velásquez, Governor of Cuba, has promised me a bargain in land and Indians. It ought to be a sound investment. Besides, as you may know, I am a familiar of the Holy Office and will make a survey for the Suprema. The Inquisitor of Jaén, our good Father Ignacio de Lora, has been chosen to accompany me. We fear that heresy needs investigating in the Islands."

At this reference to the Inquisition, a shadow, an almost palpable chill, descended on the pavilion. It happened in any company where the dread name was mentioned. A kingdom within the kingdom, a power greater than the King's, a despotism more complete than any yet invented, it paralyzed the human soul with terror. It did not represent the Catholic Church. Indeed, it represented the very reverse of Catholic, a peculiar Spanish development, narrow, local, fanatic; a parasite repudiated by traditional Catholic thought then as well as since. Not until four hundred years later would the world again be visited by a similar curse. Secret denunciation—friend against friend, child against parent, enemy against enemy—the thought of dungeon, torture, whip and stake, beggary and infamy, were the ideas which the name conjured up. No one was safe; no one was too innocent to be proved guilty. In view of the menace, many noblemen and others, who could prove the purity of their blood, their *limpieza*, free of Jewish or Moorish taint, joined the ranks of the Inquisition. These were the familiars of the Holy Office. The affiliation was valuable for many reasons; above all it gave added power and relative security.

Don Francisco cleared his throat. "Yes, I remember hearing that you are an intimate of the Inquisitor's."

Suddenly de Silva's restless eyes, forever mocking and probing, stopped as if a new thought had occurred to him. He half-closed them and nodded. "A great privilege. By the way, sir, it seems strange to me that a man of your name and fame should not be one of us. All good Christians ought to unite in defense of the Faith."

"I'm not a theologian," snapped the other.

"Nor am I. It's an honor merely to serve the Cause as a humble soldier."

De Vargas said nothing.

"Of course I regret that the Holy Office must at times use severity," de Silva went on. "But what would you have? If bloodletting and dosing are often necessary to save the body, one cannot object to medicine that saves the soul. The reverend fathers are heavenly physicians. It is wonderful, sir, to watch their patience and skill in discovering and treating the devilish disease of heresy—the worst of diseases, as you must admit. They trace the slightest symptom to its

45

roots until the cancer is laid bare. I take it, you have not attended an examination?"

"No," grunted de Vargas.

The other leaned back reminiscently with the tips of his long fingers together.

"It's a valuable experience. I recall the last examination I had the privilege of watching. It was of a woman, María Oqueda. Note how alert the reverend fathers are. It was brought to their attention that she did not eat pork and that she bathed on Saturday. You and I would have made nothing of this, but not so the learned friars. They scented disease; the woman was arrested. Before the tribunal, she maintained, of course, that pork disagreed with her and that she bathed for reasons of cleanliness. Such excuses did not hoodwink the Inquisitor. She was stripped bare as my hand—"

"Remember that there are ladies here," de Vargas growled.

"No offense, my good sir. In the treatment of this ailment, the patients are stripped—a plain fact. She was then placed on the ladder, and the cords were tightened. What an outcry, señor! You'd hardly have thought it human. But obstinate? My word! Except for screams and babble, they could get nothing from her. I spare you details which may offend the ladies. This lasted more than an hour. She was then moved to the bench and given the water torment, a curious operation. Time passed, but the zeal of the reverend fathers did not slacken. For the sake of this woman's soul, they even postponed their dinner."

Doña María was white to the lips, and Mercedes, getting up, had hidden her face against her mother's shoulder. Pedro, disgusted, glanced at his father, whose sallow cheeks were flushed.

"They got results in the end," de Silva continued easily. "The woman confessed everything they suspected. She admitted practising Jewishness in secret. No one would have imagined such a crime, for she was born Christian. You can see by that the astuteness and patience of the Inquisitor, whom God must have inspired. The woman's goods were confiscated, and you may recall that she was burned in the last auto-da-fé. God forgive her sins!"

There was a bleak silence. De Silva suppressed a smile.

"And one can never tell," he added, "at what age the disease will strike. I remember the examination of a boy of twelve. He refused to bear witness in the case of his parents and was hoisted on the strappado. They then—"

"One moment, sir," interrupted de Vargas, lisping ominously. "We have had enough of this talk. It is unpleasant."

46

De Silva looked amazed. "Unpleasant, to know that there are champions of the Faith who spend themselves to uproot the detestable sin of heresy? Don't you approve of the methods of the Holy Office?"

"I told you that I wasn't a theologian, and I have never been a hangman's valet. It ought to be unnecessary to point out that certain things aren't discussed in mixed company—details of the lazaret, the jakes, or the torture room."

"Pretty squeamish for an old soldier," de Silva sneered. "I didn't think you were so lily-livered. I'm sure the ladies enjoy it—don't you, Doña María? As for the Holy Office, it hardly seems to me that you are overrespectful."

The dike burst. Francisco de Vargas straightened up in his chair, his nose like a beak, his mouth grim, and the light of battle in his eyes. But in contrast, when he spoke, his voice was very gentle.

"Look you, sir, I'm not used to being reproved by young popinjays. Lily-livered? Before you were born, I was fighting the Moors. I have given more blood for the Faith than you have in your body. But I have fought men. I haven't stood slavering in a jail over the torture of women and children. Humble soldier of the Holy Office, indeed! As to manners, you seem to forget where you are and who I am. Do I make myself plain?"

Doña María tried to speak, but could not get a word out. Pedro leaned forward, intent and prepared. But de Silva seemed unimpressed, though his black eyes danced.

He got up carelessly. "Not quite plain, Don Francisco. Later perhaps we can clear matters up. For instance, I'm not sure why you wish to pick a quarrel with me. Though injured by this young ruffian of a son of yours, I came here peaceably and alone. It was a mistake. I should have brought witnesses."

"Injured?" exclaimed de Vargas. "Injured?"

"If I attacked two of your servants, opened the face of one and broke the arm of another, wouldn't you call it injury?"

Don Francisco stared. "What do you mean, *por Dios?*"

Pedro's time had come. He stood up a little flustered, but with his eyes level on de Silva. "Add that your men set their dogs on a girl and then assaulted her. It makes a difference."

"Oho!" interjected his father.

De Silva nodded. "Yes, I forgot. The rogues were amusing themselves with your son's sweetheart, a tavern slut from the Rosario, a notable whore named Pérez. Call it assaulting if you like. She lives by assaults."

"It's a lie." Pedro drew closer with his fists clenched.

"And having ridden down my men, he fondles the strumpet, puts her on his horse, and so back with them embracing to the privacy of the Rosario. Is that a lie too? Or did my fellow see wrong? At least the town will be amused to hear about it."

In the stricken quiet of the pavilion, Pedro was aware of his father's glazed look, his mother's distress, the pumping of his own heart. He remembered the scene with Catana at church, and how that clinched matters against him.

"So you didn't know of it?" de Silva went on. "I suppose he gave you to understand that he was hunting my slave. A fine story! I wish I knew the real truth of that part of it. And yet he calls me a liar!"

Pedro wished desperately now that he had told his parents about Catana. He would have told them, except for the ban against the Rosario and the fuss his mother had made at the church. The worst of it was the blow to his father's pride.

Francisco de Vargas got up.

"I did not know," he said coldly. "My son failed to inform me. He and I will settle that matter between us. If your men were innocent, I shall pay any proper claim. I shall report the affair tomorrow to the Corregidor and leave it in his hands. So much for that. It has nothing to do with what we were discussing—the subject of your manners, sir. If anything I said displeases you, I shall be glad to give you satisfaction at your pleasure."

"And I," said Pedro.

De Silva walked to the threshold of the pavilion and stood there a moment, a dark silhouette against the evening outside.

"I do not fight with striplings about their doxies," he answered with a half-laugh. "Or with cripples."

"Be careful," said Don Francisco.

"As to satisfaction," smiled the other, "leave that to me."

His footsteps died away before anyone spoke.

"I'm afraid," faltered Doña María. "What will he do?"

"Do?" retorted her husband. "Nothing. The man's a coward. He can do nothing against me." Then, turning to Pedro, "Did you hunt that slave?"

"Yes, sir."

"Have you an affair with Catana Pérez?"

"I have not."

"Did you visit the Rosario inn today against my orders?"

"Yes, sir."

48

"Very well, my son, for that I shall give you a sound flogging when we return to the *casa*."

— IX —

STRIPPED TO THE WAIST and kneeling at his father's *prie-dieu* in front of a gaunt crucifix on the wall, Pedro de Vargas braced himself to receive punishment. If he lived to be an old man, he would never forget that particular crucifix, which he had stared at on many such occasions. Other details of the severe, bare room that served his father as cabinet and study would remain vivid: the narrow, high-backed chairs of black oak; the table with its tall candlesticks, where Pedro had sweated at his lessons; the half-dozen leather-bound books, which constituted the family library; the rack of weapons and stands of armor, which were more interesting than anything else. But the crucifix was stamped on his mind more intimately and unforgettably.

He felt no resentment at being whipped, nor did Don Francisco flog him with any passion. It was more like receiving and administering a dose of bitter medicine. Pedro knew that he had disobeyed orders by visiting the Rosario, and that, if found out, he must pay for it. His father knew that discipline must be taught; it belonged to Pedro's military apprenticeship. It belonged also to that training in fortitude and scorn of pain which toughened the Spanish soldier.

Riding whip in hand, the elder de Vargas glanced with pride at his son's strong back, the ridges of muscles along the spine, his powerful shoulders and biceps, the small waist.

"I must attempt to make you remember that orders are orders," he said. "Have you any excuse?"

"Only, sir, that the Rosario inn was close at hand, and that I was more than hungry after hunting for the Indian. I had had no breakfast."

"Pooh!" said Don Francisco. "My dear son, reflect a moment. Often in your career you will be called upon to stand thirst and hunger for days at a time. Suppose you are sent on a foray by your captain. You must carry out the directions, food or no food. But in this case you could not even resist appetite for a few hours. I hope you understand how unmanly that was."

"Yes, sir."

"Moreover, in this case, you deliberately disobeyed. I have often told

49

you that you can never expect to command unless you learn to obey. Is that clear?"

"Yes, sir."

Pedro shifted uneasily on the knee piece of the *prie-dieu*, which was ridged in order to make the act of prayer an act of penance at the same time. The skin of his back prickled. He wished that his father would get on with it.

"Now," Don Francisco continued, "I wish to explain once more why I will not permit you to frequent the Rosario. Remember, when you become an officer, that it is always unjust to punish a man unless he knows why he is being punished. I forbid the Rosario because it is the resort of low company, muleteers, vagabonds, and bandits. It is unbefitting your name to be seen there. In such a place, you acquire bad manners and bad habits. A bad habit formed in youth is no small thing. Do you understand?"

"Yes, sir."

"Finally, I wish to ask whether this girl, Catana Pérez, is such as Diego de Silva described her. I am not a hypocrite. I have had sweethearts in my time; but for the most part they were obliging wenches and not professionals."

Pedro turned to look up at his father. "On my word, sir, de Silva lied. Catana is a strange girl and wild. More than that I don't know; but she is not a trull."

"I'm glad to hear it," said the other. "I take your word for it. De Silva has every mark of a liar. . . . And now, my son, I shall give you twenty lashes."

Pedro clenched his teeth, and the blows were laid on with clock-like regularity. They brought the water to his eyes, but not a murmur to his lips. To have cried out would have been shameful. He clamped his arms about the *prie-dieu* and stared at the crucifix.

Meanwhile, the door, which Don Francisco had locked as usual, was under siege from the other side by Doña María. If Pedro was silent, his mother was not. The punishment went on to a running accompaniment of knocks, demands to be let in, entreaties, and threats. Don Francisco might be at present in the saddle, but he could look forward to a bad half hour later. When the lamentation changed from Spanish to Italian, and he was compared to Nero of Rome and Attila the Hun, he knew that the situation was dangerous.

"Patience, my dear," he called, hastening execution; "we have almost finished." And to himself, "Heaven help me! What a nuisance women are in education!

"There," he said at last—"twenty. It grieves me to flog you, son. My compliments, by the way—you stood your punishment well."

Then, with obvious misgiving, Don Francisco opened the door to a torrent of maternal sympathy.

Mercedes de Vargas always cried when her brother was beaten. Still catching her breath, she now stood in his upstairs bedroom, holding the pot of goose grease which Doña María gently applied to Pedro's welts. In the flare of the candles, her sallow child's face looked swollen and miserable.

"On your name-day too!" she repeated.

"Cheer up, *hermanita*," he smiled. "I've had a wonderful name-day."

Doña María's mouth worked as she spread the grease. "Your father seems to forget that he is no longer in the army," she said in a pinched voice.

"It was nothing," Pedro boasted. "I could have stood ten times as much."

"Of course there was that strumpet," mused the other, as if something had to be conceded. "But we will not speak of her. I know you will not break my heart. . . . Now you must go to bed, darling, and rest."

"I don't want to go to bed."

"Please, dear."

"No! *Caramba!* I couldn't sleep at this hour."

Worse than his father's blows was his mother's babying. It was only nine o'clock. The wakeful Andalusian night had just begun. Through the open window came a babble of voices from the street, a snatch of song, the stir of the town reviving from the sun-afflicted day. Pedro had plans for the evening. He wanted to reconnoiter the walls of the Marquis de Carvajal's garden; not that he did not know them perfectly, but he had to haunt them. He had to stand in the moonlight by the gate and dream of tomorrow night. Perhaps another miracle might happen, and he would catch a glimpse of Luisa; or she might see him; or at least he could peer through the gate and try to imagine which window of the palace was hers. Anyhow the purlieus were sacred, and he was drawn to them like a moth to the candle.

"I'd only slap mosquitoes and sweat," he went on. "And I can't lie on my back."

"Very well," Doña María yielded. "Then you must wear my lawn shift. Your shirt is too coarse against the skin."

51

"It *isn't* too coarse. Men can't wear women's shifts."

"Mercedes, fetch my lawn shift—the old one."

"Oh, *Jesús María!*" he fretted. "I won't wear it, *Madrecita!*" And springing up before the shameful garment could be brought, he slipped into his shirt and doublet though they scratched abominably. "There— you see, it's all right."

"Stubborn!" said his mother.

"Thanks all the same," he answered, kissing her, and then escaped.

The little patio, with the diminutive arcades around it, was dark except for a slanting shaft of moonlight and the faint glimmer from his father's cabinet. He stole across toward the passageway leading to the grilled entrance of the house. But at that moment one of the dogs barked, and Don Francisco appeared on the threshold of his room.

"*Quién es?*" he challenged.

"It is I, Señor Father."

"What are you up to?"

Pedro cursed his luck. "I thought I would take a turn in the fresh air with your permission."

"Or without it," teased de Vargas, who now felt completely reconciled with his son. "Well, at night I suppose young tomcats must be roaming. Only, come here a minute." And when Pedro had joined him, "You'll be careful. You'll wear a sword—I see you've got your dagger—and keep to the middle of the street. I didn't want to alarm your mother, but Diego de Silva won't leave things as they are. If I read him right, he's a coward and won't send a challenge; but he has a big household. A thrust in the dark's easy, d'you see? That's the satisfaction he'll look for. Come in here and pick out a sword."

With a tingle of pride, Pedro entered the room and selected a blade from the rack of weapons. When he had buckled it on, his father added: "I suppose some men would keep you at home under the circumstances. But be damned to it! You'll never learn to take care of yourself if you skulk indoors. Now, one more thing. I've had a look from the window a couple of times. There's a man lounging up and down across the street—maybe a beggar, maybe not."

"Thank you, sir."

Taking down his hat and long cloak from their peg in the passageway, Pedro let himself out and turned right in the direction of the Carvajal Palace. A group of young fellows whom he knew passed with *holas* of greeting. When they were gone, his footsteps on the cobblestones were the only sound for a moment. Then, like an echo, he heard other footsteps behind him. Walking more quickly, he turned left at the next crossing; but the footsteps still followed and sounded closer.

In the middle of the road, he made a sudden about-face, his dagger in the left hand, his right hand on the sword hilt. A bulk in the darkness stopped.

"It's all right, *compañero*," came a hushed but unmistakable voice. "Juan García. By the saints, I'm glad you came out! God knows I'm in need of you."

<hr>

X

EVEN THOUGH the street was little more than three yards wide, there was enough diffused moonlight to see that García still wore the beard and make-up which he had purchased at Sanlúcar. But from the desperate urgency of his manner, it looked as if the watch were on his traces.

"What's happened?" Pedro faltered. "Are they after you?"

"No, it isn't that—it's worse. We can't talk here. I've got a room at the Corona. Come along."

Moonlight meditations at the gate of the Carvajal garden had to be postponed. Pedro was swept on by the man's intenseness.

"I've been hanging around for an hour," García continued in a whisper. "I thought perhaps you'd come out. If you hadn't, I don't know what I'd have done. I couldn't send you a message or call myself without somebody's getting curious, and it wouldn't do to run the chance."

They climbed uphill, threading the maze of alley-like streets and occasional groups of loungers, until a lantern showed the sign of the Crown over a broad arch, and they turned into the courtyard of the inn. An outer stairway led them up to the rooms of the second floor, which opened on a balcony running along two sides of the courtyard. At García's heels, Pedro entered a bedroom, where his guide fumbled impatiently with a tinderbox and lighted a candle. It was a barnlike, raftered chamber with an alcove for a bed at one end and with the minimum of furniture. García locked the door.

"We've got to talk low," he said, his eyes haunted.

"For God's sake, what's wrong?"

"I'll tell you. After taking this room, I waited until evening before looking up *Madrecita*. No use showing myself in the daytime. Then I went over to the Calle Santo Tomás and asked a beggar where she lived —those fellows know everybody. He gave me a queer look and made horns with his fingers, as if I had the evil eye. 'It must be this make-up,' I thought. But he took a coin I handed him, and pointed out the house —said she lived on the third floor. I climbed up the stairs, thinking she must be cursed poor. Dirty as a dunghill, it was. Brats and litter. I thought to myself how happy she was going to be . . ."

García broke off and stood staring at the candle.

"I knocked at the door on the third landing. A woman opened up. When I asked for the Señora Romero, she acted scared like the beggar.

" 'She isn't here,' she said. 'I live here now.'

"I said, 'You mean she's moved?'

" 'Yes, moved.'

"I said, 'Can you give me her address?'

"The woman looked as if she had a chill. She said, 'The prison's her address.'

"Then I got it out of her. They took *Madrecita* a month ago—the Holy Office—as a witch. People accused her—"

His voice died out. As if suddenly at the end of his strength, he took a step or two to a chair and sat down, his shoulders slumping, his big hands limp on his knees.

Though shocked, Pedro was not completely surprised. He had heard that old Dorotea Romero was a witch. Perhaps that accounted for the devil in García that took him when he was drunk. But in spite of superstition, his heart bled for the misery in the other's bull-like eyes, and he would have helped him if he could. Only in this case there was nothing to do. García might just as well have told him that his mother had died. What the Inquisition seized, it kept.

"A witch?" the man repeated. "Hell! She's no more a witch than my foot! Being brought up by her, don't you think I'd know? Regular at mass; prayers night and morning. Taught me the Pater Noster, Credo, and Ave. Used to hold me in her arms when I was sick. Used to starve so I could eat. Many's the time these hard years that I've dreamed of her. And now, because she's old, because some woman she was tending died—"

The horror of the torture room flamed in his eyes. He pressed both hands against his head, as if it were bursting.

"Perhaps they'll let her go," Pedro suggested in order to say something.

"I'm not fooling myself," returned García. "When I heard it, I hoped she might be dead." Brokenly he explained that by the grapevine method he had bought the information that she was still alive. "They'll burn what's left of her," he added. And then, desperately, "But there's one chance." He stretched his arms out. "Comrade, you've got to help me! If it was your mother, I'd do the same for you. You're the only one who can help."

García's distress excused his reference to Doña María, though Pedro winced at it—as if his mother could ever be on the same level with Dorotea Romero!

"How?" he asked.

The man leaned forward, dropping his voice to a mutter. "Listen. The Holy Office may be as holy as it pleases, but money talks everywhere. People's houses and property aren't confiscated for the sake of their souls. Believe me, the reverend fathers have the gold itch like anybody else, and I've known more than one poor devil who's bought his way out. Well, I've got money, d'you see?"

Low as García spoke, Pedro glanced nervously around. It was impious even to hear such things. It did not savor of respect for the sacred tribunal.

"But I'm hamstrung," García went on. "I'd hang to save *Madrecita,* but my hanging won't save her. Odds are I wouldn't even have sight of her in the prison if I was taken there. I can't go to the Inquisitor. *You* could."

Cold chills ran down young de Vargas's spine. He was ready to do anything in reason, but the idea of approaching Father Ignacio de Lora, Inquisitor of Jaén, with the proposal which he could see García working up to, paralyzed him.

"No, listen," begged the other. "You could. I'll wager you know him, don't you?"

"I've met him."

"You see! Then it's all the easier. And he knows you. Son of Don Francisco de Vargas. No better blood in Spain. Beyond suspicion."

Reading the refusal in Pedro's face, García clasped his hands together. "Hark you, son, for God's sake! When I saw you in the inn, I said, 'There's a lad of mettle'—the way you stood by that wench, the straight look of you. 'There's a bad-weather lad,' I said, 'that you could count on by sea or land, in march or fight.' My heart warmed to you. I felt we were born friends. You're the only one who can help save my mother. You won't turn me down!"

He saw that he was making headway, and pressed his point. The plan was that Pedro should present himself to the Inquisitor as the agent of Señora Romero's brother, a merchant of Valencia—"which is true enough," García explained, "only he's dead." The merchant, Juan García, offered eight hundred ducats in atonement for his sister's misdeeds, if the reverend Inquisitor would mercifully deign to consider the sum sufficient. In view of the fact that she had confessed to witchcraft under torture, her punishment might be considered enough. Pedro should explain that he had met García at the Corona; that the merchant, a humble man, had besought his good offices and entrusted him with the money. His responsibilities stopped there; he was acting simply as a messenger, and should disclaim any further knowledge of the merchant whatever.

"He'll know well enough why I didn't come myself," García reasoned. "He'll know that relatives of condemned heretics keep under cover. And he'll know why I picked out a young man from a family like yours to act for me."

"Suppose he wants to see you?"

"I wasn't born yesterday. Refer him to the Corona, but his men won't find me here. You can bet that he won't be surprised when they don't."

"Couldn't he make me hand over the money anyhow?"

"Yes, but not without risk of scandal."

"Suppose he refuses—"

"*Hombre!*" exclaimed García. "Suppose! Suppose! You can suppose anything. I'm simply taking the chance that he'll accept eight hundred ducats of easy money, where he expected no pickings at all. It's risky enough, but it's the only thing I can do."

Pedro shook his head. "It won't work. Father Ignacio's a man of God. People call him a saint, even though he has to be hard. He won't take a bribe."

"Call it a fine," put in García. "It's the half of all I've earned in sixteen years."

"He won't be influenced by money."

A wan smile broke through García's concern. "Boy, you've got a lot to learn about men and money. But you'll do this for me, won't you? With your name, you aren't running any risk. I wouldn't ask you if you were."

Though young, Pedro was by no means a complete fool. The Inquisition was a hot fire to meddle with. If Dorotea Romero had been proved a witch, she ought justly to be burned in expiation of so hideous a crime. What did he know about her, or about this brawny man from the Indies? Well, he knew one thing at least, that an absolute scoundrel would hardly be risking everything he had, his life included, to save somebody else, even if it was his mother. Of course, the devil might have something to do with it, but Pedro couldn't judge of that.

As for witchcraft, he wondered whether he wouldn't confess to it himself under torture. He remembered de Silva's anecdotes.

But above all, he was young. He felt no little flattered by García's dependence on him. And he had not yet learned to stifle pity in the name of common sense.

"*Bien*," he said.

For a moment García was silent. Then he got up and laid his hands on Pedro's shoulders.

"Maybe God'll let me repay you some time."

"When do you want me to see the Inquisitor?"

García's hands tightened a little. He drew one of them across his eyes.

"Night's best for that kind of an offer. So tonight. We haven't much time. I had word that *Madrecita's* hardly alive after their handling of her."

He drew out a small but heavy bag from the pocket of his cloak and gave it to Pedro.

"Here's the money. I'll go with you and wait outside."

XI

THE HOUSE of the Inquisitor of Jaén was situated on the open square of Santa María facing the cathedral, and therefore not far from the castle prison above it. Out of wholesome respect for the great man, people gave it a wide berth on summer evenings, all the more because of an armed servant of the Holy Office outside. Indeed, with the Bishop's palace not far off on the square, the entire plaza enjoyed a dour tranquillity. Its atmosphere chilled and sobered. Since the gothic outlines of the church shut off most of the moonlight, the place lay in a sort of ecclesiastical shadow.

Having left García beyond the corner of the nearest street, Pedro walked with increasing trepidation toward the guarded door of the Inquisitor. It was now well after ten and, though probably Father Ignacio had not yet retired, it was an unusual hour to call. Pedro was torn between hope that he would be refused admittance and desire to get the thing over with. More than ever, he cursed his ill-omened visit to the Rosario, which had got him into the pickle. Though he wanted to help García, he would have been glad at the moment if he had never met him.

The retainer in front of the door turned out to be an acquaintance. It was Sebastián Reyes, owner of a famous fighting cock, upon whom Pedro had won ten reals the week before in the cockpit behind the Corona.

"See His Reverence, sir?" the man answered with a stare. "Well, since it's you, I'll ask, though the hour's late, as Your Worship knows."

"On business," Pedro added in a strained voice.

"Ha?" said the man curiously and turned to communicate with another guard behind the lattice of the door.

Several minutes passed. Reyes discussed the next cockfight day after tomorrow, while Pedro sweated nervously. Finally the door opened.

"His Reverence will see Pedro de Vargas."

Like all the better houses of Jaén, the residence of the Inquisitor was built around a small inner courtyard, which contained in most instances a fountain or at least some greenery. But here the patio looked as bare as a guardroom, and as a matter of fact it served that purpose, for several armed men were on duty. Although any right-minded Christian appreciated the value of Father Ignacio's services, one could never tell when some heretic, as yet unarrested, might seek vengeance for the torture and death of a relative. It was prudent, therefore, to take no chances. Besides, in order to avoid scandal, the Holy Office conducted many of its activities at night, and the men were at hand for any sudden call.

At the end of a corridor flanking the patio, de Vargas was ushered into a long, high, naked room, with a straight-backed chair or two and a table at one end. It was lighted by a couple of sconces and a candelabrum on the table, behind which Ignacio de Lora was writing. The scratching of his pen lasted a full minute after Pedro entered. Then, rising, he held out a negligent hand to his caller, who dropped to one knee and kissed it reverently.

The Inquisitor wore the white robe and silver crucifix of the Dominicans. He was a tall, somewhat stooped man of middle age, though his short, square beard as yet contained no mingling of gray. On the other hand, partial baldness had overtaken him and left a high, domelike forehead, beneath which the low arch of his eyebrows stood out. He had a masterful nose, a severe mouth, and shrewd but unrevealing eyes. The impression he made was of cool efficiency and vigilant suspicion.

In this dampening presence, Pedro felt more ill at ease than ever.

It made it worse that for some reason Father Ignacio seemed to be inwardly amused. His grim mouth twitched in a secret, frosty smile.

"Well, young man, to what do I owe the honor of this visit?"

"If I am inconveniencing Your Reverence, I could put it off," Pedro faltered. It was hard to keep his teeth from chattering.

"No, I have a moment of leisure." De Lora sanded the page he had been writing and folded it. "How can I serve you?"

"Not me, Your Reverence. I mean, I didn't come on my own account. Matter of fact, I don't know much about it. It's somebody else I met at the Corona. His m——, his sister's a witch by the name of Dorotea Romero. He wanted me to ask Your Reverence—I mean his name is Juan García, he says, from Málaga—no, I mean Valencia. He wanted me to ask Your Reverence—he's a merchant, you know—he wanted me to ask——"

"Just a minute." De Lora raised his hand. He was doubtless used to stammering people. "Compose yourself, my son. What are you trying to say? I take it that you met a merchant from Málaga or Valencia——"

"Valencia, Your Reverence."

"Good. Valencia. Who is related to a Dorotea Romero, now detained by the Holy Office on certain charges. Is that it?"

"Yes, Father."

"Very well. Go on."

Pedro tried again and this time was able to finish on a fairly even keel. He remembered to refer to the eight hundred ducats as a fine, because the Holy Office, whomever it arrested, was never wrong; and in justice to himself, he stressed the fact that he was serving merely as an intermediary for a stranger in Jaén, whose distress had touched him.

When he had finished, the Inquisitor repressed another smile; but his eyes looked as sharp and impenetrable as before.

"Does your worthy father know of this visit to me?"

"No, Your Reverence. I have just come from the Corona."

"Hm-m. Why did not this Juan García come to me himself?"

"He is a man of humble station, who has not the honor of being known to Your Reverence. He feared that he might not secure an audience."

"Hm-m. Where is he now?"

Pedro's heart sank. "He is staying at the Corona."

"And of course you plan to meet him when you leave here?"

"Yes, Father—to give him Your Reverence's answer."

This contingency had been foreseen by García. Upon leaving the Inquisitor's house, Pedro was to return to the Corona, where he would *not* find the merchant from Valencia. Indeed, the latter would not appear at that tavern again. Having waited a suitable time, Pedro was to leave a note with the landlord, stating briefly what Father Ignacio had decided. This note itself was a blind in case Pedro had been followed. It would serve as proof that he had carried out his mission and washed his hands of the affair. He was then to return home by a pre-arranged route through the blindest part of the town. Somewhere on the way, García promised to meet him.

The Dominican's hard eyes probed an instant.

"It seems to me that you become intimate with strangers on short acquaintance, my son. How long have you known this man?"

"I met him today while returning to Jaén from the hunt for the Señor de Silva's slave. He was at the Corona this evening."

"And these eight hundred ducats—he has them, I suppose?"

"No, Father, he entrusted them to me, I have them here."

This time de Lora almost laughed. Pedro caught a glint of white teeth behind the beard.

"It's a tribute to your honest appearance, my son, and to your father's reputation, when a complete stranger entrusts you with eight hundred ducats."

"He is much concerned for his sister, Your Reverence."

Pedro by now had little hope for his mission; but the purpose of his visit no longer chiefly concerned him. More than anything else, he wanted to escape from this man and from his scornful amusement. He felt like a small mouse between the paws of an enormous cat. Though essentially true, his story, as reflected in the Inquisitor's manner, sounded like a childish lie.

"So you were to offer me eight hundred ducats—for what?"

"That it might please Your Reverence to dismiss the woman," Pedro faltered, "unless her crimes are too great. Of course I don't know—I'm only speaking for Señor García."

De Lora now actually laughed—a short bark of a laugh. It was natural, Pedro thought, that the idea of a bribe (for call it what you pleased, bribe it was) should amuse him. Bribe the drawn Sword of God! Bribe this holy man devoted to maintaining undefiled the Catholic faith! Bribe the saintly Ignacio de Lora with eight hundred ducats! More than ever, he saw how vain, how impudent the offer was, and regretted bitterly that he had a part in it. All that he could expect now was to be blasted out of the room.

But de Lora said amazingly, "Let me see the money."

Somewhat puzzled, Pedro drew the heavy pouch from the inner

pocket of his cloak and handed it to the Inquisitor, who poured a gush of gold coins out on the table in front of him. It was a great sum, greater, Pedro reflected, than Diego de Silva had offered for his father's vineyard and orchard. He had never seen so much money in his life. It was probably the reflection of the gold that lent a gleam to de Lora's eyes. Then the Inquisitor leaned back in thought, while his hand absently, perhaps scornfully, scooped up the coins, letting them trickle through his fingers.

At last he straightened up again; but instead of returning the money to the pouch and rejecting it, as Pedro expected, he set about stacking it up with the speed and skill of a business man.

"It is true that Dorotea Romero has been guilty of terrible crimes." (Ten, twenty, thirty. He examined one gold piece but found it good.) "She has confessed to witchcraft and to a compact with Satan." (Fifty. He crossed himself and Pedro did the same. Sixty, seventy . . .) "It is true, however, that she repents of these horrible sins . . ." (Eighty, ninety, one hundred. Father Ignacio swept the ten piles into a heap.) "And the Holy Office desires not the death of a sinner but rather that he should turn from his wickedness . . ." (thirty, forty, fifty) . . . "and live. Mercy must ever go hand in hand with justice."

A queer change was taking place in young Pedro de Vargas. It was not only that a glimmering of hope with regard to his mission began to dawn; but beneath this, and almost in opposition to it, he felt a strange confusion. Could it be that Father Ignacio was accepting the money, that the Sword of God was for sale, that eight hundred ducats could free from the stake a woman who would otherwise have been burned? Without knowing it, Pedro was getting older second by second, while de Lora stacked up the coins—older, less innocent, aware of money's barefaced power.

Two hundred. Another sweep of the hand. "It is only right that the Holy Office, having labored for the salvation of a sinner, should rejoice in it and release this same sinner into life." (Fifty, sixty.) "It is only just that the Holy Office should profit from the worldly possessions of evildoers, using them for pious works and thus . . ." (eighty, ninety) . . . "transferring them from the service of Mammon to the service of God. Repentance is thereby more clearly shown . . ."

Father Ignacio now fell silent. Only the clicking and occasional ring of the coins could be heard. When the eighth heap had been formed, there were five gold pieces left over, but he added these carelessly to the last heap. Then he restored the whole amount to the pouch, opened a drawer of the table, and put it inside with a golden thud.

"What can I tell Señor García, Your Reverence?"

"Ah, yes." The Inquisitor reflected. "Tell him I give my word that his sister will be released from prison day after tomorrow morning. There are certain formalities. He should be a happy man that Dorotea Romero is now in a state of grace."

"Thank you, Father."

The Dominican extended his hand. Pedro, kneeling, kissed it and prepared to leave.

"One moment, my son. It would be well to keep this transaction secret. You would incur my displeasure if you spoke of it to anyone but the Señor García. The clemency of the Holy Office might be misconstrued. I hope you understand."

"Yes, Your Reverence."

"You and I will discuss the matter sometime when I have greater leisure. It is not always wise for young men to be too obliging in the case of strangers. Meanwhile, go in peace."

Once again Pedro read a cold amusement in the other's eyes. As the door closed, it seemed to him that he heard an abrupt laugh. But at least the ordeal was over, and he had good news for Juan García. If he had lost something of his naïve youth in the house of the Inquisitor, he did not notice it at the time.

Faithful to the prearranged program, he now returned to the Corona, waited a suitable time for the merchant from Valencia, and left the prescribed note for him with the landlord. It was a ticklish business. If for any reason the Holy Office wished to lay hands on Dorotea Romero's rich relative, Pedro might be followed. But so far as he could tell, this did not happen.

Having left the tavern, he plunged into a maze of crooked streets and headed for home, keeping very much on the alert. At a dark corner, a beggar suddenly loomed up, asking for alms in the name of God and calling him *compañero*. He stopped.

"Juan García?"

"What happened?" came the whisper.

"It's all right. He took the money and promised to free your mother day after tomorrow morning." Pedro gave a brief account of the interview.

"God bless you, friend!"

"What'll you do when she's released? How'll you get her out of Jaén and keep hidden yourself?"

"I'll arrange it somehow. You forget me whatever happens. You've more than done your part." The deep voice shook with feeling. "I'll always remember it. I'd give my life's blood for you. Hurry on now."

There was a warm handclasp in the darkness; García vanished, and Pedro, with a light heart, regained his house.

XII

THOUGH TO Luisa de Carvajal next day time seemed to stand still, she concealed her impatience. Even so shrewd an observer as the Señora Hernández might have gathered that she was not especially excited by the prospect of the evening. Actually, however, she tingled with anticipation, and more than once in the course of the day she managed to slip out into the garden and follow a bypath, screened by oleanders, to a point where she could gaze speculatively at the grille of the side gate. Walls of laurel, forming a bay, half-concealed it from the rest of the garden. Here she would dream for a while before turning back to the palace.

At long last, the obstinate shadows of the cypresses, which had seemed nailed to the ground, began to lengthen. The sundial, with its absurd motto about the flight of time, showed that at least time moved. And the two ladies, who had been observing it on the terrace, went indoors to dress for late afternoon supper.

At the foot of the main stairway inside, they encountered the Marquis de Carvajal with a lackey bearing his cloak and sword. He was on the point of departure for an evening gathering at the Bishop's ard wore his usual somberly rich dress, which set off the magnificent cross of the Knighthood of Santiago.

He was a middle-aged man with a square, gray beard that had the proper uptilt of distinction. His prominent dark eyes were languid with authority. Long ago, perhaps, he had been an individual; but as time passed he had become simply the Marquis de Carvajal, an incarnate title which had absorbed its owner. If he loved money and display, as people said, these were hardly characteristic traits: they went with his position.

Antonia Hernández and Luisa curtsied; they received his bow and Luisa, in addition, a kiss on the forehead.

"Good night, my daughter. I am always chagrined at not seeing you of an evening—but there are social duties. Tomorrow night I shall ask you to attend me with your lute. Meanwhile, practise an Italian song or two, and you will not miss me."

"I cannot help missing you, my lord," she answered with perfect modulation.

"That is only natural. Be sure you pray for me. She is regular in her prayers, Doña Antonia?"

"Extremely devout, my lord."

"*Muy bien!* Good night."

He dismissed them with a graceful movement of the hand and passed on. Luisa continued upstairs, hardly conscious, because so used to it, of the empty feeling that her father left with her. Besides, it would be sunset in an hour; the thought eclipsed everything else.

Dressing took a long time that evening. It did not matter that it would be night when she and Pedro de Vargas met and that the grille of the gate would separate them. She selected one gown, then changed to another, reflecting that silver brocade showed best in moonlight. She plucked a rebellious hair from the perfect arch of her eyebrow, applied a touch of rose water to her cheeks, throat, and hands; again consulted the mirror. Her mantilla looked most becoming this way, as if it had slipped by chance, revealing the fillet of gems in her hair. The approach of evening heightened the soft pallor of her face and brought out in contrast the darkness of her almond-shaped eyes.

When she had finished, the sunset notes of birds sounded from the garden. She stood awhile at the window, half listening, gazing far off at the deepened sky. Then she rejoined Antonia.

The Marquis de Carvajal, like many Spanish noblemen of the time, had been profoundly influenced by contact with Naples, and he had laid out his garden with Italian or Sicilian models in mind. Something of Capri, something of Palermo, mingled in its general atmosphere and pattern. There was the same use of terraces, to which the hilly character of Jaén lent itself; the same billowing darkness of foliage—laurel and rhododendron, ferns and ivy—forming a screen that surrounded and isolated it. Along the center, an occasional pool reflected the guardian cypresses, and there were side paths leading to green bays, over which a moss-grown Pan or satyr presided. The small dome of a pavilion, half-glimpsed from the palace, rose among the trees; the walls of the terraces were draped with vines, so that masonry, softened by vegetation, gave an impression of luxuriant age.

In the hour after sunset, the garden released its fragrance on the

64

cooler air—the haunting fragrance of orange blossoms mingling with other flowers—as if it wooed the descent of night. Color faded from the sky; dim stars became suddenly visible; and the moon, which had already risen, proclaimed itself. The lonely diapason of frogs in the remoter pools grew louder.

Señora Hernández and Luisa lingered awhile on the terrace, leaning against the marble balustrade, then strolled down the steps, and so gradually farther on between the cypresses. It was the usual proceeding after supper. No palace servant, however inquisitive, would pay heed to them.

"Just when is nightfall?" asked Luisa, trying to keep the tremor out of her voice.

"When it gets dark," replied Antonia, "like it is now. . . . Why?"

"We wrote him to come at nightfall."

"Yes, and I'm sure he's here already."

They were approaching the far end of the garden. Luisa stopped.

"Already? Then oughtn't we—?"

"Certainly not. You wouldn't have him think that you were counting the moments, would you? He must be kept waiting. He must begin to wonder, despair."

Antonia was more than a little thrilled herself. Gallantry was exciting; it was the one really exciting thing in life. As an expert, she enjoyed all the finesse, all the strategy of love.

"In an hour will be time enough."

"A whole hour?"

"Not a minute less." Antonia slipped her arm around the girl's waist. "I know how it is, *Primacita*. But trust me, nothing helps so much as to keep a man in doubt—never quite sure. Besides, we must wait for the moon if you want him to admire you. We'll go to the pavilion and you can practise your Italian songs. That'll pass the time."

"I couldn't!"

"For two reasons, you must practise them," Señora Hernández added. "You'll be heard in the palace, and they'll know what you were doing if the Marquis should happen to ask. He'll remember about the songs. Then too, *someone else* may hear you, my rose. You sing quite well."

The lane outside the garden wandered between high walls covered with moss and overtopped by vines. It was unfrequented at this hour, and silent except for the rustle of an occasional lizard. Darkness came on more rapidly here than elsewhere, but even so it was not entirely dark when Pedro de Vargas posted himself opposite the gate.

He too was uncertain as to what had been meant by nightfall—perhaps late afternoon or dusk or night itself—and he took no chances. After the endless, languishing day, it was a relief to get to the lane as soon as possible. Now, muffled in his cloak, like a shadowy projection of the wall behind him, he stood consumed by a slow fire of expectation and impatience.

Though he did not realize it, his state of mind was partly conventional. It was the proper thing for lovers to wait and pine, to haunt the night, discreetly muffled in their cloaks. Tradition demanded it. But there was more to his vigil than this. Youth's vague idealism, colored by desire, had been brought for the first time to a burning focus. He might act like any one of a thousand lovelorn cavaliers; but yesterday morning's experience in the church, the ray of light, the upflaring of his heart toward the beauty and grace of Luisa de Carvajal, were personal and uncopied.

Twilight became night—so dense a blackness that even his cloak was indistinguishable. Between the walls of the lane, the air lay close and heavy with the cloying perfume of flowers. As long as he lived, the scent of orange blossoms would immediately recall that hour to him. Once or twice people with lanterns entered the lane, and he strolled to meet them so that they would not find him opposite the Carvajal gate. Moreover, he had not entirely forgotten his father's warning or the events of yesterday. But for the most part, he stood motionless in a waking dream.

Not until the darkness faded and moonlight silvered the top branches of trees beyond the gate did he begin to have misgivings. This was certainly nightfall, and he had been waiting a long time.

The moon grew brighter until, through the ironwork of the gate, he could see the path and space of lawn surrounded by the laurels. It had the mystery and suspense of an empty stage. Perhaps the letter had only been sent in fun. Perhaps Luisa had no intention of appearing. Perhaps she was amusing herself at this very moment with the thought of him and his foolish expectation. After all, he had been guilty of too extravagant a hope that the daughter of a grandee would condescend to unworthy clay like himself.

And now the minutes crawled past, each one emptier and more disquieting. The moonlight spent itself in vain. She would not come. He was a pathetic fool.

Suddenly a distant lute broke the silence with ripples of sound, and a voice rose somewhere from beyond the trees. By contrast with the preceding quiet, it was abruptly sweet, like the tones of a nightingale. Pedro recognized the melody as an Italian air which his sister often sang. He knew it so well that he could distinguish the words. They were by his mother's countryman, Lorenzo de' Medici.

> *"Quant' è bella giovinezza*
> *che si fugge tuttavia!*
> *chi vuol esser lieto, sia . . ."*

The recent blankness was gone. Her voice! It must be hers . . .

> "Youth is sweet, a fount upwelling,
> Though it slips away!
> Let who will be gay:
> Of tomorrow there's no telling.
>
> "Bacchus, Ariadne, playing,
> Lip to lip and heart to heart,
> Make the most of time a-Maying,
> Never roam apart.
>
> "Nymphs and other silvan creatures
> Frolic at their play.
> Let who will be gay:
> Of tomorrow there's no telling."

Silence again, but this time vibrant; the rhythm of the song continuing soundlessly after the music had stopped. He waited breathless, the refrain echoing in his mind—"of tomorrow there's no telling."

Perhaps this was all he could expect: she could find no other way to keep the tryst with him—her voice in the night, a song, a greeting. Or was it more than that—a half-promise? "Of tomorrow there's no telling." If that was her meaning, he would return here and wait tomorrow and tomorrow and tomorrow. He stood with one hand on the gate, peering into the moonlit circle beyond.

So tranced he was that Luisa de Carvajal had crossed halfway between the laurels and the gate before he was aware of her. Or rather, she seemed at first a thought picture, vague and steeped in moonlight, out of which she appeared to take form. The silver brocade of her dress and the pallor of her face against the black of the mantilla helped this effect. Then he recovered his senses only to lose them again completely.

She was here; it was not a vision.

He had prepared and rehearsed a fine opening speech, which seemed to him polished and poetic; but he could not recall a syllable of it.

Mental panic seized him. He could only stare hypnotized through the grille of the gate.

Luisa felt equally confused. Being a girl, she could have acquitted herself well enough if he had spoken; as it was, she came to a helpless stop a few feet off. The dim figure of Antonia Hernández in the background did not relieve matters.

At last desperately he whispered, *"Buenas noches, señorita."*

"Buenas noches, señor."

Then nothing. She expected eloquence, romance. He knew that she expected them. What had happened to him? It wasn't the first time he had met a girl. Usually he was as fluent as the next man.

In his embarrassment, he straightened his arm against the bar of the grillework, which he was holding, and was startled that the gate swung open. Evidently it had been left unbolted. More dashed than ever, he closed it again sharply between them and muttered an excuse.

"I didn't know it was unlocked."

"I didn't either."

In the shadow of the laurels, Señora Hernández smiled. She had done what she could. If the two young dunces didn't take advantage of the gate, there was no help for them. But giving them every chance, she now recklessly moved from sight, though remaining close enough behind the shrubbery.

"I heard you sing," Pedro faltered. "It was beautiful."

She murmured something, and he cast about for the next remark. Appalling as had been last night's interview with the Inquisitor, it was easy compared to this.

"Very beautiful."

"Did you really think so?"

"Yes."

In his prepared speech, there had been references to Cupid and holy water and Luisa's letter; there were flowery compliments and passionate avowals. That was all in ruins. He couldn't piece any of it together in a way that wouldn't sound sillier than his present woodenness.

"I know the song very well. You see, Mother's a Florentine."

"Really?"

"Yes. My sister, Mercedes, sings it."

Why, in God's name, was he talking about his mother and sister now!

He staggered on. "But not like you—nothing like." And on the point of running down again, *"Quant' è bella giovinezza!"*

"Do you sing?"

"No—that is, pretty badly. A ballad sometimes."

68

At this point he became aware that the duenna had disappeared. Somehow it made a difference. His tenseness relaxed, his blood warmed again, and thought began flowing. But he did not want to revive the speech he had rehearsed so often that day. It did not seem to fit in now.

"You were kind to send me the letter," he said, a new ring in his voice. "I never dreamed . . . It was like a miracle. After seeing you in church. I had been praying to San Pedro and the Blessed Virgin. But I never dreamed . . . Since then I've been thinking of you every minute." His hand strayed to his doublet. "I have it here," he went on, pressing the paper against his heart. "I know every word of it as well as the Pater Noster."

She drew a step nearer, her own shyness melting a little. This was what she had imagined it would be—not quite, indeed, because Cousin Antonia had said that he would talk poetically, and his words were very simple, but she had never heard any like them.

"San Pedro and the Blessed Virgin, señor?"

"Yes."

Forgetting himself, intent only that she should feel what it had meant to him, he told her about the ray of sunlight. She listened with parted lips.

"And then I knew. I knew, whether you cared for me or not, that I would always be your cavalier. It was the will of heaven for me; it meant heaven for me. I shall always serve you, always adore you, seek honor in your name. And perhaps sometime I might be worthy . . . No, not that, but still you might care for me—sometime."

Yes, now it was everything that she had imagined it would be, and more—much more.

"Why?" she breathed. "Why do you care for me?"

Why! Blessed saints! As he looked at her, the answer to that question was inexpressible. She was incarnate moonlight; she was desire and worship and beauty, ethereal and yet warm and living.

He could only answer, "Because I love you."

The benevolent gate once more opened under the stress of his emotion, but this time he did not close it. Antonia Hernández need not have worried: he and Luisa were learning fast without a tutor.

Amazing that a girl like her should forget decorum at such a moment. Instead of showing alarm or displeasure that the gate remained open when propriety demanded bars between them, she moved closer, so that they stood face to face.

"But you don't know me. How can you be sure?"

Approaching footsteps sounded in the lane, a murmur of voices.

"*Ay Maria!*" she whispered. "Quick! Come inside—they'll see you."

He shut the gate softly behind him, and they stood close together within the wall, while the footsteps passed. Her nearness, the fragrance of her dress, the silence as they waited, set his pulses throbbing. Her mantilla, slipping a little, showed the sparkle of her jeweled hair net in the moonlight and the wave of her hair.

When the passers-by were gone, he kneeled suddenly and raised her hand to his lips.

On a low stone bench within the bay of lawn and to one side of the gate, she listened while he poured himself out in the high-flown style of Andalusian lovers. The words flowed of themselves, urgent, vibrant. She listened, but was conscious too of a strange fermentation in her own mind, as if a new order of life and thought were beginning. It struck her that until now she had never possessed anything of her own; that she had been like a doll in the hands of other people. But now the doll in the silver brocade and jeweled hair net was coming to life, was taking possession of herself.

He told her about France, the invitation from Bayard. He would not have her think of him as a local stay-at-home. He would make himself worthy to be her cavalier.

"When do you go?" she asked, trying to keep the droop out of her voice.

"In autumn, Madonna." He added gallantly, "With your leave."

She counted rapidly. Two months of evenings—evenings like this.

"My father says that Monseigneur de Bayard loves tournaments," he went on. "The thought of you will give me strength. If I win, the credit and prize will be yours."

"They say that French ladies are beautiful," she put in lightly, though all at once she hated the thought of them.

"Perhaps." He had become an adept in the last ten minutes. "How shall I be able to tell? You have made me blind to them."

Half-seated on the bench, he slipped again to one knee.

"Will you give me a token, Madonna, some favor to wear? It would be my saint's relic and bring me fortune. Forgive me for asking. I know that it is too much to ask."

Even Antonia Hernández could have found nothing to improve in his manner. The hour had changed him as well as Luisa; he was not the same youth who had entered the lane.

Luisa felt caught up and swept along by a current too swift for coquetries and delays. Somehow his earnestness did not permit them.

Without hesitation, she gave him her handkerchief, a tiny scrap of cambric edged with Venetian lace. It was perfumed with rose water and had the softness of a rose, as he pressed it to his lips.

"I wish I had something better to give you, Pedro de Vargas."

Better? If he had received the Golden Fleece at the hands of the King, it would not have meant half so much. His brain reeled with happiness and pride. She had accepted him, she permitted him to call himself hers. Now there was no difficulty on earth so arduous that he could not overcome it for her; no prize so lofty that he could not win it for her. The hot blood pounded in his ears; his imagination soared like a released falcon. To express himself was impossible. When he spoke, his voice seemed strange to him.

"I will give my life for you. I would give my soul for you."

A discreet cough sounded beyond the laurels, and he regained his feet as the Señora Hernández reappeared.

"Tomorrow night?" he whispered. "Every night, I'll be in the lane."

He could barely hear the answer. *"Si, cuando puedo."*

He bowed to Antonia.

"Vaya!" she said archly. "Is it the custom of gentlemen to enter gates and to forget the proper distance?"

He appeared startled. "It is enchantment, señora. I did not know that I had passed the gate."

"Not bad!" she approved. "I see that you're a charming liar." And to Luisa, "We must go in, *Primacita*. There are lights moving in the palace. Your father must have returned."

Still dazed, still half-incredulous of his happiness, Pedro wandered back through the town, heedless of the cobblestones and turnings of the streets. The years stretched before him in a haze of gold, a limitless horizon. With love inspiring him, he could do everything—everything!

Not far from his house, a dark figure detached itself from a doorway, and at once he was on guard.

"Pedro de Vargas?" hissed a voice.

"Yes."

"I am Manuel Pérez, Catana's brother—he of the prison."

It took an instant's effort to remember.

"Yes?"

"You saved my sister from de Silva's men. I am not one who forgets. I have been here for an hour, hoping to head you off."

What was the fellow driving at?

"Head me off?"

71

"You must not go to the Casa de Vargas. It's a trap. They're waiting for you."

Clearly the man was crazy. "Who's waiting for me?"

"Those of the Holy Office. They have taken your father, mother, and sister to the Castle. With my own eyes, I saw them brought in. I heard the talk about you. Then I got away, though it would cost my head—"

"The Castle? The Holy Office?"

"Yes. Get out to the Rosario. Catana will help. You must take to the mountains. It's your only chance."

XIII

IN THE HOT DARKNESS, Pedro stared at the almost invisible face close to him. His mind, suddenly numb, refused to act.

After a long moment, he stammered: "I'm sorry, friend. I don't understand. What did you say about the Holy Office?"

Manuel Pérez repeated the incredible news. Even on a second hearing, it filtered but slowly into Pedro's consciousness. His father, Francisco de Vargas, arrested! One of the town's leading citizens, a famous man, dragged to prison! Pedro's mother and sister taken! The family house seized and already occupied by strangers, who were waiting to lay hands on Pedro himself! At a single blast, the solid world of his entire experience seemed to be blown to fragments.

Pérez gripped his shoulder. "Your Worship has no time to lose. You can get down by the east wall. Come on. Hurry! I'm due at the Castle."

Docilely, as if in a trance, Pedro suffered himself to be led on for a short distance, until at last the complete realization of what had happened struck him and he shook off the other's grasp.

"By God, no!"

"*Qué pasa?*"

Pedro clenched his fists. The monstrous absurdity of the thing beggared language.

"*Why?*" he demanded. "*Why?* What reason? They must have given a reason. What did they say, in the name of God?"

"Say?" echoed Pérez. "Is it for the Santa Casa to give an account of itself? *Señor, no!* It isn't in the habit of answering questions; it asks them." And with a touch of gallows humor he added, "I wouldn't advise Your Worship to wait for the question. Come on."

De Vargas squared himself. The thought of his family behind the walls of the prison shut out every other consideration.

"I'm going to the Alcalde, to the Bishop. They're Father's friends. They don't know about this. It's a mistake. They'll act at once . . ."

"Don't be a fool," put in Pérez, forgetting rank. "What mistake? His Honor, the Alcalde, was at the Castle when Don Francisco and the ladies were brought in. Do you think the Bishop could raise a finger against the will of the Santa Casa? I tell you once more, *señorito*, you have no time to lose."

His call last night on Ignacio de Lora crossed Pedro's mind. Could that have anything to do with it? Had his connection with the ill-omened business of García brought him and his family under suspicion? Was the Inquisitor taking that way to cover up the bribe he had accepted? The Holy Inquisition! They were impious, ugly thoughts which two days ago would have been impossible.

"I'll see Father Ignacio himself."

"Oh?" said Pérez. "In that case, I'm a fool for my pains."

The dry note in the man's voice spoke volumes. Pedro stood shifting from one foot to another in a sweat of indecision. To whom could he turn? Among his father's friends, who would be able to take his part if the highest officials of Jaén were excluded? Had he not better head for the mountains, as Pérez counseled, until influence could be brought to bear and public sentiment force a release? Perhaps, indeed, the arrest was only a mistake.

But the walls of the Castle were thick, and even more insuperable was the fear of the Inquisition. Greater men than Francisco de Vargas —much greater—had disappeared from the friendly world into the cold shadow of the Holy Office, and no one had dared to ask too many questions. The King, perhaps, or a grandee—

The Marquis de Carvajal!

On Pedro's anguish, the name flashed like a beacon. Here was the one man in Jaén who might help. He was not an official, but his word had immense weight. He stood at the summit of the social scale in the district. His power would impress even the Inquisitor. Best of all, he had served with Francisco de Vargas in Italy and called him by his first name. That he was Luisa's father did not occur to Pedro at the moment. He was simply the natural refuge in this case.

"The Marquis de Carvajal!" Pedro exclaimed aloud. "I'll go to *him.*"

Pérez drew back a step; he said nothing for a moment. Then hesitantly, "Yes, the Marquis—he's a big nobleman. If Your Worship has credit with him, perhaps— That's out of my line. Perhaps big noblemen stand by their friends against the Santa Casa. Your Worship knows best. I've got to hustle, or it's a twisted neck for me. Señor Cavalier, go with God."

He was on the point of hurrying off when Pedro caught his arm.

"Thanks, friend. I won't forget your kindness."

"Forget or remember," said the man gruffly. "I did it for Catana."

"You'll tell my parents how matters stand?"

"I'll do that. *Adiós.*"

A great emptiness descended on Pedro when the other was gone. The fellow had at least represented human helpfulness and good will. Now de Vargas found himself in an almost unbearable loneliness, like a swimmer at sea, left to his single efforts.

With a heavy heart, although painfully alert, he retraced his way uphill through the narrow, winding streets toward the Carvajal Palace. The familiar town had suddenly become alien and hostile. Every passer-by, fumbling towards him in the darkness, every beggar loitering under the overhang of a house, was a possible enemy. The scurry of rats in the gutter, the racing of scavenger dogs along the alleyways, the hunting scream of a cat, was enough to set his pulses racing.

As he approached the palace, his first confidence in turning to the Marquis faded. What if he could not obtain an audience at this hour? What if the great man had retired? Pedro knew him only formally. He was not old or important enough to insist on seeing him. But if that were impossible, where could he hide for the night?

The palace garden occurred to him as a possibility—if the gate was still unlocked. No one would think of searching for him there. And with that came the thought of his recent happiness. A half hour ago he had everything, now nothing.

He emerged at last on the quiet square in front of the palace. It was shaded from the moonlight by a few plane trees. Rounding them, he stood looking up at the stone façade, massive and formidable, its occasional windows covered with thick bars like the front of a prison. It had nothing in common with the garden behind it but seemed as detached from that place of enchantment as the Castle itself. Not a light showed; the building was wrapped in a ponderous, austere silence.

Desperation goading him, Pedro at length summoned courage enough to approach the main door and lift the heavy ring that served as knocker. The crash of it broke the stillness of the night like a musket shot. It seemed to him that it must rouse the neighborhood, and he had the sense of an echo resounding in the hollowness of the palace. But

74

nothing stirred. It took still more courage, after waiting a long while, to ply the knocker a second time.

Continued silence. Then, without warning, a sliding panel of the door jerked open, and he could make out dimly a patch of face and two eyes through the grating.

"*Caramba!*" hissed a voice. "Who are you and what do you want? *Vaya una hora de venir!* Can't you see that lights are out?"

"It's a matter of life and death," returned Pedro recklessly. "I must see His Grace."

"*Whose* life and death?"

"A friend of the Marquis—my father, Francisco de Vargas."

The porter gave an unconvinced grunt. "*Cáspita!* His Magnificence has retired."

"Just the same, inform him. He'll not thank you if you don't."

Slowly, doubtfully, the panel closed, and Pedro remained in the moonlit stillness. He did not know whether the man intended to carry his message or not. Somewhere an owl shrilled; a watchman from one of the near-by streets called the hour. Pedro stood with his heart thumping. In due time, the watchman would reach the square, would want to know who it was in front of the Marquis's door. No doubt orders had been sent out for Pedro's arrest. Standing in the glare of the moon, he was perfectly visible.

The monotonous call came nearer.

Then unexpectedly bolts were drawn, and a section of the door opened.

"All right," grumbled a voice. "Come in, but I warn you that His Grace does not care to be disturbed for trifles."

A dim lamp, held shoulder-high, lighted the servant's bearded features and showed an expanse of stone walls. Pedro followed, as the man led the way through a cavernous hall and then to the right up a curving staircase to the second floor. Here a confusion of corridors branched out.

"You're Pedro de Vargas, eh?" said the porter, turning into one of these. "Don Francisco has only one son."

"Yes, Pedro de Vargas."

He had an impression that a door on the left closed suddenly, as if it had been slightly ajar, and it seemed to him that he heard a low exclamation. But he was too absorbed by the approaching interview to think twice of it.

His guide stopped finally at the end of the corridor, parted some

75

hangings, led him across an antechamber, and announced his name to the candlelit twilight of a large room. Then he withdrew.

It was a moment before Pedro could distinguish the huge four-poster bedstead in an alcove facing him at the end of the apartment. Some pieces of richly carved furniture, a vague portrait, the oaken mass of a wardrobe against the wall, were details barely noticed as compared with the bust of the man propped against pillows within the curtains of the bed and visible in the flare of a couple of tall candles.

The Marquis had drawn a brocaded robe over his shoulders, but he had not yet adjusted his nightcap, which remained at an angle. His eyes, still blinking at the light, his square beard and hooked nose, gave him a solemn, owl-like expression. He did not, however, permit the unexpected to roughen the perfection of his manners.

"Draw near, young sir," he invited. And when Pedro stopped with a low bow and flutter of excuses outside the alcove, "No—here, if you please. The son of Francisco de Vargas has always the bedside privilege with me. That's better."

Pedro entered the alcove, bowed low again, and repeated his apologies. The Marquis gave a slight wave of the hand.

"Do not mention it. I was not asleep, and even if I had been, I am always at your father's service. There is no one whom I more affectionately admire. What is the matter that concerns him? I gathered from my servant that all was not well. It is an honor that you turn to me; it will be thrice an honor if I am privileged to help. Speak quite frankly and be at your ease."

Relief at this gracious welcome made Pedro's eyes smart. For the first time in the last hour, life seemed normal. He was once more the son of an eminent gentleman, and no longer helpless or friendless.

As form required, he sank to one knee, though the Marquis made a gesture of protest.

"*Vuestra Merced* is too good, too generous! God reward Your Grace! When my father hears of Your Grace's kindness, he will express his thanks better than I can. *Vuestra Merced*, the trouble is this."

Confidently, he now told what had happened and poured forth his bewilderment. Naturally the Marquis, knowing his father, would realize that this arrest was all a preposterous blunder. No one was a more devoted son of the Church than Francisco de Vargas—a fact of public knowledge. That he should be accused of heresy made neither rhyme nor reason. But it was not his father who concerned Pedro at the moment so much as Doña María and his sister. The shock to them might be serious, especially to a young girl like Mercedes, who had always

76

been frail. He did not know what to do, implored the Marquis's counsel.

The light of the candles turned one side of Pedro's hair to red flame, and Carvajal, who was an amateur of art, reflected that a portrait painter would have been pleased with the effect—that Venetian fellow, Titian, for example, whose work he had admired in Italy. Aesthetically interested, he looked more owl-like and benevolent than ever. When Pedro had finished his plea, he half-expected the warmhearted nobleman to rise from bed, summon his lackeys to dress him, and set out at once to effect the release of the prisoners, or at any rate to make his influence felt.

There was a long pause, during which Carvajal fingered his beard.

"My dear boy," he said at last, "believe me, you have my complete sympathy. I am more than touched by your distress. It grieves me too that Don Francisco and Doña María, together with your charming sister, should be temporarily detained. Tomorrow I have pressing affairs, but next day it will really give me pleasure to make inquiries. Meanwhile, as you say, it is probably a mistake which will clear itself in a short time."

He sipped his words as if they were honey.

"*Vuestra Merced*—" Pedro gasped.

Carvajal flowed on. "If it were a case before the civil courts, I might be more helpful; I might even be able to do something. But the Holy Office is a different matter. What right has a layman to intervene in spiritual affairs? As good Catholics, we must have utter confidence in our Mother, the Church, and render her complete obedience at whatever personal sacrifice." The Marquis raised a forefinger in admonition. "The Holy Office is charged with defending the purity of the Faith; it must protect the fold from taint. Perhaps something in your parents' lives—"

"Your Grace knows them! How could there be anything!"

Carvajal shook his head. "Ah, my son, you are perhaps blinded by natural affection. I say there may be something in your parents' lives or in yours, for that matter, or even in mine, of which we are unconscious, but which would not escape the keen eyes of our Holy Mother. In that case, we must bare our backs to the scourge and humbly beg for correction to the salvation of our souls. Yes, my son, even if that correction meant the destruction of our base and fleshly bodies."

It was plain that the Marquis enjoyed his own sermon. He spoke in a solemn cadence and turned his eyes up at the crucifix which hung facing him between the curtains at the end of the bed.

"Thus, with complete assurance, we may entrust this affair to the saintly Inquisitor of Jaén, Father Ignacio de Lora, a man who beatifies our city with his presence.[13]

Mocking echoes stirred in Pedro's mind: "Twenty, thirty, forty, fifty," accompanied by the clink of gold. He felt a growing tautness along the spine.

"If there is no guilt," concluded the Marquis, "your parents will go free. If there has been sin, you should rejoice at the expiation. Far better a temporal than an eternal punishment; far better—"

"How many go free?" Pedro demanded. "Does Your Grace know of any, guilty or not—"

"*That,* my son," interrupted Carvajal with the utmost gentleness, "is a rebellious, nay, an impious question. It reflects on the integrity of the Church. No doubt everyone, if closely examined, is guilty of sin and deserves some punishment. The reverend fathers are too conscious of their mission not to do all they can for the souls of those who come under their notice. But it has happened, I believe, that more than one has been discharged free from blame. I hope that this will be true of your parents."

Pedro's hope had turned to lead, but a growing ferment of anger sustained him. He got to his feet.

"Your Grace's advice then—?"

"Is to rely on God, my dear boy, and on the justice of the Holy Office. I shall do all in my power, all in my power."

De Vargas controlled himself, though his voice thickened. "What would *Vuestra Merced* suggest for tonight? Our house has been occupied. If I turn to an inn, I'll be arrested. I have no place to go."

In view of the fine promises, he could at least expect that the Marquis would offer him shelter for the night. Because of that, he had to keep his temper.

"No place to go?" Carvajal repeated. "My son, you have one place above all to go. You should proceed at once to the Castle and give yourself up. It will tend to show your innocence; it will be an act of filial loyalty to your father. You should support your parents in their hour of trial."

Undoubtedly there was weight to this advice. Perhaps, indeed, surrender was the best course. But an alarm began sounding in Pedro's head. Give himself up? Deprive his family of the only voice left to take their part outside of prison? He wanted to think that over.

"It's a late hour," he hesitated. "Would Your Grace generously allow me to remain here until morning? I shall then decide—" But at the look of astonishment on Carvajal's face, his words faded out.

"Young man, what you ask is impossible. It would expose me to the gravest charges. You should know that anyone who shelters a person sought by the Inquisition is considered equally guilty. Allow me to point out that it is indelicate to make a request which I must, of course, refuse."

Indelicate! A smother of heat submerged de Vargas. He thought of poor Manuel Pérez, who had risked his neck to save him, while this stuffed effigy of a grandee, his father's avowed friend, declined the most trifling help! But he mastered himself.

"I shall then take my leave, Your Grace. *Vuestra Merced* has been exceedingly kind."

The irony made no dent on the Marquis's self-satisfaction.

"You are quite welcome. It is a pleasure to advise the son of an old friend. If there is any service I can render, please call on me. And present my affectionate regards to Don Francisco and Doña María. No doubt they will soon be at liberty. I take it you are now going to the Castle—the best plan."

Pedro did not enlighten him. He felt that another minute of that honeyed voice would lead to murder. With a stiff bow and a half-smothered *buenas noches,* he turned out of the alcove.

"*Buenas noches,* my dear boy," answered the Marquis, raising his eyebrows at such abruptness. "If you will wait in the anteroom, a servant will attend you to the door. Farewell."

He pulled the tassel of a bellrope languidly; a remote tinkle sounded. Then, being drowsy, he snuffed the bedside candles himself and relaxed on the pillows. He was conscious of having graciously fulfilled the duties of his position.

But Pedro did not wait in the anteroom. He could find his own way downstairs, *por Dios;* and with long strides, jerky from anger, he followed the dark corridor towards the entrance hall. If he had been less headlong, he might have heard a light step hurrying in front of him, as if someone had left the anteroom just as he entered it; but he had nearly reached the hall landing when he was startled by a touch on his sleeve.

"Señor de Vargas," whispered a voice. "Señor, one moment."

Even in the darkness, he recognized Luisa de Carvajal and the perfume of her dress.

XIV

She led him across the threshold of a room to the side, which was vaguely lighted by a single taper. Evidently the place, a sort of antechamber belonging to a guest suite, was not used at present.

"I had been saying good night to my father when you came," she whispered. "I heard you give your name to the servant."

She still wore the dress of brocaded silver and the jeweled net over her hair, but to Pedro it seemed a very long time since they had met in the garden. His anger with the Marquis was suddenly forgotten.

"I had to know why you were here," she went on; "I listened in the anteroom. *Ay Dios,* how awful! What are you going to do?"

"I don't know," he answered dully.

Footsteps approached along the corridor. She pushed the door to and stood with fixed eyes and one hand at her throat as the lackey answered his master's bell. Then, a minute later, the servant, discovering that the light in the Marquis's room was out, returned grumbling along the gallery.

She drew a breath when he had passed. What if he had caught the glimmer of the candle in her hand! The new self which had awakened in the garden, the new pulse beat of independence, struggled against the habit of her doll-like training. What if anyone should find out that she was here in a room with Pedro de Vargas! She turned faint at the thought.

"Are you going to give yourself up?" she breathed.

He shrugged his shoulders. "Perhaps."

She would have liked to go back to her father's room, throw herself on her knees, entreat him for Pedro. He could help—she knew that; he could at least contrive to send Pedro out of Jaén. But that her father should learn that there was anything between her and young de Vargas was an idea too terrifying to contemplate. Besides, prudence told her that her suit would be useless: it would bring down the Marquis's wrath upon her, and would make matters worse for Pedro himself.

"Perhaps," he repeated. "But I'll wait till morning."

It crossed her mind that she could hide him here; there were several rooms in the palace where no one went, where he would be safe. But again the risk appalled her. Better not—

She wrung her hands. "I'll pray for you."

He was deeply moved. It did not occur to him that she could help him otherwise. The thought of himself in the prayers of Luisa de

Carvajal was enough—more than enough—a dizzy honor that restored a measure of confidence.

"If you will do that, I need nothing else."

It seemed to her that she heard footsteps again. Perhaps the doorman, waiting below, had grown suspicious, would climb the stairs to investigate.

"I'll pray for you always. You must go now."

"Yes, of course."

His green eyes were burning. She could almost feel the heat of them on her upturned face. . . . Surely there were footsteps.

"You must go . . . Hurry!"

"Listen, *querida mía*, this trouble will pass. I shall fight my way through. Then I'll come back. I'll come back with my head up. It's a vow. Remember that—and pray for me."

"I'll always remember," she whispered. "Hurry! I'm afraid . . ."

Opening the door, he disappeared into the darkness of the hall. She heard the click of his heels on the stairs beyond and the faint rattle of his sword.

Sinking to her knees, she besought the Virgin for him, praying a long time with hot, aching eyes and a lump in her throat. But somehow it brought her no comfort; she had no conviction that her prayer reached beyond the oaken beams of the ceiling. It was easy to pray.

"After all," she thought weakly, "I'm only a girl. It would have been improper to have done more. It was improper anyway. *María!* If anyone knew that I had spoken with him here! *Salve Regina!* Queen of Heaven, protect Pedro de Vargas!"

Again the prayer dropped like a pellet of lead.

After the doorman, none too graciously, had seen him out, Pedro walked across to the shadow of the plane trees and stood pondering. His glimpse of Luisa had the effect of a cordial; it heated his blood and raised his spirits. But it had not changed the thorny difficulties of his position; he had still to find shelter for the night, and he had still to decide what he would do after that. Should he give himself up, or should he follow Manuel Pérez's advice and make for the sierra? What he most wanted now was time to think.

In the darkness of the plane trees, he was balancing one course against the other when, as often happens in such cases, events took charge. Without warning, a group of men, carrying lanterns, burst into the little plaza and headed straight between the trees. The light on their corselets and headpieces, the rattle and jangle of them, denoted the watch or, at least, an armed squad of soldiers. Pedro had only a second in which to step behind a tree and to make himself as small as possible.

"I'll bet that cursed fellow was lying," growled one of the party. "Why would de Vargas be hammering on His Grace's door at this hour? It's a wrong scent."

Pedro held his breath. The posse was indeed looking for him. Some loiterer, whom he had not been aware of, had recognized him as he stood at the door of the palace, and had reported him.

"It's the only scent we have," retorted another. "Probably he got wind of something—thought the Marquis was his best chance. We'll wait a minute, then do some hammering ourselves."

They had come to a stop within three feet of Pedro, who stood glued to the tree trunk. A voice demurred that they had better think twice before interrupting the Marquis's repose. But the other, who seemed to be an officer, cut him off.

"Christ!" he swore. "I've had my orders to bring young de Vargas in wherever I found him. The Holy Office doesn't care for duke or marquis. It won't hurt to wake the porter, will it? I'd rather face him than His Reverence."

It wasn't the watch then; these were de Lora's people. The shifting lantern beams darted here and there. Pedro wondered whether he shouldn't make a break for it. The instinct of flight blotted out the thought of surrender.

"Ho! By God, who's this!"

In a flash Pedro cut loose from the tree trunk and raced for the nearest street opening.

Raucous whoops sounded behind him, and a scurry of feet. *"Al ladrón! Al ladrón!"*

With his cloak over one arm, his sword hitched up to free his movements, Pedro dashed forward headlong, aimless for the moment except to shake off pursuit. With a head start and unencumbered by armor, he had the advantage; but the men who followed were no mean runners either, and their shouts reached in front of him.

"Al ladrón!"

A group emerging from an inn blocked his road, and he had to cut back to an alleyway, thus coming almost within reach of his pursuers. He felt the fingers of one of them brush his shoulders, but a leap set him ahead again. God grant that the alley wasn't a dead end! No, it opened to the right.

"Al ladrón!"

He catapulted against two heavy figures in the dark and heard their yells mingle in the growing clamor behind. He turned left, then right, and found himself on the path that followed the inner side of the town walls. But exactly where? Yes, it wasn't far to the North Gate. If he turned in that direction, the densest quarter of the town, he was lost. His one chance lay to the east, though it meant an uphill climb. One part of the wall there was lower, and from childhood, when he and other boys had raided near-by orchards, he knew the trick of scaling it. *"Al ladrón!"* The following pack had caught sight of him in the moonlight. Panting, he turned along the upward curve of the path.

It was a grueling course. Blocks of stone, which had fallen from the neglected wall, littered the way and made running hard. The slope grew steeper. It was especially unfavorable to those who had dined and wined late, or to those of more years than agility. Without turning his head, Pedro could hear the chase stringing out; the yells were more distant, the footsteps more spaced. But do what he could, one pair of jackboots kept pace with him, sometimes nearer, sometimes farther, though a clanking sound which accompanied them showed that the man was running in his steel jacket.

"God's curse on him!" thought Pedro, whose breath grew shorter.

Up. Up. Jackboots hung on, stride for stride. If only someone did not blunder down in the opposite direction!

At last, with lungs at the bursting point, Pedro saw ahead of him the disused steps which had once served for manning the walls. His legs felt like butter, his mouth like leather. He had to make those steps. If he could once reach the top of the wall—

Tripping over a stone, he pitched full length to the ground.

Convulsively he was up at once—up just in time to meet Jackboots with his shoulder and gain room for defense. The two swords gleamed and clashed in the same moment. Mindful of the flight of steps several yards behind him, Pedro drew back foot by foot. The man followed; and, as his mind cleared, de Vargas recognized in the moonlight the features of Sebastián Reyes, whom he had talked with at the door of the Inquisitor.

"Ha! Reyes!" he panted. "Hold back, for God's love! I thought you were a friend."

"Friend be damned!" gasped the other, thrusting. "I serve the Holy Office. Give yourself over."

Pedro realized that he had perhaps a minute in which to dispose of the fellow and gain the wall before the rest of the posse came up. He retreated step by step, struggling to catch his breath, feeling the ground behind him with his heels, parrying blow after blow, with now and then a thrust of his own to keep Reyes back. The man's helmet and cuirass left only his face and arms unprotected. Shouts and the sound of running grew nearer.

In point of exhaustion, the two opponents were even; but in the science of fence, Pedro had the advantage. Not for nothing had Francisco de Vargas drilled him in every trick of combat. Alone with Sebastián Reyes, he would have had no trouble; it was cavalier against ranker. The problem, however, was one of time.

"Socorro!" the man shouted, and an approaching yell answered.

Where were the steps? Pedro groped desperately for them with his heels.

At last!

But time was gone. Around the curve of the path appeared two hulking figures, then three. Pedro hitched himself a foot up; Reyes followed, cutting at his legs; one of the new arrivals struck at him from the open side of the steps; he was vaguely conscious that another was attempting to clamber to a level above and thus take him in the rear.

Putting everything he had into one last effort, de Vargas whipped a ringing cut to Reyes's steel cap, stopped him for an instant, then backed this up with a kick that landed full force on the man's chest. Reyes came down on his hams; and at the same moment Pedro, turning, fled upward, pausing only to thrust at the face of the soldier who had gained a kneehold on the edge of the steps. The fellow toppled back. A second later Pedro reached the summit of the wall, sheathed his sword, straddled the battlement, and lowered himself to arm's length on the other side.

Footholds were here that he knew of, but he had no time for them now. Letting go, he dropped twelve feet, landed on the slope, lost his footing, and rolled several yards until stopped by a clump of underbrush.

Oaths rained from the top of the wall.

He paused a moment to shout, *"Buenas noches!"* before plunging on downhill.

XV

Outstretched on the straw which filled the shallow bedstead in her garret room, Catana Pérez found it hard to sleep. This was unusual with her; as a rule, she dropped off catlike in half a minute. Perhaps the heat of the cubbyhole, which had baked all day under the roof of the inn, or the moonlight streaming through the sashless window kept her awake. But for whatever cause, the routine of the evening—a blur of faces, jokes, oaths, wine cups, horseplay, and guitar music—drifted dully through her mind.

It was unusual, too, that she felt depressed. She had danced well and had collected almost half a peso in odd coins. The picture of herself mingled in the drift of the other pictures—herself in obscure conflict with Hernán Soler, who danced opposite her, his hawk face dark with desire, his narrow eyes fixed on her.

The conflict between them was several months old. He wanted her, demanded her. He was handsome enough, dressed gaudily, lived high. That he and his men held the mountains between Jaén and Granada, cut throats and purses, and would probably end on the gibbet, did not trouble her. So far as that went, she liked courage and dash. But she hated Soler and had no illusions about him. She knew him for a brute under his perfume and velvet.

Yet all men were brutes, she reflected—only of different kinds: some mean and niggardly, some merely savage. She liked the latter best. All men were brutes, all whom she knew. Except one.

Pedro de Vargas, the unobtainable, the never-to-be-forgotten!

She clenched her hands in a sudden paroxysm, then pressed her face against her naked arm as if to bind back the hot tears. There was only one thing she wanted, after all, one thing that made life worth living; and that was as remote from her as the cold moon. Then what did anything else matter—Soler or another? God in heaven, how it hurt under her breast, this heat of love, this ache of love!

Below in the courtyard of the inn, Lubo, the watchdog, burst into a fury of barking that stopped suddenly; but she did not heed it. The slow drift across her mind went on. Bearded faces, wine-sour breaths, leering eyes, gross caresses, and herself in the reek of it, posturing and pirouetting, showing off her body to the twang of a guitar. Tomorrow night and tomorrow after that and tomorrow again; or, if she mated with Soler, the same thing in another place until she got old and undesirable. Yet all the while, a part of her, the essence of her, unseen and unsuspected, would be escaping behind Pedro de Vargas on Campeador.

She tried now to conjure up the various times she had seen him. Staring at the ceiling, she gradually relaxed and her eyes closed.

Then, at a footfall outside her door, she was wide awake, practical, and on guard. A footfall meant usually one thing; but there was a stout bar across the door, she had her knife and feared no man.

A low knock sounded; the latch rattled. She got up and slipped on her shift.

"Who's there?"

"Sancho López. Let me in."

"Why?" she answered, alert to the ways of men.

"Hell!" returned the mutter. "Open up; I've something to tell you."

Reassured, but still on guard, Catana drew back the bar, and López entered. The first glimpse of his dark, preoccupied face set her fears at rest. He stood a moment, pinching his chin, the bristles on his face making a rasping sound against his fingers.

"It's young Pedro de Vargas," he said.

She repeated the name soundlessly.

"He's here. Something with the Holy Office. His family's in the Castle. Almost taken himself—had to fight his way out. Wants to make the sierra. I've put him in the hayloft of the stable till morning. He's badly tuckered."

She stared at López, still clutching her shift together at the throat, her eyes black pools of excitement.

"Give him some wine and victuals," the innkeeper went on. "I don't want to mix in this. First thing in the morning, see that he leaves. Hernán Soler's his best bet. But he can't stay here."

Instantly she flared up. "Are you afraid, Sancho López? I didn't think you were a coward."

"*Anda!*" he snapped, though keeping his voice down. "D'you think I'm a fool? I'd do what I could for young de Vargas, but I won't be ruined or burned for him. No Santa Casa for me! Take some rags along. He's bleeding."

"*Hurt?*"

"A scratch on the leg—nothing bad. And now I'm washing my hands, d'you see? It's your business, if you want to take the risk."

She had already picked up her skirt. "Take the risk!" she echoed, dropping the garment over her head.

"Yes. If you're caught helping him, it's the *garrucha* for you, and maybe the stake. Remember, I don't know anything. What you do with your *galán* doesn't concern me."

Galán! Lover! The word made her blood simmer. Pedro de Vargas, her *galán!* She put on her bodice, hooking it quickly, and coiled up the dark rope of her hair.

"Don't worry, Sancho López."

Barefooted, so as not to make a sound, she stole out, threaded the dormitory of snoring guests who occupied the upstairs of the inn, and

86

clambered down the ladder to the main room. It took only a minute to fill a basket with food and to slip out through a side door into the courtyard.

"*Chitón, Lubocito!*" she cautioned the watchdog, who followed her to the stable.

Inside the black, smelly place, dense with the sleep of beasts and of several mule boys who had a shakedown there, she made her way carefully toward the ladder to the spare hayloft. It was a space partitioned off from the main supply of fodder, and was the only corner of the stable that offered concealment. Climbing the ladder, she rapped gently at the trap door over her head.

"It's Catana," she whispered.

The dim rays of a lantern seemed almost bright as the trap rose and she clambered up into the loft. She said, "Hush!" and laid a finger on her lips, waiting until Pedro had again lowered the door into place.

Her heart quailed at the change in him. His usually curly hair, now matted with dust and sweat, clung in sharp points to his forehead; his face was dead white and showed hollows at the cheeks; his eyes seemed unnaturally large. He had drawn off one of his boots and laid bare a gash on the shin, where a sword had cut through during his fight on the steps. It was not much of a wound, but it had drenched his ankle and foot with blood.

"My poor señor!" she exclaimed softly. "What the devil have they done to you!"

His lips relaxed. "Not too much. Not yet. By God, you're an angel, Catana! Have you got some wine in that basket?"

He sank back on a mound of hay, while she poured him out a cup and set the basket in front of him. Then, as he told her between mouthfuls what had happened, she sponged off the wounded leg with wine and skillfully bound it up with a strip of clean linen. Sympathetic oaths in a low voice punctuated his story. When she had finished bandaging, she sat with his foot still in her lap, one arm braced on either side, her angular face intent and her mouth hooked down.

It seemed so natural for her to tend him, to sit like this sharing his ill chance, that it did not occur to either of them how strangely natural it was.

"And your fine new doublet!" she lamented, when he told her of his drop from the wall. "The lovely breeches! Had you been to a *festín* this evening?"

He had put on his holiday clothes for the rendezvous with Luisa, and now glanced down at the ruin of them.

"No," he evaded, "not exactly."

He did not enlarge on it; but she guessed, and jealousy twisted its knife in her, though her face showed nothing. She merely gazed beyond him, at the slope of the hay.

"You *are* an angel," he repeated. "I felt cursed lonely on the road from Jaén. You've made a new man of me, Catana. I'll kiss you for it."

She shrugged her shoulders. "Be sensible, señor. It's no time for kisses. Who do you think accused you to the Santa Casa? De Silva?"

The suggestion startled him. He had not thought of de Silva. Now he remembered the quarrel at the pavilion, the man's veiled threats, the fact that he was a familiar of the Inquisition. It was possible, but unlikely. No cavalier would stoop to a thing like that. Even the knife of a hired bully would have been cleaner. He fell silent, turning the possibility in his mind.

"Is she beautiful?" Catana asked suddenly.

"What do you mean?"

"I mean the girl you dressed up for tonight."

He stared at first, then frowned. That anyone of Catana's station should refer to Luisa de Carvajal, his princess of honor, as a girl, shocked him.

Catana understood. "Lord Christ!" she flared, but caught herself and looked down, then faltered, "I'm sorry."

He felt ashamed but said formally, "There is a certain great and lovely lady, Catana, whom I am privileged to serve—let it suffice you."

She felt deservedly rebuked. Indeed, if he had spoken or acted differently, he would have lessened himself in her eyes. From the standpoint of the times, he spoke and loved as a hidalgo should. If her rival had been a wench like herself, she would have thought of murder; but the greatness of the lady altered things. She knew that he should worship some highborn hidalga in that world of his which was unknown to her, that she should count herself honored by the scraps of his regard. And because her humility was sincere, they both took it for granted.

"We must make plans," she said. "You must get away from here in the morning. Do you know Hernán Soler?"

"The robber?"

"Yes."

"I've seen him here."

"He has a hiding place I know of two leagues toward Granada. You could stay with him until you decide what to do. At worst he could get you to the sea—Málaga or Valencia."

"Why should he? He doesn't know me at all."

"He knows *me*." She forced a smile. "He's a friend of mine."

"I have no money. He's not a man to do something for nothing."

"That's my business. Leave it to me. He's an *amigo muy intimo*."

At that moment she made her decision. There was no use telling Pedro, because he would protest it. All that mattered to her was that he should escape. A girl had the right to dispose of herself, and Hernán Soler would be glad of the bargain.

But jealousy, though he would not have called it such, now took its turn with Pedro.

"A fine friend!" he snapped. *"Muchas gracias!* I can look out for myself. I know the sierra."

She shook her head. "You can't live in the mountains with every door closed to you on account of the Holy Office. Hernán's your one chance. He's a good Christian, but his brother died in an auto-da-fé at Seville. He hates the Santa Casa—"

She broke off and stared sharply at the partition behind her.

"Did you hear anything?"

"No," he said.

They could not have seen the eye which had been applied to a knot-hole in the partition and at that instant withdrew. It belonged to José, the mule boy of one of the *arrieros* stopping at the inn. He had wakened at Catana's entrance, had heard voices, and with the curiosity of his age had climbed to the main hayloft for a possible peep at forbidden mysteries. But the sight of Catana and Pedro de Vargas, sitting opposite each other across a lantern, was of no interest, and he retired disappointed.

Only the usual rustling sounds rose from the stable.

"I suppose it was nothing," she concluded. "No, señor, I'll guide you to Hernán in the morning."

"The risk for you?" he hesitated.

"That's nothing."

It would have been desecration to compare Catana in any way with Luisa de Carvajal. That the one was willing to dare everything for him and the other nothing did not present itself to his mind. Luisa was not expected to dare; her value was ethical, transcendental; she existed to be adored. Between this and Catana's practical courage, there was no connection. But for a moment Pedro de Vargas felt the heat of something that was more even than adoration. It bewildered him.

"Válgame Dios!" he muttered. "I love you."

"I love you," she answered simply.

He leaned toward her. The consent in her eyes, raised to his, the softness of her lips, drew him closer.

"I love you, Catana," he repeated.

Suddenly a clatter of hoofs filled the courtyard, a clanking and ring of steel, hammering on the door of the inn, summons to open.

At once she was on her feet, alert and tense. In an instant the lantern was out, the basket hidden beneath the hay. She crouched listening beside the trap door.

Confusion started below, the snorting and stamping of awakened animals, shouts and oaths. The stable door was flung back as ostlers and mule boys trooped out to gape at the invasion.

"Cover up with the hay," she directed. "I've got to show myself. Nobody's seen you. We'll put them on the wrong scent."

Raising the trap, she slipped under it, lowered it behind her, and a moment later mingled with the throng in front of the inn.

XVI

THERE WERE about a dozen mounted men. Rugged but respectful, Sancho López confronted the captain of the troop, who sat glaring down from his saddle. To lend him support, Catana appeared, as if from the inn, and stood beside him.

"No, Señor Captain, he is not here; he has not been here this evening. . . . Yes, I know Pedro de Vargas—as who doesn't? He has stopped at the Rosario for refreshment. . . . No, I have seen no one pass on the road, Señor Captain."

"But *I* have," Catana's husky voice interrupted. "*Vaya*, it must have been an hour ago. The watchdog wakened me. I looked out and noticed a man on the road. It was bright as day. He walked fast uphill. I said to myself, 'It's no time of night for an honest traveler.'"

The news sent a rattle of steel through the troop. Sebastián Reyes demanded, "By God, what're we waiting for? That's he. It'd be pretty close to an hour ago."

"If it was he," returned the captain, "he's in the sierra by now and safe till morning."

"Unless he stopped at Juan the Woodcutter's," drawled Catana indifferently, "up the Guardia. He's hunted through the mountains and knows Juan."

The captain sat tight. He was not the man to leave one covert unbeaten for the sake of another. Besides, he knew all about the Rosario.

On the point of ordering a search, he happened to drop his skeptical eye on José, the mule boy, and found him grinning. Why? Nobody else grinned.

"You!" he barked. "Come here."

The youth's self-importance vanished. In the dead silence, he faltered forward. The captain drew a coin from his belt purse, tossed it in the air, caught it in his gauntlet. A gold coin.

"You look a sharp lad," he said. "What d'you know?"

"Nothing, Señor Captain. I—I don't know anything."

"Take a hitch on his arm," directed the other. "Jog his memory. The dog wouldn't be sniggering for nothing."

Two men, who had dismounted, stepped over to José. One collared him, the other grasped his wrist.

"For God's sake!" screamed the boy.

Slowly his arm rose behind his back. What did the arm of a ragamuffin matter except to himself? If he knew nothing, he shouldn't have grinned at the wrong time.

The captain sat tight.

"For God's sake! . . . Let me go . . . I'll tell."

He was in a hard pinch. If he did not tell, they would break his arm. If he told—

Catana watched him inscrutably over the shoulder of one of the men. She was chewing a straw.

"Going to speak?" asked the captain.

The fear of imminent pain overbalanced the remoter fear; but he lied as much as possible. To betray Pedro de Vargas was one thing—he might get away with it; to betray Catana meant at best the knife of one of her admirers between his ribs before tomorrow's sun.

She stood watching him as he stammered about the *caballero* in the spare hayloft. The gentleman had let himself into the stable and climbed the ladder. He didn't know whether it was de Vargas or not. Catana arched her eyebrows with interest and shifted the straw between her teeth. "*Diga, diga!* Well, well!" she remarked.

The troopers were streaming across the courtyard. José plucked at the captain's boot.

"The money, sir?"

He received a cut from the other's whip that sent him back with his hands to his face. When he lowered them, Catana was standing in front of him. She might have been joking for all that a bystander would have noticed.

91

"The money, sir?" she mimicked; and, removing the straw, she drew it lightly across José's throat. "Better find a priest, Joseíto. That's what you need more than money, sir—a priest."

They brought Pedro de Vargas into the inn; but, except that his hands were bound, they treated him with the courtesy due a gentleman. The captain drank his health, and Sebastián Reyes complimented his swordsmanship. When he complained of the tightness of the cords, they loosened them so that he could make shift to drink. Save for their duty, they wished him the best. No reference was made to what awaited him in the Castle of Jaén; good manners forbade it.

But Sancho López and the Rosario fared worse. Now that they had got their prisoner, the men of the Holy Office relaxed. They guzzled López's wine, devoured his victuals, and took over the premises. They might have taken him over as well for sheltering an accused heretic; but when Pedro declared that he had entered the stable without the innkeeper's knowledge, they let it go at that. López could count himself lucky to get off with horseplay—sword pricks in the behind and, when the fun grew madder, a blanket-tossing in the courtyard. Some of his guests had the same treatment.

Pedro's chief concern was for Catana, but he soon realized that he need not worry. She belonged to this element, like the devil to fire or a fish to water. She appealed to one bully against another; left them quarreling; slipped from the arms of a third to the knee of a fourth; turned the laugh on a fifth; flew into white-hot rage that took the breath from the next man; laughed, swaggered, dominated. In the end a guitar was found, a tune struck up, and she danced her audience into groggy adulation. That the Rosario, though battered, survived the evening was largely due to her.

Seated against the wall between the captain and Reyes, with the table a bulwark in front of them, Pedro half-dozed. At last consciousness split into fragments like a dream. He could see the moonlight on the fairy round in the garden; the owl face of the Marquis de Carvajal; Luisa's pale beauty lighted by the candle; the melee at the steps; the road between the olive trees from Jaén; Catana facing him in the hayloft; and now, jumbled with this, the uproar in front of him. A dream, or rather nightmare because of the cords on his arms and the dread of tomorrow.

Catana pirouetted near them, but he might have been a stranger for any recognition in her eyes. Only the professional smile. He understood: she had to pretend that she didn't know him to save her skin; but he felt terribly alone.

The windows had suddenly turned gray. It was already tomorrow.

Head-splitting din greeted the end of the dance. *"Bis! Bis! Viva la Catana!"*

"Viva!" bawled Reyes. *"Salud,* de Vargas!"

"Salud!" Pedro mumbled. He fingered his cup, then lurched forward on the table.

"By God, he's asleep," said a distant voice.

He knew nothing more until several hours later, when he wakened with his arms numb and his head bursting.

XVII

IT WAS WELL into the morning when the troopers shook off last night's carouse and got ready to start for Jaén. Seated, filthy and disheveled, on the rump of a horse, his legs dangling, his arms tied, a rope binding him to the rider in front, Pedro seemed to himself already a prison scarecrow. The sun burned down from a pitiless blue sky, adding sweat and heat to the other discomforts.

"*Oiga, moza,*" called the trooper in front of Pedro to Catana, "one more cup of water. López's foul wine has left my mouth like a pigsty."

"Perhaps it found it that way, m'lord," she drawled; but, fetching a pitcher, she filled a cup for the man and handed it up to him.

She looked pale from the night, and her black eyes seemed larger because of the hollows under them. Shifting to Pedro, they narrowed a little. The impersonal look was gone. They spoke fiercely, passionately. He knew that she was trying to convey some message.

"May I have a drink, Catana?"

"*A sus órdenes.*" She filled and held the cup high, so that, bending a little, he could drink. "*Valor y esperanza, señor!*" she added lightly.

Courage and hope! Her eyes narrowed again. It seemed to him that she stressed the last word.

The captain mounted, gave the word of command, and the little squadron clanked out of the courtyard. Looking back, Pedro saw Catana standing arms akimbo, gazing after them. She gave a brief wave of the hand; then, turning abruptly, she entered the inn.

It was a league downhill to Jaén, and because of the heat and dust, the captain rode slowly. Moreover, more people than usual were heading for the town, so much so that at times they almost blocked the highway. Peasants in holiday clothes, on foot and on donkeys, trooped forward

93

as if to some gala event. But they were in a queer humor too, a feverish humor that showed itself in forced hilarity and use of the bottle, with a sprinkling of sober faces in between. They made way docilely for the horsemen and with sidelong glances when they saw the pennon of the Holy Office, which was borne at the head of the troop.

Absorbed by his own concerns, Pedro wondered vaguely at first what saint's day it was. Then a witticism, flung at him by a yokel on a burro, recalled what had slipped his mind.

"Get a move on, heretic, or you'll miss saying *hasta la vista* to your friends."

Yes, he had forgotten. It *was* a big day. A couple of dozen men and women were scheduled to make confession of their sins in the public square and to receive penance. For some, the lash and the galleys; for some, the lash and prison; for some, the stake. It was rumored that six were to burn.

He turned faint a moment; black dots wheeled in front of his eyes. But remembering himself, he fought the dizziness off, lifted his head. He had witnessed several auto-da-fés with the indifference bred of familiarity. Now his point of view had suddenly altered, and it took no great shrewdness to understand why.

The pride of an hidalgo helped him out. He was carried forward amid the taunts of the crowd, impassive as a statue, closing his mind to the future, scornful of the present.

At last the shadow of the city gates shut off the sun. The troop plodded uphill through streets choked with people flocking in the same direction. As they drew closer to the Plaza Santa María in front of the cathedral, it was only by sheer weight of horseflesh that the riders could force a passage.

"Why not see the show?" called one of them to the captain, when they plunged into the milling crowd that filled the square.

"No, not till we've reported to the Castle," came the answer. "We'll have time later. Skirt the crowd."

But it was not so easy. The place was packed to suffocation, except for the center where a cordon of pikemen kept sufficient space clear. Brought to a halt in spite of himself, the captain looked for a crevice, through which he could wedge his way, and found none.

With new eyes, Pedro stared at the objects in the center of the plaza. There was the familiar low platform, erected during the night and standing a few steps above the cobblestones. On one side, it supported low benches, where the condemned would sit; and facing these were higher seats for the Inquisitor and the town magistrates. There, not far off, half-hidden by faggots, stood the thick, blunt posts with their blackened chains.

"*Demonio!*" chafed the captain, standing in his stirrups. But at that moment came a sound that put an end to any thought of advance.

It was a distant chant, growing steadily louder. The pikemen on the opposite side of the square, shouldering and shoving, cleared the end of the street leading down from the Castle. A hush fell on the crowd, as the diapason of the chant came nearer.

"*Miserere mei, Deus, secundum magnam misericordiam tuam: et secundum multitudinem miserationum tuarum dele iniquitatem meam.*"

Into the square, under the hot sky, slowly advanced the procession. To a philosopher, such as Germany was then producing, it might have symbolized many things: a once redeeming faith now fossilized and distorted by human corruption into the opposite of everything its Founder had advocated; a demonstration of the past, still powerful and alert to keep the New Age in leading strings. But Pedro de Vargas was no philosopher. He had been conditioned to accept humbly and in trembling the sternness of God as exercised by a divine Church. Not for him to question or protest; the very instinct of protest was in itself a proof of Original Sin. To the people in the square and to him among them, this ought, indeed, to be a joyful occasion: it manifested the victory of God over the forces of evil.

So, humbly and in trembling, he gazed at the banner of the Inquisition borne in front, and then at the column of chanting friars—white, black, and gray—of the monastic orders, and then at the shuffling procession behind. These last were the penitents. They came in single file, each one flanked by Soldiers of Christ, as the familiars of the Holy Office styled themselves. Each penitent was clad in the hideous *sanbenito*, to be worn by many of them till death, a loose, yellow garment like a nightshirt, plastered front and back with red crosses. Each had a rope about the neck and carried a long, green candle unlighted.

They limped and stumbled forward on limbs dislocated by torture. Their faces were putty gray, their hair matted; they blinked painfully in the unfamiliar sunlight. One old woman, too crippled to walk, was drawn on a hurdle, her distorted frame bumping over the cobblestones. At a pause in the chanting could be heard her shrill outcries. Most of the penitents were of Jewish or Moorish blood and had confessed to lapsing back into heresy. A few were self-admitted practitioners of the Black Art; a few were convicted blasphemers.

Hobble, hobble. They dragged themselves up on the platform, each

95

to his or her appointed place on the benches, in the order in which they would receive judgment. The old woman, still feebly moaning, was carried to her place and propped upright between two Jews. The ranks of scarecrows behind their candles looked like a red and yellow crazy quilt threaded with green. Now that they came nearer, Pedro recognized some of the faces, but was struck by the change in them. They were half-crazed men and women, only a blur of what they had been once. Fortunately, too, their minds seemed blurred, and they sat vacantly blinking at what went on.

The procession closed with another column of chanting monks and a detachment of soldiers. Then, from the cathedral, emerged the dignitaries of Church and town: the Bishop in purple, the canons and lesser clergy in their finest laces and berettas, the Alcalde and Alguazil Mayor with their badges of office, the leading noblemen of Jaén and officers of the *Miliz Christi*. Silks and velvets, gold and jewels. The crowd gaped. The peasants from the country had something to talk about for the rest of the summer. There was the Marquis de Carvajal, his beard uptilted above the Cross of Santiago on his chest, his eyes heavy with self-importance. There (Pedro's lips tightened) was Diego de Silva in black and gold. A red plume curled from the jeweled brooch of his velvet cap. Pedro knew all of them; but, concealed by the shoulders of the trooper and by the coating of dust on his face, they would hardly have recognized him. For the fraction of a moment, he expected to see his father among them.

They were only a background, however. In fact, it seemed to him that the whole concourse in the square, spectators and actors alike, was merely a setting for the white-robed figure of Ignacio de Lora. Every eye focused on the Inquisitor, as he headed the glittering procession onto the platform and took his raised seat opposite the condemned. Except for his glowing black eyes, he looked more than ever like a granite statue.

Unnecessarily the criers proclaimed silence, for everyone was now intent enough. A mass was said at an improvised altar on the platform, and then de Lora rose to preach the day's sermon. He spoke in a businesslike, penetrating voice that reached everywhere and had an effect on the mind like the probing of a lancet. He discussed heresy, God's wrath, and hell-fire. He extolled the mercy of the Church, who, by bringing souls to a state of grace and by imposing a brief and corporal penance, saved them from the eternal flames.

The voice ran on. Pedro's dangling legs felt heavier, his arms more numb. Sweat streaked his face. He tried to escape from the insistent voice by gazing up at the gothic front of the cathedral, at the roof line of houses hemming in the square.

But at one point his glance happened to fall on a man in the crowd next to the pikemen. Something familiar about him fixed Pedro's attention. Then suddenly he recognized him. It was García. Although now disguised in the steel helmet and cuirass of a soldier, the broad nose, bull neck, and bulk of the man were unmistakable.

What was he doing here? Wasn't this the morning when—? Pedro stiffened. Wasn't García's mother to have been discharged from prison this morning? Then why—?

From where he gazed, Pedro could see only García's profile, but he observed that the man was not looking at de Lora. He stood with a fixed stare turned on the benches of the penitents. Following it, Pedro noticed the old woman who had been carried to the platform, and who was being held upright by the arm of one of the Jews. Looking more intently, he recognized, in spite of the skeleton features and sparse white hair, Dorotea Romero.

She looked more like a clay-colored mummy than a woman. Her face had been contorted by pain into a mask; but some dim resemblance to her former self lingered on. Glancing back at García, Pedro saw that he did not move or take his eyes from her. Only now and then he ran his tongue between his lips as if to moisten them.

Well, this was de Lora's way. After all, perhaps he could not be expected to release the woman secretly. When it came her turn to receive judgment, he would declare her free.

Meanwhile, Pedro, forgetting his own situation, shared García's suspense. He wondered what the latter would do when his mother had been discharged. His military disguise was a clever stroke. Probably he would present himself as a soldier out of service, who had been paid by the woman's brother to take charge of her. It remained to be seen whether he could get away with it.

The sermon ended, and the crowd stirred with suppressed excitement. Even the human derelicts on the benches stirred. The supreme moment of the day had arrived.

In a booming voice, an ecclesiastic of the Inquisitorial Court summoned the penitents one by one to hear their imposed penance.

Francisco Cadena stumbled forward and lurched to his knees in front of the Inquisitor's high seat. He was shaking in every limb. Pedro knew him as a prosperous owner of olive groves in the vicinity of Jaén. He had a young wife whom he was proud of and liked to dress in the newest style. Of course, whatever penance he received, all that was now over, because everything he possessed had already been confiscated by the Holy Office. The same held true for the other penitents. They had nothing left to lose but their skin and bones.

The deep-voiced clerk reviewed Cadena's crimes. His maternal grandparents had been proved to be Jews. He had confessed to *marranía,* a lapse into Jewishness from the Catholic faith. For this deadly sin, he now felt true repentance. The Church, ever merciful, decreed the following penance, upon the performing of which she would reconcile him to herself.

The clerk paused. Cadena groveled and rubbed his hands feverishly.

"Three hundred stripes on horseback and ten years in the galleys."

Cadena still groveled. It meant only protracted death. First, the slow parade through town, half-naked, bound to a horse's back, while the executioners plied their whips. Then the rower's bench and the scourge of the overseers. Ten years.

He raised his clasped hands toward the Inquisitor.

"Your Reverence, Your Reverence," he babbled, "think . . . in the prison . . . three times the *garrucha,* three times the *trampazo* . . . Have mercy!"

De Lora made a motion with his hand. Francisco Cadena now belonged to the secular arm. One of the hangman's lackeys took charge of him, haled him back to his bench, where he sat mumbling and staring. He would never reach the galleys, Pedro reckoned.

"Panchito Marín."

An *apóstata,* a backslider of Moorish blood. He was "reconciled" at the price of two hundred lashes and eight years at the oars.

Dolores Marín, his wife. "Reconciled" for two hundred stripes and eight years of prison.

The toughs in the crowd licked their chops; the whipping of heretics made good entertainment. Pedro closed his mind to the possibility of another day several months later. . . . No, it was absurd. He wouldn't think of it. Looking at García, he saw a bead of sweat roll down the man's cheeks and drip to the ground.

"The Church, ever merciful . . . perpetual prison . . . the *sanbenito* for life . . . Iago Hasta . . . two hundred stripes . . . blasphemer . . . the galleys . . ."

The clerk's unctuous voice rolled along like an innkeeper's announcing his bill of fare. The penitents' benches were now filling up with those who had heard their sentence. Some looked unmoved, as if the capacity for suffering had been exhausted; others wept feebly; others sat shrunken and trembling. The mind of one man snapped; he

98

threshed his arms about, making faces at the crowd. And meanwhile those who had not yet heard were on tenterhooks, for the sentences of death came last. If a church painter had sought models for a "Last Judgment," the choice would have been rich. The platform exhibited a corner of hell.

"Henríquez Guzmán . . . the Church, ever merciful . . . 'reconciled' . . . to burn presently at the stake."

A higher wave of excitement swept the crowd. There were eight left. This meant that eight, not six, would burn. An unexpected bonus of two. No wonder that there was an unusual supply of faggots! The executioner began laying out his instruments, the "agony-pears," which, being thrust into the mouths of those condemned to burn, stopped their screams and thus spared the ears of too sensitive spectators.

Whether it was by chance or design, Dorotea Romero's name was read last. It occurred to Pedro that probably de Lora wished to end the proceedings with one act of complete mercy, which would redound to his reputation for saintliness. After all, the crowd would never hear of the eight hundred ducats. But the suspense was hard on García. His face had grown white; it looked as if his nerve was on the point of cracking.

At last—"Dorotea Romero." Two guards bundled the old woman forward, thrust her on her knees. The clerk detailed her crimes. She had confessed to a pact with Satan; she had attended the Black Mass; she had compassed the death of sundry people by her spells. She now repented of these unspeakable sins, and the Church, ever merciful, admitted her to penance.

"Wherefore she is now remanded to the secular arm to be burned presently at the stake."

For a moment Pedro stared incredulously at the granite figure of the Inquisitor. Surely even now he would intervene. He had taken the bribe, he had given his word. But de Lora's features looked as stony as ever. Then, in a devastating flash, Pedro understood the cheat. Was not Dorotea Romero being delivered from prison on the day assigned? A casuist, like de Lora, could maintain that the promise had been kept. And at that moment something perished in Pedro de Vargas, perished utterly, something which had given to life one of its best illusions.

But he had no time to realize that now. Dorotea, exhausted as she was, had understood the meaning of her sentence and burst into a wail of entreaty. Not the stake! If what she had already suffered could but be taken into account! She didn't beg to live, but if His Blessed Reverence would grant her a quick death—

De Lora shook his head. Then Pedro saw García step forward.

"By your leave, comrade," he said, thrusting past one of the pikemen. His uniform and casual manner made way for him. The soldier gaped, but did not try to hold him back. He strode forward, one hand on his sword, to the platform.

"A boon!" he called up to the Inquisitor. "A boon, Your Reverence!"

De Lora raised his eyebrows. "What boon, my son?"

"I am Juan Gómez, in the service of Captain de Leyva in Seville. I had leave to come to Jaén for this occasion."

"Well?"

"This woman, Dorotea Romero, caused the death of my wife, Inés, by poison. She was hired to it by an enemy. I crave the boon of carrying her myself to the stake and of thrusting the 'pear' between her jaws. Grant me this, Your Reverence, for the love of God. It is a vow I have taken."

The heavy rumble of his voice filled the square. In the silence people craned their necks for a glimpse of him. Pedro's heart stood still.

Perhaps de Lora was pleased to have this unexpected testimonial to the justice of his sentence; perhaps, too, understanding mass psychology, he perceived that the crowd sided with this bluff soldier and bereaved husband. In any case, he nodded.

"So be it, Juan Gómez. But I counsel you to beware of hatred. Cleanse your heart of rancor. The woman has repented of her sins, and in her death she will be reconciled with the Church."

He had hardly spoken before García was on the platform and had caught up the shrinking woman in his arms. Then, carrying her as if she had been a child, he stepped down to the level of the square and set off toward one of the posts half concealed by faggots. A hangman's assistant joined him.

"Pray you, brother, stand back. I need no help. It is part of my vow."

All of what happened then, Pedro could not see, for García's back was towards him. But the woman's cries suddenly stopped. García walked more slowly. To the crowd's amazement, the victim's thin arms circled his neck. Those facing him on the other side of the square, however, had seen more.

"Look out!" yelled a voice, half joking, half in earnest. "The witch is putting a spell on him. Have a care!"

De Lora, at once alert, gave an order; but so intent was everyone that not a man stirred.

García had now reached the faggots. He paused a long moment; then, bending a little, as if to shift the burden, he did something with his hands. When he straightened up, a limp form lay outstretched on the bed of firewood surrounding the stake. He stood looking down, his huge fingers still curved to the shape of the woman's throat.

Suddenly he raised his clenched fists toward the platform and roared: "Now she's safe enough, you bastards! Now you can have her!"

Making the most of the crowd's stupefaction, he hurled himself, like a mad bull, against the wall of people, and broke through it. Pedro saw a brief eddy, heard shouts and a scuffling of feet; but García had already disappeared.

XVIII

AT THAT PERIOD, the Inquisition had not yet, to the same extent as later, acquired its own special prisons, so that the Castle of Jaén was used for offenders of all classes. It afforded thieves or heretics the same accommodations.

Jaded by the events of the past night and shaken by the last scenes of horror in the public square, Pedro found it a relief at first to be alone in a cell under one of the corner towers. Sitting head in hand on the edge of a bunk filled with moldy straw, he tried to shut out the memory of García and of the execution of the condemned wretches that ended the auto-da-fé. It had all become personal with him now, so personal as to nauseate him. Not until several hours later did the immediacy of the recent sights and smells fade out into an increasing awareness of his own present and future.

Through a fifteen-foot wall, a slanting funnel, ending in a crack, allowed the passage of a ray of light intense at first but gradually dimmer as the sun moved westward. The cell had the damp atmosphere of a crypt tainted with the stench of excrements. It swarmed with vermin. As Pedro emerged from his sick apathy, the sight of a sleek rat, uplifted motionless on its haunches in the beam of light, did more than anything else to remind him of his situation. Soon it would be night, and the creatures would come scuttling out to people the darkness. Still worse, perhaps, was the complete silence of the place—no whisper of any human sound. And yet he knew that this was one of the better cells. It had light for a part of the day at least, whereas some were completely black at all times.

Uncertainty and imagination soon began working. Getting up, he started to pace the twelve-foot length back and forth. Where were his father, mother, and sister? When would he be brought before the tribunal? Of what would he be accused? How would he stand the Question? Fear of the torture grew momently like a nightmare which he could not shake off. On the other hand, he had heard of people who had been locked in to die of starvation or thirst. Perhaps that would be the way with him—for lack of evidence.

Back and forth.

The beam of light, having crossed the floor, now slanted up against the wall and fell on a line of rough scratches above the bed. *"Miserere mei, Domine."* Then, as if this were its farewell, it withdrew and left the place in darkness.

Back and forth. He must tire himself out in order to sleep. He lost the notion of time, how many hours he had been here. Now and then unconnected snatches of the past few days rose to the surface of his mind. . . . His pursuit of de Silva's Indian servant. How little he had dreamed then that the boot would soon be on the other foot! He wondered whether Coatl had got away, and winced at the thought of the scruples he had felt about helping him. The best deed of his life! . . . His resentment at García's impertinence in even suggesting the possibility that Doña María de Vargas might ever be in a like case with Dorotea Romero. Nothing to resent now. . . . His cloud castles last night after leaving the Carvajal garden. This was his castle, this hole of shame and heartbreak. Would Luisa know what had happened? Would she still pray for him? Every thought seemed ironic, bitter as gall. What was that Italian verse his mother quoted—about remembering lost happiness—Dante's verse?

All at once, as if it had been a thunder crash, he started at the sudden grinding of the key in the lock. The door banged open, and its aperture with the space behind it was blocked by the figures of several men, one of whom carried a lantern.

"You, there," said a squat, bare-armed fellow in a leather jerkin— "ready for the first chat?" He had a clanking contraption of chains in his hands, which he now deftly attached to Pedro's wrists and ankles. They were heavy and crisscrossed so as to hamper any movement. "Feel talkative, eh? Want to cough up your sins? *Adelante!*"

Grasping Pedro's arm, he half-led, half-shoved him out to the others in the corridor. They were men of the same type, square, bull-necked, crop-headed. With their hairy, naked arms and blunt faces, they looked like butchers or what they were—hangman's lackeys.

Flanked by two of them, Pedro shuffled and stumbled along the passage, which multiplied the sounds of footsteps and chains. They went down some twenty feet of steps to a lower level and followed another passageway, the lantern hovering vaguely on blank doors and sweating walls. It was more like a tunnel, narrow, low, and stifling, than a corridor. They continued on to a dead end and to an open door on the right.

"The prisoner, Pedro de Vargas," announced a soldier on guard there, stepping to one side.

"Let him enter," came a voice from within, "and leave me alone with him."

Pedro found himself in a large, vaulted room, dimly lighted by cressets. It was probably an ancient guardroom, for a fireplace occupied one end, and empty weapon racks stood along the walls. At the other end, opposite the hearth, rose a dais, such as judges used, with three chairs now empty. In front of this on the floor stood a small writing table. But these details made only a half-impression. As the door closed upon the withdrawing soldier, it was the commanding, white-gowned figure of Ignacio de Lora standing in the center of the room that held Pedro's attention.

The monk's high forehead caught the light, which fell also on his silver crucifix. He stood with his head thrust forward a little and his eyes hidden under their dark brows. Then, turning, he walked over to a high-backed chair against the wall and seated himself.

"Come here, my son," he directed. "I want a word with you."

But when Pedro, carrying his chains, stopped in front of him, de Lora said nothing for a while, merely eying the prisoner from head to foot and fingering his beard.

At last he remarked, "You look changed since the other night. It occurred to me then that we would be meeting soon. In your case, the wages of sin have not been delayed."

Until then fear had been uppermost in Pedro's mind; now it was submerged by a rising smother of hatred. He found it easy to return de Lora's stare with interest.

"Sin?" he repeated, and de Lora expertly noticed that his voice had grown older since the last time they had met. "I hope Your Reverence doesn't mean that I've taken a bribe or broken a promise. That would be unjust."

The Inquisitor's eyes did not waver. "Be careful, my son. Impudence calls for physic which you may not like. I took no bribe and broke no promise as your pertness implies. The Church accepted a fine; it released the prisoner, Dorotea Romero. What your evil imagination conceives has no importance."

An imperious wave of the hand cut off Pedro's answer. "*Señorito mio,* we are not here to discuss your opinions, but what, I take it, is of more value: your soul, which is black with evil and destined to hell. I shall be frank. Your hearty and humble repentance can alone save it—not to mention your body."

"Repentance for what?"

De Lora shook his head. "The stubbornness of sin! Well, you will learn soon enough, before the Holy Tribunal, of what things you stand accused. If you hope for mercy to yourself and your family, if you would save the souls and bodies of all of you, there is still a way of pardon left open. Take it; prove to me that your repentance is sincere; and I will do all I can for you. Otherwise—" The Inquisitor shrugged slightly and opened his hands.

"A way?" Pedro repeated.

"Yes. Tell me the whereabouts of the escaped murderer and matricide, Juan Romero, who calls himself García."

"I have no idea where he is."

"A lie. You lied to me about him three nights ago. Reveal his hiding place. It will go hard with you and yours if you do not."

"I can't tell what I don't know."

De Lora grasped the arms of his chair. "Listen. You have committed two capital crimes: first, that you did not report an escaped criminal to justice; second, that you connived with him against the Holy Inquisition. For the last time, I ask you where he may be found."

The damp air of the vault seemed to grow sultrier. The friar's lips, framed by his beard, showed a straight line; his eyes drilled into Pedro's. Then, after a silence, he got up and walked over to the small writing table.

"So Pedro de Vargas will not speak," he murmured with angry gentleness. "He makes light of the Holy Office. Like father, like son."

"My father knows nothing of this."

"We shall endeavor to find out," said de Lora. Lifting a silver bell from the table, he rang it. And when the soldier appeared, "Inform the reverend friars that it is the hour of the tribunal. Summon the other de Vargas prisoners." And to Pedro, "We do not often examine misdoers together, but in this case I think that more will be learned from a common confession."

He drew back within himself. Harsh and inhuman enough before, he now seemed to lose his individuality, to become an incarnate symbol of office. When two other Dominican friars appeared, he ascended the tribunal with them and took his place in the center. An inferior of the same order stood at the table and began arranging various papers. A guard led Pedro to the proper place before the dais.

Lastly, from outside came a confused sound of halting footsteps and clanking iron. The door opened.

"Prisoners to the Holy Tribunal: Francisco, María, Mercedes de Vargas," announced the soldier.

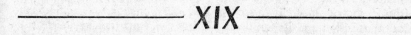

XIX

ALTHOUGH he carried himself erect as always in spite of his irons, Francisco de Vargas showed the effect of twenty-four hours in prison. His face was gray, and his thin hair, uncurled, hung lank about his neck. Similarly, Doña María's usually neat appearance had suffered. Her plump person now looked oddly shrunken and faded. Upon seeing Pedro, her eyes filled, though she tried to smile. As for Mercedes, who was little more than a child, it was to be expected that the terror of the place would unnerve her. She kept pressing her face against her mother and twisting her hands. Fortunately neither she nor Doña María had been put into chains.

Don Francisco greeted his son in a voice which showed small reverence for the tribunal; and Pedro, taking heart from the sight of him, answered in kind.

"Silence!" barked one of the guards.

"Silence yourself, dog!" returned the old cavalier. "I'll have no prison cur ordering me."

Before the flame in him, the man shrank back.

De Lora's stern voice cut in. "This is no place for swagger, Francisco de Vargas. A gag may teach you what old age has not."

But Don Francisco met the stare from the bench with his lower lip thrust out. "It would be wiser of you, Ignacio de Lora, to explain this outrage upon my family and person than to waste your threats on a man who does not fear them. I demand to know by what right you lay hands on me or mine."

Unused to such boldness, the Inquisitor found nothing to say except, "*You* demand!" But the exchange reassured Pedro in one respect: his family had not yet been put to the question; this was their first appearance before the tribunal. Probably de Lora had waited for Pedro's capture.

Without further delay, the indictment was now read by the clerk at the writing table, and immediately any need to impose silence ended. With growing stupefaction, Francisco de Vargas gazed at the clerk, while a dull red crept into his cheeks.

The indictment, involved and wordy, took a long time to read. In substance, it charged that a great-grandmother of Francisco de Vargas had Moorish blood, although she belonged to the ducal family of Medina Sidonia. His claim to *limpieza* or pure Christian descent was, therefore, invalid. This taint manifested itself in him by an irreligious attitude, shown especially in scoffing and scurrilous remarks against the Holy Inquisition and its familiars. He had even threatened one of the latter with physical violence for upholding the Santa Casa against his attacks. He had indoctrinated his family in these blasphemous principles to such an extent that his wife and daughter showed horror at the very mention of the Holy Office; while his son, inflamed by such ill precepts, had been guilty of notable crimes.

To wit: the said Pedro de Vargas on St. Peter's Day, June 29th, had fallen on two familiars of the Holy Office in the mountains; had broken the arm of one and cruelly whipped the other, all the while expressing himself in incredible obscenities against the Inquisition. That same day, in the presence of his father, he had shown an insolent and threatening attitude toward another highly respected familiar of the same reverend body. That night he had conspired with an escaped murderer, one calling himself Juan Romero or Juan García, to defeat the ends of ecclesiastical justice. He had insinuated himself into the house of the Most Reverend Father Ignacio de Lora, Inquisitor of Jaén, with a subtle intent, which had been frustrated for the moment by the vigilance of the said Reverend Father, but which had since borne disastrous fruit. On the night of June 30th, Pedro de Vargas, being called to answer for such enormities, had resisted arrest and inflicted bodily hurt upon several soldiers of the Holy Tribunal.

(*"Bravo, Pedrito!"* put in his father at this point.)

In conclusion, the indictment recorded that since their incarceration the de Vargas family, far from showing the patience and humility of repentance, had in haughtiness of word and bearing substantiated the testimony against them.

And to all these charges, credible witnesses had given oath.

The clerk, having finished the reading, sat down and prepared to take notes.

For a long minute, silence hung heavily under the vaults of the crypt, a silence both of amazement and of doom. The sting of the indictment consisted in the few strands of truth, all innocent, that it contained. Out of these, exaggerated and distorted, had been spun the whole web. But it was a web that allowed no escape.

Finally Ignacio de Lora spoke. "You have heard the indictment, Francisco, Pedro, María, and Mercedes de Vargas. It remains for you to confess these sins and to seek reconciliation with the Church through penance. The tribunal awaits your confession."

But again there was silence.

"Do you confess these sins?" de Lora demanded. "Let Francisco de Vargas, the root and source of them, speak first."

To Pedro's amazement, his father took a step forward and said, "Yes, I confess."

Surprise was not confined to Pedro; even the schooled features of the Inquisitor sharpened.

"Well?" he returned after a pause.

"I confess one crime not mentioned in the bill. Why it was not included, I do not know—perhaps because it has the distinction of being true and would therefore ill agree with the others. I confess to the black sin of refusing to sell my property outside the walls to Diego de Silva."

The words had a marked effect on the tribunal. Shocked groans escaped from de Lora's two colleagues, and the Inquisitor's eyelids drooped to a slit. The clerk's quill scratched hungrily. When it stopped, de Lora found his voice.

"You have taken that down, Father Ambrosio?"

"Yes, Your Reverence."

"It is unnecessary to point out that the prisoner's remarks are of a piece with the charges against him. In our hearing, he accuses the Holy Office of corruption and venality."

"Not yet," Don Francisco put in. "That remains to be seen. For the moment, I accuse your 'highly respected familiar,' Diego de Silva, of bearing false witness, and of perjury from motives of cowardice and greed. Let him answer it if he can."

"He will answer it." De Lora looked over the heads of the prisoners toward someone behind them. "You have heard this libel, Diego de Silva. Is it your pleasure to repeat your statement?"

From the tail of his eye, Pedro was aware of a figure striding forward, the silken footstep hardly audible. Stopping at one side of the dais, toward which he bowed, de Silva scrutinized the prisoners. He was dressed as always in the extreme of fashion: black hose and doublet, with silver slashes on the trunks and sleeves. Bareheaded out of respect to the court, he carried his velvet cap and red plume in one hand. Though outwardly grave, his insolent black eyes danced.

"Por Dios," said Don Francisco in a clear voice, "I thought there was a cursed bad smell in the place."

But the newcomer paid no attention, except for the lift of an eyebrow. He spoke to de Lora.

"Your Reverence has my testimony, given under oath. It was plainly set forth in the indictment. What need to repeat it? As for my motives, if I say that devotion to the Faith led me to prefer these charges, I hope Your Reverence will believe me. It is beneath the dignity of a Christian and a member of the *Miliz Christi* to defend himself against the slander of a desperate old man."

The Inquisitor nodded. "True."

Don Francisco gave a short laugh. "Notice, son Pedro, how convenient the dignity of a Christian is. 'Sblood! But he needn't worry. A gentleman does not stain his sword—your pardon, Doña María—with a piece of dung."

Perhaps de Silva's white face turned a shade paler; otherwise he seemed unconcerned. It was de Lora who took action. He gave orders to the burly, bare-armed man who had conducted Pedro from his cell and now stood with his mates at one side of the room.

With the skill born of habit, they made preparations. A rope was lowered from a pulley in the vault above; two wooden horses were brought forward out of the shadow of the room, and a roller operated by handspikes was adjusted between them. The lackeys then attached one end of the rope to the roller, giving it several turns to secure purchase. Weights of various sizes, with staples in them, were set down in readiness. It was the celebrated *garrucha* or strappado, and everyone present knew the use of it. A bench, like a horizontal ladder, knotted cords of various sizes, strips of linen, a ewer, and several iron instruments, were set up at one side.

This was part of the *territio,* the preface to torture, which consisted in displaying to victims the tools about to be used on them in default of a confession. It took strong nerves to look at these things. Doña María did not look, but kept her eyes on the crucifix above the tribunal, while her lips moved silently. Mercedes clung to her mother's arm. Pedro remembered the scarecrows in that morning's procession, the vacant faces. They were the products of those tools. He braced himself, trying not to think. The dankness of the place clung like sweat. It seemed deadly quiet in spite of the movements of the men setting up their apparatus.

Then Francisco de Vargas laughed again. "Clumsy stuff, Pedrito! The infidels are more ingenious. When I was prisoner to the Sultan of Tripoli, I saw a number of torments, compared with any one of which this flummery is a pastime. The Holy Office should travel for ideas."

De Lora fixed his grim eyes on the railer; but at that moment de Silva stepped in front of the tribunal and spoke in a low voice, which the other leaned forward to hear.

"You say well," de Lora nodded. "Francisco de Vargas, for the last time I ask whether you will confess the sins of which you stand charged."

"Bah!" returned the old soldier. "Confess that I'm a Moor? My blood is as good as the King's and thrice better than yours—a fact known to every cavalier in both Castiles. Confess that I'm a renegade to the Faith? The lie stinks. Confess that I taught irreverence to my family? Nonsense! My son can speak for himself; but as to what you accuse him of, I don't believe it. A truce to this! I demand the release of my family and myself."

In answer de Lora pointed to Mercedes de Vargas. "Begin with the girl. From the lips of children, we are apt sooner to hear the truth. Bring her closer before us."

Overcome with terror, Mercedes sank down, clasping her mother's knees. While one of the lackeys held Doña María's arms, another half-dragged, half-carried the child to a place directly in front of the Inquisitor, where he kept her on her feet with one arm around her waist.

Meanwhile, the mother cried, "No, Your Reverence! Pity, Your Reverence! Take *me!* She's so young! She's innocent—you can see for yourself! Good Your Reverence, take *me!*"

"Peace, wife!" Don Francisco commanded. "Would you give these dogs satisfaction?" But his face was as drawn as that of the image on the crucifix.

Pedro, straining at his manacles, tried to shuffle forward; but a guard gripped him behind. Diego de Silva smiled. The friars on the tribunal fastened their intent, hard gaze on the drooping girl.

"Mercedes de Vargas, do you confess that your father, Francisco de Vargas, by his evil precepts . . ." The Inquisitor's words fell distinct and separate like the clicking of a rosary. They came to an abrupt end.

It is doubtful whether Mercedes heard them. She hung limp within the circle of the hangman's arm.

"Apply the cords," directed the cold voice. "You may save your daughter, Francisco de Vargas, if you choose to confess. On your head be it!"

In a haze, Pedro heard his father's answer as if it were at some distance. "I will not save her by a lie, Ignacio de Lora. If you do this thing, look to your own soul."

Torture, when skillfully used, became a crescendo. It began with the flesh, passed to the muscles, ended with the bones. Its background was the helplessness of the victim. Mad with fear, the child screamed, struggled feebly, was dragged beneath the pulley.

"The cords," repeated de Lora.

The loop of the rope was passed under one arm; the girl's wrists were lashed behind her; the tightening wedge was inserted. Then they hoisted her slightly, the lackeys making a careful turn or two of the roller.

Every nerve in Pedro's body writhed. He was vaguely conscious of his mother's weeping, of de Silva's smile, of his father's haggard face, of the judges leaning forward, of the clerk sitting with his poised quill. He looked here and there in spite of himself, his eyes trying to escape.

Came a thin, sharp scream.

"Do you confess? You will save yourself pain."

Then silence.

Pedro stared at the ground. He looked up at a confused muttering among the attendants.

"Your Reverence," stammered one of them, "she has fainted."

"Revive her. You know your business."

The slender body was lowered. The bare-armed men clustered round, stooped over. "Give her air, curse you! Hand the water . . ."

At last, uneasily, his face blank, the chief of them burst his way from the group, and stood in front of de Lora.

"Your Reverence, at the first twist of the cords—Your Reverence, she's dead."

A low cry came from Doña María.

"Dead?" de Lora snapped. "Bungling fool! Have you no skill in your craft?"

"It's never happened before," the man muttered.

In the tense stillness, a voice, so altered that Pedro did not at first recognize it, spoke. "Now God has shown His mercy, and upon you all rests His curse," said Don Francisco.

The Inquisitor burst out, "Remove the body. We'll proceed." But the judges on either side of him leaned toward him, whispering. Finally he said, "Perhaps. We would get nowhere at the moment. Return them to their cells. Tomorrow night will be your turn, María de Vargas, then your son's. Think well until tomorrow night." He stared at Don Francisco. "Your turn will come last."

"No," answered the other in the same remote voice, "your turn will come last."

"By God," Diego de Silva drawled, "it seems to me that without being Moors we have got under the skin of the noble gentleman."

XX

"THINK WELL." There was nothing else to do in the darkness under the corner tower—a heat of thinking in which memory and anticipation equally mingled. And in that furnace of thought, Pedro de Vargas's youth was consumed. Out of its ashes emerged only the metal of hatred and a savage kind of fortitude, the metal of the chained tiger.

His eyes ached. It would have been a relief if he could have wept; but the death of Mercedes, the torment to which he and his parents were subjected, lay beyond tears. At times he had glimpses of the old days, that now seemed glimpses of heaven: Mercedes at her lute or facing him at table; the family together on that last night in the pavilion; his father's heartiness, his mother's smile; Mercedes again—

At times every detail of what had just passed renewed itself. At times the dread of what impended shut out everything else—the thought of his mother in the hands of the executioners and himself forced to watch. At times he writhed with self-reproach at having meddled in the affairs of the ill-omened García. Would it have made a difference if he had kept out of them? He told himself no. His father was right: the visit to the Inquisitor had merely reinforced de Silva's schemes.

De Silva!

Hatred took the form of prayer. If he might be permitted only once to close his hands around that white throat, he asked nothing more; he would be content with hell.

Out of habit invoking his patron saint, he suddenly broke off. There were no saints. As to hell, he was now in it. As to God? The blackness about him was of the grave. God? What God?

Now and then his mind from sheer exhaustion faded into unconsciousness; but it was only to sink into a welter of visions, from which the clanking and tossing of his chains awakened him.

After one of these intervals, still half in the grip of the nightmare, it seemed to him that he was no longer alone. A blur of light showed from a lantern, which was cut off by the bulk of a man, who had just closed the door. At first it seemed merely another phase of the dream; but as Pedro's brain struggled back to consciousness, he recognized the huge bare arms, bull neck, and leather jerkin of a turnkey. Having lost count of time, he gathered that the twenty-four hours had passed and that he was about to be haled again before the tribunal. He lay staring at the broad back of the man, trying to fight down a rising fit of madness.

The fellow stood motionless awhile. Then, putting down the lantern together with some other objects, he turned around. He was a monster of a man; Pedro noticed the bulging arms and thicket of black hair emerging above the neck of the jerkin. He moved slowly toward the bunk, his misshapen shadow hovering on the vault above.

"Are you awake?"

Certainly it was a dream or a trick of Pedro's crazed mind. As the man squatted down to seat himself on the edge of the bunk, his face in spite of the dimness became familiar.

"Yes."

"Then *compañero,* don't you know me?"

The breath stuck in Pedro's throat. "Juan García!"

"Who else?" rumbled the voice. "Did you think I would leave you in this hell-pot while I could raise a hand? You're the best eyeful I've had since the Indies."

"Juan García?" repeated Pedro. "How——?"

"Money." The other gave a profound nod. "Money's the key to most locks. Besides, there's Manuel Pérez. He wouldn't be able to face his sister again if he didn't do what he could. She's been stirring things up, I can tell you. But first"—García's big chest heaved—"you've got to forgive me. I've got something on my heart." And when Pedro could only stare, "God curse me for a rat! When things went like they did with *Madrecita*—or perhaps you don't know?"

"Yes," Pedro nodded.

"At first I thought you had taken the money and played me for a fool. Out of my head, d'you see—half-crazy. Then I heard what had happened to you, and I knew better. I'm sorry." García laid a huge hand on Pedro's shoulder.

"It's nothing," murmured the other. He explained how he had been in the cathedral square. "His holy, hellish Reverence played us both for fools."

García sat opening and clenching his hands. "Perhaps someday— You know why I killed her? You understand, don't you?"

"Yes," Pedro said.

"She blessed me," said García, "before I—"

He drew his hand across his eyes. Then, fumbling in the pocket of his jerkin, he brought out a key with which he unlocked Pedro's manacles. "Keep them on," he cautioned. "Others may drop in here."

Walking over to the door, he returned with what looked like a piece of sacking.

"A sword and dagger," he said, unwrapping them. "We'll make a break for it just before the hour of the tribunal. Manuel Pérez will let us out by the postern. It's a thin chance, but we'll take it together."

Pedro's heart, which had begun hammering, suddenly slackened. "My father and mother?"

"Yes, they'll come too. That's the trouble. I knew you wouldn't budge without them. I've seen Don Francisco. We'll head for the sierra, then for Almería, then for Italy. He says if we can reach there we'll be safe on account of your mother's kindred. Hernán Soler vows he can manage it." García spat. "But I'm not fooling myself. It's a thin chance."

"Hernán Soler?"

"Yes. It's Catana's doing. He's a *galán* of hers." García stood listening. "I'll push on now," he said uneasily. "The jailer's a friend of Manuel's, and he's had his pay; but there wasn't cash enough for everybody. They may wonder about the new hand."

"How can you get away with it?"

"Maybe I can't. But, for one thing, these prison lads aren't looking for Juan García in the Castle; for another, I stick to Manuel and stay where he tells me."

"But if you're spotted?"

García picked up the lantern and shrugged. "Why then, *adiós!* They won't take me alive. I've got a knife."

"Thanks," Pedro said. "I can't tell you—"

"No need," said García. "I'm not forgetting what you did for me, nor what it's cost you. We'll stand together—here or anywhere. *Hasta la noche!*"

"*Hasta la noche!*" Pedro answered.

Not until the other had gone out, locking the door behind him, did de Vargas first notice the streak of sunlight slanting from east to west through the funnel mouth of the embrasure, and realize that he had still long hours to wait.

But the whole quality of time had changed. Instead of despair, hope and with it suspense almost equally tormenting. What if García were recognized? What if someone entered to inspect his chains and found them unlocked? What if the hour of the tribunal were put forward?

A mere trifle could snap the thread of luck upon which everything depended.

He forced himself to think only of escaping from the Castle. As to the long leagues over the mountains to Almería, the difficulty of fast travel for an elderly man and woman, the constant danger of being overtaken, the risk of relying on a cutthroat like Soler, the chance of securing a ship on the coast, he kept his mind closed. It would be almost enough, he thought, to breathe free air again and to die free.

At any rate, this tremendous difference existed between now and before García's visit—the knife. Whatever happened, no one would take him back to the tribunal. His deliverance from that lay concealed in the straw at his side.

And something else there was too: in the cold blackness of his mind, the flickering of a tiny flame, a new warmth such as his careless youth had not yet known. The meaning of friendship dawned upon him, devotion of man to man, deep as the love of woman, though different. Born in the darkness of the prison, it kindled a new faith which might in time partially replace what had been lost. "A friend!" he exulted.

Hours dragged by. Once in the course of the day, a turnkey entered with food and water, while Pedro, knife in hand, tense as the spring of a steel trap, pretended to sleep.

"Wake up," said the man, "if you want any grub before the rats get it." But he did not inspect the chains.

When he was gone, de Vargas forced himself to eat in order to keep his strength up. He also walked back and forth for a while and flexed his limbs to avoid stiffness.

The ray of light followed its appointed arc, rested once more on the despairing scrawl of the unknown prisoner. "*Miserere—*" Pedro glanced at it. Superstitiously perhaps, or because of a new hope in him, he even repeated it as night fell.

Then, for the first time, he slipped off his chains; slung the baldric, to which the sword was attached, over his shoulder; fastened the knife to his belt; and, lastly, stretched out again on the bunk, with the loose irons draped over him as if they were still in place.

At least several hours remained; but his suspense increased sharply as the minutes passed, increased to an almost unendurable tension. Had something happened to García? Surely it was time. It seemed to him that he had lain stretched out there for an eternity.

In the end, when he was on the verge of panic, the key grated in the lock, the outer bar slid back, and the door opened.

"Thank God!" he began, but the words died out.

It was not García's burly figure on the threshold; the silhouette formed by a lantern in the corridor behind stood tall and thin. As it entered the cell, followed by the lantern bearer, Pedro found himself staring up at the white face of Diego de Silva.

"Put down the light, fellow. Close the door and wait outside. After talking with the old cock, I want a word with the cockerel."

The turnkey—it was the same who had brought the food earlier—knuckled his forehead. "Yes, Your Worship. It lacks a half hour until Their Reverences meet. I'll wait, Your Worship."

So, hope was over. García had failed. Despair surged back again, but not only despair. Eclipsing it, rose the lust of hatred. As Pedro stared up at de Silva, the thirst of it tingled in his mouth; his pulses beat a pæan of thanksgiving. He knew at least that de Silva would not leave the place alive. By God, yes—there was a God, and He had led the victim to the trap.

Meanwhile, de Silva, gazing down, pinched his chin. He studied the other's grim face under the thatch of bronze-colored hair, the wide, unswerving eyes, and in part read them perfectly.

Then he laughed. "Hate me, eh? Well, young Pedro, that won't last, I promise you. By the time we finish, I'll change that glare of yours into something else. Ever seen a well-whipped spaniel grovel?"

Strangely Pedro felt no hurry. Like an epicure inhaling rare wine, he enjoyed the sensation of putting off the too short moment of killing. It was almost a pleasure to scrutinize de Silva's pointed ears, the affected wisp of hair along his cheek, the bantering, conceited eyes, the foppery of his lace collar.

"Perhaps you wonder why I trouble with the de Vargas family," he went on. "They're of no consequence and hardly deserve notice. But I'll tell you. It's a policy of mine to remove whoever stands in my way, whoever offends me, even if it's someone of no importance. I never make an exception. If a young lout, Pedro de Vargas for example, strikes one of my servants, he has to pay for it. If a pretentious old fool like Francisco de Vargas prevents me from rounding out my estate in spite of generous offers, he has to be eliminated. You see, it gets around in the end that Diego de Silva does not let himself be trifled with. And soon people who *are* of importance make way for him. After that his path through life is smooth and undisturbed. That's the reason for my interest in you, young Pedro."

At another time Pedro would have felt the calculated sting of this speech, but his hatred was too complete for any further anger. In the calm of his present assurance, de Silva's words even amused him, and to the other's surprise he smiled.

"When you eliminate people, señor, you are careful not to risk your own skin—which is probably wise. Tell me some more about your policies."

It was not the effect that de Silva looked for. The coolness and the smile visibly nettled him, but he kept his drawl.

"If you mean that I do not give swashbucklers the satisfaction of a duel, you are quite right. Why should I give them satisfaction at all? My object is simply to remove them as a warning to others. Perhaps in the end even your dullness will learn that my method is thorough."

Pedro nodded. He wanted to spin the moment out as long as possible. "Yes, *caballero,* I admit your method is thorough—I'm not quite so dull as that—thorough as your dishonor, if possible." He smiled again and added, "*If* possible."

But he had gone too far. De Silva's temper snapped. The brute behind his mockery broke through, though he managed a short laugh.

"Well, *hijo,* dirty-tongued brats must be taught politeness one way or another. Get up when a gentleman speaks. You crow louder than the old carrion, your father."

Reaching out, he laid hold of Pedro's manacles with the evident purpose of jerking him up, but staggered back with the irons in his hands. And at the same instant de Vargas leaped, his grip closing on the other's throat.

Back they reeled to the opposite wall, de Silva wrenching at the hands that worked their way into his neck. More powerful than he looked, he was fighting for his life and kept Pedro at bay for a moment with arms and knees. A moment—long enough suddenly with a desperate twist to break loose. De Vargas stood between him and the door. He sprang for it, but was thrust back; and in the same instant he drew sword and dagger.

"*Socorro!*" he yelled. "Guard! You, outside there!"

Pedro had most to fear from that quarter. But no one answered. Probably the fellow had strolled off. There might be time.

"*Socorro!*"

The two swords met, grinding hilt against hilt, and de Silva leaped back from the dagger in Pedro's left hand.

"What about satisfaction now, whoreson?" jeered de Vargas. "Where's your policy and method?"

He moved slowly forward, one step after another, his eyes watchful. He had no doubt of the result. He knew that he could kill the man by sheer fury—if only he had time. That was the trouble. A minute, two minutes before the guard returned. He must strike fast.

His sword leaped at de Silva's face, avoided the parry in *quarte*, flicked to *sixte*, and ripped through the muscles of the right hand. As the sword slithered down, Pedro stepped on it. De Silva shrank back, for a moment out of reach against the rear wall of the cell. Kicking the fallen sword to one side, de Vargas resumed his slow advance. Now at the moment of success, he took no chances, even with an enemy who had no weapon but a poniard.

His opponent saw a face with hollow cheeks and above it a cluster of hair, red at the tips where the light shone through. He saw a pair of green eyes, unblinking as a cat's. And terror such as he would not have felt in open day on a fair field descended on him, terror of the burning thrust which in a moment would put an end to him. An end—

He gave a sudden gasp, his eyes on the point of the sword. "For God's sake . . ."

Within easy reach, Pedro repeated his first attack, a feint and cut, this time to de Silva's left hand, which dropped the dagger.

"One by one," he said.

De Silva raised his bleeding hands in front of his breast, his mouth working, his eyes on the door. Pedro skewered his velvet cap with its jeweled buckle on his sword's point and flicked it off.

"Bareheaded before death, señor."

"No," screamed de Silva—the words came in a babble—"you wouldn't kill an unarmed man, de Vargas; you wouldn't murder me. I was joking only. You'll go free from the tribunal."

"You have a moment left," Pedro answered. "Spend it thinking of the girl who was killed last night."

The other sank to his knees. "Mercy!"

To his relief, the dreadful point sank a trifle as if hesitating. He stared at it, hypnotized.

"Well, if you grovel—" sounded the voice above him.

But de Silva was beyond shame. "I sinned," he quavered.

"You would make amends perhaps? Secure our release? Pay a suitable fine? Make public apology?"

"Yes," breathed the man. It was well that he could not see the madness in Pedro's eyes nor the face of Mercedes de Vargas whom the boy was staring at. "Yes, everything, anything."

"Could I trust you?"

"I swear it before God."

"No, not before God," came the voice. "Perhaps if you renounced

God, I'd believe you. Renounce God, de Silva. You're a familiar of the Holy Inquisition, you're an officer of the *Miliz Christi*. Soldier of Christ, renounce God."

The point leaped up, drew close.

"I—I renounce God."

At that instant Pedro thrust the blade home, down through the man's body till the point caught on the pavement.

"Now burn in hell forever, soldier of Christ!" he whispered.

Drawing out his sword, he stared at the blank face, the motionless body at his feet.

The door opened. They could come now; he was ready. His hand tightened on the hilt of his poniard.

It was García.

"Hurry. We've got no more than a minute. I was held up."

"The guard?"

"He won't bother us—or anyone else." García's eyes were on the body. "Good work!" he added.

XXI

MANUEL PÉREZ, his unshaven face urgent and anxious, hurried the three de Vargases and García out of a small postern door opening on one of the steep slopes of the castle hill. Under a low moon, the decline looked precipitous and long. Delayed by de Silva's visits to their cells, the fugitives had practically no time left for escape. At any moment the tribunal would be summoning its prisoners, and their flight would be immediately discovered. They had perhaps a ten minutes' start until pursuit was organized. After that, nothing but speed counted, for the pursuers knew what road would be taken. Only the mountains offered a hiding place, and the mountain route only was feasible.

When he had locked the door on the outside, Pérez tossed the key away and thus prudently withdrew from the service of justice. Between him and García, Doña María was half-carried down the slope; while Pedro gave his arm to his father, whose stiff knee made hurry difficult.

At the foot of the decline, a couple of men impatiently waited with a string of horses. "By God," said one of them, "it's well you came, for in another half-minute we would have been spurring. Take a look at the Castle."

Here and there at windows and embrasures of the stone mass, lights came and went like distracted fireflies. They gave every sign of agitation and hurry within the walls. Another minute's delay would have been too late. As the party mounted, a trumpet from the other side of the Castle, clear and imperious in the still night, sounded assembly.

"We've got to race for it," said the man, "if we're to keep ahead of the whoreson troopers. It's no help to be riding with a woman."

Don Francisco, undaunted as ever, flung back at him, "What we lose in speed, we gain in honor—honor to be riding with Doña María de Vargas."

Inevitably, he at once took command; inevitably too, everyone obeyed him.

"Pedro, you and Señor García hold the rear. It's the post of danger, and except for your mother, I would ride with you. Mind you keep a good distance behind us, so that we may have timely warning of attack. These men"—he included the two strangers and Pérez—"will ride fifty yards in front of you. I'll lead with Doña María. And bear in mind the proper intervals; leave space for sword and charge. No use bunching like sheep in a pen. So forward, and God be with us!"

"*Vaya*," declared García, as he and Pedro galloped knee to knee behind the others, "there's a real hidalgo! Your father talks as if he were leading a foray. There's a captain, *por Dios!* Look how these bandit rascals obey him."

In front, with a horse between his legs, the familiar weight of a sword at his thigh, the free stars overhead, Francisco de Vargas felt his spirits revive from the desolation of the past days. Except for what had befallen Mercedes, he might even have welcomed the chance that swept him again from his peaceful moorings into the stream of action. This was his native element, and he had spent most of his years in just such nips and tucks of danger. He drew a deep breath of the warm night air.

"Talk of miracles!" he observed to Doña María. "My dear, who would have imagined some hours ago that you and I would be free of that hell-hole to try our luck again in the open! A manifest act of God and the saints—which shows that not the devil himself can keep us from Italy."

His wife, who had a stitch in her side from the unaccustomed movement of the horse, gave a breathless answer.

"This Señor García," continued her husband, "may be who he will, but he has served Pedro and us as a trusty friend, and for my own part I shall ever remain in his debt. Relax, my love, breathe naturally and go with the horse. You will soon get back to the swing of it. He spoke to me of Hernán Soler, the robber, by whose favor somehow we have these horses, and I doubt not they are birds of a feather. But after the Judases and scoundrels we saw last night, I do not cavil at an honest ruffian. By the Virgin, no! And here is something to cheer you which Pedro whispered to me as we left the Castle."

"My lord," gasped Doña María, "can we not slacken a little? I'm nearly spent."

"No, we cannot," said the other flatly; "we must win to the high sierra by daybreak. Do as I tell you and breathe deep. But listen. The cursed dog, de Silva, is dead. Pedro sheathed his sword in him when he came to taunt our son in the prison. By the Cross, I feel ten years younger for it!"

Doña María was a good woman, but the joy of the news made her forget the pain in her side.

"*Maraviglioso!*" she exclaimed. "Well done!"

Don Francisco threw back his head. "Well done indeed! And, wife, our Pedro is a boy no longer. From henceforth he's a man. He can use my war cry and carry my pennon."

Uphill though it was, they rode hard—too hard, for about a half-mile north of the Rosario, Doña María's horse cast a shoe and fell to limping. Without drawing rein, Don Francisco summoned Manuel Pérez to come up.

"Is another mount to be had?" he asked. "Or must we make the best of this? He'll be apt to go down with my lady."

"Horses enough, sir," answered Pérez, explaining that they were to meet Hernán Soler with some others of his band at the Rosario. The chief himself would escort them through the sierra.

"Then it's of no moment," said de Vargas. "But keep a tight feel of the jade's mouth, María, lest he stumble. *Adelante!*" And with a laugh, "Little I thought the other night when I was flogging Pedro on account of that damned tavern that I would soon be risking my neck in a hurry to get there!"

Thus far no sound of pursuit had reached them, but even Don Francisco felt relief when he saw a group of horsemen, black in the moonlight, waiting in front of the inn.

Their leader rode forward. He was a loose-limbed, gaunt man in complete armor, and he managed his powerful horse gracefully. A gaudy baldric, much too bejeweled, crossed his cuirass and glittered in the rays of the moon. He had a long face and a toothy smile. What stripe he was showed at once in the oiliness of his manner.

"Gracious sir and lady," he bowed, "Your Worships' servant, Hernán

Soler. I never expected the honor of devoting myself to the service of so renowned a captain, of so noble a señora."

He was clearly showing off—perhaps for the benefit of the tall girl who stood in the shadow of the archway. Don Francisco returned his compliments adequately, if not effusively; but when Soler launched upon another series of them, he interrupted him.

"I thank you from my heart, *caballero,* but we are like to be soon hard-pressed. Doña María needs a fresh mount. If you have an odd piece or so of armor for my son and me, they may be of use before dawn."

"At your command," waved Soler.

The shifting of Doña María's sidesaddle to another horse and the adjustment of armor, which was gladly supplied by several of the men to piece out a sketchy equipment for Don Francisco, Pedro, and García, took a few minutes. During the bustle, when Pedro had slipped on a cuirass and was reaching around for the side straps, a familiar, husky voice at his shoulder remarked:—

"I'll buckle it for you, señor." In the hurry, he had not seen Catana, but when he tried to turn, she added, "No, wait, you made me lose the strap."

Turning his head, he could feel her hair against his cheek.

He whispered, *"Querida,* how can I thank you for everything, for all you've done!"

"There!" She tightened the buckle. Then beneath her breath, "Stand still. Don't let on we're talking. Promise me something."

"Yes, but what do I care who listens! I'd tell anyone what I owe you. Why not let on?"

"Because I'm Soler's girl now. He might be jealous. I want him to get you across the mountains."

Pedro stiffened. "Catana? You didn't—you didn't get this help from Soler by—"

"Of course not! Be still!" She rebuckled one of the straps. "Didn't I tell you the other night about Hernán and me? *Vaya,* I love him. Promise me something."

"Anything. What is it?"

"That you'll think of me wherever you are."

"No need to ask that."

"No, I mean—" She stood a moment fingering the buckle. "We may not see each other again. You'll be a famous captain—I know it, Pedro de Vargas—when I'm hanged for a thief's trull in Jaén. But I wish— If you'll think of me a moment only, every day at the hour of Angelus? Will you?"

"At the Angelus. I swear it."

"And I'll think of you."

Soler walked up.

"That's a tight fit for a big chest," she added, clapping the breast-plate with her palm, "and hard to buckle. Well, *hombres,* will you ride?"

Soler kissed her full on the mouth—the kiss of possession. "Aye, *querida mía.* Meet me in a day or so at the place you know of. And *adiós!*"

Pedro bowed as if she had been a great lady. "God be with you, Catana!"

"And with you," she said, "always."

The little troop, grown now to some fourteen horse, cantered off. She stood in the middle of the empty road, watching it, watching one figure in the rear by the side of García. His steel cap sparkled in the moon-light. Had he already forgotten her? Would he look back once more? She clasped her hands.

"Maria gratia plena—"

He turned and raised his arm.

"Adiós, amado mío, amado mío!" she whispered.

When he had disappeared, she still looked at the turn of the road.

But suddenly a sound startled her. It came from the direction of Jaén —the distant racing of horses' hoofs.

—————— XXII ——————

IF THEY could have had the start originally planned, the fugitives might have reached the Sierra de Lucena and taken refuge in the fastnesses of the Granada Mountains before their pursuers had been long on the road. As it was, they could not hope to reach the pass without a fight; and even if this were at first successful, it would be hard to shake off pursuit. For it would not do merely to gain the mountains; they must disappear long enough to find their way undetected to the coast— Almería or Cartagena—and with luck secure passage for Italy. To be penned in the mountains would be fatal, as it would give the Inquisition time to cut off their escape by sea. After that, with a price on their heads and the province raised against them, their ultimate capture was inevitable.

Warned by a shout from Pedro, whose quick ears had picked up the sound of approaching, though still distant, horsemen, Don Francisco dropped back for conference. Like a veteran captain, he had his plans ready for the event and now communicated them to Pedro, García, and Soler.

"Look you. I remember a trail to the right not more than five furlongs ahead. We used it in the Moorish wars. It's impossible for a woman, but fair enough for men. Am I wrong, señor?"

"No," agreed Soler, "but it's better for goats. It leads west to Priego and hits the road to Puente Genil."

Don Francisco nodded. "The same. Pedro, your mother cannot take that path. She must keep to this road, and I must guard her. Half the men should ride with us. We'll press on as fast as may be. You with the others might wait for the dogs here. Hold them in play, but fall back. Then take the trail to the west. My guess is they'll follow you, thinking that all of us have gone that way. I grieve to propose this, for it means danger, and I would like my share of it, but Doña María cannot be left alone."

It was clearly the only possible plan. Soler, rising in his stirrups, selected a handful of his best men to form the rear guard with Pedro. To his credit, he did not flinch from the post himself, but the value to the elder de Vargases of his personal escort as far as the sea was too great to be sacrificed. García declared that, of course, he would stay with his friend.

Meanwhile, the little column had briefly halted.

"A word between us," said Don Francisco, beckoning Pedro to one side. "There's no use afflicting your mother with farewells. I'll tell her that you will join us beyond the pass. For myself, I know that whether we meet again on earth is God's affair. If we reach the sea, we cannot wait. You must find your own way to Italy. Whatever happens to us, your kinsman, Cardinal Strozzi, will protect you. And now bear yourself well. I'd give my life to be with you in this skirmish, but I cannot. Here they come. Shout '*Santiago y Vargas.*' My blessing goes with you!"

Their hands met in a hard clasp to be long remembered. Then Don Francisco wheeled his horse and galloped up the road. The little group of men, Pedro, García, and five others, waited. Below them the clatter of hoofs grew loud. The moon, slanting across the defile, lighted half of it.

For a first stand, the place was well-chosen. A projecting cliff, around which the road zigzagged, cast its shadow over the defenders, while anyone rounding it from below came fully into the moonlight. The sound of Don Francisco's party in front would throw the pursuers off their guard as to an ambush on the other side of the cliff. In addition, Pedro had the advantage that neither he nor any of the hard-faced rascals with him had anything to lose by fighting. Their lives were forfeit in any case, and most of them had memories of the prison and pillory, the hangman's whip or knife, the execution of friends and relatives, to avenge; whereas the horsemen from the Castle had no such cogent motives for risking their necks.

The noise of the riders came closer; a shout or two; then three of them abreast swept around the cliff.

Far up the road Don Francisco heard the onset, and his heart yearned within him. At that moment his common sense and his loyalty to Doña María underwent their hardest test.—"*Santiago y Vargas!*"—The cry floated back above the clash of swords and trampling of horses. His lower lip crept out, he half reined up; but then, closing his ears, he spurred doggedly ahead, while his wife breathed prayers to the saints.— "*Santiago y Vargas!*"—It was as if all his past life were calling to him, calling him back. He groaned and struck the pommel of the saddle with his clenched fist, but rode on.

Though trained in the tilt yard, it was Pedro's first experience of an actual melee, and he flamed with excitement. He would have given anything now for five minutes on Campeador, whose weight and spirit would have stemmed the tide more effectively than could his present sorry mount. But even so, he fared well enough. Two of the three troopers in front went down before the first unexpected charge, their bodies tangled between the horses' feet. Others closed in, jamming the road between the cliff and the opposite bank, hampered by the narrowness of the defile, a confusion and hubbub. Pedro cut and thrust, hardly knowing what he did. Perhaps his war cry accomplished more than his efforts. It was a famous shout known to all of the assailants, who gathered that Don Francisco himself confronted them. One horse, losing his footing, went down, and another piled on top. The road was temporarily blocked. The onrush wavered.

"Back!" roared García. "Back, before they rally!"

Grasping Pedro's bridle rein, he wheeled him into flight up the road at as hot a pace as spurs could wring from the horses. At the same instant, Soler's men drew off and joined them. They had covered two hundred yards before the pursuit was resumed.

"Here!" cried one of Soler's men three hundred yards further on. "To the right!" And leading down a low bank, he disappeared in a knot of pines. Pell-mell at first, they raced along the trail between the trees, then gradually slackened to a halt.

This was the critical point. Would the troopers turn from the main road after them? Or would they suspect the strategy and perhaps split their force? From what he could gather, Pedro reckoned them at fifty men. Twenty-five of these on the heels of Don Francisco would be enough.

But the chase was too hot; no one paused on the road. Shouts and then the thudding of many hoofs on the pine needles showed that the enemy had taken the bait. Pedro whooped to encourage them.

"Give them a glimpse of us," he said.

They had more than a glimpse. At that moment a man on a tall charger, riding well ahead of his fellows, burst from the trees and crashed into de Vargas's horse. Both animals went down in a flurry of lashing legs. Pinned for an instant and half-dazed, Pedro somehow gained his feet. Then consciousness blew into tatters: sensations, glimpses, blind spots. He was in the middle of a whirlpool, shunted here and there. He was flung against a riderless horse, but did not remember scrambling into the saddle. Something hit him on the head, glanced to his shoulder, but he did not feel the pain of it. Someone yelled, "Here's a sword," and thrust it into his hand. He spurred forward without knowing in what direction, shouting, slashing. The horse reared, bolted; branches whipped his face. He was out of the woods, off the trail, plunging down a dizzy hill, jumping rocks, gullies, fallen timber, hauling vainly against the bit. On, on. A rocky plain stretched before him, ghost-white under the moon. Distant peaks. The ground spun past. Then all at once his horse dropped; he plunged over its head and rolled a yard or more, his cuirass clashing against the stones.

After a while, breath and awareness crept back.

Sitting up, he found that he could move his limbs, though his left arm throbbed from a wound in the shoulder. Several paces off lay the dead horse. A gaping cut on the flank showed what had maddened him.

Unsteadily Pedro got to his feet, sheathed the sword which he had kept hold of by instinct, and looked about him. For the moment he had lost his sense of direction and could not decide where he was. But a sound in the distance brought him back to more urgent things. It came from the quarter out of which he had been riding. It was the click of horseshoes on loose stones. The pursuit was evidently still on.

Looking about for a hiding place, he could see none. The stony ground near him undulated far and wide without a break. Even if he could have hidden himself, the body of the horse outstretched and black against the moonlit ground was a telltale signal to anyone searching for him.

He stood gazing in the direction of the sound and at length caught sight of a dark figure jogging towards him across the glimmering expanse of the mesa. The rider was veering to the left and had apparently not seen him. What first struck Pedro was the man's size and topheaviness as compared with his horse, which looked like a pony carrying a mountain. Then, coming nearer, the stranger stopped all at once and let out a shattering bellow.

"Viva! Por Dios, qué no es verdad!"

"García!"

The big man slipped off his horse, as if he could make more speed on his own feet, and came lumbering towards Pedro, pulling his nag by the bridle. His heavy arms closed around the other in a bear's hug; he kissed him on both cheeks.

"Never did I expect to see thee again," he boomed—"not this side of Satan! It was the devil of a thing to leave a friend like that and ride off to hell on your own account! What ailed you?"

Pedro explained about the horse.

"Never admit it," said García. "Those bastards from the Castle will be talking about de Vargas's ride down that slope till their death day— and you tell me it was nothing but a runaway horse! That's how people get a reputation!" He broke off. "Hurt?"

Pedro was clasping his shoulder, which throbbed from García's hug. "Only a cut. What happened to the others? You did some riding yourself to follow me."

García shook his head. "No, I came after you with prudence and sanity. Even so, if I wasn't born to be hanged, it would have been my finish. I can't tell you what happened. It was everyone for himself, and everyone scattered. Soler's knaves ride well and they know the sierra, so God be with them! Besides, I drew out of it when you did, and followed to pick up the pieces."

"But the troopers—how did you shake them off?"

The other spat thoughtfully. "In such a scramble, anything can happen. Perhaps they took me for one of theirs; perhaps they didn't want to break their necks; perhaps they were busy with Soler's boys, or thought your father couldn't be far down the trail and chased after him. At any rate here we are."

García looked almost as fagged as his horse, which stood behind him, head down and knees bent. Moving a trifle, he caught his breath sharply.

"You're wounded yourself!" exclaimed Pedro.

"Wounded is right! God made me for the sea, not the saddle. I've got blisters on my rump big as ducats. Wish they *were* ducats and in my pocket," he added.

Pedro felt a pang of conscience. "*Cáspita!* You've stripped yourself for us! The jailer; Soler; money to my father for the journey—"

"Not a word of it! Call it a loan. But loan or not, if I've paid back something on account to the reverend devil, de Lora, all would be well-spent." He stood a moment transfigured with hate. "You're lucky. You leave Jaén with a part of your debt canceled. Mine's to pay, and by God I'll pay it!"

Then, wrenching himself out of the mood, he said quietly, "But we're still in pickle and have to keep going. Let's chart our course. Do you know this neighborhood?"

Taking his direction from the moon and from the mountain peaks to the south, Pedro concluded that they were over toward Puente Genil. The distant summits marked the sierra back of Málaga. That city was the nearest seaport they could make.

"And we'll never make it," declared García. "After tonight every road to the south will be watched for us. They'll reckon, I hope, that your father and mother were bound for Málaga. Besides, even if we got there, what'll we do for a ship without money?"

These were telling objections. Pedro stared blankly at the other's bluff face.

"No," García went on, "we'll do better toward the west: the Genil River, then the Guadalquivir, and so downstream to Cádiz. I've still got that bill of change I told you of—eight hundred in gold there. Damned if we'll leave that to the Jews! We can ship to Italy from Sanlúcar as well as from Málaga. And as a hiding place—*hombre!*—there's none to beat it. So tighten your belt, lad. We'll make the most of tonight. Sleep in the day, travel in the dark, rob when we must—it's a long pull, but Sanlúcar's the answer."

So, leaving García's spent horse behind them, they set out with aching limbs, Pedro's slender shadow next to his friend's broader one—two hunted men on the long road to the west.

XXIII

As MIGHT have been expected, the Marquis Luis de Carvajal took a correct view of the above events. Others, less firm in moral principle, might wish the de Vargases well or secretly admire the courage shown in their escape; but the Marquis was guided by truer considerations. Except for his rank, he owed the successes and honors of life to the simple rule of always supporting the side of authority and power. This was not pusillanimous on his part, but instinctive. He belonged naturally to that useful class of people who are born and remain unswervingly proper. It shocked him that a man of Francisco de Vargas's station should have come under the censure of the Holy Office; it shocked him still more that such a man should violently rebel against authority rather than accept its judgment like a good citizen and Christian.

At the midday table, over some cold fowl and salad, he informed his daughter and Doña Antonia of what had happened and prescribed how they should think about it. As a step in Luisa's education, he took pains to impress them with the heinousness of the offense. It gratified him that his words seemed to produce a remarkable effect. In the dark, leather-paneled room, with its straight-backed chairs and rigid footmen, one could have heard a pin drop.

"There is but one cheerful aspect of the affair," he concluded, suspending a chicken bone between his fingers. "Diego de Silva may recover from that young scoundrel's treachery. The sword was deflected by a rib and missed his heart. He is in a grave way, of course; but unless mortification sets in, the doctors have hopes for him."

A little faint, Luisa took a sip of wine.

"Treachery? What kind of treachery?" she murmured.

"The worst. The blackest." Carvajal sucked his chicken bone. "They tell me that de Silva, who is a man of deep piety and a zealous servant of the Holy Office, entered de Vargas's cell with a view of sparing him from the rigors of the tribunal. He hoped to secure a confession which might have helped the young man before Their Reverences. A deed of Christian charity. The youth sprang on him unawares and drove a sword, which had somehow been smuggled in, through his body. But he'll be brought back in chains yet, he and his father."

"How terrible!" whispered Luisa, her soft velvet eyes fluttering. For the first time, the dreadful thought occurred to her: what if Pedro de Vargas had been searched and her monogrammed handkerchief found! Blessed Virgin protect her! She felt on the point of swooning.

"I do wrong," regretted the Marquis, "to discuss such things before you, my little dove—or before you, señora." He glanced from the sweetly sensitive face of his daughter to Antonia, who looked equally distressed. "Your pardon!"

From their reticules, both ladies now drew their vials of smelling salts (indispensable to the tight-laced women of the period) and sniffed delicately. Antonia had as much need of it as her charge. She too wondered about the handkerchief and what had been learned in the prison or might be learned if Pedro were recaptured.

"He was not searched then?" Luisa asked with an artfulness understood only by the duenna.

The Marquis squeezed a half-orange over his fowl. "Not that I heard of. But you can't conceal a sword in your breeches. I tell you it was smuggled in, probably by that desperado, García."

"And you think there's a chance of overtaking them, my lord?"

"Excellent chance. Apparently they are bound for Málaga, but they will never get there. The Inquisition has a long arm, I assure you."

He finished his chicken, while Luisa and Antonia thought long, sober thoughts. Romance, glamorous in the moonlight and perfume of the garden, had hardly the substance to resist so rough a storm. Luisa was not her father's daughter for nothing; Antonia remembered her status as a poor relation.

The Marquis, having dipped his fingers in the bowl and dried them on a napkin presented by the footman, began toying with some fruit.

"Let us talk of pleasanter things," he remarked. "I believe that Diego de Silva will recover. That he may do so lies near my heart, and I narrowly questioned the doctor, Miguel Segrado, about his chances this morning." Then slyly, "It concerns you too, little daughter, so do not fail to make special mention of the good gentleman in your prayers."

"Concerns me, my lord?" said Luisa absently.

Her father eyed her with immense fondness. What exquisite beauty! It showed the blood she came from. What a pure and spiritual face! Innocent as snow. But a profound nature, like his own, a good mind.

Then as waggishly as his solemn face and arrogant beard permitted, he rejoined, "Shall I tell you a secret?" He enjoyed prolonging the suspense and consumed a grape before continuing. "It was practically arranged before this sad event, and now, if God wills that de Silva recover, it shall certainly be concluded. In brief, daughter, at his entreaty, I have decided to give you in marriage to Diego de Silva. Is that not a fine choice? Have I not done well by you?"

"Yes, my lord," she stammered, casting a helpless glance at Antonia.

But the other, equally startled, could only stare back. The ironic chance that, of all men, Diego de Silva, victim of Pedro's violence, should have been selected as Luisa's husband dazed both of them.

The Marquis raised his eyebrows. "You do not seem as pleased as I expected."

"Of course," she said, "of course—onl·· the suddenness of it."

"There's no better match in the province," he proclaimed—"none. I confess that he does not rate himself too modestly when it comes to dowry. It will cost me a pretty figure. But I have only you, and I can please my fancy. The Señor de Silva is a man of means; he stands high in the favor of the Holy Office; he is welcome at court. Since I have no son, it is time that I had a grandson. All these are on the credit side and worth the dowry. If it were not for this overseas venture—"

Thinking aloud, the Marquis frowned at his wine cup.

"Overseas, Your Grace?" put in Antonia, scenting a possible delay.

Carvajal nodded. "Speculation. These cursed Indies—a sink hole for money! He was to accompany Father Ignacio to the Islands in the interests of the Santa Casa, but cheap land and slaves were a part of it. He may waste his substance." The Marquis frowned again. Then, suddenly brightening, "But that's over, of course. The Inquisitor will have to do without him. It's an ill wind that blows no one any good. This wound may be the salvation of him. By the time he's up and married, the notion of traveling will have passed. No, all in all, he's the man for you, my daughter." The Marquis added archly, "Señora de Silva."

Luisa did not protest. Her conventional mind accepted what had to be and tried to make the best of it. After all, de Silva was a man of fashion, rather good-looking, and not too old. Her father might easily have chosen someone less attractive. If only the regrettable episode with Pedro were never discovered!

Upon returning to the mirador with Antonia, she burst into tears. "If it hadn't been for you!" she reproached.

"I know," admitted the duenna. "It *was* a mistake, my love. But I thought it would give you pleasure. I could see no harm. Who would have dreamed—!"

It is hard to be a poor relation. Suppose Luisa dropped a word to the Marquis, an innocent word apparently, as to Antonia's encouragement of romance! But no, she was safe enough. The secret was too explosive even for a word.

In her tears, the girl looked like a lovely martyr.

"Do you think the handkerchief was found?"

"No, probably not, my dear—don't worry."

"Do you think he will be captured?"

"I hope not," said the duenna devoutly.

"So do I!" mourned Luisa. "So *do* I! It would be dreadful if anyone knew about the handkerchief. We must pray for him, Cousin. I promise San Cristóbal ten candles if he escapes."

130

She raised her beautiful eyes toward heaven.

So, for one reason or another, his lady's prayers accompanied Pedro de Vargas.

In a crack of the arid land, before the sierra sweeps down into the green valley of the Genil, Pedro wakened, stretched his stiff limbs, and then, considerate of the sleeping García, sat clasping his knees and gazing toward the sunset. After a time he drew out a small, crushed object from his inner pocket and unfolded it reverently. It was embroidered with a tiny coronet and the letter "L." It retained a vague perfume of roses.

Beyond it, in his fancy, hovered a noble, sensitive face with eyes upturned to his. For an instant his angular features relaxed. Then, as if the relic were too sacred for long exposure, he raised the handkerchief to his lips and, folding it carefully, replaced it within his doublet.

XXIV

ALL OVER the world in every age, crows are of the same color. A bandit of sixteenth-century Spain might ride a fine horse and wear a showy baldric but he was still a gangster with a gangster's attitude and vices. If Hernán Soler had not lost a brother to the fires of the Inquisition, and if, all things considered, he had not thought it worth his while to convey the de Vargases safely to Almería and secure a ship for them, he would have been perfectly capable of selling them out at higher profit to the agents of the Holy Office.

As it was, he performed his mission honestly and got a discharge to that effect over Don Francisco's signature before the felucca, which they had been lucky enough to find, cleared the harbor. This was part of his bargain with Catana, who took no chances and had paid him fifty ducats of García's money on account, with the promise of a second fifty and herself when he returned. The hundred ducats alone would not have tempted him; but Catana plus the money made a difference. Besides, he had a wager with Paco Ribera, his lieutenant, that he would have the bedding of her, which could be figured in with the cash profit.

When he had seen the last of the felucca, he and his men turned into a wineshop for celebration. There were dice and women; the girls of Almería proved seductive, the wine potent, and the innkeepers hospitable, so that it was several days before he rode back exhausted and in a cold, ugly humor to the Jaén side of the mountains. From his present surly point of view, the remaining fifty ducats and Catana did not console him for his headache, nor for the news that three good men had been lost in the fight against the troopers.

He arrived at his headquarters in the Sierra Lucena about nightfall; swore at the sentry who challenged him on the trail; and dismounted with his men as the campfires were being lighted.

An overhang of rock, which formed a long, deep gallery at the base of a cliff and which had been partially boarded up to provide cover, served as Soler's chief hangout in the district. It lay at one end of a narrow valley and had a second emergency exit over a low saddle of the cliff. In front of this semi-cave, a small natural basin fed by a brook furnished abundant water. In the open part of the gallery, fires were laid and cooking was done for the forty-odd men and women of Soler's motley household. Guarded by outposts and hidden in a fold of the mountains, it was reasonably secure against the halfhearted constabulary which might be sent out against it.

Since the day after his departure, Catana had been waiting here, impatient not for Soler but for his news. She had heard, of course, from her brother, who had taken part in the fight on the road, of Pedro's and García's disappearance. That there had been no report of their capture augured well; but Soler would possibly know more. Meanwhile, she established herself in the respect, if not the affection, of the band.

Her position as the future *mujer* of the chief would have given her prestige in any case, had she needed it; but she was distinguished in her own right as a dancer and a girl of parts, who could take care of herself. Her tongue and her knife were equally ready and admired. When Paco Ribera, presuming on his rank, took liberties the first night, he came off with a wound that made sitting difficult and taught him a lesson about the new *capitana*. Then too, in case of need, she had her brother, Manuel Pérez, burly and short of speech, who during his career as turnkey had kept in with the robbers and was a popular addition to the gang. Manuel approved his sister's choice of a mate as both natural and honorable—Soler was an *hombre muy rico*—but he would stand for no affronts to Catana's virtue.

Now that the bargain had been struck, she prepared to carry out her share of it. She had been brought up to elemental facts and accepted them as inevitable. A girl, however independent, must finally belong to a man, work for him, bear children, lose her looks, and grow old: life was like that. Soler or another—it did not matter much. She was lucky in being able to turn the inevitable to some account. By saving Pedro de Vargas, she had given the years something to remember, some reason for pride.

During the days of waiting at the camp, she held aloof from the others and let them think that she was pining for Soler. Especially at evening, when the tone of a far-off bell in one of the valleys signaled the Angelus, she liked to stand on the saddle of the cliff listening to the faint reverberation and dreaming her only dream.

She was engaged in this when Soler reached camp, and the stir from below drifted up to her. Descending quickly, she greeted him on the threshold of the overhang, as he came up, carrying his saddlebags.

"Well, *amigo mío?*"

To Soler's jaundiced eye, she looked plainer and less glamorous than in the festive atmosphere of the Rosario. She wore nothing in her hair, which was also wind-blown from her walk along the cliffs. In a faded everyday dress, she seemed too lithe, too dark, too hard, too country-like. His biliousness deepened.

"Well, my friend?" he mimicked, dumping his saddlebags.

She expected to be kissed, but he looked past her, nodding to this one and that around the fire and exchanging a word with several. As the men who had been with him joined the group and their women hung on them, the clatter of tongues grew louder.

Soler spat. "Fetch me some wine," he told Catana. "My throat's dry as hell's dust."

She brought him a cup and pitcher; he half-gargled, half-drank, then wiped his mouth with the back of his hand. Evidently he felt that the need for courting manners was over.

"Well," she urged, "what news?"

"The job's done," he growled. "Help me off with this cursed armor."

Hell! he chafed, she was not half so well-favored as the Moorish slut he had had in Almería—the one with almond eyes and the mole on her hip—but in his present mood the thought of any woman sickened him.

Catana loosened the straps, her tawny cheeks a shade darker. He piled the steel pieces on top of the saddlebags.

"Take all that into our room and stow it," he ordered. Then, snappishly, "Freshen yourself up, girl. You look like a hedge clout. 'Sblood! A man might expect his wench to primp a little for his homecoming."

He found himself facing a pair of hot black eyes.

"Whose wench, fellow?" And when he did not find his tongue, she added, "I asked a question. Till it's answered to my liking, I'm no wench of yours. D'you take me?"

He turned yellow with anger, but he could not beat down her gaze.

The near-by talk quieted suddenly. Manuel Pérez, who had been joking with one of the newcomers, stopped smiling.

Though his liver burned, Soler controlled himself. "What question?" he snarled at last, his eyes beady and narrow on either side of his nose. "If you mean old Game-leg de Vargas and his wife, they got off. If you mean Pedrito, what can I tell you? It's no fault of mine what happened. They say he rode off the mountain—he and the big man. But listen to me. I'm in no mood for airs. A cursed deal I've had, with three men gone, hard riding, and nothing to show for it but fifty damn ducats. Your Grace will take orders. We'll have no shrews here. Understand?"

Catana held her right palm out and tapped it with the other forefinger. "*Bueno!* I'll take orders when I'm your woman. You say Don Francisco and his lady got off. The bargain took in Pedro de Vargas; but he's probably safe so far, and I'll admit that part of it wasn't your fault. Where's the proof his father and mother got off?"

"Do you doubt my word?"

Catana tapped her palm.

In a rage, Soler drew out the signed paper and smacked it on her hand.

"Eat it and choke!"

Catana unfolded the paper. She could not read, but she could pretend that she did, and she could at least spell out the bold, rough-hewn signature. Having satisfied herself that Soler had kept faith, she tucked the discharge into her belt. Then, lifting her skirt, she detached a purse from her garter and handed it to him.

"Now I'll take orders."

And she occupied herself with the armor and saddlebags.

XXV

In Sanlúcar de Barrameda, from the upper town where the road climbs toward the castle, a fine outlook may be had upon the beach and harbor. In front, westerly across the mouth of the Guadalquivir, stretches the long line of the Arenas Gordas that fringe the northern curve of the Bay of Cádiz; to the right extend the lovely reaches of the river, with Bonanza in the distance; the blinding white of house walls, rising tier on tier, is relieved by the sapphire and allurement of water. Giant aloes and palms are visible; gardens and orange groves circle the white town, which recalls Moorish Africa rather than Spain. The sun beats hard on Sanlúcar, maturing the grapes of its vineyards, deepening the scent of its orange blossoms, tanning the skins of its inhabitants, and producing everywhere a riot of color.

It was especially hot and colorful on that afternoon of mid-September, as two Franciscan monks gazed down at the harbor from a parapet near the church of Our Lady of the West. In twenty years, since the Admiral had sailed from Sanlúcar on his third voyage to the New World, the port had become increasingly a point of departure for westbound fleets making for Grand Canary and the Indies. Today it was alive with craft taking on cargo and readying gear for the outward voyage, the last to Santo Domingo before winter. Caravels—two- or three-masted, with cocked-up lateen yards on the mizzen—several larger carracks, some lighter brigantines, clustered in the harbor and were connected with the beach by numerous rowboats loaded or empty. But the overseas fleet made up only a part of the shipping. French galleasses, British barks, flyboats, and foists, fat-bellied traders from Holland, Italian galleys and feluccas, rode at anchor in the cosmopolitan medley. With their high poops and forecastles, they resembled a flock of sway-backed ducks.

Crews were busy with lading and tackle; hulls were being tarred; a couple of vessels had been beached for greasing below the water line. The sun played on gilded beakheads and varicolored canvas; it flashed on armor and kindled the blues, reds, and yellows of costume; it brought out the gaudy Saint Christopher on the mainsail of an incoming ship and the colored pennons of her topmasts.

The agglomeration of wooden shacks, a quarter of a mile deep, which occupied the space between waterfront and town, and which housed a community of international riffraff infamous even in that age, now hummed like a fair. Sailors, merchants, hidalgos, mountebanks, peddlers, charlatans, prostitutes, and thieves, thronged between the squalid huts. A din composed of every sound possible to human lungs floated up to the brothers of Saint Francis, leaning next to each other against the parapet.

As seen from behind by a couple of beggars lounging on the church steps, the two monks offered a droll contrast. One of them was broad of shoulder and beam, with too short a robe that displayed his big, naked calves; while the other, slender and tall, wore a habit too long for him. Though he kept hitching it up under the rope around his waist, it slipped down again and looked frayed and dusty at the skirts.

"See that caravel?" said the burly monk, pointing. "She's the *Boniface*. Her master's Jorge Santerra, a good friend of mine. She's a bitch

135

in rough weather, but seaworthy for all that. Damn me, the sight of her turns me homesick! I'll bet you ten pesos she makes port first and skims the cream off the market. Ten yellow clinkers she does!"

He scratched his thigh and continued to gaze.

The other asked, "Where's our ship, the *Iulia*—the Genoese? I don't see her."

"Over behind the French galleass," his companion answered. "There's her topmast." Then abruptly, as if to get something that was difficult to say over with, "But—well—as a matter of fact, *your* ship, not mine. Mine's the *Boniface*. Tell you the truth, I paid my passage money this morning to Santo Domingo."

"What do you mean?"

"I mean I'm not for Italy, after all."

A bleak pause. The slender monk hitched his robe. "But I thought—"

"Yes, by God, I know," the other burst out. "Devil take me for a quitter! But I can't help it. It's the feel of the west wind, maybe, or the sight of the ships, the talk on the beach. Italy's an old road; I want new ones." And when silence fell again, he added, "Don't you feel it yourself?"

The younger man nodded. "*Seguro.* Who wouldn't, in this kettle?" He jerked his chin toward the harbor. "Everybody gets the fever."

"All right then, how about your coming along with me?"

"You know the answer to that, Juan García. If Father's still living, he expects me in Italy. I can't fail him. Besides," Pedro went on, as if arguing with himself, "what's the itch that's got hold of those people down there? Gold. Why are they sailing for the Islands? Gold. What's the only thing they think about, talk about every cursed minute? Gold. Well, maybe there's something else in life."

His voice hesitated and died out. His eyes were on the west.

His companion brought a heavy fist down on the parapet. "Yes, son Pedro, and there's a lot to be said for gold. It got us out of Jaén, and it's the one thing that can get you back there—I mean on horseback, riding high, avenged, honored, reinstated, which is what you hanker for. But you're wrong about that crowd for the Islands. We talk gold, but we mean something more. Gold's the excuse."

"For what?"

"I don't know—call it urge, curiosity—I don't know."

Without realizing it, García had touched on what gave real significance to the crowded harbor. Behind this western beach lay all the past of the white race: its wars and wanderings, its unceasing nostalgia for beyond-the-horizon, its inveterate dissatisfaction with what it was or

136

had or knew. Having reached the limits of its continent, it could not stop there. Avaricious, cruel, brutal, blind, but always doing and daring, it was driven to set out on crazy planks for unknown continents, different from other races only in this, that it has been the supreme tool of the obscure, creative purpose expressing itself in life.

Pedro de Vargas responded to the vibration. Since reaching Sanlúcar, he had felt the drag of the current setting west. If he stuck to the plan for Italy, it was by an effort of will.

"*Vaya*," he muttered, "good-by will come hard, Juan García."

More than hard—unthinkable. The long road across Spain, stealing, begging, hiding, bluffing; fear and fun; robust comradeship, had bound the two men closer than brothers. And now during these last days at Sanlúcar, safe in the godless fraternity of the waterfront, monks by day, rufflers by night, rich from the proceeds of García's bill of change, they had tasted together the joy of success; they had reached the sea, out-witted pursuit. Pedro thought of the Genoese galley without García, the strange faces. Italy meant the past, the conventional. He thought with an ache of his friend heading west, of the fleet with its billowing sails and expectant decks. "Land, ho!" The new, uncharted world!

García swallowed and frowned. "I'd go with you, boy, but it's no use. What does Italy offer a plain man like me? To shoulder a pike or scratch fleas in some big lord's guardroom. I have no kinsmen cardinals to give me a leg up like you have. Sure—you wouldn't forget me, but I'd be a sow's ear. It's different in the Islands. Nobody has any kinsmen, and tomorrow counts more than yesterday. We won't talk about good-by, though—not yet."

"The galley sails in two days."

A fatalist, García shrugged his shoulders. "That's a long time, brother."

The great point about life on the beach at Sanlúcar was the unanimous antipathy to law and its agents that prevailed there. The beach had its own law—that of survival. The weakling was fair game. Everyone kept a speculative eye on his neighbor and a vigilant guard of his own purse and throat. But as most of those who frequented the shacks along the water had cheated the hangman somewhere or other, they were united by a common prejudice. No sensible bailiff poked his nose into the narrow ways between the hovels; no informer of the Holy Office kept his health in that uncongenial air; stool pigeons were almost unknown. The Brethren of the Beach furnished crews, loaded and unloaded cargoes, drifted in and out on ships, and had no truck with righteousness or its tools. Between them and the authorities of San-lúcar existed a policy of hands-off. Let a hard-pressed criminal once dive beneath the scum of that sanctuary, and he was safer than if he embraced the high altar of any church in Spain.

It was not to the credit of Juan García and Pedro de Vargas that this community accepted them without question from the moment of their arrival, dusty, hard, and tattered. Outlaws have a flair for each other. The connoisseurs of the beach knew them at once for desperate men like themselves, men with the kind of past that earned them the liberty of the waterfront. It made no difference that the hidalgo stuck out all over young de Vargas: to be a ruffian was the main thing, and no prejudice existed against noble ruffians. What counted was the cold alertness of his eyes (no longer half so young as they had been two months before), the size of his wrists, the length of his reach, the downward hook at the corners of his mouth, and his quickness of movement. He played cards or dice with distinction. A hint of danger clung to him. They called him "Pelirrojo," Redhead, respectfully.

The beach minded its own business. What bond existed between de Vargas and an old-timer like "the Bull," as García was nicknamed, or what the pair had been up to back in Spain, did not concern anybody. That de Vargas made inquiries about an Indian servant named Coatl, who had managed to sign up as gromet on a ship for the Islands a month earlier, roused a mild but not inquisitive interest. That he and García left the shacks at times, disguised in the robes of the two monks whom they had stripped on the way to Sanlúcar, did not cause remark, for it was a place used to disguises. Of course they took care that no one knew of their trip to the Medici banker's in Cádiz or that they carried the value of eight hundred *castellanos* concealed on their persons, since knowledge of that sort provoked murder.

On the evening of the day when they had stretched their legs by walking up to the church of Our Lady of the West, the Redhead and the Bull, once more in layman's clothes, took their ease at the Venta de los Caballeros in the place of shacks.

The tavern consisted of a line of sheds pieced together and completely open on the harbor side. A hundred yards from them lay the water and the far scattering of ships. As twilight deepened, it was hard to tell where the sand ended, for sand and water merged in a wide plain overarched by the evening sky. Lights began to appear on the anchored vessels. The noises of day lapsed into silence broken by isolated voices, laughter, tinkle of instruments and snatches of song. An offshore wind, languid with the smell of orange groves, sweetened the odors of tar and fish alongshore. The Andalusian night, mysterious and star-heavy, was already closing in.

A mixed company occupied the line of tables. Englishmen, Dutchmen, French, Portuguese, Italians, and even Greeks from the Levant, spoke their own languages or joined, if necessary, in the lingua franca of the ports, which was a mixture of all languages. Costume kept pace with the diversity of tongues. At the moment, a common interest in food and drink muffled the jumble of voices; but hubbub would swell later, when stomachs were filled and the dicing and fighting started.

Next to Pedro at table sat Luis Casca, surnamed "Nightingale" because of his gentle voice, which could utter abominations as if making love. He had lost one ear and wore his hair in a blob over that spot. From the lobe of the other dangled a woman's pearl earring. His handsome Sicilian face was marred by a scar from forehead to chin. Otherwise he looked like a sentimental girl, except when he used his knife.

El Moro, a spade-bearded man of few words, sat next to García across the board. He had spent five years as a slave in the Moorish galleys and had earned his nickname from that ordeal. Lacking several teeth, he had the habit of making sucking sounds with his lips. He had small, button-hard eyes. It was said that the whip marks on his back were too many to count. Both he and Casca were sailing with the Indian fleet and had been drawn to García because of the latter's experience in the Islands.

They were listening to a discourse upon how two enterprising, stouthearted men with little capital could best establish themselves in land and Indians; and how one lucky evening at cards or a successful venture to the Mainland could set a man up for life, when García, springing to his feet, all but overturned the table.

"Hola, Jorge Santerra!" he roared. "Hola, comrade!" And stopping the master of the *Boniface*, who was lumbering by, he drew him to the table. "Here's the gentleman who can tell you boys the news. He's fresh from Cuba. That's a better lay for your money than Santo Domingo. Bigger and more land. I'm heading there myself. Tell 'em what you told me this morning, Jorge. You'll take a cup of wine with us."

"Not your stripe of wine, by God," returned the seaman, for García's eccentricity in respect to water drinking was notorious. "If you can favor me with a pint of manzanilla, I'll spend a minute with you; but I'm expected for supper in the town."

The edge to this was that shipmasters, being people of consequence, did not mingle with the rank and file. It added to García's prestige that such a bigwig condescended to sit with him, and the men at near-by tables stared.

Jorge Santerra was short and squat. He wore a red scarf on his head and a landgoing hat over it, a combination which gave him a top-heavy appearance. His face and hands had the look of pale old leather crisscrossed with a web of wrinkles. His eyes, impersonal and remote, gave the impression that he was always looking into the distance.

"These gentlemen," García went on, after the shipmaster had taken a seat, "are bound for the Islands. That is, two of them are. My young pal here sails for Italy."

"Ah," grunted Santerra without comment. He intended no slight, but was plainly uninterested in Italy. His glance excluded Pedro, while patronizing the Moor and the Nightingale as men headed in the right direction.

"They're shipping on the *Ferdinand,*" García explained. "I'm telling them that the big chances lie west. Santo Domingo's old stuff. What was the gossip you were giving me from Cuba?"

Talk dropped off at neighboring tables, and men listened intently to the seaman's answer, though Santerra pretended to be unconscious of them.

"Well," he returned after drinking, "you know that Hernández de Córdoba last year discovered land twenty days west of Cape San Antonio de Cuba. Called it Yucatán. Thought maybe it was an island, but a big one, for he never got round it. Said there's a town there that they named Grand Cairo on account of its size. Stone buildings with idols in them, Indians wearing clothes, cultivated fields, and—what's most to the point—gold. In short, Cuba has nothing like it. A land of bloodthirsty people, though. Córdoba got back with twelve wounds in his body, and died two weeks later."

"Yes," nodded García, "I knew him."

"So, in May of this year, Diego Velásquez—the governor of Cuba, gentlemen—sent his nephew, Juan de Grijalva, with four ships to take another look. Grijalva wasn't back when I sailed; but one of his caravels came in, Pedro de Alvarado commanding, with reports of the voyage."

Santerra paused a moment for effect.

"Señor! He brought gold to the value of fifteen thousand pesos. Fifteen thousand pesos! Got in no time at all for a handful of glass beads. *Hijos,* the country must be lousy with gold. And it's not an island, but a continent. They heard of wonders beyond the mountains."

A deep hush followed. Several men from other tables edged closer and formed a spellbound circle. El Moro sucked at the gap between his teeth. The Nightingale's lips were moist. Pedro de Vargas's eyes, showing more green than usual, were riveted on the speaker.

"Yes, friend," Santerra went on to García, "you're right. It's the West every time. When I left Cuba, all, the talk was about the big armada that Velásquez is fitting up to take over the new land before someone else gets the jump on him. He wasn't waiting for Grijalva to come back. Everybody who could lay hands on cash or equipment was buying himself into the venture. Mortgaging, borrowing—Lord! you can get an estate with slaves at a bargain in Cuba now, if you've got ready money. As for politics—the big planters scheming for the command! They're around the governor like a pack of dogs after meat. But the talk was that Hernán Cortés would get it. He's rich and has influence with the governor."

For some reason, the name Cortés struck a familiar note in Pedro's mind; but at first he could not remember where he had heard it. Then with a pang he recalled the last family evening at the pavilion and his father's fulminations against the Indies. The ne'er-do-well son of Martín Cortés de Monroy had evidently come up in the world. Talk about a career! What could Italy offer more than this, to be Captain General of an armada out for the conquest of infidel lands? What profit and honor! Compared with taking part in such an expedition, even a place in the Chevalier Bayard's company of lances seemed insipid.

Someone was asking about Cortés.

"I don't know him myself," replied the shipmaster. "Saw him once with other hidalgos at the *posada* in Santiago, and I've carried a cargo of his hides. He made his money in cattle. A good-looking gentleman; very humorous, they say, and popular—especially with the ladies." Santerra stuck his tongue in his cheek and winked.

"But can he fight?" asked one of the audience, a flashy ruffian in parti-colored hose and with a black beard. "From what you say about Yucatán, it'll take more than a ladies' pet and jelly-belly to win it. Is he a captain? 'Steeth! he sounds like a rich slob."

Santerra emptied his cup, gave the other a glance, and said, "He *looks* like a captain." Then to García, "Thanks for the drink, brother. I'm going. By the way, the fleet sails in two squadrons. Be on board tomorrow. We leave with the ebb."

"Señor shipmaster," Pedro asked suddenly, "do you suppose the armada for Yucatán has already sailed from Cuba?"

He was aware of the question in García's eyes. He felt that the rest of his life depended on that moment. If Santerra answered yes, he would go to Italy; if it was no, if there was a chance of his reaching Cuba in time, he would sail westward with the fleet tomorrow. García wanted him, would stake him to the passage. In view of such a prospect, even his father would approve. He would send a letter at random by the master of the *Iulia*. His imagination leaped the sea to an unknown harbor, then beyond to the lands of gold. It brought him back to Spain, wealthy, famous, exonerated. It threw open the doors of the Carvajal Palace, where Luisa waited.

The shipmaster had got up, but he paused a moment.

"It takes time to fit out vessels, lay in stores, raise funds, muster a company. And Cuba isn't Spain. No" (Pedro's heart beat faster), "I hardly think they'll sail before the end of the year."

"And you reach Santo Domingo when?"

"By All Saints, God willing."

"Have you room for me on the *Boniface?*"

"I thought—"

García interrupted. *"Has he room for you! Viva!* Let me hug you! Yes, son, he has room for you on the *Boniface."*

Santerra grinned. "That settles it. *Hasta mañana, caballeros."*

Part Two

───── XXVI ─────

On a morning of late November in the year 1518, a crowded pinnace entered the harbor three miles from Trinidad de Cuba and discharged its passengers, a group from Santiago.

The report went up to the quarters of Captain General Cortés that several volunteers from Santo Domingo had reached Santiago only to find the fleet gone, and that they had chartered the pinnace to bring them on to Trinidad. Their leader was an old-timer, one of Columbus's men, Juan García, who had had an allotment of Indians and land near Isabella. It was good news too that they had brought a horse on the pinnace, a tall sorrel by the name of Soldán.

They begged leave to wait upon the General and pay their respects. Whereupon, Gonzalo de Sandoval was dispatched by Cortés to welcome them.

Sandoval met the new arrivals as they were trudging up the palm-shaded valley, and he swung from his saddle, cap in hand. They were suiting their pace to that of their horse, who was still stiff from the voyage. Sandoval's eyes took in the animal almost sooner than the men, for a horse rated high in the expedition; but he did not forget his courtesy.

"Ha, gentlemen!" he said. "Welcome to Trinidad!" Then, more formally, he introduced himself.

He was a compact, muscular young man with slightly bandy legs, curly brown hair, and the beginnings of a beard. His eyes were clear, direct, and soldierly. His voice sounded rough, and he stammered a little when embarrassed.

"The General sends his compliments and desires your attendance," he added.

García, taking a step in front, acted as spokesman. The others were presented, made a leg, and bowed.

143

A mixed group, thought Sandoval. García, the typical seaman-yeoman of the Islands, consorted strangely with the others. Señor Nightingale Casca and Señor El Moro had plainly cheated the gallows. In Pedro de Vargas, Sandoval recognized the aristocrat, a fellow hidalgo. His square hand gripped Pedro's cordially; his eyes warmed. They were about of an age, he and de Vargas.

"That's a good horse," he remarked, unable longer to put off inspecting the new mount.

"Not a patch on yours," rumbled García.

Sandoval smiled. "Well, perhaps not. Motilla's hard to beat. But this is a good horse." He poked judiciously. The sorrel bared his teeth. "Ha, bite, would he?" The sorrel tried to wheel. "Ha, kick, would he? A good horse! A horse of spirit!" He clapped his hand on the beast's haunches. "Are you his owner, sir?"

"Yes," said García—"that is, my friend and I own him together." He shot a warning glance at Pedro not to deny it. "But he'll do the riding of him. He's the horseman. No horse for me and no sore buttocks as long as I have my two legs, *por Dios!*"

It was usual enough to share a horse in the army. Sandoval laughed. "Well, gentlemen, take my advice and keep away from the dice-box. There're a good many here who'll try to win him from you, one way or another."

Walking uphill, they now came into full view of Trinidad, which already called itself a city, with its stockaded fort, its roughly built houses on the Spanish model, edging the plaza-commons, and among them a church, a tavern, and the residence of the alcalde.

The square buzzed with people, the townsfolk intermingling with seamen and soldiers from the fleet. Some strolled arm in arm; others merged with larger groups, or came and went through the doors of the tavern; bronzed veterans of other expeditions; women camp followers equally tanned and tough; newcomers from Spain; flower-decked Indian girls, plump and barelegged, at the side of white husbands or paramours; here and there the somber robe of a friar; hidalgos from country estates, with now and then a Castilian wife; natives carrying bundles on their heads; a blending of costumes and nakedness, clatter of tongues and accents.

"That's the General's banner," remarked Sandoval, pointing to a black velvet flag, edged with gold, that floated on the offshore wind in front of one of the better houses. It looked funereal at a first glimpse but showed sparkles of color on second view. Unfolding to the gusts of the breeze, it displayed the royal arms of Spain and, joined with them, a crimson cross girt with white and blue flames, having a motto in gold letters underneath.

"How does it read?" asked de Vargas.

Sandoval swelled a little. "It reads, *Brothers and comrades, let us follow the Cross with true faith, and in this sign we shall conquer.* Good-looking, isn't it? The General designed it himself. *Hola!* We're just in time for the cry. We have it three times a day. Listen."

Prefaced by an urgent roll on a long drum (the drummer plying his sticks like mad), a great-voiced crier, stationed next to the flag-pole, shouted his oyez:—

"Hear ye! Hear ye! Hear ye! In the King's name! Know everyone that the fleet now in Trinidad harbor sails by the authority of His Excellency, the Governor, to the West, for trade, settlement, and discovery, under the command of Hernando Cortés, Alcalde of Santiago Baracoa. Enroll for God and King under this his banner! Carry the light of our Blessed Faith to those in heathen darkness! Win lands and profit, gold and treasure for our gracious King, Don Carlos, and for yourselves! Join the cavaliers from Santiago, who invite you of Trinidad, you of Sancti Spiritus, and of this district, to be their comrades in arms! Eleven stout ships! Big returns for all monies ventured! Do not delay! Enlist under the banner of Hernán Cortés, Captain General!"

"We're getting to be an army," Sandoval went on when the proclamation ended. "Only three hundred left Santiago; but we're four hundred now, not counting seamen and Indian servants. Pedro de Alvarado and his brothers joined up from here. He was on the expedition with Grijalva, you know. Cristóbal de Olid's from Trinidad too, and Alonso de Avila, Juan de Escalante, Ortiz the Musician—" Sandoval mentioned other names. "I got in yesterday from Sancti Spiritus with Alonso Hernández de Puertocarrero, Roderigo Rangel, and Juan Velásquez de León. They shot off the cannon for us. More are coming. We plan to stop off down the coast and pick up others at San Cristóbal de la Habana."

"What do you think of the General?" asked García, putting his finger at once on the main point; for an expedition was a kind of military stock company, each member of it profiting in proportion to his investment; and as its leader had the functions of a general manager, everything depended on his ability. "I've known plenty of captains and generals in my time—Ojeda, Ponce de León, Nicuesa, Córdoba, not to mention Grijalva. Good men but not good enough. Never quite hit the clout, you understand. How's Cortés?"

"Wait till you've met him!" In his enthusiasm, Sandoval, who was leading his horse out of deference to the newcomers, stopped dead and tapped García on the chest with an emphatic forefinger. "Señor, there's a man for anybody's money. Doesn't let the grass grow under *his* feet, I can tell you. Sleeps with one eye open. Knows when to take a chance, if you follow me, but he looks ahead too and thinks out every detail." Sandoval grinned and slapped his leg. "Hear about the sailing from Santiago?"

"Cómo no!" said García. "Heard nothing else when we got there. Governor Velásquez tried to double-deal Cortés out of the command at the last moment, didn't he?"

"He did, and be damned to him! Call that justice, when the General has put more into this venture than anybody else? His last peso, they tell me. And that isn't the worst of it. Velásquez sends a fellow here, ordering the alcalde, Francisco Verdugo, to arrest him and send him back to Santiago. By God, the alcalde knows better! We'd sack the town. We're betting our lives on Hernán Cortés and no other. That is, most of us are," Sandoval added, "because you'll always find a few soreheads. *Hombre!* It must have been a night in Santiago! Cortés hustling the men on board, buying out the town market for supplies. Then next morning, Velásquez on the jetty: Cortés in the ship's boat. Ha, ha! Good-by, Your Excellency! I tell you, señores, you've got to get up early to steal a march on the General."

García pointed at the extra thick wheeling of Cuba's guardian buzzards over the outskirts of the town. "Slaughtering, eh?"

Sandoval nodded. "Yes, hogs. We're laying in enough salt pork and cassava bread for a three months' stretch. As to equipment, listen to the blacksmiths' shops. They're at it day and night."

They started threading their way across toward the General's quarters.

"Hola, Isabel." Sandoval smiled at a full-blown wench with an enterprising eye who stared hard at the strangers. "Seeking grist for your mill, eh? Gentlemen, this is Isabel Rodrigo, one of our ladies."

The girl simpered and bobbed. Pedro stared a question.

"Yes, our ladies," repeated Sandoval. "We've got a few in the army, some married and some in hopes of it, eh, Isabel? By God, I think they'll get more gold out of Yucatán, one way or another, than any of us."

She stuck out her tongue at him. Her gaze faltered between Pedro and Nightingale Casca. She decided on Casca and gave him an intense glance. The Sicilian answered in kind.

"Now, now!" Sandoval put in. "We're due at the General's. Business before pleasure. Be off with you, *muchacha!*" He gave her a playful smack on the behind, dodged a return cuff, and walked on. "Be careful, man," he remarked to Casca.

The other got the point and nodded thoughtfully.

Crossing the square, Pedro was struck by the number of young men in the crowd, most of them near his own age. He did not reason about it; but anyone of more experience could have told him that youth was the chief characteristic of this or any other expedition in the New World: youth with its qualities good and bad, its dash and dare, fickleness and passion; its confused motives of gold, fame, or religion, against the background of still recent chivalry; youth, credulous of rumor. From Santo Domingo to Cuba, Pedro had heard the tales of an unknown world in the West, mysterious as the planet Mars: tales of elephant-eared people and others with dog faces; countries inhabited by Amazons. Anything might wait beyond the western water.

A rumble of voices sounded from the General's house, laughter, and a scuffling of feet. Leaving Soldán and Motilla in the keeping of an Indian servant, they were about to enter when a couple of brawny fellows wearing earrings shouldered into them with never an apology and walked off singing, arm in arm. The passage beyond was filled with men, gossiping, disputing; it smelled of sweat and leather. Sandoval forced a good-natured way through the crowd, exchanging quips and greetings as he went.

So this, Pedro thought, was the moment he had imagined two months ago on the beach at Sanlúcar. Between now and then lay the discomforts and alarms of the voyage, the thousand new impressions, the landing in Santo Domingo, the hot haste to find passage to Cuba, the disappointment at Santiago, the last suspense of the chase along the coast in fear of missing the fleet after all. He wondered now if it had been worth the effort. Trinidad, the tough-looking, boisterous colonials, who were evidently to be his companions, did not attract him. Even Sandoval had the voice of a bull-herder and a homemade doublet. Not for the first time, he regretted Italy.

"Blast my guts!" roared a voice. "There's Bull García!"

A burly man, with one shoulder higher than the other, pushed forward and stuck out a hairy paw.

"Humpback Nojara!" returned García, shaking hands. "Well, well, Humpback! It's a long time since Veragua, eh? Hope we have better luck this voyage. See you when I've talked with the General."

Following Sandoval, they entered a good-sized room on the left, similarly filled with men but of a different condition from those outside.

They were evidently officers of the expedition. Though their clothes were provincial and far from the latest cut, there was still a showing of velvet and colors, steel and gold. A group at a table had their heads together over a map. Several others played cards.

Pedro wondered who was the Captain General, for no one seemed to have particular authority. Catching Sandoval's eyes, he looked inquiringly at a tall, blond man, magnificent in crimson, with a gold chain around his neck and a big diamond ring on his forefinger, the most conspicuous person in the room. Sandoval shook his head. "Pedro de Alvarado," he whispered. "A grand gentleman. You'll like him— everyone does. That's Cristóbal de Olid," he added with a glance at a dark, sinewy man overlooking the card game. "A good swordsman. And that's Juan Velásquez de León." He pointed out a thick-set, bold-looking soldier with a red beard. "Those gentlemen are Diego de Ordás and Francisco de Morla, the Governor's people." He mentioned other names.

One of the group around the map looked up.

"Ha, son Sandoval!"

The speaker was tall, slender, dark, and singularly pale; but his broad shoulders and long arms suggested physical strength. Though apparently still in his early thirties, he gave somehow the impression of being older. Through his thin beard, a scar showed reaching down from his lower lip. Facing him, Pedro met the level impact of his eyes, as he straightened up from the map. They were grave eyes, but with a friendly twinkle in them, a twinkle of personal interest and understanding. Instinctively de Vargas knew that this was the General.

"So you've brought the gentlemen." Rounding the table, Cortés held out both hands. "Señor García, eh? I've heard much of you, sir—and all good. We've been neighbors, so to speak, back in Santo Domingo. But on my conscience, haven't we met? Didn't you pass through Azúa in 1508? I was a boy then, no older than Sandoval."

"Yes," nodded García, his broad face beaming with gratification. "I was in Azúa in 1508, after the Indian revolt. Only twenty-five at the time. What a memory Your Excellency has!"

"One doesn't easily forget a man of your build and carriage, sir. I hope you're with us in this venture? Good! You never made a sounder investment, Señor García. Every maravedí you lay out now will net you a thousand. At the least. At the least, I say. Torrazas"—he nodded to a man with an inkhorn at a side table—"inscribe my friend, Juan García, on the roll of the company. Take good note of his commitment. And these other gentlemen?"

The Nightingale and the Moor, as Sandoval presented them, each received a personal welcome. They were caught up by the General's eye and made one of his fellowship. His warm, quiet voice heated them like wine. Here was no stiff-necked hidalgo looking down his nose at common people. He was a man you could talk to, a man like yourself in spite of his blood. The Moor and the Nightingale grinned and glowed.

"Pedro de Vargas of Jaén," said Sandoval.

Cortés's manner changed slightly. From bluff, he turned polished. Pedro's bow showed a breeding different from the others'.

"From Jaén? Are you by chance a relative of the famous captain of that name, Francisco de Vargas?"

As spring after winter, a golden echo from the past, the reference to his father lifted Pedro's heart.

"His son, señor."

"By my conscience!" Pedro found himself in a steel-like embrace. "Our fathers were friends, though mine never reached the eminence of yours. Alvarado, Velásquez, Ordás—gentlemen, here's a good omen! The son of Francisco de Vargas joins òur company. From the look of him, he has his father's spirit."

Salutations were exchanged. Even the group at cards paused to stare.

"Your illustrious father is well?" asked Alvarado.

"When I last saw him," Pedro evaded.

Cortés remarked, "I hope it will please you to act as one of my equerries. No doubt your merit will soon raise you to a command."

Pedro thought that he had never met anyone so winning. Cortés fascinated with a charm that made men eager to serve him, made them feel important.

"I should like nothing better, sir," he answered. "But I am with Juan García. It is entirely at his charges that I came to the Islands—"

"Nonsense, Your Excellency!" García interrupted. "The boy's independent of me, as far as that comes to. If you take him, you'll have an equerry who knows how to use his weapons."

Cortés smiled. "I'll borrow him then. Meanwhile, you and he do me the honor of dining today at my table. He can take up his duties tomorrow. I want your advice on the stores. And show me this new horse you've brought. We've room for one more manger on the flagship."

Pedro forgot his qualms of a few minutes past. A spark had passed from the General to himself. He looked at the future once more through a rainbow.

149

As for Cortés, while enlisting four new men in the army, he had added four devotees to his personal service.

XXVII

DURING the next few days, Pedro worked harder than ever before in his life. He sometimes wondered whether it did not detract from the dignity of a gentleman to oversee the salting down of pork and the lading of vats in the ships, or to dicker for poultry and cassava bread with grasping settlers of the neighborhood, or to sweat under the tropical sun on endless plebeian errands. But with a captain general who kept his eye on these and a thousand other details and who was pedantically thorough about trifles, he had no choice. If Pedro worked, he had to admit that his commander worked twice as hard; if he drudged and sweated, he did no more than Cortés himself. This was an antidote to romantic dreams of adventure. He began to learn that glory depended on salt pork and equipment, on minute planning and careful arithmetic.

"*Quien adelante no mira atrás se queda,*" as García put it. "He who does not look forward remains behind. And that," García added enthusiastically, "our General has no intention of doing, by God."

Pedro soon found that the admiration one felt for Cortés, rather than love, was the secret of his power—admiration for the man's ability, force, and vision. It was probable that a selfish unscrupulousness lay behind his charm: but, even though conscious of being used as a tool, one still willingly served him.

One of Pedro's chief duties was to stand guard over the military chest. "It shows the trust I have in you, de Vargas," the General would say. "I'd ask a wolf to play nursemaid to a lamb sooner than leave this to most of our good companions. Keep your eyes peeled. You're guarding the mainspring of the army." And tapping the box, which gave back a rather hollow sound, he added characteristically, "On my honor, you'll soon have a lot more than this to guard. My word! Tons of gold! I pledge my beard that you'll have your share of it too—depend on me —gold to your elbows."

Though busy, they were pleasant days at Trinidad, days of comradeship and responsibility. After his escape from arrest in Spain, Pedro rejoiced at being enrolled in a legitimate undertaking. He was now in the King's service, even if under false pretenses.

The fact that it *was* under false pretenses cast the only shadow upon his present life in the camp. If Cortés knew that the Inquisition was on Pedro's and García's traces, he could not compromise the expedition by enrolling them. As a dutiful son of the Church, he would be bound to arrest and hand them over. Not until the fleet had finally sailed for Yucatán could Pedro feel entirely safe.

Whenever he spoke to García about it, the latter only laughed. "Boy, we've got the Ocean Sea between us and Jaén. The Santa Casa hasn't grown wings yet. Not by a long shot. Forget it. We're in the New World."

But, perhaps as a nervous aftermath of the experience in Jaén, the dread hung on. Pedro tried to forget it, but a premonition of something impending stalked behind him. On the eve of sailing, the foreboding increased. To hide his nervousness, he wandered off by himself in the late afternoon and climbed the slope of the Vigía hill above the settlement.

At first the path wound between trees shrouded in Spanish moss, past thickets of flowers; unseen waters sounded here and there, and the voice of birds. Then finally he came out on the open land crowning the summit, a dome of sky above, the immensity of the ocean beneath. A little soothed by the exertion of the walk and by the infinite quietness, he sank down at the foot of a solitary palm and sat staring eastward over the Caribbean.

It brought back the picture of himself a few months ago, similarly seated and gazing westward from the Sierra de Jaén at the beginning of his flight with García. He confronted himself across the interval of space and time that separated one milestone from another.

At that time he had been flushed by the triumph of his escape and of his vengeance upon de Silva. Now the feeling had strangely altered. Not that he regretted killing the man—he would have killed him again without hesitation—but that he had duped the coward into renouncing God before he killed him remained an undigested lump in Pedro's conscience. His code did not justify such blasphemy as that. Strange, he thought, that the one thing which should have given him the greatest satisfaction now constantly returned to haunt him. "Renounce God, de Silva!" The echo of his own voice kept him away from mass, kept him awake at night. But was any punishment too great for the man? Was hell too hot for him? Had not God used Pedro's sword as a righteous instrument? Then why remorse?

The faint tones of the Angelus from the distant church below reached up to him and started another train of thought. He said his

Ave Maria, trying to remember something that was connected with the Angelus, something on the fringe of his mind.

Yes—Catana. He had promised to think of her every day at that hour, and in the beginning he had kept his word. A wave of longing for her passed over him. Though he had neglected to think of her at the appointed time, he had still thought of her often, and always with a warmth that was partly physical, but not merely that. A strange girl, he reflected, unlike anybody else. He owed her his life. What had become of her with that cutthroat, Soler?

The ocean, vast and infinite as the sky, shut him off from any answer. The New World was well-named. Echoes from the Old World might reach him after months, when the news they carried was long since stale; or they might never reach him. Spain and Italy seemed more remote than the figures on the moon, for at least he could see the moon. What had happened of good or ill? Were his father and mother safe? Did Luisa de Carvajal remember him?

He reached under his doublet for her handkerchief and spread it out on his knee. Inevitably his mind swung back, like a compass, to its fixed point: his one divine hour (the moonlight on the laurels of the garden, on her face), his one devouring purpose which alone gave meaning and a goal to life! If he gained her, he gained everything; if he lost her, nothing mattered. For her, the gold he might win in the West; for her, the fame.

A long shadow, advancing from the sunset, fell along the ground in front of him, the shadow of a cowl and gown. Turning with a start, he found himself looking up into the features of Father Bartolomé de Olmedo, chaplain of the army.

Taken by surprise, he lost countenance a little, returned the handkerchief to its place, and started to get up; but Olmedo laid a hand on his shoulder.

"Sit still, my son. I'll join you by your leave, and rest a moment. It's a fine spot you've chosen."

Whereupon, Father Bartolomé seated himself shoulder to shoulder with Pedro against the trunk of the palm and breathed a sigh of contentment.

He was a square, soldierly man with a scrubby beard, frank eyes, and an appealing smile. He wore the habit of the Order of Mercy. Cortés often remarked that if Father Bartolomé could not convert the heathen dogs of Yucatán, they were past praying for. Entrusted to him, the spiritual interests of the expedition were in good hands.

The friar slipped off his sandals, complaining that the thong chafed him, and wriggled his strong toes in relief.

"So you're thinking about Spain, Señor de Vargas?" he observed. "Seems far off, eh, and a certain young lady farther still?"

Shocked by the aptness of the remark, Pedro colored. Was the friar a necromancer? He shot him a nervous look.

Olmedo laughed. "*Válgate Dios,* when a young man, newly arrived in Cuba, walks off by himself and sits gazing to the east with a handkerchief on his knee, he's probably thinking of home and sweetheart. I've been young myself and not always in orders. Cheer up. You'll sail back again some day with a chestful of gold and much honor. The peerless lady will be yours. The dream will come true." He added with a sigh, "And afterwards, Señor de Vargas?"

"I don't understand."

The other retorted, "Why not? I only meant that your dream is attainable and wondered what would take its place afterwards. Another lady? More wealth and fame? Because the zest of life is effort, my son, not attainment."

Tempted out of his reserve, Pedro smiled. "Believe me, if I get what I long for, I'll be satisfied."

"Ah?" said Father Olmedo. He raised his knees and sat clasping them, his eyes on the ocean. "Well, the difference between you and me is that I shall never get what I long for."

To become a bishop, thought Pedro, or maybe even pope? Yes, it did seem a far cry for a poor chaplain.

"What is that, Father, if I may ask?"

"To know God in His perfection," said Olmedo quietly. And after a moment, "It is unattainable. And therefore I shall be happy forever in my dream. You see," the friar went on in another tone, "dreams are like carrots, and we are like mules. As long as the carrot dangles in front of our noses, we keep going, cover ground. If we catch up with it, we stop."

Unused to metaphors, Pedro digested the meaning slowly.

"How did you happen to come to the Islands, Father?"

"As a witness for God."

"To the Indians?"

Olmedo looked amused. "Yes, I came with that idea. I soon learned that the greater need was to witness to the Spaniards."

"What do you mean?"

"Why," returned Olmedo, "who is more guilty: the Indian, serving his devils through ignorance; or the Spaniard, professing Christ and serving the devil in rape and murder, cruelty and extortion?"

The friar's face grew darker.

"The Indians welcomed us like children. We destroyed them by the sword, by the lash, in the fields and in the mines. They died like flies; soon there won't be any more. We've been a plague to these islands, God have mercy on us!"

He controlled himself with an effort. "So on this expedition, I am chaplain to the army. It's my flock—of wolves," he added. "Hernán Cortés talks of converting Indians. I'm not nearly so much concerned for them as for us. By God's help, what happened here shall not happen again."

The words, harsh as they might be to Spanish pride, struck a responsive note in Pedro. Yet it was not so much the words as the ring of them, the emanation of Olmedo's spirit. He sounded actually like a good man, not good merely in the usual, but in a higher, sense; a man one could talk to—perhaps even confess to. Maybe a priest like this could be trusted.

De Vargas probed further. "It seems to me, Padre, that men like you could do some witnessing in Spain. Talk about cruelty and extortion! Holy saints! And in the Church too. I saw an auto-da-fé not so long ago in Jaén. What do you think of the Santa Casa?"

This was the test. If Fray Bartolomé sidestepped the question, Pedro would drop it; but Olmedo returned his gaze without blinking, though he fingered his beard. When he spoke, it was as if he were partly thinking aloud.

"My son, do you believe in the Holy Catholic Church?"

"I do of course."

"There isn't any other church, is there?"

"No."

"One church in Spain, England, France, the Empire, and Italy—everywhere. Every Christian believes alike. Isn't that true?"

It was before the Reformation. Pedro could answer, "Yes."

"You wouldn't like to see the Church, the mantle of Christ, torn into rags and patches, would you? Instead of one sheepfold, many folds? Would that make for harmony and peace?"

"No. But does the Santa Casa—"

"One moment. Because there are often cruel shepherds, greedy shepherds, do you think that the office of shepherd itself should be given up and the sheep left to wander?"

"No. But what has that to do with the Inquisition?"

"Everything. It was founded to protect the Faith—I say founded for that purpose. It may be that it is not accomplishing its purpose; it may be that its means are wrong; it may be that it is in the hands of evil

154

shepherds. But let me say this: not all of the Santa Casa are evil men, and not all who are condemned are innocent."

Pedro pressed his point. "Father, what do you think of the Santa Casa as it is now?"

Olmedo replied bluntly. "I shall not answer that question, my son, except to an Inquisitor himself. If that time should come——" But he broke off. "Son Pedro, let me tell you something. When we reach Yucatán, I shall preach the gospel; I shall do what I can to prevent human beings from eating human flesh and making human sacrifices; I shall overturn, when possible, the blood-filthy idols that Captain Grijalva speaks of, for it is not fitting that men should bow down before devils. But for the rest, I shall use love, mercy, and meekness, not the rack and the scourge. Judge of my beliefs by my deeds. It is how we live, not how we talk, that counts. . . . Now, let me ask you a simpler question. Why haven't you been to mass?"

Such transparent honesty looked through Olmedo's eyes that Pedro could not evade it. He felt a growing lightness. It occurred to him that the talk they had just had would have been unthinkable in Spain. Perhaps the New World meant something more than new land.

"I'll tell you, Padre," he said, "if you'll answer me one thing. What do you think of a priest who uses a confession he hears against the man who makes it?"

"That's easy," Olmedo nodded. "Whatever the man did, I think that priest is damned. Now, what's on your conscience?"

"Well, then," said de Vargas. "I, Pedro, confess to Almighty God . . ."

He told the whole story, while Olmedo listened and nodded now and then in encouragement. What he had most feared to reveal, he told simply and without fear, as man to man. When he had finished, he felt as if he had been released from prison.

"You see," he added, "I've put García and myself in your hands."

Olmedo's reply was startling. "No, my son, you've been in my hands since this morning." He drew a paper from his wallet and unfolded it. "Except for de Silva, you've told me little that I did not know; but I wanted to hear it from your own lips. . . . Can you read Latin?"

Pedro's heart had turned to ice. "Not well."

"This is an order from the Bishop of ·Santiago to Hernán Cortés for your and Juan García's arrest at the petition of Ignacio de Lora, now in Santo Domingo on the business of the Holy Office. What you have told me is set forth here, though hardly from your standpoint."

So the forebodings of the last few days had been justified. De Lora in the Islands! Pedro remembered now what de Silva had said about the Inquisitor's sailing. He and García were lost. In view of this order, Cortés and Olmedo, even if they were inclined to pity, could do nothing.

"The General handed it to me," Olmedo added. "He said that he had no time today for bishops and Latin: they were my province."

"Then he hasn't read it yet?"

"No."

Pedro got up and stood a moment gazing at the ocean. In his mind, he saw the sailing of the fleet for Yucatán without him and García. He bit his lips.

"I'm ready, Father. What are we waiting for?"

He turned to face Olmedo, but what he saw amazed him. The friar was tearing the Bishop's letter across, forth and back. When he had finished, he let the small pieces flutter down the breeze.

"So much for that!" he remarked. "The equerry who brought it wants to enroll with us. Letters can be lost. We'll be a long time out of Cuba."

"We?" Pedro repeated.

"Yes, we."

"Then, you mean—"

The friar put on his sandals and stood up. "I mean a great deal, Pedro de Vargas. If you had not confessed, I would not have destroyed that letter. Honesty covers a multitude of sins, and Fray Bartolomé de Olmedo hates injustice."

"But the General?"

"I shall tell him part of the letter—that the Bishop of Santiago sends his blessing."

Pedro knelt in front of Olmedo's brown robe.

"Father, what can I do to show you—"

"You can perform your penance, my son."

"Yes—anything. What is it?"

Olmedo said gently, "It is to take up the burden of God's forgiveness and to pray for the soul of Diego de Silva."

For a moment, Pedro did not answer. At last he said, "I swear it."

The friar laid a hand on Pedro's head and bent it back so that he could look down into his face.

"Boy, it's more of a penance than you think. God's love is a heavy burden. Remember *that* when we sail tomorrow and in the days to come."

XXVIII

IF ORTIZ the Musician had lived four centuries earlier, he would have been called a troubadour. As it was, he had the qualities and temperament of one without the name. A gentleman and good swordsman, half-owner of one of the sixteen horses of the expedition, the proprietor of a comfortable hacienda near Trinidad de Cuba, he combined with these solid assets a talent for music and song and a command of the lute and the fiddle. He had a wide repertory of old *romances* and popular airs, which inspired topical ballads of his own to the amusement and admiration of the army. A handsome man with a short, straight nose and intense light blue eyes, he was created for the joy and sorrow of women.

Pedro de Vargas, who had a respectful fondness for music and poetry, but not the least skill in them, was drawn to Ortiz by the law of opposites and sought him out with the reverence of the untalented for the artist.

On Holy Thursday, when the fleet had been two months out of Cuba, the two young men sat on the forecastle of the *capitana,* sharing the support of the mast and within the shadow of the sail, which cut off the burn of the April sun. The pitching of the bow kept others away and secured them a privacy impossible in the crowded, but steadier, waist of the ship.

Humming to himself, Ortiz plucked absent-mindedly at the strings of his lute, absorbed in the effort of composition.

"What's it going to be?" asked Pedro.

"I don't know," Ortiz murmured. "Some *serenata* or other. I got the idea this morning when the sun struck those mountains over there."

He nodded toward the near-by coast of the mainland, along which the eleven ships of the armada, scattered irregularly over the sea, were heading north. The land lay close enough for all eyes to make out the sand flats with their backing of jungle, the upslope beyond that, and at length, like clouds, the snow peaks of the interior.

> "Far in the west [Ortiz hummed],
> The white sierras bloom
> In gold and fire
> To meet the coming day . . .

Something like that. Then apply it to the lady. But I haven't got far. . . . Hell's blisters! How can a man make verse with all the noise and stench of this cursed ship on top of him? *Demonio!*" He gave the strings a resentful twang and slid the instrument between his legs. "No use."

Six feet below them in the waist, a throng of men babbled like frogs. A double row along the bulwark gazed at the land, exchanging loud comments. A dice game was in progress on one of the water casks. Barefooted, red-coifed seamen puttered as usual with gear and tackle. The three horses carried by the flagship stamped in their deck stalls. Sandoval, García, and some others were cleaning their equipment to the tune of much clanging and joking. Some of the Yucatán women, acquired at Tabasco, perched on a pile of galley firewood and held court for the lovesick; while Isabel Rodrigo and María de Vera, hard-pressed by the competition, ran a court of their own at the starboard rail. The wind from astern swept forward the smells of the ship—garlic, salt fish, horse manure, rancid oil, and the everlasting stench of the hold. And there were always occupants of the outboard seats hung over the rail as a latrine.

But the effect of crowd and commotion did not stop with the waist. Beyond rose the quarter-deck, thronged by gentlemen of the afterguard; and beyond that again, higher than anything but the masts, towered the poop deck with the General's quarters, where Cortés with the pilot Alaminos, Doña Marina, the prize of the Indian bevy from Tabasco, Puertocarrero, and a group of men from Grijalva's expedition, could be seen studying the land.

"*Animo,* friend!" said de Vargas. "Cheer up! The words will come; it isn't any noisier than usual. Until they do, give me some stanzas of that ballad about Bernardo del Carpio. You know, the one that goes:—

> "*En corte del Casto Alfonso*
> *Bernardo a placer vivía . . .*

I love that one."

Ortiz shook his head. "No, I'm not in the mood. Besides, it's such mossy old stuff. I respect the old, mark you, and at times a *cantar de gesta* suits me better than anything else. But by and large I'm modern and like the up-to-date. Why keep on about the Cid and Bernardo del Carpio when we're on a venture that's ahead of any of theirs?"

Pedro felt shocked. "I'd hardly say that."

"Well, I'll say it for you. When did the Cid or Bernardo ever start off to win an unknown continent? When did they ever fight with forty thousand howling savages like the handful of us did less than a month ago at Ciutla? When did they ever convert so many infidels as we have since landing on Cozumel Island?"

"Still, you'd hardly call us paladins, *hombre*. We aren't in that class."

"Why not? We don't have to be so cursed humble because we're alive and they're dead. How do you know that there won't be ballads about us sometime? For example:—

> "Don Pedro lays his lance in rest:
> Hark to the battle cry!
> He spurs his mighty horse, Soldán:
> A thousand pagans die.

I tell you what, Pedrito, let's make up a *romancero* of our own."

"Is that an example of it?" Pedro grinned.

"No, seriously," urged Ortiz, "let us give thought to it. Whenever anything happens—hey, *pronto,* a ballad! What do you think ought to be celebrated up till now?"

Lending himself to the game, Pedro ventured: "What about Alvarado's looting Cozumel Island before Cortés got there and the rage the General was in and how he made Alvarado's people hand everything back to the Indians?"

"No," said Ortiz, "not epic enough. You can't make a ballad out of robbing a hen roost, which was about what it came to. And Alvarado's crowd acted like boys with their breeches down ready to be birched. Nothing heroic in that."

"Well, then: Olmedo preaching the Faith and the rest of us bouncing the idols down the temple steps."

"Certainly. *There's* color and action. We'll start with that one. And we'll add that the Indians considered their devils a weak lot when they couldn't even protect themselves against Redhead de Vargas and Bull García. They became good Christians in ten minutes. Ballad number one. Next?"

"You know, I think Jerónimo de Aguilar deserves a *romance.*"

The two men glanced at a swarthy individual squatting Indian fashion in the waist not far from Sandoval. Ordained in the Church, he had been shipwrecked eight years ago on the shores of Yucatán and had been the slave of a Mayan cacique until ransomed by Cortés. He was now invaluable as an interpreter, though his Spanish had grown rusty, and he spoke with the guttural accent of an Indian. His stories of native barbarism fascinated the army: how all but one of his companions in shipwreck had been sacrificed and eaten; how he himself had been fattened for the sacrifice and had escaped. But what he liked most to describe were the erotic temptations by Indian damsels to which his master, the cacique, incredulous of his chastity, had exposed him. Faithful to his vow, he overcame the demon.

"Hm-m," pondered Ortiz. "Yes, we could make a Saint Anthony out of Aguilar. Nothing gives more of a spice to poetry than sex. . . . Well, what next? We cross from Cozumel Island to the mainland. We reach Tabasco. Now comes the battle of Santa María de la Victoria, which deserves a half-dozen ballads."

The poet struck an attitude and gave a mock-heroic lilt to his voice. "The air's a fog of sling-stones, arrows, and javelins. Seventy of us wounded at the first volley. Foot-to-foot we meet them with their lances and two-handed swords. (You know, Pedro, those cursed obsidian edges cut like a razor.) They don't enjoy our steel. Mesa lets loose his artillery. The Indian devils yell *'Alala!'* and throw dust in the air to hide their losses. They fall back to gain space for their bowmen; they come on again. Where the deuce is the damn cavalry? Why doesn't Cortés charge?"

"You know perfectly well why we didn't," put in Pedro. "We were stuck in a swamp."

"Don't interrupt. I'm talking from the standpoint of verse. . . . We're half-dead from heat, wounds, and exhaustion. We're giving ground. Then—ha!—we catch a glimpse of the horses. *'Santiago, y a ellos!'* . . . Now, you take it up. That's your part."

Pedro scratched his head. "Well, after we got out of the swamp, there wasn't much to it."

"Fie!" exclaimed Ortiz. "You've got a prosy mind! Shocking. . . . But Doña Marina," he added in a different tone—"there's something else."

He gazed aft toward the poop deck, where the graceful figure of the Indian girl stood out against the sky. She had been presented to Cortés as a peace offering with nineteen other women after the battle. He had handed her over to Puertocarrero, though, it was said, with an amorous eye for her himself. She was well-bred, finely featured, and of a pale color. It turned out that she came from the interior and belonged to another race known as Aztecs and ruled by a kind of emperor called Montezuma. Of noble birth, she had been sold as a child by an unscrupulous mother to itinerant slave dealers. Aguilar, who spoke Mayan, could talk with her; and Cortés, who missed no openings, foresaw her usefulness later on as an interpreter to her own people. She and the nineteen others, being baptized with Christian names, were now fit for Christian embraces. But she alone was called *doña.*

"We'll put her in—and at length," declared Ortiz. "Also the gold we got from the caciques. Remember, Pedro, how Aguilar got out of them where it came from? Culúa, Mexico, beyond the mountains. I knew after that we wouldn't be sticking in Yucatán. Remember the General's eyes lighting up? 'Culúa, eh? Beyond the mountains? Do you hear, gentlemen, gold beyond the mountains?' "

"Don't forget our Palm Sunday procession, Ortiz. That ought to go in," Pedro reminded him. "The Indians couldn't get over the white *teules* carrying palms and kneeling before the Virgin and Child. We must have converted a pack of them."

Ortiz yawned. "Yes, and that brings us up to date: once more on the cursed ships. There'll be plenty to write ballads about before we get to Culúa, believe me." His eyes wandered over the main deck below and stopped on a man who stood talking to the dicers around the water cask. "We've left out our villain, Pedrito. Got to have a villain in our *cantar de gesta*. There he is."

It was a broad-shouldered man with a curling black beard. He wore a gilded steel cap and a flame-colored doublet with full sleeves. Standing arms akimbo and legs wide, he suited himself easily to the pitching of the ship. He was a minor officer, Juan Escudero, a henchman of Governor Velásquez. There were rumors of bad blood between him and Cortés.

Escudero stood for something more dangerous than Indian armies, something that had been growing since the battle at Ciutla and, leech-like, was sucking away the force of the expedition. Everyone felt the spirit of mutiny flickering here and there like a half-smothered fire. It showed itself in grumbling, in dissension, in prudent forebodings, in high-sounding loyalty to the Governor of Cuba. Its source was fear— fear not only of that empire beyond the mountains, of which vague rumors had begun to filter through, but fear also of Hernán Cortés. For greatness cannot wholly mask itself; and greatness in a leader is not only inspiring but, to the timid, disquieting. Of this fear and uncertainty, the Velásquez faction in the army made the most.

Leaving the dice players thoughtful, Escudero sauntered on and stopped casually next to Sandoval.

"Tending to your equipment, gentlemen? Gad, that's sensible. I think you'll be needing it again." He spoke in a fierce, somewhat halting voice.

Pedro hitched over to the edge of the forecastle to catch what he said. Ortiz, yawning again, returned to his lute.

"So much the better," answered Sandoval.

"There're some who don't agree with you."

"Is that so?"

"Yes. We came out here to trade, didn't we?—and have a look at the land. We brought enough men to protect ourselves and to hold an outpost, not to fight pitched battles or conquer empires. That ought to be plain to anybody but a fool. We lost some men at Tabasco, remember?"

"It's the luck of war."

"Yes, young man, but we didn't come to make war. We came to trade—"

"Your pardon, sir," interrupted García, voicing the issue that split the army, "we came to settle, to colonize."

"And your pardon, sir, we did nothing of the kind. There's not a word about settlement in the Governor's instructions to Cortés."

"And there wasn't a word about anything else in the public cry. The Governor heard the proclamation. Did he correct it? He did not. Do you think five hundred good men and eleven ships sailed with the idea of copying Grijalva forth and back? I should say not."

"Well, sir," retorted Escudero, "whatever their idea, there are such things as law and obedience. We sailed under Governor Velásquez's orders, and I, for one, intend to obey them—let alone the folly of doing anything else."

Cold silence answered. Legally he was right, but law suffers from distance and salt water.

From behind Pedro, Ortiz exclaimed: "I've got it! Here you are!"

Standing up, his back to the mast, the lute properly tilted, he announced to the deck below: "Ladies and gentlemen, *A Serenata to a Lady in Spain.*" Then in a smooth baritone voice, he sang:—

> "Far in the West,
>   The white sierras bloom
>   In gold and fire
>   To meet the coming day:
>   So shall my heart,
>   O Queen of my desire,
>   At thy approach,
>   Itself in fire array.

> "Far in the West,
>   The mighty waters bear
>   Our reckless sails
>   Of venture to the shore:

Thus, borne on mightier tides,
My love assails
Thy love, adventuring,
Lady, evermore.

"Far in the West,
The echoes of our fate,
The do and dare,
Witness of God and Spain:
So let my song
A gentler witness bear
Across the seas,
To tell my love again."

A roar of applause followed the singing. "By God, Ortiz," said Juan Pilar, who was standing near by and who had a smattering of letters, "you're another Orpheus. Didn't he stand on the prow of the *Argo* and speed the ship with music toward the Golden Fleece? You ought to claim a bounty from the General."

Ortiz, gratified, slung the lute over his shoulder. "I'll do that, Juan. How much do you think he'll pay me—a maravedí?"

Bull García heaved a sigh and went on cleaning his breastplate. "Love's one thing," he muttered; "marriage is another."

Pedro, still lost in the song, stared into space.

Only Sandoval, who was tone-deaf and also a privileged character, expressed mock disapproval. "Bah!" he called out. "If you weren't such a good swordsman, Ortiz, I'd put you down as a chicken liver. This lady stuff! I've never had taste for it. What do you mean by 'Queen of your desire,' 'borne on mightier tides'? *Vete enhoramala!*"

García laughed. "Ask Pedro what he means. Since the Lady Luisa de Carvajal traded him her handkerchief for half his wits, he's been as dame-struck as Ortiz. Friend Sandoval, I share your feeling. To the devil with ladies! They do not fit into this part of the world. Use your influence on Pedro."

De Vargas continued to dangle his legs from the forecastle deck.

"Look at him!" García rumbled on. "Catana Pérez, that wench in Jaén who saved our two lives, is a pearl of a female, fit for bed, board, or march. She'd give her soul for him. But hell! She isn't a lady. You couldn't sing poetry at her."

Sandoval grinned. "How about it, Pedro?"

De Vargas thumbed his nose in reply.

163

On the afterdeck, Cortés stood with smiling, eager eyes intent on the coast. If now and then a glance took in the ship—if he was aware of Ortiz and de Vargas on the forecastle, of Sandoval and García scrubbing their equipment, of Escudero making his rounds, of the ten scattered vessels in the wake of the *capitana*—it was a casual glance that showed nothing but gaiety and anticipation.

He wore a rough woolen cap, pulled down to shield his eyes from the sun, and a seaman's cloak to protect him from the spindrift that now and then spat aboard from the following sea. Even the tropical glare had not given more than a light tan to his pale cheeks.

A gaily dressed youth, who had sailed with Grijalva, Bernal Díaz del Castillo, pointed out landmarks. A couple of others eagerly seconded him with information.

"We called the mountains yonder Sierra de San Martín, my Captain. There was a fellow in the company, named San Martín, a good soldier—"

"That river?" Cortés interrupted. "Or is it a bay, forward there?"

The pilot, Alaminos, who answered, had served not only on the Grijalva expedition, but as pilot to Columbus on his Fourth Voyage. "No, a river."

"The River of Banners," went on Díaz, not to be put out of the conversation. "The Indians signaled us with white banners."

"So, that's where you went ashore, is it?"

"Aye, sir," put in another of the Grijalva men eagerly. "It's where we picked up the fifteen thousand pesos of gold in trade for a peso's worth of green beads. They say that it came from across the mountains, from the king there."

"Ha!" said Cortés. "A rich prince. And if fifteen thousand, why not a hundred thousand, why not a million, señores? We might pay him a visit unless—"

He glanced from one to the other of the gold-hungry faces, but left the sentence unfinished and turned to look at the coast again.

"Unless what?" demanded Puertocarrero, who stood with a languid arm about the waist of Doña Marina. She leaned against him, but her handsome fawn eyes were on Cortés.

"Unless we return to Cuba, Gossip, as some of our friends require. Far be it from me to disobey His Excellency's orders. It could only be on compulsion, sirs, you understand—against my will."

His eyes, suddenly inscrutable, shifted from face to face; but the inscrutability was intentional, and his hearers smiled. They did not belong to the Velásquez party. In front of them, beyond the mountains,

a land of gold; behind them, across the sea, a royal governor. No difficult choice for stout-hearted men, orders or no orders. But of the ten
ships following the *capitana*, four were commanded by the Governor's
friends, and homesickness was spreading.

"That island there?" pointed Cortés, leaving the unnecessary unsaid.

"The Isla de los Sacrificios, sir," replied Díaz, "where we found the
heathen dogs sacrificing children to their devils."

"Wouldn't it be a sin beyond pardon to leave this country in darkness?" said Cortés gravely. "And beyond the island lies the harbor we're
making for?"

"Yes, San Juan de Ulúa."

"You know," grinned Puertocarrero, twisting up his mustache, "it
reminds me of the old ballad Ortiz was singing yesterday.

> "Here is France, Montesinos,
> And Paris, the fair city,
> And here the Duero River
> Flows down to meet the sea.

Remember?"

Cortés nodded.

"How about a new verse?" added Puertocarrero.

> "Behold the rich lands, Captain,
> As far as eye can see,
> And let not pass untaken
> The chance awaiting thee."

Knowing looks were exchanged. Cortés smiled. "I'm as good a poet
as you are, *compadre*. What do you think of this?

> "Luck of paladin Roldán,
> God grant us mercifully:
> Then do your part, brave gentlemen,
> And leave the rest to me."

He winked without winking. The teeth showed above the scar on his
lower lip. The others laughed. Disloyalty to Governor Velásquez? Not
at all. It was only verse.

"Understand, Doña Marina?" he asked the Indian girl.

She answered eagerly, "*Sí*, señor," using the two words she had
picked up.

"By my conscience," said Cortés, "we'll have her speaking Castilian in a month. . . . You know, that's an idea of yours, friend: 'Behold the rich lands.' We go ashore tomorrow on Good Friday, the day of the True Cross. If we were permitted to settle by the Governor's orders— and surely that must have been his intention, but I say *if*—we might have called our town the Rich Town, Villa Rica de Vera Cruz. It would have suited both our religion and our future. Names are important."

Filling his lungs with the offshore breeze, he exhaled lingeringly. "Ah, señores, the smell of new lands! No fragrance like it this side of heaven."

XXIX

THE memory of that last day on shipboard crossed Pedro's mind more than two months later, as he stood guard over the military chest in the teocalli or temple enclosure at Cempoala. Perhaps what made him think of it was the contrast between the bracing sea air, vibrant with sunlight, and this mosquito-laden dankness of the tropical night shut in by the pagan-smelling walls of the teocalli.

Since then the army had "compelled" Cortés to renounce his allegiance to the Governor of Cuba, and had set itself up as the independent colony of Villa Rica de Vera Cruz. It had left its long encampment at San Juan de Ulúa and had marched northward; a few tentative walls of the new city of Villa Rica had been built; Cortés had made allies for himself here at Cempoala and among other Totonac tribes along the coast, bringing them to a state of revolt against the Aztec power of Mexico. With these and Villa Rica as a backing, the march inland drew always nearer.

Pedro remembered the words of Cortés's tag to the old ballad, which had made a hit with the army:—

> Luck of paladin Roldán
> God grant us mercifully . . .

He glanced at the stout chests in the center of the room, which formed one of a line of similar rooms surrounding the temple precincts. Though half cut off by the sharp slant of the sacred pyramid outside, the moonlight through the doorway rested on the chests and gave them a dreamlike, richer outline.

Talk about the luck of Roldán! *Dios!* If a man had half the gold in those boxes, he could set himself up as a prince in Spain and marry whom he wanted. But unfortunately the plan now was to send the whole of it to the King in order to secure recognition of the new colony as independent of Cuba. Montejo and Puertocarrero had been selected as representatives, and a ship would be placed at their disposal. It was probably a good plan—it wouldn't do to have Velásquez forever on one's tail—but the price came high and hurt like sin. The whole intake thus far on the mainland, what every individual had gleaned by trade with the Indians, plus Montezuma's gifts from the still unknown inland empire. The gifts composed by far the major part of the treasure.

Pedro lingered over them in thought as he gazed at the chests. He remembered most of the inventory.

One large alligator's head of gold.
A bird of green feathers, with feet, beak, and eyes of gold.
Six shields, each covered with a plate of gold.
Two collars made of gold and precious stones.
A hundred ounces of gold ore.
Animals of gold resembling snails.
Five fans with rods of gold.
Sixteen shields of precious stones.
A plate of gold weighing seventy ounces.
A wheel of silver weighing forty marks . . .

He could still see the pompous ambassadors of Montezuma with their outlandish feathered headdresses and harlequin-colored clothes, jangling with ornaments, jade plugs in their ear lobes and lower lips. Haughty dogs, strutting too much. One of them had reminded him of Coatl and had raised speculations in his mind about the homeland of de Silva's former servant. It might be that Coatl, with his talk about marvels in the West, belonged to this same race.

Pedro could still see the ambassadors' slaves spreading their mats, heaping up these treasures, while the ring of bearded Spaniards elbowed each other for a better view.

Aguilar, the interpreter, and Doña Marina had informed Cortés that Montezuma sent his gifts and greetings and bade the white *teules* keep away from his dominions. That was funny. There had been a big laugh about that around the campfires. Send nuggets of gold to prospectors and invite them kindly not to visit the mines. These gifts made possible the bribe to Spain, made inevitable the march across the mountains.

"Friends," Cortés had argued, urging the sacrifice of the treasure, "do you think that this prince has stripped himself for our benefit, that he hasn't a thousandfold more where this came from? By my beard, gentlemen, these are but scraps and samples. And, mark you, he fears us or he would not have sent them. Now certainly we must visit him. Shall we cling to trifles which will bulk large in Spain, when we can help ourselves to this dog's treasury? Authorized by His Majesty and with a free hand here, we'll count an empire cheap at a hundred thousand pesos."

Risk all to gain all—it was like Cortés. Pedro remembered the beggarly money box he had guarded in Trinidad, and the General's promises. They had come true in part. Here was more gold beneath his nose than Pedro had ever dreamed of. But somehow he had still no share in it. His gold, as always, lay somewhere else in the future, beyond the mountains.

The trouble was that others in the army, not so willing to accept birds in the bush, looked greedily at the bird in hand. The Velásquez faction was still active. Therefore the need of a strong guard. Pedro had a mastiff with him, one of the war dogs used against the Indians; and a couple of foot soldiers, armed to the teeth, stood outside.

"One large wheel of gold" (ran the inventory), "with figures of strange animals on it, and worked with tufts of leaves; weighing three thousand, eight hundred ounces."

Pedro eyed the chest which contained it, the prize of the collection, a solid, round disc forty inches across. More than the weight of a heavy man. Doña Marina, who had learned some Spanish by now, informed him that it represented the sun, and she had thrilled over the beauty of the workmanship. But to Pedro it represented twenty thousand pesos. Twenty thousand in that one item!

The same box contained also "five large emeralds of fine water and cutting." They were of immense value and were especially designed to take the eye of His Majesty. A doeskin pouch, embroidered with feather-and-gold work, contained them. De Vargas took pride in the thought that he was guarding crown jewels. If the duty of protecting the funds of the army had once been creditable, it was now of great importance and honor. It showed clearly where he stood in the estimation of the General.

Strolling to the doorway, he stood looking out across the courtyard. It was a wide rectangle several hundred yards across, and the unbroken line of one-story buildings, which surrounded it and from which the temple attendants had been ousted, easily contained the army.

Standing in the center and dominating everything else, towered the mass of the truncated pyramid, the teocalli proper, with its steep line of steps broken by terraces, and the broad platform, with the shrines of the gods and the altar of sacrifice, on top. Dark in the moonlight, like a narrow runner from platform to base along the steps, showed a band of bloodstains left by the bodies of countless victims, who had been hurled down after sacrifice to be eaten.

A sickening taint of stale blood haunted the place. It was this, no doubt, that kept the Spanish mastiffs restless and savage. But tonight it was somewhat deadened by the smell of burning, where a heap of ashes still smoldered at the base of the pyramid. They marked the remains of the wooden idols which had been rolled down from the shrines that day by the Spaniards in their work of conversion. Tomorrow, what with fresh plaster and whitewash, a cross, and the image of the Blessed Virgin, the air would be purer. Pedro shared with everybody else the satisfaction in thus saving souls and promoting the kingdom of heaven, while at the same time pursuing fortune. Had not Saint Paul himself declared that "if we have sown unto you spiritual things, is it a great thing if we shall reap your carnal things"?

To Pedro's right, at some distance, he could see the entrance gate with the cannon posted in front of it, and he could see the gleam of the match in the gunner's hand. A sentry walked back and forth. Cempoala was a friendly city, indeed an ally; but, with Indians, Cortés never took chances. Besides, there had been some trouble that day about the burning of the idols. The Cempoalans, impressed by the weakness of their gods, were inclining towards the True Faith. Still, one never knew; and woe to the sentinel that night who neglected his watch! On pain of death, no Spaniard could pass the gate without special order.

Otherwise, the courtyard hummed with festivity. Eight Indian girls, the daughters of chiefs, had been presented to the principal captains to cement the alliance, and quasi-bridal parties were under way. The girls had all been baptized and from now on would have the title of *doña*. They each represented a dowry in lands and villages; and, as *barraganas* or accepted concubines of the cavaliers, their position was thoroughly respectable. Indeed, the blood of some of them would finally mingle with the noblest in Spain. From now on, ties of marriage would bind the coastal tribes to the army and help to guarantee its rear when it advanced inland.

From one corner, a lute twanged; the giggle of women and laughter of men sounded. In another direction, a fifer squeaked out some popular tune. Cups clashed and clattered over a toast. A good deal of pulque was flowing tonight. It might not taste like wine, but it got the same results. About the enclosure, men strolled from party to party; some natives were present, kinsfolk of the brides.

De Vargas eyed the come-and-go a trifle glumly. To be sure, he did not rank as a captain yet, but Cortés had promised him a *cacica* with a fat dowry on the first occasion and had conveniently forgotten it. He regretted the dowry, if not the girl, as he listened to the bridal celebrations. Being on duty, he was even cut out of the fun. Cursed bad luck, which the honor of guarding the treasure hardly made up for.

In the shadow of the pyramid, an obscure scuffling started and gradually approached until he could make out Humpback Nojara and a man called Gallego. They were in rollicking high spirits and had some scarecrow of a creature between them, whom they were dragging along in a sort of rough-and-tumble. Pedro could see that it was a native, but whether man or woman he couldn't tell. They came to a momentary stop beneath the stone platform upon which the treasure room opened.

Glad of diversion, Pedro barked down at them, "*Hola,* you! Don't you know the orders? Do you want to be flogged? You don't remember that the General promises fifty lashes to any man's son who touches an Indian, eh?" ("And those are the promises he keeps," Pedro added to himself.) "Lay off, I tell you!"

Like schoolboys caught in a lark, the two soldiers blinked back at him, but they kept a grip on the native. It was a nightmare figure dressed in a black robe, and with long, matted hair—evidently one of the temple priests. Pedro could see the rolling white of his eyes and the flash of teeth. He kept up a babble, which had the sound of very strong language.

"Now, now, Your Worship," soothed Nojara, with proper respect for Cortés's equerry, "orders don't apply to this cockroach. What's he doing, oozing around in the dark, casting spells, by God? Blubbering, like a baby, because his devil, Witchywolves, got burned. When his mates have had the sense to turn Christian! He's a butcher all right. Stinks like hell. You can smell him from there."

"Besides, we aren't touching him, Your Worship," Gallego put in. "Not what *you* mean. We're reasoning with him. Aren't we, *hijo?*" He gave the Indian a clap between the shoulders. "We're working on him in spite of his stink—saving his soul, by God, and may the saints credit it to us! You can't say no to that, Your Worship."

170

"Why don't you take him to Fray Bartolomé?"

"His Reverence is at the General's party. This *chinche* isn't worth disturbing him for. I hope you don't think we aren't Christian enough to deal with a bug like this, ha?"

They had had more than enough of pulque. Their high spirits might change to murder at the batting of an eye. Moreover, Pedro had no love for the priests, who cut out helpless people's hearts and splashed blood on the temple walls.

"What're you going to do with him?"

"First get barber Lencero to shear his mane off. It's stiff with blood as a board. Then we'll take a currycomb to him. Then we'll scrub him and souse the sin off him. After that, he'll want to be baptized."

"Well," grinned Pedro, "don't make too much noise about it is my advice. I'd hate to see you flogged. *Quien lava la cabeza al asno pierde el jabón y el tiempo.* At least keep quiet."

"Quiet as hush, Your Worship. *Buenas noches.* Come on, *you.*"

Pedro exchanged comments with the two sentries that shared his watch. Silence fell for a while; then roars of laughter broke from the men's quarters. But it was good laughter. The Indian dog might be having a rough conversion, but he'd be all right.

Other merrymakers passed with a shout of greeting. Sandoval and Cristóbal de Olea sauntered up. They were on the top of the world.

"Ha, Redhead! Ha, Niño!—Navarro!" (Drunk or sober, Sandoval never overlooked the private soldiers.) "Cristóbal and I have been making the rounds. Just come from the General's. 'Struth, that's a sight, Redhead. There's something to jog your liver—the Doña Catalina. What a bride *she* is! Bravest deed Hernán Cortés ever faced. Seen her?"

"Not close."

"That's close enough." Sandoval made wide, curving movements. "Ugly as sin, color of mud. And there sits the General looking politic, with a fixed smile on. You know how he looks. Gad's my life!"

Sandoval's sides shook. He planted his fists on them.

"I said to him, 'Señor, is there anything you *won't* do in the service of the Sovereigns and this company?'

"And he said, 'What do *you* think? But here's another good reason,' he said, 'for marching across the mountains, and that quickly. Anyway we leave a solid backing behind us.'

" 'Solid is right,' I said. 'Cry Santiago tonight when you charge, and the luck of Paladin Roldán God grant you mercifully!'

"So he cast his eyes up, like Saint Lawrence on the gridiron, and cried shame for mocking a public-spirited man. . . . Now we're heading for Puertocarrero's. Wish you were along."

"I'll be along in an hour," Pedro grunted. "Save me some pulque."

Olea said, "By the way, I thought Bull García didn't drink."

"He doesn't."

"Like hell! We looked in at Juan Velásquez de León's, and there was the Bull clinking cups with Escudero, tossing it down like a friar."

"Water, you mean?"

"Water nothing. He's been keeping something from us."

They walked off. "Hey!" called Pedro. But Sandoval had burst into a tuneless bellow, meant for song, and Olea joined in.

Pedro stared after them. García drinking? He couldn't believe it. In all this year together, on march and shipboard, the big man had never once yielded to his dangerous temptation. Then why should he be drinking now? Above all, why should he drink with Juan Escudero whom he hated as a leader of the Velásquez faction? The report left Pedro thoughtful and uneasy. Cortés did not tolerate brawling, and he dealt a swift, merciless justice—not to speak of the danger to García from his fellow soldiers if he went berserk. Pedro would have given a good deal to go over to Velásquez de León's quarters and take a look for himself; but, until relieved, he was chained to his post by the strictest of all rules in the army.

The night seemed quieter and more oppressive. He listened anxiously but heard nothing unusual. After a time came the measured tread of the officer of the watch, making his rounds to inspect the sentries. It was Cristóbal de Olid. Pedro could hear the challenge of those at the gate and those on guard over the arms and stores, Olid's reply, and the grounding of pikes in salute. It came Pedro's turn. Olid clanked on. In view of the suspense about García, Pedro was grateful that Cortés's *cacica* preoccupied him, for he was apt to patrol the camp himself.

Then, not an outburst of noise, but the sound of running. Instantly alert, Pedro was at the edge of the platform when a man panted up. He made out the scared face of Lazarillo Varela, one of the foot soldiers.

"For God's sake, Señor de Vargas—if you can do anything. García's gone mad. . . . He tried to kill Captain Velásquez de León. He's like a wild beast in a corner. . . . No one can get near him. . . . Velásquez's sent for a crossbowman, vows he'll have him shot. Lord Almighty! Hurry! If you can do anything . . ."

Turning to the door of the treasure room, Pedro drew it shut; and, closing the padlock with which it had been newly equipped, he put the key in his wallet. The mastiff was inside; Niño and Navarro, two absolutely trusted men, were on guard. To hell with army rules under the circumstances! He could think only of García—

"Look alive!" he said to the soldiers. "It'll be all right. I'll be back as soon as I can."

"Hurry!" urged Varela.

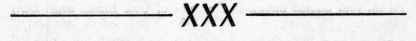

XXX

As THEY raced toward the far corner of the courtyard on the other side of the pyramid, Varela babbled something of what had happened.

"Escudero baited him for a water drinker. But he kept on the polite side. Diego Cermeño, the pilot, joined in. Stood up for García, as if he needed somebody to take his part. Which looks funny because Cermeño and Escudero are thick together. That got under the Bull's skin. He drank to show them, then kept on. They slipped out before trouble started. García went crazy between breaths, turned the table over, let drive at Velásquez—"

The platform in front of Captain Velásquez's quarters was crowded with a muttering throng, elbowing and craning for a glimpse through the vaguely lighted doorway. Sympathy was evident, because everyone liked García and sensed tragedy in what was happening. At sight of Pedro, they made way, as if for the near relative of a man at the point of death.

Beyond the threshold stood a group of tense, anxious-looking men, among whom the burly, red-bearded Velásquez stood out. He had a cut on his forehead, at which he was dabbing with a napkin, while he counted slowly in a harsh voice. Beside him stood a crossbowman, bolt in place and stock to shoulder. The room looked a wreck—trestles for the table planks overturned, stools and Indian mats shoved about, a smashed pulque jar on the floor.

Against the opposite wall, García stood at bay, his face beet-red, eyes glassy, a trace of foam at his lips. The man's gigantic shoulders were hunched forward as if he were about to attack. He wore no doublet. Somehow he had got hold of a heavy, two-handed sword, which he held stretched out in front of him, its point tapping the floor.

"I'd rather tackle Beelzebub," someone was muttering. "The Captain got off lucky."

"Five—six," Velásquez counted.

Pedro braced himself. Evidently Velásquez had given García a certain time in which to surrender, but he was calling numbers to a deaf man.

"Seven. . . . Damn you, García, I'll not have our fellows murdered by a maniac. Don't make me give the order. You can't stop a steel bolt. I don't want to kill you, you fool. Drop that sword!"

Velásquez de León might be a good soldier, but he was no psychologist. In a voice Pedro had never heard, García raged back: "Damn you and your obscenity bolts! I don't give a piece of dung for 'em. I'll slit your blasted throats in the name of God. Indian dogs! Dirty man-eaters! I'll give your hearts to Señor Witchywolves, by'r Lady!"

He started a slow, menacing advance. His delusion was plain, but Velásquez had no time for argument.

"Eight—nine. Ready, Sanchez?"

"Yes, sir."

"Ten!"

Knocked up of a sudden, the weapon discharged its bolt into the ceiling.

"The devil!" roared Velásquez. "What in hell—"

Disregarding him, Pedro stepped forward to meet García.

"*Cuidado!*" hissed a voice from behind. "Look out!"

Pedro paid no attention.

"Don't you know me, Juan? Come! You haven't forgotten Pedrito?"

"Look to yourself, Indian!"

The sword wheeled back, but at the top of its arc, it wavered, stopped. García stood like an axman delaying the downstroke. The glazed eyes quickened slightly.

Pedro stood motionless. "*Compañero,*" he said.

The blade sank slowly. García drew a hand across his face. "You're not an Indian," he growled. "Why, you're—"

He dropped the sword, threw his arms around Pedro. "Lord, boy! I knew I could count on you. This cursed jungle . . . lost my way . . . about spent. Damn savages! They'll not take *us* to the sacrifice. Shoulder to shoulder now!"

He flung loose, staring at the group in front of the door.

"They're friends, Juan."

"Where's the sword?" García was looking blindly around him. . . . "Your arm!" he said thickly. "I'm spent." His face had gone white.

Pedro caught him around the waist. He collapsed unconscious on the floor.

"Holy saints!" said Velásquez, mopping his forehead. "That was close. You've got nerve, Redhead. I'm grateful to you. It would have been a shame to kill him. But what the deuce! He was bent on murder."

The onlookers trooped in, gathered round; voices were loud in contrast to the previous hush. A bucket of water was brought.

"No," said Pedro. "Let him sleep it off. He'll be all right."

Velásquez, eager to make amends, helped carry García into a corner of the room and stuck a mat under his head. "He can stay here tonight," he added. "And leave that bucket near him. He'll have fire in his mouth when he comes to."

Pedro drew off García's boots. He found his hands trembling. Now that the danger was past, he felt almost weak from relief. Then he remembered that the danger wasn't altogether past.

Facing the others, he said: "A word, señores. You've known Juan García as a sober man and good comrade. Because two crackpots found out his weakness and made a joke of it is no cause for scandal. Will you favor him and me by keeping this to yourselves? If the General heard of it, he'd have to take measures. Understand?"

A ready murmur of assent answered.

"Hell!" said a man. *"Trim my beard, and I'll trim your topknot.* It'd be a poor thing if we couldn't do that much for the Bull. He wouldn't blab on us. Wish I didn't have more on *my* conscience than a good drunk."

"And, gentlemen," said Pedro, "not a word about me in this. I'm supposed to be on guard."

The turbulent Velásquez burst out: "What do you take us for, Redhead? Get back to your post. I'll cut the ears off of any loose-talker."

Reassured by the gang spirit in the company, which did not encourage talebearing, Pedro now returned across the increasingly silent courtyard; but he breathed freer on catching sight of Niño and Navarro still on guard in front of the treasure room. They reported all well. Pledging them to secrecy, as he had the others, Pedro told them briefly about García. Then, unlocking the door, he went inside to inspect the chests.

The mastiff, Tigre, nosed him as he entered. Everything was in order. He congratulated himself on the happy ending of what might have been a fatal mess. All that remained now was to comfort the remorseful García in the morning and to make sure that he stuck to water from then on. As if reflecting the general serenity, Tigre sank down and went to sleep.

It wanted a half hour until the guard would change and Cristóbal de Gamboa, his fellow equerry, would relieve him. About to sit down on one of the chests, Pedro stood up again. Something different in their arrangement struck him. He thought he remembered this large one as more to the left, with a smaller box on top. Probably a quirk of memory or trick of the moonlight. The six chests were all, there. Only he could have sworn—

As he hesitated, a faintly luminous zigzag on the blank rear wall of the room caught his attention. What the deuce was that? It hadn't been there before. But when he strode across to look more closely, his heart turned to water.

The luminous arabesque was simply moonlight between the irregular edge and jamb of a concealed door in the masonry, which had not been entirely closed. Except for this, no one would have suspected the existence of the door, which fitted perfectly into the surrounding stone-work.

Using the tips of his fingers, Pedro swung open the narrow entrance, and found himself looking out at an empty street behind the teocalli. Then, appalled, he closed it again and turned back to the chests. Whatever had happened, it was plain that someone had entered the room since he left it.

Various possibilities crossed his mind, as he tried the lids and padlocks. Perhaps a temple priest creeping back for some purpose of his own. But in that case the dog, who was trained to attack Indians—He glanced at the mastiff outstretched and asleep. A full meal? And yet Tigre wouldn't have taken meat from an Indian, at least not without a first challenge when the door opened. Or wouldn't he? Big, fighting dogs were often silent.

No, thank God, everything seemed all right. The lids were firm, the padlocks in place. He came to the last chest, the one containing the gold disc and the emeralds; fingered the padlocks. And at that moment, as he tried it again, one of them dropped off.

He crouched, staring, as if turned to stone, the sense of calamity holding him in a kind of vise. Weakly he tested the other padlock and found that it too was broken.

With fingers trembling so that he could hardly manipulate the tinderbox and stump of candle which he drew from his wallet, he struck a light and raised the lid of the chest. The gleam of metal beneath reassured him. Too much weight for a thief to carry, thank heaven. Then he remembered the emeralds and looked for the doeskin pouch, which had been tucked into one corner between the edge of the disc and the chest. Yes, *viva!* It was still there.

176

He drew it out—and stopped breathing. The bag was empty.

In his absorption, he did not hear the footstep behind him.

"Hm-m," said a cold voice. "Since when have you taken the liberty of opening these chests?"

Jerking around, Pedro looked up into the face of Hernán Cortés.

— XXXI —

No CRIMINAL had ever been more plainly caught in the act than Pedro de Vargas at that moment. He still held the limp pouch in one hand, his candle in the other; the golden contents of the open chest shone dully in the light; the broken padlocks lay on the floor.

"By your leave," said Cortés, taking the pouch. And when he found it empty, "Be good enough to hand over those stones."

His quietness gave a razor edge to the suppressed passion behind it.

"I don't have them, sir."

"No? Are you sure? Didn't you think this was the night to make your fortune in, while I was otherwise taken up? Well, my friend, it will be a cold night when I do not keep my eyes open for the profit of this company."

"But, Your Excellency, I had just discovered that the locks were broken—"

"Don't lie to me." The vibration of Cortés's voice had the quality of a taut bowstring. "I saw to the locks myself no later than three hours since. Have you the face to tell me that someone entered here while you were on guard, opened the chest, and departed, and that you then 'discovered' it? Do you take me for a fool?"

The truth had to come out. Damning as it might be, it was not so deadly as the charge of theft.

"Your pardon, sir," Pedro stammered, "the fact is that I was off guard for a while."

"Indeed? And why?"

Pedro equivocated. "Juan García was ill. Velásquez de León summoned me."

"When?"

"A half hour ago. I've just returned."

Cortés digested this in hot silence. Then he said: "Very well. An officer in command of an important post walks off at his pleasure to hold the hand of a sick friend. Very charitable. We'll deal with that in its place. What were your two men, Niño and Navarro, doing—not to speak of the watchdog?" He glanced at the mastiff, who had straightened up and was yawning at him. "Were they off for a stroll too? Or are you hinting that they rifled the chest?"

"Señor, no. I locked the door when I left. The dog was inside. I found the men on guard and the lock untampered with."

"Well, then—God give me patience!—would you have me believe that someone walked through solid masonry into this room and took the jewels, while the dog kept quiet? Would you palm off a phantom on me, when I find you with the chest open and the jewel pouch in your hand? Find a better tale." The cold sarcasm dropped suddenly. "Meanwhile, hand me those stones, and you can romance later."

Cortés's eyes blazed. Taking a step forward, he caught Pedro's doublet close to the throat in a steel grip.

"Do you want me to call the guards and have you stripped?"

Until then Pedro's bewilderment had half-paralyzed his tongue, but the General's words and action brought him to himself. His pride rebelled. A de Vargas was no thief. Cortés might be a hidalgo, but so was he, and his honor hung in the balance. His hand closed on the General's wrist.

"Kindly unloose me, sir, and listen," he said.

"I'm listening." But Cortés did not relax his hold. "Make it short."

Pedro played his trump card. "Whoever it was came through the door in that wall. It was ajar when I got back. That's how I knew—"

"What door?" Cortés turned his head to look. "I see none."

Nor could Pedro. He remembered now that he had closed it: and that part of the wall looked as solid as the rest.

"A moment, sir, by your leave."

Cortés dropped his hand, and Pedro, hurrying over to the wall, looked in vain for indications of the door. His fingers moved here and there between the stones, prying, attempting to get a purchase. The wall remained blank as before.

"My faith, you're a poor liar, de Vargas! It would have been likelier to have had your thief drop through the roof. At least that's not of stone."

Frantically Pedro fingered and pried, straining his nails between the cracks. "I'm not lying. On my honor, sir, there's a door—"

"Don't talk of honor," snapped Cortés. "We've wasted time enough." But he broke off in amazement. "By my soul—"

Whether Pedro had at last found the outline of the door, or whether by accident he had pressed the secret release, in any case a crack now showed, and he was able to swing back the irregular stone panel.

"By my soul," Cortés repeated. "You're right."

He looked out thoughtfully into the street, then examined the door and closed it, taking care to mark its position by several smudges from Pedro's candle.

"The mastiff?" he pondered.

"I think he was well fed by the thief," Pedro ventured—"from the looks of him."

"So it probably wasn't an Indian." Cortés picked up one of the broken padlocks. "Filed," he nodded. "The Indians have no steel."

Closing the still open chest, he walked to the main doorway. Pedro heard him questioning Navarro as to whether the dog had given tongue during Señor de Vargas's absence.

"No, my General. At least nothing but a growl or two; we thought nothing of it."

When the man had returned to his post, Cortés re-entered and, seating himself on one of the chests, fell into thought. Everything considered, Pedro wondered at the General's self-control. Others of the captains, Alvarado, for instance, or Olid, would by this time have stirred up a commotion; but so far not even the men outside knew that the chest had been opened. Cortés sat fingering his beard, his face expressionless except for the occasional glancing of his eyes. With the sense of fault weighing upon him, Pedro stood shifting from foot to foot.

He started when Cortés remarked suddenly, "I shall hate to hang you, de Vargas." And as Pedro could find nothing to answer, "But, I have no doubt, that will be the decision of the captains—unless these jewels are recovered. They are the property of His Majesty. As you well know, they are a chief item of the treasure intended to incline the Sovereigns to our petition. Be the thief who he will, you were responsible. You deserted your post without leave from me. Because of that desertion, the robbery was possible."

Step by step, Pedro could follow the perfect logic of the accusation. He could not refute one article of it, and he realized that any military court must find him guilty. A cold numbness crept over him.

"Unless the jewels are found . . ." Cortés repeated. "They were your charge. Perhaps you can recover them. I give you until tomorrow night. Until then I shall say nothing of this. But tomorrow night, you understand?"

"Your Excellency, how—"

"Use your wits. It's your affair since your neck depends on it."

A light flashed in Pedro's mind. Was Escudero's baiting of García, who made no secret of his weakness, a practical joke, after all? Trouble would almost certainly follow from García's drinking. In that case, it was natural that Pedro should be turned to. The messenger, Varela, might even have been tipped off to summon him. Escudero was a partizan of the Governor of Cuba and a reputed enemy of Cortés. He had opposed the secession of the army from the jurisdiction of Cuba; he opposed the projected march across the mountains; he opposed sending the treasure to Spain. He and Cermeño headed a group of the same stripe. Of course Pedro might be on the wrong track; but in his present straits, it seemed by all odds the likeliest.

"I'll do my best," he said. "Thank Your Excellency for the delay. Whatever happens, be assured that no one can judge me harder than I do myself. I deserve the consequences."

Cortés nodded. "Good luck to you."

"May I ask one favor?"

"Well?"

"That if I don't find the stones, if I can't clear myself, the news may be kept from my father."

"That can be managed," said Cortés.

XXXII

THE CADENCED TRAMP of the relieving guard, coming on duty, sounded in the now silent enclosure. Automatically Pedro walked out to the platform and stood at attention, as the detail assigned to his post came up. It occurred to him that it might be the last time he played this part.

"Quién vive?"

"Cristóbal de Gamboa, in command of the treasure guard."

"Watchword?"

"Santa Trinidad."

"Advance, Cristóbal de Gamboa."

The two swords rose in salute; the soldiers handled their pikes. Gamboa mounted the platform and saluted Cortés, who appeared in the doorway.

"Sir," the General directed, "you will call additional men and convey the military chests to my quarters. You will mount guard there. I have reason to believe that this room is unsafe."

"Yes, Your Excellency."

Cortés glanced at Pedro. "You are dismissed, Señor de Vargas. Your men will give a hand in conveying the chests."

"Yes, Your Excellency."

Pedro relayed the order—perhaps his last—to Niño and Navarro. Dismissed! Gamboa would think nothing, but Pedro caught the dry note in Cortés's voice. Moving off, he watched furtively the transfer of the chests from the room which he had left undefended. Even if he recovered the stolen jewels, he felt that it would be a long time before the black mark against him was canceled.

A seething hatred for the thieves who had used him as a cat's-paw possessed him. If they could fill their dirty pockets, the disgrace or death of García and himself meant nothing to them. Escudero and Cermeño: with every moment, Pedro felt more confident of their guilt. If he accomplished nothing else during his eighteen hours of respite, he vowed that he would make them pay for it.

And yet, practically considered, how? As he turned the problem over, it seemed more hopeless at each new angle. The five emeralds were easy to conceal and would no doubt be carefully hidden. They would not be carried about in the wallets of the thieves, who could expect a hue-and-cry as soon as the loss was discovered. How many men were involved in the robbery? Even if Pedro was right about Escudero and Cermeño, they were possibly in league with others, to whom they could hand on their booty. Or again, they might have acted only as decoys, while the real thief did the work.

But there was no use counting difficulties. Pedro had to follow the first obvious plan and trust to luck. It seemed to him, for lack of any better idea, that he must play the thief himself, gain admittance somehow that night to the suspects' quarters, and search their effects. The dangers of this were too plain to dwell upon; but a condemned man does not need to fear danger.

He knew that Escudero lodged in one of the temple rooms not far from Velásquez, but he was not entirely certain which, and he proceeded at once to reconnoiter. It was now ten o'clock and bedtime, for the army kept early hours even upon nights of celebration. The bridal parties in the captains' quarters had died out, leaving a drowsy aftermath of sound and a few loiterers straggling to their sleeping mats. The angles of the pyramid and of the temple enclosure, sharp in the moonlight, seemed to accentuate the quiet and the emptiness.

Pedro found Lazarillo Varela yawning on the steps of one of the apartment platforms.

"A hot night, Señor de Vargas. Going to have a look at Juan García? He's sleeping like a stone."

"No, I'm looking for Juan Escudero. Where's his place?"

Varela gave an understanding grin. "Oh, come, sir," he answered. "Nothing happened to García. All's well that ends well. It was only a prank. No use making bad blood over it."

"Just the same, I'd like a word with him. Where's he quartered?"

Varela jerked his head backwards. "In here. There're ten of us together. Only you'll not find him and Cermeño tonight; they're gone."

"Gone where? What do you mean?"

"Well," smiled Varela, "it may be they thought you'd like a word with them and they took a walk. They weren't waiting for trouble."

"A walk? Where?"

It was absolutely forbidden to leave the temple enclosure. Both for the safety of the army and to protect his Indian allies, Cortés permitted no Spaniards out of the camp.

"To Villa Rica," answered Varela. "They left before García got started."

Pedro flared up. "Don't joke with me, *hombre*."

"I'm not joking, sir. They got permission from the General. . . It's something to do with the stores. . . . They got it this afternoon, but stayed on for a part of the fun."

"You mean to tell me that they left at night to walk twelve miles to Villa Rica?"

"Yes, sir. They said it was cooler at night." Varela turned to a soldier who had come up. "Ask Panchito here, if you don't believe me. He's been on duty at the gate."

The sentry nodded. "Yes, we passed them through."

"When?"

"Maybe an hour ago."

Pedro calculated. The time coincided exactly with his absence from the treasure room. They would have had a half hour in which to circle the teocalli from outside and commit the theft. No one could connect them with it, assuming, as they probably had, that the secret doorway remained undiscovered. Likely enough, Pedro's return had been earlier than they expected. This explained the imperfectly closed door, the one saving piece of luck in the whole affair.

Suspicion of the two men had now become practical certainty; but at the same time Pedro found himself in a worse impasse than before. As long as Escudero and his companion were in Cempoala, he could have made an attempt, at least, to recover the jewels. Villa Rica was another matter. He was shut up here, while they had every opportunity to dispose of the emeralds as they pleased.

For an instant he thought of turning to Cortés for permission to follow them, but that would be useless. He was under too dark a cloud to be given so obvious a chance of escape. Of course he might accuse Escudero and Cermeño; he might even prevail on Cortés to arrest them tomorrow; and torture might accomplish the rest of it. But they were not unimportant men; they were ringleaders of a faction that Cortés was trying to propitiate. People of that sort were not easily arrested and put to the question, especially not on the word of someone, like Pedro, who was bent on saving his own skin.

No, the upshot was that he must follow them to Villa Rica without permission. Having been condemned on one count, he might as well be condemned on two. His salvation anyhow consisted solely in recovering the emeralds.

These thoughts chased through his mind, as he stood looking vacantly at Panchito and Varela.

"Too bad, sir," grinned the latter. "But believe me it's better as it is. Remember the proverb: *Hablar sin pensar es tirar sin encarar.* No use quarreling over a joke which did no harm. You'll feel cooler in the morning."

"Perhaps you're right," Pedro agreed.

He wished them good night and headed apparently toward his quarters; but, keeping in the shadow of the pyramid, he returned to the other side of the plaza, as close as possible to the treasure room. Because of the sentries at the main gate, he realized that the recently discovered secret door was his best, and perhaps his only, means of exit from the temple quarters—provided the room had not yet been padlocked on the courtyard side.

Fortunately the last of the chests had only just been removed; he could see the soldiers lugging it between them toward Cortés's apartment. Meanwhile, the door of the room stood open. Was anyone lingering inside? He would have to chance that. He would also have to chance being seen as he crossed over from the shadow of the pyramid. It could not but strike anyone as odd that de Vargas, having finished his guard duty, should return to the vacant treasure room.

With his heart in his mouth, and a heart-felt *Dios lo quiera!* on his lips, he took the plunge. . . . The room was empty.

Darting over to the wall, he began once more working at the concealed door. It came easier this time, but even so he heard footsteps approaching as he finally wrenched the panel open. Then, slipping through, he closed it behind him and sped off down the shadowy side of the street.

XXXIII

NOT A BREATH stirred the saturated July air between the white-plastered house fronts of Cempoala. By the time Pedro emerged from the Indian city, he was dripping with sweat, and he drew off his doublet before continuing across the cultivated lands circling the town. Cumbered by his sword, he hitched up the baldric that supported it so as to free his legs.

But, however hot, he did not slacken his pace. He reckoned that Escudero and Cermeño had three quarters of an hour start, and he wished to cut down that lead as much as possible before reaching Villa Rica. The question of what he would do after that presented itself, but it was useless to make plans now. He must follow events and improvise when the time came.

A few scattered natives had passed him on the street, but they gave the white man a wide berth. Beyond the town nothing stirred except the creatures of the night. A hothouse perfume of roses and other flowers hung in the air, as Pedro crossed the garden land which supported the population of Cempoala. Then suddenly he was breathing the still hotter incense of the jungle. The track meandered between impenetrable walls reinforced by the interwoven vines of wild grape or convolvuluses. Ferns brushed him as he walked, and the tricky light splashed only here and there through the upper lacework of branches. The quick rustle of small, unseen animals, the occasional plunging of a larger beast, the flutter of awakened birds, echoed the wet sound of his footsteps.

He was grateful for the moonlight, without which walking would have been almost impossible, and he prayed that it might last until he reached the more open country beyond the woods. But he by no means took it for granted. In this season of the rains, it might be shut out at any moment by a black downpour.

Luck favored him, however. He cleared the jungle and had come within sight of an Indian village, pearl-pale on a distant slope, when the moon faded out, the sky darkened, and a deluge, accompanied by lightning and thunder, cut off the view. Fortunately a small wayside temple lay close, and he took refuge there, cursing the delay.

As he stood within the entrance of the shrine, lightning flashes cut across the vertical column of the rain and brought out with momentary distinctness the hideous features of the wooden god looming above the altar. Squatting with bared fangs and glowing eyes, it had all the attributes of Satan gloating over the bowl of penitential blood left by his worshipers. The come-and-go of light and darkness gave an effect of movement to the image. Pedro felt relieved when, as suddenly as it had begun, the rain stopped and the moon flooded out again.

Returning now to the trail, he sloshed on, past the Indian village, over the rolling country beyond, through an occasional stretch of thick woods, but in general downhill as the land sloped toward the coast. At his best speed, he reckoned that he could not make better than three miles an hour along the muddy and uneven path. This meant that he could not reach Villa Rica before two o'clock.

Hour followed hour. He kept hoping for a glimpse of the two men ahead of him, but saw no one. At last, what with the dense air and fatigue, he plodded on mechanically until, roused by a salt-laden breeze, he discovered sand dunes to his right and heard the throb of the sea.

Topping another rise, he could make out the Indian town of Quiauitztlan on its hill and, on the plain beneath, not far from the harbor, the few and unfinished walls of the Spanish fort. In the rays of the waning moon, he could see too the dark hulls of the eleven ships at anchor against the silver dappling on the water.

Having reached his journey's end, the necessity of deciding the next step imposed itself. The sentinel at the gate of the still roofless fort could tell him whether Escudero and his companion had arrived. If they had, he must invent an excuse to explain his own appearance and then sometime before morning attempt to search them. It was probable that they would sleep sound after the long road. He must try to get past the sentinel without their knowing it.

But from the top of the next dune, he noticed something that completely changed his plans and indeed put a stop to any plans at all. He saw a huddle of men on the beach of the harbor, engaged in launching a boat.

Keeping out of sight behind a low dune, he ran toward them as fast as possible, his footsteps muffled by the loose sand. Out of breath, he got to a point not more than fifty yards distant, just as the boat was being steadied through the upwash of the waves.

"All right," came a voice, which he recognized as Cermeño's, "let her go."

The speaker was crouching in the stern with another man, probably Escudero, beside him. Four seamen, knee-deep in water, who had been steadying the boat, now gave a last shove and scrambled aboard. A moment later they were rowing out.

Helplessly raging, Pedro gazed after it. He had overlooked this possibility. Naturally Cermeño, as one of the pilots, would sleep on board his ship, the *Gallega*, and not in the fort. Yes, the *Gallega*. Pedro saw them pass Alvarado's ship, the *Sebastián*, and Cortés's *capitana;* they were making for the small vessel on the extreme right. Manned by Peñates from Gibraltar, who had been flogged by Cortés in Cozumel Island for stealing salt pork and who hated him in consequence, the ship was known as a focal point of mutiny. Several of the Velásquez faction had sailed with her.

As the boat dwindled along the pathway of moonlight, Pedro's hopes faded out. He had no means of following it. Inland-bred, he was an indifferent swimmer, and besides the waters were shark-infested. It was the end of his quest for the jewels. Unless he could induce Cortés to seize the two men and examine them on no better grounds than his personal convictions, the emeralds were as safe on the *Gallega* as the worms in her hull.

He lay outstretched on the sand, stiff, worn, and clammy with sweat, and took stock of tomorrow. Now he would not only be unable to restore the jewels; but in addition he had broken one of the General's sternest laws by deserting the camp without permission. There was no possible escape for him. Even if he had been willing to crown his disgrace by flight, where could he find refuge in this savage country? The only thing left now was to face the inevitable by presenting himself at the fort.

Burned out and defeated, he got up at last and followed the beach where the sand was firmer. All he wanted was to find a place to sleep in after the grueling walk from Cempoala. In this state of mind, he barked his shins and almost fell over an object on the sand which he had been too listless to notice, an Indian fisherman's canoe drawn up beyond the reach of the waves. With a vague oath, he was about to pass on when he came to a dead stop. His mind, which had been half asleep, quickened, and he looked eagerly over the small craft. It was a log which had been hollowed out by fire. The leaf-shaped paddle lay in the bottom. Here after all was a way of reaching the *Gallega*.

In his excitement, Pedro did not stop to reckon difficulties: that he had never paddled a canoe before and had no idea how to manage it; that if he upset, he was almost certainly done for; that if he reached the ship and got on board, he would be alone with a dozen men who would have no compunction about cutting his throat; that if he were hard-pressed and had to drop from the ship back into the canoe, he would surely capsize. If any of this occurred to him as he dragged the hollow log to the water, one sufficient answer presented itself: that he had nothing to lose whatever happened, and that a chance for life and for retrieving himself was better than no chance at all.

It cost him several wettings before he managed to slide into the canoe and begin a teetering progress toward the ship. He had frequently watched the Indians and now tried to imitate them by crouching low and balancing as much as possible. But the canoe, designed for two or three men, rode high and tipped distressingly at every higher ripple of the quiet bay. Foot by foot, he crept on, like a man walking a plank over some chasm, aware of the growing distance from the shore, conscious of his own helpless smallness on the expanse of water.

But little by little, the ship came nearer, her stern light showing more brightly as the moon sank beyond the inland sierras. Though only a small caravel, she bulked huge above him when at last Pedro crept into her shadow and felt his way around to her anchor rope.

This was a ticklish point, as the tide eddied about the poop and set the canoe teetering more desperately than ever. Pedro landed with a bump against the small boat which had been moored to the stern, lost his balance, and found himself under the water. He came up sputtering. The overturned canoe was out of reach; but he grasped the side of the ship's boat.

"Who's there?" came a grunt from the *Gallega's* deck.

De Vargas lowered himself as far as possible and waited, torn between fear of discovery by the man above and of sharks below. After a tense moment, the sailor could be heard padding off along the afterdeck. Pedro clambered over the side of the small boat.

Here he allowed the water to drain off him. Then, removing his shoes and belting his sword closer to his body, he pulled himself hand over hand up the anchor rope, got a grip on the deck, and worked himself upward, fingers, knees and toes, to the rail. A glance above it showed that the deck was empty. A moment later he had climbed on board.

A murmur of voices sounded not far off; someone laughed. The sound came up the companionway from the captain's cabin. Inching downward, Pedro at length had a glimpse of the end of the cabin table and of a man's back. Evidently the small space was crowded— he could see legs and knees and hands.

"So the upshot of it is," said a fierce, halting voice, "that we sail at dawn."

——— XXXIV ———

ESCUDERO was speaking. Though Pedro could not see him, he had no difficulty in recognizing his voice.

"*Hombre!*" he went on. "Won't we be a welcome sight in Cuba! Won't *we* be the pets of the Governor! When the whole armada has deserted him for a climbing double-dealer like Cortés, we show him that we're the only true men. Besides which, we put him in the way of scooping the whole pile. Ten to one, Montejo takes the treasure ship for Spain into El Marién for a last glimpse of his señora. If he does, the Governor has him like a mouse in the trap. If he doesn't, it'll be easy to overhaul him in the Bahama Channel. There's not a man jack of us but can look for an *encomienda* out of this, with broad gold pieces to boot. Let Cortés's five hundred fools have their empire if they can get it! Only a million armed Indians to conquer!" . . . Escudero laughed. "Cuba looks softer to me."

A murmur of agreement answered. Then a voice, which Pedro couldn't identify, put in: "That's all right, but what's the hurry? Cortés is at Cempoala. We could stand more water and supplies, and we can take some on tomorrow. Why not sail next day? It's a long stretch to Cape Antón."

Pedro heard the thud of a fist on the table. "Gentlemen," said Escudero, "believe me, *A lame goat takes no siesta.* If something's to be done, do it. We're safe tonight—not a suspicion. Tomorrow, who knows? And you can see yourselves taking on stores tomorrow with no questions asked, eh? Under the nose of every ship in the fleet? Very likely, isn't it? No, sirs, the cassava bread may not be very good, but we've eaten weevils before and can eat them again. We've got fish and oil. We'll run north and fill the casks at the Panuco. I'm telling you. You'll regret it unless you sail with the dawn wind."

In Pedro's mind, the theft of the jewels was by now eclipsed by this vastly more important threat. He knew how much Cortés feared that word of the army's declaration of independence from Governor Velásquez should reach Cuba before its position had been legalized by the King in Spain. It was necessary, besides, to have greater achievements to show than a few provinces along the coast. If Velásquez heard prematurely that the expedition sent out₂by him had shaken off his jurisdiction, it would mean armed interference from Cuba, probable bloodshed, and the wreck of everything that had been accomplished. Moreover, the sailing of the *Gallega* concerned not merely the loss of a few jewels, but of the treasure ship itself with the entire proceeds thus far of the venture. That in its turn entailed the loss of the King's recognition which the gold was being sent to buy.

Listening intently, however, it seemed to him that one thing in Escudero's speech rang hollow. Every ground for haste had been given except the theft of the jewels, the one compelling reason that made haste imperative. Was it that Escudero and Cermeño had taken the emeralds without the knowledge of the others? As it happened, almost the next words cleared up this point.

It was admitted that the casks could be replenished further along the coast and that prudence counseled flight. "But how did it happen," asked someone—Pedro guessed it was Umbría, a seaman who had been one of the arch mutineers from the beginning—"that you weren't able to bring a sample of the treasure with you? I thought you told us that one of the temple *papas* showed you a door. Didn't it work, or what?"

"*Por Dios,*" returned the other, "we did our best, didn't we, Cermeño?"

"Aye, aye," answered the latter. "But young Pedro de Vargas was on guard. We couldn't get him away from his post, though we tried hard enough."

"And it wouldn't have done to risk the whole project for a few pesos," Escudero added. "What difference does it make anyhow, as long as we get the whole cargo in the end?"

"It makes this difference," someone growled, "that it won't be us but the Governor who gets it. If you'd brought something along, at least we'd have had our share of that."

Escudero took it lightly. "Don't worry about your share, Bernardino. You'll have no cause to complain when we get to Cuba."

Pedro grinned. The two rogues were holding out on the others. Whatever happened in Cuba, they had lined their own pockets.

Cermeño changed the subject. "Well, if we're sailing in three hours, we've got that much sleep coming. I'm for bed."

Pedro at once started backing up the companionway.

He must somehow get to shore and warn the commander at the fort. It was Juan de Escalante, an able officer and one devoted to Cortés. Escalante would be able to take measures, provided only there was time and that Pedro could escape undetected. His plan was to regain the deck, drop below the rail and wait until the group below had dispersed, then try to get off in the small boat.

"Ho!" said a surprised voice behind him. "Who's this?"

Evidently a seaman, also eavesdropping, had mistaken Pedro in the darkness for one of his mates.

De Vargas turned and tried to shove upward, but found himself in a bear's grapple. The narrow companionway made fight impossible. The next instant both men lost their footing and catapulted down, emerging into the cabin with a crash, amid the stupefaction of the group there. They landed against the table and rolled to one side. Arching himself, Pedro threw off the other and sprang to his feet, only to face a circle of knives.

"Redhead de Vargas!" roared somebody. "By the Lord God!"

Arms pinioned him from behind. His sword was jerked out of its scabbard. His poniard disappeared at the same moment.

"Cortés's spaniel, eh?" growled Escudero. "Let me have the handling of him!" From the farther end of the cabin, he started shouldering his way toward the prisoner, his knife in hand and uptilted.

"Not so fast," said Bernardino de Coria. He was a wild blade of a man, reckless, but likable in a rakehell way. "No hurry. All in good time. Stand back, will you? How now! My word, we'll give him a hearing, won't we?"

"Cermeño!" snapped Escudero, trying in vain to get past Coria. But as Cermeño struck, his wrist was caught by the seaman, Umbría.

"Come, come," said the latter. "What's the haste? Why kill a man unheard? If it's necessary later—"

He pushed Cermeño back. Juan Díaz, a discontented priest who seconded Olmedo as chaplain, added his protest. "Calm yourselves, my sons."

Pedro thought fast. He knew perfectly well why Escudero and Cermeño were in a hurry, and he understood the advantage that this knowledge gave him.

"Thank you, señores," he said. "Before you let these gentlemen kill me, better ask what they did with the emeralds that they took from the treasure room tonight."

A tense hush fell in the cabin. The pairs of eyes which had been leveled at Pedro now shifted to the two ringleaders. A seaman, who had been holding de Vargas from behind, relaxed his grip. It would have been easy at that moment for Pedro to break loose and make a dash for the companionway, but he had sense enough to stay quiet.

Cermeño ran his tongue across his lips. Escudero laughed. "Trust one of Cortés's spies to lie! If you can find an emerald on either of us, I'll pay you for it."

His broad, blunt face looked so perfectly assured that Pedro's certainty wavered. His voice had the ring of truth. Perhaps they had already hidden the jewels. But where? Certainly not on shore, as they were about to sail. Perhaps on the ship, but they had hardly had time.

Pedro remembered a current thieves' dodge which he had heard at Sanlúcar and took a long chance.

"The emeralds may not be on these gentlemen. The gentlemen may be on the emeralds. You might begin by having a look at their shoes. But on them or under them, by my faith, they know where the stones are."

"How do you know they know?" growled Umbría. He had a crinkly brown beard, which he jutted out as if to point the question.

"Because they did get me away from my post; because the emeralds were taken while I was gone; and because the concealed door was open."

"Jesús María!" snarled Coria, showing his buckteeth. "And they talk about liars! 'Sdeath! You can understand why they wanted de Vargas out of the way quickly. By God, fellows, we'll have every stitch off them and purge them to boot."

Escudero gave in; but he laughed again, jerking his head back. The glance he shot at Pedro would have killed if possible.

"Curse you for a hothead, Bernardino! Ever hear of a joke? Cermeño and I were only fooling. Thought we'd surprise you later before getting to Santiago. What you don't expect is more of a treat, isn't it? Man, we've got five beauties with us that Master Fox Cortés intended for the King himself. Ten thousand pesos if they're worth a copper. How's that for a haul? A thousand pesos to each of us."

He did it well but met with glum silence.

"Hand 'em out," said Coria. Juan Díaz, the priest, studied the ceiling. Umbría and the four other seamen glowered. It took no mind reader to guess the drift of their thoughts.

With as good grace as the action permitted, Escudero and Cermeño removed their boots. Pedro's long shot seemed to have hit the mark. They tried to laugh it off and sneered about the thief he had been to school to.

"Set a thief to catch one," grunted Coria.

They pried off the boot heels with their knives and brought out the emeralds from the hollow spaces cut out within the heels themselves.

The glow of the stones, passing from hand to hand and held up in the dim light of the lanthorn, lessened the tension and shifted scrutiny from the two culprits. Privately perhaps everyone admitted that he would have done as much in their place. The watchful attention with which the stones were handed around spoke volumes for the trust that each member of the group placed in the next. When the inspection was over, it became a problem where to safeguard them.

"Lock them in that chest," suggested Escudero, unabashed, "and give the key to Father Juan. The holy character of a priest, señores, puts him above suspicion."

"No, thank you," said Díaz. Furtively he fingered his throat. "I'd rather not."

"Well, then," proposed Coria, "lock them in that chest and throw the key overboard. The character of the sea, gentlemen, puts it above suspicion."

He raised the lid of a heavy, iron-bound box, provided with an intricate lock. "Put the emeralds inside there. . . . Good. . . . Everybody bears witness that in his presence the jewels have been placed in the chest? Look again, gentlemen. Good! I now lock the chest, as you see"—Coria suited the action to the words, opened a porthole—"and throw the key into the water." The splash sounded. Coria added: "We'll open the chest together before reaching Santiago. It'll be a good man who can force that box without noise enough to put the rest of us onto it."

Pedro coughed. Momentarily forgotten, he became once more the focus of an uneasy, somewhat perplexed attention.

Escudero growled, "I suppose now there isn't any objection to dealing with Cortés's eavesdropper, is there?"

With folded arms, Pedro leaned against the wall of the cabin. He was playing a dangerous game and must make no false step, but he enjoyed the excitement of it.

"Deal with me?" he repeated. "Sirs, you'll have to admit that except for me, you wouldn't have ten thousand pesos in that chest."

An obscure mutter expressed agreement. He could sense that no one except Escudero and Cermeño bore him a personal grievance; but that would not save his life unless he was careful.

Coria shook his head. "You see how it is, de Vargas. Our necks wouldn't be worth a tinker's curse if Cortés or Escalante knew what we're up to. We can't put you ashore—"

"I'd pay the hangman if you did," Pedro interrupted. "Without those emeralds, I'm a dead man if Cortés has the say of it. They were taken when I should have been on guard. You know the General."

The obvious truth of this made an impression. Pedro followed it up.

"So I'm for you and Governor Velásquez. Frankly, if I could have had those stones, I'd have gone back. Now Cuba seems healthier, if you follow me."

Umbría grinned. "We follow you. How about it, friends?"

"Are you mad?" put in Escudero. "The fellow would be over the side like an eel, at the first blink. Can't you see what he's aiming at? He'd buy his pardon by informing on us. He's one of the General's wag-tails—like Sandoval."

Pedro's heart sank, for the other had read his intention well enough, but he looked unruffled.

"Señor," he said, "nothing is easier—or cheaper—than to insult a prisoner. You know perfectly well that if I had my arms and the leave of this company, I would cut off your ears. As to escape, a pair of chains will cure that until we are clear of the harbor."

"Fair enough," approved Coria. "And when we are clear, you can have your arms and my leave, brother Pedro. I'll bet my share of the emeralds on you. Anybody take me up?"

Silence followed, even on the part of Escudero. It was well-known that in fencing bouts Pedro de Vargas matched even Cristóbal de Olid and Gonzalo de Sandoval.

By majority consent, Pedro's enlistment with the mutineers was now tentatively accepted, and a pair of shackles were produced to make it effective. As the handcuffs locked, Pedro tried vainly to catch Coria's eye; he felt that he had more to hope from this scapegrace than from the others. In the wrangle that followed as to where he should be kept, Escudero urged the hold; Coria, the cabin. But the former's authority had dwindled in the past hour. Coria won the debate by asserting that a chained man was the best guard of the jewels, and for his part he thought it safer if no one who wasn't chained slept in the cabin.

"Meanwhile," said Pedro, striving again to fix Coria's attention, "I hope you'll set a guard over the companionway. It would be a pity for me if certain gentry did not wait until I have my arms."

He got a poisonous glance from Escudero, but Coria only grinned. "I take your meaning, Redhead. You'll be safe enough. I'm for sleep— if you can call two hours sleep."

The party broke up, some leaving by the door to the quarter-deck, others climbing the companionway to the poop deck. Bolts were shoved home, and Pedro remained in the darkness.

Immediately he began working at his fetters, but uselessly. Even if he had stripped the flesh from his hands, his bones were still too large to be squeezed through the iron cuffs. And with every minute, the precious margin of time was shrinking. If he could only have had a word alone with Coria! That had been his last hope. He might perhaps have won the man over.

In the stuffy blackness of the cabin, he strained and sweated. The thought occurred that even if he succeeded in escaping at that moment, it would be too late. Even if somehow he got to shore, it would take time to reach Escalante and spread the alarm. Minute by minute, the brave dream of the army, of the men he loved, was crumbling, when so little would have sufficed to save it, when he had been so close to talking himself free!

An hour gone. Outside, he heard a gromet turn the glass, chanting his call, even though there was no change of watch. Then again silence.

No, a slight sound, as if the hatch above the companionway was being cautiously raised. Then a step, slow, furtive, descending.

Escudero?

He braced himself. Someone had entered the cabin.

The shade of a dark lantern slid back and he saw—Coria.

"I think," came a whisper, "you had something to tell me. I couldn't chance it before. We haven't much time. What do you want to say?"

XXXV

IT WAS NOW or never. Coria had scented something to his advantage and was, in so far, open to suggestion. Everything depended on the next minute.

Pedro said, "I wanted to ask why you came on this expedition."

"Because I'm poor as a beggar's louse," returned Coria, "and the prospects looked good."

"Then why are you quitting it?"

"Because I'm tired of songs and promises. I got my hands on a bit of gold at San Juan de Ulúa; but *hasta la vista,* I had to fork it over to give to the King. I'm fed-up."

"So you think you'll get rich in Cuba?"

Coria grinned toothily. "Remains to be seen."

"I wouldn't count on it too much. Juan Escudero's the man who'll get rich. He has the ear of the Governor, and that's not going to be of help to you. He'll be your enemy from tonight on. Even as a friend, he's shown how much you can depend on him."

The grin faded, but Coria said nothing.

"No market in Cuba for emeralds," Pedro added. "And suppose Escudero tips off the Governor to confiscate them?"

The teeth disappeared. Coria scowled. "What. are you aiming at?"

"That you're no fool. There's nothing in Cuba for you. What do you owe to this pack of traitors on the ship, when I can show you the way to Cortés's favor and five hundred pesos?"

Coria fingered his chin. "For what?"

"For helping me stop the *Gallega.*"

"I see. Cortés gets back the emeralds. That puts you right with him. And I get the reward. Who pays it?"

"The General." Pedro was taking a big risk and knew it.

Coria lifted a skeptical eyebrow.

"Hombre!" snapped de Vargas. "Can't you see what it means to Cortés to shut off news to Cuba? As to the money, it's a good deal more than you'd ever draw from Velásquez with Escudero coaching him. That's plain."

Coria still pinched his chin. His eyes in the dim light looked like a speculative cat's. It was maddening to think how much depended on the rascal's decision: the march across the mountains, perhaps an empire. He sat weighing the pros and cons. But Pedro sensed a wavering in him. The logic was unescapable. Escudero, the Governor's man, would never forgive what had happened tonight. Whereas, Cortés . . .

"How do I know he'll pay?"

"My word for it."

"Humph!"

In spite of the darkness, Pedro could feel the approach of morning. He made a supreme effort.

"If he doesn't pay, you can have my share in the horse, Soldán. That's worth more than five hundred pesos."

"Look you, de Vargas," Coria pondered, "I'm not in this for my health. It's sometimes convenient to forget promises. What security do I have—"

"Lord in heaven!" chafed Pedro. "We haven't a notary here. What can I give but my word? You've heard of my father. I swear by his honor."

Coria hesitated a moment, then nodded. "Done!" he said. Producing a key, he unlocked Pedro's shackles, then fetched him his arms, sword and poniard, from a rack in the corner. "Now what's the plan?"

"We'll take the rigging. Cut as much as we're able. Smash the compass. If we can delay the start by an hour, we have them. When they get on to us, head for the ship's boat. Are you ready?"

Coria delayed. "We'd better take the emeralds."

"We've no time to break open the chest—not to speak of noise."

"Of course not. But, you see, we don't have to break it open."

To Pedro's amazement, he drew the vanished key from his pocket and unlocked the coffer.

"But I thought—"

Coria smiled. "As it happened," he murmured, "I threw away the wrong key."

"*Vaya, vaya!*" grinned de Vargas. "That's a lucky mistake."

"Isn't it? Of course the honor of a cavalier would have kept me from taking advantage of it. I'm from Old Castile, señor."

One by one, he looked wistfully at the stones, then handed them over.

"Well, there you are. You're the proper guardian. They're pretty but useless to a poor man—at least this side of the Ocean Sea. That was a good point of yours. No market."

Pedro dropped the emeralds into his belt purse and made sure of the buckles. It seemed unreal that he had them at last in his possession. It remained now to restore them to Cortés. Before that, he realized, some grim work might lie ahead.

Shoeless and silent, the two men crept up the companionway to the poop deck. The stars had paled within a faintly spreading twilight. It was the hour between winds before the offshore breeze started. The water lay quiet and bodiless as the sky. As yet, possibly because of the late conference that night in the cabin, no one seemed awake on the ship except the dim figure of a seaman, who stood drowsily by the rail on the main deck. Pedro nodded toward him and tapped his dagger hilt. Within the next ten minutes, at the first breath of the wind, the ship would come to life, and no time could be lost.

Like shadows, he and Coria stole down to the main deck, careful to avoid the bodies of several sleepers. Crossing to a position behind the man at the rail, Pedro struck suddenly with the loaded pommel of his knife. The fellow crumpled without sound and was eased unconscious to the deck. A sleeper stirred and grunted, then fell silent again.

Pedro heard the gnawing sound of Coria's knife at the mainmast halyards, then the jerking movement as he cut smaller cords. Hurrying forward to the foremast, de Vargas dealt with as much of the tackle as he could reach, and turned back along the deck, heading for the binnacle astern.

But now figures were sitting up or scrambling to their feet. A hoarse shout sounded. The forecastle doors swung open. A man loomed in Pedro's way as he sped toward the quarter-deck, gave an astonished challenge, was shouldered aside. Meanwhile Coria had found an ax and was raining blow after blow upon the compass when de Vargas reached him.

"That's enough," urged the latter. "Make for the boat. I'll hold them in check. Give a call when you're aboard."

Coria darted up the steps to the poop deck. Sword in hand, Pedro covered the retreat.

"Back there!" he shouted, as the first surge came at him, "I don't want to hurt any of you. . . . Well, then, take it: *Santiago! Cortés!*"

The cry rang out across the water. His sword leaped. A man fell back, cursing and clutching his shoulder.

In the surprise, the bewilderment and uncertain light, it took a minute for the crew of the *Gallega* to organize an attack; but Escudero's orders were prompt and to the point.

"Get to the deck above him," he yelled. "Cut him off. Chepito! Tobál! Fetch your crossbows. Look alive!"

Armed with a pike, he led the frontal attack himself. But de Vargas bent aside the thrust of the weapon and sent back a blow that tilted Escudero's badly adjusted helmet over one ear. Then, turning, he leaped up the steps to the poop deck, just as two men, climbing from the side, reached the same level. The bend of the rail above the stern offered a slight protection. Within it, Pedro stood at bay, while the circle of men thickened around him. From below, he could hear the thumping sounds of Coria settling himself in the boat. The latter's treason had not yet been discovered, and a shout went up for him.

"It's like the dog to let us do the fighting," Escudero raged. "Where in hell is he?"

"Here!" came an answer from the water. "Good-by, Juanito. Give the devil my compliments when you meet him. *Santiago! Cortés!* . . . Ready, de Vargas."

The confusion of this surprise gave Pedro his chance. Vaulting backwards, he dropped to the water, shot under, rose to the surface, and in a few strokes reached the boat. Helped by Coria, he floundered into it. In the next moment, Coria bent to his oars.

197

It was a heavy yawl boat and moved by inches. Awkwardly fumbling, Pedro managed to ship a pair of oars for himself.

"Pull," Coria panted. "Pull your arms out."

The pandemonium of cursing on the *Gallega* suddenly stopped. In the half-light, Pedro could see a couple of figures at the rail and the silhouette of the crossbows. Deadly weapons at close quarters, they now had a perfect target at only a few yards.

"Don't miss, Tobál," sounded a voice.

Something buried itself in the thwart at Pedro's side, pinning his breeches to the wood and searing his leg like a hot iron. The next moment he found himself in the bottom of the boat, writhing around a center of pain in his head. He heard faintly the shout that went up from the *Gallega* and Coria's fierce oath. Everything turned black, but he did not lose consciousness. He was still aware of the anguish in his head and of Coria tugging at the oars. He was even aware that at one moment Coria flattened himself. He heard the thud of another bolt. Then the faintness passed, but the pain throbbed and leaped, so that he ground his teeth together to keep from crying out.

But now another sound came from the *Gallega,* the creaking of blocks and tackle. Evidently a lighter spare boat was being launched.

Pedro forced himself up.

"By the Lord!" muttered Coria between breaths. "I thought you were sped. How is it with you?"

Mumbling an answer, de Vargas groped for the oars. He could not see because of the blood streaming from his forehead, but he could make shift to row after a fashion.

"No use," Coria grunted—"three yards to our one."

The jerky, professional oar beats of the pursuers creaked rapidly nearer. Pedro drew his sleeve across his eyes and in the now definitely clear light caught a glimpse of the boat less than a hundred yards off.

"Can you swim, Coria?"

"Yes, but swimming's no good. We've a better chance if we fight."

Pedro shipped his oars, struggled out of his doublet, and tearing off a portion of his shirt bound the strip around his head.

"I've got to see to fight," he muttered.

Coria kept on doggedly pulling at the oars. Both he and Pedro knew that they had no chance against the eight armed men. They were simply following instinct and training. The land wind now ruffled the water, cutting down their progress, though it hardly affected the pursuing boat. Pedro could see Escudero's gilded helmet in the bow, and the hard, intent face. If he did nothing else—A wave of dizziness struck. He grasped the thwart.

"Bring her around, Coria, so that they won't ram us."

The *Gallega* boat leaped forward. But suddenly, to Pedro's bewilderment, its oars stopped, tangled, began to back water. Escudero was no longer staring at him, but to the right; was shouting an order. The boat started to turn. In almost the same moment another longboat full of men came into sight, bearing down from the left in a converging line.

Coria dropped his oars. *"Gracias a Dios!"* he said devoutly.

In the stern of the oncoming craft, Pedro recognized Antón de Alaminos, Cortés's chief pilot.

"What's going on?" roared the latter, as the boats converged.

Pedro gripped the thwart. "Stop the *Gallega* from sailing." He stared blankly at Alaminos through a growing mist. "Signal the ships—"

The bottom of the boat swung up at him, and he crumpled forward to meet it.

XXXVI

WHILE THE *Gallega* was being dismantled and her crew put under arrest; while Coria, mounted on Escalante's own horse, galloped through the dawn to carry the news and earn his reward from Cortés; while later the captains at Cempoala sat in council, debating whether similar attempts at desertion to Cuba might not be made and how to prevent them, Pedro de Vargas lay half-dead in the fort at Villa Rica. Luckily or not—for opinions might differ—Antonio Escobar, Bachelor of Arts, physician, surgeon, and apothecary to the army, being but newly recovered from a flux, had not attended the troops on their diplomatic march to Cempoala and neighboring Totonac towns. He was therefore available for professional aid to the General's equerry.

It was not the policy of physicians at that time to take a cheerful view of their patients' condition. If the ailment was slight, the credit of curing it was greater; if the patient died, God's will had been done. Escobar frowned and sucked in his breath at the first glimpse of Pedro stretched on an Indian mat in a corner of the fort which had been thatched over with palm leaves. The camp followers, Isabel Rodrigo and María de Vera, fanned away at the cloud of flies settling on his head or sopped at the flow of blood with dirty clouts. Escobar frowned and sucked more ominously still when he searched the wound with his long fingernails.

"*Muy grave! Gravísimo!*" he gloomed. "What a gash! Six inches at the least. Look, women, I can put my thumb in it. And down to the skull." He tapped with his nail. "Perhaps *into* the skull. Not much hope, women—very little."

Under the probing and scratching, Pedro, though only half-conscious, writhed and groaned.

"Color of death," said Escobar, "cold sweat. Bad signs. I wish Father Olmedo were here. Juan Díaz is in the bilboes. Still, a priest's a priest and can give absolution even if he's a scoundrel. I'm afraid the good youth is beyond human skill."

"At least, Master, stop his bleeding," put in Isabel, "and the Lord love you. It's a pity to see him drain out like a stuck pig. A fine body of a man too. Look," she added, pointing to the cut straps of Pedro's wallet, "someone has got his purse already."

"Captain Escalante himself, the more shame to him—and he a gentleman," said María de Vera acidly. "He cut the purse after talking with Coria. I saw him myself. You'd think he might have left us some pickings for our trouble."

Escobar chucked her under the chin with a still bloody forefinger. "Bodies and purses are what you girls think about, eh? Well, I'll have to do my best for him, though it's a poor chance, God pity him!"

"Bah!" interrupted a stern voice from the doorway. "God pity you, Master Surgeon, if you don't do your best and if anything happens to him!" Juan de Escalante, commander at Villa Rica, took a step inside and stood arms akimbo, his smoldering eyes on Escobar. "If a soldier handled his job like you do yours, with a long face and a Lord-a-mercy, where'd he get on the campaign? Hitch up your breeches, man, and do your office. The glancing shot of a crossbow quarry isn't the worst. Stop his bleeding. You should have done it at once without dawdling."

"Hold me excused then if he dies of the shock, Your Worship. He's weak from the labor of the night—"

"Hold you excused nothing!" retorted the Captain. "Let me tell you, the General sets high store by this gentleman—not to speak of others. You'll have Bull García to reckon with if he dies. As for you wenches, I took the purse to keep your fingers out of it. Look alive now, all three, or you'll have the whip to your backs."

Thus activated, the medical staff of Villa Rica prepared to operate. From the doorway, Escobar bawled for his aide, Chávez, a lumbering giant of a man who could hold any patient on the table. He had been cleaning out the horse stalls and now appeared wiping his hands on his breech. Meanwhile, Isabel and María fetched a brazier and bellows, also a couple of irons and a pot of pitch. A rough plank table completed the equipment. Chávez then lifted the patient in his arms and dumped him onto it. Word had gone around, and several of the garrison, with a visiting Indian or two, sauntered in to look. The sun now blazed down; the cell-like space buzzed with flies and conversation.

"Strip off his doublet and shirt, *muchachas*," the surgeon directed. "He'll be the cooler. Probably he won't be needing them again anyway." Escobar shot a sulky glance at Escalante.

"I'll dice you for the shirt," said María to Isabel. "It's of prime linen. A pity he tore it."

But a cuff from the Captain silenced her.

"*Chitón, puta!*" he thundered. "Have you no shame? You'd cast lots on a dying man's belly for his shroud. I'd rather be nursed by buzzards."

In these circumstances, Pedro became deliriously conscious and looked wildly around. The heat, his half-naked condition, the Captain's cursing, the ring of faces, Chávez leaning over him, the glowing red iron, which Escobar at that moment held up and spat upon to test it, gave a scrambled impression of torture room, Indian sacrifice, and hell. He tried weakly to rise from the table, but Chávez shoved him back.

"Not so fast, señor! We haven't finished with you yet. We're only going to singe your head."

"*Misericordia!*" said Pedro faintly.

Escalante took a hand without bettering matters. "Ha, de Vargas! Pluck up a heart, *hijo*. It's this or bleeding to death, d'you see? What the devil! You're a lad of spirit." He tried a joke. "We're going to cure you if we have to burn your head off."

His words fitted in with the rest of the dream.

"Señor Captain"—Pedro struggled, his mind reeling—"if you were in this case, I would take your part. *Por piedad!* What have I done to be burned?"

"He rambles," said Escobar. "A bad sign. Is the pitch boiling? Good." He looked critically at the white-hot poker and added, "*Now.*"

Escalante seized one of Pedro's wrists and drew it back; a bystander gripped the other; Chávez shifted to the legs, spread-eagling him. As this was the position of Indian sacrifice, one of the Totonac guests uttered an *alala* in honor of the gods.

"Somebody take de Vargas by the throat," said Escobar, "and hold his head quiet. He'll jerk otherwise."

In a complete daze as to the meaning of his execution, Pedro commended his soul to God.

A soldier forced his head down. "Have a care, Sawbones. If you miss de Vargas and burn me, I'll cut your heart out."

The surgeon now lifted the glowing iron and jabbed at the open wound on Pedro's head; but, as it moved convulsively, he missed it by a half-inch. A cry and the smell of singed hair rose. The next attempt had no better luck.

"*Oh, Santa María de los Dolores!*" seethed Escalante, his face dripping. "If I did not have to hold the man's wrist, you besotted surgeon, I would bend that poker over your skull!"

With pursed lips, Escobar tried again and this time laid the white-hot iron squarely between the gaping edges of the wound.

A scream shivered up, and the hiss of blood. Pedro's body went limp.

"He's finished, by God," said Chávez, loosing his hold and running a sleeve across his forehead. "Look at him."

The patient's face was dead white. Several soldiers crossed themselves. The Indians nodded at each other in appreciation of the white man's capacity for inventing strange and cruel deaths.

"*As* I thought," remarked Escobar sagely. "You would not be warned, Señor Captain. Even my science cannot defeat the will of God. However, we've stopped the bleeding. You'll admit that it's a well-seared wound."

With startled eyes, Escalante had clapped his palm over Pedro's heart and stood for some moments in suspense. Then his face quickened.

"No, by the saints, he's more alive than you are!"

Escobar rose to the occasion. "Why not? To the man of true science, God lends a hand. Señor Captain, you may think that anyone could lay a hot iron on an open wound. Far from it. The timing must be right to the half of a second. If I had removed the iron too soon, the wound would not have been seared; if I had applied it a moment longer, the patient must infallibly have died. Know, Señor Captain, that the volatile liquor of the brain boils easily, and once it is brought to the boiling point—"

"Ho!" interrupted the Captain. "Right! Chávez, fetch me some liquor here. That native rot-gut *aguardiente* would raise the dead. We'll revive him, Master Surgeon, and then you can pour in the pitch."

Escobar protested. "The wound is well seared, Your Worship. Pitch is unnecessary."

"Nevertheless we'll have it," Escalante declared. "It can't be too well seared, can it?"

"No, sir."

"Then we'll spare no pains. We'll have no twopenny jobs in this case. Revive the gentleman."

Somebody brought liquor in a cannikin, but Escobar dissented. "Sir, we can do it better while he is in a faint. No need to tax the strength of you gentlemen with holding him."

This opinion prevailed, though Escalante vowed that he thought no effort a trouble if it would benefit so gallant a cavalier. Pedro's wound was therefore plastered with boiling pitch, which had a vivifying result and brought him screaming out of his swoon to find himself once more facing the implacable Chávez.

"What cheer, sir?" roared Escalante, highly gratified. "Take heart. The thing's over. And I'll say this for Bachelor Escobar, that Galen himself could not have wrought a sweeter job on you. No leakage now. You're caulked as tight as a careened ship. . . . Here, drink."

He rattled the rim of the cup against Pedro's teeth and emptied its contents down his throat. Then, on fire inside and out, the patient, choking and purple, was again lowered to his mat; a clean bandage, donated from the tail of Escalante's shirt, was applied to his head; and the medical staff of Villa Rica took pride to itself.

"Unless," the surgeon concluded with professional reserve, "he should die from weakness and shock, which is in God's hands."

XXXVII

WEAKNESS, a touch of fever, and Escalante's cupful of raw spirits plunged de Vargas into a dreamy state disturbed only by the flies and Isabel Rodrigo's chatter. After a time the pain in his head grew more bearable. At midday he roused enough to partake of salt-pork stew and cassava bread, washed down by a dram of Spanish wine from the precious sacramental supply. He even felt restored to the point of chatting briefly with Escalante about the events of last night, and of reassuring himself that the emeralds were safe. Escalante reported that the mutineers were in irons and would doubtless hang upon Cortés's return. Pedro drifted back into sleep again.

He was awakened late in the afternoon by a breeze on his face which contrasted with Isabel's languid fanning, and looked up to see a huge, agitated fist, pumping air at him from a palm-leaf fan. Behind the fan, equally broad, loomed the sunburned face of Juan García. It was startling to see the latter's heavy eyes full of tears, while the wide mouth suppressed evident emotion.

"*Hola,* Juan! What the deuce—"

"Silence!" whispered the other, laying a forefinger on his lips. The movement of the fan redoubled. "Silence! Do not speak. Save your strength, by God, and all will be well. I have come but now from Master Escobar. He says your life depends on quiet."

"Pooh! It depends on keeping away from him. I'm all right. But what ails *you?* The headache? How did you get here?"

García's face expressed such urgent entreaty that Pedro fell silent. "For my sake, not a word more. If you must talk, let me do it."

De Vargas smiled.

"You know what I mean," said García huskily. He ran a thumb under his nose. . . . "Ails me? Lord! A broken heart. When I woke up this morning— Such a thirst, comrade! Such a head! The devils in hell could have no worse. I say, when I woke up to find what I had done— my insults to the good companions, calling them Indian dogs, drawing on Captain Velásquez de León, making a wild ass of myself, and how you left your post to bear me aid—it was a near thing that I did not take my cursed life. Then I find you gone and the camp in a dither and the General in a rage. Then comes Bernardino de Coria spurring with news for Cortés, who calls the captains to council. But the gist of it leaks out, and that you're for death. My fault, everything my fault! The grief of it unmanned me. I sat down on the lowest step of the pyramid and banged my head with my fists. I called down curses on myself to the admiration of the army. They gathered round but could give no comfort."

García bowed his head at the recollection; his great chest heaved. Then, fiercely agitating the fan, he went on.

"Who should come up but the General himself. 'Señor García,' he said, 'nothing cures grief but action. Take the horse, Soldán, and ride to Villa Rica. It may be you will find Pedro de Vargas alive. And you may carry a letter for me to Juan de Escalante. The army returns to Villa Rica tomorrow.' So I got up, and here I am. Praise to God! I don't deserve—I don't deserve to find you still—"

He pressed his lips together and turned his face. The fan drooped. After a pause, he muttered, "Do you think you can forgive me? It seems my luck always to be landing you in pickle. I'm not asking you to speak. If you forgive me, nod; if you don't, shake. Shake's what I deserve."

This time Pedro laughed.

"Forgive you? Not for a peso! Not for a thousand pesos! Never! Damned if I do!"

García stared back uncertain. "You sound almost natural," he faltered.

"Almost. What I want to know is how much pulque you drank. It's thin stuff. I might forgive you if you drank a gallon."

Vastly relieved about his friend's condition, García beamed. "Two gallons, on my honor."

"Liar."

"It may have been three—to judge by the weight in my head. So I'm forgiven?"

"Call it that."

García put down the fan. "That skull-and-bones, Escobar, gave me the fright of my life," he growled. "Led me to think he was just keeping you breathing. Said he couldn't vouch for you. I'll kick his rump. I can vouch for you, praise God! But as for pulque, beer, wine, and liquor! Señor! I hate and renounce them. God help the whoreson who tempts me even to smell 'em!"

"Amen!" said de Vargas.

"Moreover," added García, free now to turn to his own ills, "I renounce the horse, Soldán, and curse the rascal who sold him to us. A more blistery, jag-paced beast never hopped on four feet. It's a mercy I can sit on this stool talking with you."

A swinging step sounded in the courtyard outside, and Escalante entered. He held a couple of papers in his hand.

"Coria must have given a sad report of you, Señor de Vargas." Pedro was struck by a new ceremoniousness in his manner. "The General feared you might be dying. But Escobar and I took care of that, didn't we?"

He tapped the papers he was holding. "Here's news. A ship from Cuba, Francisco Salcedo commanding, just put in at San Juan de Ulúa but, finding us gone, is making now for Villa Rica. A runner brought word to Cortés. She may come in tomorrow. She carries Luis Marín, a notable captain, with ten other soldiers and two horses. So far, good; the rest is bad. It seems that the Governor of Cuba has been appointed *adelantado* from Spain. Governor wasn't enough; he's now governor-in-chief with the right to colonize these lands."

Pedro caught his breath; García muttered an oath. The news meant that if Governor Velásquez had received this right, they, the conquerors of the country, had no right at all *except under him;* it meant that the new colony of Villa Rica did not legally exist; it meant, above all, that Velásquez must have the lion's share of the winnings.

"The General won't take it lying down," exclaimed Pedro.

Escalante agreed. "No, things will be humming from now on. The treasure ship has got to leave for Spain at once, and no other ship must leave at all until we hold the entire country for the King—for the King and not for a beggarly governor. As the General says, it's a royal domain."

As the General says had become the stock phrase in the army for settling disputes.

"You made a lucky stroke last night," Escalante added; "but we can't always depend on luck. The next ship may get away."

Pedro ruminated. "You know, as the General says—suppose there weren't any ships?"

"Yes," repeated the other, "suppose there weren't any ships?"

García, whose wits moved slowly, burst out, "No ships? What a fool idea! No means of retreat or communication?" But he broke off. Gradually his eyes lighted up. "Hm-m. No ships? Yes, as the General says, *who can't retreat must go forward.* And there're plenty with us who would like to go back. The *Gallega* crowd aren't the only ones." He smacked his knee. "By the Lord, yes! No ships! Scuttle them! Have done with shillyshally! It's a great idea; it's the only idea!"

"Spread it around," said Escalante, exchanging a glance with Pedro. "See what the men think of it."

Because of his great popularity, García was a force among the rank and file.

"Think of it?" he boomed. "They'll think well of it, as Spanish hearts should. We'll go to the General."

By this time, García had forgotten—perhaps even Escalante and Pedro had forgotten—the origin of the idea. It was now García's idea. It would be imposed on Cortés.

"Take it up with the captains," García went on to Escalante. "I'll handle the men."

The other nodded. "I'll do that. . . . Which reminds me." He handed a sealed letter to Pedro. "From the General," he continued. "It was to be returned to him in the event of your death. . . . By gad, I'll never forget you on that table, de Vargas. . . . From what he wrote me, I think I know what's in the letter."

206

Still weak from his ordeal, Pedro broke the seal with a trembling hand. What would the unpredictable General have to write him? Pardon or censure?

SON PEDRO [It wasn't a bad beginning],

Bernardino de Coria has given me what I think is a reasonably true account of your conduct in last night's affair. What he said of himself, I do not wholly believe; but he has no reason for lying with regard to you. He tells me that you promised him five hundred pesos on my part if he would assist you in preventing the flight of the ship. He says that, ever loyal to me, he would have assisted you in any case, and I accepted this assurance with thanks —and complete understanding. He tells me also that you pledged your share in the horse, Soldán, for the payment of this money.

Son Pedro, in all this, you did well and showed great prudence and management. Have no fear for Soldán, as I gladly accept this debt. Indeed, I have increased it to a thousand pesos. Señor de Coria may have to wait awhile; but, alas, do we not all have to wait until the end of our venture?

De Vargas chuckled. If Cortés ever paid his promises, the Golden Age would begin again.

Now, as to the emeralds for His Majesty, I am informed that you recovered them and that Juan de Escalante has them in keeping, so that score is canceled.

Of your desertion from camp last night contrary to orders, I will say this. Disobey any order for the sake of the army, but let disobedience be justified by success. If you had failed last night, I would have hanged you. Since you succeeded in a way greatly to the profit of this company, I promote you.

Pedro's cheeks flushed; the writing swam in front of his eyes.

I promote you for energy and initiative to the rank of captain in command of exploradores *when we march inland. You will be the eyes of the army. And may your wound, Señor Captain, be speedily mended, for we march presently. May you long live to emulate the deeds of your father, whom God preserve!*

Pedro looked up into the round eyes of Juan García, fixed on him in suspense.

"Holy Virgin!" he breathed.

"Come, boy, what is it? Speak out. No great matter, I hope?"
"Congratulations!" bowed Escalante.
"Me, a captain!" gasped Pedro. "A captain!"

———— XXXVIII ————

NEXT MORNING Pedro awakened to the sound of thunder. Or was it thunder? Boom, boom, close at hand. Boom, boom, boom, from the harbor.

Cannon. An Indian assault.

He stood up dizzily. But there was no sound of haste in the fort, no shouting of orders—in fact, nothing; a peculiar silence between the salvos of artillery. Then, fully awake, he understood. The ship from Cuba.

The recent loss of blood had left him weaker than he could have believed possible. He tottered to the embrasure in his room, which opened on the harbor, and looked out.

Yes, there she came standing in, her painted sails billowing, a bone in her teeth as she cut the water, her gilded round-tops catching the morning light, the royal standard of Castile at her mainmast. Other pennants, doubtless those of Salcedo and Marín, fluttered from the fore- and mizzenmasts. Smoke puffs floated from her sides, and a moment later came the muffled report of her answering salute.

Pedro's eyes smarted. Here she came out of the sea, a token of the world beyond its vastness, the ever-remembered world in contrast to this remote country. Cuba might not be home; but it was closer to home, was settled and secure and Spanish.

Boom!

In the new responsibility of his rank, he questioned the waste of gunpowder. But who could blame anybody? Five months of silence, of wondering about this and that, as if the ocean stream were Lethe itself. And now a sail. News perhaps of friends and parents, perhaps even a few letters; news, however old, of Europe. Of course, residents of the Islands had most to expect; but—who could tell?—there might even be a scrap of news from Jaén.

He could see the whole garrison, men and women, streaming down to the beach; García by the side of Escalante; the gunners, who had fired the salute, running to catch up. A small boat was being got out. Several Indian canoes raced toward the new vessel. She stood pointed in as far as possible, no doubt for convenience in landing the horses. Then at last came the rumble of her anchors.

At that moment, Pedro would have given anything to be on the beach. But his head swam even from the effort of standing up; his knees turned to cotton; and he just managed to reach his mat before they gave way like springless jackknives.

After a while, unable to resist, he got up and dragged back again to the embrasure. He could see the horses, who had been swum ashore, shaking themselves and taking a few cautious steps after their long confinement. The garrison and the newcomers formed a milling group on the sand, the bright headpieces of the strangers and their new equipment contrasting with the makeshift rags and tags of the Villa Ricans. Even from that distance, the clatter of tongues drifted up. Pedro could make out the lean figure of Escalante, standing a little to one side with two other men, one of whom formed a vivid spot of yellow and crimson against the tawniness of the beach. That must be Salcedo, nicknamed "the Dude" on account of his elegance. García, who had friends everywhere in the Islands, had evidently found acquaintances and was embracing and back-slapping.

De Vargas regained his mat. No fun for him in any of this. Nothing to do except languish and swat flies until García remembered him enough to drop in with a few scraps of gossip. He wasn't presentable anyway. A bandage on his head; his torn shirt, carelessly washed, still looking pinkish from the bloodstains; his breeches, ripped by the crossbow bolt, gaping indecently; his boots lost in the *Gallega* adventure and not yet replaced; his toes sticking out through the undarned extremities of his stockings.

"A lazar," he reflected. "Nothing but a lazar! Dirty as a pig! Forgotten, while everybody else enjoys himself! Hell's blisters! I look like a captain now, don't I?"

The approaching sound of voices and footsteps announced the procession up to the fort. But in his self-pitying mood, the arrival no longer interested him. Then, to his surprise, embarrassment, and gratification, Escalante entered with the two officers from the ship.

He identified them at once: Francisco Salcedo, dark, splendid, and foppish, the typical overdressed adventurer with too elaborate manners; Luis Marín, squat, bowlegged from a lifetime in the saddle, red-bearded (as were many Spaniards of the time), pockmarked, and with strangely mild ways that concealed a lion's courage.

"Captain Pedro de Vargas, gentlemen," said Escalante, introducing them, and Pedro thrilled at his new title. "You will see that the gentleman is temporarily indisposed. A recent wound"—Escalante hesitated: it was not wise perhaps to mention the mutiny so soon—"has caused the Captain much loss of blood. No, sirs, not a duel. An affair of hotheads with whom Señor de Vargas had to deal almost single-handed."

Propped up on the mat, Pedro did his best to return the compliments and express thanks for sympathy in a way to do credit to Villa Rica de Vera Cruz. He noticed the surprise in Salcedo's expression at Captain de Vargas's rags and lamentable quarters. But civilities were exchanged with grace and decorum as if the palm-thatched cell had been a palace. Of course, when it transpired that this was the son of Francisco de Vargas, the surroundings hardly mattered.

Luis Marín said, "I had the pleasure once, sir, of watching your father at the jousts in Seville. A more accomplished man-at-arms I have never seen. It does not surprise me that his son should be promoted to a command at so early an age."

He spoke with the Andalusian lisp that reminded Pedro of home.

"It's a young army, sir. Captain Gonzalo de Sandoval and Captain Andrés de Tapia, whom you perhaps know, are little older than I. . . . But, señor, since you come from Seville, perhaps you have news. Jaén isn't far off."

Marín shook his head. "No, I've been a long time in the Islands."

The call ended, they left Pedro once more to his tedium and impatience. No news. At least it was a relief that the strangers had not learned of the disgrace of his family, which would not have improved matters here. But unreasonably he had hoped for some echo from Jaén, something to bridge the gap between here and there.

In his fretful mood, it irritated him that García didn't come. He ought to realize that a fellow hated to be left out of things and was keen to hear the small talk. But the big man remained jabbering in the courtyard. Pedro could hear the distant rumble of his voice above the come-and-go outside. At last he could stand it no longer and struggled up from the mat to the door.

García was standing at the opposite corner of what might be called the plaza in jocular conversation with two of the new arrivals—one of them a stocky, bearded man; and the other a youth, dressed in black, with a cap on his head, and a white feather.

"Popinjay!" grunted Pedro, conscious of his own damaged appearance. "I'll back the army to take some of that sleekness off of him. . . . Hey, García!" he barked.

The conversation broke off. The three looked around.

"*Ya voy!* I'm coming," García shouted.

Aware that he must be making a scarecrow impression and that it did not befit one of Cortés's officers to be clinging to a doorpost and bawling for attendance in full view of the fort, Pedro tottered back to his place with as much dignity as possible.

But even so, he did not hear García's lumbering footsteps crossing the courtyard. It was a lighter tread. Apparently he had sent the page to ask what was wanted.

"Now, my word!" thought de Vargas. "I like that!"

The youth appeared in the doorway.

"The Captain desires?" he smiled.

"Nothing," Pedro snapped. His distaste for the figure in black, with the square-cut bang, deepened. "Tell Señor García, if you please, not to hurry. When he's at leisure, if he can spare me a few moments of his attention, I should like to see him."

He broke off, staring at the boy's face. A sudden fear for his own sanity struck him. Perhaps that wound—

The youth took a step toward him and smiled again, a generous, unmistakable smile.

"God in heaven!" Pedro whispered. *"Am I dreaming?* Catana! Catana Pérez!"

"Didn't you really know me, señor?"

She sank down beside him. He continued to stare, open-mouthed.

"God in heaven!" he repeated. "Catana! *Querida mía!*"

He kissed her again and again on the mouth. His eyes devoured her.

She drew her hand gently across his face. "You've changed. All burn and bone. Even a beard. And wounded. I'll have to take care of you."

He caught her in his arms again.

"You aren't real, Catana!"

His strength gave way; but to cover up the weakness that crept back, he smiled.

"Talk about *me* changed! Look at you!"

Her tanned cheeks turned darker, and she raised her hands instinctively to her hair, which was now cut square like a boy's. She drew her legs under her.

"Yes, I'd forgotten. You get so used— You see, traveling on ships—"

"But how does it happen? When did you sail? Where's Hernán Soler?"

"Dead." She hesitated a moment. "He used me badly. I killed him."

Knowing Catana, Pedro was not too much surprised nor, indeed, greatly shocked. In her world and Soler's, knife blows did not call for much comment.

"Ah?" he said. "What then?"

"I came away with Manuel. We went to Sanlúcar. It was there we heard about you and Señor García sailing for the Islands."

She added that they had crossed with the spring fleet, had drifted to Cuba from Santo Domingo, and by chance had found Salcedo making ready the caravel to rejoin Cortés. What she did not mention were the eager questionings from port to port, the tactful management, which had induced her brother to sail from Sanlúcar, follow on to Cuba, enlist with Salcedo. Perhaps, as a matter of fact, she was not too conscious of it herself. She had simply followed a current that had inevitably carried her to Villa Rica.

"Well," he said, "you've come to the right place. Catana, there's a world of gold beyond the mountains."

He told her of Montezuma's reported treasure, and she listened intently as a man would listen.

"It'll be cursed hard to leave you again," he broke off—"now that you're here. We'll be marching soon. But don't worry: I'll see that you get your share. I'll bring it back to you."

Her familiar drawl cut in. "What are you talking about, señor? You don't think I came here to sit in a flea-bitten fort, do you?"

"It's a long road, Catana; there'll be plenty of fighting. A woman—"

Met by her smile, he realized that the protest was silly. Of course other women would march: Doña Marina, the Indian, whom Cortés would no doubt take as his mistress when Puertocarrero sailed; Catarina Márquez, who kept a sharp eye on her man, Hernán Martín; Beatriz Ordás, in love with the blacksmith, Alonso Hernando; a couple of others. They would cook and wash and fight. Only the pregnant or the dolls would remain at Villa Rica. He had been thinking conventionally.

"Well then, we'll make the campaign together."

Reaching out, he took her hand. It quickened his pulse to think of the bivouacs at night, some place apart, her head on his arm, his cloak covering them.

"You know what that means, *querida mía?*"

Only her eyes answered.

"God help the man who forgets that you belong to me!" he said.

Suddenly her eyes filled. "Belong to you?" She raised his hand and laid her cheek against it. "When I think of the days and the weeks and the months! Belong to you? What I never believed possible—"

She released his hand and stood up.

"By the way, I have good news. Before we sailed from Sanlúcar, a

Genoese felucca put in. It happened to be the one which carried Don Francisco and Doña María to Italy. The shipmaster said that they reached Genoa safely, and that before he left there again he heard that they had been well received by the señora your mother's people, in some other town called Florence."

Pedro clenched his fist. *"Viva!"* he exulted. *"Maravilloso!"* For a whole year he had been haunted by the dread that after all his father and mother might not have reached Italy. "We'll see now whether that infamous charge will stick! Our cousin, the Cardinal Strozzi, will attend to that. Catana, I wager that my father is even now in Jaén, reinstated, or prepares to return there—in triumph! When this venture is over—"

His thought was no longer in the New World; it swaggered through the narrow streets of Jaén; it was rich with the gold of Montezuma; it accepted the admiration of the townsfolk; it stopped by the wide-open doors of a certain palace. The miserable, half-finished fort, his rags and weakness, Catana herself, disappeared at the moment. When he remembered them, it was still with the background of Jaén in mind.

"Any other news," he asked with studied casualness—"I mean from Jaén?"

He thought he was being impenetrable, but she understood.

"It depends. If you mean about that fine lady you're in love with, you've never told me who she is. Who is she, señor?"

Taken aback, Pedro hesitated. Why shouldn't she know? She was bound to find out in the long run. There was no possible connection between the sunburned camp follower and the daughter of grandees. They belonged to two utterly different planes.

"The Lady Luisa de Carvajal," he pronounced reverently.

Yes, she had guessed that; she remembered the episode in church. Her throat tightened, and she found it hard to keep her voice natural.

"No, I heard nothing. We left the mountains not long after you. But I did hear about the Señor de Silva. Or perhaps you have too."

"What?"

"That he didn't die from the thrust you gave him; he was getting well."

"Esplendor de Dios!" Pedro straightened up. "That devil living?"

But his first amazement was followed at once by a wave of relief. God, after all, had not permitted him to commit the unpardonable sin. It was an act of divine mercy. Now he would have the pleasure of meeting Diego de Silva again and of killing him in an orthodox manner; that is, if Don Francisco let him live. Holy Trinity, how de Silva would writhe when the de Vargases returned to Jaén! Father Olmedo would be glad to hear of this.

"Well, well," he added carelessly, "I'll make sure the next time."

He returned to the more enthralling subject. Now that he had disclosed the name of his lady, it would be pleasant to talk about her.

"You have seen the Lady Luisa, Catana?"

"Yes."

"She is beautiful as a star. She accepted me as her cavalier and gave me a favor to wear. We are in a sense betrothed. When I think of the Blessed Virgin, I think of her, Catana."

But he got no answer, and the sense of oneness was gone. He sighed. Women were queer—as if Catana could be jealous of a star in heaven!

She let silence bury the topic, then remarked: *"Cáspita,* sir, I hardly know where to start upon you. I think the breeches should come first. Take them off, and I'll see what can be done with them."

The dream light vanished. He was back once more in his naked quarters at Villa Rica.

In good humor again, she opened her belt purse.

"See, I've brought two fine needles all the way from Sanlúcar, and good woolen thread. In this country, I wouldn't part with them for fifty pesos. Now let me have the breeches."

But this intimate operation was postponed by a sudden fanfare of trumpets in the near distance and by the growing rattle of horses' hoofs. The fort sprang to life; footsteps hurried outside.

"The General," said Pedro. "Our men from Cempoala."

Getting to his feet, he stood with Catana in the doorway, so that they could watch the entrance gate.

The trumpets sounded nearer, then the beat of the marching drums; then through the gateway appeared the *alférez,* Antonio de Villaroel, mounted on a tall dapple-gray and bearing the black standard of the expedition, then the General himself with Alvarado and Olid, followed by a group of lances. Behind them wound the long file of foot soldiers; pikemen, crossbowmen, arquebusiers, gentlemen rankers with sword and buckler; the cannon hauled by natives; the baggage; the rear guard. Pennons fluttered here and there; the sunlight glanced on helmets and breastplates. Upon entering the fort, the cavaliers showed the mettle of their horses, rearing and caracoling. For an instant it was Gothic Spain rather than Indian America.

"Viva!" Catana exclaimed. "What a brave sight!"

Cortés swung from his great horse, Molinero; embraced the two new captains, Salcedo and Marín, greeted Escalante. Then, his keen eye glancing everywhere, he caught sight of Pedro de Vargas and strode over to him, his spurs clanking.

"Ha, son Pedro! It's a fine scare you gave us, but I rejoice to see that you're on the mend. You had my letter? Good! Don't thank me: thank your patron saints."

His gaze took in Catana, sharpened, twinkled.

"And who is this—gentleman?"

Pedro caught the gleam in his chief's eye and, knowing his amorousness, resolved to forestall it.

"My very good friend, Catana Pérez from Jaén, Your Excellency. She arrived with her brother on Captain Salcedo's ship. *Mi amiga carísima.*"

His arm slipped from the girl's shoulder to her waist.

Cortés understood. He pinched Catana's ear.

"*Damisela,* we've been calling Captain de Vargas 'Pedro the Redhead.' He should now be called 'Pedro the Fortunate.' "

—— XXXIX ——

EVERY COMPANY has at least one buffoon, professional or amateur, a show-off and rattlehead, who plays the clown in order to attract notice, and prefers rather to be kicked than forgotten. In Cortés's army, this post was filled by Cervantes the Mad, formerly jester to Governor Velásquez. And because a fool says anything that pops into his mind, Cervantes sometimes expressed thoughts that wise men kept secret. It was he who had warned the Governor against his choice of Cortés to head the expedition and had told him frankly: "Friend Diego, rather than to see you weep over this bad bargain you have made, I want to go along with Cortés myself to those rich lands." So, one eighth a soldier and seven eighths a clown, he became jester to the army, a perpetual chatterbox and cut-up, getting sometimes a laugh and sometimes a cuff for his efforts.

Cervantes, then, led the march on August sixteenth, the long-projected march inland, through the hot jungle lands of Cempoala, toward the mountain rampart of Cofre de Perote—toward distant Mexico. He grimaced and capered and played an imaginary flute, strutting and high-stepping, ahead even of Pedro de Vargas with his scouts, while far behind him stretched the snakelike winding of the army.

"What's itching you, man?" called de Vargas, making ready with a handful of horsemen to cover the country several miles in advance. "Save your breath for the climb. What are you dancing for?"

"A parade, valiant Captain," proclaimed the jester, who had been fishing for the question, "a parade of fools, led by Cervantes the Mad! For when all the wise men of the army turn *loco*, it behooves a madman to lead them."

Since he was waiting for de Laris, one of the scouts, who was tightening his saddlegirth down the line, Pedro continued to lead his troop at a foot pace and drew the joker out to fill in time.

"Get it off your chest, *señoritingo*," he said, with a backward glance for the missing Laris. "What's the point?"

"Luckily something that you haven't the sense to grasp, friend Redhead."

"Why *luckily?*"

"Because Escudero and Cermeño got hanged for grasping it. Because Umbría's toes were chopped off and the stumps of them fried on Master Escobar's iron for the same reason. Because two hundred lashes apiece made mincemeat of the *Gallega* seamen's backs for the same reason. No, señor, heaven preserve you from sense, which is the worst crime in this army."

Sandoval, who was riding with the scouts, broke in. "Look you, rascal, that pack of traitors was gently dealt with, as you well know. Many's the general who would have hanged the lot of them for a less cause. If you talk treason, your own back will scorch, let me tell you."

Cervantes cut a caper beyond the reach of Sandoval's lance point.

"Exactly. And therefore I do not talk sense, *caballero*. I wouldn't talk treason for the world. Tootle-oo! Tootle-oo! A parade of fools led by Cervantes the Mad!"

He drew a laugh at that. "What do you call sense?" demanded Sandoval.

"Why, sir," replied the other, walking backward to face the horsemen, "my grandmother told me that he who throws all his gold through the window is not apt to have any in his pocket. It is an example of sense, sir—or treason, as you would say—but the old lady is dead and can't be whipped for it."

This allusion to the sailing of the treasure ship, now headed for Spain, was not lost on the cavaliers, who exchanged glances.

"She used also to say," continued Cervantes, "that he who climbs to the top of a wall should not kick over his ladder, as he might wish sometime to climb down again; or that he who scuttles the ship he arrives in may have to swim when he leaves. A bit of treason, sir, which in other parts of the world is called sense."

"By the Cross," swore Sandoval, who had been ardent in promoting the destruction of the ships, "if you lay your dirty tongue to matters above your judgment, I'll have it torn out for you. How, in God's name, were we to march forward, if the chicken livers like you were forever looking back to the ships—ha?"

Ortiz the Musician, who was riding next to Sandoval, shook his head. "No, I agree with El Señor Loco. It was folly true enough. Magnificent folly, sirs, which will be to our honor. But magnificence and honor don't make sense—do they, fool? Nor does song or music."

"Not to the dead, Señor Músico," grimaced the jester. "They mean nothing to the dead."

A moment of hollow silence fell, broken only by the sucking of the horses' hoofs on the wet trail. Sandoval scowled but did not find his tongue. Cervantes, prancing backward between the jungle walls on either hand, made the most of his opening.

"When we're properly cooked and served up on Indian platters, magnificence and honor will have changed their tune. The magnificent chops of Ortiz the Musician! The honorable hams of Pedro de Vargas! Bless you, masters, what yearning and toiling over mountains toward the grave! What panting for death! Elsewhere people strive to eat; here they strive to be eaten. *Viva* topsy-turvy! Tootle-oo! I dance at the thought of the banquets in Mexico. Here comes the procession of fools led by Cervantes the Mad!"

The hoofbeats of a horse at the gallop sounded along the column. Laris arrived in a spatter of mud.

"*Vaya!* At last!" exclaimed Pedro. "*Adelante,* gentlemen!" And to Cervantes, "Go tell your jokes to Cortés and see what he gives you."

Clapping spurs to Soldán, he bounded forward, closely followed by Sandoval and Laris, with the other riders at their heels. Cervantes leaped to the side in time but missed his footing and sat down in a thorn bush to the amusement of the oncoming pikemen.

While he picked himself up, grimacing and clowning, the ranks slogged by. Being a fool, he had expressed what others kept behind their beards or passed off in bravado. There was a ticklish feeling that morning in many bellies. Now and then, as the trail wound upward, men turned their heads to look back. At what? Nothingness. Beyond the woods and savannas lay a pale vacancy which marked the sea. But the sea no longer assured retreat; it denied retreat. It was an impassable gulf and dead limit. The familiar ships, that were a bit of

Spain, no longer rode in the harbor at Villa Rica. Gone. Destroyed because they were a temptation to weakness, a distraction from conquest. Destroyed by the very men who now could hardly realize that they had done so mad a thing. In front, thousands of feet high, the mountains. Beyond the mountains, what? The army had left itself no choice but to find out. One did not have to be a Cervantes that day to feel like a fool.

Returning several hours later from the reconnaissance, Pedro halted his troop on a spur of the foothills which overlooked the entire extent of the winding column, except where an occasional coil of it disappeared in the carpet of jungle. Some four hundred Spaniards, a throng of Totonac warriors in full feather panoply, and a thousand native bearers to haul the cannon and carry supplies, made up the line of march.

Pedro smiled at the thought of the impression it would have made on his father, used to the order and equipment of continental armies. Many of the soldiers wore native one-piece cotton armor, that looked like harlequin suits. Wear and tear and the tropical sun made sport of convention. Better to survive in a wadded suit thick enough to stop most of the Indian weapons than to stifle and grill in steel. The captains and a few swells clung to Christian armor and paid for prestige in sweat, but the rank and file chose convenience.

"Well," thought Pedro of the continental dandies, "they can have their finery. When it comes to fighting—"

He clenched his hand resting on the peak of the saddle. This was his army. He belonged to it, and it to him. Since last November, he and the army had matured together, on shipboard, in battle, on the march, and in camp, its varied elements kneaded into one by masterful leadership. He would not have exchanged his place in it, his stake in its adventure, for a captaincy in the King's guard. He was proud even of its shabbiness, that after a deed of foolhardy, breathtaking heroism in destroying the ships and thereby its only means of retreat, it did not look heroic. He was proud even of its fears.

"You know," he remarked to Sandoval, "I believe that there're a good many who think with Cervantes—but they're climbing the mountains."

"Aye," returned the other in his harsh, stammering voice, "they'll climb them. I've heard that there're other mountains beyond these before Mexico. They'll climb them too. They won't be stopped by the devil, if Hernán Cortés lives. Cowards? By God, I wouldn't give a louse for a man who isn't afraid. Fear's the spice that makes it interesting to go ahead."

"Philosopher!" bantered Pedro, rattling his knuckles against Sandoval's corslet. "Well, let's take our report to the General, though there's nothing to tell him."

They dropped down to the level of the column and headed toward the rear guard, which Cortés was overseeing at the moment. As they edged past the advancing file along the narrow trail, they rode among a shower of *ha's* and *hola's* because everybody knew everybody else in the company.

Pedro threw a kiss and a grin at Catana as he went by. She was holding Ochoa by the hand. He was one of Cortés's pages, a ten-year-old boy, whose young legs were already beginning to feel the strain of the climb. Gone were the relatively fine clothes of her arrival. Instead of the cap and feather, she now wore a battered steel cap, acquired from one of the older, less active foot soldiers who had remained at Villa Rica. A dirty tabard of Indian cotton armor hung to her knees and was drawn in at the waist by a belt supporting dagger and pouch on one side and a short, heavy sword on the other. She carried the usual foot soldier's buckler and cloak on her back. As it was the height of the rainy season, her broad-toed shoes, like everybody else's, were clogs of mud. Under the curving edges of the headpiece, her lean, sunburned features stood out sharply; but they softened and lightened at Pedro's greeting. She turned her head an instant to gaze after him.

Beyond the artillery and baggage, Cortés rode at the head of the pikemen and arquebusiers who formed the rear guard. He was in conversation with Olid, his second-in-command, and with Father Olmedo. At the General's stirrup walked Doña Marina, now his mistress and ever-ready interpreter, her handsome eyes fixed on him. A group of Totonac dignitaries, half-allies and half-hostages, wearing lofty aigret plumes and varicolored cotton garments, trooped along, remote as the stone age. Except for sign language, their one means of communication with the mysterious whites was Doña Marina.

Cortés was discussing the country, which began to spread out as the trail ascended. The tropical fragrance of the lowland rose like the perfume of an infinite garden.

"It lacks but the sugar cane and orange," he was saying. "We'll have them brought from the Canaries and Andalusia. Also draught animals." As usual his thought ranged statesmanlike far ahead of the present, creating, devising. "Then, with the maize, the maguey, cocoa, and other excellent new plants with which Our Lord has blessed this land, what wealth, sirs! On my honor, I often think the produce of the soil will outvalue the gold of Montezuma." He made a gesture with his arm. "Look you, is it not like Andalusia, only richer? And these mountains in front recall the Sierra Morena and the Sierra de Granada, only they are higher. And I hear that beyond are *mesas* and *barrancas* like to those of the Castiles, only wider and deeper. We must call it New Spain, señores, the fairest name for the fairest country."

"Yes," nodded Olmedo, *"Nueva España.* And may it have all the good of the old with none of the ill!"

"Amen to that, Father! So it shall be, with the help of *Nuestra Señora* and *Santiago.*" He broke off as Pedro and Sandoval reined up. "Well, de Vargas?"

"All clear, sir, to the distance of four leagues. We noted a good camping place, well-drained and with ample water, at about three and a half leagues."

"How easily defendable?" Cortés asked. It was characteristic that even in allied and friendly territory, he marched (as the phrase went) beard on shoulder.

"Sheltered from attack on three sides, Your Excellency."

"Doña Marina," Cortés smiled at his interpreter, "ask these caciques how far three and a half leagues from here would make it to the town they call Jalapa."

"About halfway from Cempoala, my lord," she answered in her faltering Spanish, after inquiring.

"Well then, Cristóbal," Cortés directed Olid, "we'll pitch camp at the place de Vargas suggests. Give your orders. As for you, son Pedro, keep well in advance of the army. It is likely enough that the Indians this side of the sierra mean peace. But we'll not gamble on likelihoods."

With mock innocence, but loud enough to be heard by the men in front and behind, Ochoa piped to Catana when Pedro had disappeared, "Is Captain de Vargas your lover, Aunty?"

He was a precocious imp, a parentless waif, whose bright eyes and chubbiness had got him a place in Cortés's household. He handled the General's cup, carried his prayer book, and played a small role in the ceremony with which Cortés, who knew the value of display, liked to surround himself. Bullied by the half-dozen older pages and spoiled by the soldiers, he was in a fair way to perdition when Catana, who was fond of children, took him under her wing. She avenged him furiously on his persecutors, frowned the company into reticence when talk grew too broad for young ears, shielded him from such spectacles as the hangings and floggings that followed the Escudero mutiny, made him say his prayers, spanked or mothered him as the case demanded. On his side, Ochoa worshiped her; but, being a brat, he could not resist teasing.

"He is your *amante*, isn't he, *Tía?*"

Her cheeks flushed, and she pretended not to hear. Several of the men sniggered.

"Tut, tut, boy," grinned one of them, "what do you know of such matters? Why do you think he is?"

"I saw him kiss her," Ochoa announced, delighted to be the center of attention. "I saw her on his knee."

"Is *that* all? Didn't you see anything else? Let's hear, *niño.*"

The man, Alvaro Maldonado, nicknamed *El Fiero,* the Tough, was in the rank behind. Catana looked back.

"Nosing into my affairs, *bocón?*" she drawled.

There was a quality in the drawl that Maldonado did not miss and that no one missed. The grins vanished and eyes shifted in other directions. From the day of her arrival, every man in the army knew instinctively that Catana could take care of herself. The skill she displayed in knife-throwing at a target strengthened this conviction. Moreover, the respect that surrounded her did not lose in glamour by the report of Hernán Soler's killing, a deed which Manuel Pérez was too proud of to conceal.

The tough one mumbled something about a joke between pals.

"That's all right, *chico*," she answered. "I'm *camarada* to any man in this company, but my personal concerns are nobody's shuttlecock. Do I make that plain? . . . As for you," she blazed at Ochoa, "take yourself off. You're no boy of mine any more. *Vete enhoramala!*"

Shut into outer darkness, the little fellow trailed a pace or so behind, his face growing longer at each yard. In the end, he crept up and tugged at her sleeve.

"Aunty," he whispered, *"Tía querida."*

But she paid no attention except to brush away his hand. He fell back again, and after a minute his face crumpled suddenly. He burst into a thin wail, stumbling along, his fists in his eyes. Catana set her jaw and stared at the neck of Diego Ponce in the rank in front. El Fiero, who had a fellow feeling for Ochoa, gave him a nudge and a comforting wink, but the child flung away and at last disappeared.

During the next halt, Catana wandered off for a drink at a neighboring brook and was surprised upon getting up from her knees to find Ochoa at her side. He carried a stout switch in his hand and had just finished smoothing off the twigs with his knife.

"Tía querida," he said earnestly, "if you whip me, can't I be your boy again? Here's the strongest switch I could find—one that will hurt. Please—"

221

She stood a moment between tears and amusement.

"Please," he said anxiously, thrusting the switch on her and un-buckling his belt. "I'll be quiet as I can. You won't be mad with me afterwards, Aunty, will you?"

She caught him in her arms, and when he began to cry she kissed both his eyes.

"*Muchacito!*" she smiled. "Little rogue! *Tunantuelo!*"

"I ought to be spanked, *Tía querida*. I'll never tell on you and Captain de Vargas again."

The trumpet sounded the march. They went back to the trail hand in hand.

XL

THAT EVENING on the mountain slope, within the radius of his company's campfire, Botello the Astrologer, who was said to know the future, sat deep in thought. Perhaps his mind was on nothing more remote than the evening meal which Catana and some other women were preparing, or perhaps he was absorbed by the cloudy outlines of things to come. In any case, the men, awe-struck by his rapt expression, left him alone.

He was a grave, dignified person, highly respected in the company not only for his arts but for his knowledge of Latin, and because he had been to Rome. He did quite a little business in horoscopes. Even Cortés, who had a strain of superstition mingled with his hard-headed qualities, now and then consulted him. Though technically an astrologer, Botello leaned somewhat toward necromancy. It was certain at least that he had a powerful talisman, an uncanny leather thing, half a span long and shaped like a man's genitals, which, according to rumor, the devil in person had given him. It contained flock wool—for what magic purposes no one knew.

As the steam of cooking rose, Botello's expression changed and his eyes brightened. It was an excellent smell, more savory than usual. Two caldrons, hanging on a crossarm between forked stakes, bubbled over the fire and were stirred by Isabel Rodrigo; while Catana had charge of turning the spits, which supported several game birds, since known as turkeys, and a haunch of venison.

At first, the Spaniards, scornful of heathen messes, had clung obstinately to their salt pork, cassava bread, oil, and fish. Now, educated by

222

hunger, they put up with Indian fare, though sighing for beef, pig and mutton, onions and cabbages. The country provided game; even dog and lizard were edible; and such vegetables as maize, squash, tomatoes, and peppers, with an assortment of outlandish fruits, did well enough, if the deliciousness of cheese, olive oil, garlic, and other products of home, was forgotten.

His mouth watering, the wizard got up at last and walked over to Catana.

"Aren't those birds done yet, Mistress? They seem broiled to a turn."

She smiled at him. "They are so, Master; and if you'll hand me your dish here quick before the others, I'll do my best for you. But you won't refuse me a small favor afterwards, eh?" She smiled again still more engagingly. "White meat. Gravy."

"What favor?"

"Oh, nothing much. I'll tell you later." She smacked her lips and prodded one of the birds with her dagger point. "Look you—a plump wing and breast. Also a crisp, juicy slice of the venison."

Botello melted. "I'll do anything I can for you, *doncella*." He produced a small trencher from his side pouch. "Be generous with the fowl, *amiga mía,* and don't hold back with the meat. I die of hunger."

Catana winked, "It's a bargain then?" And in justice to others, she called, *"Está bien,* Isabel. Sound off!"

Whereupon, Isabel beat the iron sides of a caldron with her iron ladle and roused a hornets' nest of men with trenchers who swarmed down upon her and Catana. But already the promised wing and breast had dropped into Botello's dish, with a dripping slice of venison on top. Amid hoots of protest and shouts of *"Oiga!"* and *"Diga!"* the astrologer, like a lucky dog with a bone, carried off his prize to a quiet spot where he could enjoy it undisturbed.

Gradually the clamor and melee dwindled under the expert carving of Catana and ladling of Isabel. Silence closed in, while teeth and knives were busy. The fires grew brighter as darkness came on. A half hour later, Catana sank down by the side of Botello, finished the turkey leg she was eating, threw away the bone, and wiped her hands on the grass.

"Well, Master, did the meat taste good?"

He was in fine humor and belched contentedly.

"Excellent, Catana. I've had no better victuals in this country— though, of course, fowl should be cooked in oil with sprigs of garlic."

"Of course," she assented.

223

"And top it off with a goblet of cool white wine. Eh, *muchacha?* I wonder if I'll ever drink malaga again."

She was surprised. "Don't you *know* whether you will or not, señor?"

"Yes," he replied, becoming professional. "Of course I know. When I said 'I wonder,' it was a fashion of speech. And now, Mistress, *taz a taz;* one good turn deserves the next. What did you want of me? Your fortune in the stars?"

She shook her head. "No. That wouldn't help. If it's a good fortune, I want to be surprised; if it's bad, I'd rather not hear about it."

"Sensible," he approved. "I can tell you that Hernán Cortés himself shares your opinion. He has forbidden the casting of horoscopes until we are established in Mexico. A wise decision," Botello added gravely, "for the stars are troubled and give but two-edged answers. I would have stretched a point to please you, Catana, but I am glad to obey the General's orders. . . . Well then, what is it, if not a horoscope?"

She was silent a moment, looking down and plucking nervously at the grass blades next to her.

"I'm in love," she said finally in a low voice.

"Is it possible!" exclaimed Botello, smothering a smile in his beard, for Catana's relations with Pedro were well-known in the army.

She clenched her hand against her breast. "Ah, Master, so much in love! I want the love of a certain gentleman. I want it more than anything in the world. Good fortune or bad, if he loves me, nothing else matters."

The astrologer struggled with amusement, but his trade had taught him to keep a straight face.

"Deal plainly with me, Mistress," he said in his hollow, professional voice. "Does not Pedro de Vargas love you?"

"I don't know," she faltered. "He *likes* me—yes. I please him at times. But does he *love* me, Master; will he ever love me one tithe of my love for him? He thinks of battle, gold, fame—*por supuesto,* being a cavalier. I wouldn't have him different. He dreams of a fine lady in Spain. Let him dream of her. I don't ask—"

Her voice caught. Sentimentally Botello laid his broad hand on hers. "*Qué deseas?* It is life, my dear. Captain de Vargas is of noble blood. You cannot expect too much."

"I expect nothing," she burst out. "I only long for him. That isn't forbidden, is it?"

"You're his *querida,* aren't you?"

"I pass for it in the army. He calls me so. But not yet—not once—" She broke off, confused, and stared down.

224

"Hm-m," pondered the other, admiring her graceful figure and keen face in the half-light from the fire. "That's odd. But why do you come to me?"

She looked up eagerly. "Because I'm ignorant. You're learned and wise and have secret powers. If you could give me a charm, Master, something that would win him, that would make him care—"

With an eye to the proper effect, Botello drew himself up. "*Canastos!* Do you come to Master Limpias Botello, the pupil of the great Novara himself, as if I were a witch-bawd, selling philters! *Qué impudencia!* Have you no respect!"

Then, seeing her duly abashed, he allowed his ruffled feathers to settle and added kindly, "But, *vaya,* I've been young myself. You're a good wench and mean no harm. Besides, I admit that the meat was plentiful and well-cooked. It is true that I know charms so powerful that they would draw Prester John himself to your bed. But these are trifles compared with the works of true magic. I make no account of them."

Catana refused to be put off. "Just one, *Maestro mío,*" she pleaded humbly. "One little charm."

He appeared to hesitate. "Well, then, in your ear, for these are secret matters."

Catana drew close.

". . . change of the moon," he whispered. ". . . put some in his meat or drink. It is infallible."

The age believed in strange nostrums, and Catana, who had been brought up to the facts of life, listened as if to a medical prescription. But for all that she turned hot.

"Yes, I've heard of it," she nodded. "A girl in Jaén told me about it after she married her lover. But, señor, I could not do that, not for anything. He is too high-born a gentleman. It would put a taint upon him. It would shame him. He would never forgive me."

"He would never know, *muchacha.*"

She straightened herself. "Señor, I shall never do anything that I would be ashamed to have him know. . . . Is there nothing else?"

The magician, as if in deep thought, combed his beard. Half-honest, half-rogue, he believed in his arts, but knew that in this case no art was necessary. Therefore, why not make the most of a sure thing?

"Well," he admitted, "to tell the truth I have one charm unequaled in the world. Woman, it is mighty enough to win you the person of any man alive." Botello sucked in his breath. "It is a locket ring from Rome given me by Señor Incubo himself. But it is worth a fortune. I could not part with it."

Poor Catana sat hopelessly coveting this marvel, her eyes hungry.

"I have saved it these many years to sell to a queen," he went on. "It is singular of its kind. Ten thousand spells, I repeat ten thousand separate spells, each one potent enough to exact the obedience of ten demons, went into the making of it. I hope that the consort of the Great Montezuma will buy it of me for a ton of gold. It is worth no less."

"Could you not lend it to me, Master," ventured Catana—"only for a day?"

"No, I cannot part with it. But because of the good victuals and your kindness—" Botello hesitated. "Yes, by God, I will show it to you, though I keep it secret."

Fishing in his wallet, he brought out a small sack of cheap jewelry used in trade with the Indians, and fishing again in this he produced a ring.

It was a big gilt ring with a flashy glass ruby covering the top of it, and so contrived that the setting opened as a locket. But the reverent manner in which Botello handled it between thumb and forefinger, the way he tilted it to gleam in the firelight, robbed Catana of all judgment. She eyed the treasure with a famished longing.

"See," remarked the diabolic Botello, touching the ruby, "this is known as the Rose of Delight. I slip it on your thumb. Wait—in a moment you will feel the heat of it, such is the power it holds."

And such is the power of suggestion that Catana actually felt her thumb grow warm. She turned it here and there, unable to take her eyes from it.

"Wonderful," she murmured.

"Isn't it! A miracle. *That's* what I call magic!" said Botello. "To complete the effect and turn its energy upon the desired person, the locket must contain some element of his body, such as hair or nail parings, but he must not know of this."

Catana drew a tiny embroidered pouch of linen from beneath her doublet. It was hung around her neck with a cord.

"When I cut Señor de Vargas's hair," she explained, "he didn't know that I saved a little to put next my breast. I said three Pater Nosters over it and three Aves, but the charm did not work."

Catana removed several strands of hair from the pouch and coiled them inside the open locket of the ring. "Just to try," she explained with deep guile. "You know, my thumb's warmer than ever."

Equally guileful, Botello nodded. "Of course. What do you expect?

226

. . . Well, take out the hair and give me back the ring, *moza*. I'll let you see it again sometime."

"No." She drew away, clenching her hand. "Señor, let me keep it tonight. Do me that grace, *caro Maestro*. If you will, I'll mend and wash for you; I'll save the choicest bits in the pot. You know I have no gold, but do that much for me, and I'll be grateful to the end of my life."

A fine actor, Botello looked astounded, then touched, then wavering.

"By God, Mistress, you're a very robber. The ring is priceless. Washing and mending, say you! Pot scrapings, in return for the loan of a treasure! Well, go to, have it your way. Curse the fool I am! A kind heart will always be my undoing. Keep the ring for tonight but guard it preciously. If you lost it, the seven curses of Incubo would shrivel you up like an onion. Go to, you're a minx!"

She caught his hand to her lips. "Thank you, noble Master! Thank you from my whole heart! I'll guard the ring every moment . . ."

Absorbed in it, she got up and stood with her hand extended, then wandered off, still admiring the beautiful talisman.

Botello relieved himself with a chuckle. For the loan of a cheap ring, he would journey to Mexico in much greater comfort. The best of it was that for once he had no misgivings as to the outcome of his sorcery.

XLI

THE first day's march had not been hard, and the rain fortunately held off, so that the men lingered awhile about the campfire before sleep. A good supper, the lighter air of the upland, the beginning fragrance of mountain pine instead of the cloying jungle perfume, had put the company into a happy, relaxed mood. It was one of those evenings remembered by old soldiers when the toil and anguish of war have been forgotten.

Perhaps a dozen fires were scattered among the trees, their light intercepted by random figures. Now and then snatches of song rose above the hum of voices. In Catana's platoon, one of the men had packed a fiddle on the march and now sat scraping a tune out of the strings. When she reappeared from her talk with Botello, a shout went up for a dance.

"Hey, Catana, give us a *zarabanda*. There's a bully girl! A right Castilian dance for the honor of Jaén! Shake your hips!"

"To hell with you," she protested, still absorbed by the magic ring. "After slogging all day and cooking supper for you lazy *cantoneros* to boot, do you think I'm going to kick up my heels to amuse you? By God, have another think, vagabonds."

"Oh, come, *hermanita*," urged Manuel Pérez, who was proud of his sister's proficiency and liked to show her off. "You're not so jaded as that. Give the boys some fun. You used to work all day at the Rosario and dance all night. Are you getting old? Here's Magallanes the Portuguese, who swears we have no dancers in Spain to match the Lisbon *bailarinas*. You'll not swallow that, I hope."

"Sure she won't," someone agreed. *"Viva la Catana!"*

"Please, *Tía mía!*" yelled the boy Ochoa, eager for the glory of his patroness.

"You ought to be asleep, naughty," she answered. "Wait till I catch you!" But yielding to the general demand, she shrugged her shoulders. "All right then, if you've got to have it. Pest take you! You can't expect much from a dance in hose and breeches."

She had laid off her coat of padded armor which covered the suit she had worn on landing, now patched and stained. Her reference to breeches drew a fire of good-natured ribaldry, to which she replied in kind.

"But who's dancing against me?" she demanded. "It takes two for the *zarabanda*. Do I have to invite my own partner, gallants? I like that!"

Clowning as usual, Mad Cervantes pushed forward, cut an exaggerated bow, and kissed his fingers. *"A su servicio, hermosa señorita!"*

An arm swept him aside before she could answer.

"You're dancing with me, Catana. *Qué diablos!* Do you wonder about partners when I'm on hand?"

Pedro de Vargas had come up in the half-light of the fire without her seeing him. For an instant, she could only stare openmouthed. The ring! Having momentarily forgotten, she now recalled it. The proof of its magic stood smiling in front of her, as if Pedro had dropped from the clouds. On any other evening, she would have thought nothing of this, because they often met after supper; but tonight—

"What's wrong?" he asked. "I'm not a ghost."

She forced a smile. "You startled me, señor. I hadn't seen you. Dance? *Hombres,* you'll see how we dance a *zarabanda* in the Sierra of Jaén. . . . Remember the steps, señor?"

Pedro nodded. "I think so. Three times forward, three times back, eh? Leap and circle to begin with. It'll come to me."

Catana called to the fiddler. "Juanito, give us a tune."

The onlookers made space, some men sitting down, others standing. The firelight played on bearded faces, steel caps, and tattered clothes. Catana saw that Botello had joined the group. He smiled triumphantly at her, as if saying, "What did I tell you?" And she nodded solemnly. Juanito, the fiddler, sawed out an air, in correct time but wheezy melody.

The saraband of the period had little or nothing in common with the later slow and stately court dance of that name. It was a folk dance wild, violent, and none too proper. Bystanders clapped the beat with their hands or shouted a cadenced *aha* as the tempo quickened. Of course the theme of the dance was male pursuit and female flight, the latter being far from coy and never successful.

As Pedro advanced, broad of shoulder, light of foot, his eyes wide and intent on her, she swayed back, coquettish in retreat, then minced forward as he retired. Back, forward; then circling each other in the center, face to face. She pirouetted out of his arms. Again. Again. *Aha!* He swung her clear of the ground; she landed nimble as a cat, in perfect time. *Aha! Aha!* The dance burst into flame.

Flying sparks of thought crossed her mind. She recalled herself dancing at the Rosario, the ring of drab faces. A night's work. Lord in heaven! Compared with that, how wonderful this was! Here in this strange, wild land, one of the army, dancing before comrades, dancing with Pedro de Vargas! Life at the peak!

A dance may be swift or slow; but vibration, not movement, is the soul of it: vibration, an electric tension. Now at last she could feel his desire for her, no longer casual or partial, but concentrated and demanding. She could feel it in the gentleness of his arms even though they swung her high, in the burning of his hands on her hips, in the appeal of his eyes. She knew that she had never danced so well, with such abandon. The rhythmic clapping and shouts of the onlookers, the mad sawing of the fiddler, were an intoxicating accompaniment.

The dance grew wilder from stage to stage. *"Bravo,* Catana! Well done, de Vargas!"

Then suddenly, as it reached its crescendo, a numbing thought struck her. Mechanically she kept the beat, but her veins ran ice. Her pride turned to ashes.

The ring! It was not she who drew him to her; it was not her love. If she had been Isabel Rodrigo, the effect would have been the same. Pedro de Vargas was not free to choose; she had made him a puppet of the hundred thousand demons attached to the ring. They had brought him here, infused him with blind desire, robbed him of his will. And that was her act—to unman and cheapen him! What she had done seemed to her all at once a blasphemy.

The dance whirled to an end; she sank back in surrender across his outstretched arm. But even as he kissed her, she prayed, "Blessed Virgin forgive me!" and her lips were numb.

"Are you tired, *querida mía?*"

"No."

A congratulating mob surrounded them with much back-slapping. Suddenly Botello felt something thrust into his hand.

"What's this, *muchacha?*"

"The ring," she whispered. "Take it back."

"But you can have it until tomorrow."

"I never want to see it again!" she breathed. "I hate it. . . . But don't worry, I'll keep my share of the bargain."

She turned away, leaving him baffled by the riddle—deeper than his science—of the female mind.

At once she knew that the charm was broken. The recent passionate current between her and Pedro had stopped. It did not surprise her that almost at once Luis Avila, one of Cortés's pages, summoned him to a conference of the captains; and he left her with his usual warm smile but nothing more. It had been the magic, not she, that had fired him. He did not really care . . .

Forlornly she took Ochoa's hand. "Time for you to go to bed, *niño.*"

"I don't want to go to bed."

"Yes, you do. We'll put each other to bed. I'll tell you a story."

Ochoa hesitated. "About *brujas*—witches?"

"No," she snapped, "not about witches. I'll tell you about the little Jesus."

"Aunty, I'd rather hear about the Witch of Jaén."

"Shut up or I won't tell you anything. . . . Good night, all."

She hid her heartache at the fiasco of the evening, accepted the renewed compliments of the platoon, which was breaking up for the night, and walked off with Ochoa to the improvised lean-to of branches that served as a shelter. Crawling under it, they took off their shoes in token of undressing, and were ready to stretch out on their cloaks.

"Your prayers, little one," she reminded. "We'll say them together. Your aunty has great need to pray *Nuestra Señora* for strength and forgiveness. I confess myself to you, *chico*. I'm a vile woman."

"Vive Dios!" hotly protested Ochoa in the idiom of the camp. "I'd plant my knife in any bastard that said so—"

"Hush! You mustn't talk that way."

"And if I'm not big enough," Ochoa went on, "there's plenty of others who are: Manuel, Captain de Vargas, the whole platoon." He threw his arms around her. "You aren't vile: you're good. Why are you sad, *Tía mía*, when you danced so elegantly?"

"Be still. We must pray." They kneeled, facing each other, with bowed heads. She covered his clasped hands with hers.

They were not the only ones praying at that moment. Few in the camp were so abandoned that they did not commit their souls to God before sleeping, as men under the shadow of death. Hard Manuel Pérez in his hut close by, Maldonado the Tough, Cervantes the Jester, Bull García, became children again with folded hands.

"*Pater noster,*" Catana and the little boy murmured, "*Qui es in coelis, sanctificetur nomen tuum . . .*" And when they came to the end, "*Ave, Maria, gratia plena. . . .* Mother of God, pray for us sinners, now and at the hour of our death."

They crossed themselves and remained a moment with bowed heads. She would confess to Father Olmedo as soon as possible. She would scourge herself with knotted cords to pay for the wickedness of that love charm. Meanwhile, she felt a dawning peace.

They crossed themselves again, and she kissed Ochoa.

"I want a story," he insisted. "Please, a fairy tale."

"All right, then, I'll tell you about the Sprig of Rosemary."

He approved. "That's a nice story." But his eyes drooped.

"*En otro tiempo,*" she began, keeping her voice as monotonous as possible. By the time she got to the handsome *caballero,* Ochoa was fast asleep.

With a smile, she drew his cloak around him, for the upland air had a chill in it, and then lay down at his side. The camp had grown quiet, except for random snores from various huts and the more remote tread of a sentinel.

She stared at the vague lightness that marked the opening of the shelter. Yes, she had done well in returning the ring to Botello. But why didn't Pedro care for her? What was wrong, when he had told her that first day that she would belong to him—yes, in front of the General himself? Was she less pleasing than a year ago? Or was he bound by a vow?

The moral scruples of a later age did not cross her mind. If they loved each other, if they could not marry, their union seemed natural to both conscience and society; even the Church looked the other way.

But he might be fulfilling a vow or a penance. Perhaps she could find out—

No! *Dios!* All at once she realized what the trouble was. Her man's clothes! The fact that she marched in the ranks. Who could love a *marimacho?* When he had known her in Jaén, she was suitably dressed and feminine. That must be the reason.

Yes, a tomboy, who could take care of herself too well, who could swear and ruffle it with Maldonado himself. Repulsive to a fine gentleman like Pedro de Vargas. How could he help comparing her with Doña Luisa de Carvajal, the fashionable and exquisite? Catana wilted. Tentatively she slipped her hands to her waist, gauging its size. No stays ever made could compress her muscles to Luisa's willowy perfection. If that was it . . .

Her eyes closed.

She found herself beautifully dressed in yellow damask walking on Pedro's arm between two lines of glittering people. The fact that every now and then they paused to do a few steps of the saraband seemed quite natural. She carried her head high, felt the weight of her hair, which had grown long again. She was magnificent, admired. She floated rather than walked. Pedro admired her; she read it in his eyes. Then suddenly the dream broke into fragments—pointing fingers, jeering faces. Looking down, she saw beneath her brocaded bodice that the skirt was gone. She was wearing her frayed black hose and muddy shoes. "Catana!" they hissed. *"Marimacho!"*

"Catana."

She was awake with a hand on her knife. Someone had touched her. A vague, dark form blacked the entrance of the lean-to.

"Catana."

She would have known that whisper among a thousand, and at once her heart began racing with an excitement that was almost fear.

"Yes, señor."

"Come. Bring your cloak."

Moving quietly to keep from waking Ochoa, she crept out. To her still confused mind, it seemed part of the dream; but the arms around her felt real, and his lips were warm.

"You were sleeping hard," he whispered. "Forgive me."

She stood quivering, or perhaps his arms trembled a little.

"I've made a hut for us on the edge of the camp, where we'll be alone. I have to be off before dawn, but we have a few hours. Come, I'll show you where it is. *Muchacha mia!*" he added still more softly.

As they went, his arm was around her waist, drawing her close. She leaned her head sidewards on his shoulder.

"And I used no magic," she thought. "And he cares for me. And he loves me. Dear God! He loves me."

He was saying, "It was hard to wait. The nights have been a fever of wanting you. But not there—I knew you understood—not down there in that crowded fort, in the heat and swelter. I kept thinking of the mountains, of you and me alone—the cool night. By God, it's been worth the waiting, *querida mía!*"

He stopped to kiss her, bending back her head. And loosening her doublet, he kissed her throat.

"For our first time, it had to be in the mountains. Is it not heaven, the smell of the pines, Catana? Doesn't it recall our own sierra? It's been worth waiting for. But after tonight, always, always—"

And she had been imagining foolish things, when for her sake, for the sake of their first night, he had bridled himself, and had withheld, as if she had been high-born, to be treated with the reverence of a cavalier for a *hidalga*. She flushed when she thought of the magic ring.

"I wondered," she said, "whether these clothes—Señor, if it would please you that I made myself a dress—"

"Why do you call me *señor?*" he protested. "Am I not your *hombre?* Are we not comrades in this venture? Why don't you call me by my name? Señor!"

She faltered, "I've always thought of you that way. Since you used to come out to the Rosario. It was a brave day for me, I can tell you, when you rode up on Campeador. I can't help thinking of you as lord. But if you want, I'll try to call you"—she hesitated—"*Pedro*, señor."

He stopped again to kiss her. "*Querida*, whatever you call me will sound sweet."

"I was asking about my dress."

"Your dress?" he repeated, smoothing back the square-cut bang from her forehead. "What dress?"

"Whether you would rather have me in shift and gown than in hose and doublet."

"Why should I?"

"Because I'm so rough—You're not listening."

"Yes, I am." He slipped his arm around her again, and they walked on. "Yes, what was it you said?"

"That I wished for some pretty clothes to please you in—a clean gown—not these slubbered tights. I would not have you too ashamed of me before the captains."

233

"Ashamed!" His arm tightened. "Show me a cavalier in the army who doesn't envy me. When the gallantest high-mettled wench in the two Castiles takes me for lover, when my blood sings with pride of you, sweeting, to talk about shame? Before anyone! *Por Dios,* you ought to be whipped! Skirts and shifts on the march? Let me catch you in them! Why not face cream and perfume? You're no doll and I'm no smell-smock. You're dressed to a soldier's taste. I love you as you are." He pointed his earnestness by drawing her closer. "Which doesn't mean that I won't gown you in silks and damask when the time comes, *muchacha mía.*"

So she had been wrong again. Her mannish costume, frayed and patched, the labor and stains of the camp, made her, it seemed, even more desirable to him. He loved her for her very self. She walked beside him dizzy with happiness, proud of his masterfulness.

It had come at last, the long hoped for, the often despaired of. It had come, like a lightning flash, when she least expected it. She ached with joy and a delicious apprehension.

They followed a ledge of the hill at some distance from the main camp toward a spot where the land fell abruptly in a kind of miniature precipice. Beneath them, far and wide, the tropical lowlands spread out in the diffused moonlight, exhaling on a faint breeze the spice of their endless fruits and flowers. To the south, like a giant phantom, rose the snow-covered mass of Orizaba, and to the north the heights of the Cofre de Perote.

"Here," said Pedro, showing a hut of pine branches which had been lopped from an overhanging tree near the edge of the precipice. They were supported by a head-high ridgepole, and the entrance between them overlooked the pale distance. "Does it please you, *amada?*"

"Please me!" she echoed. "What a beautiful place, señor! It is like a fairy tale." She tilted her head back, filling her lungs with the sweet air. "What a country! I love it more than Spain."

"Hardly that!" he smiled.

"Yes, really. It seems as if it belonged to us more, to you and me. I can't find the words—"

He led her through the opening of the lean-to. "I made a deep bed, Catana." He pointed to the mattress of pine twigs. "It smells sweeter than lavender. We'll lay our cloaks over it this way."

He pressed her to him, and she could feel, without seeing it, the flame in his eyes.

"Please," she murmured—"if you'll go out a moment, I'll call you—"

In the moon dusk of the shelter, her face, transformed by the moment, looked like a much younger girl's. The protective hardness which eighteen years had given her seemed dissolved. Her lips were half-parted, and the shadows around her eyes were deep and soft.

"You're beautiful, Catana," he said. "I didn't know you were so beautiful."

Raising her hand to his lips, he lingered a moment absorbed in her; then, leaving the hut, he stood to one side where she could barely see him outlined against the sky on the edge of the ravine.

She undressed and, stretching out upon the cloaks, drew a part of them over her.

"Yes," she called.

Her heart echoed his answering footsteps.

When at last he slept, with her head still in the circle of his bare arm, she lay wrapt in a content so perfect that she feared to disturb it by the least movement. She could not waste any of the wonder of tonight in sleep, the new, ineffable happiness of lying in his arms, the feel of his body against hers, the sense of her life lost in his. A content too deep to be troubled even by desire. In the full tide of youth and passion, they had given themselves to each other fully, until desire itself had become a serene languor. If he wakened and once more possessed her, she would be content; if not, it was equal happiness to be quiet, feeling the pulse of his arm against her cheek.

Outside, paler than the moonlight, she could see the snow-clad shoulder of the great volcano sloping beyond the doorway of the hut. Now and then a stirring of the night breeze entered like a soft caress.

If it could only last, she thought, if morning didn't have to come! The sense of passing time, which gives happiness its sharpest poignancy, alone haunted her—time who takes back all his gifts. She was enough versed in life to know that nothing lasts, that nothing is ever repeated. Morning would come, then other mornings, drifting her farther away from the pine-branch hut and from these hours.

The moonlight faded into darkness. Stars appeared, but they were late stars that gave a hint of dawn. It seemed to her that time quickened like a down-flowing stream. She must waken him at the first light, as he had to ride ahead of the army, and she stared fearfully toward the east; but the star-lit sky was still unbroken.

Then suddenly a couple of bird notes sounded in the woods, and after a time others answered. She closed her ears to them. They grew louder, more insistent. A streak of gray showed along the horizon. Finally, a horse neighed.

In her fear that he should come to blame because of her, she lifted her head at last and kissed him. He awoke slowly, felt her in his arms and drew her closer.

"It is time, señor," she whispered.

"Surely not."

"Yes."

"Well then, I'll steal a half hour," he answered. "I'm hungry for you, Catana—mad for you! I can never have enough."

"Nor I—But, señor, you should go—"

"*Bella adorada mía!*"

She yielded, felt once more the wave that canceled time sweep over them.

Then, still languid from his embrace, she saw him in the dimness of the hut, drawing on his clothes, buckling his sword.

"Until tonight," he said. "I shall think only of you; I shall feel your kiss on my lips. Until tonight!"

He disappeared into the faint gray outside. Some minutes later, she heard the distant sound of hoofbeats.

Then near and far the trumpets of reveille put an end to dreams.

XLII

DON FRANCISCO DE VARGAS had never been submerged nor, indeed, too much impressed by the grandeur of his wife's Italian relatives. Even when, a fugitive and exile from Spain, he reached Florence with Doña María, to be warmly received at the magnificent Strozzi Palace in the Via Tornabuoni, he accepted the welcome as an honored guest and not as a poor relation. The Strozzis themselves had been exiles some years before and knew the ups and downs of fortune. They knew also that a renowned soldier, the friend of the Great Captain's, and a kinsman of the Duke of Medina Sidonia, was inferior to no one. Indeed, it was a matter not only of charity but of pride to shelter so illustrious a refugee.

After kissing Clarice de' Medici, the wife of Filippo Strozzi, and after embracing Filippo himself, Don Francisco and Doña María received the condolences of their hosts with simple dignity.

"Aye, Cousins," said the old cavalier, "it was a base affront upon your name and mine. You must help me avenge it. The death of our daughter—" But it was unfitting that this supreme grief should be exposed to the liveried torch-bearers in the courtyard. "No more of that tonight," he added in his rusty Italian. And tweaking the ear of a small boy who clung to Madonna Strozzi's skirts, "Who's this for a brave young colt? Piero, eh? The name of our own son. Let's have a look at you, *figliuolo*. Lord bless me! A fine lad! Big bones and keen eyes! Here's one who will do you honor, Cousins." A prediction borne out by the later fame of Piero Strozzi.

Don Francisco tossed a handful of small coins—the last in his purse—to the flunkeys in the courtyard and, offering an arm to his hostess, limped up the steps into the palace.

There, installed in a suite of high-ceilinged, frescoed rooms, he and Doña María spent most of the year that followed the flight from Spain. Through the deep-set windows, they could look out on the Duomo, which dominated Florence even more then than now; and in the other direction they could see a part of the church of Santa Trinità, where Doña María's Strozzi ancestors lay buried. On pleasant days, they could stroll between palaces down to the Arno or ride for a change to the beautiful Strozzi villa, *Le Selve,* near Signa. At Cousin Filippo's princely table gathered the beauties and wits, the financiers, scholars, and soldiers of Tuscany. After the jog-trot life of a Spanish provincial town, like Jaén, the return to Florence was more than a little bewildering until, in Don Francisco's phrase, one got back the hang of it.

But yet, overshadowing the Strozzi hospitality, Florentine magnificence, and even the suit for redress which was being pushed in Rome and in Spain, anxiety about Pedro haunted the elder de Vargases day and night.

During August, they waited confidently for his arrival and of an evening liked to make plans for his career. Should he continue on to France and to the place awaiting him in Bayard's household? Should he be trained in the brilliant court that surrounded Lorenzo de' Medici and his young French bride? Don Francisco argued for the former, Doña María for the latter. She had her eye on a daughter of the Valori family, with a good dowry and good looks, who was just the match for Pedro if the proper finesse and influence were used to catch her. With this in view, she cunningly urged that if Pedro was to become a soldier he could do no better than attach himself to Giovanni de' Medici of the Black Bands, a young man who was already the foremost captain in Italy.

But August passed, and after it September. The expected arrival did not come. Plan-making languished or sounded forced. In October the unspoken questions could no longer be kept back. Had Pedro fallen in the mountains of Jaén? Had he perished in some other way? Had he been recaptured by the Inquisition?

At night, in their square, canopied bed, Don Francisco would gently say, "Take heart, wife. No weeping. Now, now! All will be well." But often a tear would steal down his own lean face.

Once when he tried to distract her by talking of their petition to the Pope, she burst out, "Why should we care, who have lost our children? I'd rather die and be with them. What does vindication matter to us now?" And he could find nothing to reply.

It was noticed at this time that, when he considered himself alone, Don Francisco stooped and he leaned hard on his cane, though he was quick to draw himself up, underlip out and chin defiant, if he found that he was watched.

Four months had passed since the escape from Jaén. Late autumn, cold and damp in the poorly heated, cavernous rooms of the palace, shut in, and with it despair. Excusing themselves to the company below, conscious of the pity which confirmed their own fears, Señor de Vargas and his wife retired early these days, and would sit for a while on either side of an ineffective olive-wood fire keeping vigil over memories.

On one of these evenings, casually (as such things happen), a servant knocked at the door, entered, and bowed.

"A letter for Your Excellency. His lordship has paid the messenger."

Used to letters regarding his suit in Rome, Don Francisco received this one without much interest and, when the servant had gone out, laid it on the table. "I'll read it in the morning," he said. "Candlelight strains my eyes." But noticing the weathered look of the paper and the half-washed-out handwriting, he brought it a moment closer to the flame.

"What is it, sir?" asked Doña María, struck by the sudden intentness of his face.

Without waiting to break the wax that held the edges of the paper together, Don Francisco ripped them apart and spread out the letter with trembling hands.

"What is it, sir? Can't you answer? Have you lost your tongue? What's wrong?"

"From Pedro," he said in a half-voice. "From our son."

She was out of her chair and at his side in one movement, as if her plump little person had taken wings. She snatched at the letter.

"Nay, wife, nay—we'll read it together. Nay—"

Heads close, they followed the labored, schoolboy writing, their lips forming the words as they read.

"Honored Señor, my Father—Honored Señora, my Mother—"

It was the letter which Pedro had written at Sanlúcar and had entrusted to the master of the Genoese ship. Delayed by storm, forgotten in inns, sold by one carrier to another in speculation on the reward which the Strozzi address guaranteed, it had at last found its way from Andalusia to Tuscany.

When she had finished reading, Doña María dropped to her knees and lifted her clasped hands. "I thank Thee, O God! Sweet Lord, I thank Thee! Blessed Madonna, I thank Thee!"

Don Francisco reread the letter. To hide his emotion, he uttered a loud "Humph!"—but could not conceal the ring in his voice. "So that's it! The cursed Islands after all! And with that ne'er-do-well son of Martín Cortés too! A profitable venture they'll have of it no doubt! If I could get my hands on the young rascal, I'd paint his back."

María de Vargas broke off her thanksgiving. "Out upon you!" she scolded. "Shame on you for an unnatural father! When we thought him dead! When he's alive and on honorable service—that is, if he is still alive! Nero, Señor husband, was a lamb compared to you. Attila—"

"Aye," the other interrupted, in such high spirits that he could not keep from teasing her, "I knew we would come to that. If you had not so bullied and be-Neroed me when I was laboring upon Pedrito's education he would have learned obedience; he would be with us now instead of gallivanting with scapegraces beyond the Ocean Sea. Where is Bianca Valori now, not to speak of our other plans?"

"It doesn't matter." Doña María resumed her pious ejaculations. "Saint Christopher, patron of wayfarers—"

"I'm so downhearted," continued the old gentleman, his lips twitching, "that I've a great mind to give over our suit to His Holiness."

Doña María's virtues did not include a sense of humor. She rounded on him again. "Are you mad, sir? Now more than ever we must press it, so that our son may return home in honor." But noting the gap-toothed smile which her husband could no longer restrain, she said reproachfully, "You're a rogue, my lord."

He burst out laughing. "Yes, wife, to be honest, the news makes me young again. I thank God for it humbly with all my heart."

And next day his restored bearing proclaimed good news even before he boasted that his son, Pedro, had joined a renowned captain, one Hernán Cortés, in a venture of conquest overseas, from which he could expect to return with great honor and profit.

The suit for rehabilitation against the charges made by the Inquisitorial Court of Jaén proved long rather than difficult, and long only because of the distance involved between various points in Spain and

Italy. Clarice Strozzi's uncle was none other than Pope Leo himself; another kinsman was the Cardinal Giulio de' Medici, the man of action behind the pontifical throne; Cardinal Strozzi and María de Vargas were cousins. As for Don Francisco, he was distantly related to the Duke of Medina Sidonia, and the charges against him reflected on the purity of that grandee's descent. It was manifestly absurd that the kindred of such Christian princes and potentates should be accused of heresy. Apart from ties of blood, which were stronger then than now, these charges became a personal affront to pope, cardinal, and duke, so that they had a selfish interest in quashing them at once.

In addition, a political event of the first importance incidentally favored Francisco de Vargas's cause. During the first six months of 1519, the rivalry between Charles of Spain and Francis of France for the then vacant elective office of Holy Roman Emperor absorbed the statesmen of western Europe. In this election, the Pope had an important voice, and a letter from His Holiness complaining of sundry wrongs and injustices done to his well-beloved son, Francisco de Vargas, a subject and pensioner of the Catholic King, would receive more immediate attention at the Spanish court than might otherwise have happened.

Thus, the Suprema of the Inquisition at Madrid, powerful as it was, found itself under far more pressure than such a trifling affair was worth. If the de Vargases, cut off from help, had perished in the prison or auto-da-fé at Jaén, there would have been no trouble. But since they had been allowed to escape and to bring into play such capital artillery as the Head of the Christian Church and the King of Spain, not to mention cardinals and grandees, the Suprema, inflexible as a rule in supporting the authority of its provincial tribunals, was prepared for once to admit a mistake. The holy Ignacio de Lora had been guilty of no injustice, but he had apparently been deceived. Though the de Vargases themselves were not without blame in violently resisting the representatives of the Inquisition, which would have established their innocence in due time, the Suprema graciously consented to overlook this fault, to nullify the charges, and to restore all property which had been confiscated. It did more. Glad of a scapegoat, it expressed official censure of de Silva's "ill-considered and intemperate zeal." And the censure of the Holy Office cast a shadow which a man's friends were apt to avoid.

But exoneration was not enough: the case demanded vengeance and damages. For this, the Duke of Medina Sidonia, Don Juan Alonso de Guzmán, whose pride of blood was involved, made himself responsible.

Since unhappily de Silva had by now sailed for the Islands to rejoin de Lora, personal satisfaction must wait; but a suit at law was brought against him, and the small remnant of his property which he had not invested in his overseas speculation was sequestered. It was well for de Silva's peace of mind that, while adventuring in the New World, he did not know of the disaster which had befallen him at home.

All this activity took well over a year, so that Pedro and Cortés's mad army had scaled the mountains and were engaged in the desperate battles of Tlascala before Don Francisco, restored in honor and fortune, made ready his return to Jaén. He met success as he had met misfortune, too proud to wear emotion on his sleeve. To his simplicity, the outcome of his suit was owing to its justice, exactly as the election of Charles V to the Empire illustrated the triumph of right over wrong. *Of course* the Pope would sorrow over crimes committed in the holy name of the Church. *Of course* Don Juan Alonso would leap to the defense of a kinsman. *Of course* His Caesarean Majesty, the seal of whose letter Don Francisco kissed before opening it, remembered his services to Spain and was graciously pleased to extend protection. The selfish motives—family pride and political expediency—which helped Señor de Vargas more than the justice of his cause, did not occur to him. He pictured the world in the whites and blacks of his own forthright mind.

The pleasant year of exile passed. Don Francisco gave the benefit of his military advice to the Signoria of Florence, and he held an honored place among the grave and reverend elders of the city. He lamented the death of the Chief of State, Lorenzo de' Medici, and marched in his funeral procession. He rejoiced at the election of the Emperor. But since peace hung on, and no war arose to distract him, his heart was in Spain, and he planned to sail from Leghorn in September, when a final event gave a memorable close to the sojourn in Italy.

The Strozzi family, together with Doña María, were spending the hot days of late summer at *Le Selve* near the Mount Alban hills; but Don Francisco remained behind in the city. He had numerous letters of thanks connected with the suit to finish before sailing, and he also enjoyed the company of other elderly gentlemen remaining in Florence, rather than the restless come-and-go of young people at the villa.

One morning in Filippo Strozzi's cabinet, he was dictating to his amanuensis when a page boy knocked at the door and, in reply to an impatient *"Adelante!"* came in. The boy looked excited.

"A gentleman to see Your Excellency," he stammered.

"What's his name?"

"He forbade me to tell his name, Your Excellency."

"Ha, did he so?" Don Francisco's eyes kindled; his lower lip crept out. "Well then, tell him from me that I am at this moment engaged and have no time for nameless callers."

"He's a high and mighty lord," the servant faltered.

"All the more reason for him not to be ashamed of his name and to show good manners. Does he think that I am at the beck and call of any lord on earth? Let him give his name or be gone."

The page lingered. "I'll be sworn he intends no disrespect, sir. It is but his whim. He bade me say, if you refused to see him, that he has been your ancient and mortal enemy and that he had yet to learn that Don Francisco de Vargas declines to meet his enemies on f   or horse."

"Now, by God!" exclaimed the other, forgetting his stiff knee and springing up. "That's a different matter. On those terms I'll see him and welcome. Is he armed?"

"Yes, Your Excellency."

"Good!" The old cavalier shook with delight. "Hand me my sword and belt there. Señor Nameless must be a right bold and gallant fellow to come defying me under the very roof of my kinsman. Is he alone?"

"Yes, sir."

"Then, look you, boy, if he gives trouble, I want no help. Let everyone stand back. Thank God, I have had many noble enemies in my time: but if one of them comes alone to meet me, I would not have him outnumbered or put to disadvantage. I do not care to know his name now, since that is his wish—but you say he's a gentleman and of good blood?"

"Aye, sir, I can vouch for him."

Don Francisco belted on his sword and loosened it in the scabbard. Then, walking over to a mirror, he smoothed down his sparse hair; righted his gold chain, so that it lay evenly on his shoulders and showed the pendant medallion to the best advantage; arranged the folds of his doublet.

"Who would have ever hoped for such a thing!" he exulted. "Here, on a dull morning! It's like the old days. Yes, a gallant fellow. My mortal enemy, eh? Well, well."

Beyond the cabinet lay a vast reception room, tapestried and with a riot of gods in fresco on the ceiling. Having advanced to the exact center of it, Don Francisco stopped.

"Tell the gentleman that I await his pleasure."

In the entrance hall at the far end of the room, he was aware of a flutter and crowding of servants. Then the throng divided; he heard the clink of a sword, and the caller entered.

He was a tall, slender man with wide shoulders and long arms. His hair, slightly grizzled, was straight-cropped on forehead and neck. He was clean-shaven, long-nosed, and had wide-set prominent eyes, with deep wrinkles at their corners. A bold chin, a big mouth, haunted by the shadow of a smile and framed by lines slanting down from the nostrils, gave a forceful, yet pleasant look to his face. Except for a heavy gold chain of the Order of St. Michael, he was dressed simply and somberly. Walking with the careless, long stride of a horseman, he rested one big hand on the hilt of his sword, and carried his velvet hat in the other.

At the first glimpse of the stranger, Don Francisco started, then stared; his lower jaw drooped. Then uttering a loud *"Vive Dios"* he left his post in the center of the room and limped toward the newcomer with both hands outstretched, his sallow cheeks glowing, incredulous joy on every feature.

"Monseigneur de Bayard!"

"Ha, Monseigneur de Vargas!"

Whereupon the two enemies embraced, while the servant who had first announced the caller relaxed in the luxury of a grin.

"I should have known it was you!" exclaimed Don Francisco, when he had caught his breath. "No other man on earth would so have presented himself. You always loved your joke."

"Joke, nothing!" laughed the Frenchman. "Aren't we old and mortal enemies, my dear friend? Didn't I knock out your front teeth by good luck at Gaeta? Didn't you lift me from the saddle at Bisceglie a lance's length on my rump? Was I able to sit in comfort for the next two weeks? And haven't we thirsted for each other's blood in a dozen skirmishes, sieges, and pitched battles? If you don't call that mortal, what is it? But, faith, Monseigneur," he added more gravely, "it warms my heart to see you again. The brave days—ha? Friends and enemies, few of us are left."

"My lord," de Vargas answered, "I could now gladly say the Nunc Dimittis for the pleasure this gives me. That the cavalier *sans peur et sans reproche* should visit my poor self overflows the cup. I have followed your fame for years but never expected to see you again in the flesh. I thought you were in Grenoble. I never dreamed—"

"Merely a chance," put in Bayard, glad to escape from compliments. "The King's business took me to Genoa and then to Florence. When I heard you were here, I lost no time."

243

Don Francisco emerged momentarily from his rapture. "Wine and refreshment for the Lord Bayard!" he called. "At once! . . . This way, sir, by your leave. We can talk more at our ease in the cabinet yonder."

Bravely he tried to keep step with the other, but fell to limping; at which the French captain stopped to admire the tapestries and covered up his host's embarrassment. But when they were seated in the smaller room, doors closed, wine, cake, and fruit at hand, what talk!

Of course, they spoke French, because Frenchmen are rarely at home in another language; but it was plentifully mixed with Spanish and Italian. Bayard's hearty, ringing voice alternated with de Vargas's lisp.

"And this fine son of yours, señor?" demanded Bayard after several minutes. "I've been expecting him for the past six months. Is he here? Perhaps he'll ride back with me." But struck by the other's expression, he hesitated. "I ask pardon. Is it that— Surely he accompanied you from Spain?"

"No." De Vargas cleared his throat. He was torn between loyalty to Pedro and a kind of professional shame. "No."

"You mean—I hope no misfortune—"

"No—yes. Monseigneur, in view of your generous offer to my son, I hardly know what to say. The truth is"—Don Francisco gulped—"he has been guilty of flagrant disobedience. We were separated in a trifling skirmish which attended our escape. He led the rear guard and, I confess, quitted himself well. He was under orders to rejoin me here. But, sir, when he could have begun the career of arms under *your* guidance, when he had *such* an opening, what does he do but cross the Ocean Sea and enlist with a crowd of irregulars on an expedition against the Indians! Monseigneur, this is the sad truth. I am ashamed." But loyalty got the upper hand at the expense of honesty, and he added: "I believe his commander, Hernán Cortés by name, is a most accomplished captain. The boy too shows promise in the management of his horse and his weapons. But alas—"

The *alas* did not need to be explained. It covered all that Pedro would miss: the tactics and niceties of traditional war; the ordering of vanguard, "battle," and rear guard; the developing science of artillery and musketry; siege operations against fortified places; the use of horse and foot; the etiquette and discipline of a regular army. Bayard understood. He and de Vargas were professionals discussing a youth who had turned his back on their code.

For a moment the Frenchman said nothing, but took a sip of wine, his eyes absently fixed on the cornice above Don Francisco's head. In some suspense, the latter awaited his comment.

"Mort de ma vie!" exclaimed the Great Cavalier at last. "Except for his disobedience to you, I think the young *gaillard* did well. Faith, yes! The more I reflect on it, very well—though I should have liked having him among my lances."

Don Francisco's eyes brightened. "How do you mean *well,* my lord?"

"Why, he sounds like a boy of enterprise and spirit. In truth, I envy him. . . . You say against Indians? What kind of men are they? Like Moors?"

"It may be," said the other dubiously. "I've heard that some, notably the Caribs, are brave and hardy."

"Well, then, what more would you have? *Nom de dieu!* Are we not at peace? Is it not better for a gentleman to fight than not to fight? Is it not better to fight something than nothing?"

"There's truth in that," de Vargas agreed.

"Is it not the first duty of a gentleman," Bayard continued, "to acquire honor? And will your son not gain more honor in war against enemies of our Faith than in riding at the quintain in my tilt yard or chasing beggarly outlaws in the mountains of Dauphiné? *Of course* he will. He may even learn new tricks of war from the Indians to use when he returns. Time enough then to polish him off. He'll be far ahead of whippersnappers who know all the rules, but have never practised them, for the trade of arms is only learned by fighting. You must forgive him, sir, for my sake."

De Vargas beamed. With this endorsement, Pedro's adventure took on a new aspect.

"You are kind."

"Kind, no; envious, yes. I am bored, my friend. I'm a dull governor in a dull palace—little better than a bourgeois man of affairs. I attend weddings and baptisms. I hold court. Pah! Indians, eh?" He sighed. "I'd like right well to show my pennon beyond the Ocean Sea."

After dwelling on the tasteless present, conversation turned to speculation on the next war. The growing friction between Charles of Spain and King Francis promised well. But even this topic could not keep the two old soldiers very long from the past. A roll call of names: Louis d'Ars, Pedro de Peralta, Pierre de Bellabre, Alonso de Sotomayor, Berault d'Aubigny, Pedro de Paz, a score of others—names once vivid but now already faded by the passing of years, names chiefly of dead men. Bayard and de Vargas smiled fondly over one or the other; rehearsed their deeds, discussed battles, forays, and retreats; laughed often, but with a solemn undertone, as those who speak of vanished faces and days. Killed at Ravenna, killed in Navarre, killed in the

Abruzzi, killed at Marignano. The friends of their youth, the very age into which they had been born—dead and gone.

In Filippo Strozzi's luxurious study, with its books and paintings and carved cherubs, the two clean-shaven, hawk-faced, medieval gentlemen sat like discordant relics. They were old-fashioned and proud of it. They glanced with scorn at these newer fashions: this fiddle-faddle about art and poetry and useless learning; these mental subtleties that questioned even religion itself; this non-military, pretty way of building houses that could not be held against attack; this wearing of beards, which were stuffy and impractical under armor. They belonged to a simpler, more childlike age, and because of it they loved each other like brothers.

Meanwhile, Francisco de Vargas worked up to a proposal. He viewed with approval Bayard's sinewy neck, rising pillar-like from the round opening of his doublet and looking almost too big for the head it supported. He admired the Chevalier's muscular hands and thin, whipcord legs spreading out comfortably from the chair. A fighting man, *por Dios!*

"Monseigneur," he ventured at last, "in other days we have never had leisure completely to finish any of our passages of arms. Unfortunately we were always prevented or separated in the heat of battle. I have never been able, therefore, fully to enjoy your prowess. You are here for a few days. No doubt I shall never again have the opportunity. Would it be asking too much if I begged you for a meeting with lance and sword on horseback? Suitable weapons and horses can be found. I should always be grateful for the chance to observe your skill."

Bayard's eyes danced. "Three courses, eh? A few strokes of the sword if lances are broken?"

"If you would be so good. It would greatly honor me, even if I can give you but poor sport—"

"Nonsense!" interrupted the other. "My dear friend, it's the other way round. I'm too old a fox to be fooled by modesty. You know that you overmatch me. But faith, I'm tempted! It seems an age since I've had a breathing."

Then suddenly he stopped. De Vargas would never know that his crippled knee and the twelve years' difference between them crossed Bayard's mind. The Frenchman's face clouded.

"No, *ma foi*. I remember. It's impossible. Maître Champier, my physician, forbids all violent effort because of a quartan fever I had in June. I gave him my word." He added gallantly, "And, between you and me, it's God's providence that I did. I could not stand another jolt to my rear such as you gave me at Bisceglie."

So the morning passed too quickly. Due at the Medici Palace for dinner, Bayard took his leave; but Don Francisco accompanied him a part of the way.

They walked arm in arm, their servants behind them, an equerry leading the Chevalier's hackney. And people made way for the two famous cavaliers with their grave, battle-lined faces, erect bearing, and fearless eyes. Even court dandies, curled and perfumed, were impressed and gazed after them. For both were distinguished men, remarkable in this, that while growing old they remained young and gallant and undefeated.

XLIII

SINCE THE EVENING when Pedro de Vargas had told her about the miraculous ray in church which appointed her his Lady of Destiny, Luisa de Carvajal had succeeded in renewing the miracle at other times. She was quite aware of her spiritual, waxlike beauty, that brought a look of adoration to men's eyes; and the ray, slanting down from the narrow window, lent her an aureole, which lighted up her face and toilet to the best advantage. Not even marriage interfered with this casual pastime. Alonso Ponce, who had now become her *galán* after de Silva's departure, was deeply impressed by the halo and called her "Lady of the Sunbeam," which she considered a charming and distinctive title.

On an October Sunday, nearly a year after her marriage and ten months since de Silva had sailed for the New World, she drove to church as usual in the Carvajal coach with her father and Señora Hernández. Settling down to prayer, rosary in hand, she wondered whether the beam of light would descend on her that morning and, if it did, whether Alonso Ponce was there to watch. Between Aves, she gave a touch to her mantilla so that it revealed more fully the rapt and exalted expression of her face as she gazed at the altar.

Outwardly the past year had changed her only as an opening rosebud changes toward maturer perfection; but it had taught her much. It had taught her physical love at the hands of a passionate and not too delicate lord and master. It had taught her the value of cynicism as a salve for bruised illusions. It had shown her the slipperiness of Fortune and that Señora de Silva, with her dowry gone, had a much less promising

247

future than Luisa de Carvajal. Certain inherited traits, which she shared with the Marquis, had unconsciously ripened: conventional values seemed to her more valuable. Returned from her husband's house to the same mirador in the same palace with the same duenna, she could sometimes forget overnight that anything had happened. But the full measure of what had happened lay in the fact that she no longer had anything much to learn from Antonia Hernández. In experience, she and the duenna were now almost contemporaries.

The Processional had started, when a movement in the rear of the church, an indefinable stir, half rustle and half excitement, brought her head around for a backward glance. Then her eyes returned decorously to the altar; but they no longer saw the baldachin or candlesticks or the gaunt painting of Our Lady and the Holy Child. She continued to see the tall figure of Don Francisco de Vargas advancing down the aisle with Doña María on his arm.

Of course, like everyone else in Jaén, she had heard of the de Vargases' return yesterday and of the great ovation given them; but the event had momentarily slipped her mind. She knew that Don Francisco had received an added pension from the Crown, and there were rumors that the city *Cabildo* or Chapter would name him Alcalde at the next election. Her father, who lost no time ranging himself on the side of success, had spoken glowingly of this great man, to whom he had always been a devoted friend.

"But, my lord," protested Luisa, whose memory was not yet trained to sufficient tact, "a year ago you felt differently. I remember you called him—" Overborne by the Marquis's heavy eyes, she hesitated. "Didn't you?"

"It is possible, daughter. If so, I trust that you understand why. A man even of my experience can be hoodwinked by a rascal. It is true that your unprincipled husband, who deceived the Holy Office itself about the de Vargases, deceived me. I am under a cloud and am poorer by your dowry of fifty thousand ducats in consequence. But if I ever expressed anything but admiration for the noble Don Francisco, you will charge it, I hope, to the proper account and not to mine."

Instinctively she agreed with him. Allowing for the difference of age, their minds ran in the same channel. She remembered de Silva as a brute, but that was not his unforgivable crime. If he had remained rich and in favor, she could still have respected, even if she did not love, him. That he was threatened with poverty both on account of the Duke of Medina Sidonia's suit and the reckless colonial venture, that he lay under the censure of the Santa Casa, was criminal. To be married to such a criminal filled her with rebellion. Meanwhile, the de Vargases, cleared of the crime of misfortune, stood in the sunlight and deserved respect.

"I understand, my lord," Luisa had answered.

Glancing sideways now, she watched Don Francisco and Doña María kneeling down on their prayer cushions. For a moment, it seemed only yesterday that she had last seen them with Pedro and Mercedes. That they were alone recalled the lapse of time. Their clothes too reflected the difference between now and then. They were dressed in honor of their triumph. Doña María wore a wimple of the finest silk and a purple dress embroidered with seed pearls. Don Francisco, though as usual in black, had on a Florentine suit of the latest cut, its fashionably enormous leg-of-mutton sleeves slashed with gold. Under his arm, he carried a wide velvet hat with a circle of plumes around the crown.

Luisa was so absorbed that she forgot about the ray of light and even about Alonso Ponce. Her thoughts wandered to Pedro. In that far-off world overseas, he might not even have heard of her marriage. Did he still regard her as his Queen of Honor? Had he kept the handkerchief she had given him? It was significant of the change that she now hoped he had and that others knew of it and linked her name with his. Except for de Silva and her father's blundering, life could have been so different.

In contrast to the coarse and bitter experience of marriage, her meeting with Pedro in the garden, as she thought about it, was fresh and poetic. She recalled—she almost recaptured—the delicious vibration of that evening. She could smell for an instant the odor of orange blossoms, could feel the romantic mystery of the night. And once more, as then, the conventional doll-like self, so docile and trained, stirred with new life, thrilled at the glimpse of an unfamiliar possibility. The months between faded like mist; she felt again the lilt and passion of that first love.

So far as conscious thought went, the change in the de Vargas fortunes did not influence her at this moment, however much the glamour of them actually altered everything. She had no skill in self-analysis. On the contrary, it seemed to her now that she had always been true to Pedro and that they had simply been victims of ill-chance. Yes, she had always cared for him, only for him. But what was the use of memory and desire? She could never have him now.

She stared at the crucifix and clicked her beads. In the ray of light, which found her at last, she looked sublimely tragic. Alonso Ponce, worshiping at a distance from behind one of the side columns, melted with feeling. Having a taste for letters, he compared her with Dido and Thisbe and started composing a sonnet.

But for once she was entirely unconscious of herself. Examining the future, she began to find glimmerings of hope there. What if her husband and Pedro should meet in the Islands? De Silva liked to plan what he would do to de Vargas when the time came; but she felt sure that Pedro could take care of himself. Or something else might happen to de Silva. Her father, never happy on the unpopular side, had spoken of having her marriage annulled. There were several good chances then of regaining freedom. Her face did not grow less appealingly sad, but her heart beat quicker. Without praying to the Virgin for any of this, her regular prayers became suddenly devout.

That day the Bishop took the pulpit himself and preached a sermon in Francisco de Vargas's honor. He chose his text from the first Psalm: *Et erit tamquam lignum . . . He shall be like a tree planted by the rivers of water.* It was a long and flowery speech. Luisa noticed that her father nodded emphatically at every pious compliment paid to de Vargas. But her mind kept straying, and it had time to stray a long distance.

After mass, a group of notables and their ladies thronged around the de Vargases on the wide platform at the top of the church steps. The Marquis de Carvajal paused.

"Enter our coach, daughter," he instructed. "I shall rejoin you in a moment. It is perhaps as well that you defer paying your respects to our noble friends until later."

Considering the name she bore, Luisa thought that it was most decidedly as well. It alarmed her that the Marquis, in view of his connection with de Silva, should make his way through the group surrounding the fiery old soldier. In something of a flutter, she and Doña Antonia tripped down the steps and got into their coach at the bottom of them; but they were near enough to see and hear.

They heard, so to speak, the hush that greeted Carvajal's approach.

"*Virgin santísima!*" murmured Luisa.

"*Chito!*" cautioned Antonia, listening intently.

Above them on the platform, the Marquis bowed no lower than a grandee ought to bow. His beard jutted at the correct angle. He spoke in a mellow voice, rolling the words, as if he were making a public address. The Marquisate of Carvajal, the ranking title in the province, spoke through him.

"Noble Señor and Señora," he said, "let me add my felicitations to the many that attend your safe return. I have lamented your absence as well as the cause of it. I rejoice that the *nobleza* of Jaén has regained its most illustrious members. Your other friends and I are proud of the distinction—"

But he got no further. Francisco de Vargas drew himself up, nose prominent, mouth scornful. His hand, at some distance from his side, rested on the pommel of his cane.

"*Con permiso de Vuestra Merced!*" he put in with his most ominous lisp. "Let us make no speeches, Don Luis. I haven't your flow and shall come to the point. You imply that you rank among my friends? *Quiá!* Hardly!" He raised his voice a little. "Be it understood that no friend or relative, by blood or marriage, of Diego de Silva is my friend. And if anyone chooses to resent it, I shall be glad to accommodate him. While you were lamenting my absence and the cause of it, you contracted an alliance with that same cause, the murderer of my daughter. Believe me, I shall not rest while Diego de Silva lives. And I would have no pretense between you and me."

Silence punctuated the end of this. The bystanders shifted uneasily and did not know where to look.

"Holy Saints!" Luisa breathed. "I knew it would happen! I hate quarreling."

But she underrated her father's good sense. Quarrel with a man who enjoyed the favor of pope and emperor? Ask the sunflower to renounce the sun?

Carvajal did not falter; he did not look disturbed, let alone rebuffed. His face wore only an expression of solemn reproach.

"Señor, far be it from me to thrust my friendship upon any man. In my life, it has been more often the other way. When your gallant son, for whom I have the deepest affection, called on me at night and roused me from sleep to ask aid for you at the time of your outrageous detention at the Castle, I then had the honor to rank among your friends."

De Vargas blinked. "My son?" he repeated. "I knew nothing of it."

The Marquis wagged his head. "When I received him like a father, when I gave him every comfort and counsel, with the assurance of my utmost help, I then took the liberty to consider myself your friend."

In the coach, Luisa exchanged a glance with Antonia.

Don Francisco felt at a loss. The cane crept in toward his side. But when he cleared his throat to reply, Carvajal lifted a restraining finger.

"One moment, sir. I repeat that I do not impose my friendship and I shall not intrude upon you again. But you spoke of an alliance I contracted. Señor, I would have you and everyone know that that alliance exists only in name. I have long since renounced all obligations connected with it, and I look forward impatiently to the day when it ceases to exist in name as it does in fact. I was the victim of deceit, and I consider my wrongs at the hands of Diego de Silva second only to yours. If, therefore, you hold me related to him in any real sense, you do me a great injustice. Sir, I bid you farewell."

Nothing could have been more impressive. The Alcalde, Don José Herrera, put in, "Gentlemen—" But Francisco de Vargas had already laid his hand on the Marquis's arm.

"By God," he said earnestly, "if that is the way of it, I cry Your Grace's pardon: I can do no more. I spoke as an unmannerly *patán* without knowledge of the facts. May you forgive the words I uttered in haste and error!"

"With all my heart," returned the Marquis, "with all my heart."

The two old gentlemen embraced, to the vast relief of their friends.

"I shall pay my respects in the near future," said Don Francisco.

"Nay, sir, the honor of calling first is one I reserve to myself."

Bows were made and hats flourished. The Marquis stalked down the steps, bowed again, and entered his coach.

"Ho-hum!" he sighed, settling back on the cushions next to Luisa. "A right gallant gentleman, though simple-minded. Not"—he hastened to add—"that it isn't to his credit in these two-faced days. A relic of the past."

Luisa, admiring her father's adroitness, remarked, "You managed wonderfully, my lord. But was it necessary to speak in public of my husband?"

"Eh?" said the other absently, and then, giving her his attention: "*Cáspita,* yes, it was necessary. Why else did I choose that moment? Listen, my child, when a man is drowning and has a grip on you, it is necessary to knock him soundly over the head lest he drag you under. Your Judas husband is in that case, for he has embarrassed the Santa Casa and incurred the hatred of the house of Guzmán. Let him drown. I was merely knocking him over the head. Understand?"

"Yes, my lord."

"Fifty thousand ducats of dowry!" The Marquis's voice reflected his pain. "Fifty thousand ducats!"

The coach jolted downhill to the tune of Carvajal's litany. Now and then Luisa or Doña Antonia meekly nodded. But before they reached home, the aggrieved nobleman fell silent. When he spoke again, the ladies were shrewd enough to fill in the gap.

"Harken, daughter, you'll call on Doña María de Vargas after some days. I'll rehearse you."

Luisa kept the eagerness out of her eyes.

"As you will, my lord."

XLIV

UNDER the circumstances, Señora Hernández felt justified in revealing a secret to the Marquis, which, indeed, had not troubled her, but which it had once been vital to keep. Following him into the garden that afternoon, she found Carvajal moodily seated on a bench and staring with vacant eyes at a stone satyr who leered from a clump of oleanders. She remarked, not for the first time, how much older he had grown during the past months. Sometimes he had an almost bewildered expression, the expression of a man whose rule of life has backfired and left him nothing in its place.

"Well?" he said abruptly when she curtsied.

"I have something on my conscience, Your Grace, which I think you should know," Antonia began. "It concerns Doña Luisa."

Carvajal bridled. "The devil! Something unpleasant no doubt. I hear nothing else these days. Even in my privacy, people hunt me down."

"No, Your Grace, perhaps this will not be unpleasant—I can't say— though you will have to forgive me."

"Get on with it then."

Antonia was taking something of a chance in confessing her laxness as a chaperon, but she guessed rightly that the substance of her report would be welcome enough to insure pardon. As she described the meeting of Luisa and Pedro at the garden gate, Carvajal's features relaxed into indulgent benevolence. "Ah, the little rascal!" he put in about Luisa. "The young rogue!" referred to Pedro. "Naughty señora!" he smiled at the duenna.

When she had finished, he said, "I am displeased with you, Antonia." The use of her first name was a sure sign of favor. "Will you sit?" And when she was beside him, he repeated, "Yes, much displeased. A very improper señora." He patted her hand. "But youth will be served, eh? And I have to admit that I'm glad of this. So the young rogue loves her, does he? A pity I did not know of it at the time. How much it would have saved, Antonia! You did wrong to conceal it, very wrong."

With a memory more discreet than Luisa's, Señora Hernández did not choose to remind him of the water which had flowed under the

253

bridge since then, nor of what would certainly have happened if she had reported the meeting at the time.

He began thinking aloud. "The de Vargases are not rich. Their claims to dowry would be modest; they would possibly ask little or nothing. No, not rich—but in favor. That's the point. . . . You're sure young Pedro's in love with her?"

"Most certainly."

"And she with him?"

Antonia remembered Luisa's confidence after church. "I'll vouch for that."

"Then it can be arranged. We'll have her marriage annulled. I still have money and influence enough for that. And we'll build up to a more promising marriage. Let young de Vargas's parents know how it stands between him and her, hint at a union, prepare the ground for his return. Finesse, Antonia, *sutileza!* I shall need your help."

"I'm Your Grace's servant."

Next day the Marquis called at the Casa de Vargas and began spadework. It was not difficult for a man of his address and courtly experience to make a favorable impression. Besides, he had his title and prestige as a grandee to help him. Without stooping to flattery, he could still flatter with a tone of voice, an approving nod, absorbed interest in Don Francisco's remarks.

He rejoiced that so expert an umpire as the Señor de Vargas had returned to preside at the approaching *fiesta de toros* in the market place, where twelve gallants of Jaén, armed cap-a-pie and on horseback, would take part in the then exclusively aristocratic sport of fighting bulls in honor of their ladies.

"I regret that your own brave son will be absent," said the Marquis. He added with a smile, "And so, I'm sure, does my daughter."

"Indeed?" returned his host vaguely.

"Yes. From all accounts, he would be apt to win the prize, and he wears Luisa's favor, I'm told."

"Indeed?" Don Francisco stared. "Your Grace knows more of him than I know myself."

The Marquis laughed. "These young people tell us very little, my friend. It seems that your son and my daughter were mightily taken with each other. The usual moonlight and vows. I did not learn of it myself until a short time since." He shook his head. "More's the pity. What a couple they would have made!"

Having sown the seed, Carvajal left it at that. He knew that Don

Francisco would report the last remark to his wife and that they would both discuss it. Dropping the subject, he took the natural opening it left him to talk frankly about de Silva and to gloss over the marriage. This he did to de Vargas's full satisfaction.

So, when Luisa and Señora Hernández called on Doña María a week later, the way was open. Formal and cold at first in the presence of de Silva's wife, Señora de Vargas thawed in favor of Pedro's sweetheart. Facing Luisa's wistful and appealing beauty, how could she help herself? *"Pobrecita!"* she thought. "So innocent! So young!" She thought too of how she had once hoped that Pedro would pay court to so high-born a girl, even if she seemed beyond him, and how she had scolded about that trollop at the Rosario, when, unknown to her, he wore Luisa's favor. Yes, what a fine couple they would have made! The seed was germinating, for regret at what might have been is the first step toward what may yet be.

In that interview, Luisa did not need to remember her father's coaching. She could be entirely herself—indeed, more than herself, with the strange eagerness and sense of liberation which the renewal of first love brought to her. During the past week, she had felt as if she were two people: the one, familiar and conventional, mincing through the round of small duties and pastimes that made up the dull life of Jaén; the other, new, surprising, unpredictable, given to dreams and to a secret expectancy. It was this newcomer in the form of Luisa de Carvajal who called on Doña María.

This was *his* house, *his* mother. She felt a timid deference, which her pearl-pale face, dark eyes, and sensitive mouth reflected perfectly. The place seemed to her haunted by Pedro's presence, though she had seen him too little to have more than an exaggerated and half-fanciful memory of him. She behaved conventionally, of course, but with a warmth of manner that Antonia Hernández considered excellent acting. Doña María began by calling her "señora" and ended by calling her "my child."

"And the *caballero,* your son?" Luisa ventured. "I suppose you have had no news of him?"

On the surface, nothing could have been more casual—only a polite query; but the soft distance in Luisa's eyes revealed much more and captured the mother's heart.

Doña María beamed. "Not from Pedrito himself, though we hope daily now to hear something; but yesterday we had a letter from our kinsman Don Juan Alonso de Guzmán, who resides near Sanlúcar. He writes that a ship, under the command of two gentlemen, Montejo and

Puertocarrero, has just arrived from Hernán Cortés—the captain, you know, with whom our boy is serving. He says that the ship carries a marvelous treasure of gold and jewels for the Emperor (whom God preserve) and that our Castilians have found a new land far to the west which is wonderfully rich and great. A continent, Don Juan writes, and not one of the islands. He writes too that the cavaliers in command of the ship told him that our Pedro is now a captain and much beloved by the General. They have also a letter from him to us. But would you believe it?—certain officials of the Casa de Contratación, who are friends to the Governor of Cuba, have seized upon the ship and upon the effects of these gentlemen so that they are little better than prisoners. Unless we soon receive the letter, my husband plans to make the journey to Sanlúcar himself and to have a talk with the Señores Montejo and Puertocarrero. He vows he will have that letter if he has to pluck it out of the beard of whoever dares withhold it . . ."

Luisa listened with glowing eyes. Lands of gold and precious stones! Pedro, a captain! She pictured him riding at the head of at least a hundred lances through enchanted country, where gold apples grew on trees. She imagined lines of steel-clad knights, waving of banners, the gay pavilions of the camp. Did he wear her handkerchief on his helmet or attached to his pennon? What were the heathen women like?

"It's wonderful news," she sighed.

"Yes, we're proud of our son. May Our Lord protect him and bring him safe home to us!"

"I shall pray for him, Doña María."

When the call was over, Señora de Vargas could not resist clasping Luisa against her plump bosom. "Let me kiss you, my child. It was kind of you to visit me. You must come soon again. You remind me of my own daughter."

The conventional Luisa would have been concerned for her complexion and headdress during this affectionate embrace; but even after re-entering her coach, the new Luisa did not so much as glance at the hand mirror, until Antonia thrust it upon her.

"You need a touch of powder, my rose," smiled the duenna. "Here's my pomander. You were quite submerged at the end, weren't you?"

Absently, Luisa made the necessary repairs.

"If the good lady," Antonia added, "only knew how to lace, she would not be so overflowing."

"She has Pedrito's eyes," Luisa murmured. "Did you notice?"

Señora Hernández smiled again: it would be a good report she could give to the Marquis.

Part Three

——— *XLV* ———

"Is THERE any city like it in the world, gentlemen?" Cortés demanded. "On my honor, Venice is a dish clout to it!"

His captains were not apt to contradict him. None of them had been to Venice, and, even if they had, partiality for this wondrous city—a city peculiarly their own—which was now spread out beneath them would have insured agreement. But, indeed, a Venetian himself could not have failed to be impressed by the beauty of Mexico City, Tenochtitlán, under the blue of that spring day.

From the summit of the great temple-pyramid, the entire vast oval of it could be seen, an intricate pattern of square rooftops, broken by the green of patio gardens or by flowered terraces, intersected by the sapphire lines of canals and by three great avenues. Here and there, frequently breaking the chessboard level of the roofs, a wide scattering of temples rose airily on their pyramid bases. Under the deluge of sunlight, the stone facings of palace, temple, and pavement, the red or white of house fronts, the reflection from water, and the vivid coloring of gardens, released an infinite sparkle, all the more intense because of the green circle of suburbs merging at last with the blue of the surrounding lake.

North, west, and south, binding it to the mainland, the avenues of the city continued over the water in three broad causeways built several feet above the level of the lake. And beyond them the sparkle of smaller towns, like separate pearls along the shore, repeated distantly the beauty of the metropolis. Then last of all, on every side, the horizon of mountains, a gigantic cloister, shut in this beauty and shut out the world.

The men around Cortés—Alvarado, Olid, Vargas, Tapia, and others —were not especially sensitive to beauty, but on the other hand they were by no means blind to it. Besides, after five months in the city, they had not yet ceased to wonder at so magnificent a prize of their courage and luck.

"I don't know about Venice," said Olid, squinting his dark eyes against the blaze of the sun, "but it beats Seville or Toledo or Salamanca—that is, except for the churches. There's the difference. This city stinks of the devil. Aye, and the cursed quiet of it! Not a hoofbeat, not the rattle of a cart wheel! Uncanny!"

"Pooh!" interrupted Cortés, impatient of criticism. "Give us time, Gossip. Without being a prophet, let me tell you that within a year these *cues*"—he swept his hand at the circle of temples—"will be churches, with the cross on top. As for cattle and cart wheels, wait. You'll see those causeways black with them before long."

And yet vaguely Olid had expressed what all felt. Except for its canals, the city was unlike Venice; it resembled nothing in the Old World. Its beauty remained alien, unhomelike, irreconcilably pagan. Though it had the grace and vividness of a tiger, it breathed also the tiger's rankness, the rankness of raw meat and stale blood. It represented barbarism thinly concealed by architecture and manual skill, but spiritually childish; the stone age as yet unconscious of man's higher possibilities.

At the foot of the teocalli in the great central square, with its palaces, pools, and shrines, the Spaniards looked down at the skull rack, strung with tens of thousands of human skulls, the relics of endless sacrificial victims. They could see the vast heap of bones left from myriad cannibal feasts. They could see the blood-drenched stone of sacrifice, the serpent "hell-mouth" (as they called it) of Quetzalcoatl, the black-robed priests with their matted hair. They could smell the fetid odor of decayed blood that clung to the walls of the temple; and not all the flowers of Tenochtitlán disguised the stench of human excrements, used for tanning, when the wind blew south from the great market place of the Tlaltelolco district. Grandeur and beauty, brutish callousness and nightmare superstition lay outstretched before the cavaliers, who admired and partly scorned, but could never understand.

"Give us time, I say," Cortés repeated. "Why, sirs, recall what we were doing this month last year: fighting mosquitoes on the flats of San Juan de Ulúa; gaping at some paltry gifts from Montezuma; half-starving, without allies, without a base on the coast, scarce knowing which way to turn. And now—"

His arm swept the horizon. It took in not only the city, the valley of Mexico, and the guardian mountains, but the stretch of time between a year ago and now: the anxieties, schemes, crises, labors, marches, battles, victories; the founding of Villa Rica, dispatch of the treasure to Spain, scuttling of the ships, march across the mountains; the fierce campaign in Tlascala, which had been necessary to win that warlike people as allies against the Aztecs; the massacre at Cholula, which still haunted the memories of the less hardened; the ascent of the final range; the breath-taking first view of this magnificent valley with its sparkling cities. Cortés's gesture reviewed the whole crescendo of conquest.

From where they stood, he and his captains could see the great southern causeway by which, last November, they had first crossed the lake. And in the minds of all, the months since then formed an epic background. Four hundred white men taking over an empire.

Received as demigods, they had made the most of their attributes. Ruse, diplomacy, bluff, force. Pedro de Vargas would never forget the kidnaping of Montezuma in the royal palace. For self-protection and in order to dominate the country, it had been found necessary to secure the person of the Aztec emperor. Under the pretext of a call, the Spanish captains had waited on him and then had suddenly surrounded him. Choosing between captivity and immediate death, Montezuma had at last made a show of willingly accompanying the white men back to the quarters he had assigned them. After five months, he still "visited" his Spanish guests, who kept him under guard, a royal puppet and prisoner. And other memories filled in the scroll of victory. It took alertness and strong measures to buttress up the prestige of demigods.

But today crowned all. It was more significant even than the vast treasure of gold and jewels collected by Montezuma for his white masters and now stacked up in the Spanish treasure room. It atoned for massacre, extortion, and sharp practices, which the business of conquest required. For today Huitzilopochtli, Witchywolves, high god of the Aztecs, no longer sat on his temple throne. He would delight no more in the out-torn hearts of victims. His temple walls, cleansed of abominations, housed the Virgin and Child. Today in the presence of the entire company, Christ had been honored on the main teocalli of the city, and the chief cavaliers were even now lingering after the blessed sacrament of mass. To this peak they had climbed: not only the king and the goods of the heathen were in their hands, but even the Aztec gods were falling. From now on, Cortés had only to divide the spoils and transform Anahuac into New Spain.

"Yes," said Alvarado, his hard, handsome face relaxing with satisfaction, "I grant you. Close to a million castellanos of gold in a year isn't to be sneezed at. Hardly! I'll warrant you there's not the quarter of that much at home in His Majesty's coffers. We used to talk big about our prospects before sailing from Cuba; but, between you and me, gentlemen, I kept my tongue in my cheek. After the crack-up of other expeditions. By God, we're the first venture which has paid on the investment. Paid a thousand to one. If we have another year like this last—"

He twiddled the new, immense gold chain into which he had converted a part of his takings.

"And why shouldn't we?" put in Olid. "What's to stop us? These Indians?" He glanced down at the brightly dressed throng of natives in the central square. "They can't fight, but they can work. We've got them bridled in any case, with their king or *Uei Tlatoani,* or whatever he's called, dancing to the crack of the General's whip. Set them in the mines. I vow we can sweat ten million castellanos out of them by this day twelvemonth."

Father Bartolomé de Olmedo, who was carrying his vestments over one arm after celebrating mass, exclaimed angrily: *"Uf,* señores! Have we no thought but for gold in this enterprise? Is it a castellano or a cross that we bear on our banner? Is it the peso we follow in true faith and in that sign conquer? *Qué vergüenza!* There are souls here to save and treasures to win for heaven. But you talk of slavery and mines like so many Moors."

"Amen!" said Pedro de Vargas, who, since their interview on the hill above Trinidad, backed Father Olmedo on every occasion.

"Amen!" said young Andrés de Tapia, a gallant soldier, serious for his years. *"Vive Dios!* I count my chances in purgatory more improved by the last few days of temple-cleaning than by anything else accomplished on this expedition. Good night to Demon Witchywolves! *Ave Maria!"* He turned to Cortés. "We've risked something for God, as Your Excellency said when you struck the gold mask from that devil's image."

But surprisingly Father Bartolomé looked dubious. He rubbed his stubby nose with the back of his hand and coughed. Pedro recalled that the friar had never approved of Cortés's idol-breaking fervor.

"When it's time for idols to fall," he remarked, "they fall of themselves. Take care when you pull them down that you don't set others up. For my part, I'd rather see our Faith planted in men's hearts by love than thrust into their temples by force. But I'm no statesman."

"No, Your Reverence," smiled Cortés, "you're not. And history belies you. Did not Constantine set up our Church by force? Did not Carlo-magno convert the Germans by hanging ten thousand of them? And see what a Christian land that is."

"Humph!" said Father Olmedo.

Careless of the argument, Cortés once more looked out across the city.

"We'll have a count taken; but I wager we've got here no less than sixty thousand hearths. Three hundred thousand souls. A great city. And ours!" He brought his clenched fist down on the pommel of his sword. "Ours! What a jewel to place at His Majesty's feet! Was ever so mighty a kingdom won at so small a cost?"

As usual, the men about him caught his fire. They pictured themselves, small planters as they once had been, received by the King, welcomed at court, they who had given New Spain to Spain—viceroys, grandees.

"What Latin are you mumbling, Fray Bartolomé?" Cortés added.

"A verse from Holy Writ, Captain General."

"Which runs?"

"Why, sir, the Prophet Daniel says: *gradientes in superbia . . .* that those who walk in pride Our Lord is able to abase."

"Who doubts it?" returned the other. "Look you, *fraile,* for the black bile, there's nothing so good as a purge." He drew his head back, and his eyes hardened a moment. Then he winked at the others. "Well, gentlemen, remember the Prophet Daniel—especially when you're going down these steps."

And, turning, he began the almost ladderlike descent, while the others followed. As befitted their youth, Pedro and Tapia came last. Down to the first break in the steps, where a sloping terrace led round the pyramid to a second flight of steps immediately below the first. Down these to a second terrace, and so four times in all around the teocalli to its base. The Spaniards were fully armed—a precaution never omitted when they left their quarters—and the clash of steel mingled with laughter and tones of voices.

"Friend Pedro," said Tapia, "do you ever rub your eyes as I do sometimes?"

"How so, Andrés?"

"Wondering whether you or I or any of us are the same men who sailed last year from Cuba?"

"I see what you mean," Pedro nodded.

For they were not the same men; not the same happy-go-lucky

company. Indeed, it took almost an effort to remember the Cuban days. Cortés, the once popular planter, the genial manager; Sandoval, the rough country boy; Olid, typical soldier of fortune; de Vargas, fresh from Spain; Bull García with his talk (now so antiquated) of Columbus—all the captains, every ranker, had aged, had changed. One was not a conquistador for nothing. They had accomplished incredible things, had seen too much, had faced death too often, not to have hardened, deepened, become pre-eminently fighting men. Though unconscious of it, they had been forged somehow into a troop as disciplined as Toledo steel. But this sort of thing, however glorious, gives a peculiar temper to the human soul.

"Yes," Pedro added almost with a sigh, "it's true enough. . . . We'd better close up ranks, Andrés." They were now crossing the courtyard of the teocalli. "What's your opinion of this rabble? The dogs look ugly. See that bastard in the eagle helmet scowling at us?"

Two by two, shoulder to shoulder, the dozen or so men fell mechanically into close formation, outwardly ignoring the black looks of the crowd but alert as a steel trap. Their armor clanged rhythmically as they marched; the plumes on their helmets fluttered.

It was clear that the overthrow of the war god and the appropriation of his temple, even though it had been wrung from Montezuma, did not find acceptance among the hitherto patient Aztecs. As usual the throng in the square was quiet (the Spaniards were always impressed by the absence of hurlyburly in an Indian crowd), but the quiet had a sullen, menacing vibration. The muttered echo of Cortés's Aztec nickname, Malinche, sounded like a hiss. Noteworthy, too, was the presence of numerous warriors, picked men of the military orders, in traditional dress, their dark features visible through the jaws of an ocelot helmet or under the beak of an eagle. Black-coped priests were everywhere, flitting back and forth.

The Spanish quarters in the palace, or rather compound, which had belonged to Axayacatl, Montezuma's father, lay at no great distance across the square from the temple enclosure; but before the cavaliers had gone more than halfway, the quiet around them had turned to a rising mutter. Without hurrying their pace by the fraction of a second, impersonal and undeviating as a steel plow, they advanced through the crowd, which opened grudgingly to let them pass.

Mobs everywhere are inherently the same. A period of fermentation, a slow heaving, then a spark and explosion. Cortés, an expert in timing, sensed that the explosion was near and made his move at the proper psychological instant.

"Espadas, señores!" he said in his clear, level voice. "Swords!" And in the same moment that every blade leaped from its scabbard, he swept the steel vambrace of his left forearm against the chest of an Indian warrior too slow in making way for him. "Would you shoulder me, dog! Must I teach you manners!"

The hulking fellow, evidently a leader, reeled back and would have fallen except for the press behind·him.

"By fours!" said Cortés; and at once the file became a compact square.

"Vizors!"

The steel lips of the helmets shut.

"Now, *adelante* quietly, gentlemen."

It was enough. The crowd, distracted by the precise, bewildering maneuver and overawed by the terrible swords, did not reach the explosion point. Though a few yells sounded from its fringes, it opened meekly for the group, who marched on at the same steady pace to the near-by gateway of their palace. The massive doors swung open, disclosing the vast courtyard inside, the sentries at their posts, the cannon in position. They closed again, leaving the Aztecs on the outside to ferment and murmur.

"It seems to me," said Cortés, removing his helmet, "that our friends out there may be needing a lesson—a sharp one. But perhaps this show of teeth will be enough. I hate unnecessary bloodshed."

The Prophet Daniel had been forgotten.

—————— XLVI ——————

A YEAR AGO the incident in the square would have excited Pedro de Vargas as a novelty. Now it started a train of reflex professional thought. As the group of officers broke up, he remarked to Tapia:—

"You know, we could stand four or five more feet on that outer wall as well as some bastions. Eight foot's nothing to scale, especially when there're no flanking redans. I wonder the General doesn't see to it."

The "palace" of Axayacatl, a vast, irregular rectangle of open spaces and of one-story stone buildings (terraced occasionally in the center to provide an upper apartment), was surrounded by a massive stone wall. It had been honeycombed by the Spaniards with embrasures for cannon and loopholes for arquebuses, but these would be of small use at close quarters. An active man could easily leap high enough to catch a purchase on the coping; and a shove from behind would lift him to the top. In the absence of outjutting bastions, no flanking fire to clear the wall of attackers was possible.

Tapia nodded. "Yes, and take a look at the teocalli there." He pointed back at the great pyramid they had just left. Only a couple of hundred yards distant in a straight line, it dominated the courtyard of the Spanish quarters. "Did it ever strike you that slingers and bowmen up there would make this place too hot for fun? I'm wishing for the hundred and fifty men down country with Captain Velásquez de León. Perhaps we could use them better here than at Coatzacoalco."

He referred to the largest of the detachments which Cortés had sent out to explore the country. Statesman as well as soldier, the General had spent the recent months appraising resources—mines, plantations, harbor facilities. The number of Castilians in Mexico City amounted at present to little better than two hundred men. They were barracked together with several hundred Tlascalan allies; but, when it came to a pinch, it was the white force that counted.

Pedro absently rubbed his hair, which had been pressed flat under his helmet.

"And the General spoke of three hundred thousand people in this town alone." He grinned. "Well, Andrés, we need exercise. We're getting soft, *hombre*."

The young captains gazed at the mixed crowd thronging the huge courtyard within the walls: bands of half-naked Tlascalan warriors, who camped here in the open; dozens of native women (for concubines were plentiful); here and there Aztec noblemen in attendance on Montezuma; scores of slaves. The place hummed with Indian life and showed a riot of color. Only the sentries, hard and bearded under their steel caps, the gunners on constant duty at their cannon, or an occasional soldier represented the white element. In the background stretched the low, stone-faced buildings, separated from each other by irregular courts and passageways, and sometimes rising in a terrace to a second story. It was here in their long rooms capable of housing a hundred and fifty men and in their own patios that the Spaniards kept to themselves, enjoyed their women, and were waited on by their *naborías* or native servants.

"Yes, soft," de Vargas repeated. "We've been cooped up here too long. If four hundred of us could beat fifty thousand Tlascalans at Tecoacinco, we've still enough here to handle these Aztec *gallinas*."

"Send God you're right," returned Tapia. "But remember that the

Aztecs conquered this country before we came. They might surprise us. . . . *Hasta la vista*, Redhead."

Pedro returned the farewell and clanked off to his quarters, which lay in an opposite angle of the compound. On the way, he stopped to watch a fencing bout between two good swordsmen, Luis Alonso and Juan Escalona; stopped to bet a peso in a card game (the gold of the army was in constant flux from pocket to pocket); stopped to drink a cup of pulque with Francisco de Morla; and at last reached the patio upon which his room opened, to find Juan García seated on the ground between Catana's legs, getting his hair cut.

"Careful now!" boomed García. "Don't rattle Catana, Pedrito. It's a critical moment when she clips the hairs from my ears. I am most ticklish in that place, and if she cuts me—"

"Be still," said Catana, laying a firm hand on García's huge skull. "There, I got it. A whoreson long one, sticking out like a Swiss pike."

"What a picture!" smiled Pedro. "Shocking! All I can say is that it's good I'm not jealous, *amigos míos.*"

Since the end of March, Catana had put on feminine clothes— marvelous reds and yellows cut out of Indian cotton stuffs and stitched by herself. But the year she had spent in hose and doublet had left her confused. She was apt to take strides unsuitable to skirts; or at times she forgot, as now, to keep her gown below her knees.

She clipped a final point from García's forehead and brushed off her skirts.

"There you are. *Por Dios,* Soldán's mane is no thicker than yours."

Getting up, she raised her lips to Pedro for a kiss, then set about the straps and buckles of his armor, removing it piece by piece and hanging each in the right order on its appointed rack against the wall.

"Is that better, señor?"

Pedro stretched contentedly. "Much better, *pichón.*"

Meanwhile García admired his improved reflection in the small patio pool. "A good haircut, *muchacha,*" he nodded. "Here, I'll give you a buss for it."

She let him kiss her, and the three of them sat down in the shadow of the wall. Since her brother, Manuel Pérez, had fallen in one of the first Tlascalan battles, García in a sense had replaced him. The big man and Catana were devoted in a half-kindredly, half-comradely fashion. It was a warm relationship, which derived from the experiences in Jaén and from García's genius for affection. A friend to almost everyone in the army, he adored Catana as his ideal of an all-weather girl.

"There's a wench for New Spain!" he would rumble to Pedro. "There's a *mujercita* to rub shoulders with in a new country! *A fe mía,* I don't know which of you I love best. That's the thing about love: you can't weigh or measure it."

García would heave and expand with affection.

"But I know this," he added once, "if you broke her heart with your grand hidalgo ways, chasing off after some high-stepping *dama*" (he harbored a bitter grudge against the handkerchief which Pedro still carried under his doublet), "I'd—" He opened and closed his hand, staring down at the fingers.

"You'd do what?" Pedro teased.

"I don't know," the other gloomed. "I don't know. I guess it would break my heart too, comrade."

They sat on cushions in the cool of the patio wall, while servants, whom Montezuma had supplied for the Spanish invaders, set forth low tables and an array of dishes for the noon meal. Shallow braziers with live coals in them kept individual bowls hot. It was a varied menu consisting of poultry, fish, chili peppers, corn, beans, tortillas, and pineapples; thickish chocolate, flavored with vanilla, furnished the beverage.

"Blessed Virgin!" grunted García through a full mouth. "What would I give to clamp my jaws over an honest hunk of salt pork again! No work for the teeth in these messes. Ah, well, what can't be cured must be endured."

Loading her case knife with fish and succotash, Catana nodded. "Yes, Christian victuals for me too, Juan. They're chewier." She slid the food skillfully between her lips. "But just wait. This is a good country for hogs."

"Or beef," put in Pedro, cracking a turkey wing. "The General plans to bring in cattle before another year. Also grapes. No reason for us to go on putting up with pulque or this heathenish *chocolatl.* Too cursed sweet."

So, enjoying the tastiest food they had ever known, they seasoned it with the time-honored army grousing and had a satisfying meal.

Pedro related the incident in the square. Having survived the hard Tlascala campaign, neither García nor Catana took the news lightly; but their reactions were different.

"Isn't that like Indians!" the big man exclaimed. "No gratitude. We come here in all gentleness to show them how to live—stop them from eating each other, teach them Spanish ways, make them subjects of Don Carlos, the greatest king on earth, and they want to murder

266

us. It was the same in the Islands. They leave us no choice but fighting, when, if they would only settle down, everything would be happy."

Catana demurred. "They don't want to be slaves. That's natural."

"They have slaves of their own," retorted García. "But who's speaking of slaves? Servants, yes. Doesn't it stand to reason that dark-skinned *ignorantes* should be servants of Castilian cavaliers? Haven't their chiefs sworn allegiance to His Majesty, and aren't we the King's factors in New Spain? What they want doesn't matter. If they rise against us, they're a pack of rebels."

This logic was too much for Catana: it would have been too much, indeed, for almost anyone in the army.

"I suppose you're right," she faltered. "But if they should rise, they're a pretty big pack."

During the last minute, she had been growing curiously pale and now got up unsteadily.

"Siesta time, *hombres.*"

Pedro was staring at her. "Are you ill, *dulce mía?*"

"No, I'm specially happy."

"What about?"

She ran her fingers through his hair. "I'll tell you sometime."

"Why not now?"

"Oh, because—*Hasta luego.*"

Ruffling his curls again, she walked inside, her vivid dress and black hair framed a moment in the doorway.

"Catana looks dashed peaked," said de Vargas uneasily.

But García, absorbed by the Indian problem, returned an absent-minded grunt. "I'd give a thousand pesos if we had our camp on the mainland, Pedrito. Those causeways and drawbridges across the water make a nasty line of retreat. Remember how we felt about them that first day when we marched in? I was with Bernal Díaz del Castillo. We looked at each other when we came to the first bridge. 'What's in your mind, Juan?' he says. 'The same that's in yours,' I told him. 'A beautiful trap.'"

Pedro smiled. "What's the saw about crossing bridges before you come to them? That business in the plaza amounted to nothing. Why worry?"

"Because I know Indians by now," García frowned. "If they show anything, it means a lot. You wait. They run deep and quiet, quiet as this damned city."

During the siesta pause, the hush of the town, derived partly from the absence of wheeled vehicles and beasts of burden and partly from the Indian nature itself, was more obvious than at other hours. But today, imagination coloring it perhaps, the stillness seemed to have another quality—hurricane weather, hard and breathless. To alert superstition, it was as if a gigantic invisible pressure brooded over the city, perhaps the dethroned war god of Anahuac, alias Satan himself, poised to strike.

Pedro and García sat clasping their knees, listening to the silence.

"Quiet!" García repeated. "*Maldito sea!* I had a dream like this once. It comes back to me now. I was in just such a place . . ." He seemed to be groping through his mind. "I remember that all at once came a sound of footsteps running—"

He broke off, his mouth agape; Pedro's scalp prickled. For at that moment sounded a hurry of footsteps, breaking the hush between the buildings and drawing nearer.

Gaspar Burguillos, one of Cortés's pages, rounded the corner of the patio.

It took him a second to catch his breath.

"The General requires your presence, Captain de Vargas. He has been summoned to council by the Lord Montezuma. He wishes you, and the Captains de Olid, Alvarado, and Marín, to accompany him. The matter presses. You will wear light armor."

Pedro, already up, took down his casque from the rack and put it on, then unhooked the corslet from its pegs.

"Lend me a hand, will you, Juan." And when García, still shaken by the fulfillment of his dream, was tightening the buckles, de Vargas whispered, "What happened then—after the footsteps?"

"I don't know, I've forgotten."

Pedro adjusted his sword. "Well," he muttered, "we'll soon find out."

XLVII

It was a distinction to be invited to this conference, and Pedro walked more erect because of it, as he and Burguillos made their way through the irregular grouping of buildings toward the General's quarters. Since Escalante had been killed in battle on the coast and Gonzalo de Sandoval had been promoted to succeed him in command of the vital fort at Villa Rica, de Vargas ranked as Cortés's favorite among the younger officers. Perhaps the Captain General, whose proceedings were usually dictated by more than one good reason, looked beyond

Pedro to Spain and to the possible advantage that Don Francisco's support might bring him. He knew (none better) the de Vargas family connections. But if this had something to do with Pedro's rise in the General's favor, there were other more obvious reasons from the standpoint of the army. De Vargas had borne himself well and was admittedly one of the foremost captains. Even the beloved Sandoval was hardly more popular.

Conversing in a low tone with Cristóbal de Olid, Cortés stood at the foot of the steps leading up to his quarters, when Pedro and Burguillos arrived. His pale face looked unusually grave, an expression which brought out the glinting of his dark eyes. Near by, the page, Orteguilla, to whom Montezuma had taken a fancy and who had learned enough Aztec to spy on the captive Emperor, stood with a crestfallen cast on his shrewd young face.

Cortés turned to him. "This jumps with what you reported day before yesterday, *niño*, when the Señor Montezuma shut you out from his interview with the chief priests, the *tlamacazquis*, or whatever he calls them. You said then that he had changed toward you. When did this change start?"

"As I look back, my lord, it was four evenings ago, on the day when *Vuestra Señoría* broke down the great idol on the teocalli."

"And since then he has had many parleys with his priests, eh? I told you at all costs to find a means of overhearing them."

"I did my best," Orteguilla flushed; "but the council room is large; I had no hiding place, and the Señor Montezuma's guards kept me from the doors."

"Well," observed Cortés, who rarely spent time on regrets, "I doubt if your overhearing them would have helped much."

He greeted the several officers as they came up: Alvarado, florid and magnificent as always, the hawklike de Olid; bowlegged Luis Marín with his red beard and pockmarks. Last of all, Doña Marina joined them.

Cortés gave her a slight bow. "Now that we have our 'tongue,' we can wait on His heathen Majesty, sirs. . . . Orteguilla, come with us. And note well: if at any time I should hook my thumb into my belt—so—you will slip out of the council room and report to Captain Andrés de Tapia, captain of the watch, with my orders that all our company stand to arms."

Then, leading the way with Doña Marina, he turned toward the large central building of the compound, which served as Montezuma's residence.

Between two one-story wings, a flight of steps mounted to a terrace upon which the numerous apartments and patios of the Indian Emperor, his wives, and his suite, were located. Beneath the square, massive entrance to them, a Spanish sentinel stood guard; but beyond the threshold Cortés and his officers entered an Aztec world. Here the air was heavy with the smell of copal incense and flowers; here the dignitaries of the court or feudal chiefs in gaudy, varicolored garments, and wearing jade or turquoise or metal ornaments, came and went; messengers from the fringes of the Aztec jurisdiction arrived with reports; tributary caciques waited to do homage; officers from distant garrisons in their green military plumes received orders; black-gowned priests bore messages from the gods. For if Montezuma actually was the prisoner of the Spaniards, if he could leave the palace of his father only under Spanish guard, in face-saving fiction he chose to live among the white *teules* as a friend; and in fact he remained the despotic War Chief and supreme priest of Anahuac, the focal administrative center through which Cortés, master-puppeteer, could conveniently manipulate his strings.

Conducted by several Aztec noblemen, acting as ushers, the little alien group of white men and Doña Marina followed the length of the vast low-ceilinged apartment, while the throng of native courtiers drew back on either side. But the admiring curiosity of several months ago was gone. The cavaliers walked between sullen defiant walls. If they carried themselves proudly, they did not excel the bystanders in that respect. It was stare for stare, pride for pride.

"By gad, Captain Marín," said Pedro, letting his half-smile flick down the line of faces, "these dogs are in sore need of physic. Have you ever seen a more bilious pack? What dose would you prescribe?"

"Iron," laughed Marín from the corner of his mouth, "iron in the liver."

"Given externally, eh?"

But at that instant Pedro's smile faded and his glance sharpened. That tall, high-nosed fellow several yards down the line with a turquoise in his lower lip and a plug of gold in one nostril looked startlingly familiar. He wore a nodding panache of quetzal plumes, the sign of high rank, and a gorgeous featherwork corslet. But however transformed and embellished, if he was not Coatl, Diego de Silva's escaped servant, then Pedro could not trust his eyes about anyone.

Before he could catch himself, he half-raised his hand and exclaimed, "*Hola*, Coatl!" But though the dark eyes rested on his for a moment, there was no sign of recognition. The man stared, then turned away.

"Friend of yours?" Marín grinned.

"I thought I knew him," Pedro muttered, "but after all, these Indians are as much alike as peas in a pod."

The apartment opened upon a smaller apartment, where the cavaliers waited while the ushers drew coarse henequen cloaks over their finery and slipped off their sandals in order to enter Montezuma's presence abject and barefooted. Then, with eyes on the ground and bowed shoulders, they led the way through an opposite door into the council hall beyond.

Montezuma, the *Uei Tlatoani,* "he who speaks," ruler of Mexico and of the conquered provinces, sat on a low, high-backed throne at the end of the room facing the entrance. He was a slight, though well-proportioned, man of forty with a sparse beard and shoulder-long black hair. A gold crown, shaped in front like a miniature mitre, and jade earrings marked his rank, though otherwise he dressed simply. Instead of the characteristic Indian features, heavy and immobile, he had a curiously expressive face, kindly but grave and in every mood noble.

Living in the midst of them, he was familiar to all the Spanish garrison. On his side, he knew many of his captors by name and had won their affection by his generosity, tact, and princely ways. They thought and spoke of him as the Great Montezuma.

Only a few—among them Cortés and Pedro de Vargas—did not share the general regard for him. He seemed too supple, too courteous and obliging. They mistrusted his gifts and his kind speeches, considered him either feeble or false. They felt the unbridgeable chasm between their minds and his. Not all the gold he showered on them personally, not even his oath of allegiance to the King of Spain nor the treasure he had collected as tribute, atoned for the death of Juan de Escalante and the murder of several Spaniards near Villa Rica by his orders. They suspected him constantly of plot and double-dealing, unable to understand that right or wrong in the Spanish sense had no meaning for Montezuma at all. To this smaller group, he seemed only a smooth, unpredictable savage.

But today his friends and detractors alike, among the handful of officers who approached him across the matted floor of the great room, felt at once a change. The usual smile did not greet them. He sat motionless, almost statue-like, his hands on the golden-wrought arms of the throne. When the obsequious ushers had faded out, he rose

271

and returned Cortés's bow with little better than a nod; then coldly waved him toward a chair, leaving, contrary to wont, the other cavaliers standing casque on arm. His dark eyes looked as cool and impenetrable as agates.

After Doña Marina had taken her place behind Cortés, he began speaking in a measured, impersonal voice, pausing now and then to give the interpreter time to translate. The lion resonance of his tones alternated with Marina's gentle, unready Spanish.

"Malinche," he said, fixing his opaque glance on Cortés, "men fight for various things, for land and possessions or fame or to defend their hearths. But men fight best and are happiest to die for what has no price—for the love and defense of their gods."

He stopped, and Marina's voice took up the tale like a plaintive echo. When she had finished, Cortés nodded. On the point of religious zeal, Spaniard and Aztec agreed perfectly.

"Malinche," the *Uei Tlatoani* continued, "you and those with you are of the kindred of the sun. You came from beyond the sea, fulfilling prophecies that concerned the god, Quetzalcoatl. Portents foretold your coming. Who was I to resist the messengers of the gods? Though you were but few (so few that one of my houses alone contains you) and I can call to arms a thousand warriors for every one of yours, have I raised a finger against you? Though my people grieved, accusing me of weakness and cowardice, have I heeded their murmurs? When you required that I and my chiefs, chosen leaders of our nation, should accept your king, Don Carlos, as lord, did we refuse, even though we have never seen him? When you demanded tribute for this king, did I not provide you with such store of gold and jewels as no man has hitherto beheld—yes, not only the wealth of our land and cities, but the very treasure of Axayacatl, my father? Are not these things true, Malinche?"

Again Cortés nodded, adding a wave of the hand that expressed gratitude, but not too much gratitude. It implied that, after all, Montezuma had acted properly under the circumstances, and that to have behaved otherwise would have been unworthy of him.

Shifting from foot to foot, Pedro de Vargas wondered what the Indian emperor was getting at. To his youthful assurance, it was clear that if Montezuma's compliance had not been forthcoming, it would have been exacted by the right of conquest—an unquestioned right. His attention drifted to the rich ornamentation of the throne, to the marble-lined walls of the council-chamber, to the precious wood forming the low ceiling. In what luxury the unchristened dog lived!

Montezuma was saying: "Why have I done these things? From cowardice? My fame as a war chief does not point to that. Why then? Because ever, during my whole life, I have had but one end—to serve and please the gods; because it seemed their will, in omens and portents, that you should be accepted and favored. That you spoke of other gods than ours did not trouble me, for there are many gods, and often one is known by different names. That you cast down from their temples the gods of the Mayans and Totonacs did not concern us, for they were not our gods. When you besought me that you might be allowed to set up an altar to your own Lord here in this palace, I did not object. When you forbade the sacrifice of slaves and prisoners, thus depriving the Heavenly Ones of human blood and us of consecrated meat, I was still patient. Though day by day you yourselves eat the flesh of your Man God at what you call the mass, it might be that you were right and we were wrong; and as to this the Heavenly Ones were silent. But still it was not enough: you demanded more."

He clenched his swarthy fist on the arm of the throne, then relaxed it, studying Cortés's inscrutable face, as Marina interpreted.

Glancing sideways, Pedro saw Luis Marín impatiently gnawing the corner of his red mustache. Alvarado lifted a jeweled hand in front of his mouth to hide a yawn. Olid's eyes showed a yellow glint as they rested on Montezuma's crown.

It did not occur to any of them that the Aztec leader might have a grain of right and justice on his side. Such tolerance was unknown. Convinced that the Indian gods were devils, it took self-control on the part of the Spaniards to listen to such babble.

"Indeed," Montezuma went on, "your priest, Olmedo, spoke truth when he related to me what he calls *The Commandments,* one of which says that your god is a jealous god. It was not enough that at last I permitted you to place the Woman and Child in one of the temples of our chief teocalli. You must lay your hands upon our Lord Huitzilopochtli himself! You must abase and tread him underfoot! You must tear out the heart of our people—you who deny us the right of sacrifice—in order to lay that heart at the feet of your *teules!* Well, then, at last the gods have spoken."

This time Marina's translation was hardly necessary. The eyes of the cavaliers were fixed intently on Montezuma before she began to speak. They saw a new man, no longer the meek and pliant figurehead who had curried favor with them, who had supinely performed their bidding —very different from the Montezuma they had seen in tears that day when Cortés loaded him with irons to teach him a lesson, while the murderers of Escalante burned alive in the courtyard outside. The dog seemed transfigured with a new strength, purposeful, menacing.

"Ah!" returned Cortés blandly. "Ask him what the gods said. To whom did they speak?"

The question was only half-ironic. The General's companions did not find it ironic at all. They had no doubt that Satan communicated with his ministers.

Montezuma leaned forward. "To whom else should they speak but to the holy men, the chief priests of the Tenochcas?" Then, bowing his head reverently, he added: "Thus speak the gods of the Tenochcas, the Lord Huitzilopochtli, God of War, the Lord Tlaloc, God of Rain, the Lord Xipe, God of Spring, and all the other gods of my people: 'Lo, we have made the Tenochcas mighty upon earth: we have filled their granaries with food, their treasuries with tribute. We have given them victory in war and dominion over many peoples. An age long we have shielded and fostered them, while they served us and fed our nostrils with the smoke of sacrifice. But now they have turned aside; now they starve our altars; now they leave our images to be overthrown and destroyed. So, therefore, Tenochcas, hear our words. We are departing from you. You are no more our children but helpless slaves. Drought shall fall upon you and pestilence and war, you shall perish miserably from the earth. Except now, unless it be too late, you turn again to us, lay hands upon the evildoers from beyond the world, these white pretenders who are not *teules*, stretch them upon our altars, pour out their blood to us in sacrifice. Behold, we, the gods, have spoken it.'"

Marina's gentle voice sounded hurried and tense; her hands tightened on the back of Cortés's chair. The Spanish officers stood like alert statues. Only Cortés seemed unconcerned. He crossed his legs and leaned back in his chair. But Pedro de Vargas noticed that the page, Orteguilla, suddenly withdrew, and looking again he saw that Cortés had hooked his thumb into his sword belt.

"Señor Montezuma," he answered with a smile of indulgence, "you are mistaken. If I were you, I would let this brood of devils depart, and a murrain seize them! I would even hasten their going by toppling down every one of their filthy images. Do this and, on my honor, all will be well with you. Our Lord will provide the Tenochcas with plentiful harvests; He will protect them from sickness; my friends and I will shield them in war. Have done with worshiping idols, my lord, as I have told you before, and embrace the Cross. That is my advice."

If a gadfly had stung the *Uei Tlatoani*, its effect on him could not have been so marked as this speech. Even to the Spaniards, it seemed reckless. It was plainly no time to be talking conversion. But with regard to the Faith, Cortés, a diplomat in every other respect, never compromised; he took direct methods.

Montezuma half-rose, his eyes blazing, a flash of teeth between his lips. But he did not entirely rise, and an instant later he sank back. Something more potent even than his fanaticism checked and daunted him, as a beast is daunted by its tamer. He might be brave, sincere, and filled with religious zeal, but his stone-age self could not cope with the thrust of Cortés's personality. The primitive in him knuckled under to the more highly evolved man. For a moment he tried to meet the Spaniard's steady gaze, then his eyes fell.

"But why," Cortés went on, "if you wish to sacrifice us to the devil, do you warn us of it? Surprise would have been better. . . . Listen."

The clear, galloping notes of a Spanish trumpet were sounding in the courtyard. Then, one by one, other trumpets here and there took up the call. A prolonged shiver of steel throughout the compound answered.

After a pause, Cortés asked again, "Why warn us?"

Why indeed? A desire for once to abash these masterful white men? A desire for once to speak as a king, expressing the accumulated grievances of the past six months? Or was the reason which Montezuma proceeded to give the right one? His black, reptilian eyes showed nothing.

"Because I have no wish to kill you, Malinche. Because we have been friends."

"Judas!" someone muttered. "False rogue!"

Perhaps the words were louder than the speaker intended. Montezuma looked up.

"I would save you, Malinche," he went on to Cortés. "Leave this country at once; return to your land beyond the sea, and I will hold my people in check. Perhaps the gods will be appeased by other sacrifices. But leave at once."

Plainly Montezuma was temporizing. It was probable that the noise from outside had impressed him.

To his companions' astonishment, Cortés nodded. "At your command, my lord. Our mission has been accomplished. We have visited Your Highness, as our King commanded, and have secured your allegiance. We will return to him, bearing the tribute. But we have no ships, as you know, and others must be built. This will take time. Meanwhile, restrain your people—for their sakes, not ours. I should regret to harm them, but if they stir against us, I shall destroy them, man, woman, and child."

275

Cortés was a consummate actor. He spoke with an assurance that carried conviction and left Montezuma nonplused. The white men were capable of anything.

"I shall send workmen to help with the ships," agreed the Indian. "I shall do my best to quiet my people." Somehow the ultimatum of the gods had gone flat.

"Your best will not be good enough," Cortés answered, making the most of his ascendancy, "if there is trouble. See to it." He got up and took a step forward, menacing as a drawn crossbow. "I shall regret to leave Tenochtitlán, my lord; but it consoles me that, when we leave, you will accompany us."

Montezuma shrank back when the words had been translated. "I?"

"Of a truth, yes. We shall take you with us to meet our master, the King, who desires to welcome you."

He stood half-smiling while Marina interpreted. If he had decreed death, the Aztec would not have been so shaken. Forlorn in that unknown white world across the mysterious sea, a trophy for these strangers to exhibit!

"Therefore let us hasten the building of the ships, Señor Montezuma, so that we may depart together. And until then, remember that if your gods were not able to protect their idols from the fire, they are not apt to protect you in case of deceit. . . . Cristóbal, set closer guard about this prince. (Translate that, Marina.) And so, Your Highness, we take our leave in all respect and friendship."

He bowed, one hand on the hilt of his sword, and turning with his captains moved toward the door, head and beard up.

"*En conciencia,* señores," he said, loud enough for his stern voice to ring back to the solitary figure on the throne, "let us continue to risk something for God."

XLVIII

IT WAS LATE that night when the council of the principal officers disbanded and Pedro returned to his quarters. No decision had been reached because everything depended on luck. The arrival of reinforcements from Spain might turn the trick; and surely Montejo and Puertocarrero had been gone long enough to send back men and supplies. Or it might be possible, playing both ends against the center, to stir up a native revolt against the Aztecs, which would work to Spanish profit. Or something else might happen. Meanwhile, as a pacifying gesture, work on three ships would be started at Villa Rica; but Martín López, the shipwright, would not press forward the building of them too fast.

Time must be gained, in which luck could operate. The bold front maintained before Montezuma had been tempered at the council by the general appreciation of realities. Pedro was reminded of a dice game, in which he and his companions were casting mains against an invisible opponent who had every advantage. One could not get away from the fact that four hundred men were pitted against at least four hundred thousand, a skiff against an ocean, and that in case of storm, not only courage, not only cunning, but luck, in the ratio of a thousand-to-one chance, was needed. Thus far the company had had a miraculous winning streak; but every tide takes an ebb.

As he walked through the compound, lighted here and there by torches, de Vargas was struck by the difference since morning. Every available cannon stood in position, commanding the gateways. Lookouts manned the walls. Redoubled sentries went their rounds between buildings. War horses were tethered outside their riders' quarters, saddle on back and bridle on peak. Now and then the call of a sentinel: *"Alto! Quién vive? Consigna?"* rang through the darkness.

Not far from his quarters, Pedro met García, who was standing guard, his huge shadow wheeling in the flare of a torch at one of the house corners.

"So *this* was what I dreamed, eh?" he growled. "Glad I couldn't remember it! It smells like action soon, comrade. What's the news from headquarters?"

Pedro told him about the ships.

"Bah!" said García. "We didn't scuttle our ships for the fun of building others. Can't you see the General sailing from New Spain because of Indian talk! Outfaced from a prize like this! By God, it makes me laugh! But we ought to shift camp to Tacuba on the mainland."

"Maybe we will."

"And I hope not at the double-quick," García muttered.

Pedro found Catana stretched out on the mat which served as their bed. According to orders, she lay completely dressed in marching gear, headpiece and arms beside her, for henceforth until the alarm died down, no one would undress at night in the Spanish quarters. The diffused radiance of the stars through the square doorway gave a faint twilight.

277

She raised her head. "How late you are, señor! I've been lonely for you. These clothes remind me of all our campfires, the mountains, the wind. I like to remember those nights."

He placed his sword, casque, and corslet within reach, then slipped off his shoes and lay down, with his outflung arm under her head.

"We're apt to have more of them, *alma mía*," he answered, and began discussing what had happened; but gradually he realized that she wasn't listening. "Tired?" he asked.

"No. But don't let's talk about war tonight, *querido*. Let's just talk about ourselves, not the venture."

He remembered that she had looked unwell, and his arm closed around her. "*Vida mía!* God knows I would rather talk of you and how much I love you than about anything else, let alone the whoreson Indians. What cheer, my poppet? You gave me a start today at meat, you turned so pale."

"It was nothing. I told you that I was happy, happier than ever in my life."

"And you wouldn't tell me why. Is it such a secret, Catana? Come now, why?"

She was silent a long moment.

"Do you still love her a great deal, señor—I mean the Lady Luisa? . . . No, tell me truly. . . . I want the truth."

Coming at this moment, it was a puzzling question; a mind subtler than Pedro's might well have felt baffled by it. He had not thought of Luisa recently, and Catana's question turned his mind back to her and to Spain. How much did he really love Luisa de Carvajal, how much, that is, in comparison with Catana? As García had said, love cannot be weighed or measured. Pedro knew only that somewhere in his consciousness glimmered a shrine where Luisa stood aloof and alone. It was a place of dreams. The lust and dirt of the world, coarse realities, the concerns of daily life, did not enter there. Viewed from its doorway, the future became an enchanted vista of glory, poetry, and romance. It was fragrant with the scent of rose water, luminous with silver brocade and the flash of jewels in dark hair, haunted by a face with innocent, soft eyes, and by the echoes of a lute. At unpredictable moments, sometimes when he was alone, sometimes in the brawling and clatter of the camp, sometimes even with Catana, the thought of it would sweep over him like a nostalgia that was both pain and release. But now, faced by this question of comparative love, he was at a loss. No shrine for Catana! She stood knee-deep in the mire of everyday life. She belonged on the same plane with García, Sandoval,

278

and the army. Did that mean that he loved her less? Could he love anyone more?

"God knows!" he answered in honest doubt. "I'm no good at word-spinning. I love you in one way and her in another. All I know is that I love you more than my life, that you're my woman and that no one else could ever take your place. As to Doña Luisa, I love her as a cavalier loves his lady. I vowed on the altar cross to serve and honor her. But I can't explain, and you wouldn't understand."

"Yes, I do." Catana rubbed her cheek against his arm. He had told her everything she hoped to hear. His woman forever! Let the lady have his vows! Close to reality, she did not grudge Luisa the chivalrous or even the legal title. "I understand. She'll be Señora de Vargas. (Yes, señor, it is right for the sake of your name. It doesn't matter, as long as I belong to you.) But I"—she pressed her face against him—"I'm going to bear your first son. That's why I'm happy. Hasn't Our Lord been good to me!"

He crushed her to him until she ached from the pleasant pain.

"Catana! Catana *mía!*"

"Wasn't it a wonderful secret, señor?"

"*Por Dios.* I should say it was!" His voice thrilled her like music. "Let me kiss you again! *Vive Dios!* But why a son? I want a girl like you."

She half pushed him away. "*Qué vergüenza!* You'll bring us bad luck with your talk. Of course it shall be a boy. He shall have red hair and green eyes. He shall weigh ten pounds. A fine boy. Do not speak or think otherwise. I'll have Master Botello cast him a horoscope."

Lying back with her head in the hollow of Pedro's arm, she stared up at the ceiling.

"I've been a very wicked girl. *Madrecita* died too young to bring me up; I don't remember my father. Mother used to say that he was a brave and clever gentleman of the road. But they hanged him in Córdoba. It's hard for a poor girl without parents to be good, señor. Maybe that's why Our Lord has not counted it against me and has been so kind. Unless—" She paused fearfully. "Unless—"

"What?"

"You don't think He would take it out on our baby, do you?"

"Take what out?"

"My sins. I have a bad and unruly temper." She struck her breast with her clenched hand. "I curse too much." (Another blow.) "I have often neglected to attend the blessed mass. *Ay de mí!*"

"Bah!" said Pedro fondly. "You're an angel."

"A very black one. Father Olmedo spoke last Sunday about the sins of the parents being visited on the children. It made me shiver. But our boy is innocent. Besides, he's the son of Pedro de Vargas."

The latter grunted. If the salvation of the unborn child depended on his record—

"And the grandson of Don Francisco de Vargas. Is it not beyond dreams that I should be his mother—I, Catana Pérez of the Rosario!"

She thought of the innkeeper, Sancho López, of other members of the tavern household. She wished that she could overwhelm them with this great news. And her brother, Manuel. How proud he would have felt to be the uncle of Pedro's son!

"We'll call him Francisco."

"Let's. That is—" Pedro hesitated.

She understood. "No, of course. I forgot. Your señor father wouldn't want to give his name to a—to one born out of wedlock."

She turned her head away for an instant. But her happiness was too great to be darkened by a partial shadow.

"Let's talk about our son," she went on, turning back and drawing closer again. "I shall bring him up properly. Never fear that I shall spare the switch because of love. By God, if I catch him swearing and dicing as I did that young imp, Ochoa, the other day, won't I tan him! And, *querido mío,* he shall be a learned man, he shall attend the college at Salamanca." She paused thoughtfully. "Wouldn't it be safer, because I've been so bad and we unmarried, to give him to God? Wouldn't it please Our Lord? I'll bear you other sons to be *caballeros;* but our first— Why not a priest? Say yes. Maybe he'll become a bishop."

"It's well thought of," Pedro agreed. "From Salamanca, he could go to our kinsmen in Italy."

She gave a long sigh. "Think of it! Me the mother of a bishop! Maybe even a cardinal! Oh, my sweet lord, I want him to have everything I never had. All I can give him is my love for you."

"Don't talk such folly," he scolded. " 'Slife, with such a mother, he'll have a great heart in him, and a true heart, *ojos bellos!* . . . What are you doing?" He felt the pressure of her fingers, one after the other, on his thigh.

"Counting. I waited to be sure before telling you. Seven more months. May, June, July . . . It'll be December. A long time. But maybe—señor, what if it were at Christmas! What a blessing for him! What luck! Juan García must be one of the godfathers. Won't he be pleased! Only he'll spoil our son dreadfully if we aren't careful. I'll tell Fray Bartolomé de Olmedo the news tomorrow. He'll give me a spank and then a buss. Can't you see him at the christening, with his stubby nose and big fists! And Captain de Sandoval will be there, and the General and Captain de Alvarado, and all the captains and our good friends. What a christening! And I'll be standing beside you . . ."

Her voice trailed off drowsily.

"The General must be godfather too," said Pedro. "The boy must have Hernán among his names."

But she had fallen asleep, and Pedro drew the cover tenderly about her.

The excitement of the day was forgotten. He lay dreaming awhile, not of Spain, for once, and the enshrined Luisa, but of a manor house on the brow of a Mexican hill. He pictured the outbuildings and broad lands. He was riding home with his horsemen from an expedition, for it would be long before the vast country north and south was tamed. Catana stood waiting in the courtyard . . .

"Quién vive?"

The challenge of a sentry not far off mingled with his dreams. He half-awoke.

"Hernán Cortés."

The unsleeping General was making his rounds.

XLIX

ON A MORNING in early May, the page boy Ochoa beat even the sound of the joy shots. He dashed panting through the compound and yelled: "Ships at San Juan de Ulúa! Eighteen ships! Men! Guns! *Viva! Viva!*" Then, almost at his heels, came the salvos of the cannon, tooting of trumpets, racing of men.

The news was like the first breath of air to a becalmed vessel, the first relief in a fortnight of tension, rumors, menace, and sense of doom, the sense of huge coils tightening around the Spanish quarters. Eighteen ships. That meant perhaps a thousand men. With a thousand more Castilians, New Spain was in the bag. The luck of the expedition had once more pulled it through.

Pedro, who was superintending the shoeing of Soldán at the hands of Santos Hernández, the smith, grabbed Ochoa, as he ran past, and shook more news out of him.

"Stop that yelling, limb of Satan! What ships? From Spain?"

"I suppose so. From where else? The Great Montezuma called in our

General and showed him picture-writing of them. Just arrived. Eighteen tall ships. Hundreds of men. Horses. Cannon. *Viva! Viva!* The captains are all meeting at the General's. Better hurry!" He dived under Pedro's arm and disappeared around the corner, shouting his tidings and racing to tell them to Catana. The smith, who was half-squatting with Soldán's off hind-hoof in his leather apron, straightened up and followed Pedro out into the hullabaloo of the camp.

De Vargas took the steps of the General's terrace two at a time, hurried through a room of excited soldiers, passed a guard at the opposite door, and found himself in Cortés's council chamber, where a majority of the leading officers had already gathered.

But once inside, he stopped at a loss. Instead of jubilation, silence; instead of smiles, anxious faces and eyes centering on the tall figure of Cortés, who stood at one end of a rough table. Self-possessed as a rule, he was now evidently disturbed, his mouth grim, his eyes smoldering.

". . . So Señor Montezuma brought out one of those cotton-cloth rolls," he was saying. "You know the kind of pictures these Indians use for writing—smiled at me—faith, what a smile! 'See, Malinche, now you won't need those ships you're building at Villa Rica,' he said. 'Here are plenty of ships to take you and your friends home.' And, 'struth, there they were indeed—eighteen ships, though five had run ashore. Eighteen. The biggest armada ever seen in Western waters. And neatly pricked off, nine hundred men, eighty horses, twenty cannon, stores aplenty. They had landed some days ago, some days ago, mark you. 'Blessed be God,' I said, 'for all His mercies!' The dog should not know from me that there was anything amiss." Cortés broke off. "Will no one stop those fools out there from shooting off the guns? We'll need powder for other uses before we're through."

Francisco de Morla strode out into the anteroom. The chatter ceased abruptly. Like an extending ripple, silence began to spread through the compound, troubled silence.

"But what's wrong?" Pedro whispered to Andrés de Tapia, who stood next to him. "Didn't we send to Spain for reinforcements?"

"He thinks the ships aren't from Spain," Tapia shot back, "but from Cuba."

Alvarado had asked some question. Cortés answered impatiently. "Do some thinking, man! If those ships were Spanish, would not one of them at least have put in at Villa Rica? There's our headquarters, not San Juan de Ulúa, as our factors, Montejo and Puertocarrero, well know. But granting that for some reason they should all anchor at San Juan, would they not have sent a message post haste to us or at least to Sandoval at Villa Rica? Would we have to wait for news of them through this Indian?"

It was a telling argument. There had been time enough since the landing of the fleet, Pedro gathered, for a message to have reached Cortés. The captains exchanged unquiet glances.

"And here's another point," the General added. "It did not take a mind reader to see that Montezuma knows more than he tells. I'm not so dull as not to feel sarcasm, however honeyed. He kept speaking about our brothers, our brothers who came on the ships—our brothers, quotha —and smiled. Showed me the picture of the fool, Cervantes, whom we sent with the prospecting party southeast, hobnobbing with these same brothers. I'll warrant the rogue acts now as their guide and interpreter."

He rapped the table sharply with his knuckles. "No, sirs, we must not deceive ourselves. That fleet bodes ill to this company. I'll venture a peso to a maravedí that Montejo put in to Cuba in spite of our orders. Perhaps he was caught. Perhaps the gold we sent to Spain got no further. Anyway the news of our prize here leaked out, and now we have Governor Velásquez's hornets at our ears, greedy for the stakes. Was it not enough to cope with half a million Aztecs, that we should have twice our number of white *brothers* to deal with also! And thus, señores, we face the ruin of our hopes, our labor and accomplishment." He paused a moment, glancing from one to the other. "Do we face it united?"

"What's your meaning, Hernán?" growled Captain Marín, twisting his red beard.

"Why, it's simple. There may be some who might find it healthier, like Señor Cervantes, to join our brothers on the coast. Perhaps he's not so much of a fool. It's the wise man who despairs of our venture now. It's the fool who stands with me. Speak out, gentlemen. Your decision."

He knew how to strike fire from the Spanish flint. The group of adventurers about the table, each one an individualist with his eyes on the main chance, were not primarily loyal; they were gamblers. But they had the gambler's virtues: recklessness, hail-fellowship, and invincible faith in luck. To them Cortés supremely embodied these qualities. He swept men along, content to suffer, to die, or even to be mulcted of their profits, for the sake of the hotter pulse beat, the richer venture, that he offered them.

The captains expressed their decision by an indignant growl.

Cortés's eyes flashed pride. "Well then, cavaliers, I take it we stand together. God send that Captain Velásquez de León, with the hundred and fifty men at Coatzacoalco, may feel as you do! It would be a sad blow to us if he does not. But he's a kinsman to Governor Velásquez."

"By God," put in Diego de Ordás, who had been a mutineer in the early days of the expedition. "I'll vouch for him. Can you see Juan sneaking off to a crowd of Cuban white-bellies and leaving us, his good comrades, in the lurch? I can't."

Cortés turned to Olid. "Cristóbal, get off a messenger at once to Captain Velásquez and one to Rodrigo Rangel in Chinantla. Give them the news and what we make of it. Let them fall back on Cholula and await developments there, lest they be cut off separately. We must reef the sails of our enterprise, gentlemen, till the storm's past." His glance fell on Tapia. "Son Andrés, make ready to leave within the hour for Villa Rica. You'll bear a letter from me to Sandoval and make speed day and night. Pedro de Vargas, you'll be on duty as my aide for the time being. . . . *Adiós*, señores, and each of you look to the spirit of your men. No long faces, no doubts. Plenty of promises. When there's little honey in the jar, have some in the mouth, as the saying goes. But above all, let each commend this company to the favor of Our Lord."

So, with one eye on the sullen Aztecs and one on the coast, the army waited day after day, tense and on edge, while, report by report, the truth regarding the strangers at San Juan de Ulúa filtered in.

As usual, Cortés had judged correctly. It was a Cuban fleet sent to vindicate the rights of Governor Velásquez to the new lands which the expedition had occupied. Was he not the sponsor of the expedition? Had it not sailed in his name? He did not propose to be cheated of his investment. The General's surmise about the treasure ship to Spain turned out to be equally pat. Though he escaped capture, Montejo had indeed put in to Cuba for a glimpse of his estate in El Marién; and from there the news had spread like wildfire through the island. Gold, gold to the west, oceans of it! And should wealth like that fall undisputed to a pack of traitors in rebellion against His Excellency? Nine hundred gallants with hungry purses were now on the coast to debate that issue. They were commanded by the great Pánfilo de Narváez. He was there to take over New Spain in the name of the Governor, peaceably or by force. But take it over he would.

"*Pánfilo!*" drawled Catana Pérez, fist on hip among a group of soldiers. "*Pánfilo!* What a name! Makes you think of a strutting peacock, God help me! I'll bet he's a pompous wind-sack. Anyone called *Pánfilo* has to be."

"And he is," nodded García. "Talks like a voice in a vault. I know him, and he can kiss what I sit on. But there's one consolation, *hombres*, it's not a bullfrog like him who can match our fox—and no disrespect to Cortés."

The talents of the fox soon showed, and Pedro de Vargas learned another lesson in the art of war. One day three ambassadors from General Narváez appeared on the mainland side of the southern causeway. Having had the imprudence to summon the faithful Sandoval to surrender his post at Villa Rica, that officer had had them bound hand and foot, trussed up like turkeys on the backs of native carriers, and under the guard of Pedro de Solís, with twenty men, had dispatched them to Cortés. Leaving his charges in Iztapalapan across the lake, de Solís announced their arrival and told the story to the General. It sounded so much like Sandoval that Pedro, who was present, felt homesick for his friend even as he laughed.

It appeared that the names of the three unwilling envoys were Guevara, a priest, Vergara, a notary, and Master Amaya, a soldier.

"The fat-bellies got a jouncing on the *tlamemes'* backs, I can vouch to Your Excellency," concluded de Solís. "And they saw some country. It opened their eyes to the richness of New Spain. And now they sit gaping across the water at this great city and know not whether they are dreaming or bewitched. What's Your Lordship's will respecting them?"

Though the Spaniards would lose face if their white brothers entered Tenochtitlán, like bales of goods, on the backs of slaves, it seemed to Pedro that Cortés overdid it in keeping up appearances. Guevara and company were to ride in on horseback; were to be apologized to for Sandoval's barbarity; were to be given gifts; were to be shown the beauties of the city as they approached.

"Son Pedro," Cortés replied when de Vargas protested, "you've got a deal to learn about management. A spider spins his web strand by strand. Do you think four hundred odd of us can fight nine hundred with steel only? Go to!"

As a result, by the time Father Guevara and his companions, propitiated by excuses and presents, had followed the palace-lined avenue through the city, crossed the great central square, been received by the company in full regalia, been greeted affectionately by the General himself, they had shed their allegiance to Narváez like a worn-out shirt. One strand of the spider's web held them fast, and that strand was made of gold. How fortunate were the soldiers of the free-handed Cortés, who shared the booty of such an empire!

With admiration, Pedro watched the further spinning of the web during the next ten days. Much against their will, Guevara and the

285

others, heavy with bullion, went back to Narváez to sing Cortés's praises in that camp and exhibit their wealth. The Cuban armada buzzed. Why fight? There were gold and land for all, and a big-hearted general waiting to parcel it out. Why fight for Pánfilo de Narváez, who didn't part with a copper if he could help it? And why fight? asked Cortés in tactful letters to the Cuban general, aimed not so much at him as at his captains. Why not meet as friends? Of course this talk of punishment and rebels applied to the loyal colony of Villa Rica made no sense. Villa Rica, indeed, would punish any infringement of its rights. But negotiate. Come to an agreement. Why play into the hands of Montezuma, destroying a year's labor of settlement and conversion by war between Spaniards?

A diplomatic offensive.

Fray Bartolomé de Olmedo, whose priestly rank gave him immunity, carried these letters and a rich supply of gold to grease the palms of key people among the invaders.

"My son," he told Pedro on the eve of departing, "if by management or bribery I can prevent bloodshed among friends, nay, among kinsmen, it will be a good work, and therefore I am undertaking it." He sighed but added, "Would that it were possible to do this by preaching the simple gospel of peace and good will; but in this world, we must sometimes use the ways of the world to do God service."

Sauntering together, he and de Vargas had come to the apartment in Cortés's quarters which was used as a chapel, and they now stood within the doorway. The altar light and a few votive candles faintly illumined the long, low room.

"Yes," said Pedro, "and meanwhile it's good news that Captain Velásquez de León holds with us and is marching to Cholula. We'd have made a poor front without him. The General doesn't expect to avoid a fight for all your parleying, Father."

"God send he's wrong!" Olmedo put in.

De Vargas went on, "What frets me is to see the gold we've sweated and bled for going into the pockets of loons who hadn't the heart to join up with our enterprise and now come bawling for the fruit of it."

"That too is the way of the world, my son."

Pedro grumbled, "I suppose you've a list of all in Narváez's herd who have to be fattened."

"Yes, all—thanks to Father Guevara—Cubans and Spaniards."

"Spaniards? Who are they?"

The friar shook his head. "Not direct from Spain of course." He changed the subject. *"Hijo mío,* I leave tomorrow at dawn. Life being uncertain, we may not meet again. Do you remember a talk we had once on the hill above Trinidad de Cuba?"

"I'm not likely to forget it, Father—nor your kindness."

Olmedo laid his heavy hand on the other's shoulder. "God's kindness, if you please. You were guilty of black sin. Your enemy had done you a great wrong, but you sought to do him greater wrong by destroying his soul. God's forgiveness of you depended on your forgiveness of Diego de Silva and on your prayers for him. You made a vow to do this. Have you kept the vow?"

Pedro flushed. "Not recently," he shifted. "Anyway, the man's alive." Why, he wondered, was Olmedo bringing that up now?

"Since then," the friar went on, "God has protected and prospered you. Think—at Cempoala, on the *Gallega* ship that night, how often in skirmish and battle. You are a captain, high in the General's favor. You who had nothing are now rich. Think! And in return God asked only that you forgive and pray for your enemy."

"By the Cross," Pedro muttered, "I forgive him. It was forgetfulness—"

"Forgetfulness!" echoed the friar. "Mark you, Pedro de Vargas: if you forget your vow, God will forget you. At this moment, kneel before the altar and repeat that vow. And do not forget again. I'll kneel with you."

Pedro thought of the unborn child in Catana's womb. A shiver passed through him. *"Ay de mí, pecador!"* he muttered.

So at Olmedo's side in front of the altar, he renewed the vow.

But if Cortés, sleepless and untiring, spun his protective web—now with gold, now with promises, now with steel—over the land he had conquered and meant to hold, the *Uei Tlatoani,* Montezuma, in his quarters near by, did certain spinning of his own. It was clear that he had established relations with Narváez and that Aztec gold found its way into the latter's chests; clear too that he was stirring up the coast Indians in favor of Narváez. Report insisted that he had promised to hand over Cortés, dead or alive, to the invaders in return for their promise of delivering him from Malinche's protection.

"How small a thing would cure all that, Hernán!" mused Alvarado at one of the council meetings.

The General nodded. "Yes, Gossip, but patience is the virtue of our necessity. If Montezuma died, we'd have the devil loose here as well as on the coast. Even so—" He shook his head. "We're on a tightrope, *padrino.* Remember that and keep your temper till we get to the other side."

Then too, as Olmedo's letters reported, all the captains sent by Velásquez did not prove open to bribes; and some considered it wiser to take over and take all than to negotiate and share. Narváez, unmoved by diplomacy, still thundered, lightened, and marched to Cempoala. Sandoval's dispatches from Villa Rica spoke of Indian unrest and desperate measures of defense. The time had come for more than scheming. And for that, too, Cortés was ready.

"Señores," he summed up at the last council, "we have a hard choice to make, or rather we have no choice at all. It's one thing or nothing. Act, thrust, and by Our Lord's help we may clear one danger in time to deal with the next. Wait, and we're caught between the two, Narváez and the Aztecs. Therefore half of us march tomorrow. . . . You'll say, divide our force? Leave but ninety of us with five hundred Tlascalans to hold this city? What danger! Aye—bitter danger indeed! Danger for them who stay and for us who go. A handful here against thousands; a handful there when we meet nine hundred Castilians at Cempoala. Why then do we not march all together? Cavaliers, the answer is plain. Once leave this city, and we shall not lightly enter it again. Once lose this city, and we're out of the saddle of New Spain, which can be ruled only from here—our chief prize lost."

He paused a moment, then went on in a ringing voice, "So, with the help of Saint James, we take up the gage of Fortune. It may be that the Indian dogs will hold off till they see how it fares with us at Cempoala. If it fares badly, you who stay here are but dead men; if it fares well, we'll have another cast of the dice. Do I make myself clear?"

"Wonderfully!" laughed Captain Marín, who was jabbing at the table with his knife. He tossed the blade up and caught it by the hilt. "Wonderfully clear!"

"And you agree, gentlemen?"

A mutter of assent followed.

"Then I appoint Captain de Alvarado to my place during our absence." The General's eyes circled the group and stopped on Pedro. "With Captain de Vargas second in command."

"But Your Excellency—" Pedro burst out. He had been thinking in terms of the march to the sea, of head-on combat with Christians. To stay here, penned up and waiting! Why pick on him? "Your Excellency—"

"The post of danger, Señor de Vargas. And, by the way, you'll keep Juan García as your ensign. It behooves you and Alvarado to guard well our pearl of cities. I say guard it well—with wit and cunning which will help you more than strength. Guard it well."

Post of danger. The words snuffed out protest like a candle flame.

Next morning (it was early May) the company assembled after mass in the great courtyard of the compound. Polite farewells between the General and Montezuma, veiled menaces on either side, the flickering of lightning behind clouds. Farewells, not so polite, between comrades; tears perhaps, for the tough veterans were not ashamed of tears. The drums rolled; trumpets sounded to horse; the ranks fell in. Cortés swung to his saddle; El Molinero reared.

"*Hasta luego!—Hasta la vista!—Buena suerte! Adiós!*"

The gates opened before Corral riding in front with the black standard. It did not take long for the little band of horse and foot to file out. The courtyard seemed huge and untenanted to Pedro when they were gone.

―――――――――― *L* ――――――――――

NERVES. Not that Pedro de Vargas knew what nerves were, but they still functioned. Nerves that reduced sleep to fits and starts, that magnified trifles. At night the roaring of the beasts—the pumas, jaguars, ocelots, bears, and wolves—in the royal menagerie attached to Montezuma's now vacant palace across the central plaza became symbolic of encircling, savage forces. By day the murmur of the city grew to a sinister mutter of treachery and plot. What was Montezuma brewing behind the guarded approaches of his quarters? Doña Marina gently reported her fears and suspicions. And always the breathless question: what was happening on the coast? Always the weight of crushing responsibility: this queen of cities, the Aztec emperor, seven hundred and fifty thousand pesos' value in gold, to guard and keep.

"Enough food," said Pedro to Juan García one morning in mid-May, as they returned from inspecting the supplies, "enough water, enough powder. But enough brains?"

He put the question half to himself. Though often unexpressed, it was the all-important question at the back of everybody's mind. With Cortés gone, his master hand no longer at the helm, the difference in leadership was felt through every rank: by Montezuma, craftily smiling and assured; by the officers, short-tempered and covering up anxiety

289

with bluster; by the Tlascalans, who whispered of Malinche; not least by the commanders themselves, Alvarado and Vargas. Good intentions, consciousness, courage, did not make up for genius, and genius alone could cope with the situation. Everything that was done seemed tentative and imitative. It was haunted by the afterthoughts: Was that right? Would the General have done that?

Was it right, for instance, to have granted permission, at Montezuma's request, for the feast of Toxcatl, the annual dances in honor of Witchywolves and some other unpronounceable god? The festival lasted twenty days. It meant a gathering of chiefs from all Mexico and tributary provinces. Clearly the Aztecs meant to strike if Cortés lost his battle against Narváez. But if they were denied the use of the central teocalli on this occasion they might strike at once? It meant a gain of twenty days. Under such circumstances, to grant the permission, barring only human sacrifice, looked like a sort of compromise that Cortés would have made. One couldn't be sure, however.

"Brains?" Pedro repeated.

García tipped his steel cap to one side and scratched his head. "Brains? Ah, I see what you mean, comrade."

He glanced at the distant figure of Alvarado, who stood sunning himself on the terrace of his quarters. The sunlight, playing on his golden beard and splendid equipment, gave him a glittering appearance which deserved the Aztec nickname, *Tonatiuh,* Sun God. On the other hand, Pedro sometimes thought of him in terms of a glorified onion. Peel off his genial and popular manner which captivated everybody, and you came to his marvelous physique, his flawless daring; peel that off, and you found cold greed, edged with cruelty; peel that off, and what lay under it? Shrewdness, ability—or nothing?

"No, I didn't have Alvarado in mind, Juan. I meant myself, perhaps all of us. Christ! Little I knew what it meant to be a captain two weeks past. Carry out orders, lead a detachment, do a certain job—yes. But this weighing and balancing, groping, guessing! Makes me feel like a schoolboy. It's beyond me."

García grunted. "You're doing all right—as well as anybody could in your place. Don't take it to heart, *niño.* What we need here is the General. Seems a long time since he and the comrades marched, doesn't it?"

They were crossing the courtyard past a group of Tlascalan warriors, who were painting their naked bodies white and yellow. One of the number tapped a hand drum and sang monotonously, like the howling of a moon-struck dog.

"Hm-m," muttered García, "painting for war, eh? Maybe they're right. They've got a feeling for it."

"What I want to know," de Vargas went on out of his own thoughts, "is why he picked me out to stay behind—us. We'd have fitted in on the march or down there at Cempoala. There's no question about Alvarado; he's a senior captain and would have to be chosen. But for my place, why not Ordás, Morla, Marín, a half-dozen others? Why us?"

"I'll tell you," answered García in his literal fashion. "I've given much thought to the matter. The General always has two or more reasons for everything he does. One's on the surface; the rest he keeps to himself. It's in my mind that he remembered Catana's promising condition. He knew that she can't march and that you wouldn't want to leave her at this time. He says to himself, 'De Vargas would be torn two ways, half with us and half with his wench. He's a good man—none better, certainly not Ordás, Marín, or Morla. He's of more use to me in the city, looking out for his leman and the company's stakes at the same time, than he would be languishing on the march.' But he couldn't tell you any of that. As to why he chose me," García added complacently, "it's plain as my foot. He wanted a seasoned man of experience to steady you, my lad. And who in this company has more experience than I?"

Pedro laughed, but García had made a point about Catana; perhaps he was right.

"Well," he returned, "for whatever reason, here we are. Now see what we'll make of it."

They strolled over to the front wall of the courtyard, which had been heightened by a palisade since the alarm in April, discussed its merits for defense, then passed the time of day with the two sentinels on guard at the gates. Since one panel of them stood open, they crossed the threshold, standing outside for a look at the great plaza.

It was crowded today, but the first glimpse revealed a different crowd than usual. The place blazed with festival garments, the chiefs in their panaches, quilted armor, jewels, featherwork, and skins, the mighty of Mexico. There was a general thronging toward the portals of the Wall of Serpents, surrounding the temple pyramid, where rites of a religious character were about to begin. For if the Virgin and Child occupied one of the shrines on its broad summit, the neighboring shrine still contained Aztec idols, a joint tenancy which every right-minded Spaniard and Aztec alike, for opposite reasons, lamented and was bent on abolishing as soon as possible.

"How many would you say?" queried Pedro, appraising the concourse of people, while a steady stream along the avenue near at hand continually swelled it. "Two thousand? Three thousand?"

García spat judicially. "Hard upon ten, comrade, hard upon ten. What a load of gold and precious stones wasted on those heathen carcasses! If you could collect it all, it would swell our hoard by two hundred thousand pesos. Well, the time's coming. But note this. The bastards are all fighting men."

"They're unarmed."

"Aye, but when people of war meet together, arms aren't far off."

Scowling at the two Spaniards before the gates, or with eyes stonily overlooking them, the crowd along the avenue passed. Arms akimbo and legs wide, García and Pedro stared back.

Then all at once a curious procession appeared. Two youths, wearing garlands of flowers on their heads and with hair cut short, drew near, blowing reed flutes and strutting in a kind of ceremonial dance. They were the handsomest native boys Pedro had seen, perfectly shaped, finely featured, not too dark. A gorgeous retinue of pages and maidens attended them, strewing flowers, dancing and posturing. The crowd made way for them, some touching hand to ground and then to forehead, others actually prostrating themselves in evident worship.

"*Caramba!*" exclaimed Pedro. "What cursed Sodomites are these, or princes, or what the devil?"

"No, señor," said a guttural voice at his elbow, "these are gods."

Pedro shifted his eyes from the procession long enough to see that the speaker was a Tlascalan chief who had picked up enough Spanish words to make himself moderately intelligible. He had been baptized and went by the name of Bernardo, since it was impossible for a Christian tongue to twist itself around his native designation.

"Gods, eh?" De Vargas grinned. "What do you mean?"

"As I say, señor—gods, dirty Tenochca gods. May *Nuestro Señor* blast them!"

"How gods?"

Bernardo explained. Out of the jumble of words, Pedro at last got the drift. If not gods, the youths were at least incarnations. One was Witchywolves, the other Tezcatlipoca. They had been selected a year ago by the priests and had been tended, petted, and spoiled as gods should be. The pretty girls who accompanied them were part of the entertainment.

García slapped his thigh. "I'd be a god myself on those terms, Bernardo."

"Humph!" said the Indian. "Would you, señor? They go now to

death. Soon they be naked. No flowers then. Soon they break the flutes. They go up the teocalli. Soon their bellies ripped up and hearts taken out. Bloody hearts for Tezcatlipoca and Huitzilopochtli. Then people eat them. Cut off heads and stick them on the *tzonpantlis* there."

Pedro followed the pointing of the Indian's finger toward two high poles, which he had not before noticed, appearing above the wall of the temple enclosure. His smile was gone.

"Look you, Bernardo, you speak of human sacrifice, *hombre*. And that we have forbidden. The Aztecs accepted the condition when we gave them leave to hold the festival."

Bernardo shrugged. He needed no words to express his belief that the Aztecs would do as they pleased, Spanish permission or not.

"No sacrifice, no feast," he said.

The muscles stood out on Pedro's jaws. "We'll learn the truth of it and at once." His eyes fell on a black-coped native priest with white hen feathers in his hair, who was evidently late for the ceremony and was elbowing himself forward through the crowd on the avenue. "Bring me that fellow here, Juan, if you'll be so kind."

García crashed into the passing throng, his bulk shattering it. With one huge hand gripping the priest by the nape of the neck and with the other clamped on his captive's shoulder, he re-emerged like a seal carrying a fish.

A growl went up from the crowd.

"Turn out the guard," called Pedro.

The sentinels at the gate, reinforced by pikemen on constant duty beyond them, formed a hedge between the crowd and the priest, who now stood confronting de Vargas.

"Xiuhtecuhtli, Fire Lord!" muttered the people. It was Pedro's title among the Aztecs, drawn perhaps from his red hair. It implied both respect and fear. Whether because of that or because the religious ceremonies were beginning, they did not press upon the pikemen, but moved sullenly on. Only a few eddied around in an outer, scowling circle.

Pedro eyed the *papa* with distaste. He was dark, defiant, and snarling. His lips and cheeks were smeared with something shiny like honey. The white feathers in his hair stood up in the fashion of enormous bristles.

"Hark you, *padrino*," said de Vargas. "What's the meaning of those two sharp poles over yonder in the temple yard? You ought to know the purpose of them if anyone does. . . . Tell him my question, Bernardo."

The Tlascalan, frowning at the hated Aztec, haughtily translated.

293

The priest's eyes spat dark fire; he ground his teeth. At another time he might have answered discreetly, but García's handling had infuriated him. He burst into a hiss of words, then drew himself up and tried to outstare the green eyes of the Spanish captain.

"Well, what does he say?" Pedro demanded.

Bernardo licked his hungry lips. "He say—the *hijo de puta* say those poles to stick our stupid heads on after his people kill us all. *Ciertamente,* he say, they sacrifice to his gods anyhow they damn please."

Pedro's hand leaped to his knife. "Cut off our heads, eh? By the mass, he'll not live to see it!"

But at that moment, a cool demur sobered him and pressed the half inch of steel back into the scabbard. He was no longer a free agent, but one in authority. What would the General do in this case? Certainly not *that.* It was no time to resent insolence. He sighed.

A new pulse of anger shook him. Gripping the man's wrist, he lifted the arm, strong as it was, and swiveled the edge of the priest's hand against the steel gorget surrounding his own throat.

"A tough neck, *padrino,*" he laughed. "Too tough for you. Let him go, Juan."

Working his half-numbed fingers, the priest gave a final glare and turned away through the line of pikemen. García aimed a kick at him, but missed. A loud guffaw sounded from the gate.

"Too bad, Juan! What's up, Pedrito? You look like a ruffled gamecock. Trying to convert a priest? I take it you didn't prosper."

Alvarado's splendid figure filled the panel of the gate. Pedro rapped out what he had learned, and the golden smile faded.

"That's the way of it, ha?" the Captain-in-Chief rumbled. "We'll look into the matter. We'll teach the false dogs to stick by their bargain. Offend Our Lady's eyes and Our Blessed Lord's by their butcher tricks, would they? . . . Fifty men for a guard here!"

A trumpet called. There was no time lost in arming, for every man ate and slept with his weapons. Five minutes later, Alvarado, Vargas, and fifty others were marching toward the doors of the Wall of Serpents. They cut the crowd as a wedge of iron cleaves wood, scattered the gorgeous throng inside the temple yard, and found themselves before an open space reserved for the ceremonial dancing. Here, between two lines of chiefs in magnificent regalia, the black-gowned priests with their white hen feathers and honey-smeared faces were weaving a slow dance accompanied by the girls who had attended the two victims. It was a moment before Pedro recognized the youths, stark naked now, their hair hacked off, standing at one side.

As to what awaited them, there could be no doubt. Soon, among the priestly procession, they would be winding their way up the steep sides of the pyramid; would be breaking at every step, one by one, the flutes they had played during their year of divinity; would be stretched on the stone of sacrifice. They stood head up and exultant, gods about to pour out their blood for the good of the people. At the zenith of life, they were spending their final hour in a trance of rhythm, color, and fragrance of incense.

But the Spanish platoon had no training or time for mystical reflection. At one moment, the two gods stood on the brink of eternity; in the next, they found themselves the center of a steel column, which swept them out of the temple yard, across the square, and into the maw of the white men's quarters. A roar rose from behind, but the unarmed crowd could do nothing. Its leaders must take council; rites must be performed, omens consulted.

"Arquebusiers, arbalesters, to their posts!" Alvarado commanded. "Open the embrasures. Level the cannon."

But except for a hum, as of infinite, enraged bees, nothing happened.

"Well, *hijos míos,*" he beamed at the rescued gods, "you were saved in the nick of time, and I bet you're grateful. You'll tell us what these Aztecs have up their sleeves. . . . Throw a cloak over them, someone, lest they affront our ladies. *Adelante!* Bring them into my quarters and fetch Doña Marina to talk their lingo."

Catana stopped Pedro. "What's afoot, señor?"

"Nothing much, *querida.* Don't fash yourself. Only Indian stuff. We've kept those fellows from being cut to pieces in the *cu* yonder. Now we're going to examine them and find out what's happening in the city. I'll tell you about it later." He added half to himself, "I wonder how the General would handle it."

"*Pobrecitos!*" she said, eying the two youths pityingly.

In Alvarado's apartment the gods stood dazed before the awesome captains. These also were gods, and in their heart of hearts the Aztec boys believed them mighty as any. They saw Tonatiuh and Xiuhtecuhtli, Sun God and Fire God, seated in high-backed chairs with their swords across their knees, and the mysterious witch-woman, who had once been an Aztec, standing behind them. Did not the *Uei Tlatoani,* the great Montezuma himself, tremble before these *teules?*

But Tonatiuh grinned.

"Tell 'em, Doña Marina, that we're glad to have kept them alive. We take them under our protection, and no harm shall come to them.

The only service we want in return is to know what devilment the Tenochcas are up to. . . . That's the gist of it, eh, Pedrito?"

After Doña Marina had interpreted, one of the youths threw back his head and made a brief answer.

"They refuse to speak, señores," she said.

Alvarado gaped. "How? What? Refuse to speak?"

"Even so, señor."

"But, *vive Dios,* did we not save the whoresons' lives? Except for us, they'd now be butcher's meat on the way to the pot. Have they no thanks or natural gratitude? Perhaps you didn't explain to them."

"Yes, Señor Captain, I explained; they understand; but they will not speak."

"Now, God-a-mercy," sighed Alvarado, "the longer I deal with these heathen donkeys, the more they puzzle me. Do them a good turn, and it never crosses their thick skulls to render the like. The Golden Rule means nothing to them. Well then, we'll have to encourage them to talk." He shrugged discouraged shoulders and pondered briefly. "The screws or the boot? Hot irons take too long. I'll lay my money on the boot. It loosens the tongue quicker. . . . Hey, Alonso," he called to the guard at the door, "fetch Chávez with a boot. He knows how to fit it. And get a couple of men to handle these boys."

Pedro pinched his chin. He wondered what Cortés would have done. Torture seemed crude, and de Vargas, remembering the dungeon in Jaén, shrank from using it; but he could think of no better way. The survival of the garrison demanded as much information as could be obtained about Aztec intentions. The two youths probably knew.

The boot was a contraption of wooden staves bound tightly around the calf of the leg. Wedges were then hammered between knee and wood. It was very effective.

The bewildered gods were forced down upon low stools and held in position. Chávez (the one who had assisted at Pedro's operation in Villa Rica) fitted the boot to the leg of one of the captives, put a wedge in place, and raised his mallet.

"Better explain to them, Doña Marina," remarked Alvarado. "Tell 'em I don't want to break their kneecaps, but they've got to talk. If the boot doesn't persuade them, other things will."

Doña Marina interpreted in her gentle voice. The Aztecs ran their tongues over dry lips.

Alvarado nodded. Chávez came down with his mallet. A yelp, as of an agonized dog, sounded. The youth began speaking.

"He will tell what he knows, señor," murmured Doña Marina.

It was not that the Indian could not stand pain, but if he was ever to fulfill his office as a dying god, he must not be maimed. Only the perfect and unscathed were fit for the sacrifice.

"So much the better," said Alvarado. "I rejoice that he has no stomach. It saves time. Well, what does he know?"

The youth answered Doña Marina's questioning.

"He says that after the festival they will fall upon us," she translated. "Their chiefs and arms are ready. They await but the word of the gods. We have deceived them about the ships, they say: we have no intention of leaving this land. If Malinche is beaten by the other white men, let him be. If he returns here, he too shall be swallowed up. For they shall let no white *teule* live. They shall sacrifice them to the gods—all, all. They shall eat their flesh. They shall place their heads on the *tzonpantlis.*"

"Cursed thorough of them!" Alvarado grinned.

He and Pedro both laughed, to the amazement of the Aztecs, who sat staring at them. Perhaps the Spanish captains could not have done anything which would have made a deeper impression.

"We've learned little more than we knew already," Pedro observed. "It about shapes up with the other reports."

One of the youths spoke again. "They ask to be freed," said Doña Marina.

"Freed—to be cut into mincemeat?" exclaimed Alvarado. "'Slife, that's a strange boon. Why?"

"They wish to be sacrificed for their people. They wish to die for the gods."

Alvarado shook his blond head. "What fanaticism, Pedrito! What ignorance! I've half a mind to let Chávez work on them some more and make Christians of them. Chávez—"

"By your leave, Captain," Pedro interrupted, "we have more pressing things to do and to think about."

"Oh, well, have it your way," the other grumbled. He turned to Doña Marina. "As to setting them free, no. Tell them that we're giving nothing to Witchywolves, not even their carcasses. Take them off and lock them up. If they want to be sacrificed, perhaps we can accommodate them with a stake and a slow fire."

But when the room had been cleared, Alvarado fell thoughtful, staring at the rings on his broad fingers and twiddling his chain.

"Whew!" he puffed at last. "A bad prospect! I suppose I'm not more of a coward than other men, but I'm not in love with death."

He rose and walked up and down, his wide sleeves flaring, his Olympian head bowed. At last he stopped in front of Pedro.

"Cholula!" he breathed. "That's the answer. It's what Cortés would do if he were here. It's what he did there—in Cholula. Remember?"

De Vargas nodded. Who in the company could forget? He remembered how the chiefs of that hostile city on the road to Mexico had been lured into the Spanish quarters. He remembered the massacre. It had been a ruse of war, a distasteful ruse. Afterwards the city, which had been on the point of rising, lay quiet like a headless snake.

"Well?" he queried.

"Well, Pedrito. It's much the same here as there. The chiefs are here—all of them, the whole dung heap of them. We'll attend the festival tomorrow, not in formation but to view the sight, eh? Do you take me? All their nobles are inside—unarmed. I give the word—say, *Espíritu Santo*. We block the doors to cut off escape and then lay on. If we watch ourselves, not one of them should get off. A clean sweep. Then who's to lead the dogs against us? I tell you, it's the answer."

De Vargas thought it over. It was a touch-and-go situation. If the tidal wave of the city burst over the tiny garrison, how long could they hold out and from where could they expect help? The end was inevitable. If ever strong measures were justified, it was now. What would Cortés do? Then suddenly, as if from nowhere, the question presented itself: what would his father do? Don Francisco's hawk features hovered vividly an instant in his mind. His father, the soul of honor, who welcomed a fair fight, but scorned a mean advantage, however expedient, what would he do? That was more easily answered than in the case of the General. But all at once it struck Pedro that he must not try to copy either his father or Cortés. The decision was his, to be made according to his own standards and judgment. And at that moment, unknowingly, he passed a milestone in his life.

"Señor Captain," he said at last, getting up in his turn and facing Alvarado, "I think ill of the plan for two reasons. In the first place, this is Tenochtitlán, not Cholula. The people here are Tenochcas, not Cholulans. That was a small town and a soft race. This is a great city of warriors who have conquered the whole country. If you killed all the chiefs in the temple yard, there would still be plenty left to head the people. We would then have war at once. As it is, we have twenty days, and in that time much can happen. Señor Captain, I think that the plan would fail of its purpose and plunge us out of the frying pan into the fire."

This was an argument that Alvarado could follow. He fingered his beard, his eyes uncertain.

"It's a decided point," he admitted.

"The second reason has a different color," Pedro went on. "I think I know the mind of the General as well as anyone, and I know that the Cholula matter weighs upon his conscience. Nay, he has told me as much, regretting that he was overtempted to use means which reflect upon the honor of this company as Christian cavaliers. It is certain that Father Olmedo denounced the action roundly."

"He would," Alvarado muttered. "But what have priests to do with war?"

"I say that Cortés himself would hesitate before what you propose, Señor Captain. We have given permission for this festival. The chiefs are unarmed."

"I'll bet their weapons are not far off," the other interrupted.

"It may be. But does that justify us, while at peace, in falling on them with our pikes and swords?"

"Aye, if we know that they intend to fall upon us. As between knaves, the one who strikes first wins."

Pedro stiffened. "I'm not yet ready to add a knavish title to my name. Nor, in all honesty, have the Indians acted so. The Lord Montezuma in our presence threatened war. We fobbed him off with a pretext about the ships, but he promised nothing. This Aztec fellow here a few minutes past threatened war after twenty days. Are we to show less honor than these dogs?"

Alvarado's blond mask dropped. "Are you presuming to lesson me on the point of honor?"

"I'm presuming to be interested in my own honor, Señor Captain."

For a moment they stood icy and alert and silent. Then Alvarado's warm smile reappeared.

"Hark you, Pedrito, there's something in what you say. But the command here and the weight of it are mine. I'm answerable for it to the company. I do not propose to be caught napping by these rogues and I intend to strike first if that promises best. It's what Cortés would do. We'll attend the festival tomorrow and I'll decide then. If it seems likely that we can pull off the stroke to our advantage, we'll do it; if not, not. Much depends on the number there. And scruples be damned when the lives of this garrison are in the balance!"

Pedro set his jaw. "It's against my advice for every reason, sir. You can count me out of the butchery."

"You'll do your duty, Captain de Vargas."

They left it at that. With a sore heart, Pedro returned to his quarters.

"The trouble is," he complained to Catana, when they talked it over, "that it takes a smart man to treat with the devil, and Alvarado isn't smart enough. He's the kind of man who thinks he decides when events decide for him."

LI

BY THREES AND FOURS, next day, the Spaniards, duly coached by Alvarado, sauntered over to the great teocalli and mingled with the crowd inside. Only a handful to guard the gates, under the command of Juan García, and the Tlascalans, who dared not show their faces among Aztec warriors, were left in the compound. That the Spaniards were armed caused no remark, for the city populace had never seen them unarmed. The crowd did not welcome their presence, but tolerated it in a sort of scowling your-turn-next mood. Besides, the religious ceremonies of the festival drew off surplus attention.

Whatever he might have wished, Pedro could not refuse to accompany the others. He was second in command and under Alvarado's orders. Nothing had been decided anyway. Moreover, it could easily happen that the small body of men, instead of playing the hunters, might be forced into the role of hares; and in that case it would not do for one of the leading captains to be absent.

Together with Chávez, Nightingale Casca, and a crossbowman named Santesteban, he crossed the square gloomily enough, lamenting the absence of those who had marched with Cortés. The cream of the company had been skimmed off for the campaign along the coast. Pedro felt that if the captains who gathered usually at the council table had been here, Alvarado's essentially stupid plan, however plausible it looked on the surface, would not even have been considered.

The size of today's crowd did not equal yesterday's: that was the one comforting point. Whether today's ceremonies were less important, or whether the capture of the two victims had thrown a cloud over the festival, the throng of Aztec notables inside the temple enclosure did not exceed several hundred. De Vargas noted with pleasure Alvarado's crestfallen expression. Honorable scruples aside, even he must admit that the killing of these warriors, though a blow, would not cripple the Tenochcas.

"Well?" Pedro asked, walking up to the Captain-in-Chief.

The latter frowned. "Well, we'll wait. More may come. As it is, I can see some caciques here who might well be spared from troubling us. The quantity might be better, Pedrito, but the quality's of the best."

He fingered his beard. *"Por la Virgen,* I wish I knew what to do. It may be our one chance. And yet—*Mal haya!* Why did Cortés leave me in this pickle!"

Around and around, in and out, wove the dance of the warriors, a shifting kaleidoscope of headdresses, masks, prismatic patterns and colors. A cloying perfume of incense and of lilies filled the place. The thumping of drums and squeal of flutes mingled in a discord of sound, which was yet hypnotically rhythmic. In perfect cadence, every gesture and step prescribed, the chiefs were actors as well as dancers. They celebrated, no doubt, certain episodes in the lives of the gods, now to a slower, now to a faster tempo. Gradually the beat quickened, rising toward a climax; it grew hotter, fiercer, stirring the pulses of the Spanish onlookers. The savage intoxication spread. Eyes became fixed, muscles tense. The blaze of the sun, dazzlement of colors, smell of flowers, relentless crescendo of sound, acted like a drug.

Standing on the lower step of the pyramid, Pedro could overlook all of it. He felt his mind drifting, reeling in a whirlpool of sensation. The sudden voice of a speaker near at hand sounded far off, and it took an effort to steady himself.

"Señor Captain, we call on you. Now's the time. *Now's the time.* Give the word."

It was Francisco Alvarez, an officer whom Pedro disliked as a show-off and trouble-maker, a kind of self-appointed tribune among the soldiers.

"Word?" echoed Alvarado, staring at the dance, his face red, a swollen vein on his temple.

"Yes. *Espíritu Santo!* It's now or never. Let the heathen dogs have it!"

"Chitón, you fool!" snapped Pedro. He knew what the matter was with Alvarez. His own blood, whipped into foam by the drums, sang dangerously. "Cursed fool!"

The other's hand dropped on his sword. "Did you say *fool,* de Vargas?"

"By God!" Alvarado burst out wildly. He stretched his huge arms. "You're right, it's now or never. We'll have done with them. We'll give them the steel." His voice rose in a bellow above the thumping of the drums. *"Espíritu Santo!"*

The tension of the past two weeks, the rising flood of fear, uncertainty, desperation, broke its dike at the word and toppled forward in release. Like a flash of lightning, Alvarado's sword passed through the nearest of the dancers, jerked back and half-severed the neck of a second. A poniard in his other hand buried itself in a third. Roaring some kind of shout, he struck and stabbed among the gaily dressed throng, his steel helmet towering above it. On every side other blades flashed, then hacked and thrust. The beat of the drums gave place to a pandemonium of shrieks, yells, oaths—an agonized outcry that rose from the shambles, like the spirit of madness made articulate.

Rushing toward the gates of the enclosure, the Aztecs fell upon the swords of the soldiers who filled the openings. Turning toward the steps of the pyramid, they again faced a line of steel. Dashing toward the entrance of the shrines, they found the Spaniards here too on guard. Without weapons, taken utterly by surprise, the greater number had not the remotest chance. If they tried to scale the walls, they were cut down; if they begged for mercy, a blow silenced them. Relatively few escaped wounded to spread the news.

Buffeted here and there, Pedro could only look on helplessly. His first shout of protest had been lost in the explosion, and now there was nothing to do but watch the massacre, disgusted, ashamed, and sick at heart.

As the dead bodies piled up, littering the courtyard, a scramble for loot began, a plucking and tearing of gold ornaments or jewels from the corpses.

"It's mine, I tell you."

"No, by God, it's mine. I killed him."

The wranglers collided with Pedro, who, infected by the savagery around him, now saw red in his turn. Unsheathing, he brought the flat of his sword down on the head of one of the Spaniards.

The man turned with a snarl. It was Francisco Alvarez. A hot joy leaped up in de Vargas. By the saints, this was a relief! He could shut out the beastly scene for an instant and let his jangled nerves loose.

But the release was short-lived. Pedro's reputation in the company as a swordsman stopped the other even before their blades clashed. Alvarez received one stinging cut across the face and one on the shoulder, then backed away and took frankly to his heels, plunging into the mob that still eddied through the courtyard.

"Come back, obscenity," de Vargas shouted, starting to follow, when a group whirled in front of him and caught his attention. A tall Aztec, wearing the green panache and rich accouterment of a chief, had somehow got possession of a Spanish sword, with which he was laying about him and, for the moment, holding off a couple of prize-hunters. Untrained in the use of it, he could not last long, all the more as Nightingale Casca, an expert in rough-and-tumble, half-crouching behind his buckler, circled around on the lookout for an opening.

Then, as the Indian turned full in his direction, Pedro recognized the Aztec whom he had previously taken for Coatl. He had seen that face wearing the same masklike ferocity in the *barranca* near Jaén. It was the man who had spared his life and whose life in turn he had saved.

He acted on the impulse of the moment.

Springing forward, he caught the Indian's sword with an enlacing movement of his own, gave a twist of the wrist, then a jerk that disarmed him. And at the same instant, which brought them almost hand to hand, he saw that Coatl recognized him.

"Bravo!" said Casca. "But, Redhead, I claim my share. I'd have had the dog at the next turn except for you."

"And so would I," put in Santesteban. "I say it ought to be a third share each. . . . Here, I'll do the dirty work."

Expecting it, Pedro turned the blow of the dagger.

"No, *amigos,* by God, let me have him. I've taken a fancy to his equipment complete. It'll make a proper gift for Catana. I'll pay your shares—say fifty pesos each, eh? Hurry on, or you'll miss something better. I'll deal with him."

A quick estimate convinced the two men that fifty pesos each was well-paid or at least surer in stamped gold than in the form of rings, bangles, and turquoise. They knew also that Captain de Vargas's word was good. At another time, they might have been curious to see how he would finish the Indian; but at the moment the scramble for loot was too hot. Fortunately Coatl had the shrewdness to stand quiet like a man awaiting execution.

"Have it your way then," said Casca, hurrying off. "Remember—fifty pesos."

Pedro kept a grip on the prisoner's throat, sword point against his belly. He did not need to explain that play-acting was necessary.

"It's been a long time since Jaén," he said. "To think we should be meeting here, Coatl!"

The other nodded, his dark eyes searching Pedro's. The glance expressed uncertainty.

"I didn't know you were an Aztec then.".

Coatl shook his head. "Not Aztec. My land west. Friends to Tenochcas. I Zapotec."

Some tributary state. Pedro glanced toward the wall of the enclosure, a hundred yards off, and jerked his head. For a moment the coast was clear. The remaining Indians, herded in the center, were surrounded by a circle of swords, focusing the butchery and clamor. Scattered Spaniards were engaged in rifling dead bodies.

"Hark you, Coatl. Beat my sword aside. Give me a shove and make for that wall. *Hasta la vista!*"

The other lifted two fingers. "Twice," he said.

"Quick, you fool!"

"Twice, *caballero.*"

Then, following Pedro's directions, Coatl put on a convincing act— struck the sword to one side with his naked arm, twisted out of de Vargas's grip, sent him staggering back with a blow on the chest, and streaked for the wall. Leaping high, he caught the coping, lifted himself to the top, and disappeared on the other side.

Pedro ran and shouted, then with a wry smile put up his sword. He felt a twinge of superstition. What strange conjunction of their stars had brought him and Coatl twice together from across the world? Why should he twice have saved this man from death? Compulsion of circumstances. But who arranged the circumstances? What power—

"Let that be a lesson to you, de Vargas," said a familiar voice. Alvarado stooped over and, ripping a clout from a dead Indian, wiped his sword. "When you have one of those dogs in your grasp, don't give him time to say a prayer to his devils. Knock him on the head. Slippery vipers!"

In spite of his nonchalance, the Captain-in-Chief's sunniness was gone. He wore a hangdog, preoccupied look.

Pedro glanced at the pavement veined with rivulets of blood.

"Well, Señor Captain," he said dryly, "compliments on a noble feat of arms!"

Alvarado blazed up with all the passion of a tormented conscience. "Will you be pert with me, little master! Who spoke of feats of arms? A stroke of policy, yes—and to my mind a sound one. I don't care for your tone, and, by God, I'll chastise it."

"Chastise it?" echoed Pedro, his glance level. "Pick your words, señor."

"Not too carefully, my son," Alvarado retorted, the devil in him on top. "But pick them yourself. Are mutinous young puppies chastised or whipped? Or perhaps hanged? Who's the commander here?"

Pedro drew a step closer. Unconsciously, at the moment, his father's lisp crept out. "You, sir. You, sir, by all means. Who denies it? And do you take refuge behind that, eh?"

"Refuge?"

"Aye, sir. Or have you the stomach to meet me face to face? Then we'll determine this chastisement you speak of. But if not, without picking words, I'll ask you, who's the coward here?"

"Stomach to meet *you!*" Alvarado grinned. "Surely even you haven't the gall to apply coward to me."

Pedro bowed. "And the time of this meeting, Señor Captain?"

"Now!"

Alvarado snapped down his vizor. Whatever his faults, certainly cowardice was not one of them. He stepped back to gain room and drew his sword. Pedro kissed the cross hilt of his for good luck.

But at that moment a distant sound, which they had been too absorbed to notice, grew in volume and forced itself on their attention. Alvarado lowered his point.

"Wait! Harken! What the devil's that noise?"

It had the quality of an earthquake, of an approaching hurricane. The far-off rumble swelled to a roar. Both men listened a second.

"God in heaven!" exclaimed Alvarado suddenly. He sheathed his sword. "We have no time for this now. Our duty's to the company. The city's on us!"

He was already striding toward the center of the enclosure where the last piteous remnants of the Aztecs had been hacked down, and the Spaniards were busy with plunder. His voice filled the space.

"To your quarters! To your quarters! *Dense prisa! A la carrera!*"

Pulling the men off their prey, like dogs from a quarry, with a blow here, a kick there, he and Pedro spread the alarm. Several minutes later, the soldiers were streaming out of the temple yard and across the plaza toward the gates of Axayacatl's palace. There was no semblance of order. To Pedro, following in the rear, they looked like a pack of hard-pressed bandits loaded with booty, their clothes, hands, and faces smeared with blood. He followed, burning with shame, feeling a personal degradation. Where was his army, the army he had been proud of, the men he loved?

And meanwhile, down the two avenues leading into the central square, rolled slowly, because of their very mass, human torrents roaring louder as they approached—armed torrents, yelling, whistling, conch-blowing, drum-beating, the plumes of the warriors floating, like spindrift, above the surface. No more than a glimpse of this as the Spaniards plunged through the gates of their quarters. But before the last men had crowded in, the deadly rain of the oncoming storm began. Arrows and stones rattled on Pedro's helmet, corslet, and greaves. One of the foot soldiers, less well armed, pitched forward suddenly, a shaft quivering in his back. Two others dragged him through the gates.

Then, before he entered himself, Pedro de Vargas turned and, for the honor of Spain, faced the sleet of missiles, raising his arm in defiance, and, drawing back slowly, crossed the threshold.

LII

It seemed a miracle that the outer walls stood. Like a canopy of black spray, hissing above the palisades, a continuous volley of arrows and sling-stones plunged into the courtyard. Because of the din outside, orders had to be given by gesture instead of voice; even the blare of the Spanish trumpets sounded thin and remote in the enveloping clamor.

Recently ashamed of his comrades, Pedro now could not help a feeling of pride. Anarchists when it came to loot, the company met oncoming annihilation as a disciplined unit. The training of the past year asserted itself. Neither panic-stricken nor with rat-in-the-corner courage, the cutthroats of a few minutes since were again veterans, cool, determined, even gay. It was after all a relief to have done with suspense and to feel the hot breath of war on their faces.

Embrasures were opened, cannon rolled up; and their thunder added a heavy note to the howl of attack. No aim was necessary, since they fired point-blank into the mass pressing against the other side of the enclosure. Their stone balls cut lanes through the crowd which were instantly filled up. The guns were rolled back, reloaded, fired again— back and forth as fast as their crews could ram home the charges. The Indian torrent rose higher, men clambering on each other's shoulders, clutching at the palisade that topped the wall—to be met here by crossbow and musket, sword and pike, while the cannon bellowed underneath—but still clutching, still clambering, and some indeed plunging over and down to die on the steel of the defenders below.

But the garrison suffered as well. Especially the more lightly protected Tlascalan allies were exposed to arrows and slingshots, while the Castilians themselves did not escape. Wounds accumulated, and while these for the most part were not serious, they increased the fatigue which began to show as the attack went on.

Pedro met Catana, as she passed from group to group, a bucket of water in each hand, a bunch of rags stuck through her belt. She was stopped continually to the tune of, "Water here, for the love of God!" or "Bind me a clout around this bleeding, *camarada.*" Several arrows, which she had not had time to pluck out, dangled from her tabard of quilted armor.

"Will you get back to your quarters, *moza!*" Pedro shouted, raising his vizor. "Have you no sense at all!"

She teased him with a smile.

"You wait!" he stormed. "If I don't give you a ration of stirrup leather on the right place this evening!"

"Meanwhile, have a drink, señor," she answered, handing him a ladle of water. "And let me wipe your face. It's all of a sweat."

"Please go back to our quarters, *querida*. You know you ought to."

"Not for anything. I can do more good here."

He drank thirstily. Dipping a clout in the water, she sponged his face which was half-parboiled in the closeness of the helmet.

"You're such a donkey, Catana!"

"*Seguro.*"

"Be damned, if I don't make you take me seriously."

"*Caramba!* I do. But whether you beat me or not I'm not going back to our quarters."

A stone grazed her shoulder. Pedro started working at his corslet. "Well then, you'll put on my armor."

"Your armor, nothing!" she flared. "Do you think I'll let you stand naked in battle while I wear your harness? I have some decency! A pretty sight to be carrying water buckets in a suit of steel! What do you take me for!"

The figure of Alvarado clanked up. "Water, *ángel mía!*" he croaked, raising his vizor from a fiery red face. "Ah!"

He rinsed his mouth, spat out the water, then drank a ladleful.

"*Gracias,* Mistress." Glancing at de Vargas, his blue eyes twinkled. "Might as well say it as think it, Pedrito. You were right, I was wrong. The hell of a mess!" He thrust out his hand. "To the devil with by-gones!"

"*Con mucho gusto!*" nodded the other.

The two gauntlets locked. Pedro added, "But put in your word, sir, as captain, with this woman of mine to get her out of the fight. She's in no shape for it."

Alvarado nodded. "Go inside, Catana."

"Bah!"

He grinned. "You see, I've done my best."

The attack surged on, a mingled thunder of cannon and muskets, yells from ten thousand throats, blowing of conchs, defiance of trumpets. The courtyard became as cluttered with arrows and javelins as a threshing floor with straw. The bodies beyond the wall heaped up, but the assault did not slacken. The garrison, stiff, weary, and bleeding, still manned the embrasures and the coping of the wall. Two hours, three hours, passed. The sun sloped toward evening. The fight remained a stalemate at high tension.

It was Alvarado's idea to call on the captive Montezuma for help. Unceremoniously, between the chief captain and de Vargas, with Doña Marina attending, the *Uei Tlatoani* was conducted to a terrace-like eminence on the wall and induced to address the people. At the first glimpse of his revered figure, slight but stately, wearing the odd-shaped coronet of his office, a hush fell on the nearest ranks of attackers and spread through the vast crowd in the square. After hours of uproar, the silence seemed unnatural and almost uncanny.

His voice carried far. What he said, Pedro did not learn until afterwards from Doña Marina. The *Uei Tlatoani* commanded patience. The time would come, but the time was not yet. Patience. Did they think that Montezuma slept, that the gods were sleeping? Let them await the fullness of time. It would not be long. And a day of joy would dawn over Tenochtitlán. ("Words of cunning," said Doña Marina later, "and of ill-omen.")

Meanwhile, Pedro stared out over the barbaric multitude, lighted up by the slant rays of the setting sun, a medley of strange emblems, swarthy faces. A dizzy dream-sense of unreality passed over him. He recalled a snatch from Ortiz's song.

> *. . . Far in the West, the echoes of our fate . . .*

Lord! Was that day at sea only a year ago?

The rattle of his armor, as he shifted from one foot to the other, brought him back to Montezuma's voice and to the myriad of intent eyes. He thought of the handful of men in the courtyard, alone against these legions.

For the time being, at least, the attack stopped; the crowd withdrew. By the advice of Montezuma, one of his kinsmen, whom the Spaniards called the Infante, was released on the pretext of calming the people. And night came on, silent except for the roaring of the caged beasts across the square. Stiff and exhausted, the company kept vigil around its bivouacs in the courtyard.

Even Juan García felt depressed. "There's a spell on this cursed New World," he growled, sitting legs wide in front of one of the fires. "It always happens the same way. First, everything beautiful; big prospects, gold, land, Indians, a paradise for the taking. Then—crash! You wake up to find yourself in the jakes and fighting to crawl out. What prospects we had up to a month ago! And now look at us! *Jesús María!* It's heartbreaking."

"Well," grinned the Nightingale from across the fire, "who talked up the scuttling of our ships? Who was fire and flames for marching to Mexico?"

"I admit it," García nodded. "But what of most of us? Was I the only one? I say it's witchcraft. If it wasn't, who with any sense wouldn't exchange the whole New World for a nice little farm in Andalusia? A few pigs and goats. A capable woman to tend them. Quiet sleep." He picked up one of the Aztec arrows that littered the pavement and chucked it into the fire. "If Our Lord helps me out of this with a whole skin, I'll walk barefoot from Cádiz to St. Mary of Guadalupe."

Pedro couldn't help chuckling; he remembered García at Sanlúcar.

Chin on hand, Catana lay stretched out between Pedro and Ochoa. The boy had dropped off to sleep, his head on her thigh. She stared intently at the fire, the light of which flickered on her mop of black hair and brought out the angles of her face.

"'Struth, Juan!" she put in. "I know more about pigs and goats in Andalusia than you do. *Santa María!* I've still got the smell of them in my nose. As for me, cavaliers," she went on in a different tone, "if we die tomorrow, I for one will say *gracias a Dios* for the good days we've had. Would I trade our venture since Villa Rica for a chance to scratch fleas and grow old on the fattest farm in Castile? No, sirs, whatever the price! And I say *viva* now . . . *viva* tomorrow!"

From the standpoint of Pedro, who kept his eye on morale, it was the right speech at the right time. The grousing mood passed in a mutter of assent. The Nightingale fished out a pack of cards. Bull García began speculating about what was happening on the coast.

Pedro reached for Catana's hand and squeezed it. They could feel rather than see each other's eyes in the half-light.

"*Viva* you!" he whispered.

The attack flared up again at dawn. The Infante, instead of calming the people, brought them back in hotter temper, if possible, than before. Perhaps he had reported the weariness of the garrison; or perhaps it was one of Montezuma's finesses. At any rate, hour followed hour of assault.

And once more Montezuma intervened. But this time Pedro de Alvarado, drawing his dagger in full view of the crowd, pointed it at the *Uei Tlatoani's* heart. It did not need Doña Marina's interpretation to explain his meaning. Again sullenly the attackers withdrew; but they blocked every street and canal, cut the water main furnishing the Spanish quarters, burned the small brigantines which Cortés had built as an additional means of retreat across the lake, and settled down to a complete siege.

Someone discovered a spring in the enclosure itself. Food supplies were adequate. The stalemate could go on for a long time. Its ultimate solution depended on Cortés.

Tlascalan messengers were got off to run the Aztec lines and carry news to the General of what had happened. He must give help, if he were in a position to give it; otherwise the garrison was lost. After that, nothing remained but to wait.

As the aching, empty days passed, the chapel, which had been installed in the compound, received a steady flow of worshipers; and Father Juan Díaz (whose cloth had saved him from hanging after the Escudero mutiny) heard everybody's confession. Between watches, the loot of the recent massacre in the teocalli changed hands over drumskin cards. The chronic bores of the company exercised their profession on apathetic listeners. Except for worshiping, gambling, and talk, there was nothing to do; that is, nothing but stare at the chilling prospect of death unless salvation came from the coast; and of that, the hope dwindled with every silent dawn.

Then one day, while Pedro and García idled on the terrace steps of one of the buildings, Alvarado came up with Doña Marina.

"You and I are wanted by the Lord Montezuma, Pedrito. He has something to communicate. I wonder what's on the old fox's mind now. . . . Will you come?"

Since the outbreak of war, the *Uei Tlatoani's* retinue had shrunk to a skeleton staff; but there were still the obsequious ushers to conduct Alvarado, de Vargas, and the interpreter through the cavernous rooms to the presence of the Most High. This time he received them on a half-enclosed porch outside the council chamber. Suave and gracious as always, he could not hide for once a certain agitation. It might signify good or evil, and the two Spaniards watched him narrowly.

"Tonatiuh and Xiuhtecuhtli," he said through the lips of Doña Marina, "I have but now received excellent tidings from Cempoala, which I must share with you."

How had he received them? The question flashed through the minds of his listeners while the woman translated. In spite of guards and walls, Montezuma contrived always to keep better informed about distant events than his captors. But interest in what he had to say eclipsed everything else. Pedro clenched his hands to keep them from trembling. Alvarado's florid face looked a shade paler.

"There has been a great battle," said the Aztec, "a great battle between Malinche and the chief of the new-come *teules*."

He took up a thickish volume of folded *maguey* paper from the stand in front of him and opened it.

"Nombre de Dios!" Alvarado burst out. "And who won the battle? Can't he get to the point?"

"Behold," said Montezuma, handing over the volume, "the record is there in full. Let Tonatiuh read it for himself."

It was the usual pictorial report, a single incident upon each fold of the long strip which formed the book, but so conventionalized that the Spanish captain, who frowned, squinted, and turned the manuscript in every direction, could make nothing of it.

"Here, Marina," he fumed, "read me this thing if you can—devil take it!—and let's hear what happened for the Lord's sake."

He had no need to speak twice. Marina's eager eyes were already devouring the pictures for news of her lover. Suddenly her cheeks flushed.

"Nuestra Señora be praised . . ."

"Well? . . . Well?"

"Victory, sirs!" She raised her two hands, her face alight with joy.

"But the details? How? Where?"

"Look."

Forgetting Montezuma, the two captains pressed on either side of Marina, their heads bowed close to hers, their eyes following the pointing of her fingers.

"Look. Our General is at the river, Chachalacas, a league from Cempoala. He has two hundred and fifty men. There is Captain Velásquez de León. There is Captain de Sandoval. It is night and it rains. Our General speaks to the men."

"Can't you hear him!" muttered Pedro. "I'll bet he made their blood sing, rain or not. Nobody can speak like he does! So they camped at the Chachalacas?"

"No, señor. They cross the river."

"Night attack!" Alvarado reflected. "Good idea!"

"They capture a sentinel outside Cempoala. Another escapes. He carries the alarm. But Narváez sleeps. Our General enters the town. He marches toward the main teocalli. The enemy wake up. They fire the cannon. But, see, our men stand flat against the houses. Only three are killed. The others charge—it is Captain Pizarro who leads. They capture the cannon."

"Where was Cortés?" Alvarado queried.

Doña Marina examined the pictures. "It was like this, señores. The men of Narváez were too many to lodge in the chief temple as we did. Narváez had his quarters there on top of the pyramid. He stationed guards on the steps. But other captains were in other temples. All had to be taken. The General, with a few men, went from place to place."

"He would," Pedro nodded. "Go on. What happened?"

Marina pointed. "See, it is Captain de Sandoval who charges the main pyramid. He fights his way up with the pikemen. Narváez meets him. It is a fierce fight there on top of the teocalli. *Ahí!*" She pointed at the next picture, savage excitement breaking for a moment through her usual gentleness. "Look, the eye of Pánfilo de Narváez is struck out by a pike. His men carry him into the shrine where he was lodged. They bolt the doors. One of our comrades sets fire to the roof. Now all is in flames. Narváez yields; he is taken prisoner. Victory!"

Exultant oaths echoed her. "I suppose the horsemen had no time to saddle," observed Alvarado.

"But yes, señor, some escaped; others were not in Cempoala. Look"—she pointed at another fold in the manuscript—"the Captains Olid and Ordás persuaded them next day to come in. And behold"— her voice rang with pride—"there is the General seated, wearing a robe over his armor, and all the men of Narváez pay him honor and enlist under him. He greets them lovingly. Is that not glory—eight hundred of them, with eighty horsemen and many cannon, overcome by two hundred and fifty of our comrades!"

Alvarado growled, "I wish I had been there. What filthy luck to be penned in this pigsty, while that passage of arms went forward! Eh, de Vargas?"

Pedro gritted his teeth in envy too deep for words. He thought of his friend and rival, Sandoval, fighting his way up the pyramid.

"What happened to Narváez?" Alvarado added. "Hanged, I imagine."

"No, sir," replied Marina, "he is shown here in prison at Villa Rica."

The guttural, sonorous voice of Montezuma broke in, and with a start the two captains remembered him. But what he said or did now had no importance. They looked at him with the eyes of men reprieved from death through no merit of his. At a stroke, their troubles were ended; their star once more rode high. If, with four hundred men, Cortés had originally made himself master of Mexico, was there any fear that he could hold it with twelve hundred? By now the messengers from the garrison must have reached him; by now he might even be crossing the mountains westward to rescue and to avenge.

"Did I not say the tidings were excellent?" Montezuma smiled, and his smile was like the gleam of thin ice over black water. "Do we not love and honor Malinche, and rejoice in his success? We shall welcome him back with his twelve hundred valiant *teules*. Yes, he is even now preparing to march. Behold, the causeways to Tenochtitlán are open."

Marina's eyelids fluttered a little as she translated.

"And look to yourself, when he comes, Señor Montezuma," Alvarado growled. "I advise you to call off this siege, open your markets, collect gold in reparation for the rebellion of your people, and make all well against his return. If so, he may have mercy; if not, he will know how to punish. Be sure of it."

Montezuma smiled again. "All will be well, Tonatiuh. I promise that all will be very well. As I said, the causeways are open to Malinche. We shall greet him fittingly."

With wings on their heels, the two captains and Marina hastened back through the hall-like rooms to bring the great news to the garrison. Soon cannon, drums, and trumpets would be saluting the victory. Then would come the *Te Deum*. Verily God had delivered His people out of the jaws of death.

"How now, señora?" Pedro exclaimed suddenly.

On the threshold of the outer terrace, Doña Marina had stopped and was leaning against the side of the doorway.

"It is faintness, sir." The woman's tawny face looked almost white.

"Faintness? Are you unwell, Mistress?"

"No." The woman's eyes shifted from de Vargas to Alvarado, then back. "I am afraid."

"Of what?" Alvarado gaped. "Now, of all times—"

"Send a messenger," she went on urgently. "Warn our General that he must not enter this city. Let us rather join him."

The Captain-in-Chief laughed. "You are moon-struck, Marina. What ails you?"

"What I saw behind Montezuma's eyes. It was not fear. My lords, he rejoices indeed at the return of Cortés and all his army. He prepares a bitter welcome—"

In front of them, the courtyard was buzzing around a man who now broke loose and came up the terrace steps. It was Luis Alonso, who had marched with Cortés. Dust-stained but wreathed in smiles, he saluted.

"A letter and greetings from the General, Your Worships. I must

have word too with the Lord Montezuma. Wait till you hear the news!
By God, did we put them in the sack—the Narváez crowd—all of
them! What a clean sweep, Your Worships!"

He ran on, while Alvarado opened the letter. It surprised Alonso
that his news did not seem new.

"God be thanked!" said the Chief Captain. "But how did you get
through the lines, friend Luis? You notice that we've been under attack
since you left."

"By the southern causeway," the other answered. "It's wide open."
Marina's voice broke in desolately. "My lords, the trap is open."

"Well then," grinned Alvarado, his eyes on the letter, "it won't have
to wait long. Let it close! Twelve hundred Castilian gentlemen, not
counting the Tlascalans. A hundred horse. Thirty cannon. I pity the
trap."

—————— LIII ——————

ON MIDSUMMER'S DAY not three weeks later, the garrison lined the
walls of the compound to catch from far off on the southern causeway
the marching beat of drums, piping of fifes, flourish of trumpets, clatter
of horses, that announced the incoming army.

The sounds approached, distinct against the background of a vast
silence. The crowds which but yesterday had choked the central square
and avenues of the city had vanished. Tenochtitlán lay apparently
deserted.

But to the weary listeners no other music on earth would have
sounded so sweet. In spite of Alvarado's threats to Montezuma, the
siege had not been raised until yesterday. It was as if the Aztecs, having
prevented the garrison from marching out, did not wish to discourage
Cortés from marching in. Now the long vigil was over. With Cortés
once more at the helm and an army tripled in numbers to support him,
the enterprise had reached its final, prosperous goal.

The sound of the marching grew louder. Straining their eyes, the
watchers could at last see the front of the column advancing up the
southern avenue. But, as more of it came into sight, what a column!
Rank on rank of steel caps, arquebusiers, arbalesters, pikemen. And
the horsemen! Used to their own meager squadron, it seemed to the
garrison like a forest of lances.

"Trumpeters, sound off!" Pedro shouted from his vantage point at

314

the corner of the parapet. A welcoming flourish answered from the courtyard. "Gunners, blow your matches! Fire!" For an instant every other sound was eclipsed by the thunder of the salute. Then, emerging from it, the oncoming march rang louder.

Standing next to Pedro, Catana squeezed his arm. "Señor, doesn't it remind you of that day at Villa Rica when you and I—But this is much more wonderful."

He nodded. "We didn't expect it a month ago—eh, *vida mía?* Note me the appointments of these new cavaliers, the equipment! Gad, we're but ragamuffins by the side of them! Just the same, our comrades are marching in the van, as they ought. They're the stuff—"

"The General!" she broke in. "I can see him—"

"Where?"

"Behind Señor Corral with the banner."

"Yes. *Cáspita,* he's got a new suit of harness! . . . And there's Olid, Morla, Tapia, Ordás. Sandoval! By God, there's Sandoval!" Pedro cupped his hands. *"Hola,* Gonzalo de Sandoval!" he shouted, but his voice did not carry. "Ha, the good comrades!"

Catana laughed. "See there! See! If Master Botello hasn't got himself a horse. He always wanted one. It's a beauty. He's riding high as any of the captains. . . . There's Señor Ortiz. I wonder if he's made a new ballad."

Names passed from man to man down the line of onlookers. Hands and caps were waved.

"Gentlemen," barked Alvarado from the courtyard, "down here and fall in! *Aprisa!* Will you greet our company like a parcel of women on a roof? Company formation! Captain de Vargas, stay where you are and give me the signal for opening the gates."

Standing alone, Pedro watched the front ranks draw close, individual faces becoming distinct, the lance points of the horsemen on a level with his face.

"By God, there's the Redhead!" bawled the familiar voice of Sandoval. "Ha, Redhead!"

A score of gauntlets were raised, a volley of *Ha's* and *Hola's* went up from the oncoming riders. Cortés himself smiled and waved. Pedro saluted him. But at the same moment de Vargas stiffened. That cavalier on the handsome bay to the rear of his friends—the tilted eyebrows, pale face . . . And that priest with the square beard beside him on the genet? They were both staring up at him.

Fiery particles danced in front of Pedro's eyes. He went cold, then hot. His hands were shaking. It couldn't be true. A trick of the brain.

"How about it?" called Alvarado.

Pedro signaled to open the gates.

No, it was not a delusion. The pair of horsemen were real. They were still watching him—and de Silva smiled.

Diego de Silva and the Inquisitor of Jaén, Ignacio de Lora!

LIV

IT WAS CHARACTERISTIC OF Father Bartolomé de Olmedo that even the bustle of arrival did not prevent him from meeting Pedro, as the latter came down from the walls. One glance at his preoccupied face told the friar that de Vargas had recognized his two arch-enemies among the incoming troops. He would have passed Olmedo if the priest had not laid a detaining hand on his arm.

"Ha, Father!" Pedro exclaimed. "I crave a thousand pardons, but I had something on my mind." And making an effort, he added, "What joy to see you and the comrades again! My faith, you've been sadly missed!"

Gradually Olmedo's features replaced those of de Silva and the Inquisitor which were absorbing him, and he noted the leaner, tanned, worn look which the friar had brought back from the campaign.

"We've a deal to tell each other," Pedro went on conventionally. "It seems that your management didn't prevent bloodshed after all, eh?"

"No, my son; but it lessened it. The fight at Cempoala would not have been so easily won if I had not gilded certain fingers and persuaded certain people. It's clear that, for the sake of peace—at least among Spaniards—Hernán Cortés is the only possible leader in New Spain." He broke off. "But let's deal frankly with each other, son Pedro. There are more pressing matters. I know what's in your mind."

By now, de Vargas had recovered enough from what he had seen on the wall to gather his wits together; and, as he did so, his eyes sharpened. Certain points which had been in doubt were becoming clearer.

"Frankness, by all means, Father Bartolomé. Were you frank with me when you left here six weeks ago?"

The friar shook his head. "If you mean that I did not tell you all I knew, I was not frank—no."

"You knew then that Diego de Silva and this Inquisitor were with Narváez?"

316

"Yes, their names were on the list we got from Guevara."

"And that was the reason that García and I were left here, eh?"

"Yes, for your own good, my son."

"Thanks. And for that reason, you had me renew my vow?"

"Yes."

Pedro's laugh jarred. "Frankness comes better late than never. Even so, I thought you were above such tricks. But all priests are the same. They must be subtle; they must play chess with truth. I suppose you couldn't tell me why in this case. That's asking too much."

Olmedo faced him without flinching. In spite of his stubby nose, sunburned at the tip, his squat figure and dust-covered robe, he still looked impressive.

"No, not too much. And I'll tell you without subtlety. It was because I am a priest, because I hate bloodshed, and because I love you. Is that plain enough? You had taken a vow on which God's pardon for you depended. Should I let you forget it? Should I dangle temptation before your eyes by letting you go to Cempoala? As for García, I wished to save him. You and I know what the penalty is for killing a priest—here and hereafter."

Pedro stared into the unblinking, honest eyes of the friar.

"But what have you gained?" he burst out. "The men are here—penned in with us here! Is that better than if Juan and I had met them at Cempoala?"

Olmedo shrugged. "I don't know. All I could do was play for time. I gained that much, hoping that matters would clear themselves. They haven't. What happens now depends on you."

"If you think," Pedro frothed over, "that Juan and I are going to house with men who have done to death the people we loved, you're mistaken. It's too much for flesh and blood to stand."

The friar drew close and laid his forefinger on Pedro's chest. "Nevertheless, that's what you're going to stand, Captain de Vargas. There was a time when I could have handed you over to the Inquisition. Instead, I imposed a penance which you accepted and which was heavier than you thought. Now you are going to perform that penance. And if you love García, you will use every means in your power to keep him quiet. . . . Harken. Whatever you think of them, de Silva and Father Ignacio have great credit with these new men from Cuba. It touches the life of this enterprise that there be no breach between them and us. Nor will Hernán Cortés permit any. He returns in glory from this campaign. It has gone to his head. Now, more than ever, his ambition is in the saddle, and it will brush anything out of its way. A word to the wise, son Pedro."

De Vargas straightened up. "Do you think that fear—"

"Nonsense!" Olmedo interrupted. "I thought you loved your friend, Juan García. As for you, I hold you to your oath."

Through the great courtyard, now that the ranks had broken, eddied an immense jubilation: reunion of old friends, back-slapping, embraces, hubbub of voices; the newcomers strolling about, meeting members of the garrison; horses being led off to their stalls; groups forming and reforming like a kaleidoscope. From the corner near the wall, Pedro gazed at it blindly.

"What about de Silva and the priest?" he muttered. "Have you preached at them? Or perhaps we're to be the only Christians and let them choose their time to knife us?"

Olmedo shook his head. "No. It wasn't hard to make them see that you and García are in the favor of the General and of our company— that they're not masters here. They're content to forget bygones." The friar was honest enough to add, "Or so they say."

"Cursed generous of them!" returned Pedro. He stared at the pavement a moment. "Well, Father Bartolomé, the saints help me to keep my vow! It's bitter hard." He ran his sleeve across his forehead. "And I'll do what I can with Juan García—though how that will be, God knows. But let one of those *bribones* raise a finger, as I hope they will"—Pedro shook with passion—"let them step one inch across the line, and I hold myself absolved. And it will be my greatest pleasure—" He choked himself off, adding dully, "And there's an end on it."

Having got all he could expect for the moment, Olmedo nodded. But the end, as Pedro had put it, had an immediate postscript. An explosion burst out in the courtyard, a roar of voices, hurrying of feet, the swaying back and forth of a group in the center, out of which issued an animal-like raging devoid of any human tone. Then, staggering back from the group, as if thrown off by a rotating wheel, appeared the figure of Ignacio de Lora. His hands were clutching his throat; his robe was torn; and he had a smear of blood on his face. Meanwhile, the knot of struggling men scuffled round and round, opened and closed, like the staves of a barrel on the point of bursting.

With a cry of "God-a-mercy," Pedro raced toward the tumult, which widened rapidly as other men joined in.

"Get him away!" howled a voice from the tussle. "Get him out of sight!" And a couple of men, detaching themselves, began hurrying Father Ignacio toward one of the buildings.

At the same moment, the group blew apart, its several members reeling backward—and García emerged, roaring, frothing, his face crimson, his eyes rolling for a glimpse of his quarry. Catching sight of de Lora, now fifty paces distant, he bounded after him.

Pedro strained forward but could not hope to overtake García in the second or two of grace that remained. The men on either side of de Lora, warned by the shouts from behind, jumped to one side, leaving the Inquisitor alone in the path of his pursuer, who came on head down like a charging bull. Murder seemed inevitable, when, in the last fraction of time, a steel-clad figure threw itself between. Crouched low and with legs braced wide, it presented an obstacle that struck García slightly above the knees and sent him headlong crashing to the pavement. As he rose, a two-hundred-pound weight of flesh, bone, and armor landed between his shoulders and pinned him down.

It was Sandoval. His rough bellow mingled with García's raging.

"How now, *compañero!* How now, you mad fool!" And to de Lora, who stood rooted several paces away, "Get along with Your Reverence! Disappear for God's sake! . . . Ha, Redhead! And in good time, too!"

With a tremendous heave, García struggled to his knees, though Sandoval still had an arm around his throat. Pedro gripped him from the other side. But García was apparently unconscious of them. His eyes were fixed on the retreating figure of Ignacio de Lora, who at that moment vanished around the corner of a building. Then he relaxed slightly and looked around.

"Name of God!" he muttered. "Why did you hinder me, friends? Except for you, that piece of dung would have been spattered around the compound. But wait! And it won't be long either. . . . So he's joined our company, has he! That's a joke!" He clenched his huge fists, staring again at the place where de Lora had disappeared.

A vociferous, half-angry, half-curious throng surrounded them. Oaths and demands of what was up and what ailed García showered on all sides. It was noticeable that the old company tried to make light of the matter but that the newcomers were ruffled and truculent. Dirty looks started and hands fingered sword hilts. But all at once silence fell, and the crowd opened; García found himself facing Cortés.

The General was bareheaded, but otherwise in full harness. Though he said nothing for a moment, his extreme pallor, the vein across his forehead, and the hook of his mouth, denoted towering rage.

"Give me the truth of this," he said at last in a dry, hot voice. "I hope I have been misinformed. Did you attack the Reverend Father

Ignacio de Lora when he had scarce dismounted and when, thinking no ill, he was talking with a couple of gentlemen?"

García's bloodshot eyes met the black glance of the other steadily.

"Aye, Your Excellency, and I would have attacked him before he had dismounted if I had noticed him. But I was busy with the cannon. It was a mistake, I grant you. I should have waited until there were fewer meddlers about."

"For what reason, except madness, did you attack this holy man?"

The cords of García's neck swelled. Trying to speak, he could get no sound out at first. Then the words came like hot lava.

"Because that swine laid my mother on the rack; because he broke every bone in her body until she prayed him for death; because, when I bribed him eight hundred castellanos to spare her, he took the money and sent her to the stake. Reason? If that's no reason, I'd be glad of hell, provided I can tear his carcass limb from limb . . ."

The voice choked again. A mutter, half-sympathetic, half-angry, went through the crowd.

"From your standpoint, a good reason—if true," snapped Cortés in the same burning tone.

"By the Cross, it's true," said Pedro. "I swear to every letter of it."

"Who asked for your swearing?" The dark eyes flicked like a lash. "Am I concerned with this man's private feud? But I'm concerned with this—yes, in full measure—that he should flout the laws of the army by attempting to kill one of our company—let alone that Father Ignacio is a priest of God. . . . Nor is this the first time. At Cempoala, he drew his sword against Captain Velásquez and endangered the lives of other gentlemen. I overlooked it then because he was drunk. He is not drunk now; and, by my conscience, I intend to make it clear once and for all that military laws are not to be trifled with."

Though plainly in a hanging mood, Cortés curbed himself. His anger was perhaps the more deadly because he controlled it. Not that García would escape (the gallows were written in every line of the General's face), but to string him up on the spot would defeat the purpose of his execution. He must be tried and condemned. He must be hanged to a ruffle of drums in the presence of the company.

Cortés's glance singled out one of the newcomers. It was politic to hand García over to the faction to which de Lora belonged. They would not then be able to complain of favoritism to the old veterans. Besides, in the case of so popular a man as García, the comrades could not be trusted to treat him rigorously.

"Andrés de Duero," he said, "will you and some of yours take charge

320

of this man. See that he has a double weight of irons and is well guarded. We'll hear the case tomorrow."

For the first time, García seemed to be aware of his plight. "Your Excellency—" he began, but the words failed. He turned his eyes in a mute appeal to the familiar faces around him.

"Well, Your Excellency," Pedro put in, "order me a double weight of irons at the same time. Juan García and I will take what comes together."

"If it is necessary," Cortés retorted, "to teach twenty rebels the lesson of discipline, that lesson will be taught. Are you a soldier, Captain de Vargas, or not? If not, hand me your sword."

On the point of making the latter choice, Pedro hesitated. He could not help García by sitting in the bilboes with him.

"*Caramba!*" García burst out. "If you hand over your sword, I'll wring your neck. Señor General, don't let the lad make a fool of himself. He's only young and a hothead. This is my business. I don't want anyone holding my hand."

Cortés's face did not soften. "Captain de Sandoval, you can show Andrés de Duero where we keep prisoners here."

Duero picked out several of the Narváez men, drew his sword, and turned to García. "Then, sir, I am under the necessity—"

The crowd made way. García squared his shoulders. Circled by his squad of guards, he moved slowly off and disappeared between the buildings.

"Cristóbal de Olid," said Cortés to that officer, who had come up, "you will appoint a military court for tomorrow morning. You will choose officers who are neither especially friendly nor unfriendly to the prisoner. There can be, however, but one verdict. . . . And now, hark you, I have matters of importance to thresh out with Captain de Alvarado. It's been a sad mess here. Let me not be disturbed again."

LV

THE INTERVIEW between Cortés and Alvarado must have been stormy, to judge by the Sun God's red face and burning eyes when he came out. It got around that Cortés had berated him for a fool on the score of the May massacre in the teocalli. This was no doubt deserved, but it did not make for good feeling within the quarters.

Word passed that Cortés was in a seething bad humor at his sullen reception in the Valley: towns deserted or silent, no welcome, no acclaim. He had boasted great things to the Narváez captains and now had to make excuses. It was shame and fear on the part of the Aztecs, he said, because of their attack. He would mete out punishment, reconcile the people, and all would be well. But his pride burned in his belly.

Report had it that he refused to see Montezuma, the dog of a king, as he called him, who would not open his markets or furnish food. It was hinted that, drunk with his victory at Cempoala and confident in the power of his army, Cortés had put on the airs of a grandee and taken credit to himself that belonged rightfully to God.

Almost at once the joy of reunion was turning sour. Bad blood showed. The men of Narváez smarted at their defeat and looked askance at the victors. The veterans, on their side, sniffed at the new recruits.

And now this fracas about García did nothing to sweeten matters. To those with experience in military courts, his sentence was a foregone conclusion.

"By God," stamped Catana Pérez, when she and Pedro had returned to their quarters, "I don't believe it! It's but a feint of the General's. He must make a show. But *hang* Juan García? Hang one of the best of us? A greathearted gentleman like him? *Absurdo!*"

De Vargas shook his head, his eyes on the floor. After a pause he walked over to their common chest, took out his best gold chain and a fine pair of jade earrings, which he put on, then slipped a large turquoise ring on his thumb.

"Why?" she queried.

"Ordered to dine at the General's. Dinner for the new captains. Dine with Diego de Silva, Father Ignacio de Lora!" His voice shook. "Say an *Ave* for me, *rosa mía*. I can do more for Juan by keeping in with Cortés and attending that dinner than by holding off. But it's mortal hard."

Seated not far from the head of the table at Cortés's dinner for the captains, Father Olmedo watched the depressing pattern of human nature repeating itself. Something of a philosopher, he realized that this small, remote gathering represented the whole of mankind, just as a detached pool contains the essentials of the ocean. Here present were the qualities that created and destroyed empires, the same heroism and the same blindness: wisdom and courage to plan and execute; ambition and hatred to divide and nullify.

322

Rolling a bread crumb between his fingers, he reflected with what slender means the original company had wrought its great achievement. But there had been humility then, the feeling of dependence on God, the faith, however crass, in divine guidance; there had been loyalty, good fellowship, brotherhood. Now, its numbers tripled, its security assured, its goal won, it seemed to be disintegrating.

Olmedo observed the men about him: Cortés, vain of his triumph, no longer the plain, alert captain but the petulant dictator, his eyes inscrutable and scheming, as he glanced down the board. Alvarado glooming over his reprimand of the afternoon. Olid's swarthy face, reckless as ever but now with a shade of the fox in it. Sandoval, the soul of loyalty, a little downcast, evidently puzzled. De Vargas, grown old for his years, looking white and deadly, as he kept his eyes averted from Diego de Silva. And then, worst of all, the two ranks at table, Narváez's contingent facing the veteran officers, a chasm between them.

It seemed to Olmedo, who had a touch of the mystic, that Death sat at the far end of the table, balancing Cortés. For death was inevitable when vanity and human passion lined the board, as they were doing here. Why could men never learn, never see? Why, untaught by repeated experience, did they have to meet over and over again the same disaster? It was not that they did not know how to avoid it. They had known for fifteen hundred years. They had only to renounce their tiresome and malignant egos for the grandeur and freedom of love. They had only to be Christian in thought and heart. To the honest friar, it seemed childishly clear that this was the remedy for most human ills; and it lay ready at hand. For Olmedo, the ironic tragedy of human life consisted in this perpetual shipwreck within sight of the haven.

He dropped the bread crumb and looked up to find the cold eyes of Ignacio de Lora fixed on him from across the table. The man's presence added its full share to the strain which Olmedo sensed in the room. With de Lora, the Inquisition had arrived in New Spain. It was not dominant as yet, but it was there—one tentacle of the octopus feeling its way, the octopus which, it seemed to Olmedo, strained at gnats and swallowed camels.

"I've often wondered," said the Inquisitor, leaning forward with a frozen smile, "about the fate of that letter written by the Bishop of Santiago to Captain General Cortés in Trinidad de Cuba. You remember, Father Bartolomé, I spoke to you about it when you visited our camp in San Juan de Ulúa."

Olmedo shot an anxious glance toward Pedro, who was seated a few places off. Fortunately he was in conversation with Andrés de Tapia.

"Yes, Father Ignacio, I told you it was lost." The friar added significantly: "We discussed the matter again in Cempoala with His Excellency before it was decided that you should come to this city."

Olmedo's words conveyed a reminder and a warning. There had been no mincing of phrases in the Cempoala interview. Cortés had made it plain to de Lora that the latter's charges against two respected and prominent members of the original company carried no weight in New Spain.

"What you say," he had snapped, "requires an ecclesiastical court and the testimony of witnesses. We have neither the one nor the other here. Father Olmedo is in charge of the spiritual interests of our enterprise. He vouches for these two men, and that is enough for me. Hark you, we will have no brawling or feuds among us. Accept those terms or remain on the coast. Is that plain?"

"Will your Pedro de Vargas and Juan García accept them?" de Lora had queried.

"My word on it," said Cortés.

The General's anger against García that afternoon had been partly motivated by this pledge.

Now, facing Olmedo across the narrow board, de Lora smiled his frozen smile and nodded.

"Yes, you told me that the letter was lost, Father Bartolomé; but I can't help wondering how and *why*."

The friar shrugged. "It's plain that Your Reverence has had little experience with such expeditions as this, or you would not wonder so much."

"Indeed?" A slight shiver ran through de Lora, as if the cold of his passion chilled him. "No, my experience has been chiefly with men —to discern truth from falsehood. A bishop's letter does not seem to be of great importance to you, Father Bartolomé. And yet if you had not—mislaid the one in question, there would have been no attempt on my life today."

Cortés, whose sharp ears missed nothing, looked up from talking with Andrés de Duero. "Faith, I was sorry for that, as I told Your Reverence. García acted like a madman and shall certainly hang. What more can be done? Why harp on it now?"

De Lora's glance shifted slightly in Pedro's direction. "Because the next attempt may be successful, Señor General, and I crossed the Ocean Sea to serve God, not to die at the hand of renegade and ruffian

324

Spaniards. To punish them after the event will not help me. I look to your promise and to Father Olmedo's. My life, valueless as it is, is your responsibility."

Before Cortés could answer, Sandoval lowered his cup and growled: "Who calls comrades of mine renegades and ruffians! Juan García's a good Christian and a noble fellow. He's one of the boldest men-at-arms in this company. I admit he overstepped the mark today, but that he has a grievance against *you* doesn't make him a renegade or ruffian. *Vive Dios!* I should say not! Look you, Padre—"

"And look you!" rapped Cortés. "You'll hold your peace, son Sandoval, or you'll repent it. . . . As for my responsibilities, I do not need to be reminded of them. Is this the fitting place for such talk? You have my promise, Father de Lora—"

"Aye, Your Excellency," broke in Juan Buono, one of the Narváez captains, seated next to the Inquisitor, "but His Reverence makes a distinct point. He needs protection more than promises, and by God, Your Excellency, there're enough of his friends here to see that he gets it."

"Are there indeed?" sneered Alonso de Ávila from the other side of the table. "Who of them protected him today? It seemed to me that they weren't much in evidence. He'd be singing with the angels by now if it hadn't been for one of us. Eh, Sandoval?"

Cortés leaned forward intently. "Captain de Olid, take me down the names of these gentlemen. Their memory fails them. They even forget where they are. Give them attention, Cristóbal, unless they come at once to their senses."

The bickering stopped. The lower end of the table, which had grown silent and alert, resumed conversation.

Stress and strain. Olmedo thought of a boiling kettle with the steam every now and then tipping the lid.

Meanwhile, some distance off, Pedro gave studied attention to Andrés de Tapia on one side of him and to Captain de Ordás on the other. He did not look at Diego de Silva, who sat obliquely opposite, but he was nevertheless continually aware of him, of his pointed ears with their pearl earrings, of the hair jutting down along his cheeks, of his black, insolent eyes. They had met before dinner, their glances barely crossing, their faces expressionless. And Pedro felt a fierce joy, intense almost as the joy of love. He did not need to be concerned about his vow. He would soon be absolved. De Silva was merely awaiting the proper time. It would come soon. And Pedro would be ready for him. And then—oh, God, then!

Tapia was laughing about the buffoon, Cervantes, who had gone over to the enemy and had been rounded up with the others at Cempoala.

"Hombre! It's more than three weeks ago, but the fellow still eats standing up, and he sleeps on his belly. What a caterwauling he made up and down the gauntlet! We stripped him to the buff and laid on the *baquetas,* I can tell you. Kept him running till he dropped. He never had so much attention before—but not a joke out of him. It'll be a good while before he plays turncoat again."

"Yes," said Pedro, "I noticed that he looks thoughtful. I said, 'A good trip, Cervantes?' and he cringed like a dog."

"Well he may!" Ordás put in from the other side. "Have you any patience with a sneak"—he lowered his voice and glanced over at the gaily dressed Narváez captains—"who abandons his old comrades for a bunch of lettuce sprouts? Look at 'em, their points and slashes, their damask and linen, while it's a near thing that the hair on our chests doesn't show through our doublets! But we're up on them in one way, señores. They may be wearing velvet, but we're wearing gold."

Ordás fingered the splendid chain that circled his neck and passed twice around his threadbare arm.

"So here's to us, cavaliers!" he added. "And perish the *lechuguinos!"*

"But not the Castilian wine they brought," said Tapia, smacking his lips. . . . "What's wrong, Redhead?"

Pedro's eyes were on his silver platter. In spite of himself, he was listening with all his ears to a conversation across the table.

"A fine pair of earrings, Señor de Silva."

"Why, yes, I fancy them myself. A stirrup gift from my wife at parting, sir."

So the man was married. That had happened after Pedro had left. Who could have married him? Pedro wondered whether he knew her.

"By your leave," said de Silva's table companion, "I shall give myself the honor of drinking to her, señor. I have no doubt that her beauty outmatches even her pearls. . . . To the Lady Luisa de Silva y de Carvajal!"

"What's wrong?" Tapia repeated anxiously.

Pedro shook his head. The blood beat against his temples. The room blurred.

"Thank you, my friend," answered de Silva, when he had drunk the toast. "Luisa is handsome enough. I had only a short time to enjoy her, though, before the sailing of the fleet." He added with a laugh, "If she presents me with a son and heir on my return, I trust it's my own."

De Vargas shrugged off Tapia's arm, which had now crept about his shoulder.

"Name of God, I'm all right," he muttered. "Leave me alone. It's my wound from Villa Rica that takes me like this sometimes. It'll pass."

He sat bent over, struggling with himself.

Her pearls! The ones he had so often remembered from that hour in church! His lady of dreams and honor, the incarnation of what was purest and most spiritual in his life, the saint of his inmost shrine! Señora de Silva!

At that moment, though unaware of it, de Silva had his complete revenge.

Pedro's dizziness gave way to a sense of horror, like the first breath of insanity. He could not endure the torment of sitting here any longer. The presence of the two men he hated most in the world, his anxiety about García, had been hard enough to stand. But this!

He turned to Tapia. "You'll make my excuses to His Excellency, Andrés. I'm in poor fettle tonight. That old head wound, as I said. *Buenas noches.* Be sure to explain to the General."

"I'll explain. . . . Want me to go with you?"

"No, nothing to make a stir about."

Waiting until the next outburst of talk at the head of the table, Pedro pushed back his chair and left the room.

In the soft June night, he filled his lungs mechanically. The sky glittered with stars. The shadowy city, lighted here and there by the altar fires on its pyramids, lay glimmering and silent as usual. But Pedro was conscious only of a coffin-like darkness. His best friend condemned to death, his inmost Holy of Holies vacant. When the light that is in a man becomes darkness—

Not that he felt abandoned or betrayed by Luisa de Carvajal. He pitied her as he pitied himself. He knew how little she would have had to say about her marriage. But married to Diego de Silva, it was as if she ceased to exist. He could remember the image he had worshiped, but it was only a memory as of someone dead. Her pearls in the man's ears! Her body his pasture. Her name a possession which he had the right to joke about! It was impossible to worship a radiance no longer radiant. If she had married anyone else, it would have been different. It was not the fact of marriage that defiled her, but the incredible union into which she had been forced.

Taking by habit the path to his quarters, Pedro found Catana, who had just returned from a visit to García in the lockup.

"How was it at the General's, señor? Is there any hope?"

He shook his head. "Not unless we can gain time, and that's hardly possible." He added, "I wish I could die in his place tomorrow!"

Something about him struck her, and she noticed for the first time the desolate look of his face in the rushlight. But for once she misconstrued him in part.

"Don't talk that way, señor." Her voice broke. She made a rapid sign of the cross. "It's bad luck. Never call on death. *You* die?" She looked up at him fearfully. "Then what of me?" And because he did not answer at once, she caught him by the shoulders, her eyes scanning his face. "Don't you love me any more? No. Something's happened! *Querido mío!*"

The cold numbness which had bound him for the past hour lifted suddenly. He crushed her in his arms—crushed her until she could not help crying out.

"Say again that I don't love you, Catana!"

"It's back in your eyes again. But for a moment—I'm so foolish! There're only two things I'm afraid of in the world: when you talk of dying, or that you might stop loving me." She turned her head away. "Silly!" She forced a laugh. "Curse me for a goose! Lend me your handkerchief, señor."

On a sudden impulse, plunging his hand into his inner doublet, Pedro drew out the parchment wrapping that contained Luisa's keepsake, now yellow and frayed.

"Here," he said.

For a moment, she did not notice. Then she stood rigid, staring at it. "Her handkerchief? Why?"

"Why not?" he answered. "It'll serve the purpose. Keep it or throw it away. But dare to tell me again that I don't love you!"

Her eyes flamed. "Her handkerchief! Listen, *querido,* there must be no secrets between us. We will speak of it this once, but not again. What has happened between you and Doña Luisa de Carvajal?"

When he answered, the look on his face told her more than his words.

"The name has changed. She's now called Luisa de Silva."

As PEDRO HAD FORESEEN, the trial of Juan García did not take long.

Before imposing sentence, Cortés asked: "Look you, Señor García, if this court were moved to clemency, if your sentence were commuted to fine and imprisonment, would you give your word, as a cavalier of honor, to abstain from any further act against the person of Ignacio de Lora?"

Weighted down by his irons, but head up, his voice bull-like as ever, García replied: "With all respect to you gentlemen, the hell I would! As long as that whoreson and I are alive, I could not count myself a cavalier of honor if I did not seek to avenge my mother upon him."

"Do you know what you're saying?" growled Cortés.

"Sir, I do. And let me say this to boot, that whether I live or hang, I shall not rest until the debt is paid."

So impressively was this spoken that more than one of the hard captains blanched and crossed himself.

"Well then, Juan García," returned the General, "you leave me no choice. The court has found you guilty, and by the articles agreed upon by this company, you are condemned to death. For attacking a priest, who is a father in God, you are sentenced to the stake; but in mercy the court commutes this sentence to hanging by the neck until you are dead. For urgent reasons affecting the peace and welfare of this company, the petition of certain gentlemen that execution be deferred cannot be approved. Execution will take place tomorrow at twelve o'clock, that being the twenty-sixth day of June, in the year of our Lord, 1520. You have, therefore, twenty-four hours in which to make your peace with God. And may He have mercy on your soul!"

The scratching quill of Father Juan Díaz, who acted as Clerk of Court, stopped. García stared blindly at the wall above the General's head. From now on until the end, his purpose must be simply to meet death like a gallant man, without stain on his courage or embarrassment to his friends. The four officers of the original expedition, who sat on the court, frowned gloomily; the four Narváez captains looked pleased.

"So far I have spoken as judge," Cortés went on, his grimness relaxing. "I would speak now as a comrade and old acquaintance, not only here but in Hispaniola. You have laid a grievous burden upon me, Juan García. In these battles of New Spain, you have fought

329

well and boldly. You are a valiant soldier and an honest gentleman. It is no easy task for me to condemn you. But leadership is no easy task."

"You have done what I would have done in your place, Hernán Cortés," replied García. "I bear you no grudge. Where would this company be, *por Dios,* without rules! In my place, you would have acted as I have—but with subtlety. That's my regret, señores, that I behaved like a mad bull when I should have played the fox. Let it be a lesson to you, gentlemen. May you show better management than I, when dealing with your enemies, and have—"

He was interrupted by a dull boom, as of a distant cannon, followed by a hubbub of voices in the great courtyard outside. Evidently the main gates to the quarters had been slammed shut. A stir and a running could be heard from that direction. The confusion of approaching voices swelled.

In an instant, Cortés had crossed to the doorway, while the judges and audience, who had been admiring García's fine speech, crowded after him. At the foot of a short flight of steps leading down from the terrace on which the courtroom opened, they could see a throng of soldiers half escorting, half making way for, a man who staggered in the direction of Cortés, already at the foot of the steps.

It was El Moro, who had been sent that morning on an errand to Tlacopan at the end of the western causeway. He coughed as he came on, clutching at his breast, and a ribbon of blood uncurled from his mouth. He stood swaying in front of the General.

"They're in arms, Your Excellency. Thousands of them. They caught me . . . but I broke away . . . They're heading here . . . every avenue . . . canal . . . No time to lose, Your Excellency . . . I got mine all right. Christ! . . ."

He sank down and stretched forward on his face. From his back stood up the shafts of two Indian arrows.

And the city, silent and deserted since yesterday, could now be heard vibrating to an approaching sound, as of a tide past the ebb that breaks and rasps on the shingle of a beach.

While a couple of men stooped over El Moro, Cortés raised his head to listen.

He reacted immediately. "The slaves ask for the whip, do they! *A fe mía,* they'll be taught a lesson! And this time we'll be beforehand with them. . . . Captain de Ordás, you'll make a reconnaissance in force. Take four hundred men. Find out what's afoot and pacify the dogs one way or another. . . . Captain de Alvarado, look to our defenses . . ."

"Juan García?" ventured Pedro, fishing for a reprieve in the urgency of the moment.

"Remand him to the keep. We'll deal with him tomorrow as I said. . . . De Olid, see that the horses are got ready. Sandoval, have the trumpeters sound assembly."

LVII

DIEGO DE ORDÁS, who commanded the infantry, marched out to meet the Aztecs at the head of four hundred foot soldiers. In complete armor, a white plume to his helmet, he rode his gray mare, who was similarly cased in steel. He and his men made a brave show. The sun sparkled on their equipment; a light breeze fluttered the pennons; they marched with the rhythm of a Roman cohort, ranks ordered, buckler on arm, pikemen and arquebusiers at the proper intervals.

And as they passed through the gates, the Recording Angel of New Spain turned a leaf in his book.

They had not gone the length of half a street when the cyclone of such an attack as they had never seen struck down upon them. It was not merely the screaming, whistling multitudes that pressed their square—they had seen the like of that before in Yucatán and Tlascala; it was not even that they fought shoulder to shoulder and back to back in the center of a vortex—they had been surrounded before; but this was battle from above and beneath as well. Up from the canals, solid with canoes, now swarmed the warriors; down from the house-tops cascaded torrents of stones. And from all sides, panting, clutching, stabbing, sweating, wild-eyed madmen shoved in, hungry for death if only for a moment they could lay hands on one of the invincible whites.

Outnumbered a hundred to one, swamped in a sea of raging humanity, the Spanish ranks held, the wall of bucklers did not break. But retreat was necessary. Inching their way back, dripping with blood, dragging along their dead and dying, they regained the central square, only to find a howling myriad packed between them and the Spanish quarters. Still they held, still they plowed on. Ordás, bleeding from three wounds, his plume gone, his buckler pockmarked by a hundred blows, still kept his saddle, swung his heavy sword, and gave the cry of Castile. And Saint James, being called upon, lent aid, so that finally the gates were reached and the company surged through.

They were all wounded; they had lost twenty-three men; they were on the verge of collapse.

But if the returned foot soldiers expected solace and rest in the quarters, they were disappointed. Smoke volleyed here and there from buildings set on fire by flaming arrows. Without water, gangs of men, blackened, scorched, and desperate, worked with pickax and crowbar to tear down walls and bury the conflagration. Every open space was swept by a relentless sleet of missiles—from neighboring housetops, from the looming mass of the great pyramid near by, from the attacking multitude, arching their shots above the ramparts. A pall hung over the compound—dust and smoke from the buildings, smoke from the cannon and musketry, smoke shot through with patches of fire. The wounded were everywhere, but no time could be given to wounds. The dead lay where they fell.

Meanwhile, the cavalry made ready for a sortie, a steel column, with Cortés leading. The horses reared and pranced at the sting of shots felt even through the plates protecting them. Footmen clung to their bridles. The lances, still perpendicular, slanted and swayed like saplings in a high wind.

Catana, who had accompanied García's escort to the prison and had then plunged into the thick of things, held on to Soldán's bit, dodging the play of his front feet. She had a smudge on one cheek and a cut on the other. From the saddle, Pedro shouted down to her and touched his cheek with his gauntlet.

"It's only a scratch," she yelled. "It isn't anything. . . . Good luck, señor. Watch your left side."

"What'd you say?"

"Your left side, watch out!"

He roared back, "Take care of yourself, *querida mía.*"

Cortés thundered to the master gunner, "Now let them have it with all your pieces."

The explosion rocked the courtyard. The horses went wild.

"Open the gates."

Framed by the portal, a vivid picture of havoc wrought by the cannon showed beyond.

"*Adelante,* cavaliers!" Cortés gave his familiar war shout: "Saint James! And at them!"

Catana sprang to one side. *"Hasta la vista, querido!"*

Like a steel torrent, the hidalgos passed through the gate, deployed from column into line, lowered their lances, and swept forward against the shot-torn mass of the Indians. Pedro's lance passed through the skull of one man to bury itself in the body of a second. At the same time, two more threw themselves on the shaft, wrenching it from his hands. He caught the blow of an obsidian-edged *macuahuitl* on his shield and turned the thrusts of several javelins. Now and then he caught a glimpse of his companions, identified by their well-known armor, and many as yet unfamiliar, the Narváez cavaliers, concealed by their vizors. But more prominent and unmistakable than any, the pivot of the line, appeared the harness and plume of Cortés. As always, his great horse, El Molinero, kept a half-length in front of the others, wheeling, rearing, plunging. His crest rose, sank, tossed. His shout of "Santiago!" lifted itself above the clamor.

Soon the great square was cleared of the enemy, and the battle seemed over. But, probing down one of the avenues, they found that the Aztecs had not fled. Here, barring the road, were barricades; and the whistling sleet of stones and arrows from in front and from the housetops on either side began again.

Flesh and blood could not endure this fire from the house roofs. Then burn the houses; lay waste the quarter of the city adjoining the central plaza. Foot soldiers from the compound took charge of this, stormed the doors. Shrieks of women and children mingled in the yelling. Smoke clouds rose; but each house had to be dealt with separately, and the fire did not spread because of the canals.

By the end of the week, one could not recall the sequence of battles. One remembered only uninterrupted effort, noise, stench, thirst, hunger, pain, killing—lighted up here and there by some more vivid thing. . . .

The hidalgos rode out again, Cortés leading, a buckler strapped to his useless left hand which had been crippled by a stone. Crossbowmen and musketeers followed. They stormed the temple enclosure, slaughtered its defenders, and, dismounting, shields high and swords drawn, started the ascent of the pyramid. Only a hundred feet to climb, but half a mile to go. Up the first steep flight against a hail of missiles; then around the pyramid to the second flight and a second avalanche of stones, arrows, boulders, beams cascading down; then around the pyramid to a third flight and a third torrent.

Inside the walls of the compound, standing with María de Estrada, a strapping girl who had come with the Narváez people and was head over heels in love with Pedro Sánchez Farfán, Catana shaded her eyes against the white of the pyramid and gazed upward with parted lips.

"There he is! Yonder!"

Panting, sweating, their hearts racing, Cortés, de Vargas, Sandoval, and Olid lifted the weight of limbs and armor up the last steps, shouldered to a footing on the edge of the wide platform at the summit, tottered a moment, got a pace forward by the use of their swords, heard the next rank come up behind them, and plunged headlong against the wall of defenders.

So the battle raged a hundred feet above the level of the courtyard. It raged invisible to the spectators on the ground, who could see only the fringes of it, when, here and there, men locked in fight tottered on the edge of the drop, sometimes saving themselves, sometimes toppling over like dead weights, to crash and lie still at the base of the teocalli.

In spite of the odds against them, the Spaniards still had the advantage, not of courage, but of steel, discipline, physique. It was a battle of extermination. Gradually, increasingly, it reduced itself to a fringe of desperate Indians fighting with their backs to the abyss. Some were forced, others threw themselves, over; the dead and dying were hurled after them; until at the end of three hours only a steel line with bloody swords edged the brink and raised triumphant gauntlets, waving at their comrades below.

But their work was not yet finished. Turning back to the temple towers, that rose forty feet above the platform, they found that the Aztec devil-gods had come to their own again. The sacred images of Virgin and Child were gone. So, over went the idols once more. They were pushed and dragged to the top of the steps, were shoved bounding down them, while the Aztecs, watching from the central square, sent up a howl of lamentation. Then, crowning signal of defeat for all in the city to read, the shrines themselves were set afire, their wooden roofs blazing like torches. And the victorious cavaliers marched down again, forty-five fewer than before, the silver serpent winding back from the gutted temples. . . .

Meeting Cortés that evening, as he crossed the courtyard, Pedro saluted.

"A word, Your Excellency."

The General, who had removed a part of his armor for greater coolness, ran a sleeve over his forehead.

"Yes?"

"I have Juan García's parole that he will abstain from any act against Ignacio de Lora until this company is in safety. He wishes to do his part. He is a good soldier, and we need every man."

"Yes, we need every man." Cortés seemed to bring his mind back from a distance. "Well, have him out then. But make it clear to him that the sentence stands."

334

"I'll make it clear, Your Excellency."

Cortés added suddenly, "If any sentence stands except that of God, who rebukes the pride and vainglory of men." He stood thoughtful a moment. "Why is it so hard to learn that, son Pedro?" He stared at the ground and then with a nod walked on.

The council meeting that night . . . Or was it the night before or the night after? The captains filthy with sweat and dust, for there was no water for washing. Matted and streaky hair. Stained bandages. Hoarse voices. Gaunt faces. Gold chains clinking against the naked table. Cortés, one hand bound up, the other fingering his beard.

The Narváez people were bitter with an unnerved bitterness. This was the docile, serviceable population they had been promised! This was the brilliant entry into the capital of New Spain! And God reward Velásquez who had launched them on such an enterprise! And God reward Cortés who had lured them from the coast! While looking to his leadership and utterly depending on it, they still laid every blame on him. Disaster! And now what? Stay here and starve? Feed a thousand whites and five thousand Tlascalans on exploits? What of the still more valuable horses? The ration was already no more than fifty grains of maize per man. No, evacuate the city; retreat while there was still time.

On their side, the veterans rallied to Cortés, somberly, stubbornly. It was their city. They, and not these tenderfeet, had won it. It was their pride. But, after all, starve?

"Friends and cavaliers, with such stakes on the board, shall we yield the game or try one more deal? We have other cards to play."

Undoubtedly Montezuma was one of these. He volunteered to address his people. Or did he? That was Cortés's version. Others said that he agreed reluctantly, despondently, after much urging. His speaking would do no good. His brother Cuitlahua, whom on his advice the Spaniards had released to serve as negotiator, was now *Uei Tlatoani* of the Aztecs and not he. But, at any rate, once more in royal regalia—crown, robe and clasp, and golden sandals—with his guard of Spanish captains, he mounted the walls.

Pedro de Vargas remembered the like occasion a month ago and felt the difference. Once again the attackers fell silent; once again Montezuma spoke; but this was only a voice, not a spirit—an effigy, not a man. Words, flat, empty, faint, as of one compelled to speak. What had Cortés threatened if he did not speak?

No, he was no longer king. One could see that. And yet old reverence

335

held the crowd silent awhile. Then a voice shouted something; others took up the hoot. The Spaniards raised their shields in front of the king too late.

They carried Montezuma through the awe-struck throng of soldiers. His gold crown had not protected him from the sling stone, but he still wore it. A thin line of blood down his cheek stained the robe.

"Nothing of moment. A glancing shot merely."

But rumor whispered that he refused to live, tore off his bandages, sought death; that Father Olmedo worked in vain to save his soul: he remained true to his devils. Then that night, or was it the next—for there was much to be done, and recollection blurred—the Great Montezuma died.

A few of his nobles bore him out to the square between lines of mourning veterans, for he had given many a roll of cotton cloth and many a gold piece. He was an open-handed lord, and the rank and file could understand that much. A tear wasn't too great a return for a peso. As to his schemes and policy, opinions differed. But all could sense in him the tragedy of greatness brought low—the common human tragedy.

His nobles bore him out to the great square grown strangely silent and deserted; for what the Spanish sorties had not achieved, the attack of the Aztecs on their own king at once accomplished. Horrified and ashamed, they withdrew from the accursed spot and did not return. But the listening Spaniards could hear the far-off lamentation, as the funeral cortege passed among the people.

Then the *mantas*—that was also a card of the General's—the battle towers on wheels. Twenty-four hours, day and night, were spent in the building of them—hammering, sawing, nailing up their timbered sides to the height of an Aztec house. That would solve the rooftop problem. Dragged through the streets by the Tlascalan allies, their occupants, crossbowmen and arquebusiers, could sweep the *azoteas* as they moved along; or, by throwing over a gangplank, could attack the defenders of the roofs hand to hand. They lumbered off with great hopes that came to nothing. They got bogged in the canals; their wooden walls were crushed by the heavier rocks thrown by the enemy; the Tlascalans, unprotected and occupied with the hauling ropes, suffered too much.

Now, as the desperate, tumultuous days passed, and each attempt ended where it started in hunger, wounds, and thinner ranks, the inevitable choice drew nearer: escape or die. The stars themselves decreed it in Master Botello's horoscope: withdraw from the city by the last night of June or none would remain alive. And Cortés himself could not ignore the stars, especially when they and common sense agreed.

But how escape? Seven canals, their bridges destroyed, separated the Spanish quarters from the nearest, the western causeway, and three more gaps in the causeway remained beyond that. Thus ten intersections of water cut off retreat, for the Aztecs had been thorough in removing the bridges, and the Spanish lion could lash as he pleased: the trap looked tight.

The bridges! Whoever survived would at least remember them beyond all the rest. They were rebuilt of demolished houses, tumbled into the canals; of material taken from the causeway itself to fill the gaps across the lake. They were rebuilt to the tune of a howling battle at each of them; they were dearly paid for. But garrisons were posted, and the line of retreat was made good. Good for half a day perhaps. The garrison, overwhelmed, had to be rescued. It was impossible to hold a two-mile stretch against the hordes that swarmed over it. Thousands of canoes filled the lakes and the canals. Almost before the bridges were finished they began to disappear. Another day of fighting netted the same result, and the trap still held.

So at dawn the battle of the bridges began again. The seven canals were filled up with a wider shoulder of rubble. Everybody multiplied himself and fought like a Roldán or Hector. Several hundred more Aztecs were killed, a few more Spaniards and many Tlascalans. But the line of retreat stretched solid, at least to the causeway; and for the openings in that, a portable bridge was made ready. As to the thousand paces from the quarters to the causeway, that distance could be held, must be held. Moreover, for once, the enemy, either disheartened or too confident, rested from attack. Señor Santiago cause him to rest soundly! For the word passed from rank to rank that the army would march that same night.

LVIII

PERHAPS MASTER BOTELLO had never given so much of himself to the casting of a horoscope as he did on the evening of this last day before the retreat, for the horoscope which he now cast was his own. The leather talisman, stuffed with flock wool, lay on a table in front of him, together with writing materials. Bending over these, he communed with the stars—or perhaps with the devil—pronouncing secret words of power, asking questions, writing symbols, deducing answers.

It was expert magic, such as Catana Pérez and María de Estrada had never seen, and they counted themselves privileged to behold it, though the rolling of the Master's voice, the dark and terrible formulae he used, prickled their scalps. He tolerated the presence of witnesses, all the more as Catana had darned the seat of his breeches and thus restored dignity to his person which might otherwise have been wanting.

"If you must be present, women," he stipulated only, "at least be silent, or I shall call on Amadeus, the fiend, to blast you."

In the gathering dusk, a pine torch fixed to a cresset cast uncertain light on Botello's divinations. The long, bare room, once inhabited by an Aztec princess; the suspense of the oncoming night; the drizzle which had begun outside—each added an uncanny touch to the proceedings. Intent on the future, neither Botello nor the women noticed that Cervantes, the fool, had entered and stood grimacing in the shadows.

"I conjure and constrain thee, Amadeus," intoned the Master, "by all virtues and powers, and by the Holy Names of God, Tetragrammaton, Adonay, Agla, Saday, Saboth, Planaboth . . ." He added many others, crossing himself after each, while the onlookers devoutly copied him. ". . . Salvator, Via, Vita, Virtues and Powers, I conjure and constrain thee to fulfill my will in everything faithfully, without hurt of body or soul, and so be ready at my call as often as I shall call thee, by the virtue of one Lord" (more signs of the cross), "Jesus Christ of Nazareth."

Botello, as well as the witnesses, had no doubt of his magic: anyone could see that this was a mighty spell.

"I now constrain thee, Amadeus," he went on, "to answer certain questions which I shall ask. Guide thou my hand in the writing and divination. . . . Am I to die here in this sad war in the power of these dogs of Indians?"

Having made some gestures that sent a chill along Catana's spine, he took up his quill, wrote out the question, and pulling his bushy brows together made slowly a series of symbols, which he then examined with the intentness of a cat watching a mouse hole.

"Ha!" he exclaimed at last. "There's the answer. *Thou shalt not die.* . . . But once more, good Amadeus: Shall I die?"

When he had written down the first answer and the renewed ques-

338

tion, more figuring followed. A bead of sweat trickled along his nose. He drew a long breath. "Nothing could be clearer. *Thou shalt not die.*"

He set this down with a flourish.

"But once again, Señor Amadeus, once more. Will they kill my horse?" He frowned and worked his mouth over the symbols, then weighed and reviewed them. His head drooped. "Yes, they will kill it. They will kill my horse." He sighed heavily. "A shrewd blow. I spent all my winnings on him—all. A noble horse."

Catana could no longer contain herself. "Good Master Botello, while the Señor Spirit is present, ask him how it will fare with Captain de Vargas."

"And is Pedro Farfán going to marry me?" put in María.

"And how about me?" whined Cervantes.

Botello came to himself as if from a trance. "God in heaven!" he fumed. "Did not I tell you trollops to be silent! And what of you, *simplón!* Who asked you to stick your nose in! Now the spell is broken. Now Amadeus is a thousand leagues off, and it would take more conjuring than I have time for to recall him. For a bad copper, I would put the evil eye on the three of you."

Instinctively Catana made horns with her fingers. "Nay, Master Botello, I beg, do not do that. It was only a slip of the tongue. I meant no harm."

"Nor I," echoed María and the fool.

"A slip of the tongue!" Botello muttered. "Do you think it is an easy thing to raise mighty spirits out of the deep? It takes not only cunning charms, but strength of will, sweat of mind. And I am put off by the clack of jades and jokers! Ah, well, I learned the chief point: I shall not die."

"No," Cervantes jibed, "you'll live forever. But I won't. I know my horoscope. The comrades wrote it on my back at Cempoala. I'm still too sore to march, let alone run. So I don't expect to journey far from Mexico. But there's one comfort. At least they won't kill my horse."

"You have no horse, rascal," said Botello.

"Yes, and for that reason they won't kill it."

Cervantes tried a feeble caper, as feeble as the joke; but no one smiled. The chill rain, dripping outside, and the prospects of the night did not make for humor.

Botello gathered up the ciphered sheet of paper. "I'd always wanted a horse," he said wistfully. "But when you're poor—I was very proud of this one."

The wizard now looked like a schoolboy who had lost his pet thrush. Catana slipped a comforting arm under his.

"Oh, come, Master, it may turn out better."

"No, such horoscopes as that are never wrong, *hija mía*. They will kill my horse."

"And if you want the price of three horses," came a voice from the doorway, "you have only to step over to the treasure room. What are *Vuestras Señorías* dawdling here for? Haven't you heard the news?"

It was Pedro de Vargas, his hair damp from the drizzle. He had witnessed the latter part of the conjuring scene.

"And, Catana," he went on in the mock-bullying tone which she loved, "have you seen to my saddlebags and the boxes? Must I birch you for a gadding wench who gives no thought to her chores? I've spent the best part of a half hour hunting you."

She went over to him. "All's ready, señor. . . . But what news?"

"We haven't horses enough for the gold. His Majesty's fifth will be carried by seven wounded horses and one good mare under the guard of Dávila and Mexía with some Tlascalans. The rest of it— the General's and the captains' shares—belongs to anybody who wants to carry it. The soldiers may as well have it as these dogs of Aztecs, the General says."

"Wants to carry it?" gaped Botello, his personal magic forgotten for a greater, more universal magic. "And this 'rest,' worthy Captain —how much would you say?"

"Six hundred thousand pesos perhaps, not counting the jewels."

"Six hundred thousand—" repeated the wizard. "When—when can we get—"

"Now. But there's enough for all, Master. You needn't run."

The last words fell on vacancy. Botello, followed by María de Estrada, had vanished.

Cervantes pinched his chin. "A trick, a trick! What's the trick, my masters? Hernán Cortés giving away his share! He of all men, who knows best how to look after his own. Have we sunk so low? Is it then hopeless tonight? Or a trick?"

"No trick but the one you play on yourself, sirrah," Pedro answered. "The gold's yours. You can take it or leave it. But the General urges caution. There's a march tonight, water to cross, likely enough a battle on hand before dawn. Gold's heavy."

"If that's all!" exclaimed Cervantes, disappearing in turn.

"You mean?" Catana asked Pedro.

"I meant that, as usual, there's sense in what the General says. You

340

and I have got enough in our boxes if the carriers come through and don't steal it. Otherwise the best men in the army will be poor."

They were standing on the threshold of the room looking out at the thick darkness between the buildings. Now and then a gust of the mist-like rain crossed their faces.

"*Una noche triste*," Pedro grunted. "A sad night for marching. I'll not load myself down like a donkey even with gold, and don't you."

She nodded. "I've another burden to think of—worth more than gold."

He put his arm around her. "Feeling all right, *muchacha?*"

"All right so far, señor, thanks to God."

He growled, "This cursed march! If we could but have had peace till the little one came! It's hard to think of you on foot tonight and me riding. If you could manage Soldán and were in shape for the saddle, it would be the other way. At least you'll carry no arms."

"Yes, but I will, sir. A sword and buckler's nothing. I may need them before daylight. . . . Where do you march, señor—with the vanguard?"

Pedro tried to sound casual. "No, I have the ordering of the line. Be everywhere at once. Keep the companies in touch."

"What honor!" she exulted. "Why, you're almost *maestro de campo*."

"Almost—for a night. . . . Let's go over to the treasure room. We might find something to take. And it isn't likely we'll ever see that much gold again. Tell our children about it—eh, sweetheart—Montezuma's treasure?"

Picking their way through the darkness to one of the main buildings where the General's quarters, the chapel, and the treasure room were situated, they could hear a number of footsteps hurrying in the same direction. Now and then the flare of a torch revealed fragments of the enclosure and showed eager, bearded faces pressing toward one magnetic point. If the Indians had attacked at that moment, they could have carried the palace almost without contest. But except for the thronging footsteps and mutter of expectation, as the company mounted the terrace toward Cortés's quarters, the night was utterly silent. Then, more swiftly as it drew closer, the crowd trooped elbowing along the passage porch onto which various apartments opened, until it shouldered through a certain door. Always padlocked and double-guarded, few of the common sort had entered it. Many had been the speculations, the fantastic dreams, about the riches it concealed. Now unbelievably it stood open to all, and the dreams had come true.

By the light of torches which filled the upper half of the room with

341

a haze of smoke, an incredible scene was going forward. It reminded Pedro of what he had read in romances or in fabulous stories about robbers' caves. The mountains of gold which Cortés and other promoters of the expedition had promised were there—or, at least, if not mountains, high stacks of gold bars, each stamped with its value, into which grains, nuggets, and Aztec works of art alike had been melted down. There were boxes, too, containing turquoises, emeralds, jade, opals, moonstones, *chalchuites,* trinkets of mosaic. There were mantles of gorgeous featherwork in heaps, precious objects of shell or silver richly engraved. Generations of Aztec craftsmen had created the bales of treasure, strewn here and there and trampled under the feet of the soldiers.

Yes, dreams had come true with a vengeance, dreams which had launched the ships in Cuba, which had led the adventurers from Spain, which had imposed the hardships of voyage, march, and battle. For many, the object of their lives lay now within grasp, to be snatched, embraced, stuffed into wallets and bags, wrapped into bundles. Hunger, thirst, wounds, impending dangers, were forgotten in this delirious moment. The prize of life being attained here and now, what more could life give?

But there was a difference. Pedro took pride in noting that the Narváez people, the hungry pockets from Cuba, did most of the grabbing. A number of the Cortés men, the old companions, held aloof, slightly sardonic, faintly cynical. They strolled here and there looking on or occasionally, as connoisseurs, selecting a jewel or object of price, half in the spirit of a keepsake. To be sure, many had feathered their nests and wore their takings in the form of chains or rings; whereas, for the new people, this was their first great chance. But that did not account for all the difference. However dimly, the Cortés men had caught their leader's vision of something beyond gold—call it New Spain, the dream of empire. To load themselves with gold no longer satisfied them. Life had something more to give. They had grown to think of themselves as conquistadors, not gold-seekers. They thought of the march and fight ahead and remembered Cortés's warning.

Not all. There was Botello, the wise man, stuffing gold into his sack; and Cervantes, the fool, with a bar under each arm and one in each hand. And the Nightingale's person bulged with hard lumps in every direction.

"*Por Dios,* comrade," said Pedro, "by the time you add sword, buckler, and pack to that, you'll be carrying a hundredweight. Think you can make it?"

342

The Sicilian spat. "Two miles across the causeway, perhaps five to Tlacopan? We'll go no further tonight. Why, *hombre,* I'd make it with five hundredweight—when the weight's gold."

"It may be a hot five miles."

"Don't you worry. Better look out for yourself."

A confused growling and panting went up from the treasure grabbers, as each one snatched and pouched to the overflowing point, then snarled helplessly because he could manage no more. Now and then oaths and blows flared up like a straw fire; but time was too precious and the opportunity too great for quarreling.

"Talk about hogs!" murmured Catana. "Juan, you don't need a farm in Andalusia."

García, standing fist on hip, looked on thoughtfully. "That I should ever see this day!" he growled. "That I should ever see thousands of pesos under my nose and not stretch out a hand to pick them up!"

"Why don't you?" Pedro bantered. "It isn't practical, Juan."

The big man looked embarrassed. "Well, for one thing, I'm to be hanged when this is over; for another, let somebody else get something; for another, we've got to think of the company, my friend. You officers aren't the only ones with too much conscience to make pack mules of themselves when battle's in the wind. If you and the General and others can stand by watching your shares gobbled up by *bobos* who did nothing to earn them, I can stand by too. Practical yourself! Look at Sandoval."

The burly young captain could be seen across the room, half-leaning against the wall and picking his teeth. He grinned but shook his head at the rough and tumble over the gold—a professional reaction. Near by, Cortés, lynx-eyed as always, seemed impatient and uneasy. But no one could have told from the expression of either of them that practically all their winnings in New Spain were disappearing into the pouches of the rank and file. The same was true of Pedro and the other captains. At this crisis in the fortunes of the enterprise, they were playing for higher stakes than treasure.

"Pretty, eh?" remarked Bernal Díaz, El Galán, showing four *chalchuites,* the opaque green stones highly prized in Mexico, which he had just acquired. "And light. Only fools stock up with metal. I'd wager these against a fifty-weight of gold. There're some emeralds in that coffer yonder, de Vargas, if you're interested."

Pedro felt a curious languor coupled with growing nervousness. The whole affair was too unreal. After the bloodshed of the past week, on the eve of flight, it smacked too much of the hangman's feast, a final

343

debauch. It had the air of a macabre joke, ominous of death and dissolution.

Father Olmedo, stopping briefly, summed it up. "After harvest, winter; after the banquet, hunger. After this, what?"

By now the room had been swept bare of gold, the soldiers staggering out one by one with their plunder. The torches, burned to their sockets, cast a final glimmering through the place, where beautiful but perishable things lay strewn over the floor like the flotsam of wreckage.

Looking about him, Cortés gave a slight shrug. It expressed more eloquently the vanity of human wishes than many a volume on the subject.

"You're clear as to the order of the march we discussed, son Pedro—vanguard, center, and rear guard, and who goes where? We'll start breaking quarters at once to march at midnight. And no noise. Our lives depend on it." He turned to the other officers who stood grouped around him at the door. "I repeat, no noise, señores. We came with drums and trumpets; we leave like thieves in the night."

He paused, his lips quivering. Then he added, "But some of us will return."

LIX

MASS WAS SAID; and, as the witching hour approached, the companies assembled silently in the pitch blackness of the vast courtyard. Since the besieging Aztecs had withdrawn from the central plaza and its purlieus following the death of Montezuma, there was a chance that no listening ears would catch the sounds unavoidable in the marshaling of an army with its horses, baggage, and guns, no matter how much care might be taken to quiet them. The Spaniards numbered about eleven hundred, their Indian allies several thousands. Thirty cannon had to be rolled here and there; a hundred horses with noisy iron shoes had to be lined up; and no lights could be shown for fear of watchers on distant housetops. Although the thick drizzle, which discouraged the enemy from prowling, gave added concealment, the complete darkness also increased the confusion.

Next to the main gates stood Margarino and a detachment in charge of the portable bridge which was designed to solve the problem of the gaps in the causeway across the lake. Behind would come Sandoval, leading the van with twenty lances, two hundred foot, and a Tlascalan division. Then would follow the center under Cortés, with most of the horse, some foot and cannon, another division of Indians, the baggage and the royal treasure. Lastly, as rear guard, mustered the main force of the infantry under Alvarado and Juan Velásquez de León, supported by artillery and a final contingent of Indian allies.

In the black night, to get this column into some kind of initial order, and to make sure that its component parts were where they ought to be, took time. Pedro de Vargas with other officers groped here and there through the crowd, rearranging, checking up. The long wait, the soaking rain and utter darkness, drained the heart out of men in spite of the treasure they were carrying. They shifted from foot to foot or squatted in their ranks, feeling already the weight of arms and of gold-laden packs. The slipping of horses on the wet pavement, the continuous whisper of "Quiet! Quiet!" the suspense as to what the night would bring, set their nerves on edge. A kind of voiceless muttering went on: were they going to wait here forever! Why in the name of God didn't they march?

"Is it Captain de Sandoval?" whispered a voice.

"The same," he answered. "Mistress Catana?"

"Yes. I wanted to ask a favor of you, sir—if you would be so kind."

"Anything in my power, *damisela.*"

"That you'd take my imp here, Ochoa, behind you when you ride. He'd be trodden under in a melee. You're a man of luck, Captain. I believe you'll reach the mainland."

" 'Sblood we'll all reach it. Who's to stop us? These Indian dogs?"

"I don't know, sir. It's a feeling— You'll take Ochoa?"

The hoarse voice in the darkness hesitated. "Faith, Mistress, I may have to ride hard, and Motilla isn't a palfrey. Can Ochoa hang on?"

"*Cómo no!*" came the boy's treble. "Like a burr. It isn't that I'm afraid to march with Aunty, but I'd like to tell the other pages how I'd ridden behind you on Motilla. Please, Señor Captain."

"Please!" Catana echoed.

"Very well," grunted the voice. "But look out for yourself, boy. I can't have you on my mind. And off with you when we're over the causeway."

A vibration, starting at the main portals and extending backward through the ranks, began.

The familiar voice of Pedro de Vargas sounded a few yards off. "Catana, get back to your place. Take care of yourself, *por Dios.* . . . Gentlemen of the bridge, are you ready? Open the gates, there! Forward, the first detachment!"

345

Sandoval swung to Motilla's saddle, stuck out a foot, and Ochoa slid up behind him like a lizard.

"Good-by, *Tía Catana*."

"Good-by, *mozuelo mío*."

Catana had a lump in her throat. It was as if she would not be seeing Ochoa again. A ridiculous feeling, because, even in the case of attack, who could prevent so well-equipped and seasoned an army from making good its retreat? She put her depression down to the dreariness of the night, the strangeness of departure from a place to which she had grown accustomed during six months. But the funereal heaviness of farewell hung on. And of course, as she groped her way back toward the center of the column, it must be then that she would remember the ill-omened flock of birds which had recently perched on the roofs of the palace.

"*Ay de mí*," she reflected, "it is in the hands of God."

The ranks were already shuffling forward foot by foot.

"Captain Marín's company?" she whispered.

"Here," replied someone.

A horse's hoofs slithered on the pavement.

"Quiet, you fool!"

Behind the men carrying the portable bridge, Pedro rode out with Sandoval, too absorbed in the suspense of the moment for any sentimental retrospect. Were the city canals that lay between them and the lake viaduct still bridged since the day's fighting? Would it be possible to get the army out on the causeway before its retreat was discovered? If so, by transferring the portable bridge from gap to gap as soon as the troops had crossed from one segment of the dike to the next, they would be able to reach the mainland with only at worst an attack by canoes on their flanks. But if the seven canals were open . . .

Fortunately no light was needed, as they could have followed the much-fought-over avenue blindfolded. Pedro listened with his ears strained, but could hear nothing except the labored breathing of the forty men who toiled forward with the ponderous bridge, the muffled tread of the escorting vanguard, the occasional clink of a horse's shoes. Nothing. They shouldered forward into the blackness, as if the crowded city had been blotted out.

Now they must be close to the first canal. They advanced heart in mouth. Then a whisper came back. *Gracias a Dios!* The canal was still bridged. They crossed the rough surface of the rubble, treading it smoother, and so to the next; crossed that one and the next. A scout brought back the news that the road to the causeway was clear.

Viva! And still no sound of alarm. The Indian dogs, sure of their quarry and relying on the bridgeless viaduct, underrated the cunning of the Spanish fox. They still slept. It was only a thousand paces from the palace of Axayacatl to the lake, but to Pedro it seemed an eternity until Margarino's bridge carriers halted at the brink of the first gap separating the city from the viaduct beyond.

The suspense of the vanguard now took a new turn. Suppose, by some miscalculation, that the heavy gangway, which had been constructed in the quarters, did not reach across the twenty-odd feet of water? Or suppose that some unforeseen difficulty in placing it should arise?

Carrying ropes attached to one end, a number of the Indian bearers half-swam, half-forded, the intervening water; and while their fellows on the city side pushed the bridge forward, they hauled and steadied it into position on the dike. The carpenters' calculations had been correct; the timbers reached, with plenty of purchase on either side. It remained only to determine whether they could stand the stress of men, horses, and cannon. Sandoval, Pedro, and the other lances immediately put this to the test. The thudding of horses' hoofs sounded briefly from the bridge.

"Solid as a rock," approved Sandoval. "We'll be pushing ahead to the next gap, Redhead. You can tell the General that all's clear."

"Listen!" de Vargas whispered. "I thought I heard a shout."

They both strained their ears, but the only sound was the shuffle of the foot soldiers crossing the gangway.

"Probably nothing," said Sandoval. "Or it meant nothing—"

He stopped. A long-drawn call somewhere in the darkness was answered by another, then by a third.

"*Maldito sea!*" Sandoval growled. "Well—it was too much to hope that we'd get off scot-free. I'll wait for the bridge at the next gap. Speed up the column. We'll have a cloud of hornets at our ears in fifteen minutes. *Viva España!*"

His detachment marched off down the causeway. Pedro rode back to report to Cortés in the center of the column. No need for further silence or caution. The city was awaking. The first scattered cries had become a general stir, then a hum deepening rapidly in tone. All that mattered now was haste, to get the army across to the causeway and free from the tangle of the city streets and canals. The portable bridge could then be raised, and the gap it had covered would serve as moat between the rear guard and its pursuers.

347

The voice of Cortés rose somewhere in the darkness, urging speed. "Push on!" shouted the officers. The creeping advance of the column now became a hurried shuffle, the shuffle of people under too heavy loads. Ranks began to lose their form and melt into a solid block of men, guns, and horses, straining forward.

Keeping to one side, Pedro, mounted on Soldán, forced his way against the current back to the quarters, where Alvarado and Velásquez were only beginning to lead the rear guard through the gates. Then, having reassured them about the bridge, he rode again toward the head of the column, which was now crossing to the causeway.

By this time, the silence of the night had reversed itself into a roar bellowing out of the darkness on all sides. The host of hell seemed to be unleashed, whooping, whistling, screaming, drum-beating, conch-blowing. But as an undercurrent could be heard the splashing sound of thousands of paddles on the waters of the lake, converging toward the causeway. And the first gusts of arrows and stones began to rattle and sting.

Then suddenly, above all other noise, rolled a peal of thunder. At least that was the first impression of it. But the thunder became rhythmic, a continued throbbing, like giant heartbeats. Steady, terrible, it roared out a volume of sound to be heard for miles across the waters of the lagoon, conveying in its tones warning, menace, and triumph.

"What the devil!" shouted Pedro, reining Soldán back against the melee that swirled and pushed around the rear end of the bridge. "What the devil's that?"

Someone heard him and yelled. "The big drum on top of the *cu* . . . remember . . ."

Yes, that was it. Pedro recalled the huge cylinder covered with serpents' skins that stood close to the shrine of Witchywolves on the teocalli, but he had never heard it struck until now. It was more than a drum beat—much more. In the thick night, it became a slow, continuous voice, the voice of the Aztec god of war. It fell like a tocsin on the retreating army. It maddened people with its ceaseless, rhythmic thunder. It became an accompaniment, underlying everything else. Darkness and rain, confusion, fear, and clamor, merged into a storm, which found its tempo and coherence in the surging of the temple drum.

But another sound challenged, without defeating it. It was the roar of Alvarado's cannon, blasting at the city multitude, which pressed the rear guard as it fought slowly toward the bridge. Meanwhile, Cortés's center was crossing to the viaduct, along which it streamed until brought

348

to a stop by Sandoval's vanguard, halted in front of the second gap. Meanwhile, too, an assault had begun from the canoes massed on both sides of the dike.

No one could see anything—that was the misery of it. It was a battle of blind men. Out of the pitch darkness came stones, arrows, *atl-atl* javelins, thick as the fine needles of the rain; out of the darkness came clutching hands and the vagueness of white cotton tunics like pale ghosts.

Another misery was the slipperiness of the pavement, which put horses at a disadvantage. As Pedro waited at one end of the bridge for the coming of the rear guard and as the Indian attack began eddying around him, it took all his skill to keep Soldán upright. Now and then a rider went down among lashing hoofs and general confusion.

But one way or another, the center with its troops, horses, baggage, and cannon had now passed, and the first of the rear guard followed on its heels. Pedro could tell this from the war shouts of Alvarado and Velásquez as they drew nearer, and also from the battle that raged around them along the avenue and up from the city canals. At times a salvo of cannon drowned everything else. Then in the lull between could be heard the thick scuffle of hand-to-hand fighting and the rallying cries of the captains. It was as if a furnace were approaching, the hot breath of it already passing across the bridge. Pedro wondered about García, who was marching with this section of the army.

Wheels rumbled slowly over the bridge. The great voice of Alvarado made itself heard a few yards off.

"Give them a push now, gentlemen. Clear a circle about the bridgehead. Margarino, get ready to raise it when I give the word. . . . Captain de Vargas?"

"Here!"

"Tell the General that the rear guard's across and that the bridge is being sent forward."

"Hey, *compañero!*" bellowed a voice somewhere. "Good luck!"

"*Buena suerte* to you, Juan!"

Crossing the bridge again, Pedro made his way as fast as possible along the crowded dike. Though it was twenty feet wide and extended three quarters of a mile to the second gap, the several thousand troops now on it formed a dense mass hard to penetrate. Moreover, the Indian attack by canoe on both sides of the causeway had grown heavier, the rain of missiles thicker, and a continuous struggle of assault and defense was going on along the entire length on each flank. By dint of persuasion, profanity, and force, Pedro edged forward through the jostling, swaying column. He could feel a stirring of fear and tried to spread reassurance. The bridge was on its way forward; the march would be soon continued; nothing to be afraid of—they'd reach the mainland in an hour.

Hearing his voice, Catana called to him as he passed.

"Get under cover," he shouted—"under one of the cannon."

"There's where I am, señor—snug as a hen in a coop . . ."

The noise of the fighting along the embankment cut off her voice.

Finally, a blacker mass in the night, rose the clump of lances that marked the position of Cortés.

"Ha, son Pedro!" returned the General when de Vargas had reported. "That's a right comforting word. I'd begun to wonder about the bridge. Carry the news to Sandoval and then stay with him. There's nothing more you can do until we're off the causeway. We'll have to untangle the column then. *Adiós.*"

De Vargas continued his progress along the causeway until at last he reached the vanguard and found Sandoval, with Ochoa still clinging behind him, engaged in a hot skirmish, not only on his flanks but in front where the Aztecs' canoes filled the water of the gap.

"You've come in good time," chafed the young hidalgo. "In another minute, by God, we'd have taken to the water and swum over in spite of these bastards. If I could only see them! Here we've been waiting for an hour with nothing to do but kick them down the embankment and stand their fire. It's cost our Tlascalan friends heavily, poor devils!"

A javelin glanced from his helmet.

"Hey, arquebusiers!" he yelled. "Shoot all together now. You can't fail to hit, even if you can't sight. Santiago! Vargas! Sandoval!"

Shouts of defiance answered from the lake. "Xiuhtecuhtli!" someone howled, recognizing Pedro's name and adding several epithets in Nahuatl.

A volley from the arquebuses brought forth cries and the sound of splashing bodies.

"Santiago! Ochoa!" yelled the small boy, who was covering himself with a buckler.

"Keep firing," Sandoval ordered. "At least, for one of us, they'll pay with ten of theirs. Why in hell didn't we make our retreat by day! That's Botello's doing, and a damned bad horoscope. . . . Shoot all together. . . . I wish that blasted drum would burst!"

The minutes passed, spun themselves into a quarter of an hour, half an hour, three quarters of an hour. The assault from the lake grew heavier and harder to throw back. The Narváez companies, weighed down by their gold, began to crack. And the harried column swayed from side to side shouting for the bridge. But no bridge came.

"I'll ride back and see what's up," Pedro said.

But at that moment something new happened. It came with the rapidity of a cold wind sweeping forward along the column. It came at first like disembodied fear, a moan rising to a cry, swollen into a tempest of panic.

There was no bridge! Crushed down into the embankments by the passing of the army, it could not be raised. Margarino and his men were slain, Alvarado's cannon captured. A horde of Aztecs from the city were on the causeway. The rear guard had been swallowed up. The Aztecs were on all sides. No hope. *Sálvese él que pueda!*

And at once the army, as an army, vanished. It became a frantic mob, elbowing, yelling, trampling, shouldering.

"Adelante!" yelled Sandoval. "Follow me! Hang on, Ochoa!"

He slithered with his great war horse down the ten-foot steep shoulder of earth and stone into the water. The others, horse and foot, plunged after him. A tumult of splashing, grappling with canoes, oaths, blows, and shouts, sounded in the darkness.

Gripped by a fear such as he had never known, Pedro was on the point of following, when a second, greater fear drove the first one out. Catana! Where was she in the crush? What would become of her?

Turning Soldán against the torrent, spurring him, crashing a foot or two forward at a time, he managed at least to hold his own not far from the edge of the opening.

"Catana!" he kept shouting. "Catana!"

No longer like individual human beings, but merely as particles of a mass plunging helplessly from the lips of a chute, the column was emptying itself into the gap. Weighted with their gold, men sank like stone or struggled vainly, for a moment, in a tangle of baggage and bodies. Horses rolled from the embankment on top of them; while on either side of the breach the relentless canoes plied spears and clubs and arrows. A long-drawn scream rose from the water—a scream compounded of every cry which human lungs can give. And the death chute still volleyed its particles into the gap.

"Catana!"

For a moment Pedro was aware of Cortés's voice somewhere to the left. His world might have gone mad and be crashing around him, but the great captain remained true to himself.

"This way, you fools! Head toward me! The water's fordable here . . ."

But his voice might have been ten times as powerful—the fear-crazed mob could not hear it; or, if a few heard, they were swept along by the rush of the others.

"Catana!"

Doom! Doom! Doom! Doom! pulsed the great drum of the War God, roaring across the water. If it would only stop its beating inside one's head!

By now the gap had been horribly filled up. The hundreds of on-coming survivors, Spaniards and Tlascalans, could wade, floundering across on a dreadful footing of bodies, to the second segment of the causeway. They dribbled forward, so to speak, out of the pitched battle that raged on the first segment. For the Aztecs from the city and from the canoes had gained too firm a foothold to be shaken off. They occupied the dike on even terms with the fugitives, infiltrating the ranks, interlocked pell-mell, so that the causeway had become a solid writhing of agonized life fighting for itself.

LX

A SUDDEN RAGE took possession of Pedro. It had more to do with despair than with courage, but he was unconscious of either. Spurring Soldán and guiding him along the edge of the dike, where he could be surer of riding down enemies than friends, he pushed back into the melee nearest him, swinging at ghostly figures with his heavy sword.

"Santiago! Vargas!"

Holding his buckler and Soldán's reins with his left arm and hand, half-wheeling in his saddle to give greater force to the down stroke of his sword, he kept blindly on. Minutes? A half hour? An hour? Time had stopped for him. Drugged by action, he forged ahead with no purpose but fighting—

Then all at once he realized that he could see. The night was no longer pitch-black. Forms emerged: Soldán's neck and head, shadowy bodies in the tangle of the battle.

"Santiago! Vargas!"

An eagle-hooded warrior close by was locked in struggle with a Spaniard. In the faint light Pedro could make out the curving beak above the Indian's forehead and the steel cap of the Castilian. Then a broad-shouldered corslet intervened, and at the next glimpse the Aztec was down while Broad-shoulders held his comrade around the waist, evidently supporting him. But—God in heaven!

"Catana!" Pedro shouted. "Catana! Juan!"

At that instant, Soldán reared, striking out with his forefeet, then screamed and sank, stabbed from beneath. But Pedro was clear of the saddle. In a moment he had reached Catana and García, who stood back to back with a small knot of other Spaniards in what was apparently a forlorn hope.

Catana, half-leaning against García, looked up, her face haggard. Evidently, in the rout, she had stuck to her refuge under the cannon. She gave a little cry of recognition and said something that Pedro did not catch.

"Why are you waiting here?" he yelled. "Fall back, join the column."

"What column?" García roared. "We've been cut off for this half hour. It's a case of holding on till we drop. Look around you."

For the first time since the berserker mood had gripped him, Pedro took in the situation. A few scattered groups of Spaniards were making a last stand here and there. Otherwise, the Aztecs held this part of the causeway, and retreat was cut off. The Spanish dead lay everywhere, their packs broken and the fatal gold scattered about them. It was this that gave the particular group where Pedro found himself a respite from attack, for the Aztec plundering of the Spanish bodies had begun.

"There're no more of us," García went on. "Juan Velásquez is dead. Alvarado lost his horse and fell back with the last of the column. We were caught and couldn't make it."

Por Dios we will make it!" Lifting his visor, Pedro cupped his hands and put all the strength of his lungs behind them. "Santiago and Spain! Rally on us, cavaliers! This way for retreat! March all together! This way! *España! España!*"

The summons had its effect, all the more as García lent his mighty voice to it. Singly or in small squads, the remaining fighters began edging in that direction. One by one, they hacked their way through until at last the original group had grown to twenty swords, forming a compact circle. Upon this, the storm raged, but could not break it.

"Now, fall back, gentlemen. Foot by foot. No hurry. Thrust at their faces. Blind the dogs. Give them a shout. *Santiago! España!*"

Daunted by the fierce cry, which they had learned to dread, the Aztecs yielded ground, and some twenty yards were gained.

"We cut them like cheese, sirs. If they can't stand up to your voices, what will they make against steel! Let's show them what a Spanish rear guard can do with the help of Santiago!"

353

He struck the right note. A dram of *aguardiente* through their parched lips would not have had so great an effect. Foot by foot, yard by yard, they advanced, though now and then one crumpled and fell, and the circle grew smaller.

"Look you, sirs, we've reached the first gap. Now, across with you. García and I will hold them at the edge. But keep together."

Through a sheet of missiles from the causeway, hard-pressed by the Indian dugouts that did not hesitate to ram them and capsize in an effort to break the ring, somehow they got across, staggering and stumbling on the ghastly bottom, dragging up the opposite embankment to the second segment of the dike. But ten only were now left, and they at the point of exhaustion.

Happening to glance around, Pedro saw Catana swaying back and forth in the tussle, corpse-pale with fatigue, but still handling buckler and sword.

Sometimes the enemy fell back to re-form for the next rush, and the little band made relatively good speed. Perhaps because of the effort itself, the pounding of his pulses, the strain of every muscle, certain fragments of the causeway stamped themselves sharply on Pedro's mind.

In the growing dawn, he caught sight of his friend, Francisco de Morla, lying dead, a broken sword in one hand; and further off Master Botello, outstretched between the legs of his horse, giving the lie to his horoscope; near him lay Cervantes the Jester with a gaping mouth, as if frozen in a last grimace—magician and fool on the same level.

Dead men everywhere, well-known faces and many less familiar who had come with Narváez. They were tripped and trampled over by the little company plowing its way on. But the third and last gap of the causeway was now in sight.

Pedro grew aware that the attack centered more and more on him. Well-known to the Aztecs, he could hear his name shouted in a swelling volume of sound. "Xiuhtecuhtli! Fire Lord!" He was aware too that they were trying to capture, rather than kill him. Such a noted prisoner would be especially pleasing to the gods. Perhaps it was this that had preserved him. Half-blinded with sweat, exhausted, bruised, his vizor torn off, his buckler dented and warped, he could otherwise hardly have escaped the thicket of javelins and hail of blows that felled one after the other of his comrades.

"*Viva,* señores!" he gasped. "We've made the course. Look—"

A suffocating, stinking wave of human flesh, gaudy featherwork, and animal skins surged against them. "Xiuhtecuhtli!" With head, shoulder, knee, foot, sword and buckler, drawing on a last unsuspected reservoir of fury, he beat it back, and, charging in turn, cleared a circle.

"Now, cavaliers, to the water!"

Then, as he glanced around, his heart momentarily stopped. Only four were left: Catana, Juan Ruano, of the old company, García, and a Narváez recruit who at that moment, struck in the throat by a javelin, plunged forward to the causeway.

Turning his back to the Indians in front of him, Pedro dashed toward Catana, caught her by the waist.

"Keep her between us," he yelled to García.

The three of them, with Ruano, hurled themselves against the thinner line of Aztecs separating them from the edge of the gap twenty yards distant, burst through, and leaped down into the water.

He was vaguely conscious of the roar behind them; of relief when he struggled to his feet on some kind of yielding object and found the water no higher than his waist; of struggling forward, still keeping a grip on Catana, with García on the other side of her; of sinking sometimes to his shoulders and rising sometimes to his knees on the cluttered bottom; of the lilt of hope on seeing the opposite embankment lined with Spanish soldiers.

But escape would not be that easy. Pursuers were in the water behind them, and now a couple of canoes shot in from opposite ends of the gap. Pedro saw García grapple with one of these and heave it over. The other sheered off, as if choosing its moment to strike. Ruano had disappeared. With bucklers gone, but with swords and daggers active, Pedro, Catana, and García somehow waded, scrambled, dragged their way across, returned blows, shook off the eager hands and arms for a last time, reached the foot of the embankment.

Lord! Why didn't that fellow in complete armor up there lend a hand? He was evidently one of the Narváez captains; but his vizor was closed and Pedro did not recognize his harness. The men with him, a rear guard left to hold the embankment against the enemy, were also newcomers. They gave shouts of encouragement, but what Pedro wanted was the butt end of the lance on which the steel-clad captain was leaning. Too short of breath to speak, he stretched up an arm. At the same time, glancing back, he saw the remaining canoe manned by eight paddlers closing in.

"Your lance," he croaked, stretching his free arm further up and holding Catana with the other.

Then the man above him clicked back his vizor and showed the face of Diego de Silva.

Deaf to the appeal, he continued to lean on the shaft of his lance and stared down. A blow could not have been more deadly than his inaction.

The decisive second was up. Tawny, muscular arms closed around Pedro—this time not to be shaken off. Exhausted beyond effort, already bound, the three captives were dragged into the canoe.

"Name of God!" called de Silva, perhaps for the benefit of his men. "What a pity! *Lo siento mucho, de Vargas.*"

LXI

THE SEVERAL HUNDRED Spaniards and Tlascalans captured during the night of the retreat were as surely doomed as if they had been cattle herded in a stockyard. Their hearts belonged to the gods and the rest of their flesh to their captors, who would devour them in a cannibal sacrament that was fortifying to body and soul. Like cattle, too, they were graded according to value. So it was inevitable that Pedro de Vargas should take first place in this society of death. No one else equal to him in rank had been captured. As second in command of the Spanish garrison during Cortés's absence, he was well-known, much-hated, and much admired. His Aztec name, Xiuhtecuhtli, bore witness to this, for Xiuhtecuhtli or Huehueteotl, Lord of Fire, was one of the greater gods.

Inseparably associated with him in the minds of the Indians were Catana, whom they knew as his wife, nicknaming her Chantico, goddess of the hearth fire, and Juan García, known, perhaps because of his size, as Tepeyollotl, Heart of the Mountains. That the three of them were taken together seemed logical. To the symbolically-minded priests, they formed a trio somehow connected with the Aztec god of fire and not to be separated without offending him. They must be sacrificed as a unit to the divine Xiuhtecuhtli.

Conveyed by water to the vicinity of the great teocalli, they were marched through jeering crowds to the temple enclosure. There they were stripped, as befitted sacrificial victims, and consigned to a special cage in the line of cages where prisoners of war awaited their turn on the altars. The cell was especially distinguished by a placard in picture writing.

Since Pedro, Catana, and García were among the last to be taken, the cages were crowded to suffocation when they arrived; and doleful voices called to them, as they were brought more dead than living to their lockup. It was beyond them to answer even if they had heard. Numb with fatigue and despair, they were hardly conscious even of their nakedness, for what does nakedness matter to the dead? Shoved into the narrow limits of their cell, they sank to the floor in a half-stupor.

The cages were situated toward the rear of the temple enclosure and, like everything else, were overshadowed by the square pyramid of the teocalli. As their name implies, they were a series of coops intended for the human sacrificial animals, with a latticework of thick wooden bars across the front. Here, when time allowed, prisoners were fattened before the kill for the same reason that livestock is fattened. But on this occasion the gods and their worshipers alike were too starved for blood to wait on the fattening process; the sacrifices would soon begin.

The great drum on top of the pyramid continued to pulse and bellow. The central square gradually filled up with warriors back from the causeway and thousands of the city population out to celebrate the longed-for day of liberty and triumph. Already a coffle of Tlascalans were making the fatal ascent around the sides of the pyramid. A scream, piercing between two drum beats, announced the first victim; and a gaping, lifeless body rolled down the steps of the *cu* to the skilled hatchets and knives of the butchers at the foot.

A moan from Catana roused Pedro. With a flash of horror, he saw that she was lying in a pool of blood.

"God in heaven!" he exclaimed. "*Querida mía!* I didn't know you were wounded."

She shook her head, speaking through her clenched teeth. "Do not look, señor—Juan. Both of you stand in front of the bars so that no one can see." Her voice was pinched off.

"But Catana—"

"No, don't look, please. It doesn't matter if I die now." She added after a moment, "I'm glad the baby died first. Stand in front of the bars, you and Juan. . . . I'm strong. It won't last— What does anything matter . . ."

Cold with anxiety in spite of the leaden heat, Pedro and García blocked the front of the cell as best they could. They stared out through the lattice of the bars at the blank stone base of the pyramid. Now and then, between the drum beats, they could hear Catana's suppressed moans behind them. García, his eyes smoldering, tapped nervously against the bars with one of his clenched fists.

357

"If a fellow could do anything!" he kept muttering. "That's the hell of it!" And once he burst out: "A white man! A Castilian! Betray people of his own blood to these dogs! When, if he had only stretched out a hand—God! I wish I could rinse my mind of the thought of him and spit it out! That he should get away with it and live! Pedrito, I'm beginning to believe that there's not much justice in this world. I can understand how he could take it out on you and me, shameful as it is. But her!"

Pedro said nothing. What he felt was too deep for words. Besides, even vengeance seemed past caring for. He realized suddenly that he hoped Catana would die. He could not face the thought of her led out to the stone of sacrifice. Rather than that, it would be better . . .

Happening to meet García's eyes, it seemed to him that he read the same thought in them. They both looked away.

"Señor," came a wasted voice from behind, "will you bring the water ₒ ₒ . It is over. But don't look."

Trying to obey her as much as he could in the narrow space, he fetched a half-jar of water from the corner of the cell.

"If you would let me help you!"

"No—please. I can manage."

He returned to García's side. "When do you think it will be our turn?" he muttered.

The other shook his head. "Maybe right off, maybe tomorrow. There are a lot of us to kill. We'll probably be taken first or last—I think, last."

At that moment, as if to contradict him, a guard of Aztecs stopped in front of the cage, and the door was slid back. In the same instant, Pedro turned on Catana, who, half-unconscious, had twisted over to her side. But for a second his heart failed him, and after that it was too late. A noose of cords fell around his arms, pinioning them, and he was jerked to the door. At first, García's huge muscles surged against the rope; then he controlled himself. Two of the guards, entering, called Catana, but stopped when they saw the blood on the floor.

"Dead?" asked one of them in Nahuatl.

"Dying," answered Pedro, who had picked up a word or two of the language.

The guard hesitated; then, with a shrug, he ordered Pedro and García taken out and, bolting the door, marched them off toward the front of the temple enclosure.

"Señora Nuestra," de Vargas prayed, "be good to my querida and let her now die speedily. Forgive her sins and mine. Grant that we may soon meet again beyond this life. Give thy blessing to my father and mother and protect them. Amen."

The other white captives had been taken from their cages and lined up under heavy guard. Most of them were Narváez people, whose burden of gold had made them easier to capture, but some were of the old company. Bloodstained, naked, disheveled, they were hard to recognize at first.

Opposite them stood an array of gaudily dressed chiefs, eagle and ocelot warriors, green-plumed nobles; a line of barbaric shields, spears, and gewgaws. A number carried Christian swords taken in last night's battle. Some black-robed priests were gathering. A band of musicians prepared drums, conchs, and flutes.

Pedro remembered the last time he had crossed the enclosure upon coming down from the victorious assault on the pyramid. He remembered it too on the day of Alvarado's massacre. The roles had changed; the shoe was on the other foot.

As he and García took their places at the end of the line of prisoners, the opposite ranks of Aztec caciques broke into jeers, pointing and laughing at him. This scoffing acted as a tonic. On the brink of death, one final duty remained: to give them as little satisfaction as possible.

Pedro stared at them, then jerked his head and laughed, turning to García.

"Dogs' holiday, Juan."

The hooting grew angrier.

"Maybe we can nettle them into killing us with their spears. Give them a laugh."

García opened his big mouth in ribald defiance.

A tall, broad-shouldered Aztec crossed over. He was young and plainly of high rank, from the royal green of his plumes and jewels. As he came nearer, Pedro recognized him as Guatemozin, Montezuma's nephew, a fanatical enemy of the Spaniards and the Aztec General-in-Chief. The young Indian's eyes blazed with hatred, but they could not outstare the banter in the green eyes that faced them.

He made something of a speech, evidently ironic, then exultant, then menacing. In the middle of it, Pedro noticed the great gold chain around his neck. It was the famous chain of Juan Velásquez de León. He wore also a Castilian sword and fingered the hilt of it.

When he had finished, Pedro yawned. "Why, you dog, it's easy for a slave to strut when his master is tied. Give me a sword, if you're man enough, and I wager my life against the chain you've stolen that, naked as I am, in five minutes I'll shave those feathers from your head, cut off

359

your ears, and skewer your arse. If that isn't enough, we can go further into the matter."

Apparently Guatemozin understood more Spanish than Pedro did Nahuatl. His eyes flashed black fire. For a moment, he seemed moved to take up the challenge. But it would not do to tempt the gods at this point. What if de Vargas made good his boast? Instead, Guatemozin struck the captive with all his strength across the face. And Pedro laughed.

A sacrificial procession now formed: priests, caciques, guards, and some twenty Spaniards. The latter were placed at intervals between the others and driven forward at the point of spears. Drums, conchs, and flutes burst into rhythm, if not into melody, and the line advanced toward the flight of steps at the base of the pyramid.

"Good-by, Redhead," called a voice. "We'll be meeting soon. Say a prayer for me."

It was Juan Martín, nicknamed *Narices* or "Nosey," of the old company.

Pedro called back: "I'll do that, comrade. *Animo,* Nosey! *Hasta la vista!*"

Up to the first terrace of the teocalli and so around it, winding up to the summit, the white nakedness of the victims distinct from the garish costumes and black robes of the others, until at last the procession disappeared from sight on the broad top of the pyramid. Then came a wait that was hard to stand. Pedro knew that many eyes were leveled on him in a hard glee, and he kept his head up and his face expressionless; but inwardly he was praying hard for Nosey Martín and the other men up there, and for himself.

A shriek escaped the rumble of the drum; a body, without its heart, was tossed over upon the first flight of steps. It rolled down them, gaining impetus, until it stopped on the pavement of the courtyard.

The waiting priests worked quickly, beheading and flaying, for other bodies followed.

De Vargas found that it steadied him to remark to García: *"Vaya,* Juan, I wonder what Father Olmedo would have to say in defense of these Indians—or that other friar he keeps talking about, Las Casas. . . . I envy the next Castilians who have the pleasure of sticking them!"

But, getting no answer, he turned to see García staring blindly at nothing.

"How is it with you?" he added.

García shook his head. "Funny, I keep thinking of the square in

Jaén in front of the cathedral. *Madrecita* and the others. De Lora. No Indians there."

Pedro got the point. He remembered the blackened stakes and helpless prisoners. He thought too of his sister's body in the hands of the torturers. Yes, there was a certain likeness between then and now.

"*That* was in the name of God," muttered García; "this is in the name of Witchywolves. It's too deep for me, comrade. I wish I could get it out of my mind."

It was too deep for Pedro as well. On the threshold of death, best not think of it.

"Think of Our Lord"—the words came of themselves—"think of Our Lord, Juan. That's all we have left."

Including the Tlascalans, some eighty victims had now been sacrificed to Huitzilopochtli. But the Feathered Serpent, the great god, Quetzalcoatl, must not be overlooked. The scene shifted to the concave stone in front of his round temple. Another procession, containing other priests and warriors, was formed; another coffle of prisoners was detached from the dwindling line.

"You were right," Pedro said. "It looks as if we'd be the last."

García glanced at the sun. "If so, it'll be tomorrow. There're too many of us left to kill."

Pedro half-stifled a groan.

"Tonight then, Juan, if Catana's still living. I hope we can have the chance. She mustn't be brought out here."

"No," agreed the other. "Do you want me to do it, comrade?"

De Vargas shook his head. "That's up to me."

But now the cry of "Huehueteotl! Xiuhtecuhtli!" began in the dense crowd. The prisoners were herded in a new direction across the enclosure toward a broad, raised platform, upon which stood the shrine of the god of fire. It contained the usual monstrous image with a sacrificial stone in front; but the platform had a distinguishing characteristic, the living symbol of the god himself, a blazing fire, which the priests at that moment were feeding with billets of wood.

"*Por piedad!*" muttered García, who caught some of the words hooted by the crowd and understood more Nahuatl than Pedro.

"What's up?" asked de Vargas. "We're not the last after all, eh? Well, I'm not sorry. I envy our friends who have got it over with."

"No, it isn't that," García returned. "They're yelling about tomorrow. We're to be sacrificed to this particular devil. They want us to watch how it's done. Something different."

He swallowed, staring at the fire.

361

In happy excitement one of the guards struck Pedro a stinging cut across the back.

The prisoners were ranged in a half-circle about the platform. Twenty were told off, driven forward. A shout went up, which Pedro realized was directed at him. He did not need a knowledge of the language to get the gist of it. Let the white Xiuhtecuhtli look! So he would die! A flattering, eager hatred sounded in the voices. Once again he summoned his pride to meet it with a stare and laugh.

"Juan," he said, "I confess to you that my blood is water and I have no heart left. But by the help of Our Lord . . ."

He caught his breath. That man who had been driven out among the doomed twenty. Either he had not seen him before in the crowd of naked prisoners, or he had not recognized him. That stoop-shouldered man with matted beard—could that be—? At the same moment Pedro heard a breathless exclamation from García.

"Ignacio de Lora!"

What difference between nakedness and clothes, the white Dominican habit, the black cape, the silver crucifix! How different he appeared in the judgment seat as compared with standing on the hot pavement, stripped and pinioned and about to die!

He was trying to control himself, but his limbs quivered and beads of sweat showed on his body. Purplish ridges, left by the stick, marked his gaunt flanks and shoulders. As he glanced helplessly about, his eyes looked vacant, and the masterful nose had lost its meaning. His lips moved; now and then he ran his tongue over them.

"De Lora!" García breathed. "Now God—"

"Your blessing, Father," croaked one of the Narváez men, "I confess my sins . . ."

De Lora did not hear. His eyes, grown suddenly intent, were on Pedro and García. They reflected the past and present in one look of horrible awareness, then turned away.

Five men were dragged up to the platform, their feet, legs, and arms bound rigidly, so that they were incapable of movement. Usually at this time a handful of *yauhtli* or Indian hemp was thrown into the faces of the victims to deaden the coming ordeal, but no such kindness would be wasted on the white enemies. The men were loaded upon the backs of five priests who began a lumbering dance around the fire. Then, one by one, they heaved their burdens into the flames, to writhe and howl until the steaming bodies were hooked out, still living, for the sacrificial stone and knife.

Hypnotized by the horror of it, Pedro could not turn his eyes away;

362

he felt cold in spite of the heat. But when the next five were taken up to the platform, he did not look although the scrutinizing Aztecs hooted in triumph.

He wondered what García was thinking. The big man stared at the ground, mumbling. Certainly, so far as vengeance went, García could ask for nothing more complete. But strangely enough, Pedro found himself regretting that vengeance should absorb his friend at such a time. De Vargas's personal hatred for Ignacio de Lora had suddenly vanished in favor of pity. Facing together this unspeakable death in a distant, barbaric land, what did former hatreds matter? They belonged to another world, to a half-forgotten life.

"Well?" he said to García and, receiving no answer, repeated, "Well?"

"Peace, comrade." García glanced at his enemy, then dropped his eyes again. "Can't you see I'm praying for him, for all us poor sinners?" He mumbled, "*Madre de Dios,* pray for us sinners now and at the hour of our death."

The moment came; the guards closed in. De Lora, his limbs failing, was beaten and dragged up the steps of the platform.

"Mother of God," García groaned, "he is an old man and weak. I prayed God for vengeance. I didn't mean it—not this. Sinner that I am! Let him not suffer . . ."

But life clung to de Lora's fleshless body, clung as they jerked it screaming from the fire, clung to the last releasing wrench of the priest's hand.

And the gods being now duly worshiped, the remaining half of the prisoners were driven back to their cages to wait for tomorrow.

"Are you afraid, Juan?" Pedro asked.

"Not of them," García muttered, "not of them. But I'm afraid. Remember how I talked about no justice in the world? Look you, comrade, you were right. We have nothing left but our Blessed Saviour. He makes allowances for fools. God doesn't. That's what I'm afraid of—His justice."

The heavy voice shook.

"What do you mean?" said Pedro, startled by the expression on García's face. "Our Saviour is God."

"Not in that way. Listen. I prayed God for vengeance. You wouldn't pray Our Blessed Lord for that: He wouldn't listen if you did. I prayed God. I told Olmedo I had. He cited scripture to me, where God says, 'Vengeance is my business; leave it to me; I'll take care of it.' "

The big man clamped his teeth together nervously.

"Comrade, it would have been better for de Lora if I had killed him at the quarters. But God wouldn't have it. It wasn't His idea of justice. No. He planned this. Can you think of any vengeance like His? May our Saviour protect us and all men from it!"

LXII

To THEIR SURPRISE they found that an Indian mat had been provided for Catana, and a cotton blanket to cover her with. The cage had been cleaned. But they were not misled into believing that these attentions were dictated by kindness on the part of the guards. No doubt since Catana-Chantico belonged to the fire goddess she must be kept alive and in condition for the sacrifice.

Catana raised her head when Pedro and García were returned to the cage and their swollen arms released.

"God be praised!" she said faintly. "I never expected to see you again. What happened? I kept hearing cries."

"Indian deviltries," Pedro shrugged. He sank down next her. "How is it with you, dearest?"

"Well. But never mind about me." She drew her forefinger gently along an angry welt that crossed Pedro's shoulder. "*Ay de mí,* they have beaten you?"

He forced a smile. "It was nothing. My good father's riding whip used to hurt worse."

Catana's eyes, which had grown larger and deeper, met his.

"Tell me the truth—are we to die tomorrow?"

"That's the intention," he answered carelessly. "But give no heed to it, *dulce mía.* God may determine otherwise."

Still absorbed by his theological qualms, García put in a groan.

"Well then," said Catana, "we must confess to each other before dawn and make ready to meet Our Lord in the best shape we can. He was merciful to give us more time for preparation and to let us die together."

"Merciful!" García put in. "For a maravedí, I'd dash my brains out or make shift to hang myself." He stopped short. "I didn't mean that either. May God not charge it against me! Whatever I do, He'll be waiting on the other side. There's no escaping."

"Of course you didn't mean it," retorted Pedro. "Let it never be said among these Indians that two Spanish cavaliers were driven by

364

them to take their own lives. We owe that much to our names. and to the gentlemen who will sometime reconquer this city for the King. Let alone that we're the ranking officers of the company here and must not disgrace it."

García shook his head. "I'm not a hidalgo. But just the same—"

The cage doors were reopened to admit food and water, which the guards shoved in from outside, taking care not to expose themselves to the grip of the prisoners. Their service had no compassion in it; but Xiuhtecuhtli's victims had to be fed.

"Harken, you *cabrones*," Pedro called, "what's the meaning of that paper outside there?" He pointed up at the place where the sheet of picture writing was tied to the cage; and racking his brain for a word that would mean something to the guards, he added, *"Tonalamatl?"*

For a moment, the Indians stared at him through the wooden bars; then, catching his meaning, they burst into jeering explanation.

"Does it mean anything to you?" Pedro asked García.

"Not much. Something about sacrificing us to Xiuhtecuhtli and Chantico tomorrow. They kept saying 'Coyoacán.' You remember the place at the end of the southern causeway. Maybe we're to be killed there. I hope not."

"Why? What does it matter?"

"The things I've heard they do to prisoners there before killing them. Besides, remember the Chief of Coyoacán, whom Cortés had fastened to the big ship's chain. He'd be glad to see us. . . . Well, we'll find out what they meant soon enough."

But hunger now had the best of suspense. They ate the *tortillas* which the guards had brought; and, to keep their minds off tomorrow, they discussed the army, how many had escaped, what the chances were of the survivors reaching Tlascala and finally the coast.

The outlook was none too bright. Pedro summed it up: "It isn't much they can do. Two thirds killed or taken, no horses, no cannon, no powder, nothing but swords and bucklers, almost everybody wounded. It's a long way to Tlascala across the mountains. They won't get out of the Valley without a battle. And then afterwards—" He shook his head. "It's a thin chance. Of course, if the General's living, he may pull it off."

"We must pray for them," said Catana. "I love them all—I mean the old company. What good times we've had!"

Their thoughts taking refuge in the past, they sat watching the fall of evening. At long last, the temple drum had stopped, and in place of it sounded an infinite confused moan from the still crowded cages.

An endless litany: calls on God, the Blessed Virgin, and the saints; lamentation, of which no one was ashamed; the effort of the soul to prepare itself for the supreme departure. And like an answer to it, when night fell, came the roaring of the beasts in Montezuma's former palace. Excited by the smell of blood they claimed their share from the day's slaughter.

Wrapping herself in the blanket, Catana got to her knees and said the paternoster and *Salve Regina,* in which the others joined.

"It's the hour of the Angelus, señor," she said. "Remember? . . . Give me a kiss, you and Juan. Then I shall sleep. We must wake and confess ourselves before dawn."

Exhausted, she sank down again. Pedro drew the covering closer about her. Turning on her arm, she fell asleep.

"Now?" García whispered faintly after a moment.

Pedro, clasping his knees, did not answer.

"I know how it is," murmured the other. "If you want me—" He hesitated. "I'll do it. . . . But it has to be done."

"Yes," said de Vargas, "but I can't do it now—not yet. After we've confessed ourselves and prayed together, I'll do it at dawn. It's better that way."

With a nod of relief, García stretched out in his turn. The fatigue of the last day and night overcame even the dread of tomorrow, and he too slept. But for a while the fever in Pedro's brain, incandescent, consuming, defied exhaustion. He lay painfully awake, haunted by the thought of dawn.

His own death had ceased to matter. The spectacles and horror of the past day, contrary to the effect intended by the Aztecs, had left him hardened, almost indifferent. Pain, yes. But he was used to pain. A few minutes of agony and then release. He hoped to be able to steel himself and die as befitted a Spanish captain. That was a physical problem. If it had been the only one facing him, he too could have repaired his strength in sleep.

But Catana!

His mind shrunk back from the duty before him, the necessity of killing her. Fragments of the past year, little, half-forgotten, intimate things, now became a torment to remember. But he would have to go through with it. Terrible as it was, it was incomparably better than to let her suffer what de Lora had suffered. He kept flexing his fingers, rubbing them against his body, as if they had already committed the deed.

Back to the past, to the days and nights together. Once, by some obscure connotation, the thought of Luisa de Carvajal, as he used to dream of her, crossed his mind. She had been his lady of honor; she had been so designated by heaven itself. How contradictory and tangled life had turned out to be! She, the wife of Diego de Silva; he the lover of Catana Pérez. Who could decipher the will of God? Evidently the experience in church long ago had meant nothing; the vow taken on the altar cross had been only romantic vapor. But if that was so, then what of all the other impulses and tenets of belief? What of God Himself? Not what one planned, but what actually happened was God's will, he pondered. You could not be sure until afterwards.

Noticing by the vague light from outside that Catana's covering had slipped, he moved nearer and pressed his lips gently on her bare shoulder before drawing the blanket over it. Then crushed by fatigue, he fell asleep, setting his mind, as it were, to waken in a few hours.

He came to himself with the grip of hands on him and the bite of cords around his arms. At the same moment, he heard García's oaths. The thought seared his mind that he had waited too long, that now he would be unable to save Catana.

Dawn had not yet broken and they had not overslept—it was still night outside—but for some reason, probably to avoid a struggle, the guards had forestalled their waking. The next instant they were out of the cage, shivering in the colder air. Then, with a cord running from neck to neck, they were marched across the temple enclosure, into the square beyond, and so down to the canoe basin at the far end.

Catana stumbled from weakness and would have fallen except for the cord binding her to the others.

"Damn me for a fool!" Pedro muttered to himself. "Why did I wait when I had the chance!"

At the boat landing, they were corded still more tightly and laid helpless on the bottom of a war canoe large enough to contain not only them but four paddlers and guards. The latter, squatting down on their prisoners, held them still more immovable. Then the canoe glided off toward the lake.

Looking up along the back of the Indian half-seated on his chest, Pedro could see the starlight, brilliant at first, grow paler as time passed; but he could see nothing else, and, except for the repeated word, Coyoacán, he could not judge of the direction. It was about six miles across the water to Coyoacán, which he had visited seven months ago when the army had first crossed the mountains. He remembered the teocalli there, a grim, bloodstained pile.

367

As to the reason for this transfer of prisoners from one city to another, it was not far to seek. Coyoacán had lent support to the war and craved sacrifices for its local gods. Perhaps, in this case, quality made up for numbers, or perhaps more prisoners would be sent later. In spite of the discomfort in the canoe, Pedro was glad for Catana's sake that they had not been forced to make the journey on foot along the causeway.

The rhythmic dip of paddles, the tapping of water on the sides of the dugout, an occasional word of Nahuatl, were the only sounds. It came as a surprise when a chorus of hails rose near at hand and was answered by the men in the canoe. A moment later the craft nudged gently against the stone of the landing.

Yes, it was Coyoacán. In the twilight, Pedro recognized its squat outline dominated by the sawed-off pyramid of the temple. But the prisoners were given no time for more than a glance. Awaiting them stood a throng of warriors wearing ceremonial regalia—plume and bangle, jade-and-turquoise masks. They surrounded the three white captives like a pack of wolves. Words, apparently of thanks and farewell, were exchanged with the men in the canoe; and the victims, gathered up in the midst of the rout, were swept off toward the temple. But to de Vargas's surprise, the throng did not stop at the temple. It pushed on south through the still sleeping town, whooping, dancing, and evidently in a hurry to reach the appointed place of sacrifice. When Catana faltered on the point of fainting, she was swung indecorously across a pair of broad shoulders, and the pace continued. Then suddenly the town gardens ended, as if trimmed off with a knife, and black wasteland began.

It was the Pedregal, a lava stream, which in former days flowed down from one of the volcanoes at the end of the Valley. Like a dark scab amid the surrounding green, it extended fifteen square miles, a labyrinth, honeycombed with caves and threaded by blind trails. Here, if anywhere, was the appropriate haunt, the palace, so to speak, of the divinities of fire. Here the victims of Xiuhtecuhtli would be most acceptable to the god.

In spite of courage, Pedro's blood ran cold as the party, grown silent now, penetrated deeper into the maze of black basalt. The path wound between rough, jagged walls, serrated at the top. No color but the color of death. At this hour just before dawn an unearthly atmosphere, heightened by the fantastic costumes and masks of the warriors, clung to the place, which seemed to lie across the threshold of life in some never-never land of demons.

"We're in hell already, comrade," García whispered. "I wonder when we died."

De Vargas plucked up spirit enough to make a wry face. "From the pain in my feet, I'm still alive, Juan. I wish I wasn't."

It was torment indeed to walk barefoot on the sharp rocks of the trail, which cut the soles of the feet like so many knives. Observing that both prisoners were limping and scarce able to walk, sandals were provided by a couple of the band, whose feet were toughened by long custom. It would not do, Pedro reflected, for victims to appear crippled before the god.

At last they came out into an open space, formed by a whirlpool in the molten lava long ago, a small amphitheater, evidently sacred to Xiuhtecuhtli, for his grotesque statue stood on a kind of natural altar, with the grisly platform in front of it. This then was the end of the road. There remained only the kindling of the fire, a dance before the god, the final horror. And now dawn was breaking.

"They'll wait till sunup," said García, moistening his lips. "It won't be long. *Adiós,* friends. We may not have time to say it later."

Catana was lowered to the ground and stood a moment half-supported by the man who had carried her.

"Good-by, Juan. Good-by, *querido señor mío.* Only it isn't good-by. I know that."

She was interrupted by the voice of the leader of the band, a magnificently bedizened cacique wearing a skull mask. He was giving orders.

"*Nuestro Señor Salvador . . .*" said Catana.

A warrior approached with a drawn knife. But as Pedro made an instinctive movement toward her, he saw, to his amazement, that the Indian merely cut the thongs around her arms. At the same moment he felt his own arms freed.

"What's this!" exclaimed García.

The next instant three featherwork mantles were thrown over their nakedness.

"A part of the mummery," Pedro growled under his breath. "But if they think—"

He stood speechless. An Indian was holding out to him a sword. He recognized it at once. His own sword. The one that had been stripped from him at the moment of capture.

"*Diablos!*" he muttered, with a sense of dreaming, as his hands closed on the scabbard. "Do they want a fight? Well then, by God—"

His voice, rising in a lilt of joy, stopped. He found himself confronted by the skull-masked leader, who at that moment took off his headpiece. Pedro stared, gasped.

It was Coatl.

"Señor Pedro," said the Indian, struggling with long-unfamiliar Spanish, "you save my life." He held up two fingers. "Now I save yours."

The silence of stupefaction was emphasized rather than broken by a heartfelt ejaculation from Juan García, *"Qué vaina!"* He added with equal fervor, *"Qué diantre!"*

Coatl himself bridged the gap. "You forgive, Señor Pedro? I not wish to take you here. I not wish to frighten the señora. I play trick on the Tenochcas."

Pedro had his arm around Catana.

"Trick? What do you mean?"

"Listen. Before the last fighting, I speak to Cuitlahuac, *Uei Tlatoani* of Tenochcas after Montezuma. I say to him, 'Listen, I bring many men to help in this war against the white men. I ask one thing. Give me the Spanish chief de Vargas, called Xiuhtecuhtli; give me his woman, Chantico; give me his friend, Tepeyollotl (for I know you grieve, Señor Pedro, without them); give me Diego de Silva.' I say, 'Give me these *teules* if men take them in battle. Coatl ask no more. Coatl sick for their blood. This hand tear out their hearts. This hand burn them to please the fire gods.' He say, 'It shall be so. I swear by Huitzilopochtli, I swear by Tezcatlipoca, gods of my people.' He give order and writing."

The picture sheet which he had asked about crossed Pedro's mind. He was beginning to piece things together.

"I look for you in battle," the Indian went on. "I look for Diego de Silva. When I hear you taken, I turn back from de Silva to save your life."

All at once de Vargas's eyes burned. He recalled the day long ago in the *barranca* near Jaén.

"Caballero!" he smiled.

Coatl shook his head. *"Caballero* Castilian. I hate Castilians; I love my friend. Now we speak no more; we march—fast."

It appeared that the sacrifice was supposed to have occurred at noon when the sun was at its height, and that the people of Coyoacán would have attended it. Perhaps some were already on the way. Therefore, it behooved the Zapotecs to cross the mountains before the fraud was discovered.

370

"In what direction?" Pedro asked.

"Where the sun goes." Coatl pointed west. "Long march." He held up three fingers. "So many days."

"But if you could guide us to Hernán Cortés, to Malinche, he would greatly reward you, Coatl."

"Reward from him!" The Indian's eyes smoldered. Then he folded his arms. "Malinche dead. Castilians dead."

"Dead?" The word came from the lips of Catana and García as well as from Pedro.

"Dead. Tenochcas kill him at Otumba."

Terrible as this news was, it was too much expected to be open to doubt. Solemnly Pedro made the sign of the cross.

"Now we march," Coatl repeated. "We rest later."

"The señora cannot march."

"We carry her."

Meanwhile, the thirty-odd warriors of Coatl's escort had stripped off their ceremonial trappings, rolled them into bundles, and now appeared in the scantier garments of the trail. They carried shield, bow, spear, and knife—evidently a picked troop. Coatl explained that the main body of Zapotecs had returned home after the battle.

An improvised hammock litter was produced for Catana. A few minutes afterwards, the band, in single file, was winding southwestward through the labyrinth of the Pedregal.

For a time, Pedro and García walked on silently in the footsteps of their silent guides. One of the chief elements of life, the sense of a goal, even if that goal was death, seemed to have dropped out. At the moment, helpless and purposeless, they could only drift. They were reprieved from death, but life had become fog without landmarks. Behind them lay New Spain, the lost conquest, the dead companions. Before them, cut off in the barbaric world, lay what?

"How about God now, Juan?" Pedro said after a while. "Suppose you had killed yourself last night. Suppose I had—" He thought of Catana and of what might have been. "*Qué dices ahora de Dios?*"

Part Four

——— LXIII ———

THE TRAIL LEADING southwest from Cuauhnahuac (not yet corrupted into Cuernavaca) entered a world unknown to white men, an unimaginable country beyond the furthest horizon. It was almost impenetrable, a region of bare or forest-clad summits, subtropical valleys, headlong streams, narrow cañons; a region rich in precious metals, rare woods, vivid flowers, and wild life; rich too in the secrets of vanished peoples and forgotten civilizations.

After a day's grueling march from Coyoacán, up and down hill, fording streams and threading thickets, Coatl called a halt among the mounds of a ruined temple half-submerged in undergrowth. Fires were lighted, garments dried, and a ration of maize eaten. Then the Zapotec warriors filled paper-thin reeds with tobacco in token of relaxation.

Squatting against a fragment of serpent-carved wall, Coatl, who had talked little on the trail, broke silence.

"Now you are safe, señor. Tenochcas not follow here." He made a wide gesture with his arm. "This Zapotec country. Welcome to you, and peace."

Worn-out by the ordeal of the past days and of the recent march, it seemed to Pedro an effort even to voice gratitude.

"My friends and I thank you, Coatl."

"Thank him!" exclaimed García, who was massaging his tired calves in front of the fire. "That's pretty pale! When he has worked the miracle of getting us out of hell! By God, Señor Cacique, when I forget what I owe you, call me dog!"

"Not talk of debt," Coatl grunted. "Welcome in my country." He then added, "Two more days we get home."

Catana caught Pedro's eye and smiled; but the word *home* echoed dolefully in his mind. Home! How long, he asked himself, would they remain here? How long had the interpreter, Jerónimo Aguilar, who had been marooned among the savages of Yucatán, remained? Eight

372

years—until he grew like them, forgot his own tongue, painted his body, squatted like an ape. Eight years. And that was near the coast.

Mechanically his fist clenched. "Home, Coatl?" he repeated. "I seem to remember that you did not call Spain home."

The other exhaled and nodded. "I cannot send you to Spain, señor. Perhaps someday Castilians come again. I send you to them. Now"— he opened his hands—"now, except here, you die."

It was too obvious for debate. With the army destroyed, no help remained except the refuge offered by Coatl. Between this wilderness and the coast stretched leagues of enemies bent on offering any white man to the gods.

"How will you know when ships come?"

"After while I hear."

Silence descended. The twilight turned dark, and fireflies showed more vividly among the ruins of the temple. The damp breath of night thickened. Somewhere on the mountain slope above, an ocelot wailed. Pedro thought of Aguilar.

Two days later, they reached a large pueblo of cubical houses with flat roofs, spilling down from one of the lower ridges to the communal valley land. Other, smaller pueblos appeared on neighboring slopes within a circle of higher mountains. These villages, Coatl explained, were ancient seats of the Zapotec people, the greater number of whom had moved eastward to Oaxaca long ago. Looming above the housetops of the main town stood the tribal temple and, adjoining it, strung out along the ridge, the group of one-story adobe buildings which formed the *palacio* of the chief. In one of these, complete with its own terrace, *azotea,* and small, luxuriant rear garden, the Spaniards were housed.

From the terrace next morning, de Vargas and García gazed northward beyond the checkerboard of roofs at the labyrinth of mountains which they had just crossed.

"Could you find your way back to Mexico without a guide, Juan?" Pedro asked. "At a pinch, I mean?"

The big man frowned. "Not easily, comrade, though perhaps in time. It's a fair tangle, this land."

"Aye," Pedro muttered, "and a cursed long way from the coast." His thought brooded disconsolately on the distance. "Might as well be in the moon." Then, struck by an idea, he added, "But mark you. Did we ask to come here? We did not. Had we any choice? No. Then clearly it is an act of God. To what purpose, ha?"

García shook his head. "I am an ignorant man."

373

"I do not see it clearly myself," Pedro admitted. "But that there is a purpose, I know—also what we must do first and at once."

"What's that, comrade?"

"Make one of our rooms into a chapel. Set up the Cross. Pay honor to Our Lady of Rescue."

"It's well thought on," García agreed. "We couldn't start better."

In fulfillment, at least, of the divine purpose which had made them what they were, the three exiles consciously and unconsciously organized their life according to the Spanish pattern. By instinct they put first things first. Since religion chiefly gave character to Spanish life, they were careful in their devotions. Since clothes are the outward token of an inner attitude, it was not long before they called on Coatl's sewing women to furnish them with approximate Spanish dress. Since language determines thought, it was not they who learned Zapotec, but the Zapotecs who were taught Spanish. Since the dissolution of the company did not cancel their allegiance to the King, it behooved them to view this land as a future royal province, assay its resources, and plan for the day of its annexation.

"You see how it is," said Pedro: "we'll have to watch ourselves. It reminds me of the swamp in Tabasco when our good horses all but foundered that day of the battle. The earth of this country sucking us in. It may be years; but we'll keep our heads up. We're Spaniards, and Spaniards we remain."

In this effort, he was naturally the leader. Except for him, García and Catana, who lacked hidalgo principles, might easily have succumbed. But he kept them to the mark. If García yielded to the charms of native women, he was not allowed to forget that he must baptize before embracing them. Catana, who loved to dance, got a swingeing once when she participated in a stately Indian figure. Weren't the *zarabanda* and other Christian dances good enough!

Partly to combat these tendencies, Pedro insisted on teaching his two friends their letters. He got nowhere with García, who could never see the connection between sounds of speech and scratches on bark paper. Catana learned to print her name and to make words after a fashion. But the labor was great and the achievement small.

To Pedro, chafing at his exile from civilized and military life, it seemed that his companions were much too content: García, because the mines were rich and the girls amiable; Catana, because she had her lover more to herself than in the days of the company.

"You're like the Lotos-eaters in that *romance* of Captain Ulysses," he told them once.

"Who were they?" García asked.

"They were mutineers. Señor Ulysses, a notable cavalier, was trying to get his company home overseas after a war. He kept in mind his duty to the King. But they touched on a rich land where these lazy *cantoneros* settled down and went to sleep. It cost the good captain much trouble to pry them loose."

"Aye," grumbled García, who rejected the point of the story, "you've always got captains and cavaliers disturbing the peace of honest men."

Meanwhile, the chief of the Zapotecs—Zociyopi in his own tongue, Coatl among the Aztecs—held an increasing place in the minds of his guests. Not only were they dependent on him, but he impressed them personally. They stopped identifying him with other savages and accepted him as an individual. His Spanish became more fluent with practice, so that he and Pedro had frequent talks, which often became personal and intimate. Seated cross-legged on a mat, a tobacco reed between his fingers, Coatl, except for his tawny skin and the turquoise in his lower lip, seemed hardly different from any other gentleman.

"You ask me why I take trouble save your life, Señor Pedro," he remarked once when they were together on the rooftop of his quarters. "You say me not like other Indians and heathens you know. I ask why you save my life two times. You not like other Spaniards and Christians I know. Maybe someone cut out our hearts—find them alike."

Coatl enjoyed recounting his escape from Spain, the voyage to Cuba, the desperate crossing in a stolen small-boat from San Antón to San Juan de Ulúa.

"I see nothing stop me after you give that gold, señor. I surely get home. You give all you have. I see your purse empty. That bring luck to me—now to you." And noting Pedro's brooding expression, he would add, "You get home too, señor. Perhaps then you be glad remember these days."

On another occasion, Coatl asked oddly enough: "Tell me, my friend, what you want in life? You cross Great Water, fight Tenochcas, try take their land, work, suffer, lose everything, almost get killed. Maybe your god come, say, 'What you like me give you, Señor Pedro?' What you tell him?"

It took de Vargas back to his talk with Olmedo on the hill near Trinidad. The same question. He thought it over honestly but could hit on nothing truer than the usual answer.

"Well, I suppose what I want most now is success in the world. As you know, my father is a great cavalier who brought the reputation of our family to a higher point than he found it. Starting where he leaves off, I'd like to equal him if I could. That takes doing, for Don Francisco has set me a hard course. Also it takes money. If I could have had my wish, it was to get back to Spain with a good record and a pile of gold." He added gloomily, "That's over now."

Coatl made a careless movement of the hand. "In Spain, what you do with good record and gold?"

Pedro dreamed on. "Rebuild the Casa de Vargas. Be decorated by the King. Get a command in the army. A noble marriage."

With a gust of bitterness, the memory of Luisa de Carvajal crossed his mind. That too was over.

"You leave the Señora Catana here?" asked Coatl.

The question brought up a problem that Pedro always put off meeting. Catana did not fit in with the return to Spain. He realized, of course, that sometime the break must come. But until then—

A long minute passed before he answered, "I don't know."

"Well," Coatl observed, "you not want much. I think your god give it to you."

———— LXIV ————

IN DECEMBER these cordial relations with Coatl underwent an odd change. An Aztec embassy, the first in five months, appeared at the pueblo, and the Spaniards kept under cover while their enemies were present. It would not do, Coatl insisted, for the Tenochcas to learn that they had been cheated with regard to the prisoners' sacrifice, and that Captain de Vargas with his companions still lived. The Zapotecs, loosely tributary to the Aztec empire, had nothing to gain by raising an unnecessary issue with their overlords.

But following the departure of the envoys, Coatl immediately summoned Pedro to his *azotea*. He wore the circlet and plume of his rank, the embroidered mantle, jeweled earrings and arm clasps. The heavy, graven features expressed an official attitude. He raised his arm in greeting but for a while kept silent. Without being sure, Pedro sensed embarrassment and chagrin.

"What's wrong?" he asked.

A queer, veiled look crossed the other's eyes. After a moment, he answered: "Señor, we Zapotecs are few leaves on an old tree. Not

376

strong, not ready for war. The Tenochcas are many. We guard you from them, you and your friends."

Pedro nodded. "Yes, of course: we owe you our lives."

"Now they find out you here. Now they say give us back the white victims you not kill. We kill. The gods hungry. Give them back, or we come in war, burn your towns, take your young men to feed our gods."

"Oho!" said de Vargas. "Well?"

Again the shrewd look narrowed Coatl's eyes. "I say no. They leave angry. They mean war."

Pedro's heart leaped. "Mark you, Coatl, if I can't hold the passes of this country with the men we have, aye, and feed the buzzards with those dogs' carcasses, call me no soldier. On my honor, we'll singe the Aztecs' tails and send them home yelping."

"You train my men like Spanish *hombres,* eh?"

Pedro hesitated, thinking of the tough, even Spanish ranks. "Juan and I would do our best. At least they'd be trained as compared with the Aztecs, and better equipped. We'll leave them their glass-bladed *macuahuitl* baubles and get us hardened copper swords of the right shape. We'll get us fifteen-foot lances such as Cortés used in the Narváez fight. *There's* a hedge to stop even horses."

"You say horses, señor?"

"Aye, horses, let alone the Aztec dogs. Then there's the proper marshaling of the square in support of slingers and bowmen; the management of night attack that our friends from the north don't relish. We'll show them a few sleights before we're done."

"You make strong the passes?"

"Not too strong. They must be lured in and trapped."

Coatl's teeth showed. "Who can match white men! They live to kill. Your eyes happy, señor, at thought of killing."

Suddenly Pedro found himself remembering Montezuma. Just as then, he had an impression here of something under cover, though he could not define it. Why, for one thing, did Coatl not seem incensed against the Aztecs or pleased at the prospect of defeating them? The smolder in his eyes was directed rather against the bloodthirsty craft of the whites. At the moment, it appeared even to include Pedro himself.

"Aztecs call themselves warriors," Coatl added. "They children beside you."

"We do our best," said Pedro dryly. "How long, do you think, before they'll attack?"

"Who know?" shrugged the other. His vagueness sounded almost indifferent. "Maybe soon; maybe three-four months."

Pedro and García set themselves with a will to the work of military defense, in which Coatl gave them every encouragement. De Vargas enjoyed war as an art, and García was a born drillmaster. Officers were picked out and trained in the Spanish tactics. They in turn instructed others. A rough imitation of ordered ranks and evolutions was achieved. Equipment approximating Spanish weapons took the place of more primitive arms. The passes were fortified, and a strategy was worked out.

But nothing happened. Weeks became months without a sign of impending attack from the north. Except for the fun of it and that various Zapotec warriors, becoming admiringly attached to Pedro, had themselves baptized, there seemed to be no profit or point in these warlike gestures.

"By the mass, it's queer!" Pedro complained to García. "We're supposed to be training against those hounds of the Valley, but our friend Coatl never mentions them. He talks only about us Castilians—how we do this or that. I sometimes wonder whether the Aztecs made any threats. And if not, what are we stewing for?"

"Cosas de Indios!" García grumbled. "They're a crooked race. You never quite know what they're up to. But don't worry, I expect the Aztecs won't give long warning. Then, by God's grace, we'll remind them of our dead comrades. I pity the cabrón that falls into my hands."

February and March passed—nine months since the flight from Mexico. Then down from the north in April came not the Aztecs but a trickle of other Indians, wretched, desperate, and exhausted, seeking refuge in the pueblo. De Vargas happened to meet them in the valley below the town, and at first glance he could see that they came from beyond the Zapotec territory. At sight of him and García, however, standing fist on hilt beside the trail, the men cowered and slunk past. Apparently by now every white man went by Cortés's nickname, for they shouted something about Malinche and added other gibberish.

Pedro turned to one of his Zapotec lieutenants, whom he had baptized by the name of Martín and who had picked up a few Spanish words. "What did they say, those fellows?"

"They say Malinche burn their pueblo, Cuauhnahuac."

"Malinche! What do you mean? What Malinche? Are there Spaniards to the north?"

But the man's face looked blank, as one who has spoken out of turn.

378

Pedro's arm shot out. Martín found himself pinned by the throat against a tree.

"Will you speak! By God, find your tongue before I tear it out. Are there Spaniards to the north?"

He relaxed his grip enough for a word to pass. It seemed to Martín that the white lord's eyes were two gimlets boring into his brain.

"*Sí, señor.*"

"Malinche? Hernán Cortés? I say *Hernán Cortés?*"

"*Sí, señor.*"

"How long have you known this?"

Half-suffocated, the man made a vague gesture. Pedro gathered that he had known it some time.

"Did you hear that, Juan?" Releasing the Indian, de Vargas turned to García, who stood gaping. "Did you hear that?"

The other nodded heavily with a dazed look.

"The General in the north!" whispered Pedro. "It can't be!" He stiffened. "But we'll find out. Coatl has something to explain. Come on."

Surmise, suspicion, anger, billowed through de Vargas's mind. He did not notice the steepness of the winding street, the groups that melted away at the expression of his face. Upon reaching the *palacio*, he and García brushed aside the warriors on guard, crossed the series of familiar rooms and, unannounced, entered Coatl's council chamber.

They found him with two of the refugees, who were crouching in front of him, evidently begging sanctuary.

"Hold the door, Juan," said Pedro.

He walked over to Coatl, disregarding the two suppliants. He also overlooked Coatl's frown.

"I hear that Hernán Cortés is but three days' march to the north. Is this the truth?"

Met by de Vargas's cold stare, Coatl's eyes flickered, but he answered, "Yes."

"*Cuerpo de Dios!* Have you played us for fools? You told us that our comrades were killed at Otumba. You promised to send us to any Spanish company that reached New Spain. Well? What's the explanation of this?"

Coatl drew himself up. "You talk bold, señor. Remember I master here."

Pedro laid his hand on his sword. "I'll do more than talk, you false friend. I ask again, have you anything to say?"

With a gesture, Coatl dismissed the two Indians from the north, who stood cowering at one side. When they were gone, he answered: "Listen, Señor Pedro, and you, Señor Juan. I say the Spaniards die at Otumba. I think they die. I think that long time."

And indeed, as Coatl said, who could have supposed that the few hundred survivors of the Sad Night, exhausted, despairing, with no arms except sword and buckler, with only twenty decrepit horses and a rabble of Indian auxiliaries, could make good their retreat to Tlascala against the forty thousand picked braves awaiting them on the plain of Otumba?

"They warriors!" exclaimed Coatl, torn between hatred and admiration. "They warriors!

"Then, long after," he went on, "the Aztecs come—you know when, señor. They tell what happen. They say Malinche bring all east tribes against them. He cross mountains back into Mexico. They say he have more white men, guns, horses, from across Great Water. They ask help. . . . Then, señores, for first time I lie."

He paused a moment, struggling with his imperfect Spanish. "To me my people come first. I must defend them from Malinche who destroy all. So I get you and Señor Juan train my men. Therefore I lie."

"By God," de Vargas burst out, "so we've been preparing you against our own friends! Against the King's interest! It wasn't enough to keep us malingering here, deserters from the company, while our good comrades won honor in the field, but you must trick us into being renegades and traitors! A fine stroke, Coatl!"

But his thought ran more coolly than his tongue. It was unlikely that Cortés, preoccupied with Mexico and other more accessible lands, would be interested for some time in this southern region, and by that time the superficial military training of the Zapotecs would have faded. Besides, powder, guns, and steel made all the difference against arrows and copper.

"I work for my people," said the Indian. "In my place, you do the same."

The point was too true to be debated.

"But now, Señor Cacique," García put in, "what's the state of things? Are we prisoners or free?"

"Free," Coatl nodded. "I send you to Malinche. I even go with you two days' march. . . . You leave Señora Catana here?"

With a start, Pedro recalled what he had momentarily forgotten. No, he could not return at once to the army. Catana daily expected the birth of their child.

LXV

Two WEEKS LATER a new voice in the world, a little voice but furious, urgent and protesting, reached the ears of Pedro and García, who stood anxiously waiting outside the door of Catana's room.

The two men looked at each other. "Ho!" said García.

After a while an Indian girl peered around the curtain.

"How is she?" Pedro whispered.

He was for entering, but the girl pushed him back. The new voice gathered strength. He felt a queer tingle at the sound of it.

García slapped him between the shoulders. "Hoho, comrade! Listen, will you! How now! How now, eh! My word!"

The girl reappeared, drew back the curtain, and beckoned. Pedro entered, while García tactfully remained behind. Catana's angular, pale face stood out against the blackness of her hair spread over the cushions. Her eyes seemed larger and darker.

She smiled faintly. "It's a girl after all, señor. Does it matter?"

He kneeled beside her, raising her hand to his lips.

"*Amada mía!*"

"But does it matter? Are you disappointed?"

A nudge from one of the Indian women fixed his attention on the small bundle now presented to him. Holding it awkwardly, he perceived in the folds of it a wee, red face and two tiny, quivering fists. Through its wrappings, he could feel the throb of the little body against his hands. He felt curiously warm and shy.

"Lord love us!" he muttered. "Well, well!"

"You *are* disappointed," repeated Catana.

"About what?"

"That it's a girl."

Too absorbed to answer, he had reached the point of opening one of the little fists, which promptly closed on his thumb. He laughed, delighted.

"By the mass! Well, well! And every finger perfect—only so small! It's a miracle of God." Some pink toes crept out of the other end of the bundle. He discovered them and laughed again. "Look, Catana."

"Then you are not disappointed?"

"Disappointed! How so? Why? Name of God! Such a little rose! *Qué vergüenza!* It wasn't I who wanted a boy. I wanted another Catana." Then, remembering García, he shouted, "Hey, Juan, come in here. I've got something to show you."

The big man appeared, grinning broadly.

"What do you think of this for a lusty wench?" demanded Pedro. "Feel her—firm, beefy, skin like silk, eh? She's got green eyes."

García made sounds like a cooing bull. He ran his forefinger cautiously over the fuzz on the baby's head.

"And red hair, faith! Isn't she the spitting image of you! God's blessing on her!"

"You can hold her a moment."

Honored but uneasy, García stood with his mighty arms tense as if he were embracing a hundredweight. The baby, sensing danger, protested and was snatched away by the Indian woman.

"Give me my darling," said Catana. "You'll tear her to pieces between you." And when the little bundle lay in the hollow of her arm, she murmured, "Be still, *mozuela*. My heaven's treasure! Who would want anything but thee, heart's dearest!"

The two men unconsciously worshiped in silence.

With every day, tidings of the great events in the north came thick and fast. Cortés had taken Tacuba. Now he was marching on Xochimilco and Coyoacán. Nothing but the city of the Tenochcas, Tenochtitlán, remained. He held Mexico. The Tlascalans were butchering and devouring, the Spaniards burning and robbing. The Valley of Cities was a valley of flames and death.

One evening, at their private vesper service in the improvised chapel, the three Spanish worshipers recited as much of the *Te Deum* as they could remember. Once more God had performed a miracle for Spain. Out of the broken company fleeing from the Valley of Mexico had been wrought a victorious host. The martyrs who had died on the stones of sacrifice would now be avenged. The True Faith would be established forever.

"And yet," Catana observed afterwards, "I'm sorry for women and children, señor—the little ones like ours. They're as innocent as lambs. And do you recall our first sight of the Valley from the sierra of Ahualco? Lakes and white cities and green hills? Lord! It was lovely! I remember I could hardly get my breath, and even El Fiero next me crossed himself. Such a picture of heaven! I suppose it'll never be the same."

Pedro shrugged. "It's war."

There was no answer to this—at least none that she could find—but instinctively she drew her baby closer to her, as if it represented something above and beyond war.

382

A footstep interrupted them, and the stately figure of Coatl appeared around the corner of the terrace. He gave the impression of urgency but paused to exchange salutations with each in turn.

"Señores," he said, "I need help. My son ill. Our medicine men not know. Many others of my people burn with the sickness. I hear it is in the north. Your ships bring it. Maybe you know the cure."

"We aren't leeches, Coatl," Pedro answered, "but Juan García here has traveled much on ships and seen many sick men. We will go with you."

They followed the Indian to his own section of the *palacio* and into a room full of copal incense, where some women were weeping beside a mat on the floor, while two physicians, or *tepati,* squatted in front of them over the patient. A sorcerer chanted charms in one corner, thus reinforcing science with magic.

"It is fever, we know," said Coatl. "We give him medicine for it: ground roots, stomach stones of birds, powdered jewels and burnt human bone. We also bind tooth of dead man on his head, as you see. But no help."

García and Pedro glanced down at the boy's fever-racked body on which a faint rash had begun to show. They did not need any special skill to recognize what was wrong. They had seen that disease too often.

"*Viruelas,* eh?" said García. "I heard there was an outbreak in Cempoala."

The ships from Cuba had indeed brought something to New Spain even more fatal to the Indians than the civilization they represented: they had brought the smallpox.

"He's a sick boy, Coatl," García declared, "but I'll tell you what to do. Wrap him up in furs, give him something hot to drink, and make him sweat. He may go out of his head with the fire in him, but it can't be helped. It's sweat that brings out the pocks. When they show up, he'll feel better. Keep the room dark. Don't let him scratch, or he'll disfigure himself."

Pedro did not miss the chance to add, "If you'll tie a cross around his neck, it will help him more than that dirty tooth."

Within a couple of days, half the pueblo was stricken. On the whole, because of García's rough but comparatively sensible treatment, the community fared better than most. Elsewhere people, mad with fever, bathed in the mountain brooks and died like flies. Whole villages were emptied while the epidemic ranged south to the ocean. But in the Zapotec valleys, though mortality ran high, the greater number recovered.

Pedro and García, who had had the disease, went here and there, exhorting, threatening, holding things together. As superior whites, who knew the secret of the dreadful sickness, they were often asked for the charm of baptism and felt that the time was not ill-spent. To reward Coatl's kindness by leaving him at such a time would have been shameful; but Pedro got off a messenger with letters to Cortés, reporting his whereabouts, describing the richness of the country, and announcing his return as soon as possible.

In the midst of it, upon re-entering his quarters one day, Pedro found Catana crouching over the basket which served the baby, Niñita, as a cradle.

"She's so hot, señor. She won't take the breast—only cries. God! If something should happen . . ."

Pedro managed to say, "Probably nothing," but he held his breath as he walked over and looked down at the tiny form in its wrappings. Then he stooped over and laid his hand against the baby's cheek.

"Do you think," breathed Catana, "that it's . . . ?"

"No," he said, trying to conceal his fear.

"My precious! My little one!" Catana grasped the edges of the basket. "Dear Lady of Heaven!"

Her voice chilled him. "*Querida,* it is nothing. It will pass."

The baby began crying thinly, helplessly. Lifting it in her arms, Catana swayed back and forth. "Lady of Heaven," she whispered. "Mother of God . . ."

Night came on; the crying stopped, to be followed by quick, hard breathing. The fever rose. Catana held the baby in her arms hour after hour.

Standing in front of her, Pedro and García stared down; or they moved aimlessly on tiptoe about the room. They had faced death so often; but now as its shadow deepened here, they felt daunted and humble like little children.

Towards morning, Catana suddenly murmured: "Pray for her, señores, pray hard."

Sinking to their knees close by, their faces bowed upon clasped hands, they prayed as they best could, broken, clumsily. Vows to their patron saints, promises of barefoot pilgrimages to the Virgin of Guadalupe, to St. James of Campostello.

All at once, long past midnight, Catana uttered a low cry. "She's dead! My baby's dead!"

But she continued to hold the little bundle, cuddling it against her, drawing the embroidered wrap closer about it. "No, Niñita, it isn't true.

Precious! My little rose! Look, darling, look at *Madrecita* again!" Her voice hardened, sharpened.

Pedro said, "Give her to me, *querida.*"

"No! No!"

He put his arms around her. "She's mine too."

Then the desolate tears came. Gradually she released the small body. Pedro held it a moment, then placed it gently in García's arms.

He glanced at Catana. "We'll go out a moment, Juan. Come, *vida mía.*"

She hid her face against him as they went out.

And Juan García stood for a while staring blindly at the opposite wall. At last, with infinite tenderness, he stooped and laid Niñita in the gay woven basket, folding the miniature hands one upon the other. He drew the little coverlet over her and turned it back carefully, like a giant absorbed with a doll. Then all at once, flinging an arm in front of his face, he wept like a child.

They buried Niñita in the *palacio* garden under a tree with flowers resembling small, white musk roses—baby flowers. It filled the air with freshness and, swaying in the breeze, strewed the ground beneath it with delicate petals. Being handy with tools, García fashioned a rough coffin of sweet-smelling cedar. His breast heaved often as he worked, and he shook his head, thinking vague, heavy thoughts. When he had finished, he covered the small casket with a dark cloth, and Coatl's women lined it with blossoms. Niñita seemed no longer dead, as Pedro carried the open coffin in his arms to its place beneath the flowering tree. She had died too soon to be disfigured by the disease and looked merely asleep.

Coatl, solemn and stately, laid a small golden rattle near the baby's hands, and a little tortoise of gold.

"You allow, señora?" he said. "She play with them in that other land."

Then, at the edge of the grave, the coffin was closed; but Catana asked García to open it again.

She leaned down and pressed her lips against the baby's forehead. At last she said, "Now I shall always remember her—how sweet she was."

Pedro repeated what he could recall of the funeral mass. It was not much, but he knew the great comforting words: *"Requiem aeternam dona ei, Domine; et lux perpetua luceat ei."*

He slipped his arm around Catana when the coffin, finally closed, was lowered into the grave.

"It's so deep," she said. "Does it have to be so deep?"

He could feel her shrink as the earth was thrown in. At last nothing remained but a small mound of flowers, which the Indian women cast upon the spot—that and a cross upon which Pedro had carved the baby's name and the *requiescat*.

Considerately, the others moved away, leaving them alone.

"My arms feel very empty," she said.

He did not answer for a moment. He had wakened that morning to the leaden desolation which follows death, and in that desolation God had spoken. He felt sure that it was God who had brought him to a decision so alien to one of his caste, who had made it clear to him that he must choose one of two ways.

"Listen, Catana," he said finally. "Our Lord has taken the little one to Himself. All is well with her. Ours is the sorrow because ours has been the sin. Twice now He has punished us. And the sin is mine, not yours. I have not made you my wife as His law commands."

At first she looked at him fearfully, but when he paused, she nodded. "Yes, señor, we have sinned. It is as you say." Her voice caught, but she went on bravely. "Of course it would have had to end sometime. We knew that. It is best now."

"End?" he repeated. "No."

"What else is possible?"

"Are there no priests with Cortés? Father Olmedo can make us man and wife."

She stared up at him. "What is it you said, my lord?"

"I said Father Olmedo shall marry us."

A light sprung up in her eyes, then faded.

"You're mad, señor! Hidalgos don't marry camp girls. I love you— do you think I would have that? How could you return to Spain?"

"I shall not return." His hands closed upon her shoulders. "We'll stay here. It's the New World, *muchacha*. It belongs to us. Tomorrow's a bigger word here than yesterday."

"I won't have you dishonored."

His grasp tightened. "You'll do what I say. You belong to me."

"Yes, God knows I do." Her eyes filled. "But not to your hurt. I'd rather die. You feel this way now—because of Niñita. Afterwards, when you've forgotten—"

"I love only you. I'll love you always. I ask you to marry me."

Again the light shone in her face, lingered. "Señor, wait. I'll answer you when we're back with the company."

LXVI

FINALLY THE MESSENGER returned from his mission to Cortés, his eyes full of what he had seen: burning cities, warriors, cannon, ships on the lagoon, captains in armor on their barbed horses, the great Malinche, who had received him as if he had been a chief for the sake of his news from Captain de Vargas.

He touched hand to ground and then to forehead in salute, opened a featherwork pouch, and produced a bulky letter, showing a lozenge of wax stamped with blurred arms and, across it, the bold handwriting of Cortés. Pedro had not seen a letter for nearly a year. He was breaking the seal with his thumbnail, when Catana and García, attracted by the stir, came out on the terrace.

"A letter from the General!"

They pressed against him on either side as he unfolded the paper. But, in the process, an enclosure dropped out; and when he stooped for it the handwriting of the address banished everything else in his mind.

"Name of God!" he exclaimed. "It's from my father! . . . Almost three years without news! Three years! They seemed more like thirty. . . . From my father!"

Since it was already unsealed, he opened it, his eyes devouring the crabbed writing. Alcalde of Jaén . . . Doña María well—he got that from the first few lines. The letter must wait until he could read it in private. What mattered at first glance was that his parents were in good health, had been exonerated, re-established.

Having thanked and dismissed the Indian messenger, he stood with his back against the wall and spread out the closely written page from the General. Catana and García waited with their eyes intent on him.

"You could read it yourself," he teased Catana.

"Be quick, señor."

"Aye," rumbled García, "I want to know if he still intends to hang me. Let's hear, comrade."

"He begins 'Son Pedro' and thanks God for our safety, which he deems no less than a miracle."

"He's right at that," said García. "And then?"

"He bids us make all speed to him, for the war's at a ticklish point, and he needs every Castilian. 'Tell Juan García that his crime is forgotten. . . . And bring specimens of gold from this country together with a rough map.'"

"That's Cortés all right," said García. "Read straight ahead, boy, for the love of God."

Pedro faltered a moment. "He wishes us joy on the birth of our baby."

An empty silence fell. Pedro continued to read.

The letter reviewed briefly the past year, the gradual dismemberment of the Mexican empire east of the mountains, the return to Mexico, the conquering march around the Valley, the blockade of Tenochtitlán itself. Its allies destroyed or faithless, its causeways held, its water supply cut, its lagoon commanded by a fleet of brigantines, which had been carried piecemeal across the mountains (*"Por Dios, what a stroke that was!"* growled García), the queen of Mexican cities now faced the Spaniards alone.

> *But think not that the war is won* [the letter continued]. *The enemy is strong and stubborn. Our Indian friends, those from Tlascala, Tetzcuco, and elsewhere, are hard to manage and fickle of mind. At a whim, they may leave us, so that we live as men on the brink of victory or disaster. Therefore, I charge you, as one desiring honor and the King's service, to rejoin us in haste. I say in haste. You shall serve near my person as* ayudante de campo, *for we need better liaison between the forces under my command at the end of the southern causeway and those of Alvarado based on Tacuba in the west and those again of Sandoval holding the causeway to the north at Tepeyac. I have the right horse for you, a black with two white feet, newly arrived, named El Herrero.*

It brought back the old days. They could smell the army, as Pedro read, could see the pennons of Alvarado and Sandoval, the painted faces of the Tlascalans, the burly figures of the sword-and-buckler men.

> *I enclose a letter from your honored father, Don Francisco, which I opened, thinking, alas, that I should see you no more. It contains a message by another hand no doubt equally welcome,* Pedro el afortunado! [What was he driving at?] *And in that connection, my son, I doubt if it will disappoint you to hear that Diego de Silva has deserted our enterprise and returned to Cuba.*

De Vargas's heart sank. He paused to exchange a desolate glance with the others. De Silva not there! That had been one of the longed-for joys of the return—to meet de Silva again! Often Pedro had lain awake with the hot delight of imagining it.

"Diablos!" he burst out.

"When we had so hoped," grieved Catana, her eyes smoldering.

García clenched his fist. "There's justice for you! Rascal whoreson! I'd have burned him in a slow fire."

Pedro read on:—

It was politic to let him and several others depart. They had had their fill of the war and were mutinous dogs corrupting better men. But it was a hard choice, for de Silva is cousin to our enemy, the Bishop of Burgos, President of the Council of the Indies, who will lend a glad ear to his lies when the traitor reaches Spain.

Pedro was staring at the paper. He hesitated a moment, then went on in a too casual voice:—

At least I rejoice at the dissolution of his marriage with the noble Luisa de Carvajal, which your honored father reports. Therefore the fair hand which wrote you that other message is now free. . . . And so adiós.

Aware that Catana's eyes were on him, Pedro could not meet them. What other message? He reopened Don Francisco's letter and glanced down the page. Then at a couple of straggling lines under his father's signature and *rúbrica,* he turned red.

Do you remember, señor, or have you forgotten one who, praying for your glory, remembers and waits?

"Well?" asked Catana dryly.

"Nothing."

"Nothing?"

He could not help it that his cheeks burned, that the dream he had cherished so long rose from the depths. Luisa, free of the ugly enchantment which had effaced her, stood once more exquisite before him.

He excused himself and went inside to read his father's letter more carefully, lingering over the sentences where Don Francisco expressed approval of Luisa.

For there is no better blood in the two Castiles, and the lady is distinguished by beauty of person and goodness of mind. Now that she is quit of the rascal by whom she and her father were inveigled, marriage between you would be honorable and advantageous—all the more since you love each other. So, when the King's service permits, it is high time that you return here to enter a sweeter service . . .

389

He reflected that all that was over now, and at the same time he pictured the look on his parents' faces when the letter reached them that he had married Catana Pérez, a camp follower. After rereading Luisa's message, he raised it to his lips in token of farewell.

He was so absorbed that he did not hear Catana enter the room. Perhaps she had not seen the sentimental gesture, for, when he looked up, she was appraising one of his shirts that needed mending before the march.

"When do we leave for the army?" she asked.

"Tomorrow at dawn." His uneasy conscience imagined that her voice was drier and more detached than usual. "The General wrote *haste*. As I figure it, if we make speed on the trail, we might reach camp two days after tomorrow evening."

That night when all was quiet in the *palacio*, Catana got up from her mat and, stealing barefoot into Pedro's room (separate from her since his proposal of marriage), drew the letter out of his doublet. Then, tiptoeing back again and lighting a small link, she set about trying to find the words from Luisa. It was not hard to distinguish the different handwriting under Don Francisco's signature; but her skill in reading was small, and she spelled painfully, her forefinger crawling across the page.

Do you remember, señor, or have you forgotten . . .

By the time she had finished, the rush light had burned down. She crept back to Pedro's room, replaced the letter, and returning stretched out again on her mat.

After all, it was what she had foreseen and taken for granted from the beginning. If Pedro married her, he would regret forever the hidalga he had not married. Staring up through the darkness with eyes too hot for tears, Catana accepted what had to be.

LXVII

THE MORNING STAR still shone faintly when Pedro, Catana, and García, wolfing some cornbread and gulping down a brew of *chocolatl*, made ready to start. Thoughts were on the journey.

"Coatl's giving us a hundred warriors into camp," Pedro announced. "They keep rank and step. We won't make too bad a showing when we march in. By God, everybody captured by the Indians doesn't get back in that style."

"Not to speak of the gold," said García. He had divided the intake, variously acquired by gifts and mining during the year, into three equal shares and now handed Pedro one of the bags. "That'll brighten Cortés. Remember how he told the Aztec spokesman back in San Juan de Ulúa that we Castilians had a heart disease which only gold could cure?"

His chocolate cup in one hand, Pedro weighed the bag with the other. "I'd say close to four thousand pesos' weight. Half of it'll pay for the new horse and a suit of armor. Ha, darling"—he clapped Catana on the back—"you'll ride pillion behind me when we're married. Señora de Vargas y Pérez. With your share, we'll be well in pocket. Never thought you'd bring your husband four thousand pesos in dowry, did you?"

Somewhere a conch was blown. A trooping of feet and a confusion of voices sounded in the street below. Stuffing a final piece of bread into his mouth and washing it down with a gulp of the chocolate, Pedro drew the back of his hand across his lips.

"Time," he said. But getting up, he stopped at the look on Catana's face. "What's wrong, sweetheart? Lord save us! You're not the wench to have the vapors."

She stamped her foot and turned away. "It's nothing. Except we've been very happy here."

A glare of torches struck along the terrace outside, and Coatl appeared at the door. He insisted on escorting his friends for a part of the journey and was dressed for the march in a traveling cloak with a simple red band around his forehead.

"The men are ready, señores. I send carriers for your gear."

"Then fetch my sword, Catana," said Pedro, "and buckle it on me, will you, since you're my one lady. Remember that night in front of the Rosario?"

Keeping her face down, she drew the buckles to the worn marks on the belt. He eased it a trifle on his hip, fingering the pommel.

"*Y ahora adiós!*" he said with a smile at the familiar walls of the house.

"One moment, señor, by your leave—if you will come with me."

"Where?"

"To the garden."

With a twinge of self-reproach, he understood. He could not leave without another, different farewell. Already Niñita had slipped his mind.

"I'll be with you presently, Coatl," he said, following Catana.

They rounded the buildings to the lushness of trees and flowers behind the *palacio*. Dawn had begun, but clouds were gathering, and the slow wind brought a shiver of rain. The air lay damp and heavy with the fragrance of blossoms.

Silently they crossed over to the little grave and, kneeling together, prayed for the soul of Niñita, that she, who was free from sin, might live close to Our Lady. And they bade her good-by once more, as if she and the cross at the head of the grave were one.

A march of eight hours brought the party, guided by Coatl, to the first day's stopping place, Cacahuamilpa, the last of the Zapotec pueblos. It was a mere upland hamlet, but what with rain, slippery trails, swollen streams, jungle and mountain ranges, through which they had struggled, anything under roof seemed welcome at the moment.

After a change of clothes and a meal of hot fowl, peppers, and *tortillas* at the house of the local chief, Pedro sauntered out alone for a look at the weather, which had now brightened. A few rays of the declining sun, piercing the clouds, showed the country northeast that had to be covered tomorrow. He was speculating that a day's march would bring them to Cuauhnahuac and a day after that to the Spanish headquarters at Xoloc, when a shadow struck the corner of his eye, and he turned to discover Coatl beside him.

"I follow," said the Indian. "I wait until you alone."

"What's on your mind, Coatl?"

"I turn back from here tomorrow. We not see each other again. Remember in that sierra in Spain, you give me a gift at parting. Now my turn."

De Vargas shook his head. "You've paid that back a thousand times already."

But the other, with a half-smile, laid a hand on Pedro's arm. "Still, I have gift for you alone. You go with me now and see."

Mystified and curious as to what the thing was, Pedro walked along with the Indian; but his curiosity grew when they left the pueblo and plunged downhill into the rough country below.

After a while, he said, "*Vaya, amigo mío!* I have good legs, but we've done eight hours today, remember."

"It not far now, señor. If it two times so far, you not sorry."

Having reached a gorge with almost vertical walls, Coatl led the way down, pointing out footings and handholds. Opposite them, on the other side of the chasm, Pedro could see a bleak range of hills, singularly bare and grim, and he could hear from underneath a roar of cascades. In the afternoon lighting, the place made a secluded impression, which deepened with every yard down. He was glad to find himself at last on the floor of the cañon.

At this level, the gorge was lined with blossoming trees, between which the stream leaped from waterfall to waterfall. There were trees, too, having a strange golden bark and with twisted snakelike roots that made walking difficult. Occasionally birds, red, green, and blue, glanced between the sides of the valley.

Having led the way for some distance downstream, Coatl suddenly pointed at the cañon's opposite wall, and Pedro, who had been picking his way between the matted tree roots, stood staring.

In the opposite side of the mountain, an enormous portal yawned perhaps seventy feet high by a hundred and fifty wide. Though a natural arch, it looked as if built by hand.

"Cuerpo de Dios!" exclaimed de Vargas.

"Behold," said Coatl. "House of gods. Sacred. Forbidden. I, chief of Zapotec people, I only have right to enter without fear. Speak, señor, you fear?"

In the confused background of Pedro's mind, romance jostled with legend. Like Amadís, he stood before the giant's castle. Gazing at the blackness behind the vast doorway, from which came a distant muttering as of voices, he knew that, if not afraid, he was at least shaken.

But he steadied himself. "Why should I fear? If your devils are inside, we will go to them, and I shall call upon the name of Our Lord and San Pedro. What happens then will be according to their will. But you might have warned me to bring my sword."

"What use swords against gods?" Coatl returned. "You not fear, so let us enter."

Crossing the stream on a series of rocks, they reached the portal of the cavern, where Coatl, drawing out a supply of pine torches from a secret crevice in the cliff, kindled one of them with a wooden fire drill from his pouch and lighted another for Pedro. Touching hand to forehead, he uttered a few words, evidently a traditional prayer.

Pedro said, *"In nomine Patris, et Filii, et Spiritus Sancti."*

Then the man of the Stone Age and the man of civilized Europe advanced into the darkness.

By the light of the torches, Pedro could see a tunnel-like corridor slanting down, and he could feel the slope beneath his feet. Comparing great things with small, it reminded him a little of the passageway under the main tower of the Castle at Jaén. Only here a mountain was the tower, and the passageway extended five hundred feet.

393

Almost at once a swarm of bats darted around the two men, fanning their cheeks with furry wings and uttering mouse-like pipings. Everyone knew that bats were lackeys of the devil.

"Let them come," thought de Vargas grimly. "They're to be expected, for this is surely the road into hell. Let them come or change themselves to demons. Though, curse me, I wish I had my sword!"

Then suddenly, at the foot of the decline, his heart leaped to his throat.

He beheld, as far as the light could reach, a gigantic hall—but one so vast that the cathedral at Jaén would have been lost in a corner of it. To his dazzled vision, this infinity seemed encrusted with ice, frozen masses pendent from the roof, upsoaring from the pavement, wrought into huge forms and statues, a crystal world.

He had never seen stalactites and stalagmites. Only half-emerged from the Middle Ages, his mind stocked with fairy tales, his courage tensed for battle with Satan, it seemed to him a thing incredible and devilish. He and Coatl were dots—fireflies—in the glittering space about them.

Imagination soared. He saw in one mass of crystals an enormous throne, surely the high seat of Lucifer himself, but at the moment vacant. He heard, or fancied he heard, the thunderous accents of an approaching voice.

"Rivers beneath us," said Coatl, reading his face.

That might be true or not, de Vargas thought, but no river could make the sound he heard.

"This worth seeing?" Coatl went on. "I waste your time, my friend, bringing you here?"

"It is wonderful," answered Pedro gravely. "But God knows whether mortal men have the right to look at such things."

Walking forward across the vast floor, they seemed to crawl. The torchlight fell on white trees hung with diamond moss, fountains of frozen water, crystal baths to cool the heat of devils, an amphitheater crowned by a pipe organ to make music for Beelzebub, triumphal obelisks, sheeted phantoms doomed to stone, lifelike statues of lost souls.

All at once Pedro started so that the torch shook in his hand. An enormous white goat stood before them. A goat big as a horse, the very chairman of Witches' Sabbaths.

"Ha!" said de Vargas, crossing himself and relieved that the animal did not move. "Satan's image."

But at that moment something else moved. Coatl jerked Pedro back. It was a large rattlesnake, which had struck from its coil. In an instant

394

Coatl, stooping, had caught the reptile by the tail and snapped its head against the flank of the goat. It stretched limp and quivering in the circle of the light.

"Watch out," said the Indian. "Once I meet an ocelot here, but the torch scare him."

Pedro remembered Dante's adventure with the leopard. It was all of a piece with the great poet's description of hell.

"Remember how we go," said Coatl. "You come again—alone."

Pedro did not relish the thought. "I'll bring the General and my friends here. It will amaze them."

"No, you come alone."

"Why should I?"

"Because something you not see yet."

It was unpleasant talking in the vasty place. Their voices were multiplied by echoes, some loud, some faint, as if the words were passed from mouth to mouth around a circle of ghosts.

"Not see yet," came the whisper.

"Remember way lie straight to this beast." Coatl pointed to the goat. "That easy. We turn now to left. Give heed."

"Give heed," warned the echoes.

De Vargas had a natural sense of direction and now took note of turnings and landmarks. They passed along galleries, down declines, through other gigantic halls, stopping now and then to light another torch. Occasionally Coatl rehearsed him, as if everything depended on his remembering this particular route.

"It drawn here," said the Indian, showing the end of a parchment in his pouch. "But if this lost, you must remember."

Then, without warning, Coatl stopped before a natural archway.

"Here," he said.

Upon entering, Pedro saw another huge cavern hung with crystals, and in the center of it a high, white pyramid. Steps, whether natural or cut by hand, ascended toward the apex, which met the roof in an odd contorted form. It looked like a monstrous head supporting the vault, while the pyramid itself resembled a white robe, completing one giant figure. Then Pedro noticed that the steps were of a rusty color as compared with the snowy surface on either side of them.

"Blood," said Coatl. He pointed at a small, dark mound some distance off. "Bones of many men, long ago, in ancient times."

Having prostrated himself before the lowering face above, Coatl now led the way around the pyramid to a passage descending under it.

"We go down here."

"Look you, friend," said Pedro, "I have not troubled you with questions. You have shown me marvels, but there must be an end. Our torches are half-spent."

"End is here." Coatl pointed down the tunnel-like shaft. "Few paces more." Then, turning, he plunged down the sharp decline with Pedro behind him.

The torchlight fell on a hollow space under the pyramid, a bubble in the rock formation, irregular in shape, and perhaps no more than twenty feet long. Pedro, however, saw nothing but its contents.

No longer the white or crystal glittering of the halls above. Here the torches brought out a warm, yellow reflection, more dazzling and incredible.

Gold!

Except for Montezuma's treasure room, de Vargas had never seen such riches. But here they were concentrated in a narrower space. Grains, nuggets, hand-wrought ornaments in piles.

He muttered, "What's this, Coatl?"

The answer had no meaning. "Señor, this the two pesos you give me once in that *barranca* near Jaén."

"Two pesos?" echoed de Vargas.

"Gold is like maize," said Coatl. "Sow one, two grains, get many."

"I still don't understand."

"Is this not parting gift?"

On Pedro's stupefied mind, the words did not register.

"I hope it bring you good," Coatl went on. "To many Spaniards it bring evil."

Pedro turned on him. "Explain for God's love! Do you mean you're giving me this gold?"

"To you alone. That is why I say you come back here alone."

"But explain. How? Whose gold?"

He could hardly hear through the clatter of his thoughts. An ancient treasure . . . An offering to priests long ago beyond memory . . . Perhaps, even, they were priests of another race, for this god of the cavern was an old god . . . Coatl alone had the secret, transmitted from chief to chief through the far past . . . What need had the Zapotecs of this gold? They had enough in their mines and rivers.

Stooping down, Pedro ran the fingers of one hand through the precious grain, while the torch he held with the other cast yellow flickerings. Looking more closely, he could see that the treasure, when melted into bars, would not quite equal Montezuma's—perhaps seven hundred thousand pesos. A fifth of this belonged by law to the King, a fifth to Cortés, a share to the company. He could see the gold shrinking as he gazed, but still it left him rich beyond heart's desire. The treasure made him equal with any grandee. It opened every door.

"What can I say?" he burst out. "What return can I make?"

"No return." Coatl stretched out his hand. "I tell you one time your god give you what you want. We not meet again. But you go with me; I go with you. What we do for each other is seed of good or bad harvest. It is so, señor, with all we do in life." Then after a pause, he added, "Torches almost gone. It is time we leave."

In a half daze, Pedro followed him through the windings of the cavern, crossed the hall of the throne, and at last emerged into the purity of daylight. Lost in his dream, he stumbled more than once over the coiled serpent roots of the lovely trees, which seemed to writhe and close about his ankles.

He reached the pueblo after dark.

"Where the devil have you been?" demanded García, while Catana's anxious frown relaxed. "You step out for a minute and you're gone three hours."

"Walked with Coatl," Pedro answered. "He showed me a cave."

"Hell! You must like exercise!"

De Vargas said nothing. The master of seven hundred thousand pesos must guard his tongue even among those he loves. They would be the more surprised later on, he told himself to quiet his conscience.

LXVIII

BECAUSE OF RAIN and the difficulty of the fords, it took two hard days from Cacahuamilpa before Pedro, Catana, and García with their escort of Zapotecs reached the heights of Ajusco and looked down on their journey's end. The clouds having lifted toward sunset, they could view the entire reach of the Valley: at their feet, Xochimilco and Coyoacán; in the middle distance, outstretched on the lake, Tenochtitlán with its three tentacle causeways; to the left, Chapultepec and Tacuba; to the north, Tepeyac, not yet known as Guadalupe; and in the far distance on the right the city of Tetzcuco, formerly the Aztecs' chief ally but now a deserter to the Spaniards.

From one point or another in the surrounding mountains, Pedro and his two companions had often overlooked the Valley in the past and retained so vivid a memory of it that they could recall each detail of its towns and configuration. Little prepared as they were for the changes which a year had brought, its present aspect startled them.

Xochimilco, "field of flowers," once gay and glittering and fronted by its floating gardens, looked black and deserted, like a burned-out hulk. In his recent letter, Cortés had mentioned the burning of it "to punish the dogs for their resistance," a passing reference that mocked the mournful reality.

Looking farther, it seemed to Pedro that Tenochtitlán itself had changed. It appeared somehow shrunken, though its teocallis of evil memory still towered over the spread of roofs. Then he pointed out what had happened. Sections of the suburbs had been gnawed away; the buildings once standing there were gone, leaving acres of rubble, over which hung a thin haze of dust and smoke. The canals also had disappeared, being evidently filled up by the ruins of demolished houses. At a loss to understand the reason for this, he and García finally hit on the answer. It was furnished by the large camps to be seen at the end of the three causeways: one directly below at Xoloc to the south of the city; another to the west of it in Tacuba; and a third to the north at Tepeyac. The dikes themselves no longer showed gaps as before, but stretched solidly from the mainland. Apparently the siege consisted in a slow leveling of the town itself, a leveling which gave constantly wider scope for the use of cavalry and cannon, while it herded the enemy back from the lake toward the center of the city. Attack by day, a certain amount of demolition, would be followed by retirement to camp at night. As they looked, they could see a dense column of men, like ants at that distance, returning to their quarters at Xoloc, while the Aztecs, advancing from the town, harried the rear guard. The rattle of musketry, the far-off boom of cannon, marked this action.

Pedro noticed other changes. Once the lake had swarmed with canoes, the come-and-go of pleasure traffic. Now it lay empty as a blind eye. He was asking himself what could have swept it bare, when he caught sight of the obvious explanation. He had forgotten the eleven brigantines mentioned in Cortés's letter. Some five of them now appeared heading from the mainland with the evident aim of covering the retirement of the column on the causeway. Gallant little two-masted vessels with billowing sails and fluttering pennons. Their invention was the crowning stroke of Cortés's genius. They held the key to conquest by cutting off supplies from the starving city and by enfilading any attack along the causeways. Puffs of smoke leaped from their sides as they coasted in toward the skirmish. Then, after a pause, came the dull thud of the cannon.

398

The Zapotec warriors stared goggle-eyed.

"*Vaya,*" Pedro said to them, "you'll see more wonders than that before you're through. Forward, if we're to make camp before dark."

The trail descended in coils from the thinner air of the upland. Soon evergreens were left behind, giving place to cactus or to fields of maguey with their pepper trees. As the party drew closer to the lake, they encountered increasing numbers of encamped Indian bands drawn from all the different tribes of Anahuac and from the eastern plateau. They had chosen between the Aztec yoke of fear and Cortés's promises. Knowing the former only too well, they embraced the latter, prompted also by revenge and greed, but happily ignorant that with every blow for Spain they were forging their future fetters. These warriors looked askance at the unfamiliar Zapotecs, noting differences in paint and equipment. But the Spaniards needed no passport, and the party proceeded unchallenged.

As they threaded their way through the separate encampments, de Vargas identified some of the tribes. Here were Cholulans, there Tetzcucans, there Tlascalans; but the fact that many were strange brought home his year of absence from the army. Once he could have distinguished the markings and war gear of every people with which the company had had dealings.

About nightfall, through an ever-denser encampment, they reached the lines of recently built Spanish huts on the causeway at Xoloc. The sharp *quién vive* of the sentinel brought water to Pedro's eyes. It meant home.

"Captain Pedro de Vargas, reporting to the General with a hundred men."

"Whoop!" yelled the sentinel to his mates of the guard. "*Hombres!* Here are Redhead de Vargas, Bull García, Catana! Blast me!" And letting discipline go hang for the moment, Chávez of the old company teetered his partisan against the wall and flung himself at the newcomers like an affectionate bear.

LXIX

IN AN UPPER ROOM of the captured Aztec fort at Xoloc, which guarded the southern causeway, Hernán Cortés ate supper and relaxed after the day's work. Corn, beans, tomatoes, squash, and fried fish, with a dessert of Indian figs, made up the menu. As a rare treat and for the good of his leg, wounded in the recent fighting, he indulged himself with a cup of Spanish wine newly landed on the coast. Except for the page Ochoa, who thanks to Sandoval had survived the Noche Triste, he was alone.

A hullabaloo in the surrounding camp broke out, and his eyes quickened. Somebody was beating a drum. Shouts. Scuffling of feet. Women's voices chiming in. Skilled in interpreting mass noises, he concluded at once that it was neither a quarrel nor a mutiny. The drummer was clowning; the shouts reflected excitement and good temper. Still, after a hard day's fight, one didn't expect merrymaking.

"Boy," he said to Ochoa, "step down there and see what's afoot. Bring me word of it."

However, the sounds were converging on his own quarters. He caught the measured tramp of feet and instinctively looked to his weapons. It had been no more than a few weeks ago that he had foiled a conspiracy against his life on the part of certain Narváez henchmen. And who could tell when another attempt might be made?

But at the tones of a voice below, he started, smiled, and stood up. No wonder the camp was celebrating.

A moment later, Pedro de Vargas with Ochoa behind him stood at salute in the doorway, then found himself in the steel embrace of the General.

"Let me look at you," said Cortés, holding him by the shoulders at arm's length. "*A fe mía,* it's a sight for sore eyes! I still can't believe it. Back from the dead! Strikes me you've put on beef. Ah, son Pedro, the look of you reminds me of others who haven't come back, the good comrades. So many! Too many!"

The dark eyes filled. Hard as he was, Cortés kept a peculiar affection for the old company, those who had sailed with him from Cuba. It was an affection which did not extend to newer arrivals.

"*Vaya, vaya!* Sit down. . . . Ochoa, some food and wine for Captain de Vargas. I'll warrant he hasn't eaten. . . . And the father of a strapping lass, eh? Where is she, *hombre?*"

Pedro's face darkened. "Your Excellency, the child died of the *viruelas* two weeks ago, after I wrote you."

"Alas! Truly I'm grieved." Cortés laid his hand on the other's arm. . . . "And the Señora Catana? Juan García? They are here?"

"At Your Excellency's orders."

"Well, sit down. I'll see them presently. . . . Boy, didn't I tell you to fetch victuals for the captain? Are you deaf?"

Ochoa hung on. "I wanted to ask about Tía Catana, señor. Is she well?"

"Aye, well enough to spank you, *niño*," smiled de Vargas. "She's waiting to see you. What a big lad you've grown in a year!" And when the boy had gone out, he added, "Which reminds me, Your Excellency."

He braced himself.

"Which reminds me," he repeated, trying to sound natural, "that I've asked Catana Pérez in marriage."

Cortés fingered his beard. "Marry Catana Pérez, eh? Well, take a chair. Fill a cup. Yes, on my word it's true Malaga. Your health, son Pedro! Welcome back to the company!"

"Your Excellency's servant!"

But Pedro felt that his announcement had drawn a blank, and he did not have spirit enough at the moment to renew the topic.

They had much to discuss: campaigns since the Noche Triste, personalities of new arrivals from the Islands, the present state of affairs. The struggle for Mexico City had been desperate.

"I wish I had been here," Pedro mourned. "The work's finished."

"By no means is it finished," said Cortés. "You'll have your share. It looks as if we should have to pull down every stone of the city before we bring the fools to terms. Is it not sad? The loveliest town on earth. Because of these dogs' stubbornness.. I've made them every promise if they'll submit. But if not—"

He broke off, frowning helplessly at the logic of war.

"Tell me about the Zapotec country," he went on with a shrug. "Your letter spoke of gold."

It was now Pedro's turn. He outlined the resources of the western valleys in terms of minerals and timber. He spoke also of the pearl trade with the coast. Cortés listened intently.

"It sounds good. You have samples?"

"I have four thousand pesos' weight of gold with me, Your Excellency. Catana and Juan García have each as much."

"*Cáspita!*" exclaimed the General. "Hm-m, twelve thousand pesos." Pedro knew that he was figuring his own share, the King's, the company's. "Why, this is excellent. We'll make a survey of that district— and soon. You took care to locate the mines? Good, very good. Your health, *amigo mío!*"

Pedro bowed his thanks.

"You see," Cortés went on, "we have to rake and scrape to furnish a revenue worthy of His Majesty. I don't expect to recover much of the treasure we lost on the retreat. The Aztec hounds will see to it that we don't. Then there're the soldiers' claims to be met, and the captains'; our debts in Cuba. *Peste!* I wish I could lay my hands now on even fifty thousand pesos."

Two years ago, de Vargas, in devotion to his chief, would have swelled with pride to declare the treasure at Cacahuamilpa. He knew better now. Unspoken words didn't have to be regretted. If he wanted his full share of Coatl's gift, he must play a shrewd game. For the moment, he changed the subject by asking about news from Spain.

Cortés made a gesture denoting emptiness. "That His Majesty is now Holy Roman Emperor; that he finally received the gift we sent from Villa Rica; that he *even* granted audience to our friends, Montejo and Puertocarrero. Nothing more. We'll soon have to be sending other doves from our ark with other olive branches."

"Sir?"

"Falcons then—ambassadors. Good friends who can take our part against the Bishop of Burgos and his Council of the Indies—sold hand and foot as he is to our enemy, Governor Velásquez, and your friend, de Silva, at his ear."

Cortés fell suddenly to musing, his eyes intent as a cat's. Then he slapped his thigh and smiled. "By my conscience, it's well thought on! Son Pedro, you're the man. Your father is in favor, as I gathered from his letter. Your kinsman is the Duke of Medina Sidonia. You have been with us from the start and are a captain in our enterprise. You're a man"—Cortés's voice warmed, and he laid a hand on Pedro's knee—"after my own heart. A young man of energy and prudence. Nay, I love you as a son."

He had loosed all the batteries of his charm. Though Pedro knew the General well enough to take these sudden compliments with a pinch of salt and to wonder where they were leading, he nonetheless felt dizzy from the incense.

"Look you." Cortés hitched his chair closer. "When this city falls and the war ends, you will go to the Emperor. You will go to him whether he's in Spain or Flanders. You will let no one or nothing stop you, the Bishop of Burgos or anyone else."

"To Spain?"

"Aye, with suitable gifts and letters, with all the family influence you can muster. And it will be odd if you, the son of Don Francisco de Vargas, Alcalde of Jaén and captain of Spain, the kinsman of Don Juan Alonso de Guzmán, with gold to spend, mark you, and gifts to give, do not outtrump bishop or council—*provided* you reach the Emperor himself and fill his ears with New Spain."

Pedro's imagination caught fire. Himself at court! It crossed his mind too that in this way he could salvage officially a greater part of the Cacahuamilpa treasure.

Cortés added softly, "I think you can depend on the Carvajal interest as well, my son."

De Vargas started. His proposal to Catana had slipped his mind.

"Well?" asked Cortés, noting his expression.

"I'm afraid no longer, Your Excellency. Not after Catana Pérez becomes my wife."

The General smiled. "You're not serious about that."

The tone of voice reminded Pedro of a smooth stone wall. It expressed perfectly the preposterousness of such a marriage.

"But I am serious, Your Excellency."

"Oh, come! Did she give you a love charm? Have they witches in the Zapotec country?"

"You don't understand, sir." Privately de Vargas cursed himself for feeling so foolish and weak before the mockery in the other's eyes. "I love her. Our child died. It came to me as the will of God that we should marry."

How feeble it sounded! How inadequate to express the passion, sorrow, comradeship, that he and Catana had shared! Cortés cocked a humorous eyebrow.

"Dear me! Is that the way of it? Well, you'll recover. We've all had our moments."

Pedro recalled Catana kneeling beside the grave in the garden.

"I'm quite in earnest, Your Excellency."

Cortés did not answer for a long minute. The humor faded from his eyes. Finally he said, "Poppycock! Listen, man, the son of Francisco de Vargas does not marry a camp girl."

"She's been true as steel."

"What of it?" Cortés smiled again. "Son Pedro, I marvel that I waste time arguing upon so foolish a point; but I would save you from the reefs if I can. On the seas of love, I'm an old rover." He gave a toss of the hand. "Nobody can tell me much about women. I've had some of every stripe. But mark you, not one of them was worth a man's career. Leave that kind of nonsense to fairy tales."

He paused an instant, as if choosing his words.

"And mark you too, I say nothing against the Señora Catana. She's a gallant, personable wench, and no doubt loyal. What of it? Take this Indian girl of mine—Marina. Is she not gallant? Is she not true? And would I marry her for that reason, even if I did not have a lawful wife in Cuba? I would not. I would do exactly what I intend doing now when the time comes—hand her over with a good dot to one of the comrades. Why? Because a man of parts has work to do in the world of more interest and value than sentiment; and marriage is an alliance to promote that work, not to hinder it." He flashed his compelling eyes on Pedro. "Consider yourself. You are of good blood, have good talents, great opportunities. I offer you a chance which might lead far at court or in the army to the life you were born for, a chance to serve this company and New Spain. Will you shirk it, disappoint your parents, throw everything over, in order to become the husband of a gutter girl?"

Pedro reddened, and his eyes narrowed. But Cortés did not relent.

"What else is she?" he demanded. "Isn't it better for me who love you to call a spade a spade and hurt your ears than to let you make yourself a laughingstock? Have I said anything that your father would not say?"

In all honesty, Pedro could not deny it. On the contrary, he felt sure that Don Francisco would have used stronger language.

"One more thing, and I'm through," the General added. "Then you can please yourself. I know that my views of women and marriage are sound, because once only I neglected them and have smarted for it all my life. That once was enough."

He frowned at the table, his mouth bitter.

"Indeed?" said Pedro after a silence.

"Aye," Cortés growled. "My own wife, Pedro de Vargas, who waits for me in Cuba. Who cramps me at every turn. Being what she was— a girl like Catana Pérez." He shrugged. "There she is! My incarnate mistake, which has to be corrected somehow—sometime."

He sank into thought, but roused himself. "A last point. De Silva is in Spain. I'll warrant he follows Fonseca, the Bishop of Burgos, to court. *There* would be a chance to even all scores. But we could hardly use the husband of Catana Pérez to represent us before the Emperor. . . . Well, what do you say?"

Pedro's jaw set. "I intend to keep my promise, Your Excellency."

LXX

IT DID NOT take long to get back into the swing of the army. El Herrero proved to be a good horse; a suit of armor, pieced together from various sources, completed Pedro's necessary equipment, and several days' fighting across the causeway put him in trim. As aide-de-camp of the

General, his duty took him also to reunions with the comrades under Alvarado in Tacuba and Sandoval in Tepeyac. Within a week, he felt at home.

And yet not fully at home. There had been great changes in a year. Even the Narváez people were now old hands as compared with other newcomers from the Islands. The original company had shrunk into a kind of inner circle, self-conscious and exclusive, admired but envied. It was pleasant no doubt to be one of the "old" captains, but the former democracy was gone.

And the novelty of conquest had worn off. The time seemed long ago when the Aztec world of cities, palaces, and temples was like a realized fairy tale. The war had simmered down into nothing but work. Regular as daybreak, one got up, crossed the causeway, drove deeper into the city, protected the Indian allies while they demolished additional sections of houses and filled up additional canals; then fought a rear-guard action as the army fell back to its fortified camp. At this season, it rained most of the time. Soaked to the skin and tired as a woodchopper, one ate the monotonous evening rations, talked over the day's fight, and stretched out on a mat to start again next morning.

Daily the Spanish death grip tightened on the doomed city. No thrill of uncertainty as in the old days. Since the Aztecs chose rather to die than surrender, it was only a question of how much time it would take for starvation, pestilence, and attack to exterminate them in their shrinking walls.

But to Pedro, the chief difference between now and the past lay in his separation from Catana and García. His attendance on the General required quarters in the fort at Xoloc. García was billeted with other minor officers in one of the company huts along the causeway; while Catana shared a half-ruined house on the mainland with her former crony, María de Estrada, now betrothed to Pedro Farfán. Added to other changes, this scattering gave a sense of strangeness and dissolution.

As usual, Cortés drove hard. Pedro spent three days with Sandoval in Tepeyac. He had hardly returned when the General dispatched him to Alvarado. A week passed from the night of arrival, and he had not yet been given a breathing space to see Catana.

Cortés, like every other eminent leader, believed in the importance of small things. He could think in bold outline, but he was also a master of detail. The checkmate of a king often depends on the early move of an insignificant pawn. Having determined that the fate of New Spain hung on a proper representation at the Spanish court and having decided that Pedro de Vargas was the man best suited to this office, he did not propose, if he could help it, to leave so weighty a matter to the chance of Pedro's sentimental whims. Catana Pérez might be only an atom in the strain and stress of forces that would make or mar the future of the Conquest; but at the moment she was an important atom.

Therefore, one late afternoon, while Pedro was still absent, he dispatched Juan Díaz of his household to fetch Catana to him. When she had been ushered into the large upper room at the fort, and the attendants had withdrawn, Cortés, under cover of pleasant introductory phrases, studied her with the finesse of an artist.

Physically she pleased him. He liked her slender but shapely hands, which accorded with the long oval of her face. He liked too the arrangement of her hair, curving in two black bands over her ears. If her mouth was too large, it lent her character and spirit, as did the dark, heavy-lidded eyes. She had a fine bust and figure.

But he was concerned with her psychologically, and here he felt unsure. He knew how difficult it is to pry a determined woman loose from a brilliant match if at the same time she is in love with her future husband. How to set about it? Catana's reputation for courage did not suggest intimidation as the right technique. Bribery seemed equally doubtful, since he could offer nothing better than what he wanted her to give up. He disliked more sinister measures if they could be avoided. So he felt his way, alert for an opening.

At first, overwhelmed by shyness and puzzled as to the reason of her summons, she was unresponsive, until at last she ventured:—

"Is my lord de Vargas here, Your Excellency?"

"No, señora, he's in Tacuba at present with Captain de Alvarado."

"I was afraid there had been an accident," she murmured, "that perhaps that was the reason—"

"No, he's in fine fettle. Is rendering good service to this company. A man of high promise—Captain de Vargas."

He noticed her cheeks flush with the praise and her eyes kindle. By God, he had overlooked the romantic lead! He had forgotten the self-sacrifice that young fools are sometimes capable of! It was worth probing.

"Tell me one thing, señora," he went on, with a confidential smile, "what's your real feeling toward Pedro de Vargas?"

"My real feeling, Your Excellency?"

"Yes, your attitude—call it what you please."

"Why, I love him."

"Love him?"

She nodded, staring down at her hands.

Cortés laughed. "Oh, come, señora! Anything but that!"

She looked up, startled; and he thrust home his point.

"Want him, yes—I can understand that—but love?" The General waxed eloquent. "Love? Señora, love seeks to give, not to get, desires the honor and success of the loved one." He sighed. "It is rare. Indeed, yes! But such, I take it, is not your feeling toward Captain de Vargas."

Catana faltered, "I don't understand, Your Excellency."

"How now! Is it not true that you are marrying him?"

"It is true that he asked me to marry him," she breathed.

"Pooh! Don't let's quibble. He tells me that he is going to marry you. He, a man of good house, fine prospects, a man whom I had chosen to represent us before His Caesarean Majesty, marry *you!* Forfeit his career! And you tell me that you love him!"

The masterful face, pale above its beard, frightened her; but she met Cortés's hot eyes without flinching.

"Your Excellency is mistaken. Don't you think I know what he is— what I am? Do you think I intended to marry him? I'd rather die than hurt him. Your Excellency doesn't need to tell me about love and what I ought to do." Then, shocked at such plain-speaking to the Commander-in-Chief, she added, "I crave Your Excellency's pardon."

Cortés continued to stare at her, but his stare was deflated. He was like a man who, lifting his foot to mount a step, finds no step there. He had mobilized his strategy without any need for it.

"Hm-m!" he recovered. "Ha! You mean to tell me that you won't marry him even if he urges it?"

"I had made up my mind to that some time ago, Your Excellency."

"Indeed? Well then, it's good, very good. I apologize, señora. I had not expected to find you so—so"—he substituted *noble* for *easy*—"yes, of so noble and sensitive a nature. One doesn't encounter that sort of thing often. I suppose then you'll remain Captain de Vargas's *cara amiga*. And in that case I envy him."

She shook her head. "My lord Pedro does not wish it, Your Excellency. He feels that it is not God's will."

"*Qué cosa!*" Cortés raised his eyebrows. "Of course one must follow one's conscience. But his loss will be another man's gain." Struck by a sudden whim, he leaned forward and took her hand. "Even I, señora, would be very much your servant—if you pleased."

She evaded the hint as lightly as it was made. "No, Your Excellency's servant."

When she rose to leave, and they were standing face to face, Cortés said, impulsively for once: "By my conscience, señora, you are a right member of our old company. It is upon you and our comrades that I can rely. Also you can rely on me. I'll see to it, with the help of God, that you are made masters in this land—you yourself by no means least. You shall choose your own *encomienda* and villages. You'll be the forebear of an illustrious family in New Spain." He paused a moment, his eyes on the future. "Yes, we are founding a new *nobleza* here. Do not regret Pedro de Vargas too much. By blood and fortune, his ties are in the Old World; you belong to the New."

She made him a curtsy. Even Cortés could not see the emptiness behind her eyes.

Taking her hand again, he raised it to his lips. "I honor you more, my dear, than most ladies I have had the chance to meet." And with a strange pulse of feeling in his voice, he added, "Much more."

Then, opening for her, he called to the men below, "Attend the Señora Pérez."

But, riding home, Catana realized that the door which had been closing was now locked and sealed officially, irrevocably.

LXXI

WHEN PEDRO returned from Tacuba, he lost no time before calling on Catana but found that she had walked up to the pine woods above the house. Directed by María de Estrada, he discovered her leaning against a tree, her eyes on the distance of the lake.

At the sound of footsteps beside her, she turned and, seeing who it was, exclaimed, "Señor!" Then, her face lighting up with the familiar smile, she instinctively threw her arms around him.

"*Querida!*" he said. "Have I missed you! I've been nothing but the General's shuttlecock these ten days. But, by God, I'll pay myself back now. It's all arranged. Father Olmedo is marrying us tonight."

To his surprise, her arms dropped, and without answering she turned away, gazing apparently at the crumbling remnants of Tenochtitlán across the lake.

"No, señor, I don't want to marry you."

Amazement in Pedro eclipsed every other feeling. He had not taken seriously the delay she had asked for, assuming that once back in camp, their marriage was a foregone conclusion.

"*Por Dios,* why on earth not?"

Struggling with her weakness, she could not reply for a moment.

"Why on earth not?" he repeated.

There was no use telling him the truth. That would only provoke argument. Conscious of her own limitations, she wanted to make this short.

She forced herself to speak casually. "Well, señor, as Juan García says, love is one thing, marriage is another. I'd rather keep what we've had" (she touched her breast) "here, than watch it fade out. Don't you see?"

"Cursed if I do. You and I haven't been only romantic lovers: we've been comrades. That's what marriage is."

She hurried on. "Then there's another thing. We won't always be in camp. For a husband, I want someone of my own sort. No looking down or up. On account of the children, too. When you get married, you've got to think of these things."

"You never thought of them before."

"It didn't matter when we were lovers."

Pedro's astonishment gave way to hurt. "But, Catana, I've told you why we couldn't go on as we were. I've told it to Father Olmedo. He agrees with me. Are we to deny God?"

"No, señor. We could not go on as we were." It was torment to keep her eyes dry, her throat clear; to make her act convincing in spite of the voices in her mind that cried out to him. "Besides, there's this," she added, borrowing from Cortés. "I want to stay here. I feel as if this is my country. You've got to go home. You say you don't, señor; but you've got to. That's your place."

And now jealousy took a fling at him. His fist clenched.

"I'd like to know the bottom of this," he growled. "I've a mind to give you a belting and get it out of you. Look you, has some other gallant, while I've been on duty—"

"No."

"I have my doubts. Who's this husband you intend to marry?"

She had thought of no one. Improvising, she said: "Perhaps Juan, perhaps someone else. I don't know."

"Juan García! Has *he*—"

"No. He's never said a word. But he would have me if I asked him."

"*Juan!*" Pedro repeated. He balanced in a hot vacancy.

409

Would it never end? Catana asked herself. She couldn't stand much more. She wanted to press her forehead down on his shoulder and give up.

His pride got the best of it. After all, he had kept faith with her. He had been ready to sacrifice anything to do it. And she rejected him. Should he go down on his knees to her? Hardly.

"So it's your final word?" he said at last. "You won't change your mind?"

"No, señor. . . . I've told you why."

He drew himself up. "Very well, if that's your wish."

They gazed at each other across the past that lay between them. So much to be said that could not be said.

"Good-by, Catana."

"Good-by."

He turned and descended the hill without looking back. When he had disappeared, she sank down at the foot of the tree; then heard the beat of his horse's hoofs, slow at first, quicken and grow faint. She remembered the dawn in the pine hut two years ago on their march from the coast. Then the hoofbeats had marked the beginning, as they now marked the end. All that mattered in her life bracketed by a sound.

That night, Pedro informed the General that he was free to represent the company in Spain when the time should come.

"Capital!" approved Cortés.

Rumors of the breach between Captain de Vargas and Catana Pérez made a stir in the army. When the gossip reached Juan García at the end of a hard day's fight, he refused to believe it and, stalking out into the night, strode up the causeway to the square fort blocking it, where Cortés and his staff had their quarters.

"Captain de Vargas," he said to the guardsman on duty.

Being admitted, he was shown to Pedro's room, where he waited till the officers' mess was over. He waited some time. When Pedro came in at last, García felt an odd stiffness, which was all the more striking as they had not seen each other for a week.

"*Vaya*, comrade," he said, "you're so much of an officer these days that I have to get at you through walls and sentries. I've been missing you. How goes it, boy?"

"Excellent well. And with you?"

"As you see, *compañero*. Stiff from this cursed fighting every day in the city. Bruised and sore. But it won't be long now with the bastards.

I give 'em another month at the outside. After that, on my honor, I'll sleep a month by the clock."

Pedro nodded. "Yes, it's getting to the end. I suppose after that you'll settle down here? Take up some land?" His eyes narrowed. "Take a wife perhaps?"

Again the sense of ice where García had only known warmth. He swallowed and stared.

"Maybe. I guess so. Like yourself—you're settling down, aren't you, and getting hitched? I'd always figured the three of us would stick together. Which reminds me there's a fool story around—about you and Catana, that you've fallen out. Nothing to it, I know, but I thought I'd tell you."

The round bull eyes rested on Pedro in suspense. García hadn't been able to keep a quaver out of his voice.

"Fallen out—no," returned de Vargas. "We're still friends."

"*Still?* I—*Friends,* comrade?"

It was the moment that Pedro had dreaded, but he faced it now all the more easily because of Catana's reference to García as a possible husband. Once more his pride gripped him.

"I asked her to marry me, but she would not," he said carelessly.

"You mean"—García's dismay suddenly became truculent—"you mean you left it at that?"

"Certes. What else could I do?"

"You could take her by the scruff of the neck and marry her. You know that's what she wants. What reason did she give?"

"Excuses." Pedro added, coldly casual, "She spoke of marrying you."

"*Me!*" García planted both fists on his sides. "*Me!* Now, look here, boy, we'll talk straight: we've been close enough for that. *Excuses,* you said, and that's the word for it. Excuses because she loves you so much that she won't stand in your way. Deep down, you know it's that—and you accepted the excuses!"

Pedro flushed. "If you want straight talk, Juan, I'll tell you that this isn't much of your business."

"What's come over you?"

In the tense pause, Pedro's main effort was to keep his conscience at bay.

"Nothing's come over me. You talk as if I had broken my word to Catana. I did nothing of the kind. Ask her yourself."

García overlooked the denial as if not worth discussing.

"I suppose it's no longer my business what you are going to do when this is over?"

411

"I don't mind telling you. I'm for Spain on affairs at court for the company."

"Oho!" García snorted. "I thought as much. The Lady Luisa de Carvajal, the big marriage, the old-fashioned stuff! Got you in the end. For a while I thought the New World and Catana had changed all that."

Pedro reflected that there was no use debating the appeal of a career with one of García's background. He was born and remained only a ranker.

"Think better of it, comrade," the big man went on, "think better of it. Don't sell your life for trumpery. You've got the real things here: people who love you, great chances, a wonderful venture. Why, *hombre,* we're only at the beginning. Make yourself a grandee of New Spain with more leagues to your hacienda than you'd have acres at home. Make Catana your lady. Ride over tonight with Father Olmedo and marry her, I say."

For an instant Pedro felt like taking his friend's hand in agreement. He wanted to see the familiar light in García's eyes. He thought of Catana behind him on his horse, this tormented episode forgotten, the old comradeship back again, a new page turned. But on second thought, and still angry at Catana's refusal, he shook his head.

"No. . . . Listen, Juan. If you think it's a trifling venture to speak for this company before His Majesty in the teeth of our enemies, I don't agree with you. The General honors me with his confidence. I'm a Cortés man here or there. And what I do there will count here. Perhaps I'll come back some day—who knows?"

"We were talking about Catana."

A sudden anger leaped up in de Vargas. Why should García be championing her to him? What right had anyone—

"She's a good deal in your mind, Juan. Well, she's free."

Without a word, García put on his steel cap. Then he said: "You're both a good deal in my mind. The trouble is you always will be. I haven't the gift of slipping friendship off like a worn shirt. Maybe you're right with your kings and courts. I don't understand such things. . . . Good luck!"

"Thanks for everything, Juan. Curse me if I ever forget it—or you!"

The other nodded and went out.

LXXII

SEVERAL WEEKS LATER, Tenochtitlán, the once-magnificent, fell to Cortés. It lay, a heap of ruins, a charnel-house containing thousands of unburied corpses. Its overthrow was a masterpiece of military genius, valor, and enterprise. Everyone knew that it would take its place among immortal deeds of arms and felt proud to have had a share in it. Too bad that the once-glittering Valley with its palaces, gardens, cities, and temples had been laid waste, but such was war.

One by one, the captains, Pedro among them, congratulated the General and hailed the completed conquest. Cortés did not smile, but nodded gravely to each of them. He stood on the pinnacle of success, but he looked worn and haggard in the August sunlight. Perhaps, like others, he recalled the splendors of the ruined city; or perhaps the stench of putrefying bodies spoiled the keenness of triumph. So noisome was the odor that the Spaniards withdrew from their hard-won prize and moved to Coyoacán on the mainland.

"Well, my friend," Pedro observed to Sandoval, as they rode side by side across the familiar causeway, "we can lay off our harness at last. The work's done. Little we dreamed that the expedition would yield a return like this, eh, when we sighted San Juan de Ulúa? A grand success, *viejo!*"

Sandoval grinned. "Everything you say," he joked in his harsh stammer. "But you can't deny, Redhead, that the success has a bad smell."

Almost at once the army began splitting up. Detachments were sent to explore the lands beyond Mexico—to Michoacán, to Oaxaca—in all directions. The epic part of the conquest had ended; the mopping-up process, the colonizing period, began. Honduras, Guatemala, as future zones of invasion, were discussed; and chief captains, like Olid and Alvarado, made bids for this or that command. Psychologically, too, the army disintegrated, demanding pay, lands, the fulfillment of Cortés's lavish promises.

Since he was not immediately concerned in these developments, Pedro chafed to get away. Executive routine did not replace the old adventure; the more superficial comradeships could not fill the void left by García and Catana. From time to time he saw both of them, of course; but the common interests were gone. An unhappy constraint that could not be shrugged off marked these meetings, which by tacit consent grew rarer.

Meanwhile, the plans for his departure hung fire. The ruins of Tenochtitlán yielded only a pittance of gold, and the torture of prisoners, like Guatemozin and the chief of Tacuba, added little. However much Cortés and the royal treasurer, Julián de Alderete, exerted themselves, it would take months to assemble funds worthy of His Majesty, not to speak of appeasing the soldiers.

Then at last cautiously Pedro broached the topic of Coatl's gift.

"Why did you not declare it before?" demanded Cortés ominously.

"I awaited the opportune time, Señor General."

"How much is it?"

Pedro could not be definite. He had had but a glimpse by uncertain light. Some thousands of pesos.

"I've a great mind to confiscate the whole of it to the profit of the Crown and this company as a penalty for your failure to report it."

Pedro suggested that the gift had been made to him personally by a cacique independent of Spanish jurisdiction, and that Cortés might encounter legal difficulties. Besides, Pedro alone knew where the gold was to be found.

"A touch of the boot or the screws might elicit the information," said Cortés.

"And that might be a mistake, Your Excellency. Then others would know that the gold is available. Now only you and I know."

"Hm-m," the General pondered. "Yes. Well, what's your thought?"

Bargaining began, shrewd, sharp, and realistic. Seated on either side of a table, eyes veiled, mouths hard, and wits alert, they forged out an agreement. The company was to get nothing; for, as Cortés remarked, what people don't know, they don't miss. His Majesty, instead of one fifth as usual, would have two fifths. A half of Cortés's fifth would be added to the share of the Crown. Pedro held out for the remaining two fifths, arguing services and expenses. Since, without him, the gold would not have been forthcoming anyway, it did not seem too high a claim. Finally Cortés gave in. Then two copies of the agreement were made and signed, thus insuring secrecy; for it would benefit neither Cortés nor de Vargas if the company learned that it had been mulcted of its share.

On the whole a sound business deal from Pedro's standpoint. If a large weight of gold was to be transported from Cacahuamilpa to the coast and thence to Spain, it could only be by co-operation with the General. Better three hundred thousand pesos (as Pedro figured it), which would leave him an exceedingly rich man, than seven hundred thousand buried in a cavern.

But when secretly, by using the hundred Zapotec warriors whom Coatl had contributed and whom Pedro had prevailed on to remain with him, the treasure had been moved to Coyoacán, and the General realized the extent of it, he burst into fury.

"You're a rascal, son Pedro," he seethed, not without admiration. "If I had known the size of this hoard, be damned if I would have let you get off with such a figure. And on second thoughts, be damned if I will now. Hand me that paper we wrote. I'll have my full fifth, sirrah, and you'll pay another fifth to His Majesty."

Pedro respectfully declined. As it happened, he did not have the paper upon him. It was in safekeeping. And as a matter of fact, he must insist on the agreement.

"*You* insist!"

"A bargain's a bargain, Señor General."

"God help me," grieved Cortés, "that I am so beset with money-minded men and sharpers even among those of our company I most trust! Have you no feeling for the King or for me? Must even you, a hidalgo, cling to gold rather than show loyalty and gratitude?"

But when de Vargas failed to respond to this sentimental appeal except by expressions of devotion, Cortés's eyes twinkled.

"Well, *hijo mío,* devil take it, if you use as much management at court as you have in this business, you will do well. You may be a rascal, but you're not a fool. And of the two, I'd rather be represented by the one than the other. You show promise, son. I could not have haggled better myself."

Other delays followed. A ship had to be readied, the proper pilot and crew chosen. The gold, melted into bars, was furtively carried to Villa Rica under guard. January went by before Pedro at last took leave of Cortés.

After a farewell dinner with the captains remaining at Coyoacán, the General drew de Vargas into his own room and closed the door. The jovial air he had worn at table was gone.

"A final word, Pedrito," he said. "Or shall I call you Daniel? For you are sailing to the lions' den. It's no easy thing to take seven hundred thousand pesos' weight of gold from here to Spain. You travel with death. But I have faith in you. You've ripened in the last four years and mixed brain with brawn. You know enough by now, I hope, to trust no man. You'll watch that gold night and day. Everything depends on it—more perhaps than you think."

415

He paused a moment, his dark eyes lambent. Then he went on.

"Here's your problem. Granting good weather and no act of God or the King's enemies, you finally reach Spain. But will you be welcomed there as one returning from the conquest of an empire with solid proof of it in gold bullion for His Majesty? You will not. You will land in jail unless you use more sense than our first envoys, Montejo and Puertocarrero. I hear that they all but lost their shirts. As you know, any ship from hence is subject to the Council of the Indies, which has its officers in every port. The president of that Council is Juan Rodríguez de Fonseca, Bishop of Burgos. And His Grace hates our guts as he has those of every true servant of Spain for the last twenty-five years. God amend him!"

Pedro put in, "They say his sister is to marry Governor Velásquez of Cuba."

"Aye, and he has the point of view of the Governor. To him, you, I, and all our company are malignant rebels. Gold sent by us has been filched from his brother-in-law and so in part from him, since he would have had his cut of it. Add to this that his kinsman, Diego de Silva, is no doubt stuffing him with lies against us, and I ask you what would happen if you and the treasure fell into his hands. As for the gold, I grant that His Majesty would receive most of it in the end, though that would not help us. As for you and your share, you can draw your own conclusion."

Pedro grinned. "In that case, I should not long be interested in earthly treasures, Señor General."

"Exactly," Cortés nodded. "Not long. From the moment you reach Spain, my son, you must keep clear of any prison Diego de Silva has the key of. Still, you must land, and you must land with between three and four tons of gold bars. Where? How? Here's my thought on it."

Drawing his knife, he scratched roughly on the table top an outline of the Spanish coast.

"Palos," he said with a jab. "Sanlúcar, Cádiz. Now, look you, the friary of La Rábida stands here on the Río Tinto a half league seaward from Palos. And look you, here are the dunes of the Arenas Gordas running east from there to Sanlúcar."

"I know them well, sir."

"Good. Then you know that there's not a more desolate stretch in Spain. My thought is that you'll watch your chance to stand in at night. You'll land your gold below La Rábida. It's been placed in easily carried chests for that purpose. . . . By the way, I hear you're taking back some Indians."

"Yes, Your Excellency, fifteen of the Zapotecs. They are curious to cross the Great Water, as they call it, and they have confidence in me. Do you object?"

"On the contrary. They'll make a good show at court. Also, when it comes to gold, they're more to be trusted than Spaniards. They'll land with you and carry the chests up to the friary. There you'll leave those consigned to His Majesty in charge of the Father Superior, with instructions to release them only upon personal order from the Emperor. I say personal. And you'll get a signed receipt from said father that these chests are in his care. Here is a letter to him from me stating their number. As to your own property, son Pedro, it's none of my business, but if I were you I would have my Indians bury it in a place well marked by you, for to carry so much bullion through Spain needs an armed escort which you'll have no time to secure at first. And if you leave your gold with the Emperor's share, it may be difficult to claim afterwards."

As usual Pedro admired his commander's grasp of detail. In imagination, Cortés projected himself into the future and foresaw every contingency.

"The ship?" asked Pedro.

"She will anchor next day at Palos and discharge her cargo, the gold not appearing on the bill."

"Your Excellency has given orders to the pilot, Alvarez de Huelva?"

"I have done better. I have told him to take all orders from you as captain of the ship. I ought not to tie your hands in any way. But, mark you, keep an eye on this man Alvarez, and not a word to him that you're leaving the gold at La Rábida. Let him think it's buried in the dunes. He's the best pilot I could find, but mariners are a class to themselves, and it's often but a step from sailor to pirate."

"After La Rábida, Your Excellency?"

"That's up to you. I have only one piece of advice. Waste no time at La Rábida, but put leagues between you and any of the ports where the Indian Council controls. Your kinsman, the Duke of Medina Sidonia, is your best resource. Be sure to get off a messenger to His Majesty, warning him of your action, lest evil tongues busy themselves against you. Then act as circumstances require. You'll carry my letters not only to the Emperor but to my friends. You'll have your own backing. You have what's still more important, gold which speaks with the tongue of angels and greases every lock. Do what you will, only win our case before His Majesty."

Cortés broke off, took a turn up and down the room, then with a change of manner stopped in front of Pedro.

"Captain de Vargas, you and I and the rest of our company have done great deeds together. We have shared defeat and victory. The world will long talk of our wars and wonder how so few could accomplish so much. We are not saints. We have fought for profit, glory, power, but not only for these." The General stopped to kiss a medal of Our Lady which hung on the gold chain about his neck. "I dare also to think that we have fought for God and with God, since He has wonderfully helped us, that the light of the Gospel might shine where there was once darkness. Also we have fought for Spain. You and I have been comrades together in this. Now you carry the future of it with you."

It seemed to Pedro that for once he was seeing Cortés in his ultimate character. The tall, dark, lean figure towered.

"It depends on you whether we shall be permitted to consolidate what we have gained, or whether it is to be frittered away by other hands and made futile. The Emperor must acknowledge this colony, must acknowledge me as his deputy in the lands we have conquered, not Velásquez or someone else. I am not boasting when I say that I have led you well, that only I at this time can bring to good issue what we have begun, so that our labor and the loss of our comrades shall not have been in vain. I think you believe this."

"With all my heart," said Pedro.

"Therefore, I say you carry the future with you, Captain de Vargas, a future of which we can hardly dream. Can I rely on you?"

Pedro, deeply moved, raised the hilt of his sword to his lips. "To the death, my General, I swear it."

The evening was not far advanced when he went out vibrating from his last interview with Cortés. But he still had to say good-by to Catana and García and, facing this with an effort, he took his way through the winding streets of Coyoacán to the quarters which Catana shared with the newly married Farfáns. María answered his knock.

"But I thought you knew, Señor Captain."

"What?"

"That Catana left today with Juan García and the detachment for the southeast country."

Pedro stood frozen. It was a minute before he answered, "No, I hadn't heard that either of them—" His voice stuck.

"They decided yesterday," said María. "But I thought you had seen them."

In a daze, he walked back to his house, passed the Zapotec warrior on guard and, entering his bedroom, sat down absently on the bench in front of the table.

To have left without a word! At least they could have said good-by, if it was no more than a gesture. The most casual friends did as much. But that was the trouble: they and he could never be simply friends. Suddenly he realized good-by would have been meaningless. They wished him Godspeed: he knew that.

Irked by the bulkiness, he drew out from his cloak the letters that Cortés had given him and glanced at their superscriptions in the smoky rush light. "To his Caesarean Majesty, Charles, by the Grace of God" . . . "To the Duke de Bejar" . . . "To the Count de Aguilar" . . . "To Captain Martín Cortés de Monroy."

There lay the future, the fulfillment of his hopes. Why brood upon the past! He was returning to Spain rich as a grandee to marry the daughter of one. He was an envoy to the Emperor. But at the moment he felt strangely apathetic.

A folded piece of paper on the table caught his attention and, reaching out, he picked it up. At first he could make nothing of the writing inside it, for the letters were often reversed and the words misspelled. But at last he read:—

> Good-by, señor. I could not bear to say it, therefore I am leaving with Juan. May you be happy always!

He noticed a round spot on the paper, like a drop of tallow. But then he remembered that there were no candles in this country and, touching his finger to the place, he guessed what it was.

Suddenly his throat tightened. Leaning forward, he bowed his face upon his outstretched arms.

Conclusion

LXXIII

IN AUGUST 1522, there was perhaps no busier spot in Europe than the Plaza San Pablo in Valladolid. Messengers came and went; attendants of state dignitaries showed their liveries; the gaudy clothes of Flemish and German noblemen, sweating under the hot sun, mingled with the soberer dress of Spanish grandees or hidalgos. As a focal point of the colorful eddy stood the packed courtyard of a spacious house, which courtesy might call a palace, at the meeting of two streets. Here a detachment of German mercenaries, the famous *Landsknechte*, in Hapsburg colors, guarded gate and door. For Charles of Austria, now Emperor, had recently landed in his Spanish dominions after a three years' absence, during which civil war had convulsed the Castiles, and there was much accumulated business to attend to.

The confusion of plaza and courtyard, the babble of voices in audience rooms and anterooms diminished progressively as one approached the imperial cabinet where two gigantic guards with halberds stood in statuelike silence before the inner sanctum. Barred at this hour to everyone except the Grand Chancellor himself, the room was devoted rigidly to a consideration of the day's affairs.

An administrator and chiefly that, even at twenty-two, the blond young Emperor was businesslike, diligent, and competent. The sober splendor of the room reflected his masterful and earnest personality. No need for the Italian Chancellor, Gattinara, to remind him of business matters: they took precedence over everything else in his daily schedule. Seated in a stiff armchair upholstered in crimson velvet, he turned an executive blue eye on the Italian gentleman before him and asked for the morning's agenda.

He spoke in French, the tongue of his birth, and the gravely alert Italian answered in that language.

"Affairs of the Comunidades, sire. Your Majesty's pleasure regarding certain rebels captured in the late disorders. Here is the list."

The Emperor scanned it rapidly. "Clemency," he returned after a moment. "We'll get further with fines than with executions. It's money we need, not bloodshed, Monseigneur di Gattinara."

The other nodded approval and, dipping a quill into the inkhorn at his belt, presented it to Charles, who wrote a short instruction, signing it, "I the King."

"Yes, money," the young man repeated. "With Solyman and his Turks to the east, the corsair Barbarossa to the south, and my cousin of France to the north, we cannot arm too soon or too well. . . . The treasury receipts?"

"Relatively good. But if Your Caesarean Majesty is to defend Christendom from the infidels on one hand and the Milanese from France on the other, vastly more will be needed. As Your Majesty implies, no source of revenue should be ignored."

The Emperor returned the paper to Gattinara. "Next?"

"A matter relating to Your Majesty's overseas possessions. It has long waited decision. The Bishop of Burgos, President of the Indian Council, entreats that it may be finally settled."

Searching his memory, Charles found what he looked for. "You mean the claim of the Governor of Cuba—his name slips me (yes, Velásquez)—to jurisdiction over the lands conquered on Terra Firma by an expedition sent out by him under—under Hernán Cortés? A reasonable claim, it seems to me, Gattinara. Though the man Cortés writes well and sent over a sizable treasure two years ago. Still, we must have respect for law and for the royal deputies." He paused a moment. "But, *ma foi,* I know nothing of these colonial bickerings."

"It is to inform Your Majesty of the point at issue that the Bishop of Burgos craves audience together with his kinsman, Diego de Silva, who has newly returned from those parts."

The Emperor's eyes brightened. "You mean the man who was taken by the corsairs before reaching Cádiz and escaped from them by miracle? Yes, I've talked with him. He's given us valuable information of Barbarossa and his Moors."

"The same, Your Majesty."

Charles hesitated. "Is there no more important business to deal with than this squabble in the colonies?"

"We were observing, sire, that no source of revenue should be overlooked. But if Your Majesty prefers—"

"Oh, no, bring them in. I should have to see them one time or another."

A black-clad usher glided out between the German halberdiers. A gust of voices, sounding from the anteroom, fell silent. Then the guardsmen presented arms; the usher announced, "The Lord Bishop of Burgos and Señor Diego de Silva"; the doors closed; and the newcomers obsequiously advanced.

Charles extended his hand, over which the Bishop bowed low, while de Silva kneeled before kissing it. The Emperor was a stickler for etiquette, which, if backed by efficiency, is a powerful weapon in the hands of a good executive. But he lost no time in getting to business.

"We have been considering with sorrow," he said, struggling with the unfamiliar Spanish and choosing his words slowly, "with sorrow this contention between our servants, Diego de Velásquez, *adelantado* of Cuba, and Hernán Cortés commanding our forces in that part of Terra Firma known as New Spain. You, my lord Bishop, being in charge of colonial affairs, will be informed as to the rights and wrongs of the matter and can advise us. You have leave to speak."

His cool, observant eyes rested on the heavy-jowled, stubborn-looking churchman, then turned to the suave darkness of de Silva, then drifted back to the Bishop.

"Your Caesarean Majesty," began the latter, "speaks of this man Cortés as if he were a loyal servant of the Crown. Alas, it grieves me that Your Majesty should be so misinformed, and for that the fault is doubtless mine. *Mea culpa! Mea culpa!*" A blow of the palm on his resounding chest accompanied each of these exclamations. "Sire, unfortunately the reverse is the case. Hernán Cortés is an arrant traitor and villain, a man of violence and without principles, who, far from deserving the title of Your Majesty's servant, schemes only to set himself up as monarch in the lands he has wrongfully taken."

The Bishop spoke in a rumbling, angry voice with dogmatic conviction. He shook his head every now and then for emphasis. There was no gray in Fonseca's world, but only white and black—principally black. The Emperor, with his Teutonic reserve, and the shrewd Italian Chancellor sensed a partisan and exchanged glances.

"Of course you have proofs, lord Bishop?" observed Charles.

"A thousandfold, Your Majesty."

Fonseca proceeded to unload them. He did not have to invent much. It was common knowledge, he submitted, that Velásquez, Governor of Cuba, being zealous in His Majesty's service, had equipped at his own great expense an expedition for trade and exploration on the new-found coasts to the west; that he had appointed Hernán Cortés captain-general of said expedition, but with no authority to colonize; and that said Hernán Cortés had agreed to these conditions. It was common knowledge that hardly had he landed on said coasts when said Hernán Cortés—

"I know," interrupted the Emperor, stifling a yawn. "He set up a colony. I forget what he calls it—Villa something-or-other Vera Cruz. Well, I admit that he broke his word to the worthy Governor. Very irregular indeed."

"Yes, sire, and then boasted openly that he would bribe Your Caesarean Majesty—I blush at such blasphemy—to overlook, to connive at, his treason."

"Humph!" said Charles. "Did he so? Well, go on."

It was common knowledge, Fonseca continued, that said Cortés had then scuttled the ships, which did not belong to him, in order to prevent loyal adherents of Velásquez from returning to Cuba. Some of these he had hanged or maimed, all of them he had terrorized into marching inland. There he and his captains had distinguished themselves by incredible orgies of massacre and rapine, a disgrace to the Spanish, let alone the Christian, name. But when Diego de Velásquez, loyal and God-fearing, had sent Pánfilo de Narváez and twelve hundred men to assert the King's law and bring the rebels to reason, said Hernán Cortés had treacherously fallen upon said Narváez by night, had cruelly put out one of his eyes, killed divers of his company, and compelled the others to join with him.

"The fellow must be a monster," Charles grunted. "Continue."

The Bishop rumbled up and down the scale of the Seven Deadly Sins, but when he described the royal treasure, some hundreds of thousands in gold, which had disappeared on the Sad Night and which many believed had been diverted by the General to his own use, the imperial eyes hardened to blue steel.

"Some hundred thousand pesos in gold, you say?"

"No less, sire."

"Ha! . . . Well, go on."

Fonseca stamped gradually to a conclusion. "And now, Your Majesty, having lost land and treasure, he continues a hopeless fight, leading his men to sure death, because he fears rightly to face the penalty of his crimes. Sire, I ask redress for Diego de Velásquez and that he be given full power in New Spain."

"He shall have it," Charles returned. "If true, I have seldom heard a sorrier tale."

"*If true,* Your Majesty?"

Arborio di Gattinara put in, "Is it not rumored, my lord Bishop, that your sister is to marry Diego de Velásquez?"

The Bishop shot him a black look. "You imply then that I—that I who for thirty years have governed the affairs of the Indies, who have promoted and fostered them, who have built up an empire where none existed—that I, a Bishop of the Church, am lying, because my sister— Your Majesty, I ask now redress—"

The Emperor smiled. "My good lord Bishop, have patience. There are no implications. My lord Chancellor asked a random question. Well, sir?" His eyes were on Diego de Silva, who had dropped gracefully to one knee.

"A word, Your Majesty," replied de Silva in a liquid voice. "The Bishop of Burgos speaks from written report and from the testimony of credible witnesses. He speaks with righteous indignation. But let me who have seen the crimes of Hernán Cortés and of his captains with my own eyes gain the favor of your august ear. I am without prejudice, sire, believe me, a simple gentleman who sought to serve Spain in the New World and whose heart beats only in devotion to Your Majesty. *Ay de mí,* why should I have left Hernán Cortés had it been possible to serve Your Caesarean Majesty longer under his command?"

"And how was it," asked Charles reasonably, "that you were permitted to leave him? So ruthless a villain as he is pictured would have been apt to prevent it. . . . You may rise, sir."

De Silva complied as elegantly as he had kneeled. "Nothing escapes Your Majesty's penetration," he went on. "Indeed, sire, General Cortés would have prevented me if he could. But a bully has feet of clay. I had gained favor with our company, I mean that of Pánfilo de Narváez, with which I had come. I promised to lay their intolerable wrongs and grievances before Your Majesty so that, if it was too late to redress them (Poor souls! I doubt the greater number are now dead!), they might at least be avenged. If Cortés had refused to release me, he would have met more trouble than at that time he had stomach for."

Noticing the black daredeviltry in the other's eyes, Charles could understand how de Silva gained credit among soldiers. The Emperor, who was a soldier himself, observed also with approval the beautifully proportioned body which suggested effortless strength.

"I see," he nodded. "And I take it, Señor de Silva, that you corroborate the statements of the Reverend Bishop of Burgos."

"Entirely, Your Majesty, with this general exception. As a Christian, he has kept too far within the truth. He has hesitated to offend the nobleness of your imperial mind with details too foul for utterance. What if he had said that this same Cortés encourages his Indian allies to devour human flesh? What if he had described the piteous massacre

424

of hundreds of Aztec princes committed by his favorites, Pedro de Alvarado and Pedro de Vargas? A massacre incited merely by the base desire for gold, which was plucked from the Indians' quivering bodies. What if he had told of the torture inflicted on the great king, Montezuma? Or detailed the sufferings of prisoners of war, men, women, and children, branded with hot irons, parceled out among his licentious officers, enslaved contrary to Your Majesty's edicts? Sire, I am haunted by the things I have seen."

He paused to stare pensively at the floor and to let his mouth express horror and disgust.

The Emperor made a slight grimace of repulsion, but Chancellor Gattinara put in: "And yet, sir, Cortés's envoys, Puertocarrero and Mantejo, who are now in Valladolid, are men of birth and repute. They give no inkling of such enormities."

De Silva nodded. "They would not. In the first place, they left New Spain before most of these things occurred. In the second place, it is the gift of Hernán Cortés to disguise his barbarities under the cloak of expediency. He is clever as Satan, my lord Chancellor—Satan whom in all ways he resembles. . . . Take, for example, his ill-concealed hostility to the Church. There was in our company a saintly Dominican, an Inquisitor of the Holy Office, Father Ignacio de Lora. First, Cortés attempted his assassination at the hands of a ruffian, one Juan García, who, you will note, remained unpunished, although he well-nigh killed the reverend priest. Then, when that failed, he permitted Father Ignacio to fall into the hands of the Aztecs on the night of the retreat. We learned that he died, a martyr to the Faith, on the stone of sacrifice. And when he heard it, Cortés smiled."

"Faugh!" exclaimed the Emperor. "But wait, it seems to me I recall that name, de Lora. Yes, in truth! Was he not the Inquisitor who condemned the right noble Captain Don Francisco de Vargas in that affair about which His Holiness, the late Pope, took action in person? I recall too that the Duke of Medina Sidonia—Yes, Ignacio de Lora—that's the name. I'm glad that the Suprema saw fit to declare the innocence of Don Francisco and make restitution."

De Silva bit his lip. This was thin ice, and he regretted bringing up the subject. He hoped that the Emperor's memory did not extend to him. But in this, he was disappointed.

"By the mass!" Charles went on. "I wondered where I had seen your name before. You were implicated in the same affair. Were you not the one who denounced the right noble Captain?"

Gattinara said gently: "Yes, and I recall now that that was one of the reasons given for the dissolution of your marriage with the Doña Luisa de Carvajal. Is it not true?"

"Hm-m," the Emperor added. "You spoke of a Pedro de Vargas as favorite of Cortés. Is he by any chance a relative of Don Francisco's?"

At this critical juncture, Diego de Silva was true to himself. A lesser artist might have been shaken, but not he. The Bishop of Burgos admitted afterwards that he had never seen better management.

"A son, Your Majesty," he returned. And then with a shrug of the shoulders, he continued sadly: "Yes, it is the great misfortune of my life that I denounced Don Francisco to the Holy Office. It is true that I heard him utter the most shocking blasphemies and considered it my duty as one of the *Miliz Christi* to report the case. But since His late Holiness and the Suprema declared him innocent, I was plainly mistaken. Sire, I am not a grandee like the Marquis de Carvajal. I could not defend myself at Rome against the dissolution of my marriage. As a faithful son of the Church, I can only kiss the rod, as I do the feet of Your Majesty, and crave forgiveness for my sin, which reveals a blunt soldier's lack of discretion, but not—believe me, sire—a lack of religion or of honor."

The time would come when Charles of Austria would not receive such declarations altogether at their face value. But he had still enough youthful generosity to be impressed by the sincere ring of de Silva's voice. While Gattinara took a cynical sniff at his pomander, the Emperor held out his hand.

"I do believe it, sir. Your gallant conduct in the matter of the corsairs would be enough to convince me, apart from your personal bearing. Think no more of it. . . . Are there any other particulars you would like to add to your testimony regarding this man Cortés?"

De Silva hesitated. "I should prefer that the Bishop of Burgos would speak of a matter in which I might be considered prejudiced, since it relates to Pedro de Vargas."

"And that I shall gladly," rumbled Fonseca with a shake of the head. "This young man, whatever his father may be, is a consummate scoundrel, the apt pupil of his master."

"I grieve to hear it," murmured Charles, once more unconsciously put off by the other's truculence. "What has he done?"

"Your Majesty, I cite this as a final example of Cortés's villainy, for the lamentable young man in question acted on the orders of his superior. Moreover, it nearly concerns Your Majesty."

"Well? Get to the point."

But as Fonseca proceeded, the Emperor's impatience changed to grim attention.

"Sire, the so-called colony of Villa Rica dispatched this so-called Captain de Vargas to Spain with another bribe for Your Majesty. I understand it was hundreds of thousands in gold. Besides the crew, he had under his command a group of heathen savages. Having arrived at Santa María de la Rábida below Palos, said Pedro de Vargas slipped ashore with the treasure, which he buried not far from the friary to the intent of defrauding not only Your Majesty but the so-called colony which he represented. And this he did plainly in the interests of himself and of Cortés, who was privy to his action. Fortunately the pilot Alvarez and other members of the crew denounced him to our officers in hope of a reward. Otherwise, we should have known nothing."

"Hold!" said the Emperor intently. "Take me with you, lord Bishop. I do not follow Spanish so easily. You said this gold amounted to—"

"Hundreds of thousands, sire."

"How do you know it did?"

"If Your Majesty will let me explain."

"Well then, slowly." The Emperor added with an unintentional reflection on the preceding charges against Cortés, "This is important."

Once again Fonseca rehearsed the sailing and arrival of the ship with special reference to the treasure. Now and then he turned to de Silva for confirmation, since it appeared that the latter had but just returned from investigating the affair at Palos.

Charles's brow grew constantly darker.

"*Mille tonnerres!*" he burst out. "I have heard of brass before but nothing like this. I ask you again how you know what was the amount. This pilot Alvarez, Señor de Silva, and the ship's company, of whom you say you received testimony, could not know."

"But yes, sire, they knew—that there were many hundredweight chests on board and that these chests contained gold. Cortés himself instructed the pilot Alvarez to connive with de Vargas in the robbery by helping him land the treasure near La Rábida. Alvarez was then to anchor at Palos and discharge his cargo with no mention of the gold."

"Still, there may be an explanation," objected the Emperor. "If the gold was intended for us in person, de Vargas may have sent a messenger. He may be coming himself. When did he land?"

"Two weeks since, Your Majesty. Has any messenger arrived? Besides, there is another more serious development which makes his guilt clear beyond further doubt."

"More serious?"

De Silva cast up his eyes. "Your Majesty will hardly credit it, but not long afterwards, Pedro de Vargas returned openly to La Rábida. He returned with a hundred men-at-arms belonging to the Duke of Medina Sidonia, the Guzmán standard unfurled, and under the command of the Duke's own ensign. The officers of the port and of the Indian Council could do nothing. There, in plain sight of several of them, in the woods near La Rábida, de Vargas dug up ten or more hundred-weight chests, loaded them on mules, and departed. When one of the officers, taking his life in his hands, challenged him, he deigned to answer that these were his personal property, that Your Majesty had no part in them, and so adieu."

Charles turned to Gattinara. "Is the Duke a rebel, my lord Chancellor? He stood loyal during the late troubles, and have we not requited him with the castles of Niebla, Huelva, and Sanlúcar?"

Gattinara shook his head noncommittally.

"Where is this pirate, de Vargas, meanwhile?" Charles fumed. "Has no one laid hands on him?"

De Silva shook his head. "It is hard to arrest a man protected by His Grace Don Juan Alonso. Who will serve the warrant? Who has the authority? No, sire, he swaggers openly. It is said that he travels to Jaén, where his father is Alcalde. He rides, like a conqueror, with twenty-five men-at-arms and his Indians in their war plumes, while the villages stare."

"He has the gold with him?"

"Probably, sire."

It was seldom that Charles of Austria lost his temper, but at this point he sprang up. "You ask me who has the authority to lay hands on him? Monseigneur di Gattinara, you will make out an imperial warrant for the man's arrest on the charge of high treason. You will send Captain Claros de Paz with sufficient force to Jaén. And let duke or alcalde or pirate resist that warrant at their peril! Let him be brought here straight, for I shall examine him myself. I'm eager to meet the ruffian. Will you wager that we do not win back what he has stolen before he loses his head?"

Blinded by his rage, the Emperor did not observe the expression on de Silva's face, but Gattinara noticed it.

The Bishop of Burgos put in, "Sire, I ask again in behalf of Diego de Velásquez—"

"No need to ask. Is he not already *adelantado?* Are you not in charge of Indian affairs? By all means let Velásquez have New Spain, which no doubt he richly deserves as compared with the bandit, Cortés. Give immediate order."

"Your Majesty will sign the rescript?"

"When you will."

"If I may advise," said Gattinara, "it would be best to wait until the examination of Pedro de Vargas. A matter of but a few days."

"Why?" retorted Charles.

"A precaution, Your Majesty."

"Well—" The Emperor hesitated. "Well then, as you please. There can be no doubt of the result."

"None."

Faced by the glowering Bishop, Gattinara, fingering his pomander, sniffed thoughtfully and shook his head.

LXXIV

THE CARVAJAL PALACE on that August evening blazed with more candles and flambeaux than had shone through its massive, grated windows for a long time. Old Julio Brica, the major-domo, with a new white wand of office and clad in a new stiff suit of black velvet, marshaled an increased force of lackeys arrayed in spick-and-span liveries. He figured that the expense in wax and cloth would hardly come to less than five hundred pesos. But what were five hundred pesos now!

Stationing a flunkey at the grilled judas or sliding panel in the main door, he instructed him to keep a sharp lookout. "When you first see the torches of our noble guests, you will give the word. Then, Nicolás and Juan, you will take stout hold on the door rings. The rest of you," Brica continued, "will line the steps up to the main corridor, ten to a side in the order I have shown you. Is that understood? *Bien!* We must have no mistakes, mark that well, no scrambling or scuffling. All must be grace. Meanwhile, you at the judas will watch. As soon as His Excellency the Alcalde, Doña María, and Captain de Vargas dismount and are on the point of approaching the door, you will step back. At the same moment, you, Nicolás and Juan, will open. But slowly! I say slowly, without jerkiness. It must be as if our very doors paid reverence to Their Excellencies, so that, when they reach the threshold, they will find no barrier. Then, by God, bow!" Brica flashed a minatory eye at his pupils. "Tuck in your bellies. Remember the honor of our master. Let each back form a right angle to the legs. Keep that position while Their Excellencies mount the steps to be greeted by His Magnificence. We have time to practise this once more. Let us have perfection."

While Brica's last anxious rehearsal went forward, the Marquis de Carvajal loitered in his downstairs cabinet, awaiting the coming of his guests with pleasant expectancy. Like the rest of his household, he was dressed for the occasion, but in a superior splendor matching his rank. The huge satin sleeves of his short mantle crackled with stiffness. They were slashed over gold, and the mantle itself had edges of costly fur. He wore a heavy onyx ring on his thumb and the Cross of Santiago dangling from a massive chain on his breast. The excessively wide-toed velvet shoes, equally slashed upon gold, showed a powdering of diamonds. His beard, once depressed by the misfortunes of three years ago, though grayer now, had more than regained its starch and set a final patrician stamp on his appearance.

Viewing himself in a long Venetian mirror, he nodded approval. He felt that he lived up to his title. Then, having given his wide-brimmed, plume-circled hat a more arrogant tilt, he sauntered about the room fingering various small *objets d'art* but actually lost in happy meditation.

Several thoughts, all golden, drifted through his mind. Luisa to be betrothed this evening to Pedro de Vargas, who was now one of the richest men in Spain. Pedro's fortune. Three hundred thousand pesos, Don Francisco had said, and the Alcalde's word could be relied on. Three hundred thousand pesos in *gold*. *Cáspita!* What grandee could raise a quarter of that much cash? And then the wedding when Pedro returned triumphant and honored from court. The Marquis himself to the right of the altar, the Bishop officiating, the nobility of the province filling the nave. His imagination wandered on.

So impressed was Carvajal by Pedro's wealth and prospects that, without hesitating too long, he had offered to use all his influence at court in behalf of Cortés's suit before the Emperor. He had even proposed to accompany Pedro north to Valladolid and lend him the weight of his personal support. In his pleasant reverie, the Marquis pictured Pedro's success, in which he would share. It was not too much to hope that the Emperor would recognize his merit with the grant of another fief.

A watchman's distant cry recalled the hour, and he realized that his guests would be soon arriving. Pedro had reached Jaén from Seville only that day and had been met some distance outside of town by his father, by the Marquis himself, and two-score other gentlemen. But he had not yet seen Luisa. Because of this, no outside guests had been invited to witness the betrothal that evening. It was good policy, the Marquis reflected, to waste no time in making sure of Pedro before so eligible a young man proceeded to court.

Apropos of Luisa, he wondered suddenly where the devil she was. She ought to be downstairs now, and ready.

"If the silly jade," he fumed, "puts on her coquette airs tonight and keeps Their Excellencies waiting, I'll take my riding whip to her behind if it's the last act of my life."

He applied himself to the bellrope and sent up a servant in hot haste to tell her ladyship and Doña Antonia that he expected them to attend him on the moment. Then, of course, he continued to wait and mutter.

But this evening, for once, he might have spared his fidgets. If there was a lookout at the judas downstairs, a tirewoman filled the same office at the window of the mirador. Luisa did not intend to be too early on hand, but she would not for the world have missed standing with her father at the top of the steps when Pedro entered.

Meanwhile, she gave the last touches to her charm.

"Was it orange blossom or rose water you used then?" Señora Hernández queried.

"Orange, I *think*. But what difference does it make, Cousin?"

"A huge difference. I'm surprised you don't know. You see, people associate certain scents with certain hours and persons. Wouldn't you notice it if you went into a church that didn't smell of incense? And suppose Alonso Ponce forgot to put on hyacinth, wouldn't he seem different? Well, *eso es todo*. If you smelled of rose or orange blossom when young de Vargas kissed your hand that evening in the garden, and if the handkerchief you gave him smelled of it, that's your scent for *him*. He expects it now—I don't mean *thinks* of it, my love. But if you wear another scent, he'll miss something."

Luisa frowned. "Lord save us, I can't remember. It was *ages* ago." She appealed to her maid. "Sanchita, do you remember?"

"I think it was rose, your ladyship."

"Why?"

"Because Your Grace gave me your own vial half full for my nameday."

Luisa reflected. "I believe you're right, Sanchita. Yes, you're right. I did use rose a good deal at that time. Heaven reward you! I was just on the point of orange blossom. But if you're wrong, my wench—" Luisa's tender eyes hardened. "Bring me a flask of rose."

She applied little dabs here and there.

"More on the neck and breast," Antonia advised. "I'll leave you two alone of course. You won't find him as shy as he was once."

Luisa smiled and made the necessary additions. But, considering herself in the mirror, her face grew longer.

431

"I wish I wasn't so plump. You can talk about perfume all you like, but he can't help noticing the difference." She pecked at an invisible wrinkle on her throat. "I've got so old."

"My dear, you're perfection!" returned the duenna. "If you'll let Sanchita take one more hitch in your lacings, you'll be as slender as you were at sixteen. Call twenty old, *por Dios!* But you *could* stand one more hitch."

Obediently Luisa embraced one of the bedposts, while the maid untied the laces, planted a firm knee on Luisa's posterior, and threw weight and muscles into the backward pull. A slight bulge—nothing to speak of—showed above and beneath the wooden stays of the corset. Luisa gasped, but an inch had been gained.

"Magnificent!" Antonia praised. "Now talk of being plump! No, *Primacita,* you are perfection, believe me. Soldiers like Captain de Vargas want no scrawny poppets in bed. And what a skin, *válgame Dios!* Like satin." With a pair of tweezers, she removed a single hair that disturbed the delicate arch of her cousin's right eyebrow. "*So,* my love."

A voluminous petticoat reaching to the floor now was dropped over Luisa's head; then an equally long and ample dress of gold and crimson brocade, the bodice molding the corset and buttoned in front with gold buttons. A small net of garnets and topazes slightly compressed the blackness of Luisa's curled hair. Earrings and other jewels were put on. A drop of belladonna widened her eyes into black pools.

Señora Hernández glowed. "My darling, you're ravishing. I'd like to kiss you if it wasn't for the powder. Now let His Valor come! If he doesn't worship you in that gown, he's blind. *Hermosa!*"

Consulting the mirror again, Luisa agreed. "Yes, the dress is becoming. I want him to love me. I can hardly wait. . . . Dolores," she called to the girl at the window, "don't you see any lights yet? No? Tell me again how he looked, Cousin. Handsome, you said—"

Doña Antonia had been sent that morning to watch Pedro's entry into town and report her impressions. From the window of the draper's shop, she had had an excellent view.

"Yes," she nodded; "that is, in a manly way. Not a bit like Alonso Ponce of course. He looks older than he is. A little hard. Very much nobleman and captain. Nothing of the boy any longer."

"He was a sweet boy," Luisa reflected. "He sounds rather frightening."

"No, not that. But frankly, *Primacita,* I don't think he's a man to be trifled with. There was one thing I noticed. He has a big mouth, you

432

remember, and a big smile. He came riding at a footpace because of the crowd. Everybody cheering. Now and then he tossed a handful of silver and smiled. But his eyes didn't. He glanced my way, and I could see them—far-off, indifferent. Perhaps he was tired."

"I hope Alonso Ponce behaves," said Luisa. "What if he *has* been my *galán?* A gentleman ought to know when to step back."

"I shouldn't worry." Antonia's eyes danced. "He doesn't want to lose his precious life, my dear. Captain de Vargas will know how to protect his *novia* from annoyance."

"Yes," murmured Luisa, "but perhaps—" She glanced at the maid and broke off.

The duenna laughed. "Pooh! He hasn't grown up for nothing. Even if he hears of it, he'll think no worse of a little gallantry, provided it's finished. And he'll run his sword through the man who suggests that you aren't as chaste as Diana. . . . But I'm wondering," she added, changing the subject, "what kind of betrothal ring he'll give you. I'll wager it's out of the ordinary."

Luisa forgot Ponce. "I wonder too. He must be very rich. I suppose he'll have to make over part of the gold to his father." Luisa was too much like the Marquis not to regret it. "Still, I guess he's very rich, or Papa—"

"Lights! Torches!" yelped the girl at the window of the mirador. "They're coming, my lady."

With a vast rustle, Luisa and Antonia swept out of the room and down the stairs, where they met a second messenger from the frantic Marquis.

However, there was no time for scolding. With the long-prepared smile on his lips and Luisa on his arm, the Marquis de Carvajal took up position at the top of the reception stairs. The lookout at the judas dropped back. Nicolás and Juan laid hold of the door rings. The flunkeys lined the steps, prepared to bow. The doors slowly opened. Behind them showed the flaring of many torches; and out of the light, the expected figures entered: Doña María, plump and important, against the knightly leanness of the Alcalde, and behind them a tanned gentleman in gorgeous clothes by the side of the priest who would witness the betrothal; then several attendants, including a pair of tall Indians horrifically plumed.

"*Vamos!* Now!" signaled Julio Brica.

Except for one awkward back, upon which the major-domo longed to lay his staff, the household did honor to the Carvajal Palace.

LXXV

But upon Pedro de Vargas, the ordered lines of bowing servants made only a vague impression. He moved in a curious unreality that telescoped the past and present. He was the lad who four years ago had sought shelter here and had been refused. He was the fugitive who had once dreamed of such welcome as the crowning pinnacle of desire. He was the man, rich and fêted, who now returned in a triumph that beggared anything he had imagined. For a moment the various phases intermingled. The dream, too completely realized, still had the semblance of a dream.

As he mounted the broad stairs, his eyes were on Luisa. He had expected to be disappointed, afraid that memory had idealized her. But no, standing there in gold and crimson, she seemed more beautiful than his fancy had recalled, a queen perhaps rather than a princess, but more breath-taking in her maturity. Here, too, the actual left imagination behind.

On the landing, after Doña María had been received, he replied to Luisa's deep curtsy with a bow such as he would have made to an empress, a bow enhanced by the splendor of the court suit he had purchased in Seville. Then, dropping to one knee, he raised her hand to his lips.

"You see, I have kept my promise, señora."

Rising, he bowed to Doña Antonia and was warmly embraced by the Marquis.

It was a flawless scene, which Julio Brica in the background considered equal to the occasion.

Don Francisco, who had done his best that day to keep from bursting with pride, exclaimed to Luisa: "*A fe mía,* señora, you are so enchanting tonight that I would kneel to you myself. But it would be a creaky business, and I had best leave it to young joints. . . . Señora Hernández, your servant, madam." And to the Marquis: "Well, old friend, we've looked forward to this a long time; but, on my honor, it was worth waiting for."

The Marquis cordially agreed. He gave his arm to Doña María and led his guests into the state *sala* facing the entrance. It was huge, tapestried, and glimmering with candles. The parish priest followed in a sweat of humility.

Pedro was absorbed by Luisa. How had he ever been able for one moment to forget her? Surely it was by the grace of God that he had been led back through the ups and downs of fortune to his true allegiance. *Gracias a Dios!*

Of course there was the inevitable small talk. Had the voyage been pleasant? Tell them of New Spain. On that topic, he found himself talking too readily; for, though Don Francisco and Doña María drank in every word, and the Marquis combed his beard in attention, Luisa's eyes wandered.

"What funny names!" she smiled. And at another point, "General Cortés sounds *sweet.*"

It was a remark which somehow forced him to change the subject. A footman with a salver passed wine.

Then a pause came. The Marquis exchanged nods with Don Francisco. The solemn moment had struck; and, while Doña María expanded with pride, and the old gentlemen looked sentimental, Pedro took Luisa's hand. How soft it felt, how small!

"I, Pedro, will take you, Luisa, for my wife."

"And I, Luisa, will take you, Pedro, for my husband."

De Vargas motioned to one of the panached Indians, who brought a small case. He opened it and drew out a heavy gold ring set with one huge emerald. It was part of his loot in the taking of Tenochtitlán.

No amount of training could hide the dazzlement in Luisa's eyes. She held the ring up in the candlelight.

"But, señor, how glorious! How beautiful!"

"If it pleases you, it is indeed glorious. It belonged to an Aztec prince, one Guatemozin." But he could see that she wasn't listening, and he broke off.

The Marquis begged for a nearer look. An expert in jewels, he guessed at the value—between four and five thousand pesos. In contrast, the rose diamond which Luisa now presented to Pedro, thus completing the ritual exchange of rings, seemed insignificant. But Carvajal, in a whispered aside to Doña María, spoke of it as a family heirloom; and Pedro, pushing it halfway up his finger, kissed it gallantly.

The betrothal goblet was now brought. Luisa drank first, her eyes on Pedro. Then de Vargas, turning the cup to the place her lips had touched, drank in turn.

After they had kissed and the priest had given his blessing in behalf of the Church, the betrothal was complete.

Complete. It struck Pedro suddenly that by this very act his whole life was changed. Feeling the seriousness of the moment, he winced upon finding Luisa already back to her ring, turning it this way and that.

435

The doors at the end of the *sala* were thrown wide upon a supper room opening onto the terrace. With apologies by Carvajal for the simplicity of the entertainment and with compliments on the part of his guests, the company betook itself to a table heavy with wine, fruit, and silver, and lighted by massive candelabra.

Seated at Luisa's left, Pedro watched the play of the candles on her face. She was almost too beautiful. He found himself wishing that he could have found at least one imperfection.

The Marquis, silver goblet in hand, now stood up and made a speech of congratulation. It was long and polished. He sipped the words in a fashion that reminded Pedro of his last visit to the palace when Carvajal had preached on a different text. De Vargas had grown wiser since then. He saw perfectly through the shallow, pretentious man and wondered behind his polite smile how such a father could have produced such a daughter.

"I have an eye for men," said the Marquis. "It is the single talent upon which I venture to pride myself. At the beginning of my acquaintance with Captain de Vargas, I once had the honor of receiving him in my chamber. Rightly he turned to me, the old and devoted friend of your noble house, señores, for redress against an injustice which even now fills me with indignation." Carvajal paused to control his feeling. "How touched I was by his confidence! How eagerly I placed myself at his service! But that is beside the point. What I would say is that even then I clearly discerned his future greatness. 'There,' I said, 'is a cavalier born for success and fame.'"

"Why, bless my soul!" thought Pedro. "What an old cockroach it is!" He could not help glancing at Luisa, whose eyes were on the emerald. In view of their marriage, he must accept Carvajal's hypocrisy. Why quarrel with a man to whom sincerity and insincerity were the same thing? "My greatness!" he reflected. "Because Coatl handed me a weight of gold. That's my greatness."

"And so, illustrious friends," the Marquis concluded, "I drink to this happy occasion and to the union of our two houses."

At the touch of his wife's foot under the table, Don Francisco gave a start and a hurried *amen*, evidently under the impression that he was in church. With advancing years, he often grew drowsy in the evening. Then, to cover up his slip, he drank the health with a flourish and remarked:—

"On my honor, Don Luis, you have the gift of eloquence. I cannot put my tongue to such choice phrases, being only a humdrum soldier. But in plain language I thank you. May God bless our children and,"

436

he added with a wink, "bring us a strapping grandson before the year's out!"

The ladies blushed, and the Marquis smiled, indulgent of his noble friend's limitations.

Talk drifted on, with Don Francisco trying to show his son off on the subject of America. It was not difficult. Pedro's face took on a different cast when he spoke of the New World, of the company, of the beloved captains. But at last, seeing the vagueness in Luisa's eyes, he stopped.

"Ladies, my humble excuses. I tire you."

"Ah, no, señor."

"Well then, I tire myself." He glanced at the moonlit terrace beyond the threshold of the room. "To discuss old wars on such a night! Beautiful señoras, if you would invite me to a view of the garden. Remember, I have not seen it for a long time."

The old people exchanged knowing glances.

"By all means," said Carvajal. "Mars cannot compete with Cupid on such a night, nor age with youth. Their Excellencies and I will debate the past and let you young ones debate the future in the garden." He added with a twitch of the eyebrow that Señora Hernández understood perfectly, "Doña Antonia, remember your duty."

"Of course, my lord."

And of course, after a few turns up and down the terrace, she excused herself for a moment. Luisa and Pedro wandered down from terrace to terrace and were soon lost in the mazes of the garden.

It was exactly as he had remembered it: the shadowy masses of foliage, the moonlit spaces between, the heavy scent of flowers. A nightingale, hidden in some dark thicket, took up its call.

Yes, destiny had kept faith with Pedro de Vargas. From that first moment of the ray of light in church, through all the ways and days, it had led him to this hour, had crossed every *t* and dotted every *i* of the contract—even down to the nightingale. He had reached the perfect goal. Now was the time to take up the thread broken off four years ago, continue on the same tone of romance and chivalry, kneel at the feet of his Lady of Honor, and express himself in the grand manner.

But suddenly, with a queer shock, as if he had bumped up against an unexpected wall, he realized that he could not. He had seen too much, lived too hard. Here was his Lady of Honor at the end of the quest, and he hadn't the proper words for her. Destiny had done everything except restore his boyish point of view.

Clearly Luisa expected the former romantic commonplaces. She murmured: "Well, Sir Cavalier, you have kept your vow. In arms and in love you have been faithful." (She spoke her piece so tenderly that no one could have guessed how often she had rehearsed it.) "My prayers have brought you back to me."

He forced himself to answer, "Aye, sweet lady, and now I come for my guerdon."

"Alas, sir, what guerdon worthy of so high and mighty a knight?"

He said mechanically, "A guerdon of which no man on earth is worthy: your love, *reina mía*—yourself."

It was proper at this point that dramatic silence should follow. He felt inadequate and artificial.

At the right instant, she said softly, "I am yours."

He should then have kneeled, taken her hand, and burst into rhapsody. Somehow, he could only answer sincerely enough, "And I am the happiest of men."

She waited for more, but put his silence down to emotion and added lightly: "My token, sir, the handkerchief I gave you—did you wear it in battle? Do you still keep it?"

The question was natural but unfortunate. It recalled that June night in Tenochtitlán, de Silva's big ears and crooked eyebrows; the passion of that night; what Pedro would have liked to forget, that his Queen of Honor had once lain in de Silva's arms. More unfortunate still, it recalled Catana and how he had given her Luisa's token. The garden faded out. He saw only for a moment the dim sleeping room in their quarters, Catana's tanned face, darker in the half-light. He could feel her body against his and could hear his own voice, "Say now that I don't love you!" A hotter vintage than this.

The scene vanished. But Catana had entered the garden.

"You do not answer, my lord."

He lied of course. "I plead guilty, señora. We lost everything but our skins in the Noche Triste."

Naturally Luisa did not care, except that she wanted to fill these uncomfortable pauses in the conversation. She wondered what the trouble was and then instinctively she guessed. He did not know how to shift from one level to the other with her. *Cosa de risa!* She could help him there. She too had grown up and was a little tired of fine language.

But a person who has been long identified with one role should be careful about shifting to another. Better to remain ideal and aloof than to become trivial.

On a stone bench ensconced among the laurel, she talked amusingly

438

about the gossip of Jaén; coyly forbade him to frighten her with stories of battles in New Spain, but wanted to know whether Indian ladies set their caps for him; asked how he had got so rich. His account of the caverns at Cacahuamilpa interested her most.

Little by little, she drew him on. His pulses quickened. She was glad that she had taken Antonia's advice about the wider application of the rose water.

"La, my lord!" she protested feebly. "Fie, my dear lord!" But she returned his kisses.

As a Queen of Honor, Luisa had stood alone; as an amorous woman, she invited comparisons. Pedro was used to headier wine than these lemonade intimacies.

Imperceptibly the dream element of the evening shredded off. He looked at Luisa no longer as a poetic abstraction, but as a pretty coquette with a good deal of experience. He was soon to become her husband. And all at once he realized that between him and her stretched and would stretch forever four years, the flaming center of his life, in which she had no part.

He thought of Olmedo on the hill at Trinidad. "After your gold and your lady, Pedro de Vargas, what then?" He thought of Cortés on the crowning day of victory in the ruins of Tenochtitlán.

He thought of Catana.

The wooden panels of Luisa's corset cut into his arm.

"Alas, señora," he said finally without too much regret, "here comes Doña Antonia, I think. She's tactful enough to make a noise."

LXXVI

WHEN ELECTED Alcalde, Don Francisco had taken a spacious house on the Plaza Santa María, as befitted his official position, and for the time being had closed the Casa de Vargas; but the furniture of his cabinet had been brought up entire from the old house. There were the priedieu, the crucifix in front of it on the wall, the narrow black table, the high candlesticks, the rigid, high-backed chairs, the half-dozen books, the stands of armor. Nothing but the shape of the study had changed.

Into this more familiar room, the three de Vargases turned as a matter of course upon arriving home from the Carvajal Palace. It was the moment for talking over the big event of the evening before retiring. But instead of the high spirits that might have been expected, a certain constraint, emanating from Pedro, showed itself. His father eyed him curiously. Doña María, sitting down, plucked at her skirt.

"Well, I must say!" she remarked finally. "Have we been to a betrothal or a funeral? When Pedrito ought to be in the seventh heaven, he acts like a pallbearer. Not a word on the way home except about the horse Campeador you bought back for him, husband!"

"Now, now, *Madrecita!* What should I say? Can words describe her?"

"Looks can, Pedrito. At least you can *look* happy. My faith!"

"But I am happy. 'Sblood! Would you have me caper like a dancing master?"

Doña María's lips trembled. "And I who laid such store by it! Planned for it this long time, because I thought— What's happened, *querido?*"

"Nothing." Pedro flung his hands wide. "What should happen? The Lady Luisa is perfection. I am unworthy of her least smile. But, Señora Mother, marriage is a serious step. It is not to be taken lightly."

"Nonsense!"

"Nay, wife," put in Don Francisco, "there's truth in what the boy says. You wouldn't have him behave too popinjay about it."

"Words!" Doña María retorted. "A man's either happy about his marriage or he isn't. . . . *Pedrito mío,* darling, your father and I have no one else in the world to love. Don't you know how we've thought and talked of you these years and prayed for your safety and looked forward to your coming? Open your heart to us like you used—or has it changed in the New World?"

Don Francisco nodded. "Yes, speak out, son, if there's anything on your mind—whatever it is. We only want to help. Sometimes it eases a man to talk openly. But suit yourself. Your thoughts are your own. And I'm not one to go ferreting into what doesn't concern me."

Pedro hesitated. A sudden pulse of warmth throbbed under the ice which during the past months had been thickening around his spirit. Before the fire of his parents' love, he realized how much, since his break with Catana and García, he had missed the companionship of people who cared and with whom he did not have to be on his guard. But the trouble was that he hardly knew what ailed him.

"How shall I say?" he groped. "Spain has a different feel from the New World. I'm not used to it yet. It's like putting on plate armor again when you haven't worn it for a while. Life's freer, bigger, over there. I don't know."

"I'll tell you," said his father. "You feel like I did, getting back from a campaign. Missed the good comrades, the camp ways. Found life finicky."

"Something like that," Pedro agreed, warming still more. "People seem younger over there. It's as if time were starting again. Not only a new country but a new age. People don't fuss so much about show. And then, Señor Father, as you said, the good comrades. . . . But I'll get used to it. If we win our suit before the Emperor, I can hope for a command in Italy. Our kinsman, Don Juan Alonso—"

"Alack!" Doña María interrupted. "You come from your betrothal and talk of leaving for the wars. We were discussing your marriage, son. You went to the Carvajal Palace happy and come back with a long face. Why? If the marriage doesn't please you—"

"Nay, *Madrecita*, it pleases me. I would be a fool else."

"You didn't write like that on your return. Your letters from Seville—"

"Yes, I know." In a flash he realized what weighed upon him. "I know. But tonight—" The ice cracked. He couldn't help speaking. "I remembered someone I loved in New Spain. I'll always love her. I can't help it."

Doña María's gray eyes turned to *o*'s of curiosity. "Who was she?"

Pedro already regretted the slip of his tongue. How could Don Francisco and Doña María, aristocrats rigid as the chairs they sat in, understand about Catana?

"Señora my Mother, if I told you, it would only give you pain. Why talk of it?"

But she was not to be put off. "Some camp follower, I warrant."

"Yes."

"A fine compliment to the Lady Luisa—to be rated below a draggle-tail slut! I know the kind. At least it might have been an Indian princess, like the one you told me General Cortés had. Or perhaps she was"—Señora de Vargas dropped her voice—"perhaps you meant that."

"No, a Castilian girl."

"And a camp follower? Then in plain terms, my son, a whore."

Pedro gripped the arms of his chair. "Peace, señora! I'll have no one, not even you, couple that name with her. By God, madam—"

"How now!" Don Francisco put in sternly. "You'll remember to whom you're speaking, sir, I hope. . . . As for you, wife, keep such round words to yourself. What is her name to us? We would not know her."

The slight in his voice stung Pedro as much as Doña María's frankness.

441

"Aye, sir. But as it happens, you know her right well. If you will have it, it was Catana Pérez of the Rosario tavern. She came with her brother to the Islands, followed our company to New Spain. . . . Or," he added bitterly, "have you forgotten her?"

Doña María drew a sharp breath. The elder de Vargas straightened in his chair.

"Catana Pérez!" he exclaimed. "Well, by the Lord, why could you not say so at first? Do you take me for a dog? Am I the kind to forget who saved our lives? She and the Señor García. A gallant wench! Except for her, we'd none of us be here tonight."

Doña María relented. "Forgive me, son. I didn't know. I love her for her kindness. . . . Tell us about her."

Pedro's eyes blurred. He had misjudged his parents. Aristocrats, but not too rigid for gratitude.

"I thank you, Señora my Mother, Señor my Father. . . . There's not much to tell."

But gradually, as he talked, he found that there was very much to tell. The stored-up memories unfolded. The frozen silence of the past year found an outlet. He told them of the marches and bivouacs, the dangers shared, the joys and sorrow. Now and then he found it hard to talk at all.

"We had a daughter there—in Coatl's country. A sweet little one. Could you but have seen her, *Madrecita!* She had eyes like yours. She died of the *viruelas*. It was bitter hard."

A tear crossed Doña María's cheek. Don Francisco cleared his throat.

"Often I see her that way—by the grave. She would not be my wife. She thought never of herself—only of me. She said it was not fitting. Not fitting! Christ! . . . Now God knows where she may be. She went off with Juan García. A good man, a heart of gold. I suppose they married."

He paused a moment. "Love her? The word's cheap. For her and me, it had nothing to do with prattle and poetry. I'd rather say I didn't love her. Only a part of me—I don't know how to put it—a part of me—" He broke off. "That's the sum of it."

He sat gazing at the lighted candles on the table.

At last Don Francisco said, "It has been so with us, María. We have been one flesh, nay, one soul. I count that the best that life has given me."

Señora de Vargas answered him with her eyes. Then, getting up, she went over to Pedro and kissed him.

"We want only your happiness, my son. If this marriage irks you—"

He shook his head. "No, as the word's used, I love Luisa de Carvajal. We'll be happy as most. We're betrothed. I want to marry her." Seeing the pain in his mother's eyes, he added, "We'll be very happy."

He lighted a bedroom taper from one of the candles on the table, kissed his mother, bowed to Don Francisco, and bade them good night.

They sat for a while troubled. As Señor de Vargas said, "Time heals wounds, my dear; it cannot rub out scars. He'll carry this one to his death. But, like it or no, scars are the lot of every man."

—————— LXXVII ——————

EXERCISING CAMPEADOR NEXT DAY, it was perhaps not altogether accident that Pedro chose the mountains rather than the *campiña* and at last drew rein before the Rosario tavern. Like the ocean, the mind has its obscure, uncharted currents. He had not planned to visit the Rosario, yet here he was; and, being here, he turned for old time's sake into the courtyard.

At once a commotion started. Lubo, the venerable watchdog, whose powerful memory and sense of smell were the same, gave welcoming tongue and tried to renew the gambols of his prime, though in a rheumatic fashion. Other dogs, taking their cue from the chief, barked in aimless politeness. A couple of the ostlers hurried forward with broad grins, while newer hangers-on, who could not claim acquaintance with the great lord, stared and drew closer in hope of a largess. Almost everyone knew who he was, for Pedro's entry into Jaén with the cavalcade of gentlemen and the wondrous Indians had been a public event.

"Ha, Tobal! Ha, Chepito!" he greeted the ostlers. "How is it, lads? It's been a long time since the last time, eh, *hombres?*"

He tossed a handful of coins among the expectant onlookers, swung from his saddle, and clapped the two grooms on the shoulder, while at the same moment Sancho López appeared in the doorway of the taproom. The innkeeper's bullet head had become grizzled in the past four years, and his paunch had grown rounder, but otherwise he looked shrewd and businesslike as ever. He advanced beaming.

"Captain de Vargas, Your Worship, sir, welcome! Welcome to the Rosario!"

"My old friend!" said Pedro, extending his hand. "*Cómo está?* How goes it, Sancho? By the mass, but it brings back the old days to see you!"

Indeed it brought them back, as did the dark, malodorous taproom into which López ushered him. For an instant he half-expected to see the vivid figure of Catana, tankards in hand and rose in hair, materialize out of the gloom, or to hear the hot drawl of her voice. There was the table where he had first talked with Juan García, and there he had sat bound between the two troopers of the Holy Office. The pelting of memories sobered him, as he followed the innkeeper to a more private corner in the rear beyond the benches of noisy patrons. They stared at his broad shoulders and fine clothes. Then the word passed that this was Captain Pedro de Vargas, and they stared again.

Stretching his legs under a table, he relaxed, and prevailed on the embarrassed López to sit opposite him.

"No excuses, Sancho. We've been friends too long. . . . I see that custom's good. Let's have a flagon of your best, and give me the news."

"Nay, that's all on the side of Your Worship. The Rosario hasn't changed, as Your Worship sees. I grow older. Times are bad on account of the late revolts, and the mountains are full of rascals. That's all the news, Your Worship."

A buxom country girl brought wine and made eyes at Pedro, who grinned at her absently, his mind on the past.

"But first," Sancho López went on, "if Your Lordship permits, I would respectfully drink to your betrothal with Her Grace Doña Luisa de Carvajal and humbly wish long life and happiness to Your Lordships."

"Thanks, Sancho." De Vargas leaned back against the partition which formed the corner of the room. "Thanks. So you've heard of it already?"

"*Cómo no!* The town's buzzing with it."

"Yes, I suppose it would." Pedro drank, then added: "By the way, Catana Pérez would have sent her love if she had known I should be seeing you. You'll be glad to have news of her."

López nodded. "She'll never be forgotten at the Rosario. The country people have a ballad about her and Hernán Soler, and how she went overseas to find Your Worship."

"She's a great lady in New Spain, Sancho, highly honored by the company. Though truly she's a great lady anywhere." De Vargas paused a moment, then added, "The greatest I've known." A dry bitterness crept into his voice. "You see, my friend, one of the biggest jokes in life is that you learn most things too late."

But, though the innkeeper looked at him inquiringly, Pedro did not elaborate. Instead, he launched into an enthusiastic account of New

Spain: mountains, forests, plains, resources, prospects. "There's the country, *viejo.*"

"I recall, sir, that Señor García talked the same way."

"And he was right. Juan García is right about most things. Yes, there's the country."

"Do you expect to return, Señor Captain?"

Pedro stared at the bottom of his wine cup, then filled again and drank.

"No. Things to keep me here, you understand—at least in Europe. Family reasons. But curse me if it'll be easy, Sancho! It gets into the blood. You long to fill your lungs with Mexican air. You close your eyes and hear the sound of the sea on western beaches."

"Then is Your Worship staying in Jaén?"

"By God, hardly! I leave this week for Valladolid on General Cortés's business to the Emperor. . . . His Majesty has but now returned from Flanders. . . . Afterwards, marriage, Sancho. And then I hope for service against the Moors or in Italy. Catch me staying in Jaén!"

"But if you're married, Señor Captain?"

"It isn't marriage that will stop me. . . . By the way, Sancho, you recall our friend de Silva?"

"Do I recall him!"

"Well, he's at court. They say he's climbed into the saddle again. I've a long score to settle with him, *hombre.*"

López pinched his chin. "I wish Your Worship the best of luck. The man's a swine."

De Vargas showed mock surprise. "You don't tell me! I seem to remember that once—it was after the attack on Catana in the upper meadow, you recall—you said you knew something about this cavalier which would keep him quiet. Now, if you cared to tell me anything that might help, I'd be thankful."

Sancho's unshaven face had turned inscrutable. It was a moment before he answered.

"No, Your Worship. Did I say anything like that?"

"Yes, you said you knew him when he was younger and that he knew what you knew. Therefore you were safe. Surely you recall."

The other forced a laugh. "It's queer. I know nothing about Diego de Silva. Your Worship may have dreamed it."

"Perhaps," Pedro shrugged. "Well, it makes no difference. This time we'll settle accounts. I heard in Seville that he had been taken by the corsairs on returning from Cuba, that he'd stolen a small ship in

Algiers, killed several of the pirates, and got back safe to Málaga. Everybody was talking about it. I wouldn't have believed he had it in him."

López shook his head. "Maybe. I don't know. But, señor, be careful."

"*No hay cuidado,*" de Vargas grinned. "It is written: *don't teach your grandmother to suck eggs.*"

Having finished his wine, he was on the point of standing up, when a thought struck him. "Look you, Sancho, have you nothing of Catana's here? Something you could give me for a keepsake? If you had, I'd be indebted to you, friend."

The innkeeper pondered. "No, Your Worship, I fear not. She took the little she had with her."

"Think, Sancho, a knife she used, a dish—anything."

Suddenly López's eyes quickened. "By God, yes, Your Worship. Her cup, if I can find it."

"Her cup? Fetch it here! God help you if you can't find it!"

"I'll look, señor."

Pedro waited in suspense until López returned, carrying an object in his hands. It was a pewter tankard. Sancho pointed to some letters scratched on the surface.

"See—her name, they tell me, for I can't read."

Pedro gazed in rapture at the scrawled letters, inverted as some of them were: *Catana Pérez.* He fondled the cup between his hands. Her lips had touched the brim. Could he not imagine when drinking from it—

"But look here, Sancho, she hadn't learned to make the letters then." The picture crossed his mind of Catana laboring over the sheet of bark paper in the Zapotec country worlds away.

"No, señor, but she had Paco, the muleteer, who is a learned man, cut them for her. She liked ever to have her own cup to herself."

Pedro pressed it against his mouth. "I take my oath that I shall drink my night draught from no other cup as long as I live. Thanks, Sancho! Thanks!"

He dipped into his purse, but the innkeeper put out a hand.

"No, señor. The thing's a trifle. If it pleases you, I'll take nothing."

"You'll take ten pieces of gold, Sancho, which is all I have by me. I wish I could fill it to the brim. Nay, friend, it's honor I'm paying to the cup. How could I repay *you!* Here."

And while López stared at the glittering *castellanos,* Pedro's eyes were on the pewter mug. He kept gazing at it as he walked out through

446

the taproom, then put it carefully into his pouch before saying farewell in the courtyard and mounting Campeador.

But he had not ridden far toward town when he drew it out again. *Catana Pérez,* badly lettered. The muleteer was not a very learned man after all. But what did that matter? The cup represented Catana. Nothing glittering about it, nothing elegant, scarred by the rough-and-tumble of daily life, serviceable, durable, without pretense. Simply an honest cup. And yet he fancied that wine would taste sweeter from it than from any other. He fancied—

A swift scuffle of horses' hoofs startled him. He looked up to find himself the center of a ring of troopers. It was at the turn of the road beneath the Castle. Even if he had not been absorbed in the cup, he would probably not have seen them.

At once he thought of the mountain rascals López had spoken of, but he saw immediately that these men were not bandits. They wore white and red baldrics trimmed with gold, the imperial colors. Their equipment looked professional and official.

Resistance was out of the question even if he had been prepared for it. Returning the cup to his pouch, he faced an immensely broad-shouldered young man with a hard mouth and a broken nose who advanced toward him.

"Are you Pedro de Vargas? So-called Captain de Vargas?"

"The same, but no *so-called* about it."

"Ah? Well, I am Claros de Paz, captain of lances in His Majesty's Guard." The officer drew a sealed document from his belt and tapped it with a gauntleted forefinger. "I have here a warrant for your arrest."

"My arrest!"

"On the charge of high treason against His Caesarean Majesty. . . . Like to see it? Or can you read?"

Pedro, dazed, held out his hand. Yes, there it was written, signed, and sealed. No question of a mistake. He handed the paper back.

"But in God's name why?"

"How should I know? You can ask that question in Valladolid. I carry out orders. . . . Your sword, Señor de Vargas."

LXXVIII

Unarmed and with his bridle reins divided between two troopers, Pedro still gazed dumfounded at the hard-faced young Captain. He could not believe that eluding the agents of the Indian Council with the aid and protection of the Duke of Medina Sidonia constituted high treason, however irregular it might be legally. But there was no use asking questions of Claros de Paz, who obviously could not or would not answer them.

"I regret this duty, señor," the latter went on. "To arrest the son of Don Francisco de Vargas is the last assignment I'd choose. But soldiers don't choose, as you're doubtless aware."

Pedro collected his thoughts. He was favorably impressed by the tough-looking officer, who reminded him of Sandoval.

"Do you happen to be a relative of the renowned knight and captain, Pedro de Paz, who was my father's comrade in Italy?"

The other looked pleased. "His nephew, sir."

"I was brought up on stories of Pedro de Paz. My father has had a mass said for his soul on every anniversary of his death. . . . Look you, Captain, whatever you may think of me, certainly you and these gentlemen"—Pedro bowed to the troopers—"will not deprive Don Francisco de Vargas of the honor of receiving you at our house. You would not put such a discourtesy upon him."

De Paz ruminated and exchanged an undecided glance with the other cavaliers. Finally he jerked his head back. "By God, I'd like to pay my homage to Don Francisco, as we all would. Besides, we've ridden hard today from the Sierra Morena and want a breather. . . . As for you, Captain de Vargas" (Pedro noticed that his military rank had been restored), "I was told by a gentleman high in His Majesty's favor, one Diego de Silva, who said he knew you, that you were a violent pirate and freebooter. But damme if you don't seem a man, sir, with whom I would like to run a course or so and engage in other friendly exchanges. I was ordered to arrest and bring you to Valladolid. The way of it was left to me. Do you give me your word of honor that, rescue or no rescue, you will remain my true prisoner until I'm through with this duty?"

"Certes, I will," Pedro answered, "rescue or no rescue. As it happens, I was riding anyway to Valladolid, and I can think of no more agreeable company than you gentlemen."

"Then there's no more to be said," returned de Paz. "Give the captain back his sword and reins, and we'll wait on his illustrious father. . . . Damme but I'm glad of this! I've been wanting the chance to talk with one of Hernán Cortés's cavaliers. Damme, sir, I envy you the action you've seen in New Spain. And for the life of me, I can't understand this pother about the Cuban fellow, Velásquez."

Pedro, gathering his reins again, set Campeador prancing.

"I'll tell you the truth of it. . . . But, good Señor de Paz, tell me what you know about this arrest of mine. On my honor, I'm like a man in a bad dream."

The other shook his head. "And on my honor, I know nothing except that they say His Majesty is in a towering rage against you. Also I'm glad not to be in your shoes, señor, for the Emperor is not often angry."

"Did not a messenger from the Duke of Medina Sidonia arrive with a letter for His Majesty?"

"Faith, I wouldn't know, sir. . . . But, *qué diablo,* what's this?"

"This" was a cavalcade issuing from the city gates, which the little troop was now approaching. In front rode Don Francisco in complete armor and lance in hand. Behind him rode two ensigns, one carrying the banner of Jaén, the other the de Vargas pennon. Some thirty lances followed.

When word from the city gate had reached the Alcalde that a band of men-at-arms were inquiring for Pedro and were holding the mountain road, he had taken prompt action. Whether they were friends or enemies, he made ready to give them an appropriate welcome.

"Ha!" said de Paz, snapping down his vizor. "Gentlemen, fix lances! Señor de Vargas, remember your word."

"A moment," Pedro intervened. "I'll ride forward and explain matters. Have no fear of my word."

Upon recognizing his son, the Alcalde raised vizor and hand with a loud "halt!"

"Many thanks, Señor my Father," said Pedro, riding up. "But these gentlemen are cavaliers of His Majesty, led by Captain de Paz, nephew of Don Pedro, who wishes to pay you his respects." He added as casually as possible, "I am his prisoner on the parole of rescue or no rescue. The charge is high treason."

The old gentleman's face now looked blank in its turn. "But what—"

"I know nothing about it, sir. I suspect it's a stroke of Diego de Silva's. Maybe the messenger whom Don Juan Alonso and I sent from Seville, reporting that I had treasure in charge for His Majesty and that I would be shortly in Valladolid, did not arrive."

"Treason!" the Alcalde repeated. "That charge has never been coupled with our name. But"—he made an effort—"we must receive our guests. The kinsman of my old comrade is welcome." And he rode back with Pedro to the imperial troop.

Elaborate and profuse were the courtesies on either side. The newcomers gazed with veneration on the old knight, who in return dis-

449

played the stilted magnificence of chivalric Spain. Casques were doffed, fiery compliments exchanged. Don Francisco knew the families of the gentlemen-at-arms and paid honor to each. He put himself and his house at their service. He found that Claros de Paz greatly resembled his famous uncle in appearance, and he had no doubt that he resembled him even more in spirit. On his side, Captain de Paz maintained that he did not know whether he should grieve more at the nature of his errand or feel delight that the occasion permitted him to throw himself at the feet of Don Francisco de Vargas, whose name was a guiding star to all cavaliers.

Then the united companies rode back to the Alcalde's house on the Plaza Santa María, where there were renewed welcomes, compliments, and a great bustling to provide the guests with an impromptu repast.

Don Francisco and Doña María did not allow consternation to interrupt the duties of hospitality, but Señora de Vargas, pale of face and with haunted eyes, wrung her hands between times.

"What will they do to him, husband? What does the charge mean?"

"It's a heavy charge, wife, and one not lightly made. God knows what lies behind it. But I have no doubt he will be cleared. Pluck up heart, my dear. Only we must let no grass grow under our feet. See that my saddlebags are packed, for I'm riding with Pedro."

"My lord, you cannot—crippled as your knee is. It's a hundred leagues to Valladolid."

"And if it were a thousand, I'd ride. If I was sound enough to escape into Italy, do you think I'll coddle myself now when our name's attainted and our son's in need? Come, wife, dispatch. See to my bags. Excuse me to our guests for a moment. I have notes to write. Our good friend, Carvajal, will want to come with us. I must get off messages to the Duke, to other friends. Pedro's trial will not take long. He must be helped at once if help is to be of use."

So the old cavalier drove a hurried quill across paper and sent out appeals in all directions.

But in the case of the Marquis de Carvajal, who replied at once, he had a sharp disappointment. Although the Marquis had been perfectly well the preceding evening, he now excused himself on the score of gout. He would not be able to put foot to stirrup or even to ride in his coach for the next week or ten days. He lamented the stroke of ill-fortune which had befallen Pedro, but had no doubt that all would turn out well in the end. Meanwhile, he could do little, but he was entirely at the service of his noble friends. If it were not that he needed Luisa at his bedside, she would have come to bid farewell to Captain de Vargas, whom she would not fail to remember night and morning in her prayers.

"Ah," regretted Don Francisco, "I'm sorry. I counted on him."

He showed the letter to Pedro, who detached himself a moment from entertaining his captors. Having glanced through the message, Pedro smiled.

"I wonder whether he has gout in the foot, my lord, or gout somewhere else."

"Nay, son, you should not misjudge him."

Once again Pedro reflected that it would do no good to express his well-founded opinion of Carvajal. He merely answered, "No, sir, it would be impossible to misjudge him."

Since speed was an article of Captain de Paz's orders, he reluctantly declined the de Vargas hospitality for the night and insisted on leaving about midafternoon. The departure was witnessed by a concourse of people in the plaza, for news of grave doings had spread like wildfire through the town. But when Pedro appeared, equipped as usual with sword and dagger and in pleasant conversation with the troopers, rumor took a new turn. It was reported that His Majesty had sent a guard of honor to escort Captain de Vargas to Valladolid. And indeed the squadron of twenty lances, Pedro's Indians, whom de Paz accepted as Don Francisco's attendants, the Alcalde on a comfortable palfrey, several other mounted servants, the imperial banderoles and the pennons of de Vargas and de Paz, made a fine, triumphal spectacle.

Pedro embraced Doña María again in the doorway. "Don't worry, *Madrecita*. I'll be back in a blaze of glory. You'll see! . . . Nay, if you cry, *Madrecita* darling!"

The crowd burst into huzzas and *vivas* as the small company rode off, and a number trooped after it down the narrow streets to the city gates.

De Paz, his head humming from the good wine at dinner, waved his gauntlet at a pretty girl in a window and laughed. "By the saints, I wonder whether this is a pageant or an arrest. I'll wager that in all Spain the king's justice has never been more pleasantly executed."

"More gallantly, sir," Don Francisco amended.

"More admiringly, my lord," effervesced de Paz.

And so it was at the first night's stop in Linares, and so through the ten days' travel north over sierra and mesa, through La Mancha, through Madrid, through New and Old Castile. The road was enlivened by many a gay story, by Don Francisco's memories of Italy and

451

Pedro's accounts of Mexico, by military discussions, and once even by a jousting between Pedro and de Paz, which ended in mutual satisfaction, since both splintered their lances to the butt and neither could unhorse the other.

Every gentleman in the company agreed that it was a memorable, enjoyable journey. When at last the towers of Valladolid appeared across the wind-swept plain, they called forth audible regret.

"Pedrito," said de Paz (for they were now on familiar terms), "if you would speak alone with Don Francisco for a moment, now is the time. We'll have to close up ranks from here on."

Drawing apart with his father, Pedro gave him Cortés's letter to the Emperor and the equally precious receipt for the royal gold which he had obtained from the Father Superior at La Rábida.

"I'll have these fall into no hands but His Majesty's," he concluded. "A good deal could happen in the Valladolid prison. De Silva works best in the dark."

Don Francisco stuck out his lower lip. "Son Pedro, it seems to me I hear the hounds too hot on that wolf's traces for him to have much time for mischief. But be that as it may, I'll make shift to visit you in prison and assure my own eyes that nothing has happened. You have gold and I have credit enough for that."

Gradually the troop drew near the flat, unlovely city, whose walls rose higher as they approached. Don Francisco tactfully fell to the rear, and Pedro reined back to the center of the squadron so as not to embarrass Captain de Paz. In this fashion they passed through the gates and stopped at last before the squat doors of the city keep. These swung open after a parley; then de Paz, entering with Pedro, delivered his charge to Señor de Heredia, governor of the prison.

Dry, sour, and ashen-colored, the latter looked as if the hopelessness of the jail had transferred itself to him.

"Sir, what is this man doing with sword and dagger?"

"Sir," retorted de Paz, "what does any man do with them?"

Turning upon Pedro, Heredia plucked out the rapier and poniard and tossed them onto a table.

"You'll hear more of this, Captain de Paz."

"Sir, I want to hear nothing from you but what you haven't the stomach to send me. . . . Good-by, Pedrito, I sorrow to leave you in such hands."

And thrusting his broken nose toward Heredia, Don Claros paused a moment before swaggering out.

The governor turned a yellow-shot eye on de Vargas.

"Here," he said to a turnkey, "take this fellow to the tower, though I have yet to understand why a traitor should be better lodged than a thief."

— LXXIX —

THOUGH NOT LUXURIOUS, the tower room had some pretensions to comfort. It afforded light, air, and sufficient space. The bed, however moldy and verminous, boasted a canopy and side curtains. The turnkey, who had a keen scent for gold, fetched up Pedro's saddlebags and showed him every civility. In short, as compared with the warren of cells below it, the tower room could be considered an apartment *de luxe*.

But, in spite of the poet, stone walls do make a prison and iron bars a cage. The memories of other occupants haunted the place: scrawled initials, paths worn along the floor. The smell was prison smell; the dreary quality of the light, the silence, were characteristic of a prison. After the gay companionship of the road, Pedro felt the oppression of it and dreaded the coming of night.

"Yes," said the turnkey, happily pocketing a gold piece, "there's not many a keep in Spain has quarters like this for the gentry. As good as any tavern room in Valladolid. More private, too. And that isn't all. Show me the tavern anywhere that's had so many noble lodgers. Man and boy, I've attended here thirty years, and Your Grace would be surprised how many from the first families I've served. Fetched them their last meal. Took care they had enough brandy to steady them on the scaffold. Does Your Grace know—"

He ran through several names familiar to Pedro, who nodded.

"I've set their limbs for 'em when they've had too bad a time on the rack—tended 'em like a mother. Why, young Fadrique de Mendoza in the old King's time hanged himself on the crossbar of that bed. I cut him down in the morning. And he isn't the only one. Jaime Enríquez, kinsman of the present Admiral, was another. He hung from the window bars. And Don Iago de Velasco. Gentlemen sometimes get discouraged." The turnkey slapped his thigh. "Ho, ho! We laugh about it in the guardroom. Call this 'Suicide Tower'—a manner of joke, as you might say."

"Find the service profitable?" asked Pedro to change the subject.

"Only fair, Your Grace."

"Well, do what you can for me, Señor *Carcelero,* and you'll not lose by it."

"I kiss Your Grace's feet. Your Magnificence has only to ask."

"Then here's the first thing. If my father or other gentlemen should come to see me, and the visit can be arranged, you'd have five pesos a call."

The *carcelero's* lips moistened. "I'll do my possible, Your Grace."

At exorbitant cost, Pedro ate an inferior midday meal brought in from a near-by tavern. Then the afternoon hours dragged by.

He was tormented by the puzzle of his arrest. Why? What lay behind the charge of high treason? If the messenger sent by him and his kinsman, the Duke of Medina Sidonia, had not reached the Emperor, he would no doubt be charged with the theft of the gold; but it was hard to believe that the messenger had not arrived. He regretted bitterly that he had taken the advice of the Duke in not acting as his own messenger. And yet the reasons at the time seemed excellent. Charles had then barely landed, had not reached Valladolid, was absorbed by the affairs of the Comunidades. Medina Sidonia believed that Pedro's arrival at court would be attended by greater éclat if it were slightly delayed until it was prepared for by the first message and until an imposing array of backers had been marshaled. This was evidently a mistake. Both he and Pedro had underrated the vigilance and power of the Bishop of Burgos.

But it was not his personal plight that most concerned de Vargas: it was the menace to his mission. To have been selected by Cortés among all the captains, and now at the very outset to have blundered! Another case of pride before a fall. He had been too complacent over his management in landing the gold and had assumed that the worst was over when the real crisis had not begun.

The light was fading when footsteps and voices on the tower stairs roused him. Keys rattled, bolts were drawn back, and the tall figure of his father appeared in the doorway.

But when they had embraced and the turnkey, though doubly tipped, had gone out muttering that he might pay for this with his head, Pedro noticed the ominous drooping of Don Francisco's lower lip and the harassment in his eyes.

"What news?" he prompted.

"Well, Pedrito, I've been from pillar to post. It's the devil how fast friendship cools when it costs something. I could have sworn that the Constable of Castile was my friend and also Don Juan Hurtado. Perhaps I wrong them. At any rate, they were no use. I got more from

454

those two gentlemen Cortés sent back three years ago, Puertocarrero and Montejo, than from anyone else. I learned why His Majesty is so hot against you."

"You did? Well, by God, that's something, Señor Father! Why then?"

Don Francisco lowered his voice. "First, no messenger arrived. (The Bishop or de Silva may have had a hand in that, for your doings in Seville were known to the agents of the Indian Council.) Hence you are guilty of stealing His Majesty's treasure."

Pedro gave a laugh of relief. "I guessed it! So that's all! Well, sir, I have only to show the receipt of the Father Superior of La Rábida and the General's letter. That will stop the lion's mouth."

Don Francisco shook his head. "I would it might, *hijo mío*. But there are other charges."

"Other charges? How?"

"You are accused, together with General Cortés himself and all his captains, of rebelling against the King's authority in the person of Diego de Velásquez, Adelantado of Cuba." Don Francisco made a hopeless gesture. "Nay, son, the longer I live, the madder, it seems to me, grows the world."

"Rebelling against the King," Pedro burst out, "when everything we did was in his service! Rebelling against the King because we wouldn't let that fat Cuban lubber pluck us of our gains!"

The old cavalier nodded ironically. "As I say. . . . But not so loud, boy. I don't know a knave when I see one if that same jailer of yours isn't a Judas. Yes, as I say. I pass over similar charges. You are accused especially of disgracing the Spanish name by the massacre of helpless Indians in that city you speak of which I can't pronounce. You are accused of plotting the death of the priest Ignacio de Lora. You are accused of reviling the King's Majesty and conspiring with others to make Cortés king of New Spain. You are accused of inhuman cruelty to the honest seamen of your ship, who are now bought witnesses of de Silva and who swear that they sought to prevent you from making off with the royal treasure. In short, my son," Don Francisco concluded with frozen sarcasm, "you are one of the choicest monsters our nation has produced."

Pedro sat with flushed cheeks, clenched fists, and an open mouth.

"But Montejo and Puertocarrero—why are they not in prison or accused? They were Cortés's men."

"Their defense is that they left New Spain before most of these atrocities occurred. But they live in fear and are getting out of Valladolid.

455

Remember," Don Francisco added, "that the Emperor's ears have been filled with every half-truth and whole lie that the Bishop and de Silva could muster. They've spread the same thing about court. I hear too that de Silva has gained such favor with His Majesty as to set every tongue wagging. He lives in great style; has a court of his own. . . . No, my son, your crime was to have missed killing him when you had the chance. You're apt to pay for it on the block unless we can silence him." The old knight shook with anger. "Unless we can silence him," he repeated.

Leaning forward, Pedro laid his hand on his father's arm. "Not that way," he said in a low voice, "not yet. It would give support to every lie he has told."

The other nodded. "Yes, but how then? If he lives—"

"Sir, you have written to Don Juan Alonso; you have written to the Duke of Bejar. They will stand with us."

"Yes, if they come in time. Pray God they do! Pray God the trial is delayed until they do!"

There was a pause which at last Don Francisco shrugged off. "By the way," he said, "I almost forgot. As I was leaving the inn, a peddler or such like gave me this for you." The old gentleman drew out a stained and battered letter sealed with coarse wax. "I asked him what it was. He said a humble friend in Jaén, hearing of your misfortune, sent you his respectful best wishes. So I gave the fellow a coin for his trouble. Here you are."

The door bolts rattled as Pedro thrust the paper into his purse. The turnkey popped in his head. He regretted to disturb Their Magnificences, but time was up. Don Francisco gripped Pedro's shoulders, kept his voice level when he bade him good night, and limped out, leaving a heavy silence in the vaulted room.

Still dazed by the ill news, de Vargas paced up and down. So far as he could see, everything depended on gathering enough influence to act as a buffer at his trial against the force and venom of the prosecution. This in turn depended on time, on whether the trial did not take place until his more powerful backers could be assembled. But even so, the prospect looked bleak. By the intervention of Medina Sidonia and Bejar, he might get off personally with a crushing fine; but his mission in behalf of Cortés was doomed.

Spain! The career at court! The brilliant future! He glanced back at his former dreams. He remembered too his talk with García at Coyoacán. Yes, in New Spain he had possessed everything that money could not buy: friendship, respect which he had earned, unlimited scope. Here, these walls were his scope, and his life depended on the machinations of an enemy. It was de Silva who had the career at court, the brilliant future.

He paced up and down, unconsciously following the path across the floor worn by other feet. At last, remembering the letter from his well-wisher in Jaén, he drew it out and, still half-absently, having lighted a candle, broke the seal. It was evidently from a poor, unlettered person, as both paper and characters revealed. It reminded him that he had always found more loyalty among the poor than the rich.

At first he could make nothing of the drunken scrawl meandering over the paper. Then he began to recognize words, and at once his interest quickened. Desperately intent, he figured out the atrocious spelling and worse penmanship. At last, he read:—

> *Sancho López did not answer your question about a certain black dog because he fears for his life. If he had answered, it would have been this. Years ago he knew the Black Dog in Málaga. He knows that said Black Dog from poor became rich by acting in secret for the enemies of God and Spain, who make war on ships. Black Dog once visited Red Dog in his kennel across the water. Better not ask how Sancho knows, for he has long been an honest man. That this may help you is the wish of your friends. By the hand of Paco the Muleteer.*

De Vargas stared at the paper while a dozen thought sparks wheeled through his mind. Paco, the one who had cut Catana's name on the cup. So López had taken this way to answer. *"Bravo, hombre!"* Pedro's eyes blazed. De Silva in his youth an agent of the corsairs, one of those renegades who reported ship movements. *Red Dog* could only mean Barbarossa, alias Arouj or his brother, Khair-ed-Din.

This was capital news. And yet, on second thought, Pedro's exultance faded. It had been years ago. He had only the word of an anonymous writer for the fact. De Silva was in favor at court, a kinsman of the Bishop of Burgos. How could a prisoner on trial for his life make so preposterous a countercharge without doing himself more harm than good? But still—that recent heroic escape of de Silva's from the corsairs. Was it possible—

A slight noise at the door caught Pedro's attention, and he glanced around in time to see the small wicket in the upper panel closing. Evidently someone, probably the turnkey, had been watching him.

He put the letter into an inner pocket of his doublet but continued to turn over its contents in his mind.

Not long afterward, the turnkey entered with supper, which consisted of a brace of roast pigeons, a half loaf of fresh bread, some fruit, and a flagon of wine. It looked so much more appetizing than what he had eaten at lunch that Pedro did not object to the astonishing price asked for it.

"I can most heartily recommend the wine, Your Grace," said the turnkey. "It is a special Alicante fit for the lips of the King's Majesty himself."

"Why, then," said Pedro, who knew the value of keeping on the fellow's good side, "you'll do me the favor of filling a cup and drinking my health."

But to his surprise, the turnkey declined. "Ah, Your Grace, would that I might! There's no other health I'd sooner drink, and God knows such wine as that is a treat I don't have once a year. But I suffer with the gravel, my lord. The cursed physician will not let me touch *vino generoso* this month. Thanks all the same, Your Magnificence."

"Too bad," said Pedro.

He filled Catana's cup, which he had taken out of his saddlebags. But deciding to eat first, he attacked the pigeons. The turnkey, after hesitating a moment, withdrew.

It was only by luck that de Vargas, glancing at the door a moment later, observed that the wicket had been once more slid back. But why should the man want to spy on him while he was eating? He could have remained inside and watched for all Pedro cared.

Then, as if from nowhere, a shadow of suspicion crossed de Vargas's mind. It was queer about the Alicante: men of the jailer's stripe were not apt to turn down a good drink. The fellow had made a point of praising the wine. It was still queerer about the wicket. Pedro remembered his father's estimate of the turnkey. Why not put it to the test?

Carelessly raising the cup in full view of the door, Pedro pretended to drink, tilted the tankard higher, set it down at last and smacked his lips, then returned to his food. When he glanced again, the wicket was closed.

Without wasting a second, he now carried the wine flagon across the room, emptied his water ewer into the basin, and replaced its contents with the Alicante. There was no use wasting good wine in case his suspicions were wrong.

Then he returned to table and finished supper, taking care to sag a little and to yawn repeatedly. He had to make a choice of symptoms; but if the drink had been tampered with at all, an opiate seemed more likely than violent poison. Finally he slumped over on the table, head on arms but with his face turned enough for a view of things through his eyelashes.

A half hour passed. Finally he heard the faint click of the wicket, and immediately afterward the turnkey came in. But this time the man's face did not wear its former unctuousness; it was alert and professional.

Having shuffled his feet and coughed, the turnkey gave a satisfied nod. Then he drew from behind him an object which he had been holding in his left hand. It was a thin leather strap attached to a handle, and at the sight of it Pedro's scalp prickled.

It was a strangling thong, a garrote.

──────── LXXX ────────

WHEN HE HAD ASSURED himself of de Vargas's unconsciousness by looking into the empty flagon and rubbing a pudgy hand over the prisoner's hair, the turnkey set about work with veteran deliberation. He even hummed a gentle tune to himself. First, he took a sheet from the bed, twisted it into a rough rope, and made a noose at the end. Then he threw this over the crossbar of the bed, which held the canopy, tested the strength of it, and tied the other end of the rope sheet to the bedpost.

So that was the way of it, thought Pedro. First the garrote, then the noose. In the morning, another suicide would be reported from the tower room. Unable to face the charges against him, the prisoner had hanged himself, thus confirming the indictment of the prosecution as well as saving trouble and closing the case. Perhaps this explained the turnkey's accounts of other gentlemen who had been found strung up there.

Still humming, the fellow now took time to run through Pedro's saddlebags and to appropriate a pouch of gold which his charge would no longer have use for. This done, he hitched up his sleeves and, taking the leather thong, slipped it deftly from behind around de Vargas's neck, drawing the handle at one end through the loop at the other. When adjusted, the torque of the handle would be sufficient to snap the spine and crush the windpipe in a wrench or two.

But the wrench never came. Pedro's arms, outstretched on the table, suddenly locked behind the head of the turnkey, who was bending over him. Then, turning slightly so as to avoid the table and using the old

459

wrestling heave, de Vargas brought the man catapulting over his head. He now was behind the turnkey with one arm half-throttling him. A moment later, he found the proper spot on the man's jaw with his free fist and put him asleep for the time being.

When the jailer came to himself several minutes afterwards, he discovered that he was in a chair, a gag in his mouth, the sheet rope around his body, and the garrote in place about his own throat.

"So!" said de Vargas. "Now we can talk. But first let me point out that a man like you wouldn't live long in New Spain. Not clever enough. You'd be fair sport for the comrades. . . . Well? Feeling better?"

A stifled muttering filtered through the gag.

Pedro, stepping behind him, gave a slight twist to the thong, which made the man's eyes pop.

"You see, my friend, what the situation is."

Then he relaxed the garrote and, moving back in front, drew up another chair.

"I hope," he continued, "that you won't make the mistake of considering me a milksop. *Hombre,* I've killed a number of men in the past four years and all of them better men than you. If I can get what I want out of you, perhaps you'll live. Otherwise, please don't think I'm tenderhearted."

A moan through the gag and the terror in the fellow's eyes answered.

"Good," Pedro nodded. "It pays to be intelligent. There are various ways I can deal with you. For instance, I could strangle you and carry your body downstairs some place. Then who's to know who did it? Or I could make you drink the Alicante, which I've saved, and let them find you asleep here with me in the morning. I don't believe your employer would like that, or the governor of the prison. You would hang judicially. Also it would help me at my trial to have the facts published. So you see, friend rat, that you are in a bad place and that I have nothing to lose by dealing with you one way or another. You do see that, eh?"

The turnkey groaned and shut his eyes to escape the grim countenance in front of him.

"Now," said Pedro, returning to the handle of the garrote behind the man's neck, "I'm going to untie your mouth. But keep your voice low. You wouldn't think of talking too loud, much less calling for help. Then you'll answer some questions. Remember, I'll know if you lie, and that would be painful for you."

He pulled loose the knots of the gag and at the same time tightened the strangling thong.

"There you are. First question. Who paid you for this?"

Pedro could feel the movement of the man's Adam's apple, but the answer came. "The lord de Silva."

"How much?"

"A hundred pesos."

"You were to make it easy for anyone to visit me, I suppose, and you were to listen at the door?"

"Yes."

"What other instructions?"

"I was to look for papers."

Pedro congratulated himself on the forethought of leaving his papers with Don Francisco. Then he remembered the letter from Jaén. It would have been a help to de Silva to know about that.

"Have you heard when my trial is to come off?"

"Tomorrow." The turnkey winced at the sudden tightening of the thong. "It's the truth," he squeaked. "I can't help the truth, can I?"

Tomorrow! There would be no time for gathering help. If tonight's plot failed, de Silva had at least made sure of the trial.

"Now, listen, rogue. And this is the most important of all. If you help me in this, you live; if not, you die. Tell me what you know about de Silva. He works underground, and you underground rats will have sniffed something. I want a hold on him, understand? Come, speak out."

The man faltered, "I don't know anything. . . . *Ay de mí*," he croaked, as the leather tightened, "how can I tell what I don't know?"

"Think. I'll give you a half-minute."

Streaks of sweat showed on the turnkey's jaws.

"Ten seconds," said Pedro.

"Wait, Your Grace! Wait! I know who killed the messenger from Seville. They threw his body into the river. It was Tito el Fiero and his men. De Silva hired them."

"And this man Tito—where does he live?"

"On the Calle del Salvador near the market. But, my lord, if it came out that I—"

"It will not come out. If you know it, others of your kind know it. Tell me more of de Silva. What other rogue does he frequent or pay besides Tito?"

"Your Grace, I know of none."

"Think."

461

In an effort to say something, the wretch was probably fabling, but he said hesitantly, "One night I saw him come out of the house of Pablo Stúñiga."

"Who's he?"

"A rich merchant from the south, from Málaga. A moneylender. They say he's a converted Jew or a *Morisco*. But gentlemen only call on such a man when they're in trouble."

This might mean something or nothing. Don Francisco had spoken of the style maintained by de Silva, and moneylenders fitted into that pattern. But you have to have assets to raise money. Pedro had learned in Jaén that de Silva's fortune had been sunk in the American venture. Indeed, that had been the burden of the Marquis de Carvajal's grievance against him. Still, in the case of Stúñiga, his court influence might be an asset.

Feeling that he had now got all he could from the turnkey and that some of it, notably the part relating to the murder of the messenger, might be usable, Pedro considered his next step. Evidently the *carcelero* was for sale to the highest bidder. If he could now be turned into a witness against de Silva, he would be of more use living than dead.

"You know," remarked Pedro, "that I am the kinsman and friend of Don Juan Alonso de Guzmán, Duke of Medina Sidonia, and that the Duke has a long arm. He will not let the killing of his servant go unpunished, whoever is guilty. Also the Duke de Bejar backs General Cortés, whose representative I am. These are bigger men than Diego de Silva; they make safer patrons. Let us discuss matters."

Leaving his position behind the turnkey, Pedro once more drew up a chair.

"I take it," he went on, "that you are a poor, industrious man, with no special affection for de Silva beyond the money he pays you?"

"Yes, Your Grace. I have a large family."

"No doubt. Every rascal has a large family. Well, it happens that I am much richer than de Silva and, when it comes to my neck, I could perhaps use your services. Suppose tomorrow you should tell him the truth: that I did not drink the wine and remained up all night, so that with the best will in the world you were unable to murder me. You would lose nothing by that, eh?—except a mere one hundred pesos, especially as I would pay you double."

For the first time, the man's face relaxed; his eyes lighted up; he beamed.

"Ah, Your Grace makes a new man of me. I kiss your noble feet. I would let myself be cut into small pieces for the sake of your lordship."

"Gracias. But now in addition, if you were assured of pardon and patronage, it might be worth your head's weight in gold to give testimony regarding tonight's attempt."

The turnkey pondered. "What assurance have I—"

"My word of honor. Think, *hombre,* if it came to the point, I could denounce you and have you put to the question."

The other nodded. "Captain de Vargas, I am your servant."

"And you will give testimony against this Tito el Fiero?"

"Not that, Your Grace. I might as well die now as later, for death would be certain. But I will point out others who could be forced to confess."

"A kindly thought," murmured de Vargas, fighting down his nausea at the fellow. "As for other testimony regarding the man Stúñiga—"

"Anything," agreed the turnkey, "anything Your Grace desires. I have a lively fancy."

"Restrain it, Señor *Carcelero.* Keep to the truth if I call on you."

The fellow grinned. "Yes, your lordship, but I shall not understate it."

When Pedro released him from the chair, he kneeled and fawned over his new patron's hand. "Your Grace can count on me."

In reply, de Vargas lifted the pouch of gold which he had recovered from the turnkey and counted him out fifty pesos.

"A hundred and fifty more if you know what side your bread's buttered on. If you don't know, it will go hard with you."

"I have learned that, Your Magnificence."

Pedro saw him out with relief. Then, having made a pile of various articles in front of the door, so arranged that if anyone entered the noise would awake him, he stretched out on the bed.

But for a long time he remained open-eyed. Disgust at the assassin he had been dealing with mingled with the dread of tomorrow. He lay mapping out his defense, but suddenly another thought struck him. Not defense; he had nothing to defend. Everything turned on de Silva. It was not a matter of principle, but of personality. Expose him, and he had won. But the exposure had to be complete, immediately convincing, and final. Had he enough evidence at his disposal for this? No, not obvious, crushing evidence. Perhaps by luck, perhaps if he took a gambler's chance . . .

All at once he awoke to find sunlight in the room. The ordeal was close. Tomorrow had become today.

IN THE COMBINATION dining and audience hall of the palace, Charles of Austria that day followed the custom of the time by dining in public. He sat before an ample table with various covered dishes before him. At his back stood the table staff, which comprised two doctors of medicine, a court buffoon, and an assortment of pages under the direction of a steward. In front of him and around, at a respectful distance, lining the walls, was ranged the court, a mingling of Spaniards, Flemings, and Germans, whose deferential eyes rested on the plume of the Emperor's hat and on every movement of his jaws.

Businesslike in everything, Charles paid no attention at all to these onlookers. Dinner was a serious matter, to be got through efficiently and without small talk. The buffoon stood behind him as an article of court furniture, a depressed buffoon whose services were seldom called on.

The Emperor, having taken his place, cut a slice of bread into squares, each large enough for one bite. The pages removed the covers from one dish after the other (they all contained meat, fish, or fowl) and His Majesty nodded or shook his head as the whim of appetite directed. When he nodded, the pages stepped back, while the Emperor drew the dish towards him, stuck in his knife for what carving was necessary, then, raising the dish beneath his chin, used his fingers to eat with.

By God, whispered the court, it was marvelous how cleanly His Caesarean Majesty managed his victuals.

When he was thirsty, a motion of his hand brought one of the doctors with a silver flagon and a crystal cup. Charles then emptied the cup without stopping, but he restricted himself to three in the course of a meal.

The fine tapestries on the walls, and the still finer tapestry of satins, jewels, and brocades furnished by the courtiers, made a brilliant setting. Silence reigned except for the movement of the pages and now and then the cracking of a bone or a chicken wing.

Sometimes, though rarely, Charles's absorbed gaze wandered from his meat, resting an instant on one person or another; but the blue eyes revealed nothing. Today he noticed a tall figure he had never seen before, an elderly, black-clad man, straight and lean as a rapier, with a scornful lower lip and a hawk nose. He was evidently someone of distinction, for he was standing by the side of Don Iñigo de Velasco,

Constable of Castile. Charles at that time did not know the Spanish nobility half so well as he knew his Flemings and Germans. After glancing once or twice at the gentleman, he beckoned a page and asked in a low voice who it was.

"Your Caesarean Majesty, I believe it is the famous knight, Don Francisco de Vargas, about whom so much is told from the Italian wars. They say he was the bosom friend of the Great Captain."

"So!" said Charles, returning to his fowl, and the page dropped back.

After dinner, quill toothpicks were presented to the Emperor, who made careful use of them. He then rose, and the table was immediately removed, so that the dining hall became an audience room.

It was noticed that when my lord Constable approached with Don Francisco, His Majesty turned aside. It was noticed too that he pointedly overlooked the Señores Montejo and Puertocarrero when they bowed before him. And on the other hand, when he had seated himself in one of the window recesses, it was noticed that he chatted pleasantly with the Bishop of Burgos and Diego de Silva.

"We'll be meeting soon, gentlemen," said Charles. "I believe we're to have the pleasure of inspecting this young pirate, de Vargas, eh? *Au revoir!*"

Shrewd courtiers gravitated toward the happy recipients of the imperial smile. Although superficially trifling, these were important events. The warfare of years, the future of New Spain, might depend on them.

Today Charles cut short the usual hour of audience and of hearing petitions. Being informed by the Grand Chancellor Gattinara that a certain prisoner summoned by His Majesty was being held at his orders outside, the Emperor rose from the window seat and took his purposeful way out between lines of bowing gentlemen.

"You'll admit my lord de Burgos and Señor de Silva to the cabinet," he told Gattinara. "Have the prisoner brought in."

"One word, sire," the other cautioned.

"Yes?"

"Keep an open mind. Much depends on it."

"Indeed, Monseigneur?" returned Charles stiffly. "What depends on it?"

"Justice, Your Majesty—and perhaps an empire."

As an indication that he was a prisoner rather than for any practical reason, Pedro wore light arm fetters when he was introduced into the imperial cabinet. The two halberdiers in front of him stood aside, and he saw for the first time the King in whose service he had spent the past four years. The sight was not disillusioning, for Charles looked royal. At the moment the Emperor's eyes were cold as blue granite.

Then Pedro saw the lithe, poised figure of de Silva on the Emperor's left, and it took him an instant to overcome the convulsive tenseness that passed through him. The burly, truculent-looking churchman in purple, whom he rightly conjectured to be the Bishop of Burgos, interested him less, as did the lord who stood at the Emperor's right.

The halberdiers retired to the door; Pedro dropped to one knee.

"You may advance, Pedro de Vargas," said Charles, and when the prisoner stood in front of him, he added, "It is not our custom to examine rebels before their trial—we leave them to their judges—but in this case I could not resist looking at a man who has involved himself in so many crimes."

Though Pedro kept his eyes carefully turned away, he was still aware of de Silva's triumphant smile. But he answered levelly, "If my crimes have procured me the attention of Your gracious Majesty, I cannot regret them, all the more as they were committed for Your Majesty's service."

"God bless me!" Charles exclaimed. "You do not disappoint us. You steal a shipload of gold supposedly addressed to us and have the brass to claim that the theft was for our service."

"Your Majesty prejudges the case," put in Gattinara.

"There's no prejudging about it. Do our port officers not witness that this man dug up a great weight of gold in their presence and bore it away despite them, claiming it belonged to him? What more do you want?"

"The simple formality, sire, of allowing Captain de Vargas to speak in his own defense."

"Well then, speak up, sirrah Captain."

"Your Majesty, I told the truth. The gold was mine."

"Eh bien, voilà!" Charles growled. "You have it from his own lips."

"As to Your Majesty's gold, in the amount of four hundred thousand pesos," de Vargas continued, "it is where I left it on landing. It awaits Your Majesty's orders."

A different note sounded in the Emperor's voice. *"Four hundred thousand pesos!* Where?"

"At the friary of La Rábida. In the charge of Fray Tomás, Father Superior."

Pedro hoped for an effect and not in vain. De Silva's smile was gone.

466

"Four hundred thousand in gold?" Charles repeated.

An abrupt laugh cut off Pedro's answer. "Your Majesty," de Silva remarked, "may I venture a humble caution? I hope this gold exists; but as yet it exists only on the word of a man whose effrontery Your Majesty himself has pointed out. How long will it take to learn from La Rábida that de Vargas left no gold there? At least two weeks. And in that time, from my experience with this gentleman, much can happen."

Pedro smiled. "Very true, sir. Only it will not take two weeks to learn the truth from La Rábida. It will take no more than two minutes."

"How so?" demanded Charles.

"I believe my father, Don Francisco, is at court today. He has a document from La Rábida touching the matter in hand, also a letter on the same point from General Cortés addressed to Your Majesty. From my experience with Señor de Silva, I would not venture to keep such papers on my own person lest they should be mislaid."

At another time, the Emperor might have reproved this attack on a man he favored, but at the moment he was much too interested in the document from La Rábida.

"Call Don Francisco," he ordered.

The old knight entered with the dignified carriage that he maintained always. He did not look unduly impressed—indeed, he would have walked down a church aisle toward the high altar more humbly than he now approached Charles of Austria—but at the same time his bearing showed reverence.

The young Emperor, embarrassed that he had slighted him in the audience room, now impulsively rose.

"Welcome at court, Don Francisco. I have long wanted to see the good knight and servant of my grandfather, the friend of Gonsalvo de Córdoba. I regret that you come on so serious an occasion, but I would have you know that, whatever the charges against your son, they reflect nothing against you."

The other bowed over the outstretched hand. "If I do not kneel, sire, it is because of Ravenna. As for my son, I wish I had no more serious crimes than his on my own soul. But, however that may be, we stand together in all things, even in Your Majesty's displeasure."

Then, drawing out the papers he had received, he presented them. "Have I permission to take my leave?"

"Nay, stay here, sir. We may have need of you."

Charles had already opened Fray Tomás's receipt and was glancing through it.

"Look, Gattinara, the seal of the friary. Thirty-five chests, said to contain gold in the weight of four hundred thousand pesos. Let's see what the man Cortés adds to this."

And he tore open the letter from Coyoacán, his eyes racing along the closely written pages.

"Here's news. The city with the long name—fallen . . . The entire country in Spanish hands . . . A continent . . . (The fellow writes well, my lord Chancellor. I was struck by his other letter. The Caesar touch.) . . . Yes, thirty-five hundredweight cases of gold bars to be left at La Rábida . . . Equaling the royal fifth of a certain treasure discovered by Captain Pedro de Vargas plus three additional tenths donated in loving devotion by the Colony of Villa Rica. Therefore, a half . . . Said Captain de Vargas retaining two fifths. . . . *Ma foi,* you're a rich man, sir . . . Well, the letter jumps with Fray Tomás's receipt. But why, in God's name, de Vargas, did you not notify us of this? Why was it necessary to put you under arrest in order to secure information of such importance? Is it not treasonable negligence?"

"No, sire. I had no sooner reached Seville when a messenger was dispatched by His Grace of Medina Sidonia. The message stated that I brought important news and a contribution from Mexico; that I was proceeding to Valladolid via Jaén to wait upon Your Majesty who had but then landed at Santander. The Duke will vouch for this."

"What messenger? None arrived."

For the first time, Pedro stared full at de Silva, who stood pinching his chin, his face whiter than usual, his eyes elusive and yet intent.

"I believe he met with foul play. But being myself a criminal in Your Majesty's view, no charge of mine would carry weight."

This was a question as well as a statement. Charles glanced irresolutely at Gattinara, who offered no advice. Perhaps the Chancellor found a dry amusement in watching his young master extricate himself from a situation which a little heed would have prevented.

"Why, as to that," the Emperor stumbled, "clearly certain charges against you cannot be maintained. They were due to a mistake. You bring great news and a welcome contribution from New Spain. It may be we have acted overhastily—How now, Señor de Silva?"

Pedro saw a pair of handsomely brocaded shoulders meekly inclined and a sleek head bowed low, as de Silva kneeled in front of the Emperor.

"Sire, I crave punishment for myself. The fault was mine."

"No, sir. You reported the sworn evidence of the officers at the port of Palos and the testimony of seamen in de Vargas's ship. You could not do less. The mistake is not yours."

468

"But, sire, the Bishop of Burgos and I did more. We charged this man with rebellion against Your Majesty in New Spain, with blasphemous treason, with unspeakable cruelties, with disgracing the Spanish name, with conspiracy to murder a priest of God. As Your Majesty puts it, we acted overhastily. We wish now to withdraw those charges."

—————— LXXXII ——————

A SILENCE OF astonishment fell. Pedro, bewildered, could think of nothing but a big, black, devious snake. Bishop Fonseca looked as amazed as did the Emperor and Gattinara.

After a pause, Charles exclaimed, "Indeed! You withdraw the charges? Why?"

Still kneeling, de Silva lifted his head. "We would not embarrass Your Majesty. Far better that we should incur your imperial anger and that the voice of justice should be silenced than that the Majesty of Spain should be tempted to make good the boast of de Vargas and others like him that a round sum of gold, properly placed, would cover any crime they chose to commit. Therefore, we withdraw our charge. This man and his mates are not rebels; they kept faith with the Governor of Cuba; they distinguished themselves by uprightness, loyalty, and mercy; they engaged in no extortions, plots, or assassinations. They are noble cavaliers, who should be cherished and rewarded."

The Emperor fingered his beard and thrust his lower jaw out further than usual.

"I like plain speaking, Señor de Silva."

"Your Majesty, that is the trouble. The Bishop of Burgos and I are plain, direct men. We saw only a pack of villains and law-breakers, guilty of every crime. We did not see, as we ought, that any wickedness is counterbalanced by success."

It was the right note. Then, as always, Charles of Austria prided himself on his justice and fair dealing. And it did not help matters at that point when Gattinara observed thoughtfully:—

"That, Señor de Silva, is one of the truest remarks I have heard you make."

"How so?" rapped Charles. "My lord **Chancellor**, it is unworthy of you."

"It is the verdict of history, sire."

"Then let us write a new page of history. It shall not be said of a Holy Roman Emperor that he accepts a bribe –"

"Alas! Does Your Majesty mean that he rejects this gold?"

"No." Charles blinked slightly. "No, but am I wrong in believing that the gold belongs to me whether these men are rebels or not?"

"Of course it does," rumbled Bishop Fonseca. "If a thief restores part, a small part, of his ill-gotten booty, does it mean that he has absolved himself of the theft?"

The Emperor nodded. "That's the right answer, Monseigneur di Gattinara."

"Sire," returned the Chancellor, "we were speaking of rebels, not thieves. If Cortés were loyal, what would you have him do that he has not done? He presents Your Majesty with a great country, conquered by a handful of men against millions; he sends a king's ransom in tribute. These are not the acts of a rebel."

"Precisely," injected de Silva, who had risen and stepped back again next to the Bishop. He smiled coolly, his dark, arrogant eyes on Gattinara. "Precisely. As I said, Cortés is not a rebel. He is a successful man. Whether he is called viceroy or king of New Spain hardly matters. He rules there and scorns any other authority. Witness Narváez and the loyal gentlemen he has maimed or murdered. He presents His Majesty with a great country and at the same time keeps it for himself. When he could have sent forty million, he sends four hundred thousand as a sop to avoid trouble. These are the ways of success."

Charles fingered his beard again. "Forty million?" He was still young enough to believe in any figure from the New World.

"Aye," returned de Silva. "Cortés has had the pillage of a hundred cities. On the night of the retreat, I saw him toss away hundreds of thousands in gold to the common soldiers. I do not recall that he was able to save a *blanca* for Your Majesty's treasury."

"Ah, *Nuestro Señor*," de Vargas prayed under his breath, "is there no fire in heaven for this dog?"

But what fire there was seemed directed against Pedro himself. The Emperor's hard blue eyes were leveled on him.

"Look you, gentlemen," said Charles, "we have had enough of this. We do not appoint royal governors to have their authority mocked. We do not appoint ministers of our lands beyond the sea"—he glanced at Fonseca—"to have them ignored by Hernán Cortés or Pedro de Vargas. My lord Bishop, you and Señor de Silva have preferred charges against this man. He must face them. I have directed Don Fadrique Enríquez, Admiral of Castile, to appoint judges, who now wait to begin trial."

So, Pedro reflected, it was as his father had feared. The great news from Mexico, the offering of the gold, were not enough to clear him.

The power of the Bishop of Burgos, entrenched for thirty years, could not be so easily defeated. He, a newcomer, a young man, was no match for such an official. And what sort of trial could he expect with this great influence against him? He could not deny that he and the rest of the company had rebelled against the Governor of Cuba. He could not deny that he was second in command at Tenochtitlán at the time of the massacre, and it would do him no good to affirm that he had protested against it. He shared the responsibility with Alvarado. As for other charges, it was his word against de Silva's, with this difference—that he was discredited and de Silva was in favor. No, he had no hope in defense; his one chance lay in attack. And now was the moment.

"Your Majesty," he put in, trying to keep his voice steady but conscious of the crisis, "may I ask one question?"

"We have heard enough," Charles began. "We have no time. No, my lord di Gattinara, there are other matters—"

"Sire"—Don Francisco had stepped forward—"if I have ever rendered any service to Spain, if there is any memory of it, hear my son."

Charles frowned impatiently. "Well, then. But let him be brief. What is the question?"

"Your Majesty," Pedro went on, "does not the character of an accuser affect in some way the credence given to the charges he makes?"

"Yes, and if you refer to the character of your accusers, I would say that it confirms their charges. Of his lordship of Burgos, I need not speak. Of Señor de Silva, I shall point out that he is not only vouched for by the Bishop, but has served me well already in sundry matters. Does that answer you?"

Pedro's heart beat fast. Everything depended on the next move.

"It does; but let me speak to the point. I pass over the fact that this man has once before denounced me and that his empty charges were not only dismissed by His Holiness the Pope and by the Suprema of the Holy Office, but that Your Majesty himself took action to the same effect."

"A theological matter," put in Charles, "concerning your venerable father as well as you."

"And yet, sire, one false denunciation on whatever matter does not recommend the next one by the same man. . . . I pass too over the fact that this person"—Pedro found it difficult to use de Silva's name—"joined our company in the ranks of Pánfilo de Narváez and therefore plainly may be considered a prejudiced witness. Nor do I press the point that he sneaked off to Cuba after our defeat when he thought the enterprise was doomed—though I'll wager a thousand pesos that he would give his soul now to have hung on until victory. I shall not speak of his betrayal of me and of two of my comrades on the night of the retreat, which is still more discreditable, for I have only my naked word to prove it."

"Come!" snapped the Emperor. "We want no oration."

"It will be no oration, Your Majesty," Pedro went on. "Therefore, at this time I mention only the disappearance of the messenger from Seville, though I have evidence that a hired bully of Valladolid, one named Tito el Fiero, killed him in this man's pay."

"Sire!" de Silva burst out furiously, though with a new tremor in his voice. "Am I to stand here—"

"Patience," Charles smiled. "You'll have your turn later. . . . Well, de Vargas, have you done with your *passings over* and *not mentionings?*"

"Aye, Your Majesty." Pedro felt terribly alone, as he prepared to make the decisive cast. No turning back after this; it was all or nothing, success or ruin. "Aye, Your Majesty, for there is a last matter of greater importance. I charge this man with being in the pay of the corsairs, a spy of Barbarossa's, a renegade and traitor to Your Majesty and Spain."

"By God—"

De Silva's rapier was out, and at the same moment he flung himself at Pedro, but not so quickly that he did not find himself blocked by Gattinara.

The Emperor had sprung up. "You, sir! Do you forget where you are! Do you draw a sword in our presence! Except that I admit the provocation was very great, I would hand you over to the guards."

Controlling himself, de Silva returned the blade to its sheath. He was dead white, and his hands were trembling.

"Flesh and blood cannot stand some things."

Charles pointed his outstretched hand at Pedro. "If you fail to make good that charge, God have mercy on you!"

De Silva put in, "Your Majesty, do not let him soil your ears—"

"I shall make the charge good," said Pedro, giving rein to his luck with an unspoken prayer. "First, let me ask this man whether some years ago at Málaga he did not act as an informer for the corsairs and receive large sums for his services. And I should add that I have a witness in Jaén to prove it."

De Silva had the look of one drowning. "Sire, the keeper of a disorderly tavern, Sancho López—"

"At least, he seems to know the witness," remarked Gattinara.

"Next," continued Pedro, "I would have him narrowly questioned by some able seaman on his escape from Tunis. He claims to be a soldier, not a sailor. How then was he able, after slaying the crew, to bring a felucca single-handed to Málaga? He knows nothing of the sea. Let him explain how he laid his course, handled the sails. He says, I hear, that the ship was wrecked not far from Málaga. Is there no wreckage? Were there no witnesses? Has he been cross-examined on the said miraculous escape?"

"As to that," de Silva struggled, "have no fear. I'll explain—"

"Lastly," Pedro concluded, taking the final chance, "it is to be asked where this bankrupt villain draws his funds for the state he keeps at Valladolid—"

De Silva gave a harsh laugh. "Is this not childish—"

"And in that connection," Pedro added, "I would call as witness the turnkey of the prison whom Diego de Silva paid to murder me last night. He will give evidence not only about that. He will show that this man frequents the house of a so-called Málaga merchant, a *Morisco*, who should be put to the question, one Pablo Stúñiga."

Whatever de Silva's faults, lack of decision was not one of them. Before the guards at the door could cross their halberds, he had passed them. His voice sounded in the anteroom, as if he were in pursuit of someone. A roar of confusion rose on the outer stairs. A moment later came the clatter of a horse's hoofs from the courtyard.

After orders for pursuit had been given and the excitement was past, the Emperor reseated himself. He turned first to Bishop Fonseca.

"You vouched for this man. What have you to say?"

But for once the Bishop of Burgos had lost his tongue. "Nothing, Your Majesty," he stumbled. "I—I renounce him."

Gattinara struggled with a smile behind his beard. "And what becomes of the charges against Captain de Vargas," he queried, "when the sole witness to most of them has—shall we term it—withdrawn?"

"*Cré dieu!*" Charles brought down his fist on the arm of his chair. "You should have advised me in this, my lord Chancellor."

"Sire, may I submit in all humility that management of perplexed cases is learned not by advice but by experience? Your Majesty trusted de Silva. The rule for princes is to trust no one very far."

Charles nodded. "I believe I shall profit by the lesson. . . . Remove the irons from Captain de Vargas. It may be a case of pot and kettle; but, with the pot gone, the kettle is no longer called black. Well, sir, Charles of Austria makes his apologies."

When the fetters had been taken off, Pedro advanced and, kneeling, raised the Emperor's hand to his lips.

"May I ask a boon, Your Majesty?"

"Two, if you like."

"That the trial proceed. Not mine alone, but that of General Cortés and all our company." Suddenly Pedro found himself quoting. "As the General says, we are not saints, Your Majesty. Nor are we devils. We were desperate men, fighting a desperate fight, and in the heat of it we made mistakes. I beg Your Majesty to judge us by our accomplishment. We have given to Spain an empire which awaits only Your Majesty's orders. The boon I ask is the appointment of an impartial council not chosen by the Bishop of Burgos—men who have no interest but justice. Let them determine the merits of Velásquez and of our General. I pledge my honor, sire, that loyally we shall accept the verdict."

"Not much of a boon," Charles returned. "After today, no other course would be possible. You shall have that trial, Captain de Vargas, and that impartial council. . . . You may rise." But when Pedro stood up, he added, "Tell me one thing. Are all the captains of Hernán Cortés like you?"

Pedro stammered, "Sire, I was one of the youngest. They should not be judged by me. Take Sandoval, Alvarado, Olid, Marín, Dávila, Tapia —a dozen others. I am not worthy to be mentioned among them."

"Indeed?" smiled the Emperor. He turned toward Gattinara and Don Francisco. "Do you believe that, gentlemen? Well, we'll put it to the test. I'm giving you a boon you haven't asked for, Captain de Vargas. You can have the task of bringing Diego de Silva to justice— alive or dead."

LXXXIII

IF CHARLES OF AUSTRIA had made Pedro an officer of state, it would have been as nothing compared with the warrant received within the hour, authorizing him to seize the person, dead or alive, of Diego de Silva and commanding all loyal subjects to assist in the arrest. He took immediate council with his father, when they were at last free from congratulating friends and alone at the inn where Don Francisco had been stopping.

The old gentleman emptied a measure of wine and thumped the table. "By the mass, I wish I were younger! *Por Dios,* I wish I could

474

ride with you on the traces of that carrion! Alive or dead, ha? My dear boy, you'll forget the first two words, I hope, when you overtake him. But watch yourself. He's an eel and a fox in one."

"I see it this way," said Pedro. "He'll head north. My fear is that he's halfway now to the French border. The mountain passes are so many holes in a sieve. We can't plug them."

Don Francisco shook his head. "I disagree. We're on the eve of war, and Castilians will find cold welcome in France. I say look to the ports. He'll head for Africa. Where's home for a renegade except among his friends, the infidels? He'll turn up on the east coast or on the south coast east of Gibraltar."

"The port officers are being warned," said Pedro. "Señor di Gattinara took order for it—also to notify inns and trumpet the reward. Meanwhile, the chase this afternoon lost him in the city itself. The guards at the gates have seen no one like him pass. It may be that he's gone to cover here for the present."

"You spoke of a Tito el Fiero and the Moor, Stúñiga."

"They are covered, sir. I'm expecting news about them at any moment. I've summoned my rascal turnkey, who may know something."

But the news, when it came, was blank. El Fiero and his mates had vanished. So had Stúñiga. The turnkey did not appear. A search by the city watch found his body with the throat cut not far from the prison.

"Poor scoundrel!" exclaimed Pedro. "He merited no better. And yet I promised him protection."

Spain is an ideal country to play hide-and-seek in; ideal, that is, for the party in hiding. Weeks became a month. Now and then, on the strength of a report, Pedro would lead a hunt in one direction or another, only to return baffled at the end. It seemed to him that a needle in a haystack would be easier to find, for at least one could know that the needle was there, whereas by now de Silva might easily have escaped from Spain. Indeed, for a time, de Vargas was the hunted rather than the hunter. Twice his mail shirt turned the dagger of a hired assassin. Then even these attempts, which encouraged him to believe that de Silva might be still within reach, stopped; and he had to admit a complete stalemate.

Meanwhile, Don Francisco returned to Jaén to reassure Doña María and to publish the good news from court. He had much to publish. With the Fonseca influence excluded, it did not take the reviewing council long to decide between the claims of Cortés and the Cuban governor. The enormous fact of the conquest silenced even Spanish legalism. What had Velásquez, what had any other colonizer in the New World, to show in comparison with this? The court and soon the whole of envious Europe rang with the deeds of Cortés and his company, which had added new glory to Spanish arms. That the actual conquerors should be denied recognition and reward in favor of a man like Velásquez who had lent only his name and a small investment to the enterprise was too great an absurdity for even the most pedantic to accept.

Called now and then to witness before the council, Pedro played his part in this exoneration and reaped his share of the laurels. As the power of the Bishop of Burgos declined to nothing and the star of Cortés rose higher, no longer were the Cortés men overlooked at court assemblies. They stood now in the full noon of imperial favor.

Before a group of friends, including the Marquis de Carvajal, who had been invited for the purpose, Don Francisco described the scene of Pedro's knighting.

"You will forgive my partiality, señores, but I consider this the crown of my life. You should have seen my son, gentlemen. I tell you he bore himself well and gallantly. Nay, many remarked on it. In addition His gracious Majesty conferred on him the Cross of Santiago and has promised him the command of fifty lances in Italy. But, sirs, to my thinking, this is not the best of it." Don Francisco paused here for effect. "I had it from the Grand Chancellor himself that my boy's general, Hernán Cortés, has been justified in every act, that he's to be appointed governor, captain general, and chief justice of New Spain, that his officers and men are to be honored and rewarded. My lord di Gattinara vowed that this had been owing to Pedrito's management. What's a Cross of Santiago compared with that—to have rendered stout and loyal service to one's captain!"

But, in view of all this glory, Don Francisco and his friends would have been puzzled could they have seen Pedro's moody expression that same evening as he left the palace in far-off Valladolid. He had temporarily taken a house in the city and now rode back to it through the dark September weather with hardly a word to his brand-new squire, Cipriano Dávila, and none to his link-bearers. Swinging wearily from the saddle, he nodded to his Zapotec retainers on guard and trudged upstairs to his bedroom.

He felt as if the last smile, bow, compliment, reservation, and politic remark, had been pumped out of him. Good Lord, how tedious, how boresome! He could not rid himself of the sad philosophy that here in Spain everything could be bought. Not a man at court, the Emperor included, who was not somehow for sale in terms of pesos. Where would the honors of Cortés and of the company be now if gold had not been forthcoming from Mexico? And would a deserving but poverty-stricken de Vargas have been knighted and decorated? His disgust included himself. He too had sold out, he as much as any.

A page relieved him of his stiff, wide-sleeved cloak and then of the tight, brocaded doublet.

"Ah-h!" he breathed, stretching his arms.

He remembered how Catana used to squire him when he came in from some duty, and how he would then take her on his knees and lean his cheek against her. It seemed ages ago. The poor page did not know why his master stared so coldly at him. To curry favor, he brought a letter which had just arrived from Luisa de Carvajal but earned nothing more than a grunt. Pedro dropped the letter unopened onto the table. No need to open it. He knew by heart the phrases it would contain, the sugary little repertoire. There had been no letters at first. Now that he had become His Excellency Don Pedro, they arrived daily. He felt cynically indifferent: they too belonged to the pattern of everything else.

"Fetch me my night draught, lad," he said. "Then get along with you."

The boy went out and returned with a silver flagon, which he dutifully tasted, a custom not without its practical value. Next he opened a special leather case and produced a pewter tankard, which his master insisted on using every evening. He handled it carefully, feeling sure that there was some witchcraft in the strange characters carved on the side of it.

"God give Your Excellency a good night."

"He's the only one who can do it," Pedro returned dryly. He noticed for the first time that the lad somewhat resembled Ochoa, Cortés's page, and, reaching out, he pinched his ear. "Good night yourself, little knave," he said—a kindness that sent the boy off happy.

The deuce of it was that Pedro could see no end to the weariness and the boredom. After court, his marriage; after his marriage, the military conventions of a regular army; after Italy, the court again. Well, he yawned, he had asked for it.

But an old Latin tag haunted him tonight. *Et in Arcadia ego*. It had been a wild, fierce Arcady he had known, but how fresh and free it seemed now, as he looked back!

The Emperor had hinted that he might be the proper man to take the good news to Mexico, but de Vargas had not been receptive. The surge of longing was tempered by the realization that he could not recapture the old life by returning to the scenes of it. Better launch out into something entirely new where he would not be forever reminded of the past. The past belonged to Catana and García.

Strolling over to the window, he stood looking into the darkness that covered the garden at the rear of the house. A flurry of dead leaves brushed the panes and brought a shiver of autumn.

In Mexico now, it would be the end of the rainy season, good marching weather. Expeditions would be pushing out. Much talk of fabulous mines, new empires. He wondered what Sandoval was doing. And, thought following the well-worn paths, he found himself again with the company.

Old faces seemed peculiarly vivid tonight, men he hadn't remembered for a long time. Most of them dead. Ortiz, Escalante, Manuel Pérez, Master Botello, Juan Velásquez, Francisco de Morla—many others. An old song woke in his ears, Ortiz's song.

> *Far in the West,*
> *The white sierras bloom*
> *In gold and fire . . .*

He had forgotten some of the words, but the tune filled in the gaps.

> *Far in the West,*
> *The mighty waters bear*
> *Our reckless sails . . .*

God! *That* was living. Whereas this—His clenched hand relaxed.

His comrades had not lived to see the victory, to gather the gold and the fame. Not like himself with his title, decoration, and treasure. But how was he luckier than they, who had gone down in the heat of living? What did he have more than they; that is, more that counted for happiness? For the first time, he actually understood what Olmedo had meant in that talk of theirs long ago. The dream, not the realization; effort, not fruition; battle, not victory—these were life.

Returning to the table, he filled the pewter tankard, his thoughts reverting to Catana. It seemed odd that all he had of her was this poor cup and the few lines she had written him in Coyoacán—these and memory.

Having drunk, he sat turning the empty tankard between his hands, rubbing his thumb over the scratched letters, his mind adrift. Then, all at once he looked intently at the cup as if he had never seen it before. *Catana Pérez*. The edges of the letters were sharp. They must have been newly cut, for otherwise they would have worn smooth after four years of tavern use. But Sancho López had said that this was Catana's former cup, which she had had marked by Paco the Muleteer. Had the innkeeper lied to please him? Was it Catana's cup after all?

Then, struck by another idea, he opened the little amulet pouch that hung around his neck and took out the note she had written him at Coyoacán, holding it close to the candlelight and studying the letters. A sudden pulse quickened in his forehead. The same letters were reversed here as on the cup. He had never been able to teach her to make a proper *n* or *p*. But then—but then, if she herself had cut these letters on the tankard—why then—

Springing up, he fumbled among his papers in a leather writing case and retrieved the note he had received from Jaén, signed Paco. Here too the same letters were reversed.

But God in heaven! . . .

Could he believe, on such evidence, that Catana was in Spain, that she had been at the Rosario, that she had written him the all-important letter about de Silva? Common sense rejected the idea; wishful-thinking embraced it. A new flood of life boiled through him. He stood an instant eying the paper. Then before he knew it he had opened the door and was shouting for his squire.

Cipriano Dávila appeared, wide-eyed and sword in hand, under the impression that his master had been attacked. Pedro's expression startled him.

"Look you, my friend," said de Vargas, "see that our horses are saddled and ready for the road at dawn. See that there are mounted servants and led horses enough—at least two spare mounts for each of us. We'll be traveling fast."

"Where to, my lord?"

"Jaén. Damn the city gates, or we'd be off this hour! Still, I must write to take leave of His Majesty."

"No bad news, I hope, sir?"

"The best news perhaps. We'll find out in Jaén."

479

LXXXIV

OFTEN DURING THE next four days, Cipriano Dávila, stiff and saddle-galled, wondered what the news had been that kept them riding as if the fate of Spain depended on it. But Pedro offered no information except that he was taking one chance in a thousand and wouldn't risk his luck by talking about it. He rode silent for the most part, his eyes on the distance in front. When he spoke at all, it was generally in reference to possible short cuts or other details of the journey. He did not, however, ride like a fool who spends all his resources on the first flurry, but showed the skill of a good trooper in husbanding his horses over hard terrain, letting them out when the footing warranted it, inspecting their hoofs at every halt, seeing to it personally that they were well-fed and well-tended at night, with their legs bandaged. Young Dávila, an apprentice in the career of arms, both groaned and congratulated himself on belonging to so expert a captain. Here was a cavalier you could learn from, and his respect for Pedro grew with every blister.

In view of the size of the party (they were eight mounted men in all, with six led horses) and the roughness of the roads, they could do no more than twenty leagues a day, and that meant riding from dawn until well past sunset. But at night in the country inns, after Dávila had stretched out, he would be drowsily aware that Don Pedro was still up, pacing the floor as if fatigue meant nothing to him, and as if a night's sleep for horse and man were merely a weakness that had to be put up with.

Toward the end of the third day, they were well into La Mancha, with the peaks of the Sierra Morena in the distance across the plain.

"We'll halt at Alcázar de San Juan," Pedro decided. "We've broken the back of the road, with sixty leagues behind us. The devil's in it if we don't reach Jaén this time two days hence." His spirits mounting at the thought, he added, "Then, *hombres*, you can sleep your heads off —or drink 'em off, if you like."

They covered the two miles to the village and clattered into the courtyard of the *fonda* Mariana. But Pedro had hardly entered the common room when a voice out of the semi-darkness exclaimed: "Holy saints! My dear boy! What a miracle! How does this happen? What good fortune you are here!" And de Vargas saw a square white beard approaching him through the twilight.

For an instant, even after his eyes had adjusted themselves to the dimness of the room, he hardly recognized the speaker. It was the

Marquis de Carvajal. His beard and hair were disheveled, his clothes disordered; the arms he threw around Pedro trembled.

"*Ave Maria!*" returned de Vargas, though none too cordially. "That I should find you here, my lord! How is it with Your Grace? What's happened, in the name of God? Your Grace looks distracted."

Carvajal sank to a bench and took a deep breath. "Ah, my son, and who wouldn't look distracted who's been for two hours in momentary fear of death! Fortunately I saw him first and managed to get upstairs, where I lay hidden." The dust on the Marquis's clothes suggested that he had been under a bed. His next remark confirmed the notion. "There was only a plank between me and the devil. Two hours long I had to listen to him. My rascal lackeys ran off; though that was as well, or my livery would have been recognized. I had just taken heart to come down when your horses filled the yard, and I thought he was back."

"But who, *por piedad? Who?*"

The Marquis shook his head. "I'm no longer equal to these alarms."

"Take me with you, Don Luis. Who are you talking about?"

"Why, my ex-son-in-law, de Silva. May God—"

"*De Silva!*" Pedro stood rooted. "De Silva?"

"Yes, and may God—"

"Which road did he take, do you know that? We didn't meet him. I say, which road?" And laying no gentle hand on Carvajal's shoulder, Pedro shook him.

"The road to Jaén."

"*Jaén?*"

"Yes, with fifteen roughs, each of them harder-looking than the next. At first I thought that their object in riding there was to assassinate me or perhaps your father, but that does not seem to be the way of it. I could hear de Silva talking to one whom he called Tito. They will not enter Jaén, being in fear of your father, the Alcalde. They plan to put up at the Rosario. For some reason, they are in fury against the innkeeper, Sancho López, whom they vow to burn at a slow fire and then destroy the inn. They are heading for Granada and the sea."

De Vargas strode to the door. "Cipriano!" he called to the squire, who was busy superintending the stabling of the horses. "Saddle again. We're pushing on."

"Your Excellency, the horses are spent."

"Spent or not, we're riding them. Unpack my armor and help me on with it. See to your own. Let the men look to their weapons. By the mercy of God, Diego de Silva is on the road ahead of us. . . . When did he leave here?" Pedro asked the Marquis.

"An hour ago. I felt too weak to move—"

"An hour ahead of us," Pedro relayed to the squire. "We're no men if we can't cut down that lead. Chances are he'll put up for the night at Herencia three leagues on, and if we watch ourselves we can take him off guard. Remember there's a thousand pesos reward on his head. I'll add another thousand if we catch him."

Dávila and the servants sprang into action. They all had taken part in other hunts for de Silva and were hardly less keen than their master. This must have been the reason for the haste from Valladolid, Dávila reflected; but he wondered why de Vargas had kept so quiet about it.

Pedro felt a hand on his shoulder: he had forgotten the Marquis.

"But, my boy," quavered Carvajal, "you're not following that devil with but seven men. I told you he had fifteen. Stay here till morning and raise help from the Knights of St. John. They have a commandery here."

"Yes, and let the fellow put more space between us! No. He'll halt at Herencia, but he may not stop there. The mountains begin at that point. If we miss him at Herencia, we may lose track of him. Have no fear, Your Grace, a surprise adds numbers to the attack, as General Cortés used to say."

"And what of me?" Carvajal demanded. "Is this courtesy to leave an old man, abandoned by his servants, in an evil hostel, when the reason I am here is to be of service to you?"

Dávila clanked up with Pedro's armor. Pedro lifted his arms to facilitate the fitting of the cuirass.

"Service to me?"

"Of course. As soon as I could drag myself from bed, I set out to lend you my help at court. My word is ever my bond. It is to insure the continuance of your good fortune that I have undertaken this grievous journey. With my constant presence, protection, and advice, you will secure even higher honors than His Majesty has already conferred. Instead of knighthood, perhaps even a marquisate or a county. You have wealth. By skillful management, a proper sum to the proper person—"

"Tighten the gorget, Cipriano," de Vargas directed. "Never take chances on the throat. A lucky thrust there, and the game's up."

"You're not listening," snapped the Marquis.

"On the contrary, Your Grace, I'm all attention. You were saying a bribe here and a tip there under your direction might get me a *condado* or a *marquesado?*"

"Yes, we must not stop with knighthood. You should manage your

482

cards at court to the best advantage. You need a councilor of experience like me. Ah, if it had not been for the cursed gout, I should have been with you sooner, and your affairs would have taken an even better turn."

"No doubt. . . . The pauldrons, good Cipriano."

"Therefore, surely," Carvajal persisted, "you will give me your company this evening. And we shall consider matters: whether I should continue on to Valladolid and there await your return, or whether I shall go back to Jaén under your escort."

"The vambraces, Cipriano."

Carvajal drew himself up. "I am not accustomed to inattention. When you are at leisure, I shall expect to have your ear."

The Marquis reseated himself with great dignity on the bench. The arming proceeded until finally nothing remained to put on but the casque.

"Now have one of the men help you, friend Dávila," said Pedro, "and look well to the joints in your harness. We may have hot work, if God gives us luck."

Then, with his casque under one arm, he turned to the Marquis. Actually, so far as Carvajal was concerned, he had reached the breaking point. Did the old timeserver take him for an idiot? Any fool could see through his present maneuver.

Perhaps if Pedro had not been absorbed by the thought of de Silva, he would have been less direct. But the need for haste set him on tenterhooks. He had no time for flourishes.

"Well?" he said.

"My boy, as one who is soon to occupy the position of a second father to you, I have the right to demand your deference and command your attendance. I have explained why you should remain here this evening." The Marquis added a hint of the direst threat he could imagine. "Your union with my daughter is not yet consummated. I should be loath to have anything arise which might affect it. As you see, I have made a considerable sacrifice in your behalf."

"Then, sir," returned Pedro, "I shall be frank. I value your sacrifice as it deserves: at the weight of a counterfeit *blanca,* or perhaps at the weight of your daughter's prayers, which are the only help I have had from your house. Go to Valladolid or return to Jaén as you please. I have more pressing matters to consider. But do not ever again, my lord, treat me as an imbecile who accepts false money for good coin and is grateful. In short, sir, you command neither my deference, my attendance, nor anything else of mine."

483

Amazement and shock struck Carvajal dumb. He could only stare back at Pedro. It was not until the latter had slipped the casque over his head and was on the point of turning away that the Marquis found his tongue again.

"Indeed, sir? And the betrothal? Do you think that vows once taken can be daffed aside on a whim? That my daughter can be insulted and disgraced at your pleasure, ha? The law will have something to say to that."

Dávila entered. "We're ready, Your Excellency."

An odd gleam showed in de Vargas's eyes. He knew that the Marquis would be open to a financial proposal; but he was damned if he would make one. Instead, a hankering which had beset him for a long time seemed on the point of fulfillment.

"The betrothal stands, if you please," he returned. "That's your affair."

And, reaching out, he indulged himself by pulling the Marquis de Carvajal's beard.

"Take note of that, Dávila. And now, by God, we'll spur."

LXXXV

ILL LUCK ATTENDED the pursuers from the outset. They had not covered the nine miles to Herencia when Campeador cast a shoe and another of the horses went lame. An autumn drizzle set in, which made the going no better; so that it was at a shamble that the little troop entered the outskirts of the village. Here Pedro called a halt, while one of the men went forward to reconnoiter the inn. He returned to report that a party of *caballeros* had indeed stopped for a drink an hour and a half ago, but had then turned up into the mountains.

Confronted by an impossibility, de Vargas was forced to give in. Fatigue, night, weather, and unknown roads were all against him. He reasoned that de Silva, who had probably been hiding in one of the mountain ranges south of Valladolid—perhaps even in the near-by Montes de Toledo—had fresh horses as compared with his own, and that Tito el Fiero was enough in touch with other bandit leaders to insure a safe passage for their party through the sierras. Probably they would not hit the main road again until they had crossed the Sierra Morena and were in sight of Jaén. This meant that, while Pedro followed the highway, de Silva was taking short cuts which would increase his lead. The one chance was that, not knowing himself to be pursued, he would ride at a more leisurely pace. But one could not count on that, and the cost of failure to reach Jaén before him came too high to think of calmly.

"Why is de Silva breaking cover just now?" Dávila wondered that evening, as they talked things over in the wretched little tavern. "He's had over a month to get clear."

Pedro shook his head. "Man, I hate the fellow as I hate hell; but, to do him justice, he has the wits of fox, wolf, and snake in one. Go to earth until the hue and cry dies down, then make a dash for it. He has a better chance that way than when the hunt was hot."

Two long, anxious days followed. For the sake of speed, a selection was made from the available mounts; but even so, the party seemed to Pedro to crawl. And though he inquired at each crossroads, he got no news of de Silva's troop.

It was only at Linares, fifteen miles from Jaén, that they once more picked up the scent. Yes, a company of armed horsemen from the mountains had passed through two hours since. They had taken the Jaén road.

Two hours since and fifteen miles to go and darkness again falling. Pedro and his squire took council together under the eaves of the tavern yard. No fresh horses could be procured except at a prohibitive cost of time. The servants, less well mounted than de Vargas and Dávila, had to be left behind.

"Well then, *amigo,*" de Vargas concluded, "I'm riding on. You can come if you please, but I advise against it. Two against fifteen was considered big odds even in the company. I'll not think the less of you—in fact, you'll be showing sense—and it's not your quarrel."

The squire's answer was a laugh. "I thought Your Excellency knew that my name is Dávila."

Pedro clapped him on the shoulder. "I apologize. I ought to know that men of your house never stay behind."

Having bid farewell to the servants, de Vargas swung into his saddle. "So then, Cipriano, *adelante.*"

The rain had stopped, and the sky had broken into scattered clouds with a silvering of moon between. But the road was dark, so that the riders kept alert for any stumble on its uneven surface. They leaned well forward on the horses' shoulders to ease them of the weight of the armor as much as possible.

It was ten o'clock when the walls and towers of Jaén showed vaguely to the right, and for a moment Pedro hesitated. Should he add another half-mile to the distance from the Rosario by riding to the city gate, rousing the watchmen, and calling for reinforcements? That would mean not only farther to go, when every furlong made a difference to the jaded horses, but it meant a loss of precious time. So, deciding against it, he kept straight on along the mountain road.

At this point, Campeador and Dávila's horse showed signs of collapse. They had covered three hundred miles from Valladolid in five days of poor weather and hard roads. They had been under saddle today since before dawn. Faced now by a steep climb, they came to a jog, then to a stiff walk.

"We'll hold up a moment," Pedro said desperately. "After that, if we kill them, they'll have to make it."

Reaching back to the cantle of his saddle, he unhooked a flask of *aguardiente*. "Here, Dávila, pour this into them. It may do the trick." And while the squire, forcing open the jaws of the horses, emptied the flask, Pedro sat on edge with impatience.

"Friend Cipriano," he went on, "in what lies ahead (that is, if we're not too late) we must use our wits as much as our steel. Unless they're idiots, a troop like that, bent on such work, will have outposts to ward off surprise. I look for a couple before we reach the inn."

Fired by the brandy, the horses could now be worked up again to a labored gallop. Breathing like bellows, they got within a half-mile of the Rosario, when suddenly three riders, edging out from the blackest side of the road, seemed undetermined whether to challenge or to head toward the inn.

"Ha, *hombres!*" Pedro hailed. "The Señor de Silva and Señor Tito, are they at the appointed place?"

"Who are you?" returned one of the fellows.

Pedro and Dávila rode up. "Friends from Valladolid, and a damned hard chase we've had. We've good news for the gentlemen. That dog de Vargas has got his. Our friend did for him."

"Fernando, you mean?"

"Aye."

They were now close together, knee to knee. Pedro had loosened his mace from his saddlebow.

"You'll be welcome," said the other. "There're lively doings at the inn. I'm surprised the place isn't on fire yet. Cursed luck that I'm missing—"

"*A ellos!*" shouted Pedro, swinging his mace sideways just under the man's steel cap. At the same moment, he spurred Campeador, lifting him to his haunches and bringing him down on another rider, who sank with his horse to be trampled under the war steed's hoofs. Dávila had buried his poniard in the third fellow's face.

"Bravo!" said de Vargas. They spurred on, leaving the wreckage behind. "We'll see how that trick works in the tavern courtyard. No doubt there's someone on guard there."

Pedro's heart was in his mouth as he neared the Rosario. It looked to him curiously dead and sinister under the broken clouds. Drawing close, he thought that he heard a commotion inside; but he was evidently mistaken, for a moment later the place seemed wrapped in silence. Then with a mutter, half-oath, half-prayer, he turned through the archway into the courtyard.

It contained a number of horses tethered under the eaves of the surrounding sheds, but he could see no attendant until, glancing toward the lighted windows of the common room, he noticed a figure peering in. So absorbed was the man that he did not turn to look when Pedro and Dávila dismounted. Evidently he assumed that they were a couple of the outposts. When he did turn, it was too late. Dávila's heavy sword nearly severed his neck.

A muffled cry, followed by an outburst of oaths and laughter, broke the stillness inside the tavern. Paying no attention to the sprawling body of the man whom Dávila had dispatched, Pedro and the squire in their turn now peered through the window.

Beyond a tangle of overturned or broken benches and tables, which, together with a couple of outstretched forms on the floor, bore witness to the desperate fight that had just taken place, de Vargas's eyes fixed themselves on a center of light, where a roaring fire swept up the chimney of the great hearth. In front of it, forming a semicircle, Pedro could see the backs of some ten men seated or standing; but instantly his attention was drawn to two dangling figures that evidently absorbed the group of onlookers.

Swung up, each by his wrists, to a beam that crossed the projecting canopy of the hearth, a couple of men hung just beyond the reach of the flames. Since their feet did not quite touch the floor, the involuntary writhing of their scorched legs gave the impression of a grotesque dance that excited the merriment of their tormentors.

"Go it, Sancho!" sounded a rough voice from the circle. "Lift up your heels! By God, for a fat man, I'll say you're nimble!"

Obviously de Silva was making good the threat that Carvajal had overheard of burning the innkeeper at a slow fire. The clothes of the victims had not yet caught but were already smoking. As Pedro looked, one of the bodies swung around, and he recognized dimly the features of Sancho López. The huge broad-shouldered figure who hung beside him was unmistakable. In the next instant, a deep voice of helpless rage brought Pedro's heart into his throat.

Juan García!

Then de Vargas caught sight of another form slumped over a table, which had apparently served as a barricade. The face was hidden, but he could see the dark hair and limp hands.

Catana!

His guess had been right, but he had come too late.

An icy madness possessed him. It sharpened all his faculties and focused them. He stepped back from the window.

"Look, Dávila," he said tonelessly, "there're two doors to the room. You take that one; I'll go in here. And, mind you, raise a yell as if you were ten men, when you open the door. Put the fear of God into the bastards. Whatever happens, remember de Silva—he mustn't get away. Now, then, both together!"

Fascinated by their pastime and a little drunk, the toughs in front of the fire were caught unprepared when the two doors crashed open at the same instant.

"Santiago y a ellos!"

Instinctively Pedro gave the shout of the company. A second later he had crossed the room, converging with Dávila upon the startled group before it had time to face around.

"Santiago!"

De Vargas had been reckoned a great swordsman even among the swordsmen of Cortés, but tonight passion turned him into something more. His broad battle blade—ax and sword in one—rose, wheeled and sank, as if it had been no more than a rapier. Two men went down in the first moment. He hammered the clenched steel gauntlet of his free hand on the head of another. His sword crashed through a fourth man's pauldron, through flesh and bone. Reaching García and López, he cut them free with quick jerks of his dagger, paused an instant over the motionless form of Catana, then turned again upon the panic-stricken ruffians, who were scuttling toward the doors.

But where was de Silva? Had he somehow slipped past? Had he been out of the room? Where was Dávila?

Emerging from beyond the threshold, a couple, locked together, reeled back toward the center of the room; and Pedro saw his squire grappling with a tall figure in light harness. One steel arm was about the other's waist, but de Silva's grip immobilized Dávila's sword hand, while the former's dagger could find no mark on the squire's cuirass. Then, with a trip and a twist, de Silva got his opponent off his feet and fell on top of him, his knife poised above the young man's vizor slit.

Pedro sprang forward with a shout. But the blow never fell. Instead, a bench hurled by someone from behind caught de Silva on the side of the head, throwing him off balance for a second; and in that second Dávila, rolling over like a cat, locked his gauntlets around de Silva's throat.

Pedro was dimly aware of García, followed by Sancho López, hurtling past him and out through the door in pursuit of the remaining bandits. The vizor of his helmet, which had been cut loose during the fight, slanted in front of his eyes, and he paused in exasperation to tear off his helmet, calling at the same time, "Hold, Cipriano! You've won the reward, but leave the dog to me!" And prying loose Dávila's grip, he hauled de Silva to his feet.

For an instant, the two foes stood facing each other, the years of hatred and treachery between them, between them too the consciousness of Catana's motionless body at the near-by table.

"Remember," said Pedro half under his breath, "when I made you renounce God in order to save your pitiful life? Eh? Remember? I thought I had paid you then for my sister. But you lived to run up the score. I wanted you to roast in hell then. I suppose if I set you to roast before that fire now, I could make you curse God again. It's well for you that I've taken a foolish vow. So now pray for your soul if you have one. I tell you pray."

De Silva's white face seemed impassive. Then a sudden grimace convulsed it. "Pray yourself, you obscenity!" he snarled and, leaping forward, plunged his knife point down on Pedro's bare head.

The steel bit in, but a backward jerk turned the blow into only a gash across the forehead. Though half-blinded by the rush of blood, de Vargas could still see well enough to swing his sword with every ounce of strength behind it against the angle of his opponent's neck and shoulder.

De Silva staggered, sank to his knees, then plunged forward. It took an instant to free the blade from the already lifeless body.

"God's justice," said de Vargas. "You've witnessed an execution, friend Dávila."

LXXXVI

PEDRO SHEATHED his sword and stood looking down at de Silva, but at the moment he did not think of him. He thought of Catana. Vengeance and, indeed, everything else seemed unimportant.

"Señor!"

Startled, Pedro turned and, hardly believing his eyes, saw Catana supporting herself with one hand on the table edge. Her lips were parted, her cheeks white. He gazed at her as if she were a vision.

"Catana!" he breathed.

The smile he had thought of so often lighted her face. "I wonder if I'm dead and in heaven," she faltered. "It was a bad knock I got when the fighting started."

He was already in front of her. At the sight of his face, she exclaimed:—

"*Ay María!* You're hurt!"

"It's nothing. It's you—"

But before he could finish, she drew a kerchief from her belt pouch. "Sit down, señor, and I'll bind up your head."

"Rubbish! It's you who need tending. I want to know—"

"Sit down, *querido*. How can we talk, and you blinking from that cut?"

Straddling a bench, Pedro obeyed. Suddenly he felt as if they had never been separated. It was so familiar, the touch of her fingers. He caught one of her hands and kissed it. Then, when the bandage was finished, he sprang up and took her in his arms.

"Sweetheart!"

Her head sank on his shoulder. "It's been so long, señor."

"Long? An eternity! But I've a lot to settle with you, *muchacha*. Why did you come back to Spain after leaving me?"

"Because of you."

"Well, in that case, *por Dios*, why did you hide?"

"Because of you."

"Hell! Can't you explain, dammit!"

Catana looked past him. "Yes, señor—but who is this gentleman?"

Pedro had forgotten Dávila, whom he now beckoned to and introduced. The young man bowed, his eyes curious. The words "Señora Pérez, a member of the company," did not explain either his master's excitement or this tall, sunburned girl in boy's clothes.

"What's happened to Juan and Sancho?" Catana asked anxiously.

Pedro replied with a jerk of his head toward the courtyard.

The uproar was subsiding. A last flurry of panic-stricken hoofbeats dashed out through the archway, pursued by a bellow of jeers and maledictions. Then a moment later a deep voice sounded beyond the threshold.

"Ah, the cockroaches! We scotched all but three of them. By God, Sancho, the rascals got their bellyful at the Rosario! But, man, it was a close call! If it hadn't been for those cavaliers—"

And the bulk of Juan García filled the doorway. His big face was beet-red. His touseled black hair stood upright. He carried a blood-stained ax in one hand and a sword in the other. But at the sight of Pedro, both sword and ax thumped to the floor. He stood speechless a moment, then, stretching out his arms, he roared, "Ho, by the saints! Who else could it have been! Now, by glory!" and came on like an avalanche.

He folded Pedro in an embrace that bent the cuirass. He kissed him on both cheeks, and ended by rubbing his hair back and forth with the palm of one hand.

"By glory!"

"Hey!" protested Pedro. *"Misericordia!"*

"I knew it was you," García announced. "That is, I'd have known it if I'd had time to think—even with your vizor down. Lord! I'll never forget that yell when you came in! . . . How did you happen to turn up tonight? Ha, comrade! Comrade!"

He had reached the pommeling stage, regardless of his bare knuckles on the steel of Pedro's harness.

"Hold, for God's love!" laughed de Vargas. "It's lucky I'm in armor. But how is it with you and Sancho—after the fire, I mean?"

"Still alive, boy. Still alive, as you see, thanks to you. It was a near thing, though."

He broke off to throw an arm around Catana. "I thought you were sped, lass, when that dog felled you with his knife hilt." And exploring with one finger, he added, "You've a bump on your head like an egg." His glance rested on de Silva's body across the room. "But I see that the whole reckoning's paid. . . . Comrade," he went on apologetically, "we were taken by surprise. We did not put up a fight worthy of the company."

"It seems to me you did well enough," remarked Pedro, eying the wreckage of the room. "Exactly what happened?"

Between García, Catana, and López, the story was told: the sudden clatter outside, the inrush of armed men. Taken unawares and without

491

weapons except their knives, the chosen victims had been overpowered after a brief but sharp resistance. ("The girl and I got two of the rats anyhow," put in García, extenuating the defeat.) There had been only a few guests that evening. Terror-stricken, these, together with the servants, had been herded down into the cellar.

"Then it went as Your Excellency saw," added López. *"Ay de mí,* I'm a ruined man. My furniture! My crockery! And who'll ever stop at the Rosario after this? A sad name, it will have."

De Vargas laid a hand on his shoulder. "Take heart, Sancho. I'll foot the expense, with five hundred pesos to boot. After your service to me, I could do no less. As to the name, my friend, it hadn't so much to lose that it can't recover. Fetch up your guests from the cellar, fill their bellies free of charge; and they'll spread your praise through Andalusia."

"But now," demanded García, "I want to know how you came to be here tonight. I ask it again. And I want to know how it feels to be a *Don* and an *Excellency* and a *Commander of Santiago,* by God."

"I want to know more than that," de Vargas answered. "I want to know whether Catana's your wife."

The grin vanished from García's mouth. He frowned. "What do *you* think?"

Catana smiled, and Pedro needed no other assurance.

"I think you're a fool, Juan, to have missed a chance you'll never have again."

"A fat chance!" rumbled the other.

"But I want to know still more," continued Pedro, his eyes on Catana. "And it's going to cost someone a whacking if she can't satisfy me. . . . Sancho, light candles in the back room. I've a word to say to this wench. And let no one interrupt if they hear sounds of grief."

"That's the talk!" approved García.

When he had closed the door of the room, Pedro stood looking at Catana, trying to realize that it wasn't a dream.

Then he burst out, "Well, Mistress, have you nothing to say?" But belying the roughness of his voice, he caught her to him and held her a long while, until her hair was ruffled and her face red.

She looked down before the blaze in his eyes. "I wish I was wearing the beautiful dress I bought in Seville, not these things." He smothered her voice again. *"Amado mío!"*

"But can't you explain?"

"You don't give me a chance."

492

He sat down and drew her upon his knees. "Now."

"Well, señor, you ought to know. I couldn't stay behind when you left New Spain. I had to be where I could see you sometimes. I couldn't live else. And I thought just seeing you wouldn't hurt, if you didn't know I was here. Juan and I heard of a trading ship when we were in the southeast country. We reached Jaén before you. I saw you ride into town."

"You did! But, Catana, the New World? You said you wanted to stay. You refused to marry me. I don't understand."

She half-smiled. *"Don't you understand, querido?"*

"Yes, I was a fool not to make you marry me at Coyoacán."

"No, señor, you'd have done wrong if you had, and I was right to refuse. But, listen. I heard your talk here that day with Sancho López. Until then I intended that you should never know I was in Spain. But your tone of voice—ah, señor, it told me more even than the words. I could hear that you weren't happy. Then I decided that after your marriage, when you sailed for Italy, I should be on that ship. We would make the campaign together."

She stopped. "Who told you I was here? How did you find out?"

"You told me." He paused to kiss the surprised droop of her mouth. "I'm probably the world's poorest schoolmaster, and you're the densest pupil. At least there's no worse writer. All I had to do was compare your letters to me. I was dense myself not to have thought of it before."

She flushed a little. "And I so proud, believing it was well-written."

"Well-written enough to save my life. Except for you, Catana *mía,* it's odds I'd have given work to the headsman in Valladolid."

"Then who cares if I'm not learned!" She put both arms around his neck. "Señor, you'd better give me that beating you promised. I'll be crying anyway in half a minute for happiness."

They were too absorbed to notice that the latch rose cautiously, and an exploring eye peered in. Then García flung open the door with éclat.

"Now, that's the way it should be!" he proclaimed. "And it shouldn't ever have been any other way."

Pedro stood up with one arm still around Catana and embraced García with the other. "I cry quarter. But be noble, Juan. Don't crow over me. You were right and I was wrong, and so to the devil with bygones!"

"It's easy said," the other grumbled. "Here we are, like fish out of water, when we ought to be taking up land in New Spain. And you've got to marry the Lady Luisa, now that you've gone this far. With lodgings for Catana on the side. None of this would have happened except for your stubbornness. She'd be your lawful wife instead of a kept woman, and we'd all be grandees in Mexico."

"I don't care," said Catana, fist on hip.

"No, you wouldn't," García returned. "You haven't sense enough. But what about me? The gold we put by in Coatl's country won't last forever. What'll *I* do?"

"Plenty," Pedro nodded. García's words recalled him from the happy present to the still happier future. "We all have plenty to do, and fast. Maybe you don't know that I've been appointed by His Majesty to take the imperial rescript to Cortés."

"*What!*"

"Aye. So we'll ride for Seville as soon as the men I left at Linares have caught up. Then I must go back to Valladolid to receive His Majesty's letters and collect my Indians. I could never face Coatl without them."

"But that means—" The incredible news filtered slowly through García's dazed mind. "*Does it mean you're sailing for New Spain, comrade?*"

"I hadn't supposed the General was any place else."

"But then—then—" García drew a deep breath and let it out in a roar. He lifted both fists above his head and brought them down on the table. "Then—New Spain! Holy saints! The three of us! Carrying the great news! The comrades! The General! I can't—I can't take it in! Blast me, I—"

He stopped short and his face fell. "But the Lady Luisa? You're betrothed. It's as good as married. What'll you do—"

"That reminds me." Pedro turned to Catana. "Where's the dress you bought in Seville?"

She pointed to a chest in the corner. "There."

"Well then, strip off those things and get into it."

"But why, *querido?* It's late—"

"Because I want you to, Mistress. That's reason enough."

"Well, of course—"

Pedro and García turned their backs. There was a hurried sound of undressing, a thump of shoes taken off.

"But I'll give you another reason," Pedro went on. "It's that no priest will marry you in breeches."

"Priest!"

"Yes, priest. There's one in the village down the road. We'll pull him out of bed by the big toes if necessary."

"Priest!" Catana gasped. "Why?"

"Because you know very well I vowed not to sleep with you again until we married; and if I don't sleep with you tonight, I renounce salvation."

"Señor, you can't break your pledge to the Lady Luisa! You'd be dishonored. I didn't mean to interfere—No, señor, God forbid! I can't let—"

"*Chitón!*" Out of patience, Pedro turned on her. Unfortunately she had got no farther in her change of clothes than a shift much too short for protection.

"Please!" breathed Catana, fumbling in the chest for her petticoat.

"Please!" he fumed, unbuckling his belt. "I'll give you something to say *please* about, Mistress. You're taking it on yourself again to tell me what to do and what not to do. I'm going to settle this once and for all. If I have to turn you under my arm, so be it." And suiting the action to the words, he grasped Catana in the position indicated.

"Señor, I didn't mean—Ho! Alas! It isn't proper—ouch!—before Juan. *Ay de mí!* I'll do anything . . . you want . . . if you'll only let me . . . San-ta Ma-ría! . . . put on my petticoat."

"Well, then, remember." He released her and turned his back again.

"That," observed García, "is what you ought to have done a year ago."

Pedro agreed. "Yes, and I'll know better for the future. Juan, see that the horses are ready."

"All I meant to say," Catana ventured in a small voice after García had left, "was that I love you so and that a great marriage—Nay, I didn't mean it."

He had turned again, but this time he found her in yellow damask that set off the blackness of her hair and eyes.

He stood gazing a moment.

"*Reina mía!* You're beautiful!" He strode to her; then, dropping to his knee, he pressed her hand to his lips and laid his cheek against it. "God! How I love you! I wish there was some other word."

She pushed his hair back from his forehead. "You mustn't kneel, my lord. Please. . . . But you can help me fasten the back of this dress. . . . You really like it?"

He fumbled awkwardly with the buttons. Then, noticing a movement of her hands, he frowned. "Did I beat you so hard?"

"No." She turned her head to kiss him. "It was nothing. . . . To think of me! Married to you! Señora de Vargas! . . . Are we sleeping here tonight?"

"I should say not. A bug-ridden sleep we'd have of it. No, *dulce mía,* we're sleeping at my father the Alcalde's."

She swung around, her face pale.

"My dear lord, not that! I wouldn't dare! I'd die of shame! Please, don't make me—"

"I certainly shall. You're riding with me on Campeador. As for shame, don't speak that word again. You and I are sleeping at my father's house. It's where my wife belongs."

——— LXXXVII ———

A FLUSTERED COUNTRY PRIEST, torn between fear of the Bishop, whose office he was usurping, and fear of García's big fists, married Pedro and Catana in the parsonage of the near-by hamlet. García acted as best man; Sancho López gave away the bride; and Cipriano Dávila served as an additional witness.

When it came to the ring, Pedro slipped off the heavy signet ring from his thumb and dropped it loose over Catana's finger.

"Never you mind," he whispered. "I'll have it made tight for you."

"But it's your coat of arms."

"Your coat of arms too, *Doña Catana mía.*"

He could see her lips repeat the new title, *doña.* Then she smiled faintly and shook her head.

"Do you take this woman?"

Pedro intended no irreverence, but the priest started at the loudness of his answer.

And after the final blessing, when they kissed each other, it was as if they had never kissed before.

"My dear lord!" she whispered. "My dear, dear lord!"

"How now!" roared García at last. "Are you going to stand there forever? Aren't the rest of us to have a chance, by the mass?"

Congratulation of Pedro and the kissing of the bride began. Everybody made the most of the opportunity and kissed her until her lips burned.

"*Jesús María!*" she laughed. "*Pobre de mí!* I'm so scratched by the beards of you *hombres* that my mouth feels as if it stretched from ear to ear. *Sangre de Dios—*"

She caught herself and shot a troubled glance at Pedro.

He pinched her ear. "You'll never stop cursing, sweetheart. It's the brand of the company."

The priest brought wine, and healths were drunk. Sancho López

496

presented a tankard. "If Doña Catana will do me the honor," he bowed.

"*Doña Catana?* Didn't you bring me up, Sancho? What's become of Long-Legs?"

The innkeeper shook his bullet head and grinned, but he answered, "That's a long time ago, your ladyship."

His heartiness held a new note of respect. Except that she took it as a tribute to Pedro, Catana wasn't sure that she liked it.

"Well, to me," put in García, "you're still Catana Pérez of the army, the lass who cooked my meat and washed my shirts and held my head on her knees when I was in the bilboes. With all respect to His Excellency here"—he rapped Pedro on the chest—"that seems more of a title to me than any damned *doña.* . . . But what's the lay now, comrades?" he went on seriously. "I take it Jaén will be too cold or too hot after this to hold you. We start for Seville when?"

Pedro grinned. "Seems to be in the stars that whenever you and I leave Jaén, we leave it in flight. You and Cipriano will meet Catana and me a league out of town on the Córdoba road at s' up day after tomorrow."

"Hey?" returned García. "Meet you and Catana? A   staying at the tavern?"

De Vargas tried to sound casual. "No. Do you think I'd ?   off without the blessing of my parents, without presenting my wife? *Cáspita!*"

García shook his head. "I suppose not. But if I know your honored father, the Alcalde, it's not too sure we'll meet on the Córdoba road day after tomorrow."

"Pooh!"

"Pooh, nothing. Suppose he doesn't approve of"—García coughed —"the change of plans? You might end in the clink, my boy. He has the power." The big man added significantly, "Why not leave Catana with me, at least until—"

"No! From now on, Juan, I'm not leaving her with you. We're going to take what comes together. How about it, *querida?*"

She laid her cheek against his shoulder.

In the upward spiral of his happiness, it seemed to Pedro that their ride through the warm night was much too short, though they rode at a walk. Catana's arms were around him, her thumbs hooked in his belt; her hair brushed his neck. Even the uncertainty as to what reception he would be given at home could not overcloud these radiant facts. He realized that to present Catana as his wife, in view of the betrothal to Luisa, demanded more consideration from his parents than had his confessions six weeks ago. He was proposing to leave them in a pickle of embarrassment, while avoiding it himself. But the present was too absorbing for him to be concerned even by the immediate future.

"Please don't trot," Catana had said after a hundred yards from the parsonage.

"Why not? You won't fall off. It'll make you hold me tighter."

"I'll do that anyway, but please don't trot. Alas!"

He pulled up. "What's wrong?"

She hesitated. "You ought to know."

He laughed and, detaching her hand from his belt, he bent low enough to kiss the palm, then continued to hold it, interlacing his fingers with hers.

"That was a blessed strapping I gave you, *alma mía*. I thank God for it. Otherwise, you'd still be hemming and hawing and worrying about me. It cleared your mind of the great-marriage stuff. As if your little toe, a single hair of you, didn't mean more to me than all the blazons of the world! I've learned that at least. Do you know what I wear under my shirt, eh?"

"No, my lord."

"That last letter you wrote me at Coyoacán. By the mass, it's been read often enough since then! But now—*vive Dios!*—to have you back again! And my own wife! Before God and man! My own señora! Lord, you'll get little sleep tonight, Mistress. . . . Did you ever think of me?" he added provocatively. "I'll warrant you didn't, you false slut."

She pressed her face against his back. "Not once, not a single time, curse me else!"

"How! What do you mean? It's well for you you're behind me."

"I mean just what I say, *querido*. How could I think of you once when I thought of you always, every minute?"

He hooked his reins over the peak of the saddle and turned. "I can't go another moment without a kiss."

Campeador philosophically stopped at this point and took to cropping grass by the roadside. It was several minutes before the slow progress was resumed.

"Señor," she said, her arms closer around him, "do you think it's possible that Our Lord might send Niñita back if we prayed very hard? Of course I'd have to bear her again. But do you think Our Lord would?"

"Faith, I do," said Pedro. "Hasn't He brought you back? Hasn't He always been good to us? Let's pray Him for it tonight."

But for the most part, the ride passed in a silence much more eloquent than words. Pedro de Vargas could not have expressed the infinite horizons that seemed opening before him any more than one can put music into speech. When he spoke again, the tone of his voice rather than his words expressed him.

"By God, we'll take up land southwest of Cuernavaca. We'll import cattle. I say there's more in livestock than in gold. Besides, we have enough gold. Juan García must live near us—he and others of the comrades. That way we can make a head against any Indian upflare. I'll build you a great house, *muchacha,* and you'll give me kids to fill it." Her arms tightened, but she didn't answer. "What are you thinking about?" he added.

"Partly of you," she said, "and partly of your parents. We're almost at the city gate. Señor, I'm so afraid."

"*You* afraid! You'd thumb your nose at the devil. What are you afraid of?"

"Your señora mother. I think I'm even more frightened of her than of Don Francisco. They're such great people, and I'm only—"

"You're my wife, remember that. Don't worry, *querida,* we'll manage."

And yet now that the ordeal was close, he began to feel more than a qualm himself. If his father took a stand against this marriage, it might come to more than a tongue-lashing. Pedro feared only two people in the world, Cortés and Don Francisco de Vargas.

It took some time at the town gate before the keeper opened. The watchmen were calling one o'clock when Pedro stabled Campeador in the mews behind the de Vargas house. Then he led Catana across a rear garden and through the back door to which he had the key. By this time he felt a trickle of cold sweat under his armpits.

The house was utterly quiet as they reached the central patio and started climbing the stairs to the second floor. Only some night tapers were burning.

"I'll take you up to my room," he whispered. "Then we'll see what's to be done."

But in the upper corridor, a page, sleeping athwart the threshold of Don Francisco's door, started up, gaped at Catana, and faltered a greeting.

"Lights here," said Pedro, bracing himself and entering his room.

When the astonished page had brought a candle, Catana gazed at the unfamiliar walls, at the canopied bed. Her knees felt weak.

"I believe I'll sit down."

Pedro took one of her hands. "Why, you're cold as ice, sweeting. Nay, do not fear. If I had thought—"

"Back in Jaén are you, *hijo mío!*" exclaimed a familiar voice at the threshold. "Back, and no word to announce you! By good luck, I happened to be awake. Nay, are you hurt? That bandage . . ."

The voice stopped on a breath, changed its tone to steel.

"By'r Lady! I seem to be intruding. What woman's this?"

—— LXXXVIII ——

IT DID NOT IMPAIR the dignity of Don Francisco de Vargas to be wearing a skullcap of velvet, which he put on at night, and a dark chamber gown. He looked like an old falcon in the robes of a judge. His black eyes challenged on either side of his beaked nose; his lower lip drooped.

"Well?" he demanded, while Pedro was searching for his tongue and Catana gripped the sides of her chair. "Well?"

Glancing at Catana, Pedro came to himself.

"I have the honor, Señor Father, to present my wife, Doña Catana de Vargas y Pérez."

Self-controlled as he was, Don Francisco could not help a start. It was a moment before he breathed, *"How!"*

Pedro burst into explanations. The old gentleman continued to stare at poor Catana, who would have been happy if the ceiling had fallen to hide her from those piercing eyes. When Pedro stopped, Don Francisco took a step toward her.

"Catana Pérez!" he said in a voice which might mean anything.

At that, Catana's nerve failed. She dropped to her knees in front of him.

"Forgive, Your Excellency! Forgive! It was my fault. I shouldn't have come back. I couldn't help it. I only wanted to see my lord again, not to have—not to have this happen. Don't blame him, Your Excellency. Forgive—"

Terror made her speechless when she felt herself gripped under the arms by two hands of steel and lifted to her feet. Terror then changed to blank amazement when Don Francisco, having held her a moment by the shoulders at arm's length, drew her to him in a hug, and kissed her on both cheeks.

"By my honor!" he said. "By my honor! Forgive, *hija mía?* Forgive what, in God's name? That you saved my life and honor? Nay, better, that you saved the lives of my wife and son? That you loved the scapegrace and bore him a child? That you are back to give him happiness and mettle again? I thank God that I can now thank you for everything!"

If Catana was gradually reviving into a bewildered happiness, it was Pedro's turn to be surprised. He had expected at best a resigned, if benevolent, pardon, not enthusiasm. For a moment, he wondered whether his father really took in the circumstances.

"We were afraid, sir," he hesitated, "we feared, because of my betrothal to Doña Luisa, that you might be angry."

"Ha? And why? You were pledged first to Catana Pérez. If she would have you and you did not marry her, you'd be a knave. Also a fool. Any man can see that she's worth two of the other. Body with spirit to match, something for a man to count on. What more does a soldier want?"

But at that Don Francisco turned, limped to the door, pushed the staring page boy out of the way, and made for his room, calling, "Wife! María! Out of bed with you!"

Catana leaned against Pedro and took a deep breath.

"Señor, I think I love him almost as much as I love you."

Later, when Doña María, to Catana's great embarrassment, insisted on her privilege of undressing and bedding the bride, Pedro related the events of the evening and discussed plans with Don Francisco. The news of de Silva's death was received with grim exultation and further heightened the old gentleman's good humor. As to the Carvajal marriage, Pedro for the first time told the truth about his interview with the Marquis four years ago, when he had appealed to him for help, and described their recent meeting at Alcázar de San Juan.

"Humph!" said the elder de Vargas at the end. "I wish I'd known this before. The old fox would not have made such a fool of me. Pulled his beard, did you? Good! Nay, you can leave him to me. He'll keep silent enough."

Don Francisco approved too of his son's return to New Spain. "You've made it your country, Pedrito. Your friends are there, and the Emperor's service goes forward. Your wife would not be happy in Spain. . . . Though hard it is to say good-by."

"What of you, my lord? Could you not join us, you and *Madrecita?*"

To Pedro's surprise, the old cavalier's eyes brightened.

"Faith, who knows? After my office here expires, who knows? You are all we have. Also I would see your children as they come along.

New Spain is plainly different from the scurvy Islands. Did not my lord Bayard himself express the wish to show his pennon there? In short, we'll consider it, my son. It's well thought on."

Meanwhile, the state bedroom had been aired and lighted; the bed had been made with Doña María's finest sheets; and now that the sleepy serving wenches were gone, Catana laid her head on Doña María's plump bosom and cried from happiness.

"Never have I been so frightened, Señora Mother. I thought you would hate me because of my lord Pedro and would blame him because of me. I know right well who I am and what he is. But you and His Excellency are saints from heaven."

"No saints, my dear," said Doña María. "We are old and have only our son, and we love him. It broke our hearts to see him grieve for you. He would never have been the same. Is not his happiness more to us than anything else? Besides," she added, stroking Catana's hair, "it's easy to love you."

Catana put her arms around the older woman's shoulders.

"I've never had a mother. Come to us in New Spain, so that I can serve you and have you near me when I bear your grandchildren. Señora, we're going to have many children—as many as God will give us. Come to New Spain, *Madrecita querida.*"

Doña María's eyes filled. "Perhaps, if my husband consents." She said more firmly, "I'll make him. . . . And now, daughter, it's time to put you to bed. Pedrito will not be denied very long. Come."

She unbuttoned Catana. The dress was slipped off, the petticoat, the shift.

"No stays, *hija mía!* And breasts so haughty! Who would ever think you had had a child! Such a figure, too; skin like marble. I'd have thought you were darker."

"It's the tan of my face and arms, señora, and my big gipsy mouth. But by a miracle of God my lord puts up with me."

Doña María kissed her. "I don't wonder he's mad about you." Then, noticing the marks of the belt, she exclaimed, "Has someone beaten you?"

"Yes," Catana said simply, "my lord Pedro whipped me well because I didn't want him to break his pledge with the Lady Luisa. He would not be gainsaid. He's strict with me, but I love him the more."

"And he you," nodded Señora de Vargas. "He can't keep his hands from you, one way or the other. Well, I've had my beatings too. They break no bones, and we manage our men just the same. Get into bed, child."

When she had put out all the candles except one at the bedside, she leaned over and drew Catana to her.

"You'll rule him, *hija mía,* have no fear of that. You'll rule him with love and wisdom. I know it. But he will never know. That's our secret."

"Will you bless me, my lady?"

María de Vargas made the sign of the cross.

"My blessing now and forever."

A knock and a voice sounded. "Aren't you ready yet? Name of pity!"

Catana slipped down under the covers. Doña María smiled and opened the door.

. . .

From the top of an undulation in the Córdoba road, Don Francisco de Vargas, mounted on his saddle mule, gazed westward at the small band of travelers receding in the distance. Long rays from the early sun, which had just lifted a crimson shoulder above the summit of the Sierra Magina, brought them into brilliant focus. He could still make out his son's pennon on the lance carried by Cipriano Dávila and an occasional glinting from the steel caps of the servants who had arrived yesterday from Linares. But his eyes were fixed on the three riders in front: García, broad-shouldered and top-heavy on his mule; Pedro, centaur-like, a part of his horse; and between them, Catana, riding sidesaddle on another mule. The old gentleman could no longer see the fluttering white plume on the hat which Doña María had given her, but it still fluttered in his mind's eye. Vivid too were the sunburned face, expressive mouth, and the parting kiss he had had of her. A right cavalier's girl, his thought commented.

He leaned forward, his eyes following them with keen tenderness. Youth, he thought. The New Age, an age turned westward across the Ocean Sea. How different from his own! How unimaginable! And yet from the rear guard of the past he bade the future God-speed. The stage might change; the actors might wear other costumes; but the essence of life remained. Courage, honor, love, would blossom in the New World as in the Old. That was what counted after all.

On the edge of a slope, beyond which the road disappeared, the little party drew rein and turned; he could see them waving back at him. Drawing himself up in the saddle, he raised his gauntlet in salute and blessing and farewell.